D1189116

Anita Burgh was born in Gillingham, Kent, but spent her early years at Lanhydrock House in Cornwall. Returning to the Medway Towns, she attended Chatham Grammar School, and became a student nurse at UCH in London. She gave up nursing upon marrying into the aristocracy. Subsequently divorced, she pursued various careers – secretarial work, a laboratory technician in cancer research and an hotelier. She has a flat in Cambridge and a house in France, where she shares her life with her partner, Billy, a Cairn terrier, three mixed-breed dogs and three cats. The visits of a constantly changing mix of her four children, two step-children, six grandchildren, four step-grandchildren and her noble ex-husband keep her busy, entertained and poor! Anita Burgh is the author of many bestsellers, including *Distinctions of Class*, which was shortlisted for the RNA Romantic Novel of the Year Award.

THE AZURE BOWL

Daughters of a Granite Land
BOOK ONE

Anita Burgh

ORION

An Orion paperback
First published in Great Britain by Chatto & Windus Limited in 1989
This paperback edition published in 2000 by
Orion Books Ltd,
Orion House, 5 Upper St Martin's Lane,
London WC2H 9EA

Third impression 2001

A CIP catalogue record for this book
is available from the British Library.

Printed and bound in Great Britain by
Clays Ltd, St Ives plc

To the memory of
Elizabeth Rose Vincent

Part One

Chapter One

1

Alice Tregowan's upbringing had been unconventional. Her mother, Etty, hated her. George, her father, seemed unaware of her existence.

It had not always been this way. There had been a time when Etty was as involved with her children as any wealthy young mother was expected to be in England in 1881, that is, she took a dutiful if lukewarm interest in their clothes, manners, health and diet. Each day, at teatime, they were brought to her boudoir to play as she lay, languidly beautiful, on a chaise, resting before the inevitable fatigue of another evening spent with society.

The degree of play was controlled by how exhausted their mother was. If not too tired, she had been known to read to them, to play a game of spillikins or, if she was feeling very relaxed, they might have a round of 'Happy Families'. But often she was too tired and would lie, eyes closed, her hands crossed limply on her body – a voluptuous body, released for a few short hours from the constraints of her stays, and now comfortably covered with a lace and embroidered peignoir.

At such times the children were expected to 'play' quietly. The problem was that the room held such a jumble of furniture that movement was severely restricted. Small tables proliferated, each with its clutter of boxes, silver-framed photographs and ornaments – all far too precious for the children to touch. It was as if there were not a material or metal known to man that was not represented in this room. Jade and malachite vied with onyx, lacquer with bronze, crystal sparkled, mother of pearl glowed. Iron and brass supported. Lace, chintz, brocade, silk and satin, ruched, bunched and swathed, competed for attention. The curtains at the large windows were half drawn, the shades were down, for Lady Tregowan was afraid lest one shaft of sunlight mar her alabaster complexion and cause a freckle to appear. Always a fire glowed, winter or summer, making the room so hot that even the fronds of the palm in the corner wilted.

Alice was afraid of this room, and of doing damage in it, as she was afraid of her mother. To society Etty was a beautiful, gracious, witty, laughing woman. To her children she was a puzzle. One moment she was engrossed in what they had to say, the next irritated beyond endurance and pushing them from her. One minute she could be laughing, the next screaming at them to leave her alone. Alice did not enjoy her daily visit to her mother.

In their London home, at the top of the house, beneath the great glass dome, the children had their suite of rooms – a day and a night nursery, a schoolroom, their nursemaids' rooms and sitting-room, and a tiny kitchen for making toast and hot chocolate. There were walls, lined floor to ceiling, with cupboards full to bursting with clothes, the best that the White House shop could supply. Every toy that a child could want was there.

Here, in total control, resided their nursemaid Queenie Penrose with her two nursery assistants. Queenie, with her ample body and breasts as soft as the softest feather pillow, whose large good-natured face with round cheeks shone red as any apple. Queenie, whose neck smelt of soap and biscuits, was warmth, security and love.

Very occasionally their mother appeared in the nursery – rustling in her silks, glittering with jewels, expensively perfumed and exuding graciousness like a visiting queen from a far distant land.

From the barred nursery windows, if they stood on

tiptoe, they could watch the activity in the square below, the hours of the day marked out by the arrival of the delivery men. First the clang of the churns as the milk, fresh from the cows in Hyde Park, was ladled into tall white enamelled jugs, held by the kitchen maid. The rat-a-tat-tat of the postman. The meat boy with his hand-cart that squeaked. The calls of the old flower seller, the fisherman, the shrimp man, the pretty fruit girls. The rattle of the hurdy-gurdy with the monkey that bit. And, as winter drew in, the bell of the muffin man with his hat as flat as a board.

Most evenings, once Queenie was safely in her room with her jug of stout and her penny dreadful, Alice and Oswald would steal from their beds and crouch on the stairway. They would peer through the balustrade and the wire mesh suspended in the stairwell. The mesh had been placed there the day after Oswald had dropped a toy train over the side, missing a footman's head by inches. Far below, the gas lights, in their ornate brass chandelier, hissed. As if through the wrong end of a telescope, the children watched the comings and goings of their parents' friends. The women's dresses swished and swirled, their overskirts frothy with frills, ribbons and flounces of lace which, caught back into full bustles, swayed like giant, brightly coloured bells. The guests formed ever changing patterns on the black and white marble floor like a giant kaleidoscope.

When the Tregowans travelled to their large estate in Berkshire, the children followed with their retinue. Here they were kept strictly to their own quarters but the nurseries were even larger and they had the freedom of the park, the river and their ponies.

Fairhall was the name of the house. Once it had been a classically proportioned Georgian house, built by an earlier Tregowan after destroying the original Jacobean mansion. Georgian it had remained until this generation of Tregowans, with their love of the modern, had had the house redesigned. The perfect proportions had been swallowed up by flying buttresses, battlements, pointed arches and pepperpot domes. Only inside might an observant visitor have noted a classical arch, a remnant of a cornice, or a fine chimneypiece which had escaped the destruction.

In this house there were no small rooms. Each room seemed grander than the one before. No expense had been spared on their decoration. Ceilings were heavily plastered and then painted in crimson and blues with liberal coatings of gold leaf. Wood was carved and curved into every conceivable form of animal and mythical creature. Huge oil paintings were commissioned from the latest artists. Befitting the rooms, the furniture was on a grand scale too – a sideboard as tall as a tree, a dining-table to seat a battalion.

During most of the year, the house stood in quiet, grotesque splendour, but when the newly fashionable house parties descended, it came to life and seethed with people. Etty and George liked to entertain on the grand scale and did so with practised ease.

George Tregowan was as proud of his new house as he was of his wife. A man of great physical attraction but with limited intelligence, he would, with a bemused expression, watch his beautiful wife flitting amongst the assembled company. Etty could outwit him at every turn but he only marvelled at the quickness of her mind. To him, she was like a beautiful, clever child whose every whim he wished to satisfy and whose fluctuating moods he benignly forgave. They were unfaithful to each other in the discreet manner which their society demanded. He had his son, and so he was complaisant about her adventures. He did not think or speak of love; such matters were beneath his manly dignity. But, if many women shared his bed, his loyalty remained with Etty.

Once a year, in early spring, the family and Queenie, Etty's maid, George's valet and Phillpott, the butler, would travel across town to Paddington and climb aboard their personal coach for the annual visit to their estate in the West Country.

Their coach was added to the regular train in which less important individuals travelled. Alice loved this journey, the excitement of the great train huffing and hissing in the station impatient as she was to begin. The coach was furnished in red plush and gilt, the woodwork of the shiniest mahogany. Tiny oil lamps glowed, the golden bobbles on their shades swaying with the rhythm of the train. It was like a miniature house on wheels where, in the small galley, Phillpott would heat up their already prepared meals.

Alice enjoyed the journey so much that its completion was only made bearable by the prospect of seeing Gwenfer again. Both she and her brother agreed: Gwenfer was their favourite home of all.

Gwenfer. Had one not known of its existence one would never have realised it was there, tucked as it was between the two giant cliffs which the wind battered and at whose feet the sea lashed and sucked voraciously, hungry to steal more land. On the cliff top there were no trees, for there was never time for them to root deeply enough to withstand the gales of autumn and winter. Only the broom and hawthorn kept a tenacious hold on the poor soil. But by spring and summer, those same barren cliffs were ablaze with the colour of the wild garlic, the periwinkle, foxglove and a hundred other flowers. Then they came alive with bees, butterflies and dragonflies, their improbable colours added to nature's gaudy summer palette. Across the landscape the tall chimneys of the tin mine pump-houses seemed to strut, arrogantly and noisily.

A narrow road criss-crossed the scrub and led through iron gates which never closed, flanked by gateposts surmounted by the great stone falcons which had stood there for centuries. The road snaked perilously down the granite sides of the cliff, twisting and turning to reveal, far below, a valley. Purple, pink and white rhododendrons lined the roadside. Mophead hydrangeas stood waiting their turn to flower and wild rhubarb plants, with stems as thick as an arm and taller than a man, promised shade beneath their giant leaves when the summer finally came.

In the very beginning it had been Gwenfer cottage, then farm. In medieval times it progressed to house and then manor but now, having grown, its size an indication of the Tregowan family's fortunes, it was known the length and breadth of the land simply as Gwenfer. George Tregowan might, like his forebears, have been tempted to extend it further had its position not prevented him. The house filled the head of the valley, embraced protectively on each side by the towering cliffs. Built of the same granite the building appeared to be an extension of the rocks.

Etty came to Gwenfer on sufferance. It was too far away from London and society. It was also too small for her needs. Those intrepid friends whom she could persuade to travel such a distance had to be restricted in number to fifteen, whereas Etty felt that a successful house party needed at least thirty people.

It was fortunate for the house that it was not her favourite – thus it had escaped Etty's 'improvements'. The panelling remained in position, the plasterwork was original and the great stone fireplaces, plainly carved, still stood in the high-ceilinged rooms. She was not sufficiently interested in its interior to refurnish it, so the designing flair of Mr Waring and Mr Gillow had not been called upon and the furniture was much as her husband's Elizabethan ancestors had left it. So great was her lack of interest that Gwenfer lacked the clutter of the other houses. The walls remained white, the only colour coming from the tapestries and family portraits. There was no gas so the great wall sconces remained and oil lamps glowed warmly. The long, mullioned windows to the front of the house faced on to wide terraces of informal gardens which Etty had not bothered to have landscaped. These gardens cascaded wildly down to the floor of the valley where a small river tumbled towards the sea. Even when the ocean was shrouded in fog, even on the calmest day, its sound could be heard in each room of the house, a persistent background noise, as breakers crashed on to the boulders, and spray flew through the air to mingle with the river.

With the sea, the wild gardens and the moors, for Oswald and Alice Gwenfer was a paradise.

This life, for Alice, changed dramatically the day that Oswald drowned.

Everyone was in agreement that what subsequently happened was unfair, since Alice had not been with Oswald when, against all orders, he had ventured out on to the rocky point at the mouth of the cove to fish. The greedy sea, with one rogue wave, had scooped the young child effortlessly off the rocks and there was no one to hear his cries. For three days the sea had played with him before returning his bruised and broken body to the shore, as if it had tired of and had no further use for him.

Lady Tregowan's broken-hearted husband tried the impossible – to soften the blow of telling her that her firstborn had been found, dead. The housemaids scuttled to their rooms and, weeping, hid their heads under their pillows in a useless attempt to shut out the sound of their mistress's dreadful grief. Etty's screams echoed through the long corridors, swirled down the dark oak staircase and reverberated around the great hall to be absorbed into the thick granite walls, there to join the other cries of joy and pain the house had collected from Tregowans long since dead.

Alice, barely five years old, was perplexed, afraid and unhappy. Too young to grasp the finality of death she waited patiently for her older brother to return. She waited huddled in a corner of the hall, forgotten in the ensuing panic, and was fearful of the terrifying noises coming from her mother's rooms. And she was unhappy for, instinctively, if not with understanding, she knew that nothing would ever be the same again.

In the church that stood on the cliff, buffeted by the Atlantic gales, positioned as if in defiance of the very elements which God had created, the family vault was opened and, in the presence of his father, the local nobility, the servants and a scattering of miners, Oswald's small coffin joined those of his ancestors.

The funeral was barely over when Etty instructed that her bags be packed and her carriage ordered. She swept down the staircase swathed from head to toe in deepest mourning, her sorrow seeming to make her smaller, and, with no word to anyone, stepped into the carriage. She sat rigid, her face a ghostly blur through the thick folds of the veil. She looked straight ahead and did not see her daughter's white, tear-streaked face at the window of the great hall.

'Don't leave me,' Alice cried, hammering with her tiny fists on the thick glass. But her mother did not hear.

The coachman's whip cracked and the unwieldy, old-fashioned carriage began to move. The horses' necks arched with the strain, their hearts beating almost to bursting point as they hauled the heavy coach to the top of the hill.

Etty did not look back.

That evening, unusually, George asked to see his daughter. He stood in his study, his back to the fire, a large glass of whisky in his hand, and looked at the doll-like creature before him, with her long blonde hair caught in a blue bow. Large, solemn grey eyes studied him in return. They both felt awkward. To Alice, her father was a handsome giant whom she rarely saw and could not remember talking to. To George, Alice had been his second child, a daughter at that, whom he rarely noticed. His interest had been invested in Oswald, and now Alice was all he had.

'Alice, your mother is not well,' he started, bluntly.

'Oh, Papa, no.' The small face creased with anxiety.

'She will be well again. Then we shall send for you,' he added, hurriedly, afraid that the girl was about to cry.

'When, Papa?'

'I'm not certain.' He turned his back on her and studied the fire and Alice knew that she was dismissed.

From the window of her room, the small white face watched once again as this time her father climbed into the coach and she heard the coachman's whip crack.

'Off to London, I be bound.' Queenie sniffed in disapproval as she bundled her charge into her arms and hugged her.

2

Queenie was wrong. George's coach sped across the moor and headed towards Bodmin and the estate of his sister Maude Loudon.

Maude and he had once been inseparable but since his marriage, ten years ago, the relationship had cooled. Maude had not approved of Etty. For the sake of peace, Maude could have pretended an approval she did not feel, but that was not this woman's way, and with characteristic bluntness she had made no secret of the fact. She knew she was right, that her brother had made a dreadful mismatch and that Etty was an empty-headed creature who would bankrupt him given half a chance.

There could not have been two more disparate women. Etty lived for society. Her passions were her clothes, staying beautiful, gossip and men. In contrast, Maude had dedicated her life to husband, children and hunting – not necessarily in that order. Not for Maude the modern

11

practice of delegating control of the household to a steward and a housekeeper. Maude knew daily the state of her larder, how many bottles of jam and preserves stood on the stillroom shelves, and she herself counted the sheets and pillow cases. It was Maude who kept the great ledgers of household expenditure in immaculate order. Maude ruled her small empire efficiently. She knew who on the vast estate was ill or in trouble. She knew the names and birthdates of all the children born since she had come to Loudon House. Her tenantry worshipped her, her children feared her.

For twenty years she had cared for her husband Marmaduke, Marmie for short, and everything that was important to him. In that time she had presented him with eleven children, nine of whom had survived. What little time she had to herself was devoted to the hunt. She would boast with pride that there was not a bone in her body she had not broken at some time in the field, some more than once. It was her hope that her life would end, quickly and cleanly, on the hunting field. Now forty, solidly stout, contented that she did her duty, there remained no vestige of the pretty, slim girl who had left Gwenfer all those years before.

As his coach approached Loudon House, George wondered what he was doing here. Etty would be furious if she knew his plan. He felt apprehensive as the carriage rolled nearer to the sister of whom he had always, if he were honest, been afraid. What would his reception be? He wondered why he should turn to Maude with his problems. His handsome features were marred by a frown as he thought deeply – not a normal pastime of George's. Blood, that was it. Blood was always thicker than water, everyone knew that. This conclusion cheered him, and the frown disappeared.

He was less sure of this when half an hour later he stood in the drawing-room of Loudon House and faced his sister – ten years older and ten years larger – with the same unfriendly but self-satisfied expression he remembered from his last visit.

'George, my dear fellow.' Marmie broke the awkward silence and stepped towards George with his hand held out in welcome. He had missed George these past years – a good shot, fine company, a capital chap to get drunk with was Marmie's opinion of his brother-in-law.

'Marmie, old sport. You look just the same.' Gratefully George grasped Marmie's proffered hand.

'You too, George, old man.'

'When you two have ceased this mutual admiration, perhaps George will have the courtesy to inform us what he is doing here after all this time,' Maude said, sharply – so sharply that the camaraderie between the two men was immediately broken and they stepped back from each other with furtive, almost guilty, expressions, like young boys who have been found with their fingers in the biscuit barrel.

'I'm in a bit of a fix, Maudie,' George began. Maude stared coldly at him. 'I've come to ask your advice,' he added quickly.

If there was anything that Maude liked better than to give advice, it was to be asked for it. She smiled at her brother, a small smile – the merest twitching of her lips; Maude was too expert in the ways of the world and of her brother to give him a more expansive one. Instinct told her that he wanted something.

Maude fussily settled George into a wing chair in front of the blazing fire. She knew well, from experience, that comfort was essential for the imparting of confidences. George settled back in the chair. He accepted a large whisky from Marmie and stretched his legs towards the warmth of the fire. He began to relax as he felt the tension of his responsibilities gradually fade. He had been right to come: Maude would arrange everything just as she had when they were children.

Maude selected a chair opposite George, a large

13

commodious chair which only just managed to accommodate her magenta-clad bulk. Since George said nothing, Maude took the initiative.

'I heard about Oswald, George. A dreadful tragedy. We were both so shocked. But I thought it best, in the circumstances, to stay away. Not of course what I wanted, but then,' she paused, 'the situation was not of my making.' Maude was not yet prepared to relinquish completely the animosity between them.

'Your letter ... thank you, very kind ...' Maude waited impatiently for George to begin, her plump fingers drumming on the edge of her chair. 'It's Etty,' George said suddenly, looking at Maude with anguished eyes.

Maude immediately stiffened and sat rigid in her seat, her ample breasts heaving as she took a deep breath to steady her nerves. Her husband nervously refilled the glasses.

'I doubt if there is any advice I can give you about that particular person.' Maude's voice was steely in its coldness.

George saw the rancour in his sister's face and knew he could never discuss with Maude his great fear for his darling Etty – stupid of him to think that he could, he realised. Helplessly, these last few days, he had watched in despair as Etty sank deeper into an ocean of grief from which he seemed unable to rescue her. He had found himself remembering the frequent swings of Etty's moods which had so often exasperated, but equally had delighted, him. But now the thought had crossed his mind that perhaps these moods had been a warning of darker things to come. He took a large sip of his whisky; there was no point in confiding these thoughts to Maude.

'Well it's not Etty, really. It's Alice.' He had the satisfaction of seeing Maude relax again in the big chair.

'Alice?'

'Etty is mourning deeply for Oswald. She doesn't want ... it's difficult for her ... It seems it's still too painful

for her to see much of the girl – for the moment, at least.'
He finished his explanation with a rush.

Maude sucked in her lips which could have meant
disapproval or understanding. Unsure which it was,
George waited but his sister said nothing.

'Alice is alone at Gwenfer, Maudie. I have to get back
to Etty and I feel I should not take the child with me at
the moment. I don't know what to do, and that's the crux
of it.'

'Has the child had mumps?'

'Mumps? I've no idea, Maude. I should have to ask her
nursemaid.'

'We have mumps here. Half the children on the estate
are down with it; two of mine have got it. If the others
catch it, it could be months before we are out of
quarantine and then I have to take Letitia to London for
her coming-out.'

'Letitia a debutante? Good God, is she that age
already? How time flies.'

'Yes, George, time does fly and nieces and nephews
grow up,' Maude said pointedly as if to blame him for his
absence. 'She's seventeen, past the mumps, I hope. We
have great expectations for her. But, as I was saying, if
Alice has had mumps, she can come immediately. If not,
then she should wait until it's all over, which will not be
until late summer at the earliest. Can her nursemaid
manage until then?'

'Then you'll take her?'

'But of course.'

'I don't know how long it will be for, Maudie. I don't
know how long this sadness of Etty's will last ...'
George shrugged his shoulders with a helpless expression.

'The duration is of no importance, George. For ever, if
necessary. Alice is our niece, it is our duty is it not,
Marmie?'

'Goes without saying George, old boy. Blood and all
that ...' Marmie said gruffly. He was saddened at

15

George's news; he had always had a soft spot for Etty, pretty little thing. Empty-headed, for sure, but who wanted brains in a woman? And what a bosom. Marmie wiped his forehead with a large white handkerchief – why, just thinking about the woman brought one out in a sweat . . .

'That's settled then.' Finally Maude gave George a large smile. What she would have liked to add was that she held nothing against Alice, the child could hardly help having Etty for a mother. Even more, she would have liked to say that she realised she was taking on the child for life. Maude had always suspected Etty's high spirits of being a sign of an overheated brain. But seeing the dejected slump of her brother's body, Maude for once refrained from speaking her mind. 'You'll stay the night, of course?' she said instead.

3

The sea was seeping through the rock. Reuben knew it was there; he could smell it. Despite the dust, the heat, men's sweat, the stench of their fear, it was there. Reuben's gut knotted another turn. For twenty-eight years, since as a lad of eleven he had gone proudly underground with his father, he had lived with this stomach-churning terror – every hour of every shift of every day that he had worked.

Tentatively he put his hand up to touch the rock above him to gauge the extent of the seepage.

'Thanks be to Jesus,' he muttered as he felt along the rock and decided it was safe to continue.

Each year it grew worse. As the lodes on land were exhausted so the tinners were burrowing further and further under the sea, the risks daily becoming greater, with only the rock between them and the mighty weight of the Atlantic, pounding above their heads. Reuben had no love for the sea. Like most men who lived close to it, he feared it. Reuben had known too many men who had drowned to regard the sea as anything but an enemy. There were tin levels that Reuben had worked where he could even hear the sea above him – those were the worst of all. He had complained to the mine captain who had laughed and told him it was only his fanciful nature, that no one could hear the water through the rock at that depth. Reuben knew better. It was just feet above him, waiting for him, biding its time until it would suck him away.

Reuben paused, adjusted the candle stuck on to his helmet with a lump of clay and shouted to his own son, Paul, who was new down the mine and newly keen, that it was croust time. Reuben opened up his kerchief and carefully holding the pasty it contained by its ridge, so as not to dirty the part to be eaten, divided the food. He peered at the innards but the light was too dull and so he sniffed it. He cursed with disgust as he smelled only onion and potato, no meat again. Paul tucked his share into his pocket and crawled back along the level to join his mates.

The older men sat in silence as they ate. They were exhausted, too exhausted for the jokes and chatter that the younger lads would be enjoying and which they had enjoyed when they were young and fresh like them.

Reuben sat alone to eat. He had never been popular. There had been a time, when he was younger, when he had cared about the way the others avoided him. But that was long ago; now it did not bother him. Still, after all this time, it puzzled him, though. It had nothing, he knew, to do with his work, in that he was respected and trusted. Sometimes he wondered if it was because of his fear of the sea and the fact that he did not join the others in the fishing. He would have liked to, when the red mullet came in and the whole community, called by the look-out, rushed to the boats and the beach, and the bonfires were lit and everyone joined in the excitement and the celebration. But Reuben's fear of the water was such that even to see it from the cliff top made him apprehensive. For Reuben knew that was where he was to die. But he did not have the words to explain And, had he been able to communicate his dread, he might have had to endure their laughter. Sod the lot of them, was Reuben's studied verdict on the problem.

He knew that time was running out for him. At nearly forty he had done well to keep going. He had had his share of accidents but nothing too serious, not like some of the poor bastards – legs crushed, senses knocked out of their heads from falls of rock. His time was nearly up, though; already his body complained at the intolerable contortions he had to demand of it. Each morning he found it harder to get going, to set his limbs moving. Stiff limbs meant risk – risk of not getting away from danger fast enough, risk of ending up entombed down here for eternity. Reuben was never sure which he hated more, the sea or the dark, damp mine. Not much to choose between them, he thought, as he wrapped the remains of his pasty in his kerchief and, in the dark, felt with his hands for a dry spot to store it. He called for Paul.

His pick swung. Hours to go and then the long crawl, the endless walk to the ladders, and the climb – some said 300 feet, others 400. Whichever it was, the climb was enough to finish a man at the end of his shift, Reuben thought. There were mines where the management had installed automatic man-machines for lifting the workers from the workface, but not this mine, not for them such luxury while that bastard Tregowan was the main shareholder.

The pick swung. If Reuben hated the mine and the sea, there was something he detested still more strongly. Tregowan. At the thought of the man Reuben spat a great gob of phlegm and dust. Reuben loathed Tregowan

18

and the other venturers. He hated the fat, rich pigs who drank and ate on the proceeds of his labour and his fear.

Reuben stood in the Miners' Arms, as usual slightly apart from the other men of his shift. They were all caked with dust and sweat. As the heat of the room permeated their damp clothes, from each man a haze of steam rose like plasma.

The room was long and narrow; the walls were stained a deep ochre yellow from years of tobacco smoke. A large oil lamp hanging in the centre of the room swung drunkenly in the draught each time the door opened. As it swung it gave off fumes which mingled with the smell of sweaty bodies beneath. The bar was a long trestle table on which stood a barrel. A couple of candles, stuck into empty bottles, glowed feebly, their light making little impact on the general gloom.

At one end the young miners played shove halfpenny, joked and arm-wrestled. At the other end, Reuben's shift huddled together and the talk was subdued and worried. Nathan Zennen had heard a rumour. Despite their fatigue they clustered around him, deep frowns on their grimy faces. The rumour had to be listened to: Nathan's wife's cousin's daughter worked at the mine captain's house.

''Twas Mrs Johnson's maid told the cook who told our Emmie that they'm talking of closing down the Creamer and Crossways levels,' Nathan announced, sucked deeply on his blackened pipe and waited for the effect of his news.

'What now? Why that would be the end of Bal Gwen.' There was a mutter of disbelief.

'They'd have to close ee down.'

'Seems like, 'less us gets more tin out or finds copper.'

'Bugger. There bain't no copper there. Dig as deep as you likes below them lodes, but that copper all be gone,' old Dibden growled and spat on to the sawdust-covered floor.

'What do they buggers think we'm doing down there? Scratching our arses? If there were more tin to be got out, wouldn't we be doing it?' Hendon Trelawn asked angrily. Reuben listened and took a swig of beer from his pint pot.

'What do they fat bastards know about mining, anyway? Counting money, oh aye, they'm good at counting money!' Nathan's spit joined Dibden's on the filthy floor.

'Them close they down, where them going to get the tin from then? Answer me that. We'm got to have tin. Everyone knows that. Trewlin and First lodes can't go on for ever,' Hendon said aggressively.

'Perhaps they'm moving out,' Nathan suggested darkly.

'Moving out . . . ?'

'Where to . . . ?'

'Don't ee talk draft . . .'

A chorus of noisy scepticism was raised at such an idea.

'Perhaps they'm thinking of putting their monies in Malaya, more like, where the poor chinkies work for less than we do,' Nathan explained.

'Malaya? I bain't heard of a mine called Malaya.'

''Tis a country, Hendon, you dolt. Out east somewhere. I's read about it. Seems there's tin and copper there a-plenty. And the labour is dirt cheap, truth be told,' Nathan explained patiently, sucking on his pipe all the while.

At this information from the only member of their group who could read, the men fell silent. You could not argue with the reading of things.

Reuben looked morosely at the jug of ale, his third, which he had until this moment been enjoying and which he had intended should last him the evening. Although he hated the mine, the thought of no Bal Gwen seemed impossible. The Bal had been there since anyone could remember. Reuben's father and grandfather had been down it before him. Like as not, every great-grandfather he had had since time began had worked that mine. The rhythmic booming of the pump engines reverberating across the moor had been the backdrop to all their lives. Its ceasing would be akin to the sea falling silent, Reuben thought, and downed the rest of his ale in one great draught.

'I'm off,' he grunted to no one in particular, not wishing to hear more.

Outside in the empty street, he leaned against the wall of the pub, looked up at the heavens and cursed God. If only he had been able to overcome his fear of the sea. The other miners had their boats; they could supplement their earnings with fishing. But Reuben's fear was too great and he had given his share of their boat to his brother, and had shrugged when Ishmail sold it to raise his fare to sail to America. Why had he not listened to his brother who had tried to persuade him to go with him, telling him that tin mining here was dying? But Reuben had only laughed, had said that this was where he was born and this was where he would die. It certainly looked as if he would die here now, but of starvation not of old age. 'Bloody Tregowan,' he cursed and aimed a stone at an emaciated dog which dared to cross his path. The stone missed, which made Reuben curse even louder. His mother had been right. He should have taken up his rightful option on the allotment, grown his own vegetables, raised a pig – as many did. Reuben's reasoning had been simple enough – he worked hard enough down the mine, he had no intention of breaking his back to dig the land, at the end of his shift. A reasonable attitude when work was plentiful, not so now with unemployment staring him in the face. Maybe, if he went to the mine captain, he could take out another option. He spat – that would mean waiting for dead men's shoes. 'Bastard Tregowan!' Reuben had felt a moment's pity for the man last month when he heard that Tregowan's lad had drowned. Now he was glad, now he hoped that Tregowan himself would fall into the sea and be sucked away.

He made his uncertain way down the cobbled street and struck off across the wastelands which led to the mine cottages set some way from the village. In other communities miners were respected craftsmen, but not on Tregowan's land. Here they were kept apart as if the village were ashamed of them.

The rickety front door crashed open as Reuben kicked it viciously, making the fragile hinges even more vulnerable. He blundered into the downstairs room of the two-room cottage.

'Food,' Reuben bellowed.

Nervously Ada Blewett ladled out some of the weak soup, more water than sustenance, from the large black saucepan which stood bubbling on the cast-iron range. She placed the bowl and slice of bread in front of her husband.

'What's that?' He glared across at his wife, her body heavy with child, her breasts sagging over the swollen belly, her face grey with fatigue, fear and lack of food.

'Soup,' she replied, nerves making her voice shake.

Reuben slid his spoon about the plate as if attempting to identify its contents. 'Soup, call this dish-water soup?' he shouted at his cowering wife. 'I work my bloody guts out and you expect me to eat slop like this.'

'But, Reuben, I've no money,' she wailed.

'Money! Money. You'll have less bloody money from what I hears.' He lifted the spoon to his mouth and sipped noisily. 'Christ!' He spat the contents of his mouth across the table. In one movement, spoon, plate and soup flew across the room. The plate caught Ada's forehead, the spoon her mouth, and the hot soup soaked into the clean but faded dress which strained over her stomach.

'It's got too much bloody salt in it, you useless bitch,' he roared. With one heave he overturned the table. Reuben lurched across the room at his wife who already had her arm up to protect her head from the blow she knew was coming, and had known would come even as Reuben sat in the pub.

Ada was used to Reuben. Every week, sometimes twice, he beat her. She waited like an animal, almost hardened to the pain after so many years of abuse. It was almost as if Ada did not mind. It was as if Ada accepted it, unquestioningly, as her lot. She understood her husband, understood his frustration – how hard he worked for so little in return. She knew the dreadful dangers he faced each day; she knew the fear that wormed inside her man. And she knew that each day as he grew older the fear was increasing. With so little money for them all, she could have been forgiven for resenting the amount he wasted on beer. She did not, she understood; what else was a man to do?

With her arm up Ada stood and waited for the ritual blow to fall. It caught the side of her head. Her two youngest sons, cowering in the corner of the room, screamed and their father aimed a kick at them. He stumbled as they escaped the room and his fury. Mary, his only daughter, stepped forward and with astonishing strength for one so thin attempted to stop her father.

'Leave my mam alone,' she screamed, pulling at her father's coat as blow upon blow rained down on her mother. Reuben turned and aimed his clenched fist at her.

The beating would probably have remained a normal one if Ada had not turned quickly and instinctively to protect her daughter. Her large belly unbalanced her and she fell to the floor. That was when Reuben began to kick her with his heavy boots.

Mercifully for Ada she lost consciousness almost at once and was spared the agony of further kicks aimed at

23

her stomach, as Reuben vented his resentment at the prospect of another mouth to feed.

In the half light Ada came to, to find her children screaming above her, fearing that she was dead. As Ada opened her eyes their screams subsided into sobs of relief. A great pain made her wince as she tried to move. The pain came again, and then again, sharper and more intense each time. Ada was sure that the child within her was fighting to live.

'Quick, Paul, get Mrs Rosslyn,' she gasped to her eldest son. The boy sped from the cottage and away across the rough land to the village.

Mrs Rosslyn did not arrive in time. A few great pains later Ada grasped Mary's hand.

'It's coming, girl, I can't hold it.'

'Oh, Mam, wait, please, wait,' Mary begged.

Ada screamed and from her body, slipping out on to the dirt floor, a baby emerged, three weeks early and crying louder than any child Ada had produced before.

'Mam,' Mary said with wonder. 'It's a girl.'

It was as if the sight of a sister after so many brothers made Mary come to life and take control. She ordered her brothers to stop standing there, gawping, and to go and get water from the pump in the alley. She took the scissors from the kitchen drawer and searched in the box on the shelf for some string. Quickly she tied the cord in two places and, with eyes closed, deftly sliced through the cord. She took a stiff sheet, grey with age, from the cupboard, gently wrapped the baby in it, and handed the child to her mother.

'Oh, Mam, a sister,' she said as if unable to believe such a miracle.

'If the poor mite lives,' Ada sighed.

'Her'll live, Mam, just listen to her bawling.' Mary laughed.

Ada slumped back, a fresh pain racking her body, as

Mrs Rosslyn bustled into the room in time to inspect the afterbirth.

Mrs Rosslyn and Mary tidied Ada as best they could and made a temporary bed for her on the floor of the overcrowded room. Both knew the futility of trying to wake Reuben who was sprawled across the only bed, in his own vomit.

'The bowl, Mary.' Ada pointed to the bowl on the mantel. Azure blue and with bright red roses painted on the side, it was the only pretty thing that Ada possessed. It reminded her of happier days when Reuben had loved her and had won it for her at the Feast Day fair at St Just. Mary handed her the bowl and took the baby in her arms. Wearily Ada searched for money.

'No, Mrs Blewett. I don't want no money. I did nothing. I can't charge for nothing. Mary here was the midwife, by rights, wasn't she?' The large, good-natured woman smiled at them both. 'Look at her, proper little mother already.'

Mary, thin but tall for her ten years, her lanky hair falling forward, sat on the end of the bed rocking the baby in her arms and crooning to it.

'What shall we call her, Mam?'

'You delivered her, Mary, you choose,' her mother urged.

Mary looked at the baby a long time, thoughtfully. 'I'd like to call her Ia.'

'That's a pretty name, Mary. You don't hear it used that often these days,' Mrs Rosslyn said. 'That's a saint's name I'll be bound.'

'It's pretty, isn't it? And she's going to be pretty too, so she ought to have a nice name.'

Mrs Rosslyn looked uncertainly at the baby. Beauty was not marked in the Blewett family, she thought to herself. She collected her bits and pieces, made her farewells, and bustled out as busily as she had come.

*

Ada was not to know then that the beating was the best thing that could have happened to her. That particular beating had rendered her sterile. In future, when Reuben clumsily sought her body in the night, she would be able to relax. There would be no more mouths to feed.

4

At Gwenfer, Alice, who had not had mumps, awaited her parents' summons to return to London. She knew nothing of her father's visit to Bodmin. But the spring became summer and the summer slid into early autumn and still the telegram did not come.

After the first few weeks Alice no longer missed her parents, who had always been shadowy figures in her life. She did not lack for company for she had Queenie and the two nursemaids, the housekeeper and the cook. And there were the housemaids, the footmen, the grooms, the gardeners. Alice had a small army of people to care for her and lavish attention upon her.

But Oswald was a different matter. Alice longed for her brother to return. Each night she prayed to God to let him come back to her. She would wander down to the sea, alone, and sit on her favourite rock – at a safe distance from the water, for one thing she had learned from Oswald's tragedy was that the sea that she loved was never to be trusted. Although Oswald's body lay in the vault of the church, Alice knew that his spirit was still here at the place he had been happiest. She knew this with a certainty which she never questioned. She would face the promontory from which Oswald had been swept away and she would talk to him. She told him what she had had to eat, what silly things Queenie had said, the jokes she had heard. She would talk of inconsequential things, but also she would tell him of her loneliness, and her worry that perhaps their parents had forgotten her.

Sometimes talking to him made her cry but she learned that, when she did so, she always felt much better afterwards. Gradually she came to terms with the fact that Oswald had gone for ever but, able to talk to him as she was, she began to feel happy again.

When in September a summons came it was not to her parents but to her uncle and aunt's house near Bodmin. Alice's bags were packed and the child was almost sick with excitement. She could not understand why Queenie and the maids were crying as they helped her into the coach. Alice was not crying, for Alice was away on a holiday.

Until the letter came, Alice had known little about these relations, except that they should never be spoken of. Now she learned in detail of an uncle and aunt and, better still, nine cousins, from Letitia, newly engaged, to Gladys, at five her own age. She had never known other children, apart from her brother, and, while she felt shy of meeting them, she was excited by the prospect of making friends. Amongst them there might be one who could take the place of Oswald.

At Loudon she was ushered into the drawing-room where everyone awaited her. She looked shyly at her uncle and aunt. She saw her uncle's kind face between the largest mutton-chop whiskers she had ever seen and she knew she liked him. She looked at her aunt, saw the tiny black eyes in the lard-like flesh, saw the thin mouth and the heavy jaw and knew that here was a person to fear.

She curtsied politely. She shook hands with her cousins. The older ones smiled kindly at her; Letitia even kissed her. The younger ones giggled and the youngest poked her tongue out behind her parents' back. Alice was nervous as she tried to answer her aunt's probing questions all of which seemed to do with her mother.

Alice was relieved when they were all dismissed from the drawing-room. She joined the line of the younger children who formed an orderly crocodile and, led by the nursery maid who had been waiting outside the room, made their way upstairs to the nursery wing.

The nursery here was not like her own. There were no pretty curtains at the windows, no pictures on the walls, and there seemed to be very few toys. The chairs were hard; the floors were bare boards. The bed she was shown was of iron with a coarse grey blanket on it, whereas her own bed was painted white and had pretty muslin curtains and a white eiderdown. To Alice it seemed a most depressing place. Worst of all was the chief nursemaid, heavily moustached, who stood waiting for them, looking as stern as her aunt.

They were served tea of bread and jam with water. No cake or tarts, no hot chocolate – Alice had had no idea that people could eat so miserably. She did not know that Maude Loudon had strict theories on bringing up children: she treated them rather as she did her horses – she had them fed, watered, mucked out. If they misbehaved, a good hard talking-to or, if necessary, the whip usually put matters right.

The meagre tea finished and cleared away, the children drifted off to their different pursuits. Alice was left alone with the two youngest. No sooner had the nursemaid slipped out of the room than Gladys, the youngest and the one with whom Alice most hoped to be friends, kicked her.

'We don't want you here,' Gladys lisped. 'Why have you come?'

'You know why she's here, you dunderhead. Her mother's gone raving mad and hates her, that's why she's here. Worse luck,' Gladys' brother Albert said in a sing-song voice.

Alice might not know what to say but she knew what to do. She looked from brother to sister unsure which to attack first, and decided on the brother. She jumped at him, kicked him hard, punched him as Oswald had taught her and knocked him to the ground where he lay with a look of intense surprise on his face. She then

28

swung at his sister, spat at her, scratched her face and tore a lump of hair out with one vicious tug.

'My mother is ill. She's not mad, and don't you dare say she is,' she hissed through clenched teeth. 'I'm not staying here,' she shouted as the door flew open and a gaggle of nursery staff swooped in, followed by the remaining brothers and sisters. The noise of screaming and arguing was so deafening that Alice began to be fearful of the chaos she had created.

'What did you do that for, you ungrateful little bitch,' the nursemaid said, grabbing her and painfully twisting her wrist. As quick as lightning Alice kicked the woman's shin, at the same time sinking her teeth into the hand which was hurting her. 'You spiteful little cow. You're coming to the mistress right now.'

Followed by the indignant family, Alice was pushed and pulled along the corridors to her aunt's room.

'Silence!' her aunt immediately ordered. Everyone stopped talking and shouting. 'Now will someone explain to me the reason for this cacophony?'

'She scratched me and pulled my hair. *And* she hit Albert,' Gladys accused.

'And why should she do a thing like that? You tell me, Alice.'

'I want to go home. I don't like it here.'

'You can't go home, this is your home now,' Maude explained patiently. 'I promised your father that you could come and live here whilst your mother is so ill – for ever if need be.'

It was this information that made Alice start to scream. She was shaken and shouted at, but still she screamed. The doctor was summoned and she screamed even louder. Eventually she was taken to the night nursery and, although it was still light, was unceremoniously put to bed. Only when the door closed did she stop screaming – exhausted and with a sore throat for her efforts. Looking about the room she wondered what was the worst thing she could do. She picked up the jug of water from the washstand and threw it over her bed. Then she wrapped herself in the blanket and lay on the floor, quietly sobbing her longing for Queenie.

In the morning, upon finding the bed damp, the nursery maid slapped her. Alice was beside herself with fury – no one had ever struck her. She hit the nursemaid back. The irate nurse sent for the senior nurse who, in turn, sent for her mistress. As soon as her aunt appeared, Alice began to scream again.

For several days Alice refused to eat, and screamed at every opportunity. At night she soaked her bed with the jug of water. Maude Loudon was at a loss. With all her experience of children and horses she found she could not control Alice. She complained to her husband that her brother should have told her his daughter was mad too. Nobody thought to ask the child what her problem was; all they did was to shout at her to behave herself. Even had they asked, it might have been impossible for Alice to explain – they might have understood her need for Queenie, and her fear that she would not get her parents' message when it came, but it was unlikely that Maude would have had the imagination to comprehend the child's need for Oswald's presence. He was always at Gwenfer but Alice found she could not reach him here.

At the end of a week a triumphant Alice, quiet now, but very tired, was returned to a jubilant Queenie.

'I'm never leaving you,' she vowed to her nursemaid. She settled back into her old routine. She waited.

5

On leaving Gwenfer Etty had travelled to London. When George arrived there he found consternation amongst the staff of the London house. Etty's behaviour was strange, to say the least. She would demand food at any time of the day or night. She might request roast beef for breakfast and then order bacon and eggs in the middle of the night. Rarely was the food eaten. She refused to sleep in her bed but instead spent the long nights sitting bolt upright on a chair, a fur rug wrapped about her – the strange thing was, as the maid remarked, that, when she dozed, she never fell off it. At times she would howl like an animal, so loudly that passers-by in the street would pause and look up at the windows of the mansion. She began to look drawn and ill.

Belowstairs her ladyship's madness became common talk. There were a few who were sorry for her but the majority, especially those who had daily dealings with her sharp tongue, felt it was time she pulled herself together. So difficult had she become that even the housekeeper and the steward – individuals far too grand normally to be involved with belowstairs gossip – had been heard to agree. But worse, the servants from other great houses had begun to gossip about her too, as rumour followed rumour on the belowstairs grapevines. One brave footman enquired of her staff just how mad Lady Tregowan was. It did the status of the Tregowan staff no good to be associated with such talk.

At first, because of the period of mourning required by society, only the household was aware of the extent of the problem. That was until the morning she decided to walk in the park, and in front of her horrified maid's stare began to undress, dancing across the lawns, throwing her discarded clothes as she did so, and singing in a strange tuneless wail. The maid quickly wrapped her own cloak about her mistress and hurried her home. That was when George decided it was better if he removed his wife to the privacy of his estate in Berkshire.

It seemed a good decision. Once at Fairhall, there was a slow but marked improvement in Etty's behaviour. For three weeks there had been no scenes. No one dared to say that perhaps the worst was over for fear that her

31

ladyship should suddenly deteriorate again. It was as if the entire household was holding its breath.

George allowed himself to hope when his wife had ordered her dressmaker to attend her. Admittedly she did not order new clothes in mauve and grey, as etiquette would now allow. Instead all her new clothes were in deep black – he feared her mourning might last indefinitely. But then she suggested a small dinner party, with a few of their closest friends. The evening passed without a hitch, Etty was really quite vivacious, he thought. But best of all, finally she had begun to talk about her daughter again.

Christmas was approaching and it was Etty who suggested that Alice should be sent for. Everyone, from her husband down to the scullery maid, awaited Alice's arrival as a hopeful sign that things were, at last, returning to normal. The household breathed again. A letter was dispatched to Queenie.

Alice was the only person who was not surprised – she had always known she would be sent for. With her retinue of nursemaids she caught the train for London. This time there was no private coach; instead they travelled in the public carriages just like everyone else. Queenie sat with a large basket on her lap, not trusting the net of the parcel rack. Queenie was always uneasy on these journeys, muttering that such speed was unnatural and bracing herself at each bend of the rails for them all to be flung to destruction. She never saw Brunel's great bridge across the Tamar. As the train approached the bridge, Queenie would close her eyes and not open them again until they were safely across on the other side.

Alice had no such fear and would have liked to be allowed to hang out of the window all the way to London. Queenie always vetoed such exciting notions with tales of people blinded by the cinders from the engine or, worse, having their heads lopped off by passing bridges.

Alice looked forward with pleasure to the moment when Queenie decided it was time to eat. Queenie would not countenance their getting off at Truro Station and eating there – 'I likes to know where my food's coming from' was the reason she gave. Instead, the contents of the big picnic basket were shared out between them. Alice thought this food and the fact of being allowed to eat with her fingers were far more fun than the formal meals she had when she travelled with her parents. At every station the guard would come to check that all was well, and each time he gave Alice a barley twist. This was by far the best way to travel, she decided.

At Fairhall Alice immediately examined her rooms. She was happy to be reunited with toys that, in the passing months, she had forgotten she possessed. She was surprised to find that her brother's fort had disappeared, together with its hundreds of lead soldiers. She was disappointed. On the journey she had planned how, at last, she could play with it. Oswald had never let her touch it, but now he could not stop her. There was no sign of his books, his butterfly net; even his rocking horse was absent.

In the stables she found her pony, grown fat from lack of exercise, but Oswald's black pony was nowhere to be seen. When she asked where he was, the groom looked sideways like a lizard, she thought, and then suddenly found something of great interest about his shoes while he sucked long and hard on a piece of straw.

'Sold,' he eventually lied gruffly. It was not up to him, he later reasoned with the other grooms, to tell the little girl that her mother had ordered the poor beast to be shot. Nor did Queenie tell her that all Oswald's toys had been made into a bonfire, watched by the estate children who looked on with awe and longing at such treasures. Seconds later, before their astonished eyes, the flames ate them, so that they later wondered if they had imagined the toys in the first place.

The toys had gone, and the pony had died, so that no other child should know happiness with them – that was Etty's mad reasoning.

On this first night in her parents' home, Queenie took great care in dressing Alice. Her petticoats had extra starch, the trim on her pantaloons had been ironed at least three times before it met with Queenie's approval. Her long blonde hair had suffered the curling tongs and now hung in large fat ringlets. It was dressed with a large red bow which matched exactly the sash of her new broderie anglaise dress.

Alice was shaking with anticipation. Not only at the thought of seeing her parents again, but, since it was Christmas Eve, she was hoping to find there a Christmas tree with presents piled high underneath it. Last year was the first time the family had followed the Queen's fashion and had a Christmas tree ablaze with candles. Alice had thought it the most beautiful thing she had ever seen, more beautiful, even, than the pile of presents at its base.

There was no tree. That was the first disappointment.

'Mama, Papa,' she called happily, her excitement far outweighing the shyness she normally felt with her parents. She raced across the wide drawing-room towards them.

Etty leaped from her seat, her hands shooting out defensively as if warning the child away. She stood rigid, an ugly grimace twisting her fine features.

'Etty. Quietly,' her husband said gently, stepping forward and putting out his hand to catch her arm. She reacted as if stung and angrily shook his hand away.

'Merry Christmas, Mama. I brought you a present from Penzance.' The child smiled innocently.

Etty said nothing but backed away from her daughter, who advanced on her holding out the prettily wrapped box she had decorated herself.

'Merry Christmas, Alice. It is lovely to have you here.' Her father stooped, swept her up into his arms and kissed her firmly on the cheek. Etty watched them, like an animal at bay, her lips pursing rhythmically as if preparing themselves for words she wanted to say.

'But, Papa, there's no Christmas tree. Last year we had a tree. Oswald and I loved it . . .'

From Etty issued a long, high-pitched shriek. She stared venomously at Alice for what seemed an age.

'Dear God, why could it not have been you?' Etty screamed and crashed to the floor, a heaving, sobbing heap of black crepe and jet beads.

George swore, strode quickly across the room and transferred Alice into the arms of Queenie who stood stock still, her face a mask of horror. As she took the child she seemed to come to life.

'There, there, my little angel. Don't ee fret. Queenie's got ee,' she whispered to Alice as she cuddled her to her ample breast, carried her out of the room and swept up the long staircase to the nurseries, her face red with indignation.

Such a fuss they made of Alice in the nurseries. She was given the biggest, most comfortable chair to sit on. She was given a whole box of chocolates, when normally not one chocolate was allowed before dinner. She sat straining her ears, trying to hear what Queenie was whispering to the other maids over at the far side of the room. It must be interesting, judging by their wide-eyed expressions. But all debate ceased when the door opened and her father strode into the nursery. The three women bobbed their curtsies.

'I've called for the doctor to come, Queenie.'

'Just as well, m'lord.' Queenie's indignation was emboldening her.

'As for Alice, I think it's better for all concerned if she returns to Gwenfer with you.'

'Yes, m'lord,' Queenie stiffly replied.

'In the morning, perhaps?'

'Tomorrow's Christmas,' she said staunchly. 'The little one has looked forward to it for weeks past.'

'I intend to return to London tonight. What would there be for her to do here?'

'She could join us, m'lord.'

'In the servants' hall?' George frowned at the irregularity of such an idea. He shook his head, unable to make a decision 'Do what you think best, Queenie. Make sure she's happy and has everything she requires. And don't let anything upset her. She's had enough disturbance.'

'I'll see to that with pleasure, m'lord.' Queenie was surprised by the concern which Lord Tregowan appeared, at last, to be showing for his child.

George turned towards the door. 'Just one more thing, Queenie. Keep her away from the first floor, do you understand?'

'Oh, m'lord!'

'Did I do something wrong, Papa?'

'No, Alice. Your mother is still unwell. I shall come and visit you in the spring. You will be safe with Queenie here.' He glanced almost guiltily across the room at the stout woman.

'I miss Oswald too,' Alice said quietly.

'Yes, yes, Alice, I'm sure you do. We all do,' George said, his voice strangely thick and muffled. Quickly he turned to the door.

Alice was given her supper and was then hurried off to bed. As she tucked her up Queenie told her of the fun they would have tomorrow, but Alice could only feel sad since it seemed that Christmas was not to be as she had hoped.

'I didn't mean to make my mother angry, Queenie.'

'Course ee didn't, my handsome. What a thing to say!'

'Does she wish that I had drowned?'

'My, what put such silly notions in your head? Course her didn't, my beauty. Her loves her little one. Just like Queenie loves ee.'

'Are you upset, Queenie?'

'Me upset? No. What gave ee that notion?'

'Because when you are upset or angry, you always sound Cornish. You don't otherwise.'

'Well I never. What a head you'm got on you,' Queenie laughed and bent to kiss her, then lit her night-light and softly closed the door behind her. Alice waited for a while and, when she judged the coast was clear, slipped from her bed, crept along the nursery corridor and listened at the door of Queenie's sitting-room. She heard not only Queenie but the butler and the housekeeper, too, which in itself was strange – she had never seen either of them on the nursery floor before.

'Miss my Christmas, go back tomorrow? Not likely, m'lord! I told him straight. Bloody cheek expecting us to travel all that way back tomorrow just as we'm got here. 'Tis not right. I told him plain.'

'I don't know what the others will say, having the child with us for our celebration.'

'There's naught else to be done, Mr Phillpott. Otherwise it means one of us missing out and I's not having that. We work hard looking after that little scrap all year as it is . . . what with the responsibility . . .' Alice heard mutterings of sympathy. 'In any case, Mr Phillpott, the rest'll do what ee tell they.'

'Poor little mite. It's so sad. She's such a sweet thing. Carrying on like that as if it were all her fault.' Alice heard the genteel voice of Mrs Duncan, their housekeeper. 'She probably wished she could do the same as she had done to that poor little pony.'

'Lawks, Mrs Duncan, you don't think she'd try anything, do ee? He did say as we'm not to go near the first floor. Her isn't violent, is her?'

'I wouldn't like to guarantee anything, Miss Penrose. That I wouldn't. I've never seen anything like these carryings-on in all my years in service, and that's the truth.'

37

'What's he thinking of? That's what I'd like to know.'

'What's he to do, Miss Penrose? Lock her up in an asylum – we all know what those places are like. It wouldn't be right for the likes of her. We all thought that Miss Alice's coming here would improve matters; but it seems to have made things worse – she hasn't been this bad for weeks.' There was a rustling as Phillpott leaned forward conspiratorially. 'In point of fact, it probably suits him at the moment. From what his valet says, it seems he's taken a fancy to a young actress from the Drury – no doubt that's where he's off tonight.' Phillpott spoke so softly that Alice had to strain very hard to hear, and found she did not really understand what they were saying.

'Good God, Mr Phillpott, what a pickle!'

'You can say that again, Miss Penrose.'

'What I was thinking coming up on that there train is, if she could fall for another baby, maybe that'd do the trick. Especially if it was a boy.'

Mrs Duncan snorted. 'Not much chance of that, Miss Penrose. Not with him anyway, not from what her maid tells me. You understand, the sheets . . .' Mrs Duncan coughed delicately into her handkerchief. 'Mind you, if she could get over this and go back to her old ways, it wouldn't matter who the father was if it did the trick, would it?'

'But the title, Mrs Duncan . . .' Mr Phillpott sounded shocked.

'I don't care about the title, Mr Phillpott. I don't give a fogle for the title or whose bastard gets it. What's to do, that's what I want to know?' Queenie huffed.

'You look as if you're dead stuck, Miss Penrose.'

'I don't mind that, Mrs Duncan. I love that little mite. But how can I bring her up to be a lady, I asks?'

'Care for another port, Miss Penrose?'

'That would be most welcome, Mr Phillpott, I must say. I'm still in a dreadful state, I's telling ee . . .'

Alice heard the two younger nursemaids returning up the back stairs from their supper. Quickly, but reluctantly, she slipped back to her bed. She lay staring at the shadows made by her night-light on the ceiling. It was strange. She felt dreadfully sad, with an ache inside her and a lump in her throat. But she could not cry. She thought she would like to cry . . .

The next morning, to her surprise, Alice awoke to find herself in Queenie's room and bed, Queenie's fat arms protectively about her. And, when she awoke, Queenie did not sound Cornish any more.

Chapter Two

1

For three years Alice's life at Gwenfer was much as before. The large household of staff remained but with only the young child to serve.

The main part of the house was shrouded with dust-sheets which were only removed when, each spring, her father came to visit. Then, for a short time, the house came to life, guests arrived for dinner, and there was hustle and bustle which excited Alice. She thought her father came to see her and she looked forward to these visits.

'Come to count his money at the mine more like,' she overheard Queenie say, and for the first time in her life she was angry with her and told her not to speak about her father in such a manner. Queenie, taken aback by Alice's spirited defence of her father, found herself apologising to the eight-year-old.

The first year he came, Alice asked after her mother. On his subsequent visits she did not enquire.

Once her father had departed for London, the dust-sheets were brought out again and the main house was shrouded in ghostly emptiness. Only in the nurseries and the servants' quarters was there any activity.

Alice's routine never varied. Each morning Queenie supervised her washing and dressing. Queenie had a cousin at St Just who made up her dresses from patterns Queenie had sent from London. Alice's wardrobes were full – with matching hats and jackets, dresses in muslin, cotton and velvet. Her buttoned boots were in calf, silk and satin. And Queenie spent hours sewing lace trim on to her petticoats and night-dresses.

Each Sunday the carriage waited at the front door and Alice and Queenie went to church. Alice was aware of the keen interest that was shown in her by the local community. She noticed the sly glances. She took pleasure in the envious stares of the other girls as they eyed her clothes. She, in turn, was appalled at how drably everyone but she was dressed. Alice felt very important on Sundays sitting alone in the Tregowan family pew.

Once a week they went to the vicarage for tea. Alice looked forward to this particular outing. The vicar had three children for her to play with. Their sitting-room was shabby but warm and comfortable and here the children could play as boisterously as they wished. Mrs Hadley, the vicar's wife, never seemed tired, never told them to be quiet, never pushed them away – she smiled benignly at them while she served tea to Queenie. Alice adored Mrs Hadley and wished that she could have been her mother.

Knowing how Alice felt about the family, Queenie had to steel herself to explain to Alice that the Hadleys would be moving away. The vicar had been promoted, she said as cheerfully as she could, and was off to help in Truro now that the splendid new cathedral was nearing completion. Alice burst into tears at the thought of this impending loss. She cried more at the prospect of losing Mrs Hadley than the children. It was only when Queenie pointed out that the new vicar and his wife would no doubt be equally kind and charming, probably with a large family too, that she stopped wailing.

Alice waited impatiently for the new vicar's first Sunday. In church, in the place of a young and smiling Mr Hadley, stood a thin, gaunt, middle-aged man, Mr Reekin. It seemed to Alice that Mr Hadley and Mr Reekin talked of different Gods and she had thought that there was only one. Mr Hadley had talked of a kind God, of a paradise they would all go to one day – which made Alice happy, able to think of Oswald already there and waiting for her. He preached of forgiveness and always of love. Mr Reekin, on the other hand, climbed into the pulpit and stood for a full minute as he sternly surveyed the assembled congregation for the first time. With a loud bang he brought his fist down on the pulpit, making the great golden eagle, whose outstretched wings held the giant Bible, shake. He began to shout and he glared at them so ferociously that they all began to shift uncomfortably in their hard seats. He hectored them about a vengeful God, of hell and damnation. He frightened Alice into rigidity and sowed in her young mind the seeds of many nightmares to come.

'Popery,' muttered Queenie. To Queenie, any deviation from the Low Church she regarded as the only form of worship was thus labelled with the bigotry of centuries. It was a foregone conclusion that such fiery evangelism would not be to Queenie's taste. She shepherded Alice up the aisle and through the subdued congregation. And those about her murmured agreement.

At the door the vicar waited, unsmiling, for his flock. His clothes were old and smelt of must. Looking at the grimy fingernails of the hand he proffered, Alice stubbornly put her hands behind her back and refused to shake it.

Worse was to come when they were invited to tea and for the first time they met Miss Reekin, the vicar's sister. She was thinner than her brother and with a bitter line where her lips should have been. She had the yellowed complexion of one who had spent many years ministering to the natives of the colonies. Alice sat beside her, bolt upright as she had been taught. The stuffing of the horsehair sofa penetrated through the three petticoats that Queenie made her wear. If the vicar smelt of must his sister smelt of vinegar, Alice thought. She was alone with them for, upon their arrival, Queenie had been summarily relegated to the kitchen for tea.

'Out to tea' should be fun, this was not. No sooner had the tea been poured than the questioning began. Did she read her Bible? Did she say her prayers? Did she give money for the heathens? Did she know her catechism? Did she know what happened to little girls who did not?

'No,' Alice said in a whisper, wishing Queenie was with her, and unable, in her nervousness, to swallow the dry cake.

'God takes note. He knows what all his creatures are doing. He is all-seeing.'

'Yes, Miss Reekin.'

'And if you transgress God's laws, Alice, what will become of you?'

'I don't know, Miss Reekin.'

'You will be doomed to hell, there to burn for all eternity.' Miss Reekin's thin body became rigid with emotion, her voice shrill 'Can you imagine that?'

'No, Miss Reekin.' Alice's voice shook with fear.

Miss Reekin crossed the sparsely furnished room and returned with a large book. It fell open with ease at a particular page. 'Look at that,' she ordered. Alice found herself confronted with a painting of hell in all its horror – the victims seeming to scream out of the page in their agony. She looked up, wide-eyed with terror, at her tormentor.

'Look closely, child. That is hell, Alice. That is where sinners go.'

'I don't want to go to hell, Miss Reekin. I've done nothing wrong.' Alice felt that at any moment she was about to cry.

'Think again, Alice. Are you sure? Have you not lied? Have you not taken something that was not yours?' the vicar intoned, loudly, as if he were still in the pulpit.

43

'No, I have not,' Alice's indignation at such a suggestion gave her back her voice. 'I'd never do anything like that. I'm a good girl. Queenie says so.'

'Beware of pride, Alice. Pride in yourself is an equal sin in the eyes of the Lord. A wicked sin.'

Brother and sister loomed above her, leaning towards her, their eyes glinting with a strange excitement. Alice jumped up, her plate clattered to the floor, and she pushed past them towards the door.

'I don't like it here! Where's Queenie?' she asked looking wildly about her. 'Queenie,' she wrenched the door open and shouted out into the hall. For one so large, Queenie could move quickly when needed, and this was one of those occasions. She appeared in the hall, took one look at Alice's tear-stained face, grabbed her coat and in one smooth movement slid her arms into it, and jammed her own hat on to her head.

'Time we was off,' she said in a tone of voice that brooked no argument. 'Now thank Miss Reekin and the vicar here for your nice tea.' Within seconds she had Alice safely outside the house and standing on the path. Queenie looked up at the windows, sniffed, and marched Alice down the path towards the carriage and there sat, her back ramrod stiff with anger. 'Now, you tell Queenie what happened.'

'They said I would burn in hell for ever and ever if I sinned. When I said I hadn't, that I was a good girl, they said saying that was a sin.'

'Lawks!'

'I won't, will I?'

'Course you won't, my handsome. Good girls like you go straight to heaven.'

'I don't like them, Queenie. They're strange, and they smell, and they frightened me.'

'Mad, more like. All that sun out in they there tropics got at them, no doubt. Well, that's settled. We shan't be going there again,' Queenie announced emphatically.

Alice settled herself comfortably against the woman's warm bulk, and hoped she could forget the picture.

Since they no longer went to tea, they also stopped going to church. Alice missed the admiring glances but this was well compensated for by not having to see the Reekins.

The vicar did not give up easily. Both he and his sister called, ostensibly to enquire after Alice's health since she had not been to church for over a month.

'We've been going to chapel,' Queenie lied.

'Do you think you should, Miss Penrose? After all the child was baptised in the church,' the vicar enquired coldly.

'His lordship has given me total responsibility for Alice,' Queenie replied, equally coldly.

'In matters temporal but surely not spiritual,' Miss Reekin said, tartly.

'I knows nothing of temporal nor spiritual. I just knows his lordship told me, "Look after her, Queenie, and keep her happy. Don't let nothing upset her." That's what he said and that's what I does.' Queenie stood, arms akimbo, in defiant mood.

'I think you go too far, Miss Penrose. I am certain Lord Tregowan did not mean you could decide on something as important as the child's religious upbringing,' the vicar lectured, legs astride, thumbs deeply buried in his waistcoat pockets.

Queenie's answer was a silent, angry glare.

'We shall be writing to his lordship, Miss Penrose. I think we should warn you,' Miss Reekin said with an unpleasant twitch to her mouth, which was the best she could manage in the way of a smile. 'Then we shall see what sort of authority you have.'

'Write as many letters as you like. I doubt as you'll get any replies. If that's all? I have duties to see to even if you don't.' And with one of her biggest sniffs, Queenie bustled from the room, leading Alice by the hand, and leaving the reverend pair speechless with anger.

To salve her conscience she did take Alice to the chapel for a couple of services. But the chapel was bare of pretty things to look at and Alice sensed that the glances at her clothes were ones of disapproval rather than envy. The nonconformists had never been part of Queenie's life nor had she ever bestowed her approval upon them, so after a couple of Sundays she announced that they would not be going any more. Instead, each day, Queenie read Alice stories from *A Child's Illustrated Bible*, where the pictures held no menace for her, and, at night, Queenie guided her through her prayers. This was to be the extent of Alice's religious instruction.

Once a month shopping trips were made to Penzance. After the quiet of Gwenfer Alice enjoyed the busyness of the town.

Their first visit was to Septimus Woodley, the family lawyer. The shelves on the walls of his dark office were covered with large deed-boxes, each with the Tregowan name upon it. He would give Queenie a brown envelope with money in it for Alice's needs. In return Queenie would give him the small ledger book she kept in which she noted all their expenses. Mr Woodley rapidly added the figures, checking that they tallied. Each time he did this with such speed that Alice would tell him how clever he was. This information always produced a smile from the normally dour man, who would open a drawer and produce a tin of barley sugar twists – just as she had known he would. Next, he always pretended to have lost the small velvet purse which he gave monthly to Alice. The purse contained a golden sovereign which was hers alone and Alice, giggling, would help him search his untidy desk for it. They always found it.

This visit over, Alice and Queenie would walk slowly down one side of Market Jew Street and then up the other. From there to Causewayhead – each shop window was carefully studied for any new additions since their last visit. They then retraced their steps to shops where an item might have taken their fancy. Alice was never content until she had spent all her money. She would buy material and trim for her doll's clothes, more shells for her growing collection, and always they visited Shakerley's the chemists to buy sweet-smelling soap and sachets. Amongst her monthly haul of shopping there were gifts for her nursemaids, chocolates for Mrs Malandine, the housekeeper at Gwenfer, and a bottle of sherry for Mrs Trelawn the cook, who had once confided to Alice that she was 'very partial to a drop'.

The shopping finished, they would go to Queenie's favourite restaurant, Chudleigh's, in the Greenmarket. It was always full of Queenie's friends and relations, for she belonged to one of the largest families in the area. Wherever they went – shop, tea-shop, hotel – always there was a member of the Penrose family. Queenie would sip her tea and gossip. Alice played with her shopping and, barely noticing, accepted a multitude of kisses and hugs.

Each time they went on these trips the coach would clatter past the church, through the cobblestoned village, past the granite school, with its bell tower, where Alice always craned her neck in the hope of seeing children at play. A couple of hundred yards outside the village they would roll past rows of back-to-back cottages, their fronts separated by a cobbled alley. From the coach the granite cottages, each with its thatched roof, tiny windows and small fenced front garden, looked pretty. There was always a handful of women gossiping and a gaggle of children playing. Alice liked to imagine how cosy life in one of those little cottages must be – sitting with a mother and father beside the glowing hearth, or playing with brothers and sisters.

'Who lives there?' she would often ask as they passed by.

'The miners. I've told you before often enough. Why do you always ask? Nasty rough folk, you don't want nothing to do with they,' was Queenie's invariable answer and she would pointedly look away from the cottages and study the view from the other side of the coach. Alice did not believe they were nasty folk; she believed that someone with whom Queenie had quarrelled must live there, for Queenie was always falling out with people.

After three years of this routine, it was the servants themselves who changed Alice's way of life. First, it was the footmen. With no house steward and no butler, they were unlikely to learn the skills of their trade, and could not hope for preferment. Idle and pleasant though their life at Gwenfer had become, they had to look to the future, and one after the other the footmen resigned, having found places in houses where the arrangements were more conventional.

The house steward in Berkshire, upon hearing of this exodus of staff, studied the books and decided that replacements were hardly necessary with only Miss Alice in residence. Footmen from one of the other Tregowan houses could travel down with his lordship on his annual visit.

Without footmen the housemaids became restless. Now there was no one to flirt with, there were no high jinks in the servants' hall. And how were any of them to achieve their goal of being ladies' maids, when there were no ladies to attend to? All but one decamped to other estates where there was more life and better prospects.

One of Alice's nursery maids eloped with a fisherman. This unsettled the second, who promptly ran away.

There was much blustering and posturing on Queenie's part. 'It wasn't right . . .' and 'How am I supposed to manage . . . ? and finally, 'That's it. There's nothing for it, I shall go meself . . .' But of course she did not go, how could she ever leave the child who had no one else to love her? she asked of anyone who would listen.

Mrs Malandine had no thought of leaving. She enjoyed the peace of Gwenfer and, middle-aged, she appreciated her light workload. Mrs Trelawn, the cook, was content enough. Apart from these two and Queenie, of the original indoor staff only one housemaid, a scullery maid, the boiler man and a boot boy were all that was left.

It was a logical progression, then, when Queenie, breathless from her ascent to the nurseries, carrying a heavy tray with Alice's lunch on it, declared:

'This is stupid.'

As Alice ate her lunch, she watched curiously as Queenie packed a selection of her clothes, a basket full of toys and her own possessions. Then they both decamped to the back of the house and the staff quarters.

It was an arrangement which Alice enjoyed from the very start. The huge kitchen with its vast black and brass range was a warm and friendly place. Along the length of one wall was a great pine dresser whose many drawers held all manner of exciting treasures – fish slices, nutmeg graters, lemon presses, flour sifters, string; these objects now became Alice's preferred playthings. On this dresser were arranged, in descending order of volume, a long line of copper jelly moulds which Alice delighted in being allowed to clean. She would sit at the long, scrubbed pine table watching Mrs Trelawn as she deftly prepared the roasts, filled the pies, stuffed the birds, marinaded the fish and made the pastry for the meals they all ate together in the stillroom. It was not long before Alice was helping her. She learned to roll the pastry, then to make it. She decorated the pies. She cored the apples and sliced them thin as paper, she chopped the mint, she made the gingerbread men.

Of an evening, in the servants' hall, Alice would play Snap with the boot boy, or with Flo the remaining maid. She taught them spillikins, and together they would draw. Queenie taught her to sew. And, best of all, after supper, each evening Mrs Malandine would teach the nine-year-old Alice to read and write.

Her bedroom was situated directly over the servants' hall, so that at night, as she waited for sleep, she could hear the others talking and laughing beneath her. It was a much cosier way to live.

2

Alice had lived contentedly with the servants for four years.

Ia Blewett was seven. She did not know she was, birthdays were of no significance in her environment. What mattered was one's size and strength and how soon it would be before one could go out to work.

The family was smaller now. Paul the eldest had sailed away to America to join his Uncle Ishmail. For over a year they had waited for news. Ia's mother had fretted and worried about her son, not knowing if he lived or died. But finally the longed-for letter had arrived. They had had to wait for Mary to return from her work in the Miners' Arms, to learn the contents, for Mary was the only one of them who could read or write. She had to read the letter aloud so many times that it soon became creased and tattered. It was a short letter, misspelled, full of crossings-out and ink blots, but, importantly, it told them that Paul was well. He was no longer mining but working in a factory.

'What's a factory, Mam?' Ia asked.

'I'm not sure, Ia, but it do sound grand, don't it?'

Then, the previous week, her beloved sister Mary, after a violent argument and a beating from her father, had run away, no one knew where, and that added to the burden of worry which beset her mother.

Isaac, her youngest brother, had been ill for months with a bad chest, and was now too weak to work. He spent his days lying on a bed in the small sitting-room, coughing and sweating.

The miners' fears had been realised and the mine was long since closed. A mere handful of men were kept to work on maintenance and the futile task of trying to save the workings from flooding. Only Jacob, in the family, was lucky enough to find employment at the mine.

Ia played in the dust in the alleyway between the cottages oblivious of the flies which buzzed about her. With a stick she was drawing patterns in the soil and thinking about her family. If only she were older and bigger, then, with Mary gone, she could have taken her sister's cleaning job at the pub, which would have helped. Instead, she felt useless as she watched her mother becoming older and more bent each month. The stick swished across the pattern she had carefully made. She hated her father. She hated him so much that she wished that the roof-fall, which had smashed his legs to pulp five years ago, had killed him. It was her father's fault that Mary had left. Mary had always been kind to Ia and looked after her: it had been almost like having two mothers. It was Mary who had helped their mother the most, in the house and with money. Not like Jacob who, Ia knew, lied about his money to their mother. The lack of money was always with them. Occasionally her mother would manage to get some washing to do, the odd scrubbing job, but most of the time hunger stalked the family.

When the accident had first happened, Ia had felt sorry for her father as he lay groaning on the bed, the deep wounds in his legs causing him agony as the pus had formed and evil-smelling liquid seeped through the bandages. There had even been talk that one leg might have to be cut off. But it had been saved. After three months Reuben was back on his feet, with a fearful crutch to support him, which he used as a weapon to beat them all. Since he could no longer work, all he did was shout at his family, lie in bed or hobble up to the pub with the few pennies he had beaten out of his wife.

Ia looked closely at a great black beetle, lying in the dirt on its back, its legs waving impotently in the air. She looked at the beetle and thought of squashing it, just as she wished she had the strength to squash her father. She lifted her foot, paused, then bent down and gently turned the beetle right side up, smiling as it scuttled away.

'Ia?' her mother called. Ia turned into the cottage. 'Ia, I'm off to the big house. I'll be back for tea. Tell your dad, when 'e gets back.'

'Why you'm going there?' Ia asked curiously. She had seen the gates that led to the big house, but she had never seen the building itself.

'I've a job for the day. They needs someone to do some scrubbing.'

'Can I come?'

'No. I don't know as how they'd be too pleased if I turned up with a young 'un.'

Ia watched her mother walk up the alleyway and make off across the scrubland towards the cliff. She settled back to drawing with her stick, but within five minutes she was bored and set off in the direction her mother had taken.

She slipped through the gates and into the lush undergrowth so that no one could see her. She could hear the sea far below her, and made her way towards it.

Down in the cove Alice sat upon her rock and faced the sea, her back to the land. She was twelve and had reached that point in childhood when the adult she was to become made fleeting appearances on her child's face. It was evident that she was going to be beautiful, that her bone structure was fine, that her profile would be perfect and that her large grey eyes were to be one of her best features. Her hair was thick and silvery blonde and she wore it long and loose. But her fine eyes wore a guarded expression. This was no longer the clear-eyed, innocent look one would have expected in a girl who had wanted for nothing. But then Alice had wanted. She had never suffered materially, but as she had grown so she had become more aware of her parents' abandonment of her. Apart from Queenie, who in the world loved her? Now that so little work was done in the mine, her father had ceased his annual visits; in fact he had not been for two years. Alice had had to come to terms with the fact that Queenie had been right and it was only the mine he had come to see, not her.

Living as she did with the servants, she had learned many things. She had discovered that her father was rich. The mines were his. Six mines he owned, in total. Four he had closed, including Bal Gwen; only Bal Etty and Bal Fair, twenty miles away from here, were being worked. She had learned that her father was feared and hated. This information had not shocked her, when she had overheard it, it was as if they talked of a stranger – for she no longer knew him. She had learned how to recognise, from the sly glance in her direction, when a choice piece of gossip was about to emerge, and know that it would never be said in front of her. So she had resumed her old habit of listening at doors. In that way she had learned that her mother was now totally mad, kept locked in a wing of Fairhall with iron bars at the window. Having the run of Gwenfer's library she had read *Jane Eyre*; she knew of Mrs Rochester's suffering and would wonder how much her mother suffered. Occasionally her feared Aunt Maude visited. It was on one of these visits that she overheard her aunt and Queenie discussing the possibility of madness being handed down to the children of such people and since then, at night, she would lie awake and wonder if she, too, one day might go mad and be locked up with keepers as her mother was. She would wonder what it was like to be mad and completely distanced from people – and she feared it.

She disliked these tours of inspection by her aunt. Luckily for them all, Maude never came unannounced, so there was always time for the nurseries to be returned to a semblance of normality. Beds were made up, clothes hung in wardrobes, books lay open as if recently left there. Aunt Maude would never have countenanced her niece living in the back quarters with the servants. Alice quickly realised that the visits were not out of interest or affection but were another duty which her aunt demanded of herself. She would arrive in a flurry, inspect Alice's rooms, her wardrobe, check her exercise books and question her on her health and routine. She would bustle through the kitchens, inspect the provisions, take a dish of tea and then prepare to be off. On each visit she punctiliously asked Alice if she would not prefer to move to Loudon and each time Alice, politely, declined.

Upon her return to Loudon, Maude would write a lengthy report to her brother George. Each time she wrote she would point out that the lack of a governess for the child was a scandal, that Alice seemed bright and appeared to be educating herself – a situation which could not continue. Each time George Tregowan meant to do something about a governess but each time something else turned up and he was able to forget. For the truth was that George did not like to dwell too long on the matter of his daughter. The last time he had seen her she had looked far too much as Etty had done before the madness of her mind had penetrated her beauty and reduced her to a scrawny, prematurely aged harridan. Once he had visited Etty daily. Now he could not bring himself to enter her rooms – bare of furniture, lest she hurt herself – with their barred windows, and the sour smell of incontinence. In fact he was rarely in Berkshire these days; in London, he found it easier to forget about Etty. There he had the distractions of society and a succession of comely women who were only too happy to flirt with him and even to clamber into his bed.

Thus, over the years, the happy-go-lucky child slowly disappeared. Alice became quieter and more thoughtful. She would spend hours in her father's library, reading anything and everything. She enjoyed learning. She now took little interest in clothes, and though she would dress up for her aunt's visits, she was happiest in the plain cotton dresses which Queenie, on her insistence, made for her. Around her shoulders she would wrap a shawl as each day, rain or shine, she went walking or riding. A stranger seeing her could have been forgiven for thinking that she was a servant's daughter rather than Lord Tregowan's.

Alice was not discontented, however. She had everything she wanted at Gwenfer; she was happiest there, and could no longer see the point of going elsewhere. She could walk and ride for miles and still be on her father's land and she had the friendship of the staff. Alice loved the countryside. She liked nothing better than to sit quietly and watch the merlin jinking in the air, the pitched battles of the seagulls with the crows. She enticed the squirrels to eat out of her hands. And, unknown to the huntsmen who regularly hunted the cliff top, she had made friends with a fox which she regularly supplied with food.

Her favourite spot of all was still the great slab of rock, at the entrance of the cove, its base indented and smoothed by the years of rain-water washing upon it. From here she could see the two things she loved the most – her house and the sea.

She had long ago forgiven the sea for taking Oswald. In a strange way she understood. How could the sea have resisted him as he must have looked that morning, with the bright sunlight playing in his hair, which the wind must have lifted, and his beautiful face alight with excitement as he fished from forbidden territory? Of course, the sea would have wanted him all to itself, she thought.

This July morning, Alice looked at Oswald's rock and sighed.

'Oh, Oswald, how different everything could have been . . .' she said aloud.

The sound of a twig breaking made her turn round. Standing under a large rhododendron 30 feet from her, stood a child, with dirty and bedraggled hair which, had it been washed, would have been as blonde as Alice's own. The frightened eyes were the same grey as Alice's. Her feet were bare and her legs, beneath the short, tattered skirt, were scratched and bloody with weeping sores. The young girl looked shyly at Alice, reminding her of a startled animal. Then, abruptly, she shook her head, flicking her long hair over her shoulder in an almost defiant gesture and stood and stared at her.

'Hallo, who are you?' Alice broke the silence but the girl stood there sullenly. 'Why don't you come and sit here? It looks hard but it's quite comfortable.' Gently Alice held out her hands. She was unused to company and normally did not search it out, but she found that she wanted this girl to join her. Still the child stood silently but one foot was lifted in the air, wavering uncertainly as if she might be about to take a step. 'Would you like some of my lunch?' Alice unwrapped her bundle and spread the food on the rock, using the kerchief as a table-cloth. 'Do come . . .' The girl looked at the food and then at Alice and then back to the food. Alice picked up a soft buttered roll and held it towards her, very much as she did when coaxing her fox. As quick as lightning the girl ran forward, grabbed the food, stuffed it into her mouth and then began to back away. 'Have some cheese,' Alice said quietly. Again the girl darted forward, her movements as swift as a dragonfly's. This time Alice hung on to the cheese. 'Sit down. Then you can have it.' Obediently the child sat on the ground at the foot of the rock. As the cheese followed the bread with equal speed Alice laughed, unaware, in her ignorance of hunger, of its dreadful pain. A chicken breast was quickly gulped. 'My goodness, you are hungry, aren't you?' The child nodded. 'You have the cake. I'm not hungry.' Alice was serious now, at last realising that the little girl was starving.

The girl stared with disbelief at the sponge, golden yellow and oozing with strawberry jam and clotted cream. She took the cake and looked at it suspiciously, sniffed it, and then a small pink tongue gingerly licked at the jam. Glancing up at Alice she smiled with delight at the taste, stuffed the cake into her mouth, swallowed and then burped, loudly.

'You should say, "I beg your pardon",' said Alice, sounding like a miniature Mrs Malandine.

'Why?'

'Because people do when they make a rude noise like that. It's polite.'

'What's rude about it?'

'Well, it just is, you see.' Alice was less sure of herself now.

Ia shrugged her shoulders, grinning broadly. 'Beg your pardon,' she said in her heavily accented voice.

There was another silence. Alice was not used to making conversation and knew even less how to talk to other children.

'My name's Alice. What's yours?' she said abruptly.

'Ia.'

'Ia? I've never heard that name before.'

'It's mine,' Ia said defensively.

'Yes, yes, I'm sure it is. You're very pretty,' she added quickly, afraid that her new acquaintance might run away.'

'Is I? Mind ee, so's ee.'

'Thank you.' Alice blushed with pleasure at the compliment. 'But you're supposed to say *you*.'

'What's wrong with ee? Everyone says un.'

'Nothing's wrong with it except it's not right,' Alice laughed at her own confused sentence. 'Where do you live?' she asked, preferring to change a subject on which she was getting muddled.

'Up along.' Ia jerked her head towards the cliffs.

'What are you doing here?' Alice asked and immediately regretted the question as she saw Ia's alarmed expression.

'I don't mean no harm. I wanted to see where me mam was. She's scrubbing up at the big house.' Ia played with the sand, looking slyly up at Alice as if making up her mind about something. 'Who was you talking to just now? There bain't no one else here.'

'Talking? Me?' Alice blushed fiercely. For a moment she said nothing, unsure how the child would react to the truth. She looked closely at Ia who stared solemnly back, her grey eyes alert with intelligence and what Alice thought was a look of sympathy. 'My brother, Oswald, that's who I was talking to.'

'Has 'e gone to America? My Paul, 'e's gone there, but sometimes I talks to 'e. I stands up on the cliff and I tells him everything.'

'No, my brother is dead. A long time ago . . .'

'That's not nice for ee.' Ia stood up suddenly, brushing the crumbs from her skirt. 'I's going now,' she announced.

'Do you have to go?' Alice was disappointed.

'Got ter see me dad.' And as swiftly as she had appeared she left.

Left on her own, Alice felt suddenly lonely, a strangely new emotion for her. Thoughtfully she made her way back to the house. She entered the back door. In the stone passageway was a woman on hands and knees, scrubbing the floor. She was unaware of Alice's approach as she concentrated on pushing the large scrubbing brush rhythmically back and forth, with hands which were red and chapped. She paused only to push back a wispy strand of hair and to reload the brush with soap from the hard, bright yellow cake beside her. Alice stepped neatly past the bucket, and was half-way along the passage before she stopped and turned back.

'Excuse me, are you Ia's mother?'

Abruptly the woman stopped scrubbing and nervously dried her hands on her overall. Once again she brushed away the recalcitrant hair and, with tired eyes full of alarm, looked up at Alice.

'I be,' she replied in a soft, uncertain voice. 'She bain't been no trouble? I told her her wasn't to come . . .' She scrambled quickly to her feet.

'No, she's been no trouble. I was curious, that was all. I shared my lunch with her.'

'That was kind of ee, miss. But don't ee let her be a trouble.'

'Well,' Alice said awkwardly, unsure now what to say. 'Mrs Trelawn is expecting me . . .' and she sidled away along the wall, confused by the bob the woman had given her – no one else ever did so – and almost fled to the safety of the kitchen.

How like her Ia she was, and yet how unlike, Ada Blewett thought as she picked up her scrubbing brush.

'If right were right . . .' she said softly and resumed her task.

'What's the name of the woman scrubbing the passage, Queenie?' Alice asked as she burst into the kitchen.

'That's Ada Blewett.'

'She's so thin.'

'They're all thin,' Mrs Trelawn, the ample cook, laughed; thinness was never likely to be her problem.

'I met her daughter Ia. She's starving, Queenie. You should have seen how fast she ate my lunch. It gave her indigestion.'

59

'They're all starving, more's the pity. It's the mine closing down – there's no other work to be had. I gather her husband was hurt in a mining accident and she's other children too.' Queenie sucked her tea through her teeth and wondered whether to have another slice of seed cake. 'These are hard times, Alice,' she sighed, as she decided to have another slice after all.

'Could we not give Mrs Blewett more work?'

'I try to share what work there is amongst the women, Alice,' Mrs Malandine explained. 'It wouldn't be fair to single one of them out, now would it?'

'I don't know the others, Mrs Malandine,' Alice said briskly. 'I'm going to feed them.' She crossed to the dresser and from a drawer pulled a table-cloth which she opened out on the pine table. From a speechless Queenie she took the remains of the seed cake and placed it on the cloth. A loaf of bread followed and some biscuits from the tin with a picture of Queen Victoria's Golden Jubilee which she and Queenie had bought last year. She raced out to the cold room and took two chickens from the shelves. In the dairy she selected a slab of freshly churned butter and a lump of cheese. She returned to the kitchen with her haul.

'I'm going to need a basket for all this.'

'How about some vegetables then, or maybe a bottle of his lordship's best port?'

'What a splendid idea.' In her excitement Alice was oblivious to the sarcasm in the cook's voice as she raced from the kitchen. 'Where's the port kept?' she asked, returning with a basket full of fresh vegetables.

'No, Alice. Mrs Trelawn was only joking. Port's not for the likes of they. 'Twouldn't do at all, would it, Mrs Malandine?'

'Reuben Blewett would drink the lot and then probably murder them all,' Mrs Malandine retorted.

'You can't give them all that food, my girl. That's our food . . .' Mrs Trelawn's face was twisted with concern.

But Alice was not listening as she humped the heavy basket out of the kitchen. 'Queenie, stop the child, won't you? I'd planned they chickens for our supper tonight.'

'She's a lesson to learn here, Mrs Trelawn. Don't you fret,' Queenie replied placidly. Heaving herself from the chair she lumbered across the kitchen to listen at the door.

Mrs Blewett had laboriously worked her way along the passage nearer to the kitchen. Alice plonked the heavy basket down on the stone floor beside her.

'Mrs Blewett, would you like to take this food back for your children and husband?' Alice said with a sweet smile. Ada looked up at her with her exhausted eyes. She stared at the basket. As she looked from the food back to Alice, her hand shot to her mouth, then tentatively towards the food and finally dropped sharply to her side.

'Thank ee, miss, but no thank ee.'

'I beg your pardon?'

'I said no thank ee.'

'You don't want it? But I want to help you.'

'We'll manage, miss. My wages is sufficient. I knows you means well, miss. But we Blewetts don't take charity from no one.'

'Please, Mrs Blewett, I didn't mean to offend you. It's just that Ia and I . . .' Alice was close to tears.

The woman sank back on to her knees and continued with her scrubbing but not before taking a last lingering look at the basket. Back and forth went the scrubbing brush. Alice stood silent and perplexed.

'Perhaps, in that case, you could manage to work for us more often, Mrs Blewett. Say every day?' Ada looked up at her sharply. 'You would be doing me a favour, Mrs Blewett. There's so much to do and poor Queenie gets so tired.'

Ada smiled. 'Why thank ee, miss. That would suit very well.'

Alice lugged the basket back into the kitchen. All was

silent. Mrs Trelawn was making a cake. Mrs Malandine was reading *The Cornishman*. Queenie was innocently concentrating on her mending. No one said a word.

'I'd better put these back, then,' Alice said despondently and walked slowly to the pantries.

Queenie winked at the other two women. 'That's a lesson the young woman's learned well. The gentry do have a hard time understanding pride and charity.'

3

Each day Alice packed enough lunch for two and sat waiting on her rock in the hot summer sun. But Ia did not come. There were days when Alice, strangely, felt that the girl was there watching her secretly. She always left the food, and the next day it had always gone, but, she reasoned, it could have been the wild animals which ate it.

Alice had all but given up hope when, silently like a wood spirit, Ia appeared and stood, at a distance, solemnly staring at her.

'Hallo,' said Alice shyly. 'I thought you weren't coming back. I've got a strawberry tart for you today.' Alice held out her hand in welcome. This time, Ia skipped towards her and fell with enthusiasm upon the food which she gobbled rapidly. She leaned back against the rock, and belched, loudly.

'Beg your pardon,' she enunciated carefully, grinning broadly and obviously very pleased with herself.

'How old are you, Ia?'

'Dunno.'

'You must know how old you are. Everybody does. I'm twelve. I shall be thirteen next February.'

'Next year I'll be going-to-work sort of age.'

'You'll be too young to work, next year,' Alice said, shocked.

'No, I won't!' Ia replied defensively.

'What will you do?'

'Dunno. Should have gone to mine, but there bain't no work there now. Perhaps up at the pub, I dunno.'

'When's your birthday?'

'I bain't got one of they.'

'Don't be silly, everyone has a birthday – with presents.'

'What's a present?'

'It's something nice someone gives you, because they like you. Especially on your birthday.'

Ia laughed loudly. 'Well, I bain't had one of they, I can tell ee.'

'*You*, not ee,' Alice said automatically. 'If you haven't got a birthday, then we'll have to make you one. Today is the eighth of July, so we'll make today your birthday.'

'Thank *you*,' Ia said carefully.

'And this –' Alice picked up the book of Tennyson's poems that she had been reading earlier. She searched in her basket for a pencil. 'And this will be your first present.' On the flyleaf she wrote 'To Ia on the occasion of her birthday from her friend, Alice' and beside it she printed the date. She handed Ia the book. With wonderment the girl fingered the finely marbled endpapers, sniffed the fine calf binding and traced the gold of the title.

'Cor, miss. Thank ee, I means *you*,' she giggled. "Tis a beautiful thing,' and she clutched the book to her thin chest. 'Do you work?'

'No, only at my books.'

'When'll you start?'

'Never, I suppose.'

'Everyone works.'

'Not everyone, Ia.'

'Don't be daftie, you have to work to eat. How do you eat?'

'My father sends money.'

'Ah, I sees. Where's he work?'

'He doesn't either.'

'Well, I never did. That's strange.' Ia shook her head, perplexed 'Which way's America?' she asked suddenly.

'Out that way, a long way.' Alice pointed to the west. 'A long way across the sea.'

'How far beyond the Brisons?'

'Thousands of miles past the Brisons. All those miles means days in a ship.'

'That's where I's going, one day. When you's old enough you can go in they ships, don't cost a penny.'

'Really? Who pays the fare?'

'Dunno. But it's true. That's where I think our Mary's gone. You get on they boats and then when you'm gets there you'm gets a job. Some go to Australia, but me, I's going to America. Our Paul's there. He says you don't get the pain there.'

'What pain?'

'This un,' and Ia pointed to her stomach. 'Mind ee, I bain't got 'e today,' she giggled.

'Can you read?'

'I's learning. Sometimes I goes to the school, but I hates that Mr Featherstone. 'E 'urts when 'e 'its,' she said with feeling.

'He hits you?'

'If you'm gets it wrong. Then 'e 'its, and it bloody 'urts.'

'Ia!' Alice was shocked at her use of a word she had only ever heard the groom use. 'That's dreadful.'

'Mind ee, 'e don't hurt like me dad does.'

'Your father hits you too?'

''E 'its everyone. I 'ates 'im. I wish 'e'd die,' Ia said in a quiet voice which made the statement all the more chilling.

'That's a terrible thing to say, Ia. Really wicked. You know what the Bible says?'

'No, what do ee say?'

'"Honour thy father and thy mother,"' Alice quoted and then blushed as she realised that she could hardly claim to honour her own parents. Nowadays, apart from a quick prayer at night to keep them safe, she rarely thought about them. But then, she consoled herself, she did not go around wishing them dead. 'And the Bible isn't a person, it's a book, God's book. Now you're going to say you haven't seen a bible.' Alice feared she sounded pompous and giggled nervously.

'That's right. Bain't you clever?' Ia grinned mischievously.

'Do you go to church?'

'Not likely. That place smells, so does that there vicar, a 'orrid man. And all them dead bodies – my mam says it's not a healthy place to be.'

Alice laughed. 'Would you like me to teach you?'

'What?'

'All the things I know.'

'What do you know?'

'Not much but more than you,' Alice said with a smile. She found that she desperately wanted Ia to agree for she wanted this girl to be her friend. It was as if she suddenly realised how lonely she was.

'What do I need learning for?'

'It could help you when you get to America.'

'Do you think so?' Ia leaned forward eagerly.

'Of course. If you can read and write you're sure to get a better job. In a shop maybe.'

'A shop? I'd like that. When will ee teach me?'

'We'll start tomorrow, you can come when your mother comes. Go right to the top of the house, and I'll be waiting for you in the schoolroom.'

That evening Alice was busy. She swept out the schoolroom, unused since she and Oswald had played at schools, just as she planned to do with Ia. She sorted out her first reading books, her alphabet bricks, the abacus.

She sharpened pencils, sorted out exercise books, and at the back of the cupboard found the old globe on which she would be able to show Ia where America was.

The next morning, Alice waited, seated behind the big governess's desk. In front of her lay the register she had ruled out last night, with Ia's name neatly printed in it. Her wait was interrupted by a commotion out on the landing.

'You're not going in there,' she heard Queenie shout.

'I is. Miss Alice said as how I could.'

Alice hurried to the door. 'Queenie, let her in. I've promised to teach her all I know.'

'Not looking like that she isn't. Look at her,' Queenie said, holding Ia at arm's length. 'She's filthy, and she smells. She's probably alive.'

'Don't be silly, Queenie, of course she's alive.'

'Lice, young woman. That's what I'm referring to. Come here,' and she yanked Ia towards her. Deftly Queenie parted the hair on Ia's scalp. 'Just as I thought. Look.' Queenie sucked in her cheeks with disapproval. Alice stepped forward and peered at Ia's head. Between the strands of hair an army of lice were in the process of scattering in panic away from the light and Queenie's prying fingers. 'Alive she is.' Her fat fingers delved into the hair and emerged triumphantly squeezing one of the offending creatures.

'Queenie?' Alice looked at her nursemaid in horror. 'Isn't there something we can do?'

'Come with me.' Still holding Ia at arm's length Queenie marched towards the old night nursery. 'Get Flo and Sal to bring up hot water,' she ordered.

Alice ran downstairs in search of the housemaid and scullery maid. Together the three young women man-handled the large kettles, which were always bubbling on the range, up the back stairs to the nurseries.

'Sal, get the bath and you, Flo, get the towels.' Queenie was issuing orders like a general.

The housemaid looked with disgust at Ia who stood, shivering with fear in the corner as far away as she could get from Queenie. 'I begs your pardon, Queenie, but I's not waiting on the likes of her,' Flo said with a defiant sniff.

'You'll do as you're told, my girl.'

'I won't.'

'Flo, do as Queenie says. Now,' Alice interrupted. Flo was so surprised at the authority in Alice's voice that she dropped her a quick bob before scuttling out of the room with Sal, both complaining bitterly, to fetch the bath and towels.

A large towel was laid on the floor, the bath placed on top and the hot water poured in.

'We'll need plenty more hot water, girls. And the large enamel jug in the washhouse,' Queenie instructed. This time they did as they were told, without argument, if ungraciously. Queenie bustled out to return a few minutes later with a pile of Alice's old clothes, which she began to hold up against Ia, gauging the size.

'Right, Ia. You take your clothes off.'

'I bain't taking my clothes off for no one, so there,' Ia said, clutching her thin arms about her as if to protect her ragged dress.

'You can have a nice new dress if you do,' Alice said temptingly in a wheedling tone.

'I likes this un.'

'But it's got holes in it.'

'What if it has,' Ia snapped defiantly.

'If you want to continue to see Miss Alice, you take them clothes off and you has a bath. Otherwise, out,' and Queenie pointed dramatically to the door. Silently Ia removed her clothes.

'Oh, Queenie, look.' Alice pointed. Across Ia's thin buttocks were livid lash marks. All over her body sores glistened with pus. 'Oh, Queenie,' Alice repeated, distressed.

'It's cruel, he'm a wicked man. Poor little love.' Queenie's cheeks puffed out with indignation. 'You've been scratching they there flea bites, haven't you?' Ia nodded miserably. 'Alice, you go to the door, and take the water from the other two. I don't want them in here gawping and talking about what they see. None of their business.'

Ia complained loudly when she was finally lifted into the water and screamed shrilly when Queenie attacked her hair with the Lysol. Alice was kept busy ferrying the jugs of water across to the bath. Half an hour later Ia, wrapped in a towel, sat with her head over a piece of newspaper while Queenie patiently combed her hair with a fine-toothed comb. The lice and nits fell in hundreds from her head; those still alive Queenie pounced on with relish, almost, Alice thought, as if the woman were enjoying the grisly task. The hair cleaned to her satisfaction, Queenie gently spread calamine lotion on the sores and an hour later a transformed Ia stood before them, in one of Alice's old dresses.

Ia's blonde hair shone and cascaded on to her shoulders. She was beautiful. Ia stood in front of the long mirror, and squealed with delight when, for the first time ever, she saw herself.

'Bain't I blooming lovely?' She smiled up at them.

That night Queenie sat Alice down for a serious talk. Alice knew it was to be serious for only on such occasions were Queenie's hands devoid of sewing or a slice of cake. Instead her fingers were spread out on the table before her.

'You should forget her, Alice. I know you mean kindly but it's cruel really.'

'I don't understand.'

'She's gone home to that hovel they live in. She's already reinfected with lice, I'll be bound. It isn't right,

Alice, what you're planning on doing, especially with the likes of her . . .'

'I know what's not right, Queenie. It's not right that she has those things in her hair and mine is always clean. It's not right for me to have so many clothes when she has rags. It really is not right that I don't know what it's like to be hungry and she knows nothing else.' Alice sat back surprised at the depth of her feelings.

'Be that as may be,' said Queenie, equally surprised by Alice's outburst, 'but don't you see, my girl, there's nothing you can do? There's always been them as have and them as don't. Just thank your lucky stars that you're one of the fortunate ones. You can't change the way of things. No one can.'

'I can't change the world, I realise that. But I can help one little part of the world – and that's Ia.'

'And what about all this reading and writing you're planning on? What good do you think that's going to do the girl, filling her head with useless nonsense like that? She's got to live in her world. She can't live in yours.'

'But if I teach her, then when she goes to America on the boats she'll get a better job.'

'The boats? Dear God, my girl, them boats take out girls to be skivvies and that's if they're lucky. Most, as far as I hear, end up . . . but never you mind. That's not for your ears. And what about them lice, I asks you? You'll think twice if you catch them from her, now won't you?'

'We can check her hair every day. We can keep washing it. Keep her clothes clean. I'll do it, I'll look after her. Don't you see, Queenie, I've got to help her, I need to do something.'

The older woman sighed. 'Bless you, Alice. You're a good child. I've often worried as maybe, me not taking you to the church and all, you might turn out a wrong un. I was foolish to think such a thing. Seems you could teach that vicar and his sister a thing or two about Christian goodness.' She looked at Alice's anxious expression. 'Oh, very well, if it makes you happy. But it'll end in tears, mark my words.'

Ia was clever. She learned at a speed that surprised Alice who was now kept busy in the evenings reading up her books so that she had something new to teach Ia the next day. As Ia learned, so did Alice. Some days they were in the schoolroom, on others they would wander the cliff top or along the shore – investigating the rock pools, watching and identifying the birds, picking wild flowers to press.

Alice no longer felt the need to speak to Oswald these days. Ia completely filled the void he had left. She found that she could not remember a time when Ia was not a part of her life. She had forgotten the emptiness she had suffered before Ia had wandered into her life and into her heart. For she had grown to love her only friend. They both longed to be allowed to live together and not to have to part each evening. But each time Alice tentatively suggested that Ia should leave her family and move to Gwenfer, Queenie emphatically quashed the notion. As they looked alike, so their minds came to be in tune. What one liked or disliked so did the other. They knew they looked like sisters and many were the times they wished they were.

Ia, at first intimidated by the large house, now felt completely at home in it, almost as if it were her own – a situation which did not meet with approval belowstairs. Like a little governess, Alice taught her how to eat correctly and Ia learned that food could be a pleasure instead of merely a necessity. She celebrated Christmas with Alice at Gwenfer. For the first time she had presents to open, lovingly wrapped by Alice, and while Alice was out riding Ia mounted the pressed flowers they had collected, determined, too, to have something to give.

Ia soon knew and quickly appreciated the feel of velvet, silk and fine linen, and when they went shopping it was she not Alice who could immediately recognise inferior quality. She took pleasure not just in looking at but in stroking the delicate bone china and took to wandering about the house, her head on one side, solemnly studying the paintings. She became used to the feeling of space which the large rooms of Gwenfer gave her. More and more she felt that Gwenfer was her true home, not the stinking hovel on the cliff which she returned to at night. In Ia was sown and nurtured a love and a need for beautiful things and in her also grew realisation of how unfair life was, in that Alice should have so much and she so little.

For three more summers the two were inseparable.

4

Then one day, in late summer, Ia did not come. Alice waited patiently for an hour and then walked down to the rock to see if she were there. The thought that Ia might be ill was of no comfort. If it were illness which was keeping Ia away, it must be serious, for she had never missed a day in the past. She had come with frequent colds. She had hobbled in with a sprained ankle. One day she had arrived stiff from one of her father's beatings and with a black eye which, to Alice's admiration, she had joked about.

'Has Mrs Blewett said that Ia is unwell?' Alice asked on the second day.

'That woman hasn't been to work for over a fortnight, Mrs Malandine is not pleased, that she isn't,' Queenie replied.

'Then I must go and see.'

'You'll do no such thing. Remember what happened to you the last time you went snooping around up there? Stones, that's what you got. No, you keep well away.'

The next day Alice could wait no longer. Pretending

that she was going to her rock, instead she slipped around to the stables and saddled her horse.

As she approached the cottages Alice's heart was thumping beneath her cotton dress. Queenie had not exaggerated: the last time she had come here she had been humiliated. That had been long before she met Ia. That day she had been riding the cliff top and out of curiosity had decided to take a closer look at the cottages which had always fascinated her as a small child. At the sound of her horse, a gang of boys had appeared. She had smiled politely and said, 'How do you do.' At first they had sidled towards her with what she took to be an equal curiosity. She was not prepared for the stone which came flying through the air and missed her head by inches. Angrily she had ordered them to stop and had announced who she was. At this information a hail of stones was unleashed. Her horse's ears pricked back, and he reared in panic. It had taken all her strength to stay in the saddle. She wheeled the horse around and galloped back to the stables. She had not intended to tell Queenie, but one of the grooms had found out and told her. That night, still shaken by the experience, she had promised never to go there again.

Now, here she was, disobeying her nurse and wondering if perhaps she should have asked the groom to accompany her.

No gang of boys appeared as she nervously coaxed her horse towards the cottages. The horse remembered their last outing too for, ten yards short of the houses, he stopped dead and refused to move an inch further. She slipped down from the saddle, tethered him to a field gate and walked the rest of the way.

Everything was quiet. There were no groups of women gossiping, no children playing. The smell was the first thing she noticed. A fetid animal smell, but not at all like the pleasant smells of the stables and home farm she was used to.

She knew which house was Ia's, the girl had written her a story about her home; 'third alley along and four houses in' she had written in her round and confident hand. Alice entered the third alley and tripped on a rock. When she looked down, she saw with horror the reason for the stench. In the middle of the alleyway ran a gully which, after six weeks of drought, was dry of water. Instead, all along the runnel lay human faeces crawling with maggots and flies. With an expression of disgust, Alice lifted her skirts high; at each step she took, a cloud of flies billowed up in front of her before settling back to their greedy task. Two dogs, unnaturally still, watched her, struck with inertia by the heat of the sun. Only their eyes watched her progress down the alley.

She knocked on the door of the fourth house. There was no reply. She pushed the door. As it creaked and gave way, she stepped gingerly into the darkness. The stench of human excreta overwhelmed her. She stepped quickly outside, and leaned against the door jamb fighting the sudden wave of nausea. She gasped for fresh air but instead inhaled the contaminated air of the alleyway. She gagged. Frantically she searched her pocket for her handkerchief, and with relief breathed in its sweet lavender scent. She re-entered the cottage, the tiny scrap of lace held to her nose her only protection against the evil odour.

As Alice's eyes became accustomed to the gloom, she saw that she was standing on dirt, dirt packed hard by years of footsteps, but dirt none the less. The only floor covering was a tiny rag rug which stood in front of the small greasy range in which no fire was lit. On the mantel stood an azure-coloured bowl that reminded Alice of the colour the sea sometimes was in the cove. Crudely painted with red roses, it was the only ornament of any sort that she could see. To one side was a rickety table, one leg of which was supported by a brick. Around the table stood up-ended wooden boxes which served as chairs. A small cupboard, one door askew on a torn hinge, was the only other piece of furniture. The tiny, glassless window was covered by a scrap of sacking, light filtering weakly through its holes. There was no sink, but a bowl was piled high with dirty crockery on which a bluebottle lazily harvested what it could find. The buzzing fly was the only sound until, from above her head, Alice heard a cough.

Carefully she climbed the stairs conscious of how broken and dangerous they were. Tears of distress filled her eyes at the conditions in which she found her friend living. She should have known, she should have been here to check, she should never have allowed Ia to live like this. She would take her home with her, she thought, as cautiously she picked her way to the top of the stairs where there was almost no light.

In the bedroom the smell was worse. Her handkerchief, still clamped firmly to her mouth and nose, could offer no further protection – the stench had won. In this room there was no window, only the darkness which made it seem she was stepping through a blanket.

'Ia,' she whispered. 'Ia,' she repeated urgently.

'Alice, is that you? Thank God you've come.'

'Where are you? I can't see anything.'

'Where's the bloody candle?' She heard Ia curse as she fumbled in the blackness. There was the sound of a tinder-box being struck and the stub of a candle was lit. 'Can't keep it on long, 'tis the only one left,' Ia's voice hoarsely whispered.

In the flickering light of the candle Ia's face peered up at Alice. But it did not look like Ia. Her face was gaunt, her eyes blazing with fever. Around her mouth fresh sores glistened and her expression was twisted with pain.

'Ia, what's wrong with you?'

'My head's the worst, Alice. I feel there's a little man in there with a hammer.' Ia attempted to laugh, but she winced instead. 'And my guts hurt something chronic.

74

Look.' Weakly she lifted her shift and Alice looked down on Ia's thin form, her stomach swollen, the skin taut like a drum. 'I can't shit, Alice – begging your pardon – if only I could.' She tried to smile. 'Jacob, he never stops . . . Christ, my poor bloody head.'

'Hush, Ia, don't try to talk. Lie still, there's a good girl.'

In reply, Ia hauled herself on to one elbow, the effort making her pant. 'It's my mum, Alice, she's real poorly, she's been groaning there for days now, and Isaac's very bad . . .'

'Lie still, Ia. I'll see to everything,' Alice said with a confidence she was far from feeling. She picked up the candle and crept across the room. Holding it above her head, she looked down on Isaac. Isaac, always the thinnest and weakest of them all, was now even thinner. A bright red rash dotted his chest and stomach. She covered him gently with the one blanket which he threw back fretfully. Beside him on the bed Ada Blewett tossed feverishly, clawing at the air with hands like a bird's talons.

'Reuben, Reuben, is that you?' The clawlike hand, hot with fever, grabbed Alice's arm. 'Oh, Reuben . . .' she sighed.

'It's Alice, Mrs Blewett. I'll get help.'

'I knew you would help, Reuben. I knew you'd come back . . .'

'But, Mrs Blewett . . .'

'I'll take the blue one, Reuben, the one with the roses painted on the side. Oh, 'tis a pretty bowl, Reuben my love. You'm good to me, Reuben. Give that bowl to me here.' She let go of Alice's arm and held her hands out, cupped ready.

'Here you are, Ada,' Alice said, placing the imaginary bowl into the woman's hands. Ada's fingers closed gently about it. She began to croon, rocking her hands and then holding them up to the candle-light as if examining the bowl.

''Tis the most beautiful bowl in the world, I'll keep 'im always. I loves you, Reuben.' She smiled up at Alice, but in her agony the smile became a grimace.

'I love you too, Ada,' Alice knew she had to reply. Quietly the woman went back to sleep. Alice became aware that her skirt was damp. She looked down to see that the sheet was covered in pea-green faeces, flecked with blood. She wanted to be sick. She slipped from the bed. As she turned, holding her candle aloft again, she looked down upon the dead face of Jacob.

'Ia, where's your father?' Alice whispered urgently.

Ia's grey eyes focused on Alice, and through the pain and the fever flashed with anger. 'Up the pub, where else?'

'Be patient, Ia, be brave. I'll be back as soon as I can.' Alice raced down the stairs, this time ignoring their fragility. She looked about the room for a tap; there was not one to be seen. Grasping the only saucepan she could find, she went outside. Up the alleyway a boy was lounging against the door of a cottage, idly throwing pebbles at one of the dogs which was too weak to move.

'You,' Alice shouted at him, 'come here.' He sidled suspiciously towards her. 'Where can I find water?' Lazily he pointed up the alley to a pump. 'Can you ride?' He nodded. 'I've no money on me, but if you'll go to the big house and ask Miss Penrose to come here, quickly, I'll give you sixpence.' He turned his back and began to walk away. 'A shilling, I'll give you a shilling if you'll go.' At mention of the shilling he turned to face her again. 'Thank you,' Alice said with relief. 'Tell Miss Penrose, I need sheets, soap and towels, some buckets. Tell her to bring broth.' The boy walked away from her. 'Candles, lots of candles. And matches . . .' she yelled at his disappearing form. She relaxed only when she heard the sound of her horse's hooves.

Alice stood in front of the water pump in dismay. Beneath it was a trough full of stagnant green water with a dead rat floating on the surface. At her feet lay a cat, half eaten by maggots. She swished the flies away from her eyes. With the dead cat in the way there was nowhere to put her saucepan. She balanced it on the adjoining wall which led to a privy from which oozed a thick, malevolently smelling stream. With both hands and much effort she pumped the handle up and down. It seemed an age before any water appeared, at first a small brown trickle and then faster, until finally the water emerged cool and crystal clear. With one hand she kept the pump going, holding the saucepan under it with the other.

She ran back to the cottage with the water slopping about in the pan. She looked frantically about her for kindling to make a fire but could see none. In desperation she ripped the filthy peg rug into strips – it was so old it tore easily. Then she began to break up the boxes from around the table. She needed matches. She looked anxiously up the stairs: Ia had used the tinder-box, so there were obviously no matches, but she had no idea how a tinder-box was used. With a shaking hand she pushed her hair back out of her eyes. She should go upstairs and comfort Ia until Queenie came, but she could not. She was afraid. She was afraid of their suffering – but most of all she was afraid of Jacob, lying dead. Despising her own weakness she forced herself to start climbing the stairs, just as a commotion outside announced the arrival of Queenie. With relief Alice ran down and went outside to greet her.

'Thank God you were so quick,' Alice said.

'What a pigsty,' Queenie complained, as she looked about her with distaste, clutching her skirts high out of the filth. 'I thought I told you you weren't to come here? This lad fair made my heart stop. I thought something had happened to you. Don't you ever disobey me again, young woman, else . . .'

Alice did not give her time to finish the threat. 'Please, Queenie, not now. It's the Blewetts. I think that Jacob's dead. And Ia's ill and in such pain. And her mother, her mother's gone mad ...' She clutched at her nurse, dragging her towards the cottage.

'Lawks, what a to-do. Well, one thing's clear, this is no place for you, Alice. You get on that there horse and you goes straight home.'

'I'm staying here.'

'You'll do as I says.' Queenie puffed up with indignation.

'Where am I to put these, Miss Penrose?' The coachman panted towards them, weighed down by his load of bedding.

'You'm owe me a shilling.' The boy popped his head around the coachman's bulk, clutching a large bucket in his hand.

'You bugger off.' Queenie aimed a cuff at the lad.

'Have either of you got a shilling? Have you, Mr George?'

'A shilling? You promised him a shilling, you'm more money than sense, that's to be sure.' Queenie's voice rose dangerously, and Alice heard the Cornish creeping in, a sure sign that her nursemaid was growing agitated. She rounded on the boy. 'If Miss Alice promised you'm a shilling, then a shilling is what you'm'll get, but you'm going to have to wait for it. Now be off with you. Put the blankets in there, Mr George.' She indicated the open doorway of Ia's cottage and followed him in.

With Queenie's stout body, the large coachman, Alice, and the paraphernalia they had brought with them, the room was full to overflowing. 'Now, Mr George, you stays here a minute, while I find out what's what.'

Under Queenie's weight the steps groaned ominously and Alice and the coachman both held their breath as the nurse made her way with effort up the narrow stairs. Two minutes later she was making the difficult descent.

''Tis bad,' she announced, sucking in her cheeks with concentration. 'Mr George, if you'd be good enough to go and fetch Mr Penwith.'

'Mr Penwith?' the coachman said in an almost inaudible whisper.

'Yes, one of they boys, stiff as a poker. Looks to me as if he won't be the last to go neither,' she said ominously. 'Then when you'm done that, if you'd be so kind as to go back to the house. I've a mighty list of things we'll be needing. Get soap, Lysol, scrubbing brushes, new mattresses – three will be sufficient – bring oil lamps, kindling, coal, bread, milk and some cheese – this'll be hungry work. And bring Sal back with you, not Flo, she'ms too stuck up for this 'ere.' The coachman on his way, she turned to Alice. 'Now, you get along to the doctor and get him to come here quick. Then you go to the chemist and ask him for a good dose of ipecacuanha. Understand?' Alice nodded and turned to go.

'Alice.' The girl looked back at Queenie. 'You did right to come, my lovely.'

Outside the cottage the boy was still holding Alice's horse and muttering about his shilling. For a moment she thought he had ideas of holding the horse for ransom. Tetchily she grabbed the reins and was soon urging the horse up the road to the village. Her first call was at the chemist's. She ordered the ipecacuanha, and told Mr Phillips to dispense it quickly. Then she asked for ten shillings in small change in such a peremptory way that it quite unnerved Phillips who was used to a far more gentle maid than this. He was quick with the medicine and just as quick to enter the ten shillings in his ledger. She wrapped the money in her handkerchief – she felt she might have need of it before the day was out.

Three minutes later she was pounding on the doctor's door. She did not know the doctor since she had never been seriously ill in her life. But she had seen him at Gwenfer, once when Flo had had a fever and on another occasion when a groom had sprained his leg. The door was opened by a young maid, little more than a child.

'The doctor is having his lunch. If you would kindly leave a message he will see to you when he has the time,' she said in the sing-song voice of one who had learned such a message by heart.

'I need to see him now.' Alice pushed past the maid into the dark hallway. 'Which is the dining-room?'

Such behaviour was beyond the girl's experience. She stood open-mouthed and speechless with horror as Alice pushed open door after door until she found the dining-room.

Dr Flinders, fat and florid, was enjoying his boiled mutton. A large napkin billowed over his corpulent frame, mutton fat dribbled down among the valleys of his many chins. At the other end of the table his plump wife was similarly engrossed but with better success at containing the meat juices in her mouth.

'Miss Tregowan,' the doctor said, lumbering to his feet, surprise etched on his face.

'Oh, Doctor Flinders, thank goodness you are here. I need you urgently. It's an emergency.'

'An emergency, Miss Tregowan?' he said, concerned.

'Yes, doctor, the Blewett family. I fear they are all dying.'

The doctor subsided into his chair and picked up his knife and fork as if about to eat again.

'Doctor, you must come now!'

Carefully he laid down his cutlery and looked across the table at Alice. 'The Blewetts of this world can wait, Miss Tregowan.'

'If you don't come it could be too late.'

'When I've finished my luncheon, Miss Tregowan, and after I have made my other calls.'

'But, you don't understand . . .'

'My husband understands very well, young woman. If the Blewetts aren't dead yet another couple of hours will

80

make little difference. If they should die, they would have done so in any case,' Mrs Flinders said in a rich baritone voice which rumbled up from her full, well-fed stomach.

'How do you know? Are you a doctor too, Mrs Flinders?' Alice snapped angrily.

'Well, really! Such rudeness.'

From his voluminous coat the doctor produced a small blue notebook. He opened it, one fat finger going down a long list of names. He looked up at Alice. 'The Blewetts are not part of the medicine scheme,' he said smugly.

'What medicine scheme?'

'Each family pays an insurance of sixpence a month. The Blewetts appear not to have bothered. They are not my patients.'

'If Mr Blewett did not pay the insurance, then why should his wife and children suffer just because he is stupid?'

'Unfortunately, that is the way of the world.'

'So you won't see them?'

'I did not say that, Miss Tregowan. I said after my luncheon and after I have seen my regular patients.'

'Good God, if it's money you are worrying about, take this,' and angrily she threw the ten shillings' worth of small change on to the table from where they rolled all over the floor.

'Really!' Mrs Flinders exclaimed again, her vocabulary apparently distilled into this one indignant word.

'It's not the money, Miss Tregowan,' Doctor Flinders blustered, 'it's the principle of the matter.'

'I have no patience with your principles, doctor. But I'll tell you this, if you don't come this instant, I shall make certain that you are no longer the mine doctor. I realise there's little work for you at the mine at the moment, but I have heard that my father is considering reopening it. Then you'd be sorry.' Alice was lying: she knew nothing of her father's plans.

Muttering ominously, the doctor hauled himself to his

feet. He collected his bag, ignoring his wife's objections, and, with a thunderous expression, let himself out of the house and climbed into the buggy which stood ready harnessed in the roadway.

Alice and the doctor had barely cleared the main street of the village when the doctor's door opened again. Mrs Flinders bustled out and walked quickly to the vicarage to report this most interesting morsel of gossip to her friend Miss Reekin.

The doctor remained with the patients less than five minutes. He emerged, wiping the sweat from his brow with a large handkerchief, to confront Alice.

'There's nothing to do there, Miss Tregowan. I suggest you take yourself to the church – that is if you know where it is – and pray for your strange choice of friends,' he said pointedly.

'Doctor!' But the doctor was hurrying up the alleyway back to his buggy and his boiled mutton.

A red-faced puffing Queenie appeared. 'You useless old fart,' she screeched at his retreating form.

5

'What do we do now?' Alice asked anxiously as they watched the doctor disappear.

'Calls hisself a doctor! We'd be better off with the farrier.' Queenie's normal high complexion was made redder by her anger.

'Did he say what is wrong with them?'

'I'm afeared 'tis as I thought. 'Tis the typhoid.'

'Why didn't he treat them?'

'He says they'm too far gone.'

'But doctors can't just leave patients to die.'

'That old buffoon can. Do you think you can ride to St Just? There's a new doctor there, a Doctor Salmon. He's young I hears, but then beggars can't be choosers.'

As soon as Alice was away, Queenie and Sal fell to. With the help of the coachman they cleared out the pathetic bits of furniture from the downstairs room. They laid the Gwenfer mattresses on newspaper, for want of anything better, and made them up with fresh clean sheets. One by one they washed the patients, dressed them in clean night-clothes, and Mr George gently carried them down the rickety stairs to be laid on the clean beds.

'Get they dirty mattresses and all that soiled bedding outside, Sal. Then burn the bloody lot.'

On the waste ground a huge bonfire was soon burning.

Reuben Blewett lurched past it towards his cottage outside which his furniture, such as it was, was stacked.

'Cor, bugger. What you'm doing?' he demanded of Queenie.

'What you should, by rights, be doing, Reuben Blewett, looking after your family instead of being at the Miners' Arms getting drunk,' Queenie snapped back.

'You bloody interfering old bag of blubber.'

'You stop that filthy talk, or I'll wash your mouth out with carbolic soap, and that's a promise.'

'You'm no right. They'm my things.' Reuben had stopped blustering and was now wailing.

'They things'll come to no harm here. No one's likely to steal them.' She looked sternly at the man, noted the unfocused eyes, the sway, and decided that he was in no fit state to take in the information that his son was dead and his wife likely to follow. 'Now out of my way, Reuben. You better find a quiet corner to sleep that there beer off. When you'm in a fit state, I'll tell ee what's what.'

Through the haze of alcohol which was befuddling his brain, Reuben looked at the stout, large-boned woman in front of him. He would dearly have liked to hit her, but even in his drunkenness he realised that Queenie was not the sort of woman he could hit and get away with it. He stared at her blearily, and slouched away. When he was a good distance away he turned and let forth a string of expletives in her direction. 'Sticks and stones,' shouted Queenie in response. Let the interfering busybody get on with it, he muttered to himself and made his way unsteadily across to the field where he fell asleep beneath the hedge.

In the cottage, Queenie gently bathed Ia's brow. 'At least you can breathe a bit more free in here, my beauty,' she comforted the child.

Mr Penwith's cart arrived, with a coffin on the back. Assisted by his son he unloaded the coffin and they entered the cottage. Penwith looked enquiringly at Queenie who, using her large body to screen Ia from the sight, nodded up the stairs.

It had been difficult for the men to get the wooden box up the stairs, it was almost impossible to get it down. Mr Penwith slipped, the coffin teetered, Queenie moved quickly to help steady it, and Ia saw the fearful sight. She screamed. In a trice Queenie turned back to comfort her.

'There, there, my lovely. Don't you take on. 'Tis only a silly old box.' She hugged the girl against her large soft bosom.

'No. It's not true. Not my Isaac,' Ia cried out in despair.

'No, my love, it bain't your Isaac. See there he be, sleeping like a little angel.' She pointed across to the adjacent mattress.

'Jacob?' Ia looked up at Queenie. Her eyes, already full of the pain of her illness, clouded with the added pain of grief.

'I'm afraid so, Ia. We was too late to help 'e.'

'But Jacob's so strong. And he works, Queenie, he works for all of us . . .' Ia began to sob as the men finally managed to manoeuvre outside the plain pine box containing her brother.

Alice arrived back from St Just with the new doctor, in time to see Jacob being loaded on to the back of the cart.

'Where are you taking him?'

'I've a shed back of my place. I'll put 'e there. Miss Penrose said as to get him out of the house.'

'A shed? You can't put him in a shed.'

''Tis the only place for the likes of 'e, what with nowhere in the house like,' Mr Penwith replied politely.

'Take him to the church. Put him in the Lady Chapel,' Alice ordered.

'The church? I can't put 'e there. What's the vicar going to say?'

'I'll deal with the vicar, Mr Penwith.'

The doctor and Queenie emerged from the cottage; both looked grave.

'Is it the typhoid, doctor?' Alice asked.

'I'm afraid so, Miss Tregowan. Is your father here by any chance?'

'No, he's in London. Why?'

'I want that water pump dismantled. That's the cause of the problem. It's been known these past twenty years that water contaminated by human effluent causes this disease. It seems the information has taken longer to reach these parts. These poor people have been poisoning themselves.'

'It's been like this as long as I can remember, doctor,' Queenie volunteered.

'And no doubt with this illness frequently recurring?'

'Why, yes. And twenty years ago we had cholera,' she added helpfully.

'So this could all have been prevented?' Alice asked.

'Yes, Miss Tregowan. With good sanitation, clean water . . .'

'Then my father killed Jacob.'

'Alice, what a dreadful thing to be saying,' Queenie protested.

'If these cottages are your father's responsibility, yes,

then in a manner of speaking he is responsible,' Doctor Salmon replied – not that his lordship would necessarily see it in that light, he thought to himself.

'What needs doing?' Alice asked brusquely.

'Immediately, as I said, that pump to be dismantled – the handle chopped into splinters and burned. This alleyway to be scrubbed out with disinfectant. And as many containers as you can muster full of clean water, from Gwenfer, I suggest. No doubt the water is pure there.' Alice chose to ignore the doctor's rebuke.

'And in the future?'

'I'd like to see that privy razed to the ground. New sanitation, a maximum of two families to each privy. A new water supply. And ideally these cottages, with all their vermin, burned to ashes.'

'I shall see that all this is done, doctor.'

He looked at the slight, beautiful girl standing in front of him. Her fine grey eyes looked uneasily at him. She is ashamed, he thought, and her shame gave him hope for the future, if not for the present. For the young doctor was a realist, and asked himself what a young slip of a girl could do to rectify this slum? 'I sincerely hope so, Miss Tregowan,' he said firmly but he chose to smile kindly at her and her grand ideas.

Alice turned to the young boy who still lurked, waiting for his shilling. 'You go and get the mine captain, tell him I sent you, and tell him to come with as many strong men as he can find,' she ordered. The boy took off quickly, cannoning into the vicar who had just turned the corner. He bore down upon them, a look of thunder on his thin face.

'On whose authority was that corpse deposited in my church?' he demanded without preamble.

'Mine.'

'Then I suggest, Miss Tregowan, that you make other arrangements.'

'That "corpse", as you call it, is young Jacob Blewett.

There's other sickness here, we could not keep him in the house with the rest of his family so ill.'

'He's not staying in my church.'

'"Your" church, vicar? I believed it to be God's church and, after Him, to belong to the people of this parish.'

'These people were not part of the community, they were outsiders. They never attended my church.' He put special emphasis on 'my'.

'The Blewetts have lived in the parish for centuries, Mr Reekin. If they did not attend your services, is it any wonder? What sort of welcome would they have received?'

'Of course they would have been welcome . . .'

'Really, Mr Reekin? Are you sure of that? Welcomed in their rags? Welcomed with their lice? With their suppurating sores?'

'If they had cleaned themselves up to enter God's house . . .'

'Good, Mr Reekin. At least it is God's house now. Tell me, Mr Reekin, how often have you visited the people in these cottages, how much pastoral care have you shown them? What charity have you given them?'

'I might ask the same of the Tregowans, Miss Tregowan?' He smiled an unpleasant, triumphant smile.

Alice flushed. 'I cannot speak for my father. For myself I confess a dreadful, unforgivable ignorance. But had I known, Mr Reekin, I would have done something about it. Did you?'

The doctor and Queenie had stood pivoting their heads back and forth as they had listened to this verbal battle. A small smile hovered about the doctor's mouth – perhaps he had misjudged the girl, he was thinking. Queenie stood, grinning proudly.

'Be that as it may. I want that body out by nightfall. Penwith's shed is perfectly adequate . . .'

'"Suffer the little children . . ."' Queenie interjected.

'Don't you be insolent with me, Miss Penrose. It is only

87

now becoming clear what damage you have been doing these past years.'

'You have Jacob moved from the church and tomorrow I will go to see my godfather, the Bishop of Truro. I warn you,' Alice threatened.

'And I had better warn you, vicar, that I fear this is an epidemic: God knows how many lie ill and dead in the other cottages. It would seem likely that Jacob will not be lying alone,' the doctor added quietly.

'Queenie, what can we do to help the others?' Alice asked, turning her back dismissively on the man of the cloth.

The vicar swung round and made his way back up the alley. Queenie hugged Alice, 'Oh, my maid. Am I proud of you?' She beamed. 'But as to here, there's naught for you to do. Best be getting back home, there's a love.'

'But I want to help.'

'Miss Tregowan, I think your help today has been of inestimable value. I agree with Miss Penrose: I think you should go home and rest, we don't want our champion falling ill, do we?' The doctor smiled gently at her. In a way Alice was relieved. Suddenly she felt exhausted, as if the putting of one foot in front of the other would be too much for her.

'I must see the mine captain first. Then I'll go.'

Alice slipped into the cottage to say goodbye to Ia. She kissed her friend on the forehead and smoothed her hair.

'I have to go now, Ia.'

'I wish you would stay.'

'I know. But I've a lot of things to do. I'm going to make your life so much better, Ia. I may not be able to see you for a day or two, but I'll be back – that's a promise.'

On the way out she met the mine captain and gave him orders to clean up the alleyway and to dismantle the pump. Wearily she turned her horse towards Gwenfer. As she entered the gates she realised that she had forgotten the boy's shilling.

*

Reuben woke up feeling chilled as the sun began to lose its daytime strength. He hobbled back to the cottage on his crutch. Queenie took him to one side and, as gently as she could, told him that Jacob was dead. Reuben's first thought was to wonder where on earth he would get his beer money from, with the best wage-earner dead and only his wife's wages from scrubbing for them to live on. When Queenie told him that Ada was not expected to last the night, he simply did not believe her. Ada was as strong as an ox. She had never let him down; she would not do so now.

'Bugger the lot of you, trying to frighten a fellow silly,' he bellowed at her and limped his way to the place where he felt most secure – the Miners' Arms.

The doctor, Queenie and Sal were now joined in their task by a group of women from the village. Some were genuinely distressed and full of guilt that they had not acted sooner. However, amongst their ranks were a few who liked nothing better than a good catastrophe to counter the boredom of their lives. Miss Reekin and Mrs Flinders were not among either group. The help of these new volunteers was greatly needed. The doctor had been right; of the twelve inhabited cottages, the fever was in eight. That night there was much to do.

As the evening advanced, Reuben became progressively drunker. His money was gone but, feeling sorry for him, the other men forgot that they normally had nothing to do with him and were soon plying him with drinks.

'Time' was called. Reuben said a fond good-night to his new friends and began to weave his way uncertainly across the scrubland. He had made this trip a thousand times, but never as drunk as this. In the moonless night he stumbled on a rock, cracked his head and sank into unconsciousness.

At about dawn his long-suffering wife gave up her own painful struggle. It was as if the kindness that was finally being shown her had allowed her to relax, but in so doing she had loosened her fragile hold on life and death had slipped in to take her. As she died she whispered one word: 'Reuben.'

When Reuben finally regained consciousness, his head ached. Unaware that he had cracked his skull on a rock he blamed the beer. Stealthily he made his way towards his cottage. He stopped in his tracks – another coffin was being carried out and loaded on to Penwith's cart. Most men would have felt anguish at the sight – Reuben was angry. What did Ada mean, dying and leaving him alone? Now what was he to do? Where was the money to come from? He watched the capable form of Queenie supervising the loading of the plain wooden box. Interfering old bat, he thought. 'Sod the lot of them,' he muttered. 'Let them sort the muddle out.' He turned his back on his home and hobbled away across the cliff and from the problems that would beset him if he stayed.

In the early morning Queenie and the doctor sat sipping tea, well laced with brandy, and debated what to do with Ia and Isaac since there was no question of Reuben being able to care for them. The doctor was fairly confident that, while both were still very ill, they would survive.

'I think they should be taken to the workhouse at Truro. Penzance is too close,' Queenie announced.

'That is if Truro will take them. They are not its responsibility.'

'If you had a quiet word with the right people, I'm sure you could arrange it – an important person like you,' Queenie smiled slyly at him.

'It is possible that it could be arranged. But would that not upset Alice? She seems very fond of the girl.'

'Her's too fond, that's the problem, doctor. It's not right. She can help the girl now, but in eighteen months, why, she'll be off to London to become a fine lady. What's going to happen to poor little Ia then? Her heart will be broken, that's what.'

'Hearing that explanation then you are right, Queenie. I thought you were concerned only for Alice. But as you point out . . . Perhaps Truro is the solution. But what will you tell Alice?'

'I think 'twill be better, and kinder, in the long run if I tells her that Ia died, just like her poor mam,' Queenie said and took a sip of her tea.

6

The following morning Alice sat on the train to London. It was hot. The first-class compartment was full, and Alice's request that the window be opened had been met with shocked horror by two of the passengers – obese matrons whose silk dresses were stretched so tightly that their bosoms resembled large pink and green balloons. She had noticed the women's looks of disapproval when they boarded the train at Truro. It had not taken her long to work out the reason, which was the way she was dressed. In a simple cotton dress, and an undecorated straw bonnet, she must have looked like Flo's sister rather than her mistress. Alice smiled and was rewarded by stony-faced expressions. She realised that she was wasting her time – let them sweat in their snobbish indignation that she, apparently a serving girl, should be travelling first class with the likes of them.

Flo's excitement, charming at first, had begun to grate on her nerves. When, last night, Alice had told Flo that she wanted her to travel to London with her, she had been surprised at the girl's hysteria. Flo, for all her affected ways and air of superiority over Sal, had, it transpired, never been further than Penzance.

What with the heat, the malevolent stares of the two women and Flo's chatter, it was a relief, at each stop, to leave the carriage and to walk a while on the platform in comparative peace. She began to wish that she had not brought the girl with her, but knew that this would have enraged Queenie. She would be angry enough when she was given Alice's note; the thought of Alice travelling unattended would have made her apoplectic.

Just after Plymouth Flo, exhausted with excitement, fell asleep at last, giving Alice much-needed time to think. The long train journey would enable her to marshal her thoughts and arguments. As the train trundled relentlessly nearer London and her father Alice began to have doubts about the wisdom of her actions. Last night, in the heat of her shame and anger, this trip had seemed the only possible course of action. Now, she began seriously to worry about what she would say and what her father's reactions might be. As his daughter she felt she had a right to confront him, but since their relationship was so distant she wondered if he might think her behaviour presumptuous. But then, she argued, she was a Tregowan too, and as a Tregowan she had no choice. But what, she thought suddenly, if he were not there? She knew that he lived by society's rules. It was August, might he not be in Scotland for the shooting with the Prince of Wales? She began to wish that she had had the foresight to telegraph her arrival.

It was late evening when the train finally pulled into Paddington. Once more her clothes were to prove a disadvantage since the porters ignored her as they made for the more elegantly dressed passengers.

'There's nothing for it, Flo. We'll have to carry our own bags.'

As they passed the great locomotive she stopped and thanked the sweaty and coaldust-covered driver and his fireman and tipped them both handsomely just as she had seen her father do all those years ago.

Several times she lost Flo in the crowds – the girl would keep stopping to gaze about her open-mouthed like a congenital idiot. At the hackney carriage rank they had a long wait. The drivers were in no haste to have two simply dressed country girls as fares. Alice found herself growing increasingly irritated by such attitudes. Provided she had the money to pay, she thought, she had every right to a cab. But at last one hansom cab driver took pity on them. He refused the large, heavily moustached man who had pushed past them, with a cheery 'Sorry, guv, these young ladies was first,' as he helped them into the cab. It was the first time that Alice had travelled in public transport and it was an experience she did not enjoy. The interior of the carriage was small, uncomfortably upholstered and stuffy compared with the coaches to which she was used. It also smelt unpleasantly of unwashed bodies and stale cigar smoke.

The cab pulled to a halt in front of Tregowan House, her father's large London mansion close by Hyde Park. Light blazed from almost every window and people could be seen moving about inside. Her father was at home.

A grey-liveried footman opened the door to her knock.

'I'm Alice Tregowan,' she announced.

The young footman looked down from his lofty height, and sneered. 'Oh yes, and I'm Mr Gladstone. We've enough for tonight, thank you very much.' And he began to close the door upon them.

'I beg your pardon. I *am* Alice Tregowan. Let me in,' Alice said shrilly, at the end of her tether.

'She is, you know, Miss Alice, I mean. You'm'll be in for it like as not,' Flo interceded but to no avail. The great door swung shut. 'Cor, what do we do now, miss?'

Alice banged the falcon-head knocker sharply, several times.

'Bugger off.' The footman's head appeared. Through the crack of the door Alice saw the imposing form of her father's butler crossing the hall.

'Phillpott,' she managed to shout before the door was slammed shut, to be reopened a second later by Phillpott.

'Why, Miss Alice,' he smiled.

'What a relief to see you, Phillpott,' Alice said as she swept past the footman.

'See, I told 'e,' Flo stuck her tongue out at the footman, who looked suddenly sick and seemed to have shrunk in stature.

'His lordship is dining, Miss Alice. If I could get you some refreshments. In the morning-room perhaps?' Phillpott said, unperturbed by the sudden arrival of his master's young daughter whom he had not seen for several years.

'No, thank you, Phillpott, I'll go straight to my father. It's important I see him immediately. I haven't much time.' And she sallied forth across the large marble-tiled floor towards the dining-room.

'But, Miss Alice . . . May I suggest that first you . . .' Phillpott, abandoning his normal dignified glide, almost ran to catch up with her. To Alice's surprise he looked agitated.

'No, thank you. I need to see him now,' Alice replied breezily as she turned the handle of the tall mahogany door which led into the dining-room. She entered, closely followed by Phillpott.

A large party was dining. A heavy haze of cigar smoke filled the room. The table was littered with the remains of food, as if bread and cheese and nuts had been thrown with abandon. Empty bottles lay everywhere, wine stains soaking into the fine damask table-cloth. Several chairs were upturned. A heavy guttural snoring rose from a prone figure by the door. Despite the presence of port, decanters and cigars, there were women present – women in revealing, low-cut dresses and with heavy paint on their faces. One woman's head was flung back, her eyes closed, while a man toyed with the nipple of one of her breasts which was exposed. On the table a young girl was dancing – wearing the thinnest of chiffon shifts over her naked body.

Alice knew that her mouth hung open, that her eyes were wide with horror, that a blush covered her from head to foot, yet she felt rooted to the spot. As if in slow motion, her father, at the far end of the table, stood up.

'Alice?' he queried as if not sure whether this young woman were his daughter or not.

'M'lord, I'm sorry. Miss Alice insisted, I could not stop her . . .'

The girl had stopped dancing and was trying to cover her nakedness with a napkin she had grabbed from the table. One or two of the women laughed loudly, as if they found Alice's embarrassment amusing.

'I beg your pardon,' Alice mumbled, turned and, with as much dignity as she could muster, quickly left the room.

'Miss Alice, I'm sorry, I did try to warn you.'

'Of course you did, Phillpott. It's my fault. I should have sent a telegram.' Alice's voice now was crisp and efficient as she spoke to the servant. 'You spoke of refreshments. Some tea would be nice and perhaps a sandwich. And would you see that my maid is looked after and given a bed; she is very tired.'

'Miss Alice.' The butler inclined his head.

In the morning-room, Alice sat down heavily on the nearest chair. She shuddered and closed her eyes, trying to blot out the memory of the scene. She did not understand. Was it usual for people to dance half naked on tables? Was it normal for women to uncover their breasts and let men play with them? She shivered as she recalled the expressions she had glimpsed on the men's faces as they had watched the young woman dancing: their eyes glittered, their mouths hung open in a way which Alice found frightening. This couldn't be normal behaviour, she was certain. Then, who were these people? Surely they could not be the 'society' whom people referred to when speaking of her father. Aunt Maude, she knew, came every summer to London for the season in 'society'. Alice could not imagine her being part of such a group, not for one minute. The very thought

brought the glimmer of a smile to Alice's lips. She wished
Queenie were here – she would have explained it all.
Alice sighed: this was what came of rushing in to see the
father she barely knew.

The door opened. Her father entered, closely followed
by Phillpott with her tea and sandwiches on a tray which
also carried a glass and decanter for her father. George
crossed the room and quickly kissed her on the cheek.
The atmosphere was relieved a little by Phillpott who
fussed about her with the tray of refreshments. But finally
there was nothing left for Phillpott to distract them with
and he withdrew, leaving her alone with this stranger.

'This is a surprise, Alice. I received no . . .'

'I didn't send one.'

'It might have been better had you telegraphed.'

'Yes, Papa, I'm sorry, I should have thought.'

'Next time.'

'Yes, Papa, I shall.'

A silence descended. She had known this was going to
be difficult but it was worse. She found she could not
remember any of the speeches or arguments she had
rehearsed in the train. Her father took a long time
pouring himself a drink.

'I had . . .' she said at the same time as George started
with 'I'm sorry, Alice . . .' They both looked at each other
and laughed; the tension eased a little. 'After you, Alice,'
he said.

'No, please, Papa, you first.'

'I was only going to say that I'm sorry you arrived
unannounced. I would have made arrangements . . .' He
looked at the floor, and Alice realised that he was as
embarrassed as she.

'I understand,' she said, blushing furiously, and understanding nothing.

'So why are you here? Is it an emergency? Is your nurse
ill? Are you finally bored with Cornwall?' He managed a
weak laugh.

'No, Queenie's very well, thank you. And I can't ever imagine being bored with Gwenfer. But, yes, we do have an emergency.'

He leaned forward and, at first tentatively, but then with an ease which surprised her, she began to tell him of the typhoid epidemic, of the Blewetts, of the hideousness of their suffering.

'Most unfortunate,' he said, when she had finished. He sat back in the large wing chair. 'But these things happen, Alice.'

'But they need not happen, Papa,' she said with feeling, and at length began to tell him what Dr Salmon suggested.

'Let me see if I understand fully. This Dr Salmon of yours, he wants a new water supply and a new sewerage system laid. New cottages built?'

'Yes.'

'And who's to pay for this massive undertaking?' He laughed again, but this time a short, cynical laugh.

'Well, you are, Papa, I suppose. I can't think of anyone else who would.'

'But, my dear child, this will cost hundreds of pounds.'

'I expect so.' Her voice reflected her disappointment that he was not taking her seriously, that he clearly dismissed her as a child with a hare-brained scheme. But she persisted, determined not to return until she had persuaded her father to help. 'I'm certain, Papa, that we could keep the cost down by using the local men. I am sure they would be willing to help for almost nothing. And Dr Salmon would be only too happy if we consulted him on health matters. I'm sure we could do it at a reasonable cost.'

He laughed at her eager innocence. 'And why should I?'

'Because it's . . . our duty.' She had been going to say 'your duty' but at the last moment she changed the word.

'Indeed? These men no longer work for me. I feel no

obligation to them. Are you aware, Alice, that I charge them no rent? Am I, on top of housing them free of charge, supposed to support these people merely because they will not support themselves? Good God, what is the world coming to?' He was beginning to bluster in self-righteous indignation. Alice felt she was approaching this the wrong way but she did not know how else to persuade him. She took a deep breath.

'But they can't support themselves, Papa, and that is our fault. Now that the mines are closed there is no other work for them. You must remember how poor the land is at Gwenfer. They used to be able to grow their own vegetables, and raise a pig. But now things have reached the point where, having eaten their pig, they cannot afford to buy another one. And if they sell the pig, what do they eat? And their seed strains get weaker and there's no money to buy new seeds, so there are no vegetables either.' She paused, looking at her father earnestly. 'Then they starve,' she added, quietly.

George shook his head at the speed with which Alice argued. He looked at her sitting across from him, at the eager, excited face, her blonde hair catching the light from the gas mantle, the fine bone structure of her face. It could have been Etty sitting there all those years ago, busily tying him into knots with her arguments, persuading him that she simply had to have the diamond bracelet she had seen in Garrards, and that Fairhall desperately needed a new conservatory.

'Good God! So, apart from building new cottages, I'm now to buy seeds and pigs as well?' He threw back his head and laughed loudly. Alice felt hurt that he should be amused.

'It *is* our responsibility, Papa. For 800 years we Tregowans have lived there, employed people, relied on their labour. We have grown rich and they have grown poor. We cannot suddenly stop caring for them. They look to us, and they are finding us wanting. I was ashamed yesterday when I saw those hovels. For the first and only time in my life I was ashamed of my name,' she said, tears glistening in her eyes. 'And it need not be charity. They don't want charity, I've tried that. They want work. There's still tin in the mines: they could be made workable again. I'm told the flooding has not gone too far. And . . .'

'Oh, my God, now the mine!' He slapped his thigh and he laughed even louder.

Alice stood up and angrily faced her father. 'I didn't come all this way for you to laugh at me. I came because, like me, I thought you would be ashamed and want to do something. I'm sorry I wasted your time, Papa.' She turned towards the door, unable to see it through the tears that were blinding her.

'Alice,' he called, 'I didn't say I wouldn't help.'

She turned back quickly, hope rekindling. 'You will?'

'Perhaps something should be done about those cottages. There's no point in neglecting property so that it eventually falls down. And if your doctor is correct in his assessment, then, very well, new water pipes shall be laid. But the mine is a different matter, Alice. There is no point in talking about matters of which you know nothing. It has been closed too long: it could not now make money. In any case the cost of opening it up would be prohibitive.'

'Money! You sit there talking about money, Papa, and I am talking about lives,' Alice said, pink now with agitation.

'Alice!' Her father stood up, frowning. 'I do not like the tone of your voice. You will apologise at once.'

Alice looked stubbornly at her father. She did not see why she should apologise; she had spoken only the truth. But then, she thought, if she antagonised him too far, how would she get the cottages improved? 'I'm sorry, Papa,' she said, looking intently at her hands rather than at him.

'I should think so, Alice. You appear to think that money is unimportant. How do you think you live, how do you imagine expenses are paid, young woman? Because I don't throw it away on wild schemes. Have you any idea of the enormity of our expenses?' he asked, sharply.

'But our expenses are enormous because of the way we choose to live – each in a different house,' she countered with a courage she was far from feeling. 'We choose, but these people have no choice. They live like animals . . .'

'Am I to gather from this conversation that, in the cause of economy, you would be willing to give up Gwenfer?' he said, smiling cynically at her.

Alice stopped short. That was not a consideration which had entered into any of her arguments. Gwenfer was so much part of her life that she could not now imagine living anywhere else. But then she thought of Ia as she had seen her yesterday. 'Yes, Papa, I could give up living at Gwenfer. I could live in a cottage there, with Queenie, quite happily if necessary.' Her voice was firm and she stood up and looked defiantly at her father.

George studied her face hard and then looked for a long time into his glass. Alice waited impatiently, biting back words: she sensed that her father was reaching a decision and that she must remain silent, hard though it was.

'I'll have my agent obtain estimates for the building works. I will not build new cottages, I can tell you that now, but perhaps a few improvements will be possible. As for the mine – old miners always say there's tin a-plenty. Why, they would promise you gold if they thought it would mean you would open up the workings again.'

'But, Papa, I'm sure it would cost almost as much to repair the cottages as to build nice new ones . . .'

'Alice, do not try my patience too far. There will be repairs or nothing.'

'Very well, Papa. But, if you don't trust the miners, perhaps if you had an engineer . . .'

'Alice!'

'I'm sorry, Papa.' She lapsed into silence but her mind was racing. Later perhaps, if she came to London more often to see him, perhaps then she could persuade him to change his mind.

Suddenly he smiled at her. Her enthusiasm was really rather endearing, if misguided, he found himself thinking. And she looked uncannily like her mother. 'Your Aunt Maude said I was ruining you, letting you live the way you've been doing. It seems that it's more likely to ruin me,' he said, but there was a tone of indulgence in his voice which made Alice laugh with him.

'Your aunt says you need a governess. Do you?' he asked abruptly. He did not like to think of Etty any more.

'A governess?' Alice's eyes lit up. 'Oh, Papa, that would be marvellous. I love to learn, but there is so much that I cannot teach myself. Please, Papa, that would make my life perfect.' She clutched her hands together with excitement. 'But if you do find me one, could she be good at mathematics, please?'

'Mathematics? What on earth does a young woman want with mathematics?'

'I've been able to teach myself so much, but I need help with mathematics. And I've read in the newspapers that women can go to university now, just like men. I would so love to go to university, Papa.'

'University?' he almost shouted with astonishment. 'I have never heard of anything so outlandish.'

'But, Papa, more and more women are attending them these days.'

'We are not talking of other women, but of my daughter. Good God, girl, we'd never find a husband for you if you became a bluestocking!'

'Very well, Papa,' she said demurely, fearing that if she

101

continued talking about university, she would not even get a governess.

'That's more like it,' he muttered as he poured more whisky for himself. 'The lawyers will get on to Gabbitas, Thring at once.'

'Gabbitas, Thring?'

'A company which will find a suitable governess for you.'

'Papa, you cannot imagine what joy that will give me.' She would have liked to cross the room, fling her arms about him and kiss him. But she did not, for she felt she did not know him well enough.

'How long are you staying then, young woman? Am I to have the pleasure of your company for a week or two?'

'Papa, I'm sorry, I have to return tomorrow. I promised I would go straight back, you see. I'm needed there. But perhaps I should go first to Berkshire to see Mama.'

'No, Alice,' George said firmly. 'That would not be wise. It is better that you should remember her as she was. She would not know you. She no longer even recognises me.'

'If you say so, Papa,' Alice said, evident relief in her voice. She had not wanted to go, but had thought that after so long perhaps she should.

Later, alone for once in bed, George thought about his daughter. A beauty she had turned out to be, though that was not surprising with Etty for a mother. But what spirit. She had stood up to him well. He liked spirit in a woman – spirited but at the same time knowing when she risked going too far. Extraordinary that she should be so, when one thought of her upbringing. He really should have done something about her before. He had been neglectful, but she seemed to have come to no great harm. Pity she should have seen his guests, though. He wondered what she had made of them. Perhaps he should have said something to her about them, tried to explain. But how did you explain people like that to a daughter you barely knew? And how to explain to an innocent virgin that he was bored, and that out of that boredom debauchery had crept into his life? He turned over on the pillow. There were aspects of his life these days which he himself did not like to dwell upon.

Alice could not sleep either. She would have liked to stay longer. She wished she knew her father better. He seemed harder than she remembered, as if he no longer cared about other people; she wished she could change that in him. And who were those strange guests? And why had that girl been dancing half naked . . . ?

The next morning, Alice and a complaining Flo took the train to Penzance. Flo was full of the wonders she had seen, the miraculous gas lights – no filthy oil lamps to clean here. One of the housemaids had shown her a marvellous machine which sucked the dust up out of the carpets. She had let Flo work the bellows as they lugged the heavy machine about the room. She couldn't wait to tell Sal about it: imagine not having to drag out carpets and beat them. While Alice stared out of the windows, Flo chattered on about the wonders of the bathroom where water gushed from the taps, and the privy where everything was simply flushed down a hole. Best of all though, Flo had liked the footman, Frederick, the young man who had at first refused them entry – he was not nearly as snooty, she said coyly, as he had at first appeared. Flo had seen that there was another life beyond Cornwall and she resented her mistress dragging her back so soon to Gwenfer.

7

The train arrived late at Penzance. The evening was hot and oppressive, the air so leaden that people felt they had to fight to breathe. They scoured the skies anxiously, hopeful of any sign of a storm.

Wearily Alice and Flo climbed into the ancient Tregowan coach which had been waiting over an hour.

'I want to see Ia, Mr George. Stop at the cottages please,' Alice ordered as she settled herself in the back of the coach. Before they were half-way along the Promenade both she and Flo were asleep.

Alice was woken by the coach stopping. They were at Gwenfer.

'Mr George, you didn't stop. I specifically asked you to.'

'You'm were so fast asleep, Miss Alice. And 'tis too late. They others all be asleep by now, I be bound.'

Alice was too tired to argue. Exhausted, she mounted the stairs. The old coachman was probably right; she would get up early to see Ia, she thought, as she prepared for bed.

From far out in the Atlantic a great storm swept in. The waves in the bay crashed on to the rocks and clawed their way up the great cliffs, their booming reverberating through the valley and echoing against the walls of the old house. The windows shook as the wind screamed around the house, searching in its wildness for a chink in the armour. The trees in the valley bent double as if curtsying to the storm. The sky was rent with streaks of crystal-blue lightning.

Over the valley, across the cliff, through the county, the storm relentlessly forged its way, wilfully destroying roofs, trees and even men in its progress across the land.

High in the west wing of Fairhall, in the bare room beneath the pepperpot tower which was Etty Tregowan's prison, May Prior peered anxiously out of the barred window. It had been too hot for man or beast – she was certain a storm must be brewing. May feared storms. Not for herself, but for the effect they had upon her charge.

For any wildness in the weather released the demons which lurked just beneath the surface of Etty's insanity.

She could see nothing in the unseasonal darkness. 'Black as Nooker's knocker,' she muttered to herself as she turned back into the room. Etty sat at the table, playing with the doll which was her favourite toy. She dressed and undressed it, then dressed it again. She was crooning in a tuneless voice a ballad of her own making. She smiled up at May and offered her the doll.

'Yes, there, my pet, what a lovely dolly you've got.' May stroked the dolly's bedraggled hair, almost as bedraggled as its owner's. 'Hungry, Etty?' She smiled at Etty. She had long ago ceased calling her 'm'lady'.

'Hungry, I's hungry,' Etty said in a childlike voice which, coming from her woman's body, sounded eerie.

May crossed the room and tugged the bell pull. From the only cupboard she took Etty's spoon and one for herself, two tin mugs and two wooden platters. At a quiet knock on the door, she recrossed the room and, from the chatelaine at her waist, selected the keys which unlocked the several large locks in the heavy oak door.

'You all right, May?' the burly footman asked. 'Everyone reckons there's a right storm brewing up.' He poked his head tentatively round the edge of the door to look at his mistress still crooning her incomprehensible song.

'She seems quiet enough for the moment. But I 'ate a storm.'

'Do you want me to come and sit with you?'

'I don't know, Thomas. Trouble is, anyone else in the room does unsettle her so. Tell the truth I don't know which is worse for her – a storm or you sitting there. I think we're all right for the time being. We'll see how things are when you come back for the dirty dishes. Oh, and, Thomas, you couldn't bring me along a pint of beer, could you?'

'May, you know you're not . . .'

'Oh, go on, Thomas, don't be a spoil-sport. Who's to

105

know? You all gets your beer, downstairs. It ain't fair, me stuck up here never seeing a drop of it.'

'I'll do me best,' he said with a grin. He had always had a soft spot for May: he liked them big and there was no doubting she was about the finest woman he had ever clapped eyes on, with her huge hips and fine muscular arms.

May took the glass jug of milk, poured it into their mugs and returned to the door. She took the tray of food and handed Thomas the jug. Carefully she locked the door behind him.

'Cor, look at this, Etty. Cook's done us proud tonight.' May looked with distaste at the food she was sharing out between them. Minced chicken, mashed potatoes and puréed vegetables, followed by jelly in paper cups. What May would not have given for a slab of roast beef. At one time they had had normal food, but since the day that Etty had tried to choke herself on a lamb chop, everything had been mashed and minced. Watching Etty shovelling food into her mouth with her hands, there were times May thought it was a pity the poor soul hadn't succeeded. But then, she reasoned to herself, that would have put her out of a job.

'Use your spoon, Etty,' she said automatically. She said it at every meal, but she might as well have saved her breath. Etty always ate with her fingers.

May had been looking after her for nearly nine years. In that time she had been able to take only a few days off; if she were not there Etty went berserk. It was quite touching really, she thought, spooning jelly into her mouth. She was not complaining; Lord Tregowan paid her double for her pains. It might be a lonely life, but she was comfortable, warm, and her generous wages were piling up untouched for she wanted for nothing. When it was all over, May intended to get a nice little pub somewhere. She had noticed the way Thomas eyed her, and had a feeling that he'd be only too willing to join her.

At the beginning it had not been lonely work. In those days Etty had talked! How she had talked. She had told May of her life, the lovers she'd had, the wickedness they had got up to. There was many a nobleman May could ruin if she ever set her mind to it. But, as the years had slipped by, so Etty had slid mentally back in time. From womanhood to adolescence to childhood, until now she was like a toddler. May hoped she did not choose to slip further back and become a baby – big as May was, carrying Etty would be difficult. And what if, having become a baby, she wanted to be newborn? Then what? Would she die? It didn't bear dwelling on really, May thought, as she picked at her teeth.

May did not like Etty but, on the other hand, she did not dislike her. Etty was her job, that was all. A job which was helping May to fulfil her ambition for a nice little business all of her own.

Their supper finished, May rang the bell again. The wind had risen considerably but still Etty seemed completely unaware of it. Thomas reappeared, this time with a ewer of hot water and the promised beer.

'You're a pet. I'll thank you properly one of these days,' she flirted, as she exchanged the dirty dishes for the beer.

'Best watch her with that beer pitcher,' he warned.

'Don't you worry. I won't take me eyes off her. If I needs help I'll ring.'

May undressed Etty, washed her and put her into a clean night-dress. Then May took her hand and led her to the cage in which her mattress lay.

'Dolly, want my dolly,' Etty lisped.

May looked at the woman, at the pleading in her eyes. 'Oh, all right, just this once, only you didn't ought to really.' And she picked the doll up from the table.

With Etty safely locked in her cage, May took her knitting from the locked cupboard. It was only really safe to knit once Etty was in bed. She settled in the easy chair, put her feet up on the stool and, between sips of beer and a little knitting, she kept glancing across at Etty who was soon fast asleep.

Lulled by the beer, May began to nod. The beer was strong and because she had little of it these days May was soon oblivious of the storm that was now whipping about the park in a frenzy of destruction.

At the first snore from May, Etty's eyes snapped open. She looked across at her sleeping nurse and smiled. She was a fool, Etty had long ago decided. That Thomas was a fine specimen: Etty would have had him between her legs in no time at all. Quietly she pushed the covers back. She picked up her doll. With a quick wrench she pulled the head off and from its inside carefully removed the eyes. She separated the wires which held them together and made them open and close. Then silently she rolled across the floor to the gate of her cage. She paused. Still May snored and the wind outside was on her side, deadening any sound. Deftly she inserted the wire into the padlock and with deep concentration manipulated it until, with a click, the lock sprang open. On her bare feet she moved across the room. She bent to pick up one of the knitting needles and with one sharp lunge impaled May through the heart. May grunted. Etty stood back and, her head on one side, looked at her, disappointed. She was dead already. Etty had dearly wanted May to know that she was killing her.

She tore the chatelaine from May's belt. She knew exactly which keys to use and soon the door which had imprisoned her stood open. Etty paused again, relishing this moment as she looked out and saw the staircase which would lead her to freedom.

Singing softly a tuneless dirge of her own making, she tripped down the stairs. The house was in total darkness but Etty did not mind: she remembered exactly where to go.

In less than five minutes she was out. The wind

scooped at her hair, at her night-dress, as Etty danced wildly across the lawn, enjoying the fresh air, relishing the wind and her freedom. As a sheet of lightning lit the air, Etty shrieked with joy and her dance became wilder. Thunder rumbled across the sky and Etty rolled on the grass in ecstasy. The damp grass felt cool against her burning skin. Over and over she rolled, down the bank and into the water. She gasped, and then stood up. 'Water,' she crooned, dipping her hands into it, throwing it across her face, her hair, massaging it into her breasts and between her legs. That was it, that was what she wanted. She looked up at the sky, she threw her hands above her head. 'Oswald,' she screamed, and slipped beneath the black, fast-flowing water.

8

The following morning, exhausted from her long journey, Alice found to her shame that she had overslept. It was nearly noon before she had washed and dressed and was down in the kitchen. She raced in, apologising to Mrs Trelawn, and asked if she might have some bread and milk which she began to devour with a healthy hunger. Suddenly, a loud sniff issued from Mrs Trelawn. Alice looked up, surprised, in time to see a large tear plop into the stuffing Mrs Trelawn was preparing for the chicken in front of her.

'Mrs Trelawn, what is the matter?'

'I can't be saying, Alice.'

'You can tell me. Please, what is it?' Alice moved to stand beside the woman and put her arm about her. 'Mrs Trelawn!'

'Oh, 'tis too cruel.' The cook collapsed on to a chair and began to sob. Alice began to feel afraid.

'Something's happened. Something dreadful. I must go

to the cottages immediately.' She turned towards the kitchen door.

'No, Miss Alice, please.' Mrs Trelawn held out her hands towards her. 'You'm to wait here. Queenie said.'

'But why won't you tell me what's wrong? You must tell me.'

'Please, Miss Alice, don't ask me to. Queenie'll be here directly. Mr George went to fetch her when we heard you stir.'

'It's Ia, I know it's Ia.' Reluctantly Alice turned back towards the pine table. 'I should never have gone.' She picked at the stuff of her skirt, her heart pounding, a dreadful foreboding making her feel nauseated.

She looked up sharply as, with a noisy bustle, Queenie arrived. Her fears were heightened at sight of Queenie's tear-stained face.

'There there, my handsome.' Queenie's arms were about her and Alice collapsed already sobbing on to Queenie's ample bosom. 'Does her know?' Queenie asked over Alice's head to Mrs Trelawn.

'I bain't said a word,' Mrs Trelawn said between her sobs.

'I wish I had not gone, Queenie. I should have been with her. I'll never forgive myself for not being with her.'

'Now, my little one, you'm not to blame yourself for that, what could you have done? 'Tis probably for the best. You can't see that now, but you will, my little one, Queenie promises you.'

Alice stood back from Queenie, her face etched with horror. 'How could you say such a thing? How can it be for the best? My friend, my dearest and only friend.'

'Oh, my lovely, 'tis of your mother I speak. The poor soul, last night . . . out of her torment at last.'

'My mother?' Alice looked with amazement at her nurse. 'Did you say my mother?'

'I'm sorry, Alice.'

A slow smile spread over Alice's face. 'Ia – I must see Ia.' And she raced from the room light-headed with relief.

'Well I never, Mrs Trelawn. Did you see that? Not a word about her poor mother. She's bewitched by that Ia.'

'Oh, 'tis shocking, Queenie, there bain't no doubt about it.' Mrs Trelawn wiped her eyes with her voluminous apron. 'Is Ia there?'

'No, her left this two hours past.'

'What you'm going to say to the maid about her?'

'I don't know, Mrs Trelawn, and that's the truth.'

Alice did not wait to harness her horse but raced up the drive oblivious to the heat. She ran until she reached the cottages. Only at the entrance to the alleyway did she slow to walking pace. Everything was quiet, just as it had been that fearful day when she had discovered Ia ill. She reached Ia's cottage and pushed the door open. The cottage was bare. She called Ia's name. There was no response.

Outside once more she looked anxiously to left and right. Not a soul was in sight. A door opened and Dr Salmon appeared. Alice ran up the alleyway towards him.

'Dr Salmon, wait for me,' she called. The doctor waited for her to join him. 'Doctor, Ia's cottage, it's empty. What has happened?' She grabbed at his sleeve as if to prevent his walking further.

'I'm sorry, Alice, but Ada Blewett's dead.'

'Oh, dear God, no!' Alice exclaimed.

'And Reuben Blewett's vanished.'

'Poor Ia. Oh, Dr Salmon, she must be in such distress. I must see her. Where is she?'

Dr Salmon looked for a long time at his shoes; he patted the knot of his cravat; he bent and picked up his medical bag, and he coughed.

'Dr Salmon . . . what is it? Why will you not answer me?'

'I'm sorry, Alice, but Ia is no longer here.'

'She's gone away?'

'I did not say that, Alice.' He looked at the men dismantling the privy.

Alice, with dawning horror, stared at the doctor who seemed incapable of looking at her. 'You mean she's dead?' Alice's voice rose sharply. 'No, I won't believe that. Tell me it's not true, please tell me it's not true.'

But the doctor did not reply. He began to walk to the end of the alleyway, hating himself for what he had done and hoping to God that Queenie was right.

Like a wild creature Alice rushed past him, a dreadful scream coming from her lips. 'Ia . . .' The name trailed from her as she ran from the cottages and out across the scrubland.

'Alice . . .' he called helplessly.

Across the cliff and through the gates she sped. She did not follow the drive but fought her way through the dense undergrowth. Trees and shrubs lashed at her though she felt nothing but the pain inside her, the pain which she felt was destroying her soul. She broke free of the plants and raced along the river bank, barely aware of stumbling and falling. She ran as fast as her legs would carry her, as if by running fast enough she could outdistance what had happened – make it all disappear. She skimmed past her rock. Scrabbled across the boulders, making, all the time, a strange mewing noise. When she reached the end of the promontory, she stopped: there was nowhere else to go.

The strange noise too had stopped. She stood silent at the point where Oswald had stood nine years ago. Then she had had a family; then she had felt loved. But Oswald had left her and then her mother had gone too. Always, she now realised, she had hoped for her mother's return. There was to be no return. Her mother would never love her now. She looked up at the sky and screamed, blaspheming against the God who was supposed to dwell there. Then she called for Ia, with all the pain of her great loss in her voice.

The clear green water sucked and slapped at the rocks at her feet, making its own music. She listened to that music for only a moment.

'For the love of God, take me, too,' she cried and jumped into the restless sea.

A large wave scooped her up, tossed her to another which threw her playfully to a larger one which gently, as if she were a baby, laid her on the sand of the cove.

The sea did not want her.

9

It was Dr Salmon who found Alice. At first he feared she was dead but when he examined her a shallow sigh escaped from her lips. He scooped her into his strong arms and ran with her to the house.

Queenie saw him coming and at sight of the dripping wet, apparently lifeless figure in his arms, she collapsed into an unprecedented faint on the floor of the great hall.

The doctor had two patients.

Queenie was quickly revived with sal volatile and bundled off to bed with the stern instruction that she had been overworking and must rest. She did – for two hours before she was up and fussing over Alice.

Throughout the rest of the day the doctor feared for Alice's life. He called to her; he chafed her hands. He made Queenie hold her hand and beg her to return. He was certain she could hear; in fact he was equally certain she was conscious. It was as if the girl did not want to live and in feigning death was willing it to come to her.

Through the long night he and the nursemaid coaxed and cosseted her. After first admonishing Queenie for not being in bed Dr Salmon had finally conceded defeat. The stalwart woman was not going to leave her charge even if a thousand doctors told her to do so.

At about three in the morning Alice finally opened her eyes. She smiled at them.

'I'm sorry,' she said almost in a whisper and sank into a deep and natural sleep. Dr Salmon felt the tension leave him too.

He and Queenie were sitting at the kitchen table drinking warm milk laced with rum. Queenie had finally relinquished care of Alice, for the time being, to Mrs Malandine.

'She has to be told the truth about Ia, Queenie. It was a dangerous game we were playing.'

'I didn't say naught about the girl,' Queenie said, quickly.

'No, I know you didn't. It was my doing. But then I did not know the child's mother had just died, too.'

'Fat lot that seemed to concern her.'

'We don't know that, Queenie.'

'All she could think of was that Ia. Wrong it is, real bad of her.'

'Perhaps her extreme reaction to the news about Ia was an indication of her feelings for her mother.'

A loud snort was Queenie's response.

'You will explain in the morning?'

'Will you be coming to see her, doctor?' Queenie ignored his question.

'I fear not. The Tregowans are Dr Flinders's patients. It would not be right of me to usurp his position.'

'I think she'd rather be seen by you.'

'We'll see what her father says. When's he coming?'

'Day after tomorrow, with her ladyship's body. A sad home-coming to be sure.'

Alice stood in the great hall with Queenie beside her and waited for her mother to return. The hall was decorated with urns of arum lilies whose sickly sweet scent was to fill her with horror for the rest of her life. The windows throughout the house were shuttered, the paintings swathed in black, the mirrors turned towards the walls. A wreath of laurel with long black satin ribbons hung on the large oak door. Candles glowed in the wall sconces of the darkened hall even though outside the sun was shining benignly. The long table in the centre of the hall was draped with black crepe, large candles stood at either end, and the table was strewn with more lilies and laurel. The house and Alice waited.

She heard the coach arrive, but she did not move. The heavy, ornate coffin was carried in by six men whose muscles bulged, whose brows poured with sweat. It was laid with reverence on the prepared table. Her father stood beside her, his head bowed, and they waited while the lid of the coffin was removed.

Alice looked at a stranger. An old woman, wrinkled and emaciated. It could not be her mother, she thought, through the clouds of laudanum administered earlier by Dr Flinders. She stepped forward dutifully as her father did and stared down at the face of the mother who had never loved her – and she felt nothing. She had buried her mother already, there in the sea where Oswald's soul rested. Nor did she grieve now for Ia – the laudanum saw to that. Alice felt and acted like an automaton.

Queenie was worried. While the girl was drugged, they had no problem but what was to happen when she ceased to take it, she wondered, what was she to do about Ia? Had Alice reacted in a normal way to the news of her mother's death Queenie would not have had this struggle of conscience. She would have told her Ia was well and in the orphanage in Truro. But the knowledge that Alice had thought more of a poor village child than of her own flesh and blood was more than Queenie could countenance.

There was much debate around the kitchen table as to what Queenie should do. It was Mrs Malandine who took matters in hand, sought out Lord Tregowan and told him what had happened. George sent for Queenie.

'You acted quite properly in the end, Queenie. A most unsuitable arrangement. I cannot countenance my daughter having such a girl as an intimate friend.'

'No, m'lord.'

'I cannot imagine how you let it come about in the first place.'

'I'm sorry, m'lord.'

'Well, we will say no more about it. It is better that Alice should continue to think that the girl is dead.'

'Yes, m'lord. Thank you, m'lord,' and exonerated from guilt, Queenie returned to the kitchen.

George himself walked about with a long and gloomy face. But it was an expression bred only of convention. Had he had someone to confide in, he would have spoken only of his relief that Etty's agony was over. He would have explained that she had been as dead to him for many years. He might even, in his cups, have confessed his pleasure at being free of her at last. For George hoped to marry again and firmly expected that time and a willing young woman would provide him with an heir.

For a week Alice continued to take the laudanum prescribed for her and for a week after the funeral her father stayed on at Gwenfer. But once the seven days were up he felt restless and anxious to return to London. Though he would not be able to move freely in society for another year, there existed that hinterland he inhabited where his mourning would mean nothing. It was that life to which he wished to hasten back. Out of courtesy he asked his daughter if she would care to return with him, sending up a silent prayer, even as he asked, that she would decline. He need not have worried: Alice wished to stay at Gwenfer. She knew she was drugged – she wanted not to be. She knew she had to come to terms with Ia's death and she believed that only here would that be possible.

Her father left. Alice refused her laudanum dose. As she battled to return to normality, she began to come to terms with the loss of the one friend she had had in the world. She spoke to no one. Many were the times, despite his lordship's instructions, when Queenie almost relented and told her the truth.

Chapter Three

1

The arrival of Philomel Gilby saved Alice's sanity.

For two weeks after her father's return to London Alice kept to her room and she barely ate. Once she had made the pronouncement that no one was to mention Ia's name in her presence, she refused to talk. Alone, she was haunted by the fearful images of hell she had long ago been forced to look at by the vicar's sister. When she slept it was to dream of Ia in torment. When awake it was to do battle with these fears. She would rationalise that, if there was such a hell, her sweet friend could not have sinned enough to be there. But in sleep the nightmares returned. She needed help and counsel but her grief prevented her talking of her mental agony.

Long were the conferences in the kitchen. Queenie's greatest fear was that Alice might go mad like her mother. Mrs Malandine took a far more pragmatic view by pointing out that Alice had never been as moody as her mother. 'Leave her alone to come to terms' was her studied opinion. Mrs Trelawn, a warmer soul altogether, was all for Alice being told the truth. But the house-keeper, who had never approved of the relationship in the first place, argued that his lordship should be obeyed in such a matter. Mrs Trelawn finally decided that such business had nothing to do with a cook, and kept silent. And Queenie fretted.

Upon the arrival of the governess, Miss Gilby, common courtesy forced Alice to come downstairs and to make an effort. The governess was not the easiest person to take to on sight. At her creation, nature seemed to have been in a mischievous mood. Her left eye, small and brown, was straight but her right eye, large and blue, was crooked. The cast of this right eye made it appear as if it were trying to see its counterpart, an impossible task given the size of Miss Gilby's nose. It was a nose of noble proportions, far more suited to a Roman emperor than to the small visage of an English governess. And, although she had a prettily shaped mouth, it never quite managed to close over her large, jutting teeth. As if her face were not unfortunate enough, her shoulders had a strange bulbous shape that verged on being a hump.

Philomel Gilby feared life. She was afraid of the heat but fearful of the cold. Cities caused in her an agony of worry. She was terrified by the sea, yet the countryside held untold terrors, too. She would never go near a horse, and dogs were also to be given a wide berth. Food was a vexatious problem and she survived on a diet of bread, warm milk and the occasional soft-boiled egg. This annoyed Mrs Trelawn who took the rejection of her food as a personal insult. Miss Gilby had lived for years in the governesses' hinterland, neither servant nor family, and it would have been difficult to know who frightened her most – the masters or their butlers. She had the patiently resigned air of the genteel middle-aged woman who knows that love has passed her by.

Given such disadvantages, Miss Gilby had from an early age immersed herself in learning. Orphaned in her early twenties, with no money and no home, she had been forced to seek employment. It was then she had discovered that she loved to teach. Any subject in this woman's hands became of interest. Within a week of her arrival Alice was happily engrossed in history and literature. They had begun Latin and French. A fine musician, she had quickly controlled Alice's self-taught piano-playing, and soon her repertoire was growing.

Though a modest water-colourist herself, she was still to inspire Alice's greater talent. She was an avid reader of the political scene, and taught Alice of world affairs which few others in this West Country backwater had heard of. Botany she could elucidate, the other sciences and mathematics she preferred not to dwell on – they were too fearsome to contemplate – but that was the only academic failing of this paragon.

Miss Gilby found the living arrangements at Gwenfer rather unusual. But since she prided herself on her adaptability – with a slight leaning to the Bohemian – she quickly took to the life belowstairs.

Enough young women had passed through her hands for her to be able rapidly to assess Alice's potential. She set to with zeal to repair the damage of the young woman's neglected education.

Alice's social conscience was a rare discovery in one of her class. Miss Gilby was proud of her own slightly risqué radical leanings, which until now she had had to keep secret from her employers. Now she found herself able to discuss at length with Alice the dreadful injustices of life.

The girl was obedient and obliging; on only one matter would she not comply with Miss Gilby's wishes – she refused to go to church. Alice had been quite blunt on the subject. There was no God, she said, and there was no logic for God's existence. What sort of God would have allowed her brother to drown, her mother to go mad and her best friend to live and die in squalor? In a way, deep inside her, in that part of one's being she found it best not to explore too closely, Miss Gilby agreed. But given her all-consuming fears, Philomel trudged off to church each Sunday as an insurance policy – just in case.

For six months the two women worked. Each night Alice went to bed exhausted. With her mind full of new things the nightmares of Ia began to fade. If she was not happy, at least she enjoyed a degree of contentment that she had thought would never be possible again.

While she was pleased that Alice seemed to have recovered, Queenie was not happy with the situation. Alice spent so much time with the governess that Queenie felt she rarely saw her now. Queenie would sit in the kitchen with her large sewing basket on her lap, a cup of tea at her side, and sulk.

Alice, immersed in the new excitement of learning from so fine a teacher, was unaware of the situation. Philomel, well versed in the rivalry rampant belowstairs, sighed.

Philomel knew well that it would not take long before the baleful glares and the insolent silences of Queenie would be followed by more tangible attacks. She had to wait only a fortnight.

She was grateful when upon her return from a particularly long walk with Alice, Queenie had invited her to take a cup of tea. Fatigue had made her drop her guard and she happily accepted the proffered cup only to find it seasoned with salt. The following evening the sheets on her bed were damp, which involved Philomel in a most uncomfortable night on a chair. Then her possessions began to disappear, always to turn up in the most unexpected places. So her needlework appeared in the flower-bed, the novel which was so engrossing her was found amongst the dirty linen and, most vexing of all, her diary disappeared altogether.

Compassion, however, was one of this remarkable woman's many virtues. She understood the love which Queenie felt for the girl; she understood the fear that her presence had aroused in the nursemaid's heart. Philomel was able to forgive. And she had lived so long with the 'slings and arrows of outrageous fortune' that she knew she could survive the campaign. She was quite right. As the little governess's time at Gwenfer lengthened to a year, and a second Christmas came and went peacefully, it seemed that Queenie had come to accept her.

Upon her seventeenth birthday Alice was summoned to Septimus Woodley's office.

'Are we too much of a young lady to enjoy a barley twist?' He grinned at her, his yellow teeth glinting in the weak February sunshine which filtered through the dust motes filling the air.

'I hope I never grow too old to enjoy them, especially yours, Mr Woodley,' she replied. Though she had long outgrown them, she would not have cared to hurt his feelings.

'Well, to business,' Mr Woodley announced, once the barley sugar had been dispensed. He took down one of the great deed-boxes boldly marked TREGOWAN. 'So, Miss Tregowan. I have good news to impart. Your father has waived his right over your mother's estate and you are therefore the sole heir.' He rustled in the box and produced a large document. 'This is your mother's last will and testament. In it she has stipulated that upon your seventeenth birthday you are to receive her jewellery and a legacy of £3,000. The rest of her considerable fortune is to remain in trust for you until you reach the age of thirty. Your father is to administer this estate and to give you such income as he sees fit – well, I can't foresee any problems there, Miss Tregowan, can you? A most generous man, your father, is he not?'

'Good gracious, Mr Woodley,' Alice said weakly, rendered almost speechless. 'I had no idea that my mother had a fortune to leave me.' Since her mother's death there had been times when she had felt guilty that all her mourning had been for Ia. However, she had doused that guilt with the thought that her mother had never cared for her. Now she was faced with the knowledge that her mother had cared sufficiently to leave her all she possessed.

'Indeed. Your mother's family were extremely wealthy: she came to her marriage with your father very well provided for.' What strange people these aristocrats are, he thought to himself – imagine the young woman having no idea of her mother's wealth. Still it was none of his business. 'However,' he dug into the deed-box, 'here is a bank draft for the £3,000 to which you are entitled immediately. Perhaps, with a little of it, you would like to buy some pretty things. Then, I suggest, you permit me to advise you on safe investments for the remainder.'

'Tell me, Mr Woodley. Did my father ever instruct you to obtain estimates for the repair or rebuilding of the miners' cottages at Gwenfer?' Alice spoke briskly. She was more than a little annoyed by the lawyer's patronising tone.

'He did, Miss Tregowan. When he came down for your poor mother's funeral, if memory serves me right.'

'And what happened?'

'Oh, it was too expensive. In the circumstances, I believe he decided to leave well alone.'

'I see,' Alice said, fighting to hide the anger she felt. That her father had not fulfilled his promise to her should not have surprised her. Once a week she had made a point of riding that way, always in the hope that work might have begun. Several times she had written to her father to ask when repairs were to commence but her father had not replied.

'What were the estimates?'

'What a strange thing for a pretty young lady to want to know.' Mr Woodley stopped tidying his papers and looked up.

'I should like to know, please,' she said smiling and trying not to show her fast-mounting irritation.

'I should have to look up the exact amounts but I think it was in the region of nearly £400. A considerable sum of money, Miss Tregowan.'

'And to rebuild?'

'Of course, that would be substantially more.'

'How much?'

The lawyer sucked in his cheeks and shrugged his shoulders; a cloud of dust shaken from his old jacket joined the dancing dust in the shaft of sunlight. 'I'm not a builder. But, with building costs today, you must think in terms of £60 to £70 for each cottage. At least double the sum for repairs, if not considerably more.'

'Then use that money.' She pointed to the bank draft which still lay on his desk. 'Get builders to draw up plans immediately.'

'But, Miss Tregowan, what will your father say?'

'Need he know? He never comes here, except for funerals, it seems. I understood that this is my money to do with as I wish.'

'Yes, Miss Tregowan, but to waste it on such a project . . . ?'

'I don't regard it as waste, Mr Woodley. It is what I want and I would appreciate it if you would put these matters in hand for me. If you do not wish to, then I shall take the bank draft to Mr Bolitho's bank across the road and ask them to arrange matters for me.'

Mr Woodley's brain worked rapidly. Here sat the next generation of Tregowans – with her mother dead and no male heir she would one day be the richest woman in Cornwall. He thought of the commissions, the fees he might lose in the future should he antagonise her now. 'Whatever you wish, Miss Tregowan,' he said, smiling unctuously at her.

A week later the astonished inhabitants of the miners' cottages were informed that new accommodation was to be built for them nearer the village. As each new cottage was finished, a family would be moved. The old cottages were then to be razed to the ground.

Several months later, when the work was complete,

Alice stood with the villagers and watched the fire devouring the old houses. As the orange flames caught hold in the 'third alley along and four houses in' the tears poured down Alice's cheeks. At last she felt that she had buried Ia.

2

Ia Blewett bent forward over the great sink of steaming water. The muscles in her upper arms bulged, making her stick-thin forearms look deformed as she manhandled the soaking sheet on to the scrubbing board. She liberally coated the scrubbing brush with soap.

'Blewett, less soap,' shouted Mrs Drew the overseer.

'And how on earth am I supposed to get this clean without? You miserable old toad,' muttered Ia into the steam.

'What did you say, Blewett?'

'I was telling myself that I must remember to use less soap, Mrs Drew.' Ia flashed a smile at the woman who, mistrusting Ia, her smile, and the beauty of her face, glared back.

'Be sharp about it. When you've finished that, get over to the steam room and help with the folding,' Mrs Drew ordered. Ia sighed; she could never get on the right side of the woman. Some of the other overseers melted at her smile, which years ago she had learned to use to her advantage, but not Mrs Drew.

Ia bent to the task in hand. She worked efficiently and with a speed surprising in one so young and thin. She was tall now, far taller than most girls of twelve. The authorities presumed she was over thirteen and she had not disabused them of this idea – the older they thought she was the sooner she would be free of this place. Her hair, when not damp from the steam, was still strikingly blonde, even though she rarely saw the sun. The large

125

grey eyes wore a guarded look now, always on the watch for trouble that might be brewing, alert for the easiest escape route.

It was a constant puzzle to Ia why she was still in the workhouse orphanage. Most of the girls had been placed in service by thirteen. Since everyone thought that was her age she should have a job by now, but still no one had said anything about her moving on. Only last week, in bed – the only place the girls were free to talk – her friend Jinny had suggested that perhaps she was still here because she worked too fast and they wanted to keep her permanently. Jinny had pointed out that there were women who had been here since birth and no doubt would die here too. Maggie Smith in the kitchens for one, and Flora Brown the simpleton – neither of them had ever lived anywhere else.

'I'm not a simpleton,' Ia had hissed back.

'Didn't say you'm were. No need to be so touchy. When I get to thirteen, I wouldn't mind staying. 'Tisn't that bad, and outside could be worse.'

Ia had lain awake staring into the darkness, amazed that anyone could contemplate living in this place for ever. It was like a prison and they were prisoners, except that they had never done anything wrong beyond being born in the wrong place to the wrong people. The girls spent a lot of their time talking about 'outside', and debating what it was like. None of them knew: most had come here as small children and their memories of what life was like 'outside' were dimmed by time.

Ia, of them all, because she had been older when she had arrived, had the sharpest memories. Made sharper too by her contact with another world in the shape of Alice Tregowan. Planted firmly in Ia's mind was the notion that, unless you were one of the lucky ones – like that bitch – 'outside' had been a dismal place where hunger, dirt and disease lurked. It was a measure of the misery to be found in the workhouse, however, that she never ceased planning to get away. If she wasn't chosen to go before the selection board soon, she knew she would have to run away. It was pointless to ask when she was to be selected – that would indicate to the authorities that she was discontented with her lot and would ensure that she was never put up for selection.

It was not dirty in the workhouse and illness was treated quickly by the visiting doctors; there was even a hospital ward for the really sick. But it was cold, it was dreary and oppressive, and there was no privacy – even their weekly baths were taken in pairs. Talking amongst the girls was discouraged; only at night, with the lights out, could they whisper to each other. She was not hungry. They were fed – but what food! Skilly and gruel and hard-baked bread, with a slice of fatty meat on Sundays for a treat. It was only at Christmas that they had anything resembling good food. It seemed that then the local population assuaged a mass feeling of guilt: money poured in to provide turkey and plum pudding. But as soon as the festive season was over, the corporate guilt disappeared for another year. Without doubt the Christmases here were better than any she had had at home, but nothing could ever match the Christmases she had shared with Alice.

Ia turned on the hard pallet and sighed. Some days she'd rather not eat. She smiled, remembering her picnics with Alice. The chicken breasts, the cakes, the lemonade. Her mouth filled with saliva at the memory. She forced herself to stop thinking as the image of the food made her stomach ache. She longed for Gwenfer. At night she would lie dreaming of it. She would pretend she was walking through the rooms and she would test herself to see if she could remember each painting, each ornament, each sword. She always could. No good came of thinking of those days: that was all in the past. It might as well have been a dream. But she found it hard not to remember that other happier time. From Alice she had learned to be dissatisfied. She was left with a hunger for learning that was never eased since there was no teaching in this place and no books apart from the Bible. And because of Alice, she spoke differently from the rest of the girls, a handicap which when she first arrived had landed her in many fights and beatings. The easiest thing would have been to revert to her old accent but this Ia refused to do. She was proud of the way Alice had taught her to speak. She compromised by swearing with the best of them. She found that her cursing had eased this one particular problem. The only favour the Tregowan girl had done her, she decided, was to leave her with a deep abiding mistrust of everyone. It had served her well in the two years she had been here. Despite her harsh thoughts, a tear rolled down her cheek and soaked into the straw-filled pillow.

Ia often cried when she thought of Alice. But they were bitter tears. For the first six months Ia had waited every day for Alice to come to collect her. So confident was she that she would tell the other girls she was only here for a short time. They had sneered. She had lashed out and, as a result, had spent many hours in solitary confinement, with bread and water. When Ia cried now, it was always at night, in the dark, and she had trained herself to cry silently.

In the daytime, she had learned to control her feelings. Ia rested her arms on the wooden rim of the sink and surveyed her life. She was not staying here, that was for sure – how would she ever get to America if she did? But how, on the other hand, could she get a job outside if she ran away? One needed references for jobs, she was certain.

She lugged the great basket of clothes out to the yard. The basket was so heavy that she felt her arms would be pulled out of their sockets or that her guts would rupture. In the yard the washing-lines crisscrossed and, when the sheets were billowing in the wind, Ia liked to pretend she was on a sailing-ship travelling away from the drudgery of her life. She looked up at the top of the high wall, where the sun shone on the shards of glass set in the top, as much to keep the inmates in as to keep others out – but who would be mad enough to climb in? She laughed to herself as she bent to pick up the sheets. It was such a small, mean patch of sky that she could see. Its very smallness always made her think, by contrast, of the great swathe of the sky on the cliffs at Gwenfer. She looked up at the building opposite, where the orphaned boys lived.

She waved. 'Hallo, Isaac,' she said almost gaily. It was her own little ritual when she hung out the clothes. She had not seen Isaac since she had arrived here. The intermingling of the sexes filled the authorities with such fear that even church services in the chapel were separate. She wondered if he was big now, if he was healthy, for she was never able to get news of him.

'Blewett, what are you mooning about? Get on with your work, girl, or it will be a report for you.' Mrs Drew's voice thundered across the yard.

When she had hung the last sheet on the line Ia made her way to the steam room. Of all duties she most hated working in the steam room. The heat from the ranges along one wall, where the flat-irons heated, was intense. It had its own peculiar noise created by the insistent hissing of the steam, and the thudding of the heavy irons as they were pressed down on to the fabrics. Fear in this room was a tangible thing. Woe betide any girl who scorched her ironing. The girls' cheeks were red from holding the iron as close to their skin as they dared to gauge its heat before slamming it down on the cloth while sending up a silent prayer that there would be no burn marks. Many of the girls' cheeks were scarred where they had miscalculated and had burned themselves.

It was not only orphans who worked here but some

women from the workhouse itself. Ia despised these women as they shuffled around the high-windowed room, with expressionless eyes and mouths which never smiled. These creatures had given up all hope, which Ia refused to do.

Across the room Ia saw Jinny and made straight for her.

'Sheets?'

'Thousands of they buggers, look.'

Together they began to fold the sheets. They stretched them, tugging as hard as they could to straighten them to be ironed. Then they walked towards each other to fold them. As they got closer they grabbed the opportunity to whisper.

'Ia, have you heard? Sally Banks is in the infirmary.'

'So? I never liked her. What's wrong with her?' Ia bent to pick up the bottom of the sheet.

'They say she's very ill, that's what's wrong.' The two ends of the sheet were joined. They returned to the pile for another.

'She wouldn't be in the bloody infirmary if she wasn't,' Ia hissed as she walked forward with her end of the sheet. 'With what?'

'Don't know, but Aggie says she was screaming fit to bust and the sweat rolling off her. Doesn't look good for her according to Aggie. But it could be good for ee.'

'What do you mean? What's it got to do with me?'

'She's up for the selection that's what. So there's a place going empty if she don't get better . . .'

'Blewett. Mills. Get on with your folding and stop chattering,' the gimlet-eyed chief laundress screamed at them.

Ia's brain was racing as she continued, silently, the minuet of sheet folding. How could she get on the selection board? That night in bed, for the first time in her life, Ia prayed to a God she did not know and a God to whom she had never given a thought.

The next morning at breakfast Ia's name was on the list for the selection committee. This day she would have no work. Instead she was to bathe, wash her hair and dress in the garment reserved for Sundays, before presenting herself in the warden's office at three o'clock. Ia felt sick with apprehension.

3

Ia stood in the governors' committee room, completely in awe of her surroundings. She had never been here before. The fine oak panelling, the highly polished furniture, paintings on the walls, the bowl of flowers – it was as if she stood in a different building from the one she had lived in for so long. It even smelled differently.

The three members of the selection committee stared at her. The matron was a fat, cold woman long embittered by life. There was a younger woman with a sweet and gentle smile and the prettiest hat Ia had ever seen, with a great, brightly coloured feather which must have come from a mystical bird, she thought. The third was a gross man with a face as red as beetroot, and more chins than Ia would have thought possible to fit on to one face. He studied his hands at length. These hands seemed to give him much pleasure for he smiled smugly at them. They were fat hands, like large white uncooked sausages – sausages wearing a heavy gold ring that dug deep into the flesh, and with nails that shone as if polished.

Ia stood awkwardly and wished that someone would speak. The younger woman smiled at her but said nothing. The matron frowned and the two women looked at the man in the middle as if waiting for him to start the proceedings.

His study of his hands completed, he looked up at Ia from tiny black eyes almost concealed in flesh. A small mouth within his large beard opened a mere fraction.

'Name?'

'Ia Blewett.'

'Ia? What sort of ridiculous name is that? What's wrong with a sensible name like Jane or Mary?'

'I don't know, sir.'

'You'll have to change that.'

'Yes, sir,' Ia said, unable to keep a hint of resentment out of her voice.

'No one will want you with a name like that,' he explained gruffly. 'Call yourself Fanny. A good name, Fanny.' The matron nodded as if agreeing; the young woman stopped smiling.

'How long have you been here, Blewett?'

'Two years, matron.'

'And have you been happy, here, my dear?' It was the woman in the feathered hat who asked her this. Ia warmed to her, and the way she had not called her Blewett, but not sufficiently to be able to tell the truth.

'Yes, thank you, ma'am,' she lied.

'So, you want to be a scullery maid?' the fat man enquired, taking a large gold watch from his pocket and studying that with as much concentration as he had previously given to his hands. A thin skin of sweat had broken out on his face. He did not look straight at Ia.

'Yes, please, sir.'

'Did you always want to be a scullery maid?' the woman in the feather hat asked.

Ia did not know what to answer. Was it a trick question? If she said no, she wanted better things, would they reject her? If she said yes, would that show lack of intelligence?

'I'll do, happily, whatever God wishes of me,' was her inspired answer.

'Good, good,' the man rumbled and this time looked at Ia with a strange glint in his eye which unnerved her. He wiped the sweat from his forehead with a large white handkerchief. Inconsequentially, Ia wondered if she had laundered it.

The three heads were bent towards each other and a whispered conversation took place which she could not hear. 'Passed!' the fat man bellowed, as he scribbled on a piece of paper. Ia stood transfixed as he handed the paper to her.

'Take the paper, Blewett. Go next door. Mrs Drew will see to you.'

Ia bobbed a small curtsy. 'Thank you,' she whispered and escaped from the room as fast as she could, her heart almost bursting with happiness. She looked at the piece of paper. 'Mrs Tresek' she read, with an address in Lemon Street. And in the top right-hand corner was a number.

From a pile of wooden boxes, Mrs Drew selected one marked with the same number as was written on her paper, 147. She picked up a pile of clothes. 'These are for working in, Blewett, and this is your underwear. The dress you've got on is for Sunday best.' She stuffed the clothes into a cambric bag. 'You keep the cloak too.'

'Yes, Mrs Drew. Thank you.' At that moment even Mrs Drew seemed generous.

'Let's see that paper.' She read it. 'My, aren't you the honoured one? The chairman of the governors, no less, has chosen you.'

'That man in there?' Ia asked with sinking heart.

'Lovely house they live in. Just across town. Not far. Here's your shilling.'

'My shilling?'

'You always gets a shilling when you leave and start work.'

'Thank you.'

'Mrs Tresek will pay you quarterly for your labour. Eleven pounds a year and half a day off a week. Do you understand?'

'And half a day off a week,' echoed Ia wonderingly.

Mrs Drew looked up sharply. 'What do you mean by that?' she asked suspiciously.

'All that money *and* time off, it sounds like paradise, Mrs Drew.'

For the first and only time Mrs Drew smiled at Ia. 'Well, I expect you'll have to work hard for it.'

'I don't mind hard work, Mrs Drew, you know that.'

'Right, now, what have we got in this box here?' She took a large key and opened it. She pulled out a book. 'Poetry,' she said dismissively. 'Not much use to a scullery maid.' Ia looked at the book; her first instinct was to leave it there. What did she want with a reminder of the Tregowans? But then she thought she might sell it, so she slipped it into the bag of clothes. 'My, isn't that pretty,' said Mrs Drew as she carefully lifted out an azure blue bowl gaudily painted with red roses. Ia's hand shot to her mouth.

'My mam's bowl,' she said with disbelief, a slight catch in her voice.

'That's all there is, I'm afraid. That's all you came in here with.'

Ia took the bowl and clutched it to her. 'Thank you,' she said breathlessly as if the woman had given her the bowl as a present. She had never expected to see it again.

'Well, good luck, Blewett. Keep off the gin and don't oversleep, that's the best advice I can give you.' She almost laughed as she waved the girl out of the room.

Ia stepped out into the corridor, clutching her bag of clothes and the bowl. She looked down the length of the polished corridor to the large green door at the end, by which sat the porteress. She stood savouring this moment before taking that first step towards freedom and her new life.

'Ia,' a woman's voice called from behind her. Ia froze; it was so long since any adult had called her by her first name. She swung round.

'Yes, ma'am,' she said to the woman in the feathered hat.

'Hallo, Ia. My name is Mrs Hadley, I'm Canon Hadley's wife. I should like you to take my address, in case you ever need help or advice.' She smiled sweetly.

'Why thank you, ma'am,' Ia bobbed a curtsy.

'You are very beautiful, Ia.' Ia blushed with pleasure. 'But beauty can be a dangerous thing. Be careful, Ia.' The woman glanced nervously at the committee room door. 'Be very careful . . .' she repeated. Ia stood waiting, for the woman looked as if she were about to say more. She smiled again. 'I wish you well, my dear,' was all she said. Ia thanked her and resumed her walk down the long corridor.

Mary Hadley watched the beautiful child. Even as Ia Blewett had walked into the committee room she had sensed something different about her. It was not just that lovely face; there was a brightness, an intelligence, in her eyes which caught one's attention. And when she had spoken, it had been with an educated voice. Altogether different from the orphans they normally dealt with. Mary Hadley sighed and wished she were not such a coward. Alderman Tresek should not be allowed to take these girls into his house. He had unnatural appetites: the whole of Truro knew that, but because of his wealth and great political power nothing was ever said. She had allowed that beautiful child into his clutches, and she despised herself. How she longed to be back in a country living, away from the politics of a cathedral town. She went back to the committee room for the tea and cakes which the matron always served on these occasions.

Ia reached the porteress who rose from her chair to open the door.

'Goodbye, Blewett. Now watch yourself, girl. No funny business. We don't want to see you back here next year pregnant and in the workhouse, do we?' The porteress leered at her, making a mental note that within the year this one would be back.

'Would it be possible for me to go over to the boys' house to say goodbye to my brother?'

'What, Isaac Blewett? Didn't they tell you?'

'Tell me what?'

'I'm sorry, dear, Isaac died in the influenza epidemic, last winter.'

'No one told me,' Ia whispered.

'Now, that they should have done. Would you like to sit down here a moment? You look white as a sheet,' the porteress said, suddenly concerned.

'No thank you,' Ia said, wildly pulling at the heavy door.

'Here, let me help you. 'Tis a heavy door.' At last the green door swung open and Ia, momentarily blinded with shock, stumbled out into the open. It was hot. She felt dizzy. She leaned against the wall taking deep breaths of what should have been sweet freedom. She crossed the gravel path and sank on to the grass, trying to assimilate the news of Isaac's death. Her grief turned to anger that no one had seen fit to tell her. He might have been ill and calling for her . . . She dug out a large clump of grass with her hands and hurled it forcefully at a flower-bed. How dare they treat us as less than human, how dare they, she repeated to herself. A tear rolled down her cheek and she quickly wiped it away. She must not cry – not in the daytime; her grief would have to wait.

'What's wrong, Blewett? Playing truant already?'

Ia looked up, shading her eyes from the sun, to see above her the corpulent shape of Mr Tresek, the chairman of the selection committee.

'Nothing, sir.' She scrambled to her feet and remembered to bob.

'Enjoying the sun for a minute, were you? You didn't get much sun in there did you, my dear?'

'No, sir.' She managed a wan smile.

'Such a pretty little thing,' he said quietly and, to Ia's horror, one of the sausage fingers stroked her cheek, feeling like a damp wodge of dough against her skin. 'Now, run along to Lemon Street, Blewett. Or shall I call you Fanny? I shall see you later.'

Ia picked up her bag of clothes, packed her bowl carefully amongst them, and swung the bag across her shoulder before scuttling away. Out of sight behind a tree she put down her bag and lifted the hem of her skirt to wipe her cheek where the chairman's fingers had touched her.

That's what Mrs Hadley had meant. The chairman had plans for her, wicked plans.

'That's what you think,' she said aloud. She knew about men; she had heard her father forcing himself upon her mother enough times. She had listened to the gossip among the girls in the orphanage. The thought of those fat white hands and what they might do to her made her shudder.

'No, you won't. You dirty old bugger!' She swung her sack up over her shoulder again and walked out of the workhouse grounds. Outside she enquired the way to the west and marched rapidly down the street, up the far side – out of Truro and away from Bernard Tresek, Esq.

4

Under the sweltering August sun Ia toiled up the hill out of Truro. She wanted to put as big a distance as possible between her and the town before nightfall. She stopped at a crossroads. She looked at the signpost. Penzance. The town was close to her village of Gwenfer. She turned towards that road, her heart lifting at the thought of seeing Gwenfer again, the familiar faces, the cliffs . . . She stopped dead – but if she went there they would find her. No doubt they would assume that was the logical place for her to go; Gwenfer would be the first place they would look for her. 'To Falmouth' she read, but that was only a few miles, too close to Truro and the orphanage. It would have to be Bodmin. She sighed to herself, seeing from the signpost that Bodmin was over twenty miles away. And what if they were looking for her already? On the road she might be seen. They would lock her up again or, worse, make her work for the chairman. There was nothing for it: she would have to make her way skirting the outside of the city through the fields until she was safely past.

Three hours later the sun was setting and Ia was tired. Her legs ached from tramping through the fields, clambering through hedges, climbing fences and stiles. Tomorrow, she decided, it would be safe for her to walk on the comparative comfort of the roadway.

She spread her cloak on the ground beneath a large oak tree, took her work clothes out of the bag and put them all on. She giggled at the strange figure she must present with so many clothes on. She wrapped the cloak about her and, using the bag as a pillow, settled down to sleep, thankful for the fine weather.

She was woken just before dawn by a damp drizzle. Already she was soaked and chilled to the marrow. She lay there for a few moments wondering what to do and then decided she would be better off walking through the rain than lying here and getting stiff in it.

All that day and into the night she walked, a resolute walk, looking neither to left nor right, ignoring the coaches which sped past covering her with mud and spray from the road. As she walked, she formulated a plan. Bodmin was big, she was certain, otherwise so many carriages would not be going in that direction. She would find work, she would save every penny and then, in six months or a year, she would go to Plymouth and get a passage on a boat to take her to America. Then she would search out Paul or her Uncle Ishmail and best of all her sister Mary who, Ia was convinced, had made her way there, too. Then she would no longer be alone.

The decision filled her mind with such excitement that she forgot the wet, the cold and the hunger pains. Her hunger she determined to ignore, in any case: she had decided that the shilling from the orphanage would be the foundation of her savings. She would eat when she got a job and not before.

The following morning she was less sure. The pain in her stomach was acute and she knew she must look like a tramp, her dress and cloak filthy from the mud. At this rate she would never find work. She stopped at a stream, washed and arranged herself as best she could, using her fingers as a comb through her tangled hair. Some early blackberries hung over the water; with delight she devoured the lot. At least the rain had stopped. It was a beautiful summer's morning as she took to the road again.

She did not get to Bodmin. Rounding a corner of the road she saw an inn. At the front of the building stood many carriages and people were milling around. With so many vehicles it must have many customers, she reasoned, and if they were busy, she stood a better chance of getting work. She slipped round the side of the inn, to the back door, ignoring the ribald remarks of the grooms. She knocked but when no one answered she let herself in and found herself in an empty corridor. A smell of freshly baked bread and roasting meat filled the air, making her feel faint. She leaned against the wall for support.

'Hallo, you'm the new girl?' A large, jolly-faced woman had appeared from one of the doors. The big apron she wore was covered in flour, as was most of her face.

'Yes,' Ia lied quickly.

'I need you, my maid. 'Tis a mad-house here today. 'Tis always the same on market day. You come along with me . . .' and she waddled up a steep flight of stairs

139

with Ia close behind. Up they went into the attics. ''Tis very small, but 'tis clean as a whistle.'

Ia all but gasped at the room into which she was shown. Flowered curtains flapped at the open window. Two beds were neatly made, covered with brilliant white counterpanes. On a washstand stood a bowl and ewer.

'Get cleaned up and get yourself back down to the kitchen, sharpish. The dirty dishes are piling up something shocking down there.'

'Mrs . . .'

'Bottrell, Amy Bottrell. And what's your name, girl?'

'Ia Blewett. But . . . Mrs Bottrell, I have to confess, I lied downstairs. I'm not the new girl. But I'm desperate for work and I can work hard – you'd never regret taking me on.' The desperation she was feeling showed in her eyes as she looked anxiously at Mrs Bottrell.

The woman stood, fat arms akimbo, and studied her. 'That's good of you that you told me the truth. But then 'twas silly to lie in the first place, wasn't it?'

'Yes,' Ia replied, shame-faced. 'I don't normally. It's just I don't think I could face another night sleeping in the open . . . that's what made me lie.'

'Run away?'

'Yes.'

'Are they looking for you?'

'I don't know.'

'Who you run away from?'

Ia took a deep breath. 'I was at the orphanage in Truro. I got a position with the chairman of the governors but, well, I didn't trust him, the way he looked at me, and he touched me . . .' Ia shuddered.

Mrs Bottrell's face twisted with distaste. 'There's some evil old buggers around. Get washed and down you come, girl.'

'You mean I can stay?'

'Three shillings a week and your food. Any tips are yours. No time off until October, then you can have a half day a week. Now, quick about it, dinners are due out.'

Ia tidied herself and raced back down to the kitchens. Soon she was up to her elbows in soap suds.

Mrs Bottrell might have a jolly face but in the kitchens she turned into a tyrant. She screamed, she shouted, she swore, she threw saucepans, she beat the meat, and she clipped her assistants round the ears. Then, when the lunchtime rush had subsided, she became again the friendly person she had been before. By three o'clock they were sitting down at the kitchen table to the best food Ia had eaten for years. Great bowls of soup with fresh bread, then steak and oyster pie, followed by strawberries and a large bowl of clotted cream. Ia had never dreamed that working people like herself would have food such as this to eat.

John Bottrell, the landlord, was as fat and as happy as his wife. Their son, also John, was rather simple and his job was to help the ostler Paddy to care for the horses. There were three girls, apart from Ia, working in the kitchen. And there was Sarah who helped the landlord in the bar.

As they ate, the new girl arrived. She was a thin, scared-looking creature. Even the kindest of souls could never have called her pretty. John Bottrell took one look at her and had a whispered conversation with his wife. They both looked so hard across the table at Ia that she found herself blushing with confusion.

'I could do with more help in the bar and at the tables, Ia. You'll do.'

Ia tried not to look too eager. She had already worked out, while she was washing up, that three shillings a week was less than she would have earned in Truro and she was unlikely to get any tips if she were working, unseen, in the kitchens.

'She'll need a better dress than that. Lend her your

141

spare, Sarah, till we get the material and she can make her own.'

That evening, her hair washed and rippling down her back over the tight-fitting gingham dress which Sarah had lent her, Ia was a sensation in the bar. Mr Bottrell was pleased with her and the patient way she dealt with his more lecherous clients – men with the heat on drank more. He'd known what he was about when he'd decided on Ia for the bar instead of the other new girl.

It was hard work carrying the heavy platters of food. As the evening wore on the kitchens seemed to be a mile away from the tables she was serving. Her arms ached from carrying six tankards full of frothy beer at a time, from tipping up the barrels when they were running out. And she was weary too from having to parry the groping of the customers, pretending a goodwill towards them she did not feel.

At half past one the landlord took pity on her and suggested she went to bed. Wearily she climbed the stairs. As she reached her room, the door of the next room opened and Sarah came out with a man.

Ia had been working at the inn for a month. She had her own dresses now, two of them – one for wearing, one for the wash. Whilst everyone was kind, she had not made friends. The new girl, Sue, with whom she shared her room rarely spoke and Sarah frightened Ia. There was a hardness about her which reminded Ia of some of the overseers at the orphanage. So, although she was surrounded by people, she was often lonely and would frequently find herself thinking of Jinny and wishing she were here with her.

She was used to the work now and no longer found it so tiring. She had even schooled herself not to react to the groping and fumbling of the guests. She had been quick to learn that if she let the men feel her, she usually received a tip, all of which joined the orphanage shilling and her wages in the blue bowl which had belonged to her mother. Every night men suggested she take them to bed with her; each night she joked as she refused their offers.

'Why don't you entertain?' asked Sarah, one evening in a lull.

'No, thank you.'

'Too good for it or what?'

'No, it's not that. Not yet, I'm not ready.'

'Ha! The men wouldn't agree with you. Right little cock-chafer you are. Mind you, I'm not complaining. You hot 'em up, and I gets the trade.' Sarah laughed. 'Sooner you gets rid of your virginity, the richer you'll be.'

Ia said nothing, but concentrated on polishing the glasses. And I'd end up looking like you, she thought, eyeing Sarah's pallid complexion, and the cold sores on her lip which never healed. Ia was not naive. She had watched Sarah, seen the threepenny pieces change hands and knew deep inside herself that eventually this was what she would have to do if she wanted more from life. She realised that a future in service was out of the question now: without references no respectable household would take her in. And while she was happy enough here, she had no intention of working in a public house all her life. Ia wanted to be surrounded by beautiful things.

Her plans were changing too. In the bar she heard much talk of London. London, it seemed, was even bigger than Bodmin. One man had told her you could walk for days and never get to the end of it. But, they told her, money was to be made in London. More money than normal folk dreamed of. They talked of guineas to be earned and she had dreamed of pence.

It was her fare to London she worked for now; America could come later. That and enough money to keep her going until she was on her feet. She had learned

143

that the more she giggled and flirted, the more she slapped their hands, shrieking 'Naughty', the more they wanted to grope her and the more farthings she got for her pains. A farthing a feel and threepence for the real thing seemed to be the going rate. But Ia had begun to dream of guineas.

Come next April she would leave, she decided. For London.

5

In her eighteenth year Alice should have been presented to London society. Instead, she stayed at Gwenfer. She had received a letter from her father asking if she wished to make her debut. When she had replied that she did not feel ready, George was relieved that his pleasures were not to be curtailed by the arrival of his unworldly daughter in his London house. They agreed to postpone the event until she was eighteen.

In truth she had no desire to be a debutante, not ever. She did not want to leave Gwenfer, where she felt too much needed doing. She determined that if she could avoid going to London altogether, she would. She did not want to find a husband, and certainly not the kind she would meet during the season. Undoubtedly such a man would have his own estate where, if she married, she would be expected to live. She wanted to live at Gwenfer, was determined to die there.

Alice was constantly busy. The new cottages finished, she ordered the building of almshouses for those in the community who could no longer care for themselves. She had the school, which had become seriously run down, repaired. She was shocked by the lack of books and materials in the building and had it restocked. She no longer asked or expected her father to help; it was her own money she used. In addition, she bought a herd of cows whose milk, pale golden in summer, was made into butter and clotted cream which they sold to the new hotels opening in Penzance. Summer visitors were now beginning to flock there in increasing numbers and Alice looked about for further ventures for her villagers. A small enterprise was started to make souvenirs for the holiday-makers – copper Cornish pixies, little boxes, ashtrays. The creamery and the craft factory were run by the villagers; the profits were shared amongst the workers. Alice took nothing from either. For the first time for a long time the name of Tregowan was revered.

Mr Featherstone, the schoolteacher whom Ia and others had feared, became ill, which gave Alice the opportunity she had been longing for – to get rid of him.

'Miss Gilby, would you consider running the school in the village? You won't want to spend the rest of your life teaching me.'

'Me? Good gracious, Alice, I've never given such a thing a thought. I'm a governess not a schoolteacher.'

'You're a teacher of genius, Miss Gilby. I don't think your talents should be restricted to just one person.'

Miss Gilby patted her tidy hair and almost simpered. 'I don't know if I'm capable.'

'A house goes with the position. It's a dear little cottage, close by the school. The garden could be lovely. And it would be permanent, Miss Gilby.'

Philomel Gilby had a lot to think about in bed that night. Time was moving on. Alice had just celebrated her eighteenth birthday and in a few months would be away to London where she would need her no longer. Miss Gilby had already begun half-heartedly to look at the announcements for teaching positions though a change was not a prospect she relished. The endless moving about the countryside and having to meet new people, was a constant torment to her. Alice's suggestion was attractive, but against it was the idea of small children. Miss Gilby had always found them difficult and, though she could never admit this to a living soul, she was afraid that they would laugh at her and her strange appearance. She was unnerved by the thought of rough, village children, and particularly boys. However, a permanent position, one for life, with a house of her own was all too tempting ... In the morning she gratefully accepted Alice's offer.

It was Miss Gilby who finally persuaded Alice to go to London for the season. She pointed out that though the balls and the dinners might be irksome, the concerts would not be. And Alice could go to museums and art galleries which until now she had only heard of. London's cultural life seemed much more inviting to Alice than its social life.

Miss Gilby had persuaded her to go because she was concerned about her charge. She was too quiet and withdrawn. Happy when she was learning, a sadness crept over her when she was not. Miss Gilby had at first assumed that this sadness was caused by the death of her mother and was surprised to learn that it had something to do with a village child – a child who had so affected Alice that she would not allow anyone to mention her name in her hearing. Philomel was shocked. Radical as she was politically, hers was very much a theoretical radicalism. When it came to day-to-day living, Philomel had rigid views of what was proper: this relationship certainly did not fit within those bounds. Alice had mentioned the child to Philomel only once. Mrs Malandine and Mrs Trelawn seemed to think this a good sign; Miss Gilby was not so sure. She had learned from personal experience that being able to talk of one's loss was a help: she had never had anyone to talk to about the death of her own beloved parents and she knew how deeply she still mourned. Perhaps a change of scenery and the excitement of the season would help the young woman.

*

It was March. In April Alice was to travel to London with Queenie in attendance. Philomel had always been a fascinated observer of human nature and was quietly amused to notice the change in attitude towards her from Queenie who now felt that she was, once again, in the ascendancy.

Madame Delamere of Truro had been summoned to Gwenfer by Mrs Malandine who knew about these things.

Alice was sitting on her rock in the early spring sunshine and had quite forgotten the time. She had long ago taken up her old habit of coming here when she wanted to think. A flustered and puffing Flo appeared.

'That Frenchie woman's up at the house waiting for you, Miss Alice.' Since their trip to London, Flo always called her 'miss', the old familiarity had gone for ever.

Alice skidded into the room that had been her parents' bedroom, her hair dishevelled, her feet bare.

'*Je suis désolée, voulez vous m'excuser, madame?*' Alice smiled apologetically at the short, black-clad woman who was waiting for her. The woman clucked her tongue so that Alice was uncertain if she was forgiven or not. 'It was such a lovely day, I lost track of the time, watching the sea and the birds.'

'Watching the sea won't find you a fine husband, mademoiselle.' The woman continued to cluck, as with birdlike motions, and with Queenie's assistance, she helped Alice to undress and handed her clothes to the downtrodden assistant she had brought with her. 'Please to hold yourself straight, mademoiselle,' she ordered as she expertly measured Alice, who stood in her simple shift. 'I see you wear no corset,' Madame said disapprovingly. 'Please ask your maid to fetch one for you, mademoiselle.'

'But I don't possess a corset.'

Madame looked horror-struck and agitatedly fanned herself with a swatch of material. She snapped open the locks of a large travelling trunk she had brought, delved amongst the contents and came up with a selection of corsets. 'If mademoiselle would be good enough to try one of these . . .' she said, as she wrapped round Alice's slim figure a confection of pink silk and lace and threaded the eyelets. She began to tighten the laces. Alice stood uncomplaining. She pulled harder and Alice felt the breath being pushed out of her body. As the laces were pulled tighter, Alice felt as if her internal organs were being squeezed out of her.

'Please, madame, that hurts.'

'As they say in my country, it is necessary to suffer in order to be beautiful, mademoiselle.' She flicked her tape measure about Alice's waist. '*Enfin*, eighteen inches. No young woman should enter society unless her waist is eighteen inches or less.'

'I'll stay at eighteen inches if you don't mind,' Alice said with a wan smile, thinking she had never felt so uncomfortable in her life.

From the trunk Madame selected a white satin dress which she helped Alice step into. The dress clung to the front of Alice's body. The material of the skirt was swathed back across her hips and caught up into a bustle at the back. Across the bustle were four cabbage roses made of matching silk. Alice could hardly believe her reflection in the cheval glass. Queenie's large bosom seemed to grow to twice its size with pride. Alice grinned; she looked ridiculously like a woman.

Madame's head was twisted on one side as she studied Alice. At last she smiled. She was pleased with what she saw. Here was a creature worthy of her skills. Had she not, as she was fond of asking everyone, dressed the Empress Eugenie? This was not strictly true. Madame Delamere had once stitched the hem of a dress for the empress when working as an apprentice to a dressmaker – not, unfortunately, in Paris but in London – when influenza had decimated the experienced workforce. Nor had she ever crossed the Channel to the land of haute couture and her knowledge of its language was limited, to say the least. But the story was so often repeated that she now believed that she had dressed the empress and, if she was not French by birth, all her sentiments and her imagination were unmistakably French.

She made a good living from her salon in Truro. Most of the ladies of the county came to her for their gowns, but none was as beautiful as this Tregowan girl. Too often the client's bust was too heavy, the waist too thick, and the hips were never of this season's shape. Their daughters, too, lacked the style and carriage of this young woman, and taxed all Madame's ingenuity. Madame Delamere regretted that she rarely had the opportunity of dressing the quality who went to London, or to dear Mr Worth for their gowns.

'I regret, mademoiselle, that time will not permit me to arrange a complete wardrobe for you, as I should have wished,' she fretted, an hour later, as Alice stood amongst the cascade of silk and satins which had been conjured out of the trunk.

Alice looked in disbelief at the two ball gowns and five other assorted outfits. 'But how much more will I need?' she asked.

'The belle of the season must have at least ten ball gowns, ten tea dresses, ten afternoon dresses. At least four costumes of linen for the country, and four outfits for Ascot. And you will need hats, shoes, parasols and of course lingerie. Oh, such fun it would have been for me to create all this for you.'

'It sounds an awful lot of clothes just for one person,' Alice ventured doubtfully.

'Your appearance is your greatest weapon, mademoiselle.' Madame Delamere arched her brows grotesquely at Alice.

A week before she was due to leave a letter arrived from

her father to announce that he had remarried and that he and his wife were looking forward to her arrival.

In the kitchen the consensus was that he should have waited a bit longer.

The following day Alice sat at the stillroom table with the others as they finished their Sunday lunch.

'Where's Ia buried?' she suddenly asked.

Everyone laid down their knives and forks with a clatter and looked at her as one. 'I'd like to put up a beautiful headstone, perhaps one with angels on it. She would have liked that.'

'What do you want to do a thing like that for?' Queenie said sharply.

'Because I loved her.'

'People like that don't have graves like the rest of us,' Mrs Malandine said stiffly.

'What do you mean?'

'They lie in paupers' graves.'

'I don't understand.'

'They just have numbers, if anything at all. Sometimes several are buried together.'

'Queenie, why didn't you tell me this?' Alice said, turning accusingly to her old nurse. 'I must find her. If her grave doesn't carry her name it's as if she never existed.' Alice's obvious anguish distressed Philomel.

'Oh, my, 'tis hot in here, isn't it?' Queenie said, fanning herself with her napkin. Her normally high colour was tinged now with magenta. She rubbed her chest. 'I ate that good dinner too quickly, Mrs Trelawn.'

'You all right, Queenie? You'm looking a funny colour.'

'I'm feeling a bit queer, Mrs Trelawn. Well, more than a bit . . .' Queenie clutched at her chest. 'Oh, lawks,' she sighed. She put out her hand towards Alice and stared at her with eyes that seemed to be struggling to focus. 'Oh, my handsome . . .' Her eyes glazed. She slumped to one

150

side and slid from her chair on to the floor with a heavy thud.

They all rushed to her side. Flo screamed and for her pains received a sharp slap from Mrs Malandine. Sal stood wide-eyed with horror. Philomel wrung her hands.

'Queenie, Queenie, are you all right?' Alice knelt beside her and gently cradled her head.

'Sal, go into the kitchen and get one of they pheasant feathers I uses as a garnish. Bring it here with matches. That'll bring her round. She's fainted with the heat,' the fat cook said cheerily.

'I'm afraid it's too late, Mrs Trelawn. I'm afraid she's gone,' Mrs Malandine said as she dropped Queenie's wrist.

'Gone?' Alice said, hysteria rising in her voice. 'Speak English, woman. What do you mean?'

'I'm sorry, Alice. I'm afraid she's dead. Her heart must have . . .' Mrs Malandine said helplessly.

All eyes turned to look at Alice, fearful of her reaction.

'She'll get cold, she hates the cold. Could you cover her, please,' Alice said quietly, got to her feet and walked quickly from the room.

'Flo, you follow her, we don't want her doing what she did last time,' Mrs Malandine said ominously.

'I don't think there's any question of that, Mrs Malandine,' Philomel said coldly but added in a quiet but purposeful voice, 'Where do you think she has gone to?'

'There's a rock in the cove, Miss Gilby, her always goes there when her's upset,' Mrs Trelawn advised her.

Philomel made her way gingerly through the garden, staring anxiously to left and right, as cautious as any jungle explorer. She went down the valley to where, in the distance, she could see Alice sitting on a large rock. She paused for a moment, collecting her thoughts and admiring her charge whose lovely face was profiled against the azure blue of the sea. Quietly Philomel approached her. She said nothing, but put her arms about Alice and held her closely. Alice sat silent in her arms. Philomel stroked the young woman's hair, surprised at the warmth of feeling she experienced as she held her close, not a familiar sensation for the little governess – to be in such close proximity to another person.

'I can't cry, Miss Gilby. It's as if I have no tears in me, no grief. But, oh my God, I have a terrible rage.' She looked up at her governess with anguish in her eyes.

'My poor Alice.'

'I never had a mother, you see, Miss Gilby, she was my mother. She loved me so and now, now who will there be to love me? I feel so alone, so dreadfully alone.'

'You have all of us, we . . . I . . . I . . . love you, too.' Miss Gilby stuttered over the unfamiliar word.

'What do I do, Miss Gilby? Why Queenie?'

Philomel sat for a full minute composing her reply. 'I know your feelings, Alice, and I shall not insult your intelligence by saying that these things are sent to try us. I can't tell you why Queenie died. There's nothing I can say to help you through this grief. But you should realise that, because of your love for her, she has not gone for ever. She will always be alive in your heart.' She gazed out over the sea for what seemed a long time. 'There are some of us not as fortunate as dear Queenie.'

Alice took Philomel's hand, 'Please, Miss Gilby, don't say such things. *I* shall always be grateful to you, I shall never forget you.'

Delicately Philomel wiped a tear, first from her blue eye and then her brown. 'Oh, silly me, I am supposed to be comforting you.' She gave a weak smile.

'I can't go to London. I have never wanted to. Now I certainly won't go.'

'Oh, but you must, Alice.' Miss Gilby fluttered with disapproval. 'Queenie was so proud of you. You were her little girl, and she was about to see you launched on the world as a beautiful woman. It was to be the culmination of her work. You must go for her sake.'

'Her little girl . . . ? Oh, Miss Gilby, how will I ever replace her?' And at last the tears for Queenie began to flow.

6

At the front of the train, in the luxuriously upholstered first-class carriage, Alice sat feeling uncomfortably restrained in her new travelling costume. The whalebones of her corset had lodged somewhere in the region of her ribs and were digging into her unmercifully. At this rate, she thought, it was going to be physically a most unpleasant summer. Nor was she used to wearing a hat, albeit a small, snappy creation from Madame Delamere. She kept fiddling with her hair, which Flo, with much giggling, had dressed up that morning. Alice was so used to it flowing about her shoulders that the nape of her neck felt strangely naked. She knew that young girls were supposed to be excited by having their hair dressed up, their skirts lengthened. She was not: she wanted to be as she had always been, in fact she did not think she even wanted to be a woman.

The train slackened its hurtling speed, slowing down to cross the great iron structure of the Tamar Bridge. Alice felt a great sadness as she remembered how dear Queenie had always closed her eyes at this point, fearful of the height. If only Queenie were there with her instead of Flo, then the thought of this summer might have been bearable. As if the season were not bad enough, the prospect of meeting her new stepmother filled her with apprehension. No doubt she would be like Aunt Maude and equally bossy.

Alice walked out into the corridor to stretch her legs. A

153

corridor on the train seemed to her a distinct improvement and would make the nine-hour journey much more
comfortable. Near Exeter they lunched on the picnic
packed by Mrs Trelawn – succulent crab from the cove,
feather-light chicken vol-au-vent and fresh fruit.

At the back of the train, on the uncomfortable wooden
seats of the third-class carriages, Ia unwrapped her
kerchief and took out the pasty which Mrs Bottrell had
insisted she bring with her. For the umpteenth time she
reread Mrs Bottrell's note recommending her to her sister
who ran a public house in Barnet – wherever that might
be.

Alice stood amongst the crowds on Paddington Station
and looked about hopefully for her father. Surely he
would be here. Flo had counted the cases a dozen times
and was now engrossed in a battle of insults with the
porter who had immediately come to their assistance.
Better than last time, Alice thought, smiling to herself.

'Flo, go and see if the carriage has been sent for us. I'll
stay here with the luggage.'

At the ticket barrier the first-class passengers milled
about, a brightly coloured throng, the women's clothes in
every conceivable fabric and colour. Bonnets were
trimmed with ribbons, fruit, birds' feathers, every conceit
of the milliner's art, which added to the kaleidoscopic
effect. From the rear of the train a crowd of third-class
passengers surged along the platform, a crowd dressed in
black, grey, brown and dun-coloured clothes like birds of
another species. They scrambled past and over the piles
of expensive leather baggage and the gaily rimmed
bandboxes, their possessions in bags and sacks which
they carried slung over their shoulders.

Alice stepped back to let the tide of people swarm past.
Amongst them, walking resolutely with her head held
high, giving the impression of a courage she was far from
feeling, was Ia. She had never seen so many people, nor

heard such an unholy noise in her life. Ia was terrified but was hiding it well.

As she walked Ia peered into the first-class carriages. She envied the comfort she saw, the thick cushions, the handy tables, the lamps, the wood panelling, the curtained windows. Bet their bums didn't ache, she thought. One day she would travel that way. One day it would be the only way she would consider travelling.

Ia's step faltered. Ahead of her stood a tall young woman who was strangely familiar. Ia stood staring at the woman, unsure – it had been so long. But the carriage, the beautiful profile, the fine blonde hair were the same. It was Alice Tregowan. But a different Alice, taller, more beautiful, wearing a cream velvet suit with an elegant matching hat. Ia felt anger swelling inside her as if the emotion had taken a physical form. Her chest felt clogged with it and she had difficulty in breathing. She fought to calm herself when what she most wanted to do was to cross the platform and strike Alice hard across her beautiful face. And then to scream at her of the pain of rejection, the loneliness, that she with her thoughtlessness had caused – to let her see the bitterness which she had sown in Ia.

'You bitch,' Ia muttered to herself venomously, making the man in front swing round to stare at her with astonishment. For the moment she had to content herself with that; anything more might lead to an arrest and a return to the workhouse.

As Ia came abreast of her, Alice turned to talk to a young maid who had run up to her. Ia passed her by.

Chapter Four

1

'Alice! At last we meet!' Across the wide expanse of her father's drawing-room, Alice looked up from the book she had been studying, to see a small, pretty woman tripping towards her. The woman's hair was a mass of bobbing curls in which diamond stars twinkled. The large, improbably blue eyes were set in a perfect heart-shaped face. She held her heavily embroidered skirt slightly lifted, the better to show her tiny feet on which she moved with small, childlike steps. She was dressed for the evening in a low-cut dress from which swelled her full, alabaster-white breasts. Long strings of pearls were surmounted by a fine diamond choker. She was dressed as a woman yet she had the face and manner of a young girl, and Alice had to remind herself that her stepmother was two years older than herself. 'Alice,' she lisped, putting her arms out in greeting. 'Oh, you are so tall, you lucky girl. Little me will have to stand on tippy-toes to kiss you,' she trilled and kissed the air somewhere in the region of Alice's chin.

Lord Tregowan stood to one side beaming with pleasure at the scene. 'Welcome, my darling Alice,' her uncomprehending ears heard him say; he had never used such a term of endearment to her before.

'Alice, I've been so excited about your coming. I told Georgie you'd be such a friend for me. A sweet playmate. Didn't I, Georgie? Dear, sweet Georgie wanted to rush me off to Rome for our honeymoon. But I insisted on being here when you arrived. I simply had to be here for your season. It's my duty to my daughter, I said.' She

156

giggled and danced an excited little step, clapping her small hands together. 'We've so much shopping to do, Alice. So much money to spend . . .' she trilled.

'Hallo, Papa,' Alice said as her stepmother paused for breath. 'And stepmother,' she added awkwardly.

'Oh, Georgie,' Lady Tregowan shrieked. 'I will *not* be called that. Too ageing. No, no, Alice must call me Daisy Dear, as all my dearest friends do.' Alice noticed with amusement that in her agitation Daisy's lisp vanished altogether.

'You must dress for dinner, Alice. We are to dine with the de Greys. They will be most helpful to you.'

'If you don't mind, Papa, I am very tired. It was a long journey. I would much prefer not to dine out tonight. I would be unable to hide my sadness . . .'

'Sadness! Why are you sad? You can't be. I won't let you be sad,' Daisy insisted, clapping her hands again.

'My nursemaid died.' Alice found it difficult to say, as if putting it into words made the fact irrefutable.

'Dear, dear. You can't let a nursemaid ruin your season.' Daisy laughed shrilly.

Alice looked at her stepmother and decided she did not like her. She looked at her father but he was smiling inanely at his wife. 'It *was* a long journey, Papa,' she said, desperate to be excused. She had been given a year to mourn the mother she did not know and a mere two weeks for the nurse she loved. 'Please, I shall be happy with a sandwich and a glass of milk.'

'A sandwich!' Daisy gave a tiny shriek, and then clapped her pink-nailed hand over her mouth as if horrified. 'In my house, you shall dine,' she said magnanimously, ringing the bell for Phillpott.

'Really, Daisy, I'm not hungry.'

'But you must eat to keep up your strength – a big girl like you. And it's Daisy Dear. Otherwise I might be confused with that old Daisy Warwick and that would never do, would it, Georgie?' She smiled at her husband, arching her eyebrows. He grunted with the contentment of a man well pleased with life. Alice stood, feeling huge and gauche beside this new relation.

She wished they would hurry and leave. Her stepmother's chatter was giving her a headache. Her body ached in the unfamiliar confines of her stays. It was another ten minutes before Daisy, looking at the small diamond-encrusted watch she wore on a gold chain around her neck, with the pearls and the diamond choker, exclaimed at the time and at last they left. Alice had a strange feeling of *déjà vu*.

As soon as she heard the front door slam, she crossed the hall to the baize door at the back of the hallway. She slipped through and down the iron-railed stairs into the basement. Here the walls were painted a dull green, and the stone floors were bare, in bleak contrast to the opulence upstairs. She remembered which way to go, but had she not, the clattering of pans and the buzz of talk would have guided her. She entered the large, steamy kitchen. Green-painted like the corridor, it had only one small window which was barred. The room was a hive of activity as her dinner, obviously at short notice, was being prepared.

'Hallo, everyone,' she said loudly, to be heard above the noise. 'I'm Alice Tregowan.' Silence was immediate as the staff stopped what they were doing and stood staring at her. She smiled at the woman wearing a large white apron over her dark blue dress. 'I just came to say, Cook, that I don't want anything to eat – just a sandwich and a glass of milk in my room, please.' No one said anything. 'Well, good-night,' she said uncertainly.

The only answering 'good-night' came from the scrawny little scullery maid, who blushed furiously at the glare she received from the cook for her pains.

As Alice closed the door on her way out she heard a loud, irate voice say, 'Bloody cheek, coming into *my* kitchen.'

Alice leaned for a second against the closed door and remembered the warm welcome of the kitchen at Gwenfer. It seemed that here she must remain firmly in her place upstairs: not for her the warmth and chatter of the kitchen.

Alice retraced her steps and climbed the stairs, past the drawing-room floor, and on up past the floor where her parents had slept and her mother's boudoir had been, and where her own new room was situated. She went on upwards, past the guest bedrooms, and up to the old nursery floor. She paused at the top to look over the banister. The wire netting was still there. She smiled, remembering the times she and Oswald had stolen from their beds to watch the crowds below. The hall beneath looked the same; the only difference was that the comforting hissing of the gas in the chandeliers had been replaced by electricity.

She opened the day nursery door and flicked the light switch. Still unused to this wonder of modern science, she switched it off and then on again, enjoying the silly sense of power it gave her. She looked about the room. Nothing had changed: all their toys were still exactly where they had left them. The room looked as if its child occupants had merely gone to bed and would be back in the morning to resume their games. The London nursery had been spared Etty Tregowan's vengeful destruction.

She breathed in deeply: it still smelled the same, the same sweet smell of lavender bags, chalk, linen and milk. And here, Queenie's presence was a tangible thing. She crossed to her large dolls' house, and opened the door. The family of dolls were still in residence. She bent down remembering how, as a child, she had longed to be small enough to climb in with them. This evening, young woman though she was, this feeling was almost overwhelming. She picked up the doll that had once been her favourite and from which she had been inseparable, and hugged it to her. She switched off the light and, still holding the doll, returned to her bedroom.

The high-ceilinged room had been recently redecorated and carefully furnished. She could not remember the room having looked like this: it must have been done for her. Flo had already unpacked her clothes and a fire glowed in the grate. Beside it, on a small table, stood her sandwich and a glass of milk.

With difficulty she struggled out of her clothes. Perhaps she should not have sent Flo to bed as soon as they arrived. In future she would need Flo to help her undress, she realised. With relief she removed the hated corset and stretched with pleasure and a sense of liberation. She put on one of her plain white night-dresses and curled up in the chair to eat her sandwich and drink the milk. She sat looking at the glowing coals, holding the doll to her. An image from earlier in the evening came back to her. The watch, of course, the watch, the pearls, the diamond choker had belonged to her mother. She had seen her mother glance at that watch so many times when she was tiring of her children's company.

She leaned her head against the silk upholstery of the chair feeling suddenly very tired. There was a pain inside her which was real and had nothing to do with illness. She longed to be home at Gwenfer.

2

Within an hour of leaving Paddington, Ia was hopelessly lost. She had asked several people for directions to Barnet, but either she was stupid or they had lied. She was not only lost but dazed. She had not realised that so many grand buildings existed, side by side. Gwenfer was big, but these buildings stretched as far as the eye could see. There was nothing like this in Truro, nor in Bodmin. They ought to be included in the seven wonders of the world that Alice had taught her about, she thought, as she cricked her neck to peer up at them and the sky beyond.

Her feet were beginning to hurt. On her shopping trip to Bodmin, with her savings, she had not only bought material to make her new skirt and blouse for this adventure, but a smart pair of high-ankled boots, neatly fastened at the side with black shiny buttons. Now she wished she had worn her old shoes, but they were deep in the bag she was carrying and she had no intention of unpacking in the street.

Every street was busy. The wide roads were full of hansom cabs, the horses snorting and pawing the road with impatience whenever the traffic came to a halt. Amongst the cabs were the carriages of the rich, emblazoned with arms and shining from hours of the coachman's polishing. Disappointingly, there were few open carriages, since rain threatened. She could not see into the broughams, as she would have liked, to see the clothes of their occupants.

She stopped to press her nose against a shop window. She had never seen such treasures. There were gowns made from materials she did not know the names of and in richly glowing colours. One dress had impossibly intricate gold thread work, she saw a shawl that looked more like a spider's web, and shoes in satin which made her new boots look dowdy.

At a jeweller's display further on she was fascinated at the array of sparkling stones. One day, she resolved, her eyes wide with wonder, she would have such jewels – a necklace like that blue one there and a ring with a large red stone like that one, or did she prefer the green? She laughed. 'I'll have the lot,' she said to herself with some amusement.

At a grocer's she could barely bring herself to look, but curiosity got the better of her. The window was full of great hams, whole cheeses, a slab of butter sculpted into

161

a huge wheatsheaf. The smell of freshly ground coffee filled the air, wafted into her nostrils, and reminded her how very hungry she was.

A thin drizzle began to fall. The rain settled the dust but made the smell of horses overwhelming. The grey pavement changed into a shimmering silver strip. The whole street was suddenly full of the sound of clicking and thunking as umbrellas were hurriedly unfurled, and with the birdlike cries of women, fearful that their slippers and dresses would be spoiled, peering anxiously up and down the street on the look-out for hansoms or for their own coaches. For a while Ia stalked along behind a man whose umbrella was so large that it shielded her as well as him. But when he turned into a doorway, she strode on in the driving rain.

As she trudged, the fine large buildings began to thin out. The shops were not as grand, and there were fewer fine carriages. Here there were villas, at first large but diminishing in size the further she walked, until she began to worry that somehow she had reached those outskirts of the city which she had been told it would take days to find.

As the light faded, Ia amused herself by peering into the houses. Each one was different; each, to her, was opulent, a microcosm of another world.

A totter's cart rattled by, the scrap iron clattering about in the back. A mangy dog sat on the tailboard and eyed Ia with a doleful expression as the increasing rain plastered its remaining fur against its thin body. Looking at the dog's wet coat, Ia put her hand up to her own hair and found it soaked. She wondered if she looked as bedraggled as the dog.

The cart stopped. The driver, a middle-aged man with a sack around his shoulders for protection, swung round in the seat.

'Wan' a lift?' he shouted.

Ia looked behind her to see whom he was shouting at, but there was no one else near. 'Me?' she asked.

'Can't see no one else looks as if they could do with one.' He grinned, showing the serious lack of teeth in his mouth.

'Thank you.' Ia ran to catch up with him and hauled herself up on the seat beside him. The dog immediately clambered over the old baths and buckets in the back to give her a welcoming sniff.

'Bugger 'orf, Domino,' the man growled. The dog cowered.

'He's doing no harm. You're a nice dog aren't you, Domino? That's a strange name for a dog.'

'Won him in a game of dominoes. Was daft enough to take the silly bugger.' The dog wagged his tail, aware that he was being talked about. 'Still, he's good company.' He clicked his tongue and the undernourished horse, in sad contrast to the fine carriage horses she had been admiring, wearily began to pull the cart again.

'Is this your job?' She nodded to the old pots and pans.

'What's rubbish to the nobs is money to me. Where yer going?'

Ia took Mrs Bottrell's note from her pocket. 'The Prince of Wales, Barnet,' she read carefully.

'Cor, love us, yer going the wrong way.'

'Oh dear, I'm not am I? I've been walking for hours. I'm tired out.'

'Going to a job there, was yer?'

'Yes. My last employer recommended me to her sister. I was to work in the bar,' she said proudly, afraid he might think her merely kitchen help.

'Fancy Whitechapel?'

'Where's that?'

'Just along here. Yer mean you've never heard of Whitechapel?'

'No.'

163

'I thought everyone had heard of Whitechapel what with the Ripper an' all.'

'The Ripper?'

'Yes, Jack the Lad. Ripped the girls open he did, threw their innards out.' He laughed loudly at the look of horror on her face. 'Everyone's heard of the Ripper,' he boasted.

'Not where I come from. Have they caught him?' she asked anxiously.

'Na, but he's stopped this past five years so he must be dead. Where you from then?'

'Cornwall.'

'Nar, I ain't heard of that.'

'Everyone has who lives there.'

He roared with laughter. 'That's good, miss. Very good.'

'I need work, though. So I have to go to Barnet.'

'A pretty little thing like you won't have no trouble getting work. I knows the very place. My brother, he's got a big boozer. He'll take yer on, if you smile nicely at him.' He leered at her and his fetid breath whistled through rotten teeth.

Ia recoiled from the stench. She found that she was twisting her hands together in her lap. The man was being very kind and yet she felt frightened. Perhaps it was his teeth, she thought to comfort herself. But she was used to bad teeth and stinking breath – there had been no adult in her village with a full set of teeth, and at the orphanage she had been unique in having all of hers.

'Thank you,' she said finally, for with night falling, what choice did she have?

The cart finally halted outside a large public house from which came a babble of noise and singing. She followed the man in, and was almost knocked sideways by the malodorous smell of damp clothes and overheated bodies. Through the bar they went and out to the back where Ia was introduced to his brother Bert Fowler, a mirror image of the carter.

'You worked in pubs before?' he barked.

'Yes. Not as big as this one, though.'

'A pub's a pub. You strong?'

'Oh yes, Mr Fowler, I know I'm thin but you'd be surprised how hard I can work.'

The man eyed her up and down. 'Start at five, finish at midnight unless you're on special duties.'

'I don't mind what I do, how long I work.'

'Well that's handy to know, I must say.' Ia noticed that the gas light gave his skin a strange green look. 'Five shillings a week and I takes half of any other earnings. I'm strict on that. You mess me about and you're out on yer ear, understand? What you called?'

'Ia Blewett. I won't mess you about, Mr Fowler, I promise.'

'Right. Well you looks fair done in tonight. Best run along to bed and start fresh in the morning,' he said almost kindly. 'Gwen,' he bellowed. 'Gwen! Where the hell is the girl? Gwen!'

'Here Mr Bert, evening Bob.' Gwen, a dark-haired girl of fifteen or sixteen, appeared. She wore a pretty blue dress which showed her full figure to advantage. And she had a broad smile that enlivened a rather plain face.

'Gor blimey, Gwen, wot happened to you?' the carter, Bob, said with a grin. The girl's hand shot up to her face and she gingerly fingered her livid bruised eye.

'Right corker, ain't it?' she said good-naturedly. 'John-nie Flocks gave it me,' she announced almost with pride.

'Reckon he's gorn on you, Gwen my girl.'

'Reckon so, Bob.' Gwen giggled.

'Gwen, this here's a new girl, Ida. Take her up and find her a bed. Put her in wiv Sybil till I finds out more. She looks fresh to me.' He turned his back on them. Ia picked up her bag and followed Gwen from the room.

'Where yer from?' asked Gwen over her shoulder.

'Gwenfer, in Cornwall.'

'Cor lummie, where's that?'

'A long way away, by the sea.'

'I've never seen the sea, just the bleeding river. Johnnie says he might take me to Margate if I behaves meself.'

They had reached the top of a narrow flight of stairs and entered a darkly painted corridor with a row of heavily varnished doors on either side.

'The sea is lovely. Always changing colour. I miss it.'

'Blimey, you talk posh!'

'Do I?'

'You on the batter?'

'I'm sorry?' Ia smiled, not understanding.

'On the batter. You know, the game?'

'What game?'

Gwen shrieked with laughter. 'Cor blimey, a ruddy cherry pie! Going wiv men, that's the batter. Where've you been? Well if you don't know wot it means you ain't done it then, have you?'

'Well, no.'

'How old are you?'

'Fifteen,' she lied.

'You've hung on to it long enough, ain't you? You'll soon get popped here, that's for sure.' She looked along the corridor, grabbed Ia's arm and spoke to her in an urgent whisper. 'Listen, Ida. The old man'll get at least three guineas for your cherry wiv your looks. He'll tell you he got a quid and give you ten bob. You hold out for thirty bob. He'll pay up. He won't want no trouble because he'll get good money for the first few months, whilst yer still tight, see. But once you're popped and you loosens up then the money is less. You see?'

'But . . .'

One of the doors opened and Gwen brought her finger up to her lips. A plump woman, her dress crumpled, smiled a sad smile at them and made her way along the passage towards the stairs down to the bar.

'That's old Jilly. She won't last here much longer. She must be down to sixpence a go. The old man don't want to know at that price. There ain't enough in it for him, you see, what wiv the laundry and the lights . . . He'll throw her out on the streets now, I should think.'

'How much will she earn then?' Ia found herself asking with fascinated curiosity.

'Fourpence a go, enough for a bed in them flea-pits called lodging-houses. Hardly worth it, is it? Me, I want to be out of the bash by then. I've high hopes Johnnie'll ask me to move in wiv him. You're lucky to be here, Ida. We gets a lot of shift mongers down here looking for jam tarts.'

'Shift mongers? Jam tarts? I don't understand.' Ia looked bewildered: this was a foreign language.

'Toffs, that's the shift mongers, they like the excitement, makes a change from the West End. Jam tarts, that's us, of course.'

At the far end of the corridor she opened one of the doors and showed Ia into a dreary room. There were four beds with dark blankets, four pegs on the wall and sacking at the window.

'This is where Bert puts the skivvies. As soon as Bert's made his mind up about you, you'll get yer own room. Come and see mine.'

She took Ia's hand and led her to the next room. Here there was a square of carpet, a large double bed, a commode, a dressing-table with a mirror and flower-patterned curtains at the windows. There was a strange, unfamiliar and musty smell to the room.

'Loverly, ain't it?'

'It's very nice.' Ia paused. 'Do you mind, you know, the men?'

'No, why should I? Course there's some as I don't go much on – the old fat men, those who take ages and the really smelly ones. But sometimes I'm lucky and get a really nice, posh toff. You'll be all right, you'll get the best. Bert'll see to that.'

'But, Gwen, I don't want to.'

'You what?' Gwen said with disbelief.

'I've got plans. Plans of my own.'

'Well, I 'ope I'm not around when the old man finds out. What's the point of hanging on to it? You've got to get rid of it sooner or later, and what else is a girl like us to do?'

'Gwen?' Bert's voice bellowed up the stairs. 'Get down here. You're wanted.'

'Here we go. Get along to your room, Ida, there's a pet.'

Ia made her way back to her room. She took her night-dress from her bag, carefully placed her precious azure blue bowl on the dressing-table, then turned down the blanket on the one bed which did not look as if it was occupied. She settled back on the plain ticking of the mattress, her head on the hard uncovered pillow. She was perturbed by what Gwen had told her. She had no intention of doing what Bert wanted. But she could not ignore those wages – who ever heard of anyone earning so much in one week? She would just have to explain to Bert and hope he would understand. When Ia did 'it' she was determined it should be with a gentleman. She had doubts if one of Gwen's 'posh toffs' would be the real gentleman she wanted.

Through the thin wall she heard Gwen's shrill voice welcoming someone, the rumble of a man's voice in reply. Gwen was laughing. The bed creaked. Ia closed her eyes hoping that sleep would come so that she need not listen. But as the noises from Gwen's room grew louder sleep became impossible. Gwen was sighing, and then she cried out as Ia heard the unmistakable sound of flesh being beaten. Gwen screamed, she was crying, begging for mercy. Ia sat bolt upright in bed, clutching the blanket to her in terror. The thumping of the bed-springs was so loud she thought the bed was about to fly through the wall, and all the while Gwen was screaming and moaning. Then everything was quiet. Ia could hear the thumping of her own heart. Suddenly she heard Gwen laugh and begin to talk naturally. Gwen's door opened and shut and then there was silence again.

Five times she heard Gwen return to her room. Once it was quick, once it was slow, once there was no sound, and twice Gwen was beaten.

Sleep finally came to Ia. The young girl slept fitfully, surrounded on all sides by the bestial sounds.

3

The following morning Alice woke early and rang for her breakfast which was served her by a strangely respectful Flo. Alice chatted to her but there was little response.

'Are you all right, Flo?'

'Yes, thank ee, Miss Alice.'

'You seem very quiet.'

'I've got me responsibilities to worry about.'

'What are they?' Alice asked, trying not to smile at the seriousness of the girl's expression.

'That Frenchie maid of her ladyship's says as I'm to get your dress ready for this evening and that your hair is to be dressed perfectly, else I'm for it.'

'I should not let my stepmother's maid, French or otherwise, order you about, Flo. You work for me.'

''Er be so grand though, Miss Alice. And she bain't no fool. She knows as I'm not really a lady's maid.'

'You do my hair beautifully. Better than I could ever manage. You suit me very well.' Alice smiled kindly at her.

'But 'tis the responsibility, Miss Alice. If you'm look a rare old mess tonight, then it's all my fault.'

'What is so important about tonight?'

'Didn't you'm know? Didn't they tell ee? You'm dining at Marlborough House, with the prince and princess, that's where you'm dining. And young maids don't get invited there, so it's a very particular honour, that's what that there Frenchie says.'

'Why aren't young women normally invited?'

'That Frenchie says it's because the conversation and what like isn't suitable for a young maid's ears. And the prince don't like dining with unmarried women – that's what her do say.'

The memory of her father's dinner party flashed into Alice's mind. Surely it would not be like that, not with the princess there.

'Oh, Miss Alice, you'm eating with the likes of they! Who'd ever have thought it at Gwenfer?' Flo's eyes widened at the wonder of it all.

'Good gracious. I suppose I should be excited. But I'm sorry, Flo, I'm not. So I shouldn't worry, if I were you.'

'Oh, Miss Alice, you are a one.' Flo laughed, her easy familiarity returning.

Once she was dressed Alice wondered what to do with herself. Her father had already left the house and according to Flo the new Lady Tregowan was not to be disturbed until noon.

To while away the time Alice read a little, then wrote letters to Mrs Malandine and Mrs Trelawn and a longer one to Miss Gilby. But it was still only ten o'clock. She left the letters on the side table in the hall for Phillpott to weigh and post. Through the glass of the front door she saw the sun shining and decided to take a walk.

The rain of the night before had left the air clean and there was a freshness about the city which she had not expected. She remembered where the park was, where Queenie used to take them each fine day, and she set off in that direction. The day was so lovely, the park so beautiful, that it was more than two hours before Alice returned.

An agitated Flo was pacing up and down the hall.

'Oh, Miss Alice, thank goodness you'm back. Lady Tregowan is in a dreadful temper. You'm to go to her bedroom immediately.'

It felt strange to Alice, entering her mother's room after all these years to find another woman in it.

'Alice, there you are, you naughty, naughty girl.' Daisy was sitting up in bed, the great cloud of silk and lace pillows making her look even smaller. Her blonde hair was loose and lay about her shoulders in a tumult of curls. Perched on the top of her head was the merest wisp of a lace night-cap. 'Such thoughtlessness.' She gave a little frown.

'I'm sorry?'

'My dear, you've been upsetting the household. Mrs Longman, my cook, is beside herself with indignation. She tells me you cancelled dinner and then went into her kitchen. Such naughty temerity.'

'Well, I wanted a sandwich.'

'Then you should have rung the bell for Phillpott. What *were* you thinking of, Alice dear? One simply does not go into the servants' quarters, whatever next?' Daisy twittered.

'But I did at Gwenfer. I lived with the servants at Gwenfer.'

Daisy fanned herself with a white ivory and ostrich feather fan. 'Don't tell me about the dreadful things dear Georgie allowed you to do. I've told him he must have spoiled you dreadfully. You are not at Gwenfer now, my sweet. You must behave in a seemly way. I've never set foot in any of my kitchens. Good gracious, what would the staff think if I did?'

'I'm sorry, I didn't realise.'

'And where *have* you been all this time? I have been quite beside myself with worry.'

'I took my letters downstairs, and the sun was shining so I went for a walk.'

'A walk! Are you telling me that you went for a walk, unaccompanied?' Daisy screeched, her little girl's lisp quite forgotten.

'Why, yes.'

'Did the servants see you?' She lowered her voice.

'I don't know. Does it matter if they did?'

'Of course it matters. They have their standing to consider, too. You must understand, Alice, that whatever we do reflects upon them. Fortunately, no one seemed to know where you were, even that milkmaid you brought with you from Cornwall. Thank goodness you're not known in society.' She shuddered with relief.

'But at Gwenfer I often went out alone. Sometimes I would be out all day. Why should I stop doing that just because I'm in London?'

'You must stop it. Immediately.' Daisy's fanning of herself was now almost demented in its agitation. 'You could ruin all your prospects, compromise yourself ruinously.'

'Last week I rode where I wanted, walked where I wanted. I haven't changed . . .' She laughed.

'I think we've heard quite enough about your gypsy ways at Gwenfer. Last week you were a child. Now you are about to become a woman. And you are my responsibility. It is my duty to see that you make a good match. I can assure you that you won't do so if you continue to wander about the streets unchaperoned.'

'It sounds quite ridiculous to me,' Alice said, trying to keep her tone light.

'It is not ridiculous. It is –'

'"– The order of things",' Alice interrupted dryly.

'Are you being impertinent?' Daisy asked sharply.

'No, Daisy. I'm sorry if I sounded so. I'm bemused. It all seems so peculiar to me. How can I be free as a bird

172

one week and then, when I'm supposed to be grown up, I become virtually a prisoner.'

'A prisoner? Now who's being ridiculous? And it's Daisy Dear, not Daisy. I told you last night.'

'I'm sorry, Daisy Dear,' Alice said, feeling stupid. She found the name her stepmother insisted on as ridiculous as the new rules and regulations.

'Well now. I'm glad you're going to be sensible. Gracious, I do feel very grand telling a big thing like you how naughty she has been.' Her laugh was a gay tinkling affair. 'Now, for tonight, what shall you wear? I'm so looking forward to seeing your wardrobe.' Lithely she slipped from the bed, wrapping herself in a robe which matched her night-dress but which had even more lace cascading from it. 'Véronique,' she called. Her maid appeared. 'Come, Véronique. You will have to dress both of us until we find Miss Alice a suitable lady's maid.'

'*Oui*, m'lady,' the maid replied, impressing Alice with her ability to bob a curtsy and walk at the same time.

'Flo is adequate for me,' Alice protested.

'Don't be silly, Alice. What can a country girl like that possibly know about such matters? And your hair. Just look at your hair, the imbecile doesn't know what she is doing.'

Alice patted her smooth hair which Flo, that morning, had neatly pinned up. 'I should hate to hurt her feelings.'

'Well, perhaps she can help Véronique in little ways,' Daisy said, fluttering her hands with irritation.

Ten minutes later the contents of Alice's new wardrobe lay on the floor.

'These are dreadful.' Daisy stamped her foot. 'They look as if they were made by a cobbler. These styles are simply years out of date.' She stamped her foot again. 'Bustles! Good gracious, Alice, no one has worn a bustle for ages. You'd be the laughing stock of London in such grotesque clothes.'

'I thought they were very pretty,' Alice said, almost feeling sorry for Madame Delamere.

'That, my dear Alice, is because you know nothing of couture. You have been too long in the country. Your father has behaved very badly towards you.'

'It was my choice to stay in Cornwall. I'm sure I had only to ask to come to London . . .' Alice said loyally, and immediately wondered why she defended him.

Daisy sighed and gave her a pitying look. Véronique clucked her tongue in sympathy. 'Well, you certainly cannot appear tonight. So much is obvious. I should never be able to hold my head up in society again if you appeared in one of these outlandish creations.' She kicked at one of the ball dresses disdainfully. Alice felt an overwhelming sense of relief. Daisy looked Alice up and down critically. 'You're far too big to wear anything of mine. I shall just have to say you are indisposed. Do you realise that not to attend could mean social death?' She glared dramatically at Alice. 'And your stays are impossible! Just look at the size of your waist, it is huge.' The cornflower-blue eyes grew large with astonishment.

'I feel as if I can hardly breathe,' Alice complained, red-faced now with indignation.

'Véronique, send round to "Madeleine's" and ask Madeleine herself to be good enough to come at once. Since there is no time to go to Paris, we shall simply have to do the best we can. And then go round to the corsetière, Véronique, and arrange a fitting. Then there's your hair.' Daisy eyed her critically. 'It's so dreadfully straight – it will never do. Véronique must use the curling tongs and you must have a fringe, everyone has a fringe this season.'

'But I don't want a fringe. I don't think it would suit me at all.'

'Tut! It's fashionable, that's the importance. Oh dear, I feel quite exhausted . . .' and she fluttered from the room, with Véronique in flustered, sympathetic attendance.

Alice looked into the mirror. 'Big!', 'huge!', 'enormous!' She studied her image, the tight little waist, the swelling breasts.

'Fiddlesticks,' she said and pulled the bell for Flo to help her out of the hated stays.

4

For a week Ia had been helping in the kitchens. Every time the door opened, she heard the noise from the bar and longed to be part of it. She was afraid to say anything to Bert Fowler, though, in case he might misinterpret a request to work with the customers. She was not popular in the kitchens, through no fault of her own. She was too pretty, that was the problem. The staff behind the scenes were either women who had been prostitutes but whose looks the way of life had destroyed so that now no man wanted them, or they were women who had been born deformed so that no man had ever wanted them. Ia's long blonde hair, clear grey eyes, full mouth and fine bones were objects of hatred amongst her workmates. She was lonely and there were times that she felt like going back to the comfort of Mrs Bottrell. But always the ambition for beautiful things, which had burned in her too long to be discarded now, prevented her from running away. That and the thought of the five shillings that would be hers, come pay day.

'Excuse me, Mr Fowler, but this is only three shillings.' Ia showed the coins to Mr Fowler who sat at the table in his private sanctum, a large ledger in front of him and a money box from which dangled a set of keys.

'So?'

'You told me it was to be five shillings.'

'That's when I thought you was a whore.'

'But . . . you didn't say anything about that. I thought you wanted a worker and I'm a good worker.'

'I've got as many workers as I need. It's whores I'm short of.' He looked up at her slyly, at the same time making a pile of two shining shillings in front of him.

'I'm sorry, Mr Fowler, I can't.' She looked with longing at the money before her.

'Not for, say, six shillings?' And he added another shilling to the pile.

'No, Mr Fowler,' Ia said firmly, averting her eyes from the silver.

'Tell yer what, Ida. I likes yer. I'm a fool to meself but all right. You're going to 'ave to do it some time or other, but I'm prepared to wait. Four shillings, there, I can't do fairer than that. You are a good worker, I'll give you that.'

'Thank you, Mr Fowler. Four shillings is fine.'

Ia quickly scooped up the extra shilling and escaped from the room before he could change his mind. Bert Fowler leaned back in the chair, filled his black pipe with tobacco and contentedly began the ritual of lighting it. He was unbothered. She'd change her mind; he'd seen the way she had looked at the money. Bert prided himself on his understanding of people – no one could want money as badly as that little girl and not come round to his way of thinking.

A month had gone by. The unpleasant atmosphere in the kitchen remained, but Ia now worked with the comfort of knowing her savings were growing every day. When she went to America it would be as a proper paying passenger – she'd heard a lot about the boats from the other girls by now and the dreadful conditions of those who went free and in steerage. She would travel in reasonable comfort. With savings she could bide her time when she arrived and get a decent position instead of being bonded into employment. She wanted to be independent.

Each night Ia was first to bed. When she was alone she

counted her money. She knew exactly how much was there – two pounds, three shillings and fourpence three farthings – but touching it, counting it, gave her such pleasure that it had become a nightly ritual.

Then, one night, she discovered that she was threepence short. The knowledge made her feel sick. Frantically she crawled over the floor combing every inch of the room in her desperate search. She ripped the blankets off the bed, she moved the dressing-table. It had gone. It had been stolen.

That night, Ia lay awake for a long time seething with a desire for revenge. The other women came to bed – fat Sybil, smelly Phoebe and skinny Ruby. It had to be one of them, she knew: each of them hated her enough.

The next day in the kitchen, she watched the actions of the others like a hawk. When Sybil sidled out of the room, Ia quickly asked the cook's permission to go to the lavatory. She sped upstairs and, as silent as a wraith, crept along the corridor. She gently pushed open her door just in time to see Sybil turning from the dressing-table on which stood Ia's bowl.

'You thieving bitch, you put my money back! I saw you.' Ia sprang across the room, grabbed her precious bowl and peered anxiously into it.

'I ain't got your bleeding money, hoity-toity cow.'

'You have. Don't you lie to me, you thief!' She replaced the bowl and spun around, grabbing Sybil by the hair with one hand and punching her in the stomach with the other. Sybil bent double, coughing and spluttering as much with indignation as pain, since she was three times Ia's size. Ia tugged at the hair again, swung her round, wound her leg round Sybil's and brought her crashing to the floor, where she leaped on her and began to bang her head repeatedly on the wooden floor. Sybil's screams for help brought first Gwen running, then four of the other girls, all of whom began to take sides, screaming and yelling either for Sybil or Ia.

Ia was blind with rage as she beat the woman. Suddenly she found herself wrenched backwards by the collar, and unceremoniously pulled to her feet.

'Wot the bleeding hell's going on?' Bert shouted above the caterwauling women.

'She stole my money.' Ia pointed an accusing finger at Sybil.

'Did you, Sybil?'

'I did no such fing, Mr Bert. Bloody cheek,' Sybil blustered as she hauled herself to her feet.

'Sybil?' Bert Fowler bellowed. Sybil coloured and looked shiftily at the floor. 'Sybil, you give it here. You know what I told you about this nasty little habit you've got.'

Still looking at the floor, Sybil dug into the pocket of her greasy skirt and produced a handful of pennies. Bert grabbed them and handed them back to Ia who quickly replaced them in her blue bowl. 'You're a fool, you are. You don't trust no one in this world, understood? Money you keep locked up, not left around for thieves like this.' He aimed a swipe at Sybil who neatly ducked and raced for the door. 'Right, all of you, out. I wants to talk to Ida here.'

The show over, the others sidled one by one out of the room, leaving Bert and Ia alone. Bert crossed the room, shut the door, and stood in front of it.

'Right, Ida. I've waited long enough. I've lost me patience, you can't play the blushing violet no longer. Tonight yer gets it – no more messing about.'

'I bloody won't.'

'Oh yes, you bloody will. Wot you think I am, a bleeding charity? This is a whorehouse not a nunnery.'

'I've done nothing wrong. I work hard. You can ask Cook.'

'I have girls queuing up at the back door to do that work. I can get as many as I wants. I wants you on the game, tonight, understood? Gwen'll find you a dress, show you how to look . . .'

'I'm sorry, Mr Fowler, but I explained my position before.'

'Too good for it?'

'No, Mr Fowler, I'm not too good for it, it's just that your clients aren't good enough for me.' Ia stood squarely facing him, shaking her hair back with anger.

'And who the bleeding hell do you think you are? You wouldn't last five minutes out there. You'd be back here, within the month, begging me to take you in again on *my* terms.'

'I wouldn't beg you for anything even if I was starving.'

'That does it! The loss is yours. If you won't sell your cherry, then I'll take it for meself,' and he lunged across the room to grab Ia. In one movement he swung her on to the bed, flicking her skirts back and rapidly unbuckling his belt.

Ia lay wide-eyed with terror as she saw the large man with his huge swollen member bearing down upon her. Then she smiled.

'Ah, changed your mind, have yer? Seen me, haven't you? You'll never see a bigger one than that, my girl.' He nuzzled his mouth into her neck.

'Oh yes, Mr Fowler, you are so big,' Ia whispered. Sliding her hand down she took hold of him in one hand, raked her nails along his penis and with her other hand screwed his scrotum.

'You fucking whore . . . ' he bellowed. He leaped off her and rolled on to the floor, holding himself in his agony. 'I'll kill yer for that, I'll fucking kill yer,' he roared.

Ia jumped nimbly over his writhing body, snatched up her bowl, stuffed as many of her clothes as she could grab into her bag, flung her shawl around her shoulders and ran, as if the furies of hell were behind her, out of the room, down the stairs, out of the pub. She ran and ran until she was certain she was out of Whitechapel.

<h1 style="text-align:center">5</h1>

'Just look at all these clothes, Flo,' Alice said with a marked degree of exasperation as Flo entered the room, carrying yet another dress-box. Alice was standing already surrounded by dressmakers' boxes, tissue paper, a welter of ribbons and a sea of white silk and satin.

'How on earth is one person expected to wear all of this?'

Flo surveyed the scene. 'Someone like 'e, Miss Alice. You'm a grand lady, and no mistake.'

'I don't feel like a grand lady, Flo. I fear I'm a dreadful disappointment to my father. The truth is, I would much prefer to be back at Gwenfer. I dream at nights of feeling the sea wind in my hair, that I'm watching the kestrels, eating Mrs Trelawn's saffron cake –' She was interrupted by a great sob from Flo, rapidly followed by a flood of tears. 'Flo, my dear, what is the matter?'

''Tis 'e talking about Gwenfer. I'm so sick for Gwenfer, Miss Alice.' And another river of tears coursed down her face.

'Poor Flo. I've been so engrossed in my feelings that I haven't been thinking about you. I'd no idea you were unhappy.'

''Tis all a dreadful let-down. I was so happy when you'm told me I was to come. I thought London would be paradise, all that there excitement and everything. But the staff, they'm so stuck up, they laughs at the way I talks. And they'm sound funny to me. And I hate that Véronique, she makes my life hell . . .'

'Then you shall return to Cornwall tomorrow. I can't have you being unhappy.'

'Miss Alice!' For a second Flo's face was filled with

relief. Then she frowned. 'But I can't go. I couldn't leave
'e alone here, you'm miserable too.'

'Nonsense. What's the point of us both being miserable
if one of us can be happy? It's only for this summer and
then I'll be back too.'

'But what if you'm get engaged?'

'I've no intention of getting engaged or married. I want
to return home. No man is going to prevent me from
doing that. No, Flo.' Alice held up her hand as Flo was
about to protest again. 'I'll ask Phillpott to make the
arrangements for you. You'd better go and pack.'

So far, Alice had endured a month in London and the
full season was not even under way, yet. This month,
instead of being able to go to the art galleries and
museums Miss Gilby had recommended, every moment
of Alice's day was dedicated to the preparations for her
début.

These preparations involved Alice in standing rock still
for hours at a time, while seamstresses swarmed about
her, pinning and tucking. Her hair was daily tortured, by
the curling tongs, into curls which were pinned up at the
back of her head in an elaborate cascade. She had resisted
the fringe that Daisy had wanted. It might be all the rage
for this season but Alice was equally adamant that she
did not wish her hair cut and frizzled into what, to her,
was an unbecoming fashion. She couldn't help admiring
Daisy Tregowan's energy. Once she appeared from her
room at about noon, she was a ceaseless whirl of activity.
Daisy was dedicating herself to her stepdaughter's launch
into society.

Apart from the fittings, which Daisy liked to supervise,
there was endless shopping to be done. Shopping with
Daisy, a perfectionist in matters of attire, was wearying.
Many a shopkeeper's face twisted with anxiety when
Lady Tregowan appeared in his establishment. If a
leather was not supple enough, if a bonnet was too plain,
if a trim had a fault in it, Daisy would make a scene. If a

replacement was not immediately available, then she would sweep from the emporium, vowing never to return. It was a fretful time for all concerned.

Alice never saw a bill and, of course, money never changed hands. But the expenditure on both their wardrobes was mounting rapidly. Alice would think of the cost and found she could not be comfortable with it. On their return from the theatre, opera, or a dinner, Alice had seen the starving beggars in the streets, the shoeless children, the huddled forms attempting to sleep in doorways and in the park. She had noticed young girls, with brightly rouged faces, with skirts shortened to display their ankles, flitting about the Haymarket – she was too innocent to know what trade they plied, but instinct told her that, as Queenie would have said, they were up to no good.

She made one attempt with her stepmother to stem the flow of money.

'I really do have enough, Daisy Dear. Perhaps instead of spending more we could give some of the money away to those beggars we see?'

Daisy's cornflower-blue eyes appeared to double in size. 'What on earth for? They'd only spend it on beer.'

'They might spend it on hot food.'

'Of course they wouldn't.'

'You don't know that, Daisy Dear. It just seems so wrong to me that we have so much and they have so little.'

'What ridiculous things you say! If we did not buy our lovely things, how would the seamstresses survive? The shoemakers? Good gracious me, Alice, you talk most alarmingly at times. It's overfamiliarity with the servants that gives you these strange notions. Now, what shall we wear tonight?'

It was the only such conversation they had. Alice felt that there was no point in further discussion with her stepmother.

Alice hated the long, elaborate dinners she was expected to attend. To be plucked from the solitude of Gwenfer into nightly having to make polite conversation with strangers was more than she could bear. She had not thought of herself as a shy person, but with these people she found she was. She did not know what to talk to them about, she found she could not understand their jokes, and was incapable of joking in return. The gossip meant nothing to her since she did not know of whom they spoke. The young people she met reduced her to the same sullen silence. She would sit praying for the meals to end, feeling gauche and unlovely as her stepmother sparkled further along the table. In addition, she found the unaccustomed ten or eleven courses of rich food more than her body would tolerate. But at least everyone behaved themselves normally and there were no dancing girls!

Finally, with some trepidation, she asked Daisy if, until the season proper started, she could be excused dining every evening. Perhaps just once a week? she timidly suggested. Annoyed by her tongue-tied stepdaughter's embarrassing lack of social grace, Daisy agreed with alacrity. Daisy's hasty acceptance of this arrangement only reduced Alice to greater shyness and awkwardness in company.

If it had not been for her daily, chaperoned walk in the park, Alice felt she would have gone mad. Now she would not even have Flo to walk with, but would have to take Chantal, the new French maid her stepmother had chosen for her. At least she could use the time to improve her French.

Alice was not to know that one of the huddled forms she passed in her carriage at night, was Ia. In the weeks since she had left the pub and Bert Fowler, Ia's life had become intolerable.

When she had raced away from Whitechapel, she had

had no clear idea of what she was going to do. As evening fell, she found a pie and eel shop, which was warm and cheap. Once she had eaten they did not seem to mind her staying there. But, at eleven, the proprietor had, with finality, removed the salt from the table and wiped the marble top with a damp cloth.

'We're closing now, ducks. Sorry. Ain't you got nowhere to go?'

'No. I didn't think about where I could sleep tonight.'

'It's raining out there, love. You can't sleep in the street tonight, that's for sure. Got any money?' Ia nodded, suspiciously. 'Nip along to number 45, it's a lodging-house. If you're quick you'll get a bed. After closing time, you won't – they fill up fast as a bucket.'

'How much will it cost?'

'Sixpence a double, fourpence a single. You'd save a penny sharing.'

'I don't think I like the idea of sharing.'

'Can't say I blame you, love. Don't know who you'd land up with, do you? Take my advice. Strip the bed, and take this newspaper and wrap yourself in that – that way the bugs will have a job finding you.' She laughed good-naturedly. 'And sleep with your possessions under you. It's safer.'

'Thank you very much, I'll do that. You don't by any chance need any help, do you? I work very hard.'

'I'm afraid not, lovey. There's just me hubby and me, and business is slack. Life's hard, ducks,' she said as she closed the door behind Ia.

Ia found the lodging-house, which had beds free. The dosser in charge showed her into the dormitory. It was a long room with upwards of sixty beds in it and mattresses laid on the floor between the beds. Across the room was slung a sturdy rope. She asked its function and was told for twopence a night she could lean on it and sleep as best she could. She counted out the fourpence for her single bed.

Left alone she readjusted the flimsy screen that stood by her bed; it would give scant privacy for it was open at the top and bottom and had huge holes in the side. She recoiled with disgust at the vermin that scuttled blindly for shelter as she stripped the wooden bed of its filthy grey blanket.

She put on all the clothes she had managed to bring with her, and, wrapping herself in newspaper, hid her blue bowl between her legs. She was exhausted and fell asleep at once. By one o'clock she was wide awake: a crowd of noisy singing drunks had appeared. The rest of the night was to be punctuated by their singing, swearing and fornicating. Fights broke out and people vomited. Ia slept little.

The next day she looked for work but it was impossible to find. Using the sun as her guide she moved further to the west of the city, where, she had been told, things were better. By evening the busy streets became even busier. The public houses were filling up, music and laughter flowed on to the streets, buskers appeared singing and dancing, one man had a bear that danced to his flute. Ia found she was enjoying herself.

'Bugger orf, you cheeky cow.'

Ia felt a sharp stab in her back and pitched full length into the gutter. She looked up to see two young girls standing over her, hands on hips. Their skirts were looped up showing ankles in tight, leather boots, their faces were heavily rouged. On their heads they sported pork pie hats with bright red feathers, set at a rakish angle on their exuberantly curled hair.

'This is our pitch,' one hissed at her.

'I'm sorry, I'm trying to find the West End.'

'Ha! Much luck you'll find there, dressed like that. Get going or we'll call our fellers. Want a beating?'

'No, no, I'm going.' Ia scrambled to her feet, clutching her bag. She ran and did not stop running until in front of her she saw a large park where she slumped exhausted on the grass. The night was unseasonably warm, all around her she could see the shapes of sleeping people and more shapes arriving to settle down. She covered herself with her shawl, put her sack under her head and joined them.

She spent her days in search of work. Some days she was lucky and might get a couple of hours washing up in a pie shop or pub, most days there was nothing. At first, in the evenings, she had wandered the streets looking at the sights but too often she was attacked by prostitutes or propositioned by men. So on fine nights she would go early to Hyde Park and, wrapped in newspaper, her bundle of possessions beneath her head, she slept. When it rained or was too cold she braved the discomfort of the lodging-houses.

With little work, and a week of bad weather, her meagre savings were disappearing at an alarming rate. She was frequently hungry now as she tried to do without food. Her clothes were becoming bedraggled from being slept in. She managed to keep clean by going daily to the public bath-house to wash – but that was becoming too expensive.

On a beautiful May day, with the daffodils in bloom, and the sky a wonderful blue, Ia sat in Hyde Park and saw none of it. Her fine face was marred with a frown of worry – she could not go on like this. She could not face the pub and Bert Fowler. She did not have enough money to return to Cornwall. It seemed that the only thing left was to go back to the East End, to forget her dreams of gentlemen, and to take the first man who asked for her body.

The park was full of people strolling about making the most of the sudden change in the weather. Young children rolled their hoops and bounced their balls as their nannies huddled on the park benches and gossiped and fussed over their younger charges in their high-wheeled baby carriages. Young lovers walked hand in hand oblivious of everything but each other. Old men and women watched them and remembered with longing another age and their own youth and past loves.

Ia watched the passing parade and felt sorry for herself and her proud plans. A gentleman she had wanted but what gent would want her now, bedraggled and daily getting thinner. She looked critically at the clothes of the young women and envied them their finery and knew instinctively how much better she could look in clothes like theirs.

In the orphanage, at the Bottrells' inn, her dreams had seemed so simple and possible. She had had no idea how hard life in the city could be, how lonely one could feel surrounded by so many people.

A beautiful young woman approached. Dressed in white and with a pretty white parasol, which shaded her face, she was chatting to a maid who accompanied her. Ia admired her carriage, the proud way she held her head. She must remember that, just in case one day she had a silk dress like that and a pretty parasol to shield her – how one walked was important. If one walked like a queen, as this young woman did, then one was treated like a queen for the crowds stood back to let her pass. She came nearer, changing the parasol from one hand to another, and Ia saw her face. It was Alice Tregowan. Ia huddled on the grass and watched her. Her mind was a mixture of emotions – not least of them was envy. The couple passed by, not sparing a glance for Ia. Why should they? She was just one of hundreds of poor people who crowded on the grass as if apologetic for their own existence.

Ia got to her feet. At a safe distance she followed Alice across the park, out of the gate and up Park Lane. She was twenty feet behind them as they crossed a square to the large house in the centre. Ia watched them being admitted. She ran across the grass, skipped down the basement steps and knocked on the door.

The door was opened by a footman in shirt-sleeves. Ia

thought he was the most handsome man she had ever seen in her life.

'Excuse me, is there work here?'

'Clear off.'

'Please.' Before the door was slammed in her face she had time to smile, the smile that she knew made men look at her again – when she wanted them to. 'I'm from the Tregowan estate in Cornwall, Gwenfer. I was hoping you might need help in the kitchens.'

The footman paused, eyeing her up and down. 'From Gwenfer? You'd best wait here a minute.'

Ia stood in the area for what seemed an age before the door reopened. 'You're to come this way,' her handsome footman ordered. She followed him through to the kitchen.

'You really from Gwenfer?' the cook asked suspiciously.

'Yes, truly.'

'You don't sound as if you are. Pity that Flo isn't here, she'd have told us. Do you know Miss Alice?'

'Not personally, I've seen her of course about the estate,' Ia said. 'But she doesn't know me,' she added quickly.

'What's the name of the cook at Gwenfer?'

'Mrs Trelawn.'

'And the housekeeper?'

'Mrs Malandine, and Mr George is the coachman.'

'That's right. Well, you'd best clean up. You can have a month's trial as the second kitchen maid. Fanny will show you where you sleep and what to do.'

It was not what Ia had planned, but here she would be safe. She would bide her time, recoup her savings, until she knew a little more about how to survive in London.

Chapter Five

1

Ia climbed wearily from her bed, fumbled in the half light for her clothes, and dressed as silently as she could, for fear of waking Fanny. Fanny was the senior kitchen maid and, as such, had the luxury of another half hour in bed.

Ia tiptoed along the attic corridor and down the back stairs not daring to put her shoes on until she had reached the basement. Very quietly she opened the kitchen door and put on the kitchen light. She always did this as quietly as possible: it amused her to see the floor of the kitchen a heaving mass of panicking cockroaches as they scuttled out of the light and into the safety of their dark corners. It also amused Ia to switch the light off and on again several times – she could not get over the miracle.

She crossed the kitchen and stood wanly staring at the huge range, the lighting of which was her responsibility. It was a responsibility that she approached with dread each morning. To Ia this cooker was a cantankerous, filthy monster. She was convinced it had a life of its own, so she always spoke to it politely in order not to antagonise it. Each morning her routine was the same. She would clean out the grate and riddle it. She blacked the grate and polished its brass rod and knobs. She laid the paper and kindling. Then she added the coal. Some days it roared obligingly into life; on others it sulked and belched smoke at her and would only condescend to catch light when she had wept sufficient tears over it.

'Right my beauty, are you going to light for Ia this morning or not?' she said aloud as she fed in its own

189

black brand of food. Her hands shook as she lit the match to put to the paper. Her hands shook every morning for, if the range was not alight and the water boiling by the time Cook appeared at six thirty, Ia was in for a scolding. Bad temper would smoulder in the kitchens for most of the day, which put her in everybody's black books.

This morning, with a comforting 'whoosh', the cooker lit. 'Oh, you wonderful old girl, there's my angel.'

'You'll get locked up in the loony bin if you go on talking to it like that.'

Ia looked up from her kneeling position to grin at Jim the boot boy who, like her, had early morning duties to attend to. 'It can be a right old bugger,' she whispered.

'Shush, it might hear you.' He laughed. 'Any chance of a cuppa?'

Ia carried the enormous kettle out to the scullery and put in enough water to make their tea. In the month she had been here, Jim was the only kind person she had met. The cook, Mrs Longman, could not have been less like Mrs Trelawn. On some days Ia thought she must be mad, the way she screamed and threw things about the kitchen. When she had a knife in her hand and one of her tempers came on, Ia was filled with a gut-watering fear. The butler, Mr Phillpott, was such a lordly creature that Ia was convinced he was unaware of her existence. The housekeeper, an austere, cold-mannered woman, noticed only the cook, the butler and her especial friend, Véronique, her ladyship's maid. The gaggle of housemaids talked and giggled with the footmen. She had noticed several of the footmen glancing slyly at her when they thought she was not looking, but they did not deign to speak to her. Fanny, the other kitchen maid, was glorying in her sudden promotion and dedicated her life to making Ia's as unpleasant as possible. That left Jim, and no one but Ia and Fanny appeared to talk to him either.

There were days when the unfriendliness almost drove Ia into boasting of her friendship with Alice. She never did. Who would have believed her? She realised now that at first she had hoped that someone on the staff would recognise her from Gwenfer and would mention her to Alice – her pride would never allow her to approach Alice herself. But among the staff there was not one from Cornwall. She had recognised the butler from his occasional visits with his lordship but, of course, the butler was unlikely to remember her.

'Here you are, Jim.' She placed his cup of tea on the table and smiled at him, the smile which made Jim's legs go wobbly every morning.

'You ain't half pretty, Ia,' he said shyly, blushing furiously. Emboldened by his courage, he tentatively put out a hand to touch her face.

'Jim! Don't be a daftie.' She shied away from him, but immediately regretted her sharp tone when she saw his expression change to one of hurt. 'I like you, too,' she added hurriedly. She did like him, but not in the way he wanted her to. For Ia was in love for the first time. She knew at last the heart-pummelling feeling as 'he' approached. He was Frederick, the footman who had let her in on the very first day she had come here. And he was one of those she had noticed looking at her with that special look in the eye. But he had never spoken to her since that first day and she was too much in awe of him to say anything. So she had to suffer the agony of seeing him each day – not allowed to speak to or go near him.

But when Cook screamed, when Fanny pinched her, when the washing-up seemed to grow by the minute instead of diminishing, when the potatoes had more eyes than flesh, when her hands were raw and bleeding from the soda in the water, when Ia thought she could not stand this life a moment longer – then Frederick would pass by, and Ia knew she had to stay just to be close to him. In bed at night before she went to sleep, she no longer dreamed of America and of her life there; now her dreams were full of Frederick.

Ia laid the cook's tea-tray. She swept the floor, counting the dead cockroaches – twenty, a good haul. She filled the large kettles and put them on the range. Then she joined Jim at the long, bleached white pine table for her own tea.

'You don't like it here, do you?' he asked.

'Not much.'

'Where was you before?'

'In a pub, in Whitechapel.'

'There's money to be made in pubs. I wouldn't mind a job in one.'

'You two ain't supposed to help yourselves to tea. I'll tell Mrs Longman, that I will,' Fanny announced as she entered the kitchen, glancing immediately towards the range.

'Oh, come off it, Fanny. We always did, before you got so bleeding grand.' He grinned at Fanny.

'Don't you talk to me like that, Jim Trotter, I'll tell on you. What I did makes no difference. She shouldn't and that's that.' Her mouth set in a spiteful line.

'Come on, Fanny, she's done the range, the kettles are on, the floors swept, Cook's tray's set. Leave her alone, Fanny. You're turning into a right sour apple.'

'I'll sour apple you, you filthy little guttersnipe.' Fanny aimed a swipe at him; grinning, he ducked.

'Fancy a kiss, Fanny, fancy a fumble?' Jim leaped up from his chair, grabbed Fanny, pinned her arms behind her back, and planted a kiss full on her lips. 'There, ain't that better than being a naggle?' He laughed, winking at Ia over Fanny's head. To Ia's surprise, Fanny slid on to a chair, a silly smile on her face.

'Oh, you are a terror, Jim, and no mistake. Maybe I'll have a cup meself, Ia, before I goes and wakes the dragon.'

Ia looked with interest at Jim and Fanny. The change in the girl had been quite dramatic: maybe she was in love too. Ia hoped so; it might make her easier to work with.

Fanny disappeared with Mrs Longman's tea. Ia laid out on the table the bacon, sausages, eggs and bread that would be needed for the staff breakfast. Half an hour later the cook appeared. Longman was an unfortunate name for her since she was barely five feet tall and almost as wide. It always surprised Ia that such a loud voice could belong to one so short. She and Fanny almost stood to attention as they awaited their instructions.

2

'Fanny! Ia!' Both girls dropped what they were doing and rushed to Mrs Longman. 'We've thirty for dinner tonight, fifty for a reception and late supper after. Fanny, you prepare the vegetables – potatoes, carrots julienne, broad beans, artichokes, celery – make sure you get the grit out this time, girl. Then there's the salads to wash. And I need vegetables for the stock. Then get on with the fruit – I'm hoping for some early strawberries from Fairhall. But squeeze two dozen oranges for the jelly, and I'll need apples for the compote. Three dozen lemons for the sorbet. Now where was I?' The cook pushed her hands, agitatedly, through her hair, and took a deep breath. 'Ia, you wash the dinner service. You'll find it in the third china cupboard along. Don't break nothing. If you do, you're out, understand? When you've done that, help Fanny. Then when you've both finished come to me. This is a big night.'

'Who's coming?' Fanny boldly asked.

'None of your business, girl. Now off with both of you and get going.'

Both girls turned to their tasks. 'Jim,' Mrs Longman bellowed. 'Get those turbots back to the fishmonger and you tell him, Mrs Longman's compliments but if he thinks I'm serving them, he's another think coming. You tell him there's plenty of other fishmongers. Stop by Mr French's and tell him I need another half dozen quail.' She turned to the table. 'What you standing gawping for, get on with you.' She threatened Jim with her soup ladle and he scarpered quickly from the kitchen. 'Ia,' the cook screamed. Nervously Ia approached her. 'When you've done the china, get along to Frederick and Robert and tell them I want that silver so as I can see my face in it.'

Carefully, making half a dozen trips, Ia carried the dinner service to her scullery and equally carefully she washed and dried each piece. It must be an important dinner: in the four weeks she had been here they had never used this service before, she thought, as she held up one of the plates, which had the Tregowan arms embossed in the centre, heavily encrusted with gold. Uppermost in her mind, however, was the thought that soon she was to speak to Frederick.

The china stacked, Ia went in search of the footman. She could find him nowhere. Finally, plucking up courage, she went along the downstairs corridor where the male staff slept, as far away from the female staff as possible. She knocked softly on the door.

'Hallo.' Her heart lurched at the sound of his voice.

'Frederick, I . . .' She stood, only her head peering around the frame of the door.

'What you doing here? It's out of bounds to the female staff. They'll have your guts for garters,' he said, adjusting his cravat. Shyly Ia peered around the room taking in the magnificent blue velvet uniform, heavily braided with gold, which hung on the wall. For the first time she was aware of the interesting smell of pomade and tobacco.

'Cook says she wants you and Robert to clean the silver until she can see her face in it.'

Frederick threw down the brush he was just about to use on his jacket. 'Who the bloody hell does she think she is? We take our orders from Mr Phillpott, no one else. You tell the fat bitch that,' he said, angrily. Ia's eyes filled with tears. 'Come on, duckie, don't cry. Come here.' He held his hand out towards her. 'Come on, I won't bite you.' Ia looked over her shoulder up the corridor and quickly slipped into the room, and shut the door behind her. Frederick handed her a large white handkerchief. 'Don't let the old cow upset you. Have a good blow and give us a smile.'

Ia looked up at him gratefully and smiled.

'Jesus!' Frederick exclaimed, staring fixedly at her. Ia wondered what she had done and the smile began to disappear. 'Don't stop smiling, Ia, whatever you do.' Gently he lifted Ia's chin and, leaning forward, kissed her firmly on the lips. Ia felt her legs buckle as a bolt of pleasure shot through her. She had never been touched like that before. No one had ever kissed her, never – not even her mother. He stepped back and looked long and hard at her. Her work-roughened hands flew to her lips and touched them. She looked at Frederick with a soft expression in her eyes that, had she but known it, made her look even more beautiful.

'And don't tell anyone I did that.' He laughed as he slipped into his jacket.

'No, Frederick,' she whispered.

'Can you get off this afternoon?'

'No, I don't think so. It's pandemonium in the kitchens.'

'My, that's a big word for a little girl. Try, just for an hour.'

'I don't think I can,' she said with anguish.

'I'll wait for you by the bandstand in the park. You'll make it,' he said confidently.

Ia could not remember getting back to the scullery. She leaned against the sink, her heart racing, a strange excitement in the pit of her stomach. He had known her name, she thought with wonder. He had known she existed. She was in a daze of happiness as she prepared to help Fanny with the vegetables.

Ia worked at double her usual speed. Even Mrs Longman complimented her on her efficiency. By four, the lunch dishes were washed and stored away. All the preparations for the dinner had been made.

'Mrs Longman? Could I?' Ia twisted her hands nervously. 'Would it be all right if I just nipped out to the shops for a minute?'

'The shops, what do you want with the shops?'

'It's me mam's birthday,' she lied. 'I'd like to get her a small present.'

For the first time, Mrs Longman smiled at Ia. 'Well, there's a good girl. Not many think of their mothers these days. Yes, Ia, that will be all right. You've been a good girl today. But only an hour, mind.' And Mrs Longman settled down with a slice of madeira cake and a cup of tea with a large measure of whisky in it to give her strength, as she was fond of saying.

Ia flew up the stairs to her room, quickly threw some water on her face, brushed her hair, and changed into her orphanage Sunday best which, as the food here was good and plentiful, was now a little too tight across her burgeoning breasts, but it was the best she had. Within minutes she had raced downstairs, afraid that Cook might change her mind, out of the door, across the square, dodged the traffic on Park Lane and was hurrying into Hyde Park.

Just short of the bandstand Ia skidded to a halt, gasping for breath. About her a throng of people paraded – smart top-hatted gentlemen, and elegant ladies in pretty gowns, topped by outrageous hats. Round and round the bandstand they promenaded as if they were on a carousel.

'Ia, over here,' she heard Frederick's voice calling her. He was crouched beneath a bush. 'Over here, you dolt. I don't want no one seeing us, not with you looking like that. Haven't you got something better to wear?'

'No, it's all I have. I had a skirt and –'

'If you want to be seen with me, you're going to have to get something else, that's for sure.'

'I don't get paid for another six weeks. That's what Mrs Longman told me,' she replied, flushing with shame and disappointment. Looking at him she saw the reason for his reaction. He looked devastatingly handsome in a black suit, a crisp wing-collared shirt with a fancy tie and pin and a snappy bowler on his head; and to her astonishment, she saw across his middle the gold of a fine watch-chain. What glorious creature like him would want to be seen with her, looking as she did? She hurriedly straightened her too short dress and crouched under the bush with him.

'Well, I'm not walking out with you looking like that, and that's flat.'

'I've got my small savings.'

'Then I suggest you spend them, that is if you ever want to see me again.'

'Yes, Frederick. You're right. I'll get the material and make myself a new dress. I'll buy a bonnet too,' she said, eagerly.

'You do that. Blue. That'll suit you.' He kissed her quickly on the mouth. 'I'm off.'

Before she could think what to say to stop him he had ducked out from under the bush and was lost in the milling crowd. Despondently, Ia made her way back across the park, worrying about the thought of spending her savings. Still, she reasoned with herself, she could replace the money when she was paid. This thought cheered her and the memory of the resplendent Frederick made her smile. By the time she descended the basement steps she was singing.

It was half past one before Ia, exhausted after the long evening, finished scouring the last pot. She dried her hands, switched off the light and left the kitchen to the cockroaches.

'Psst . . .'

Ia peered along the gloomy corridor, the only light coming from a single bulb at the far end.

'Ia, here,' Frederick whispered.

Ia sped along to him. He grabbed her hand and whisked her into his room.

'But, where's . . . ?' His mouth bore down upon hers and silenced her questioning. His hands were feverishly searching her body – first her breasts, then he lifted her skirts and his hands began to creep up her legs.

'Where's Robert?' she managed to gasp.

'Out with his doxy. Don't worry, he won't be back for ages.' Frederick's voice sounded strange and thick. 'Open your legs, there's a good girl.'

She did as he asked. It was as if she no longer had any control over her own body, it was as if his hands were guiding all her actions. His hands found what they had been seeking. A soft moan escaped from Ia, as he gently kneaded her. Wordlessly she allowed him to lead her to the bed and lay her down upon it. She nestled her head into the pillow, smelling the unfamiliar odour of men, and liking it. She sighed. Frederick flicked her skirts up, tore down her drawers and then flung himself upon her. In silence, and roughly, ignoring her cries of pain, he began to penetrate her. He spoke once, cursing the resistance he found. Then, with anger, it seemed to Ia, he crushed his body down on hers pushing further and further into her so that she felt full of him. He bounced wildly upon her, forcing the breath out of her body. Suddenly a great moan escaped from him, his body

198

seemed to shudder and, with no warning, he slumped down upon her and lay silent.

Ia looked wild-eyed at the ceiling not knowing what to do, and fearful that he was dead.

'Blimey!' To her relief he eventually spoke. 'That was a turn-up. I'd no idea you were a cherry. Who'd have thought it?'

'I've been saving myself for a gentleman.'

'A gentleman. That's a laugh.'

'I think you're a real gentleman, Frederick,' she said shyly.

He stood up suddenly, took her by the hand and pulled her to her feet. 'Sorry about your drawers. You'd best not wear them next time.' He laughed. 'Now, off you go, doll,' and he playfully slapped her on the rump. 'Not a word to a soul, mind, else we'd both be getting the order of the sack.'

Ia slipped silently up the stairs aware of an unfamiliar stickiness between her legs. Fanny was asleep. As quietly as possible, Ia wet a flannel and washed herself. She was alarmed to see the flannel covered in blood. She hoped that was normal. She changed into her night-dress, blew out the candle Fanny had left burning, and slipped into bed.

In the darkness she lay looking at the ceiling unable to believe the happiness she felt. She could barely believe that it had happened, that Frederick had wanted her. A fine man like that. Everything about him was perfect, even his name; only a gentleman would call himself Frederick instead of Fred. With her fingers she examined herself, searching for the bruises she was certain must be forming. It was not the act that made her happy, it was the fact that he had chosen her. She had found it rather frightening, and it had all been over so quickly. Men paid for that? Daft buggers, she thought smiling into the night.

She turned her head into her pillow. She would not mind spending her money now. She would spend all of it.

Who needed to go to America? She planned her blue dress, wondering if she could afford lace to trim it. Why, maybe she would get married in it. She wondered, dreamily, as sleep came to capture her, how many children they would have and what they would call them.

3

The special train ground to a halt at Radwood Station. A long line of carriages awaited them, each drawn by perfectly matching grey horses, each coach emblazoned with the Earl of Radwood's crest. The cavalcade made its way out of the station yard, down the main street of the pretty Berkshire town and out across the meadows, drenched in June sunshine, that led to Radwood Castle.

Over a month into the season, Alice was becoming more used to large parties in the grand houses her parents frequented. But, as she looked out of the carriage window, she decided that, apart from the palace, this must be the grandest of all. Ahead lay a great house which with its many wings, towers, battlements and a drawbridge over a moat on which swans serenely swam looked more like a child's representation of what a castle should be, than an architect's concept.

Alice was a little more relaxed now. She had, to her surprise, begun to enjoy some of the parties. This was largely because, with the season under way, the circle she met was much wider than her parents' tight, sophisticated social clique. That affected circle still made her feel ill at ease. She found them rather threatening and yet did not know why. And the way that conversations ceased as she entered a room made her uneasy. One would have had to be blind to be unaware of the infidelities being played out. It was as if all of them were on a roundabout of illicit liaisons.

Dancing had not been one of the skills that Miss Gilby

200

had taught her. But she had a natural grace and rhythm that, she hoped, masked her frequent mistakes. She preferred talking to the older men and women than the girls of her own generation. This was primarily because none of the girls had the least interest in the arts, politics and literature that interested Alice. In return the young girls found Alice too dull to bother with and too serious for her own good – but then, Alice had not had their pampered youth in which to grow shallow and flighty.

She had met many young men and, while they were better informed on the subjects that interested her, she was aware as she talked that they looked at her in surprise and backed away from such 'unfeminine' interests. Certainly she had not met anyone who could be considered a prospective husband. As she had no desire to find one, she was not unduly perturbed.

This visit to Radwood Castle was to be her first introduction to a large house party. And in three weeks' time was to be her own ball.

The carriages swirled into the large courtyard of Radwood Castle. An austere butler and a housekeeper patiently shepherded the laughing and chattering group, who all knew each other, into the enormous entrance hall. There was so much marble in this hall that a whole quarry in Italy must have been plundered for its decoration. Dusty and tattered battle standards hung below the high ceiling; large deerhounds lolloped up in greeting. The confident voices of the group bounced off the walls and echoed along the long corridors, making it sound as if there were a hundred of them instead of thirty.

'Tell me, you must be Alice Tregowan?'

Alice turned to find a tall girl, with a kindly rather than a beautiful face, smiling at her. Her hair was a reddish gold that sprang from the combs which were meant to hold it in place. The cameo brooch at the lace of her high collar had come unfastened, and the buckle of her large silver belt had slipped slightly off centre. Her brown eyes twinkled with a joy of life and her voice had a delightful husky tone to it. She had the friendliest face of anyone Alice had met this season.

'Yes, I am,' she smiled back. 'Excuse me,' Alice said awkwardly, 'but your brooch is about to fall off.'

'Oh, rats. It's always doing that. Silly thing.' Instead of repinning it she ripped it off and stuffed it into her side pocket. 'I've been so looking forward to meeting you, Alice. I'm Gertrude Granver, Lord Radwood's daughter.'

Alice held out her hand, and was about to speak when the girl added, 'And call me Gertie, please.' She gave Alice a firm handshake. 'Come up to my room.'

'Should we?' Alice looked nervously across the hall to where Daisy Dear was engaged in conversation with a large, imposing woman, with more than a slight moustache. Lady Radwood she presumed.

'It's all arranged, I told my mother I was stealing you the moment you came. I hear you are incredibly intelligent. I am too, so I am sure we will have lots to talk about.' She spoke matter-of-factly, with no conceit, and then laughed a loud uninhibited laugh that made everyone turn in their direction. Alice found herself blushing furiously but Gertie was totally unperturbed.

Gertie led the way up an imposing stone staircase guarded by ranks of suits of armour. Along a bewildering number of corridors they sped. Gertie had perfect posture that made her appear as if she moved on wheels, which Alice envied her. The walls were covered in paintings and where there was no painting a tapestry had been squeezed in. Chairs, which no one ever sat on, lined the route, below bookcases holding books which no one read. On every available surface were ornaments, bronzes and busts. It was so like Fairhall and the London house in its clutter that Alice thought with longing of Gwenfer with its austerely furnished rooms and the space that such an arrangement gave. Finally Gertie stopped, opened a door and showed Alice into a pretty and uncluttered set of rooms. Large windows overlooked the water-meadows and the Thames flowing through the park.

'Oh, I love *these* rooms,' Alice exclaimed.

'Marvellous, aren't they? I had such a battle with Mama, but I cannot abide overfurnished rooms. Finally, she said if I wanted to live like a nun, that was my business,' Gertie smiled. The smile lit her face, and Alice could not understand why, at first, she had not seen that the girl was lovely. 'Why on earth have we never met before, Alice?'

'Well, I usually spend all my time in Cornwall – to my stepmother's horror.'

'And I was in Italy, of course. My poor Mama was unwell, so we had to stay and I missed the beginning of the season. Not that I minded, I never wanted all this anyway. I'd much rather have stayed there.'

'How wonderful. I wish I could go to Rome. Did you see the Bernini fountain? Did you see Michelangelo's Pietà?'

Gertie, with such a willing audience, embarked on a long lecture on her tour, producing large leather-bound books full of postcards, water-colours she had done, and general souvenirs – opera programmes, tickets, restaurant receipts. Alice leafed through the books, envious at what she saw.

'I'm going back, you must come too,' Gertie said replacing her scrapbooks on the table. 'Why don't you live with your parents?' she asked, boldly.

'It's my choice,' Alice said, in the hurried way she now used to explain the strange arrangements of her life. 'I prefer Cornwall, I couldn't imagine living anywhere else.'

'I do understand. That's how I feel about our place in Sutherland. That's why I've set my cap at Basil Frobisher: he's only a baron and Papa and Mama are furious, but he owns a magnificent estate in Ross and Cromarty. I don't believe in love, you see, but since I have to marry someone, I've decided that the location of his property is as good a recommendation as any.' Gertie laughed her delightful, gurgling laugh. 'What about you?'

'I don't want to marry, not unless I find someone who is willing to come and live at Gwenfer with me.'

'Not much hope of that, is there? If he would, then he wouldn't have his own estate would he? Your father will never let you marry a younger son. It does all seem so ridiculously unfair. Have you met the Duke of Ruling?'

'Yes, he's extraordinarily handsome, but, well, he doesn't seem very bright, does he?'

'That's the trouble with dukes, they all seem to be so stupid. He's the one whom Papa wants me to catch, but . . . no thank you. At least Basil has a passion for art and the opera.'

There was a shuffling and giggling outside the door, followed by a knock, and a cluster of young girls fluttered into the room. One girl's face was vaguely familiar and for some strange reason made Alice feel uneasy. Alice was introduced to Gladys Loudon.

'But, Gladys, I thought you came out last year?' Gertie enquired.

'I should have done, but ever since my aunt died – Alice's mother – we seem to have been in mourning, first for her and then for a whole string of relations.'

'You two are cousins?' Gertie looked in astonishment from one to the other.

'Yes, but we haven't seen each other for ages, have we, Alice?' Gladys smiled unpleasantly at her.

'No.'

'Last time, Alice tore my hair out and hit me,' Gladys said with a laugh.

Alice remained silent.

'A real terror weren't you, Alice?' Still Alice said nothing. 'What was the argument about, cousin, I can't remember?'

'Nor can I.' Alice looked at the spiteful face of Gladys

and knew that she was about to tell. 'Should we, perhaps, go to our rooms to change?' she asked in as even a tone as her mounting anger would allow.

'I remember . . .' Gladys looked mischievously at the others. 'Didn't my brother say your mother was mad? Wasn't that it?'

The other girls gasped, Gertie looked concerned, and Alice's mouth set in a hard line. 'Mind you, she chose the right time to die, didn't she? For you I mean – there was still plenty of money and the jewels . . .' Gladys arched her brows. Her friends leaned forward eagerly, amazed at Gladys's boldness.

'I don't know what you mean, Gladys. People don't *choose* when to die. She had been ill for a long time.'

'Oh, really, Alice.' Gladys laughed unpleasantly. 'I'm sure it was expected, but not in the way you mean.'

Alice turned away. 'Gertie, could I be shown to my room? I should like to lie down before dinner,' she said with dignity.

Gertie leaped to Alice's defence. 'Miss Loudon, you have no manners,' she said before ringing for the maids and sweeping out to show Alice to her room personally.

As she dressed for dinner, with Chantal's help, Alice was very quiet. What had Gladys been trying to say? Had her mother *chosen* to die? But, if she had, then why was she buried in the family vault? Alice knew that suicides could never be buried in consecrated ground. Would her father tell her? Could she ever ask such a question?

She thanked Chantal, took a last look in the mirror, wishing, not for the first time, that she be allowed to wear a colour other than cream or white. Reluctantly, she went down to the large drawing-room, intending to keep as far away from Gladys and her coterie as possible.

The room was already crowded. She looked about anxiously for Gertie. Across the room a man was staring at her. Modestly Alice looked at the carpet, but something made her look up again. She felt a strange excitement which made her feel breathless. He smiled at her and her unfamiliar sensation intensified. She found that she was blushing.

4

Chas Cordell, champagne glass in hand, looked across the room of yet another English country house, and saw without doubt one of the most beautiful young women he had ever set eyes on. She noticed him and, looking down, blushed charmingly. He continued to stare, willing her to look up. She did; he smiled. His smile had a devastating effect upon women, and he knew it.

'Who's the pretty blonde girl, over by the door?' he asked his friend Gordon Ffetherting-Smythe.

'Which one? Some days they all look the same to me in their virginal white.' Gordon guffawed.

'The one with the spectacular pearl choker.'

'You're wasting your time there, old sport, Gal just doesn't seem to be interested in men. The original ice maiden.'

'I'd still like to know.'

'Alice Tregowan. Father's a baron but filthy rich for all that – tin mining mainly. He's just married that delicious Daisy Fielding – now there is a woman.'

'What happened to her mother?'

'She died a few years ago, mad as May butter. Rumour has it she killed herself – old boy hushed it up, I've heard. It's probably just as well she doesn't appear to be interested in men – gossip like that, a lunatic in the family, well, I ask you, who wants to know? Mind you, maybe her money will ease that little problem for her.'

'Nice for her in the circumstances to have a little of her own, then,' Chas said with studied lack of interest.

'Little! Her mother was enormously wealthy. And she's Tregowan's heir: his son died years ago. That is unless Daisy Dear obliges with a new son. Mind you, what she has will be nothing to a fellow like you.'

Chas smiled a small, enigmatic smile. It was a mystery to him how the rumour had started that he was rich; but it had done so. Once he had discovered the doors that opened to him because people thought him a millionaire, he had done nothing to disabuse them. And what man could resist the attention of the pretty girls pushed his way by their scheming mothers?

When he had arrived in England with one letter of introduction to Lord Chisholm, he had worried about how long he would be able to support himself, yet, since that date, he had been fed, wined and accommodated in the utmost luxury, so that he still had almost all his money intact. The English fascinated Chas: they pretended that money was vulgar – a subject never to be mentioned in polite society – and yet they seemed obsessed with it and talked of little else. A young debutante could be the most beautiful woman on earth, but without money she might just as well have been a shop girl. He had lost count of the conversations, similar to this one, he had had with Gordon and his other friends about a girl's background.

'Do you know her? I'd like to be introduced.'

'Oh yes, of course, I know her,' said Gordon, as if the question were stupid, since his family knew everyone of any importance.

Crossing the room to meet Alice was a lengthy business since introductions had to be made, friends greeted, but at last they stood before her.

'Miss Tregowan,' Gordon bowed. 'Might I have the pleasure of introducing to you my friend Chas Cordell from America.'

Alice held out her hand in greeting. 'Mr Cordell, I've never met anyone from your country before.'

'How fortunate for me, Miss Tregowan, then there is less chance of my boring you.'

His smile unnerved Alice. Her logical mind told her that a smile could not possibly make her pulse race at such an alarming rate. He was handsome, with hair as blond as her own, clear blue eyes and shoulders far wider than any other man in the room. But then there were many handsome men here . . . 'I'm sure you are incapable of boring anyone,' she found herself replying, to her own astonishment.

To her regret, dinner was announced and of necessity they were separated. If she moved her head slightly forward and to the left she could just see him along the great table at which they all sat. She found it difficult to concentrate on the conversation of the gentlemen to her left and right. Her mind was wandering to such an extent that she wondered if she were becoming ill.

The lengthy, elaborate meal was finally over. The ladies withdrew. Alice avoided her cousin who sat to one side of the drawing-room with her gaggle of friends, constantly eyeing Alice, and giggling.

'I do think your cousin is abominably rude,' Gertie said taking a seat beside her. Her exuberant hair was once again escaping from its pins, and her pearls had managed to become knotted. 'Would you like some barley water?'

'No thank you.' Gertie waved the footman away. 'I agree with you, Gertie. Gladys was unpleasant as a child, she doesn't appear to have improved.'

'It's a shame one cannot choose one's relations as one chooses one's friends.'

'Do you know Chas Cordell?' Alice asked as casually as she could, preferring to get off the subject of her cousin.

'Handsome, isn't he? I gather he's a very rich American. He's a friend of my brother's. Good Lord, I sound like your dreadful cousin!' She laughed. 'Do I detect some interest from my new friend who said she never wished to marry?'

'Gertie, don't tease me, I was just enquiring.' But her deepening colour betrayed her.

Lady Radwood had decided that the party was too small for the ballroom to be opened up, so the footmen had removed the furniture and rolled back the carpet in one of the large salons. The younger members of the party trooped along the corridor as a small orchestra began to tune up.

Alice sat on one of the gilt chairs fearing that Chas Cordell would prefer to go and play billiards, or that he had left, or, looking about the room, that he would ask one of the many other and far prettier girls to dance.

'Miss Tregowan, do you polka? If I might have the honour?'

'Not very well, I'm afraid.'

'No worse than I, I am certain.' Chas smiled at her and led her on to the dance floor. She did not know why, but she had never danced better in her whole life. After the polka they danced a waltz; she would have liked to dance another but propriety made her refuse. Instead of leaving her as she had expected, he stood, as if on guard, behind her chair. Gertie introduced her to Basil Frobisher, a large good-natured-looking man, with the clear eyes and reddish skin of one who spends much of his time in the open air. Gertie was right: he knew a great deal about art and, to Alice's intense pleasure, so did Chas who enthusiastically joined their heated discussion of Mr Ruskin's work.

Convention decreed that the young ladies had to be in bed before midnight. Reluctantly Gertie and Alice said good-night.

Alice found she could not sleep, a new experience for her. Her mind was spinning with memories of the evening and the image of Chas's face, as over and over in her mind she retraced their conversation.

*

The next day he was not there. Most of the young men had gone to a cricket match in Windsor. Alice wondered what Chas would make of the bizarre game. She spent the morning in Gertie's room talking as she had never done before with a girl of her own age. She had a friend, she realised with mounting pleasure. Immediately before luncheon she was summoned by her stepmother.

'Alice, dearest. Just a teeny-weeny little bit of advice from your stepmother,' she trilled. 'Don't dance too frequently with an admirer – it simply isn't done.'

'I don't understand, Daisy Dear.' But her heart was racing for she knew very well what her stepmother meant.

'You should not appear too eager, Alice. Don't be silly, you know exactly what I mean.' She peered anxiously at her beautiful face in the mirror. 'Good gracious, Alice, do you think that is a horrid wrinkle appearing?' she shrieked.

'No, Daisy Dear, I don't. It's a shadow.'

'Thank goodness. The thought made me feel quite faint. Now, where was I? Yes, this dashing young man from America. I'm sure society is the same there, Alice. You must not appear too forward: it will frighten him away. Good gracious, I made your father's life a misery for months, by keeping him dangling.' She laughed merrily. 'You must do the same.'

'It's not as you think, Daisy Dear. Mr Cordell and I are interested in the same things – art and music. I really don't think he has any other sort of interest in me.'

'There is only one sort of interest. And Mr Cordell certainly shows it for you, my dear. Of course he is most charming and, from all accounts, very well provided for.'

To Alice's relief Daisy dropped the subject of Chas and went on to discuss their gowns for the evening. Eventually Alice was free to escape and return to Gertie.

All the young women rested in the afternoon, which Alice found irksome. She would have preferred to take a long walk by the river, or to read in the library. It would have caused too much trouble to disobey, so she spent a restless afternoon, quite unable to sleep, and longing for the moment when she could change into a tea-gown and go down to join the men.

As soon as the men arrived, Chas made straight for Alice's chair. She felt certain everyone was talking about them, and she felt a secret pleasure at the envious stares she received from Gladys and her friends.

That evening Alice swept caution to the wind and danced nearly every dance with Chas.

The following day, as the house party disbanded, Chas sought her out.

'Might I call on you in London, Miss Tregowan?'

'I should be honoured, Mr Cordell,' she replied, resenting the social strictures which prevented her from calling him Chas and saying how she longed to see him again. 'I'm to have a ball in three weeks, at Fairhall, my father's house in Berkshire. Perhaps if you are not engaged elsewhere . . .?'

'Miss Tregowan, I should be more than happy to attend.'

'I'll arrange for an invitation to be sent you,' she replied, amazed at her own forwardness.

5

Alice was in despair. She had last seen Chas on Thursday; each day since then she had expected him to call on her. He had not come. She would have preferred to wait at home just in case he should call, but Daisy would not hear of it.

'Let him call and not find you in. It will be salutary for him. My "At Home" is on Thursdays; he is sure to attend. If he does not, then we were mistaken,' Daisy advised crisply.

For six days it had been a very despondent Alice who accompanied her stepmother on visits – to the shops, to 'At Homes', to dinners, to a concert. But at least she now had a friend to confide in – and Gertie was convinced that Chas would reappear.

She was certain that Gertie kept her sane during this time. Whenever she could escape from her stepmother it was Gertie's company she sought. Together they would visit museums and art galleries. Gertie knew so much that Alice was envious of her superior education. But Gertie was also fun and they teased and giggled with each other as any eighteen-year-olds would do. Alice felt free to confide about Chas. And, equally important, she was able to talk of her grief at Queenie's death and found that Gertie understood her sadness for her nursemaid. In a matter of days Alice felt she had begun a friendship which would last her for the rest of her life.

It was Thursday afternoon when Daisy Tregowan was 'at home' to guests. No invitations were given; people came if they had calls to return, to pay their respects, if there were flirtations they wished to pursue, and largely to see who else was there. An hour had passed and Alice had all but given up looking at the clock. The room was crowded with equal numbers of men and women – for this was the time that assignations were safely made. About the room the gentlemen's hats and gloves lay on the floor beside them, an indication that they visited only for a short time and were about to leave. This was done to placate irate husbands, should they appear, though this was unlikely since those same husbands were undoubtedly visiting someone of interest in another house. Only newly wed couples arrived together.

Alice had reached the point of wishing that everyone would go so that she could escape to her room and at least have the privacy to think about Chas, to try to remember his voice with its fascinating accent – so strange, but attractive, to her ears. She liked to touch the gowns she had worn when dancing with him, knowing that he too had touched them. Everything that was happening to her emotions had come as a shock to her. She wondered if this was love. She was having difficulty coming to terms with this state of affairs; she had long denied to herself the possibility that there could ever be a man she would love. And he was completely the wrong man for her. The last thing she wanted was to go to America. But, like millions of women before her, she was having to learn that where love was concerned all past plans, all ideals, simply melted away in the face of the fierce heat within her.

'Miss Tregowan.' She had been trying unsuccessfully to concentrate on the conversation of an old friend of her father's. Alice jumped at the sound of his voice, manners forsook her, and leaving the man in mid-sentence, she swung round to face him, her face alight with joy.

'Mr Cordell, what a pleasant surprise.' She beamed with pleasure, thinking how dull he made all the other men in the room appear.

'Miss Tregowan, I trust I do not impose myself upon you?'

'Mr Cordell, you are not imposing yourself at all. It is our pleasure that you honour us with your company.' She shook her head with frustration at this obligatory dance of polite words. 'I feared you were not coming,' she blurted out, hoping that no one heard her.

'I have fought with myself all this week, wishing to see you so much but afraid you might not wish to see me,' he replied, in an urgent tone.

'Oh, I did. I truly did!' She laughed up at him. He looked at her lovely face and had to use every ounce of control not to bend there and then to kiss her full on her delightful mouth. He smiled his warm, slightly crooked smile, overjoyed at the naturalness of her reaction. He glanced about the crowded and noisy room.

'Is there nowhere we can talk?'

Alice noted her stepmother, across the room, safely involved in a flirtation with a Guards officer. 'I'll go out; you follow me in a moment. The morning-room will be empty,' she whispered and quickly skirted the crowd to slip out of the door.

They had ten precious minutes of each other's company before Alice insisted on returning to the drawing-room in case they were missed. These were minutes of sheer joy for both of them. Chas looked at her with wonder: her blonde beauty was such that she seemed to shimmer in the cool, shaded room. Later she could not remember what they had spoken of. She remembered laughing and she knew she had flirted – she, who had thought she did not know how, had teased and flirted easily with a man! They did not touch, but they longed to. And this longing filled the room, making the atmosphere seem charged – like the air before a storm. To touch would have been bliss, but not to do so was exquisite torture.

She had entered the room a woman who thought she might be in love; she left it certain.

6

For ten days Alice saw Chas every day. They walked in the park, they rowed on the Serpentine – always chaperoned by Chantal who, being French, prided herself on her discretion in such matters. To Alice's joy her father appeared to approve; he had even gone so far as to invite Chas to join them in his box at the opera. Chas was at every dinner she attended, and at the various balls. Several times they had managed to hold hands; once they had managed to snatch a quick, chaste kiss.

Alice, while deliriously happy to be in love, found it also a very uncomfortable experience. Her heart seemed out of control and always within her she felt a tension that she did not understand – a tension that sometimes when he was with her she found almost unbearable.

Alice had started the season concerned at what she saw around her in London – the poverty, the misery with which the city abounded. It had been impossible for her to ignore the huddled bodies sleeping, wrapped in newspaper, in the street when she returned from a ball. Selecting food from yet another sumptuous buffet she would suddenly remember the starving multitudes outside and her pleasure would disappear. She would sip chilled champagne and think of the women who were beaten black and blue by drunken husbands, and her pleasure in the champagne would evaporate. She would happily dance the night away and then, as she left a ball, the sun already glinting over the roof-tops, she would glimpse the strained, tired face of a maid or footman, and her guilt that their labour was required for her to enjoy herself made the glittering ball seem suddenly tawdry.

But now? Now that Chas had come into her life, all she thought about was him, and her, and him with her, and all the guilt and pain she had felt vaporised as her love deepened. It was as if, in this world, only they existed.

It was Daisy's novel idea to hold Alice's ball in the country. Always eager to be innovative, she had decided against London. Her friends had objected to the inconvenience of the journey and that they would be able to attend only one ball that night instead of the customary two or three. Precisely so, Daisy had thought: on this particular night there was to be only one ball that mattered – Alice Tregowan's ball. The acceptances had been slow to come, and she had worried briefly that she might have made a social mistake. But, finally, the reply she had awaited most eagerly had come. The Prince of Wales would be attending. Now able to send out instructions that orders were to be worn because of his presence, she found that the replies came in an avalanche.

215

Those she had overlooked, or those she had decided to snub, were virtually begging at her door. Daisy was becoming adept at manipulating society. They were heady and powerful weeks for her.

For a week Fairhall had been in turmoil. The start of the preparations for Alice's ball had been a thorough cleaning of the house from top to bottom. Once the house was spotless, the china, the silver, the linen were all inspected, polished, washed, stacked and counted. Grass was cut, paths raked, trees tidied and flowers cajoled into bloom. So great was the workload that the majority of the staff from the London house had been sent to Fairhall.

Daisy had instructed professional florists to decorate the ballroom, the dining-room and the seating areas. The meeting of these men with the head gardener became fraught as the decorators issued their demands.

'I've done the best I can. If them flowers be blooming on Thursday, well and good. But if they ain't, there's bugger all I can do about it. You'd best speak to him up there,' the crusty old gardener informed them, pointing heavenward. In panic the decorators ordered cartloads of flowers from London, just in case.

As the week progressed, the food began to arrive. Ia had never seen so much, nor had she ever seen kitchens so busy. The cool room, the pantries, the bakery and the dairy began to fill with food. Great tanks of water were filled with fat lobsters which climbed over each other in their fruitless bid for freedom. Crayfish, langoustine, salmon, oysters and trout languished in water, awaiting the same fate. Turbot, sole and halibut were stored in ice. Chickens, turkeys, geese, ducks and quail were plucked by the dozen. Sides of beef and whole pigs were marinated and dressed.

Ia thought she had never seen such a genius as Monsieur Alphonse, Lady Tregowan's French chef. He had created castles of jelly, cathedrals of blancmange. Ice sculptures which took her breath away were being carved.

The day before the ball a line of gardeners appeared bearing every vegetable and fruit in season. Ia's fingers were red from hulling and picking over the strawberries, raspberries, loganberries and redcurrants. But Monsieur Alphonse was a pleasure to work for. He never shouted, he ruled his kitchen calmly and with courtesy. He gave his instructions quietly and precisely, and in consequence order emerged effortlessly from the original chaos. Had it not been for Frederick, Ia would have liked to work here rather than in London.

Each bedroom had been allocated, every inn and hotel in the neighbourhood had been taken over. Daisy had asked Alice how many rooms she required for her friends, but when it came to the count she decided that she had only one real friend – and Gertie was to share her room.

For this ball Daisy had ordered the most breathtaking dress of the season for Alice. The heavy white satin underskirt was covered with a flowing overskirt of finest silk chiffon. A small army of seamstresses had worked for weeks to sew the thousands of seed pearls and diamanté that decorated it in the shapes of a dozen different flowers and butterflies. The overskirt was caught at the back of the waist by a large silk cabbage rose from which a cataract of finely pleated chiffon fell in a long train. The sleeves were tight at the wrist but flared up into enormous gigot sleeves at the shoulder – the latest rage. The tight-fitting bodice, rigid with more pearls, was cut far lower than any other dress Alice had worn. She loved the dress but hated her hair which, on Daisy's insistence, had been curled by the heated tongs into the fashionable curls which Alice insisted on calling a frizz. Once Daisy had left her room she had had Chantal pin real white roses on to her hair, so that the chignon was a mass of sweet-scented blooms with diamond clips scattered amongst them. About her neck she wore the pearl choker with diamond clasp which had belonged to her mother and which, so far, was the only piece of that collection she had been permitted to wear.

Chantal stood back. Alice studied herself in the long mirror: she saw how her grey eyes sparkled with excitement and knew she looked beautiful. She could hardly wait for Chas to see her.

Alice slipped downstairs; there was still half an hour before the guests would arrive. She peered into the ballroom. It was a room which Alice disliked – too grand, too carved, too large, an unsuccessful attempt by her parents to re-create a medieval banqueting hall. But tonight it had been transformed into a white garden. Garlands of flowers were looped across the rafters and trailed down the walls. From great white china vases flowers cascaded on to the floor. For the first time, Alice thought, the room looked beautiful. She inspected the dining-room. Champagne glasses gleamed, the large silver punchbowl was full. Long tables were swagged with still more flowers. The food was a work of art. She thanked Monsieur Alphonse who, with a large bunch of parsley in his hand, was garnishing to the last moment.

Alice passed through the green baize door which led to the passageway and the kitchens. As she opened the door the blast of heat rocked her. She looked about at a scene of apparent devastation as an army of kitchen maids helped, for once, by the housemaids, endeavoured to clear up before the washing-up began.

'Excuse me,' she said from the doorway. 'Excuse me,' she said more loudly to be heard above the hubbub. The maids turned to look at their young mistress, staring in wonder at her magnificent dress, and at her beauty. In unison they bobbed their curtsies and Alice felt uncomfortable. She had never become used to their curtsies, it always made her feel awkward.

'I wanted to thank you all for your extremely hard work this evening. I fear there will be the most dreadful amount of washing-up,' she smiled. 'I am sorry.' Across the room her eye was caught by a tall, blonde girl, who stood sideways so that only her profile could be seen – yet she seemed to be looking slyly at her. There was something familiar about her. Something strangely familiar . . .

'You look a picture, Miss Tregowan,' a maid said shyly, and Alice turned her attention to her.

'Thank you, I think it is the dress rather than me.' She laughed, 'I've asked Phillpott to make certain that you all have a glass of champagne tonight.' One or two murmured their thanks but most seemed too much in awe to speak. 'Well, thank you again,' Alice said awkwardly.

'I'll say this for her, she's a real lady that one,' said one of the senior housemaids as the door closed. 'You don't get many as bothers to thank us.'

'She looked like a princess,' a little scullery maid said dreamily.

'To think she thanked *us*,' said another.

'She's not as perfect as she seems,' Ia said sharply, as she lugged a tray of crockery towards the scullery. 'Judas!' she muttered as she stacked the dishes. Alice had seen her, she was sure of it. She leaned against the sink and allowed the wave of rage that Alice's betrayal caused in her, to subside. She had once loved Alice. She had loved her more than anyone in the world. But now? Was it hatred she felt? Would her anger ever leave? She poured the soda into the sink and turned the taps on. No, she did not hate her – at least she did not wish her dead. But she hurt inside from Alice's neglect. It was the pain of being deserted, the pain of finding her trust had been misplaced. She swilled the green soap in its small metal basket through the water to raise a lather. She plunged her hands in. She would never forgive Alice, she could not. One day, she did not know how, but one day she would taste the sweetness of revenge for this desertion.

By nine o'clock the house party dinner was over and the staff moved in to clear the debris. Alice had longed to sit beside Chas but such a dream had been vetoed by Daisy, who had placed her beside the guest of honour – a German prince related to the Royal Family, whose English was so limited that Alice regretted that Miss Gilby had had time only to teach her French. A long way down the table she could see Gertie and the younger members of the party enjoying themselves. She saw with anger that Gladys had been seated next to Chas. Momentarily she feared what the girl might tell him – but she rejected the thought: Chas would never believe ill of her or of her family, she was certain. Then she noticed Chas whispering to her cousin, who flicked open her fan and smiled suggestively over it. Alice suffered a bolt of jealousy, another emotion which was new to her and which she was, for the time being, unable to identify.

The ball began. Chas was the first to ask her to dance. She was to receive many compliments that night but his were the most important to her. She danced with the Duke of Ruling and was amused to realise that he was smitten with her. Then it was the turn of the Earl of Stanby, a clumsy oaf who trampled her feet mercilessly. Lords and Honourables paid court as they danced with her until the duke's name came round again on her dance card – and, all the while, every part of her was longing to be dancing only with Chas. Each time she floated around the ballroom, she looked for him, wondering with whom he was dancing. But he stood at the edge of the room, his eyes never leaving her.

At eleven, forewarned by look-outs, Alice stood with her parents at the top of the steps awaiting the arrival of the royal party. Daisy felt faint with relief. When the message had arrived earlier that the prince was not to dine with them, she had been mortified in front of fifty diners. Then the ball started, and still he had not arrived; she had been afraid that she was to be shamed in front of a thousand guests. It would have been impossible not to notice the pitying looks of her arch-enemies, the whispering that had started. But her faith was vindicated – here he came.

Up the drive, heading a long cavalcade of carriages, came a horseless carriage – the noise was deafening as it coughed, spluttered and lurched its way towards the house, a cloud of evil-smelling smoke billowing out behind. Those carriage horses which witnessed its arrival reared and whinnied with terror. Daisy clapped her hands over her ears most fetchingly.

From the automobile the prince alighted and, with surprising agility in one so portly, mounted the steps beaming with bonhomie.

'My dear Tregowan, Lady Tregowan, Miss Tregowan, my apologies! We wanted to make a grand entrance.' He laughed loudly, gesturing to the machine. 'It would have been much faster by carriage – this machine stopped, and took my coachman an hour to restart – but not nearly so exhilarating. Tregowan, I recommend one to you,' he boomed in his slightly guttural voice. Daisy and Alice sank in deep curtsies. As she rose, Alice was aware of his blue eyes regarding her boldly. He took her hand, and seemed to hold it for ever. The prince looked her up and down and said, 'Delightful, Miss Tregowan,' in a voice which made Alice look down quickly with confusion.

'Your Royal Highness,' she managed to utter.

From the other carriages a crowd of men had raced, each anxious to be as close to the prince as possible, each jostling for the best position.

'Is my cousin Prince Fritz here?'

'Yes, Your Highness, my stepdaughter and I had the pleasure of dining with him.'

'Great fun, dear old Fritzie, isn't he? Such wit!' The

221

prince did not speak as such, but bellowed, and Alice felt that he must be speaking of a different dinner companion from the one whose company she had just endured.

A very proud Daisy Dear, her head held so high that she almost looked tall, escorted the prince and his party into the ballroom. The music ceased. In a rustle of silk and satin, the miniature medals of the men glinting in the light from the great chandeliers, the assembled company sank as one in curtsies and low bows. The prince beamed like a pleased headmaster at his pupils' excellent behaviour.

'Please, we are informal tonight,' he said, waving his hand airily. Daisy felt she would burst with pride. The greatest compliment a society hostess could receive was the prince's announcement that the evening was to be informal in his company. George and Daisy led the prince and his party to the room set aside for bezique. The music began again.

'Miss Tregowan, please can we talk? I need to speak to you, urgently.' Chas was by her side.

She looked at her dance card: each dance had a name beside it. 'I shouldn't really. I should be dancing. Look, the Duke of Ruling is next.'

'I detest the duke, with all his money and land. I am fearful each time I see you dancing with him.' He had a despairing look on his face as he spoke. Alice saw the duke making his way across the ballroom towards her.

'Quick, this way,' she said, taking Chas's arm and throwing caution to the wind; she led him out along the corridor towards the conservatory.

The large conservatory, built by her mother, was heavy with the scent of jasmine, tuberoses and gardenias. In the centre a fountain trickled and fat carp swam lazily in their marble pond. The orange, lemon and palm trees were arranged so they formed private bowers, each furnished with chairs and small tables.

'Miss Tregowan, please may I call you Alice? I hate

this formality. In my country I would have been calling you Alice for weeks now. And I long for you to call me Chas.'

'I hate it too,' she said in a low voice.

He took her hand. 'Alice, my darling,' Alice's heart, always unstable in his presence, gave a jolt. 'I must talk to you and I'm afraid that what I have to say will make you angry with me.' He ushered her to a chair in one of the bowers furthest from the door, and sat opposite her. Taking her hand he looked at her for what to Alice seemed an age. For the first time Alice felt apprehensive. He looked so anxious. What could it be? Perhaps he was already married? At the thought, her white kid-gloved hand shot to her mouth. No, he would not have deceived her. Maybe he had done something wrong and was in trouble with the authorities.

'Alice, I love you.'

'Oh, Chas, I love you too.' She said the words slowly, relishing each one of them. 'I thought you were about to confess something dreadful.' And she laughed with delight at his declaration and at her previous fears.

'But that is not my confession, Alice.'

Alice felt she was on a high-flying swing as her elation once more became anxiety.

'Alice, I want to marry you.'

'Oh yes, please,' Alice blurted out, her emotions hurtling back to excitement so that she quite forgot the conventions of such matters. Again her gloved hand shot to her mouth. 'Oh dear. I'm not supposed to say that, am I? I'm supposed to leave you in a torment of indecision.'

'You're like no other woman, Alice. You're so natural, you say what you think. You're like me. We were never meant to be imprisoned by society's conventions.' He lifted her hand to his lips and kissed it gently and again studied her silently, so that her fear began to mount again and she sat rigid in her chair. 'I have no money, Alice, that's my confession.'

Alice's body relaxed and she smiled broadly. 'What a relief, Chas. Money is unimportant. It's our love for each other that matters. I have money enough for both of us.'

'I think it might matter to your father. And in any case I would have to make my own way. I'm not the sort of fellow who would allow his wife to support him.'

'Fiddlesticks! Does it matter which one of us has the money? I don't think so. And my father likes you.'

'Because he thinks I'm a Yankee millionaire, my darling, that's the only reason.'

'No, Chas . . .' But even as she spoke she felt a shiver of apprehension. She knew that in her father's circle money, if never discussed, was, all the same, of paramount importance.

'You see, when I first came here, I had a letter of introduction to Lord Chisholm and honestly, Alice, I don't know how it happened but everyone took me for a rich man, and I just let them continue to think it. I mean, I've had a wonderful six months, it hasn't cost me a penny.' He laughed but it was a very strained laugh. 'If only I had been honest right from the start and explained that I had nothing.'

'But then we would never have been allowed to meet, Chas,' Alice said logically. 'But,' she smiled at him, 'you *look* so rich.'

He laughed, a more relaxed laugh this time. 'I've always appreciated the better things in life. My father was a shopkeeper, he did well – well enough for me to go to Yale. I suppose it was there that I picked up my liking for expensive clothes and what we call the high life. When I left college, my father would have liked me to go into the business – I wish I had now. But I didn't. I did several jobs but I couldn't settle at any of them.'

'What work?' Alice interrupted, wanting to know everything about him.

'I worked in a firm of brokers for a short time – a friend's firm, but I decided the office was not for me. I sold champagne for a while, but I regret I drank more than I sold. Then I sold jewellery for six months. But I couldn't settle. So, I thought, I had better join my father. But what I didn't know was that his business had gone from bad to worse, and he was made bankrupt.' Alice put out her hand to take his, her face etched with concern.

'Then, out of the blue, an aunt I had never met died and left me $2,000. I looked at my father and how hard he had worked all his life, finally for nothing, and I thought, that's not for me. So I got me this fine wardrobe of real dandy clothes and a ticket for Europe. And that's it. Chas Cordell is an imposter.'

'Did you not think to give the money to your father?' she asked, filled with concern for the poor man who was to become her father-in-law.

'I did, I did,' Chas said hurriedly. 'He wouldn't take it. Refused it outright.'

'Do you want to return to America?' she asked anxiously.

'I don't mind one way or the other. But I have to find work or else your father will throw me out. Mind you I reckon he'll throw me out anyway when he hears all this.'

'But I have plans, Chas.' Her voice was bubbling with excitement as she explained about her inheritance, about Gwenfer and her longing never to leave the house she loved. Hurriedly she told him of the farm he could manage – if he wanted. She explained about the near-empty stables where they could breed horses – if he wanted. She told of the closed tin mines that could be reopened – if he wanted. 'So, there you are.' She sat back in the chair, her eyes sparkling.

'Oh, Alice . . .' His arms were about her and Alice was being kissed for the first time in her life. She clung to him knowing there could never be another man for her.

'I'll speak to your father tomorrow.'

*

225

When they returned to the ball Alice was aware of the censorious glances that were cast in her direction, but she did not care. She had not compromised herself. How could she have, when it was Chas she wanted to marry?

That night, in bed, after she had told Gertie all that had happened, Alice wept softly into her pillow, tears of sheer joy.

At four o'clock, Ia, her work finished at last, made her way to the bed in the attic she had been allocated. There was no chance of finding Frederick: she did not even know where he had been billeted. But in any case she was too tired. She had two hours before she must be up to start the breakfasts. There were fifty for luncheon and thirty for dinner – work was far from over for Ia and the staff.

She blew out the candle, lay on her hard bed, turned her face into the pillow and wept – tears of sheer exhaustion.

7

To say that Chas Cordell had been thrown out of the house, the next day, by Lord Tregowan would be something of an exaggeration. But there was no doubting that the young man had been requested to leave and in such haste that he had not even been allowed to say goodbye to Alice.

Alice, meanwhile, had been in her room with Gertie, nervous with excitement, awaiting the summons to the family drawing-room to discuss the engagement and wedding plans.

It was a young girl made even more beautiful by the knowledge that she loved and was loved in return who opened the door of the drawing-room. She walked into a room full of sombre atmosphere. Her smile quickly disappeared, her happy mood could not fail to be pierced by it.

She had spent most of the season avoiding her Aunt Maude, whom, even had it not been for her childhood memories of her, she could not like. Today avoidance was impossible for there sat her aunt, resplendent in purple satin which matched the high colour of her cheeks. Alice looked around apprehensively – Chas was not there; Daisy was sitting to one side crying quietly, but prettily, into a small handkerchief. Her father looked thunderous and her aunt likewise. It was the presence of Aunt Maude which filled her with foreboding, for it was as if the big guns of the family were lined up, her aunt being the biggest.

'Pray explain to us, Alice, why you encouraged that young American,' her father said without benefit of greeting.

'We are in love. He has asked for my hand.'

'I am only too aware of that. And a more unsuitable match I cannot imagine.'

'I thought you liked him, Papa.'

'That was when I thought he was suitable.'

'Now he is not suitable?'

'He is worse than that, he is a charlatan, an imposter. No one will receive him now.'

'Because he has no money?'

'Precisely. I could scarcely believe my ears when he stood there,' he pointed dramatically to a place on the carpet, 'and had the audacity to ask for your hand while explaining that he was penniless.'

'At least he was honest with you, Papa.'

'Don't be insolent, Alice. I have sent him packing. With luck he will be in France or on his way back to America by tomorrow. You are to forget him.'

'Forget him,' Alice's voice rose. 'I can't forget him, I love him. I intend to marry him.'

'Oh, Alice, how could you do this to us? What on earth

227

is the prince going to think?' Daisy sobbed from the depths of the chair in which she was hunched, rather like a frightened little girl, her handkerchief clutched to her mouth. Alice almost expected her to start sucking her thumb.

'Quite honestly, Daisy Dear, I don't care what the prince thinks,' Alice announced and Daisy closed her eyes in horror at such a blasphemy. 'I have done nothing to be ashamed of. I did not know about Mr Cordell's financial situation until last night, and it makes not a jot of difference to how I feel. Society liked him well enough when they thought him rich. Well, I am not as hypocritical as your society.'

'Such talk will help none of us, Alice. You have behaved foolishly. How could you be so indiscreet as to disappear with him last night? Can you imagine what everyone is thinking and saying?' Aunt Maude broke in.

'It would not have been so indiscreet if he had been the millionaire you all thought him.'

'Alice, apologise to your aunt.'

'I'm sorry, Papa, I can't. I love him. The fact that he has no money is irrelevant. I have money.'

'What sort of man would allow himself to be kept by his wife?'

'I can name quite a few who were here last night,' Alice replied in a reasonable tone.

'Alice!'

'And you could have been the Duchess of Ruling . . . Oh, you silly fool. Don't you see that you are compromised now? No one who is anyone will want you now.' And Daisy began to weep again which brought her husband to her side to comfort her.

'I don't want to be a duchess. I want to be Mrs Cordell. I did not ask to come here in the first place. I was happy at Gwenfer.' Alice felt dangerous tears begin to prick the backs of her eyes. She did not want to cry; she had to keep control.

228

'Ah, Gwenfer. I always said you would rue the day you left the child there, George. Hobnobbing with the servants – she has acquired a skivvy's mentality.' Maude Loudon scowled.

'The servants at Gwenfer are good people. They are loyal and honest, and I love them.'

'How could you be so ungrateful to your father, Alice?' Maude Loudon creaked in the chair with exasperation.

'My father insisted I came for my début. Well, I came. The whole object of the exeicse was for me to find a husband. Well, I've done that, too.'

'I have never in all my life been spoken to with such insolence. Oh, my poor George, I see Etty's blood here. And where will that end?' Maude looked soberly at Alice.

'My mother has nothing to do with this.' Alice glared at her aunt.

'Hasn't she?' Maude gave one of her tight little smiles.

'Maude . . .' feebly George admonished his sister.

'Bad blood will always out,' she continued.

'Like Gladys?' Alice said, almost hysterical now.

'Alice!'

'Alice! Alice! Alice! You can Alice me all you like. I have found the man I wish to marry, Papa. And I intend to do so.'

'Go to your room, Alice. Perhaps, Daisy Dear, it would be best if we curtailed the season and took Alice to Rome.'

'Oh, Georgie, what a wonderful idea, you are so clever.' Daisy smiled bravely at her husband through her tearful eyes.

'I'm not going to Rome. I'm getting married.' Alice stood her ground.

'And how do you think you could survive?' her father asked, unpleasantly.

'We can live at Gwenfer. I have Mama's money, I need nothing from you. And then there is my mother's jewellery.' Alice looked pointedly at her stepmother who, as always, was decked with diamonds and other gems. Daisy nervously fingered the choker at her neck.

'Alice, you should be ashamed of yourself speaking to your dear, loving father in this way.'

'Loving father? Loving father?' Alice's voice rose hysterically. 'Aunt Maude, what loving father? Papa would not have cared if I had lived or died these past thirteen years. When did he come to see me? When did he show love? Oh, cheques yes, money yes, but was that just to salve his conscience? He has no feeling for me. I have been brought here to make a good marriage for his satisfaction, for his standing in society, not for my well-being. My coming-out has been lavish in the extreme, but he spent that money because it suited him and amused his empty-headed wife!' Alice shouted back. 'I owe my father *nothing.*'

Aunt Maude lumbered to her feet, puce with indignation. Daisy began to howl.

'Alice, go to your room immediately. You will stay there, you will take your meals there. You are to see and speak to no one. We leave for London tomorrow and then we shall travel to Rome at the first available opportunity. There we shall consider your future. Now get out of my sight,' her father added coldly.

Alice sped from the room and raced up the stairs praying that she would find Gertie there.

'Gertie, thank goodness you're here.' Alice finally burst into tears.

'Alice, what has happened?' Gertie's face was creased with concern.

Alice blew her nose and explained rapidly. 'If I write Chas a letter, will you get your brother to deliver it to him immediately? We are going to London tomorrow and I think probably to Rome the following day. I have to see him, Gertie, I love him so much. We have only a short time . . .' She rushed to her desk and quickly wrote the letter, angrily dashing tears from her eyes as she wrote. All she could think to write was that she would meet him at six in the morning, the day after tomorrow, outside the London house. 'We'll have to elope, Gertie, there's nothing else to be done,' she said dramatically as she gave Gertie the letter, which her friend slipped into her pocket.

At that point Gertie's stony-faced mother entered the room and shepherded her out, as if Alice had a disease her daughter might catch.

Two days later as dawn broke, Alice, who had not slept, crept from her bed. The night before, the maid had packed her cases ready for Rome. The trunks were too heavy so she could manage only two of the smaller cases. Lastly into a leather bag she tipped the few items of jewellery she had been allowed to wear. She had thought of writing her father a letter but had decided finally that she did not know what to say to him. She sat on her bed and nervously watched as the hands of the clock moved round to six. What if he did not come, what if he had already left? she asked herself as she quietly drew the bolts on the front door.

The street was empty. Alice stood with her luggage beside her on the pavement and peered anxiously up the road. A noise from the area steps made her jump. She swung round. She could see nothing but was certain she had heard something. Picking up her bags, she backed up the front steps and hid behind the pillar of the portico, and nervously peered round it. In the area someone was moving. She dared not be seen by one of the servants: word would spread instantly. Again she leaned forward and standing on tiptoe looked down into the area steps. At sight of a maid's cap and blonde hair she relaxed a little. The girl climbed up, systematically sweeping each step, until she stood at the top of the area. She leaned her broom against the black railings which she then began to dust. Alice edged round the pillar as the maid laboriously dusted each metal rung. She returned to her broom and vigorously began to sweep the pavement. Then she stopped and leaned on her broom, looking up and down the street. Alice, still trapped behind the pillar, watched the girl and was struck by how pretty she was even in her dull uniform. A delivery boy rode past and whistled. The maid lowered her head, rather like a nervous animal. The action made Alice feel uneasy, as if somewhere she had seen this girl before, as if she knew her. The girl looked up the street sharply as a carriage swung noisily around the corner. Alice could see her profile now – of course, it was the kitchen maid who had attracted her attention at Fairhall the night before last. Alice shivered, suddenly aware of the early morning chill.

From the carriage window Chas's head appeared, his face alight with pleasure at seeing Alice. He leaped from the carriage, bounded up the steps, scooped Alice into his arms and kissed her. Letting go of Alice he bent to pick up her two cases. Alice, bold now that Chas was with her, tripped down the steps, past the maid who stood with open mouth leaning on her broom, which clattered to the pavement as she jumped with surprise.

'Good morning,' Alice smiled as she spoke to the startled girl and hastily climbed into the carriage. Chas jumped in beside her, the whip cracked, the horses reared and, with Chas's arm about her, Alice was speeding away to a new life.

Ia watched the carriage disappear up the road in a cloud of dust. What was Alice up to? How beautiful and happy she had looked. How excited she had been. Was she eloping? What a romantic thing to do . . . Ia sighed and picked up her broom and idly, this time, brushed the pavement. Lucky Alice . . . She stopped dead. Lucky Alice, it was always the same. Lucky, rich, with lovely homes and beautiful possessions. She had everything and now a handsome man who loved her enough to run away with her. Ia's eyes half closed like the eyes of a cat as she looked up the road where the carriage had gone. Well, she hoped he was a real bastard, one who would make Alice's life a living hell and wipe that smug smile off her face. Ia's one regret was that she would not be there to see her misery.

Ia looked at the railings she had just cleaned, now coated with dust from the coach.

'Bloody Tregowans. Rot the lot of them,' Ia muttered as she dusted the railings again.

Part Two

Chapter Six

1

Alice stood at the window of her hotel bedroom and watched the tangle of traffic below. Each day she spent hours watching New York which after three months still fascinated her. At any hour it was busy. There was an urgency in the movement of the carriages, the hand-carts, the many horse-buses, and even the pedestrians seemed to walk faster than in London. It was noisier too, much noisier – people talked loudly, shouted in a confusing babble of different languages. Even the horses' hooves seemed to her to make more noise.

The whole city appeared to be a huge building plot: Alice was reminded of children who, having built a tower with their building bricks, immediately knocked it down and began again. Few old buildings survived; those that did so huddled, appearing afraid, as the destruction continued about them. She became used to seeing a house, once one of a row, now standing in isolation like a solitary tooth in a gaping mouth – but never for long, soon it would be surrounded by new, taller buildings. As the price of land rose so the pressure to build upwards had begun. She had become accustomed to the tall buildings of London but nothing could have prepared her for these towering blocks which seemed to defy gravity. She had been shown one building of thirteen storeys which, she was convinced, would surely fall down if the wind blew hard enough. But there was no style of architecture that could claim to be totally American. The architects looked to ancient Europe for inspiration. So the new houses of the rich were Italian palazzi or French châteaux; even the more modest buildings were adorned with Greek columns, Roman friezes.

For some time the difference in the light had puzzled her. There was a quality to it that amazed her with its peachy glow until she looked in the atlas and saw how far south she was in the hemisphere.

She had presumed, so far from Europe, that shopping would prove difficult. Nothing could have been further from the truth. Alice doubted if there was anything that one could buy in London or Paris which could not be obtained here.

Sometimes she found the noise of the city irksome. At those times she would find herself thinking of the peace of Gwenfer on a perfect day, with the merest breeze, and the sea gently lapping the rocks, and she would be consumed with a desperate longing to be there, from which came a feeling of emptiness, of a particular loneliness that Chas could not fill. It was then that she needed Queenie. She sighed and peered down at the bustle far below her. There was so much confusion in her life and her emotions that she wished she still had Queenie to turn to. For she knew that, if she had not always liked the advice that Queenie gave, it was honest advice. How strange it was that, so far from home, she rarely gave her mother or father a thought but her old nursemaid appeared repeatedly to her in dreams.

She rearranged the curtains, pleating the heavy damask neatly into its ornate tie-back. Luxury was everywhere. This hotel was the epitome of it. It was furnished throughout in black mahogany, which Alice had never seen before but which gave it a striking elegance. The carpets were the thickest she had walked on, used as she was to the priceless, fine woven, antique carpets of her father's houses. She particularly enjoyed bathing here: the water gushed from the faucet – she took pride now in using new, American words – always piping hot and apparently inexhaustible. Like a child, she delighted in

238

standing beneath the shower, the water falling over her in a forceful cascade. She had only once had a shower in England, at Gertie's house, but there the water had trickled out, lukewarm, and it had been an uncomfortable experience. Here she was never cold, the radiators were almost too hot to touch – in dramatic contrast to the tepid ones to be found in the few English houses which boasted central heating. The food was as good as any creation of Daisy's Monsieur Alphonse and there was an even more bewildering choice. And George Tregowan would have been more than impressed by the selection of fine wines available. She was not sure what she had expected; certainly not a primitive life-style, but neither had she thought to find this degree of sybaritic luxury.

Perhaps what delighted her most about this hotel was the knowledge that Mr Dickens had stayed here. She liked to think he had slept in her bed and often when she walked the long corridors she wondered if his feet had stood on these selfsame carpets. Had the lift been installed then? Probably not, so he would not have had the childish thrill she had, several times a day, of riding up and down in the plush gilt cage.

She looked at her watch and frowned. It was already eleven. Sometimes she wondered what on earth Chas did all morning. No matter what time he said he would come to collect her, he never appeared before noon. She touched the window, it was cold. The glorious Indian summer they had been enjoying was now over and late October was becoming bitter. She needed warmer clothes. The cases she had taken in her haste had contained only a few summer clothes. These were becoming sadly bedraggled with too much wear and were too lightweight for the autumn and fast-approaching winter.

She was in a quandary. She had exactly five pounds left. Since she had never in her life bought any clothes for herself, she was unsure if it would be sufficient. In any case, she did not even know how much that would be in dollars. She wished now she had had the sense to bring more money with her. But she had flown without once thinking of such mundane practicalities as how they were to live. Money and love were not good companions, she thought, smiling to her reflection in the window. Now, however, despite her love for Chas, she frequently found herself worrying about this very subject. This hotel must be expensive. Chas had been honest with her about how much money he had – it could not last for long. Things would be easier when Chas got a job, she comforted herself.

Not that Chas ever complained of the expense. He was generous to a fault. There was this hotel, the flowers and chocolates and he was always bringing her little presents of scent or handkerchiefs – all small tokens she treasured. Then there were the many restaurants to which he took her. The first time she had set foot in a public restaurant had been so exciting. She found that the bustle, and the comings and goings of the diners, added entertainment to eating. And there were their many trips to the theatre and to the opera, all of which she knew must be eating into Chas's legacy.

She loved going to the opera at the recently built Metropolitan. It was not just the music, though of course that was wonderful. No, it was that she was allowed to stare, something totally forbidden her in London, but which here everybody did. The objects of their interest were the occupants of the 'Diamond Horse-show' as everyone, rather racily she thought, called it. These were the lower tiers of boxes where only the richest sat and where, therefore, the most spectacular jewellery was displayed. From the orchestra stalls where they sat, they would consult the diagram presented by the management which indicated who was sitting in which box that night, and then it was quite permissible to raise one's opera glasses and to gawp with the rest. Chas had pointed out Mrs Astor, Mrs Vanderbilt, the Goulds and others whose names meant nothing to her but whom Chas explained. He seemed to know everything about everyone – who was arguing with whom; who was in love with which one; who was unfaithful; by whom they were dressed, what it had cost; what they ate and, most important, how much money they had. It seemed that in America the amount of money one had was of far greater importance than one's breeding. He knew to the last dollar the worth of the jewels on display as if the cost had been publicised which, as far as she knew in this uninhibited land, it might well have been. From never speaking about money or even thinking about it, both of which English society would have considered vulgar, she was thrust into one that seemed obsessed by it. After the initial shock she had found Chas's interest in the subject rather endearing and totally honest.

It was still strange to her, however, to be an outsider looking on at the famous 'Four Hundred' of American society when, had she not run away, she might, as her father's daughter, have been a welcome guest among them.

Once the summer was over, she had read in the social columns that the important families had returned from their sojourn on estates in Newport for the start of their season. In passing she had mentioned to Chas that William Astor was a great friend of her father's from his many trips to Europe. Chas had immediately suggested that she write to Mrs Astor, introducing herself. Alice had been dubious of the wisdom of this, pointing out that she should really have a letter of introduction but that, in any case, she had no desire to join the social circus again. Chas was insistent, however, so she had written. There was no reply. What Alice did not know was that Mrs Astor's daughter, though married, had run away last year with a man. Errant daughters were hardly likely to be welcomed in her drawing-room at the moment. Chas had been bitterly disappointed by the outcome, almost childishly so, Alice found herself thinking with surprise. Now Alice was embarrassed when she saw Mrs Astor at the opera, illogically fearing that the woman must know who she was.

'Look at them,' Chas had stormed one evening. 'You a lord's daughter, and they're not prepared to accept you. And to think one day you'll be as rich as they are.'

'Please, Chas, stop,' she admonished him, aware that people in adjacent seats were taking a sudden interest in her.

If the cream of New York society did not want to know her, they had their own friends, young and carefree like themselves. Their days followed a pattern. Chas would call for her and they would meet their particular group for lunch at one of four restaurants they frequented. After lunch, she and Chas would go shopping or walk in the park or visit a museum. In the evening they would again meet up with friends for dinner, usually at Delmonico's, which would be followed by a new experience for Alice, a visit to a club, where they would dance and drink most of the night away. They were all very nonconformist, she thought. Several of the other girls wore make-up, two of them even smoked. And, in public, the girls would frequently touch their male companions, stroke their faces, put their arms about them and even kiss them. Such behaviour between unmarried couples shocked Alice.

Roger and Delaware were Chas's best friends and were always accompanied by Beth and Caroline. With their brittle sophistication, these two young women intimidated Alice. They talked of little but clothes, stores, hairstyles and where next to eat and be seen – certainly the latter was of greater importance. Both were pretty but it was a prettiness marred by the set of their mouths and a hardness in the eyes. Wherever they were, they never ceased looking around at who was there and with whom. Each new entrant to the room was appraised with a swift stare reminiscent of the canniest merchant in the bazaar. In a second the newcomer's dressmaker, jeweller and thus her worth had been noted. They reminded Alice of exotic but predatory birds. In turn, she was aware, they thought her somewhat priggish and too serious for them. Her inability to laugh at their jokes annoyed them particularly – Alice rarely understood what these jokes were about. There were times when she wondered if she really should be part of this group. She knew with certainty that Queenie would not have approved. And their company made her long for Gertie.

If she had doubts about his friends, she had none, however, about Chas. He was perfect – well almost. There were times when he was quite snappy with her and she could never think of anything that she had done to justify this irritability. It happened usually late in the evening and frequently when he said 'good-night'. She would hold her face up to his for a kiss and he would be quite abrupt, when kissing her cheek and almost pushing her away. She found this hurtful but since in the morning he was his usual happy, considerate self she always forgave him and thought no more of it.

It seemed more than three months since Chas's carriage had sped away from her father's house to Tilbury, there to join the luxury steam yacht belonging to John Waddell, an old friend of Chas's from his broking days. Alice had known luxury but this yacht astounded her. Once in the plush salon with its thick carpet, its carved panelling, its elegant curtains pulled across the portholes, its large and comfortably upholstered chairs and couches, it was only the motion of the vessel which reminded her that she was on a ship. The food served in the beautifully appointed dining-room, the table ablaze with silver and crystal, was as good as any she had eaten on shore. And her cabin was a misnomer for the elegant stateroom with its four-poster bed, its fire in the grate and the delightful adjoining mahogany and marble bathroom that led off it. Arriving in such luxury, Alice had been horrified at the sight she had seen when they had berthed in New York. Standing at the rails with the Waddells' party she watched the steerage-class passengers being disembarked from the two large ships alongside into smaller boats, to be transported to Ellis Island. After anything from eight to fourteen days at sea they had looked exhausted and afraid. Alice had instantly felt guilty about her own comfortable crossing. The others had laughed, enjoying the spectacle from the security of their luxury.

'They look so dirty and ill,' she had said.

'You don't get much comfort for ten dollars,' her host had pointed out. 'And it prepares them for Ellis Island,' he said, roaring with laughter.

'Ten dollars! Is that all it costs?'

'A bargain, they shouldn't complain. It used to be twenty.'

'What happens at this Ellis Island?' she had asked.

'Oh, it's great fun to see. We'll arrange a trip for you,' John Waddell had said. Seeing her concerned expression he hurriedly explained that their party would not be required to land there.

Two days later Alice had been appalled as she entered the great echoing immigration hall on Ellis Island with her rich and elegant friends. The hubbub was deafening as the thousands of people incarcerated there shouted, argued and pleaded in a dozen different languages. They clutched, as if for comfort, the pathetic bundles in which they carried their worldly possessions. She saw only one man strut proudly past carrying a leather case – perhaps a symbol of prosperity and importance where he came from. And then she watched him reduced by the hectoring officials to another shuffling, dejected member of the herd. No one was allowed to feel important here. She noted how raggedly they were dressed, how dirty and wretched they appeared after their long journey. She could not help but be aware of their smell. And she was distressed by how defeated they all looked at the start of this adventure. She watched the immigrants being shunted from one official to another, saw them being numbered. In their bewildered acceptance they reminded her of dumb animals being herded. With horror she saw their eyelids being opened with what looked like a button-hook and at intervals a T was chalked on an immigrant – she thought of animals in Cornwall being marked for slaughter. She noted other letters and, asking what they meant, was told that each one indicated a disease which the doctors had diagnosed – H for heart disease, L for rickets. The worst of all were the T for trachoma and a circle with a cross in it denoting simple-mindedness, both of which were indications of certain deportation. Diagnosis? In a matter of seconds these doctors made decisions which brought misery and despair upon these people and shattered their dreams with one stroke of the chalk. She turned away unable to watch as families were torn apart, guiltily remembering the ease with which she had entered this golden land and with which she had been persuaded to come and sightsee. She tried to shut her ears as she heard them begging, attempting to bribe the officials. She had seen enough. She declined to see them being interrogated in another hall, so she missed seeing the joy when eventually the lucky ones, clutching the precious piece of paper which gave them the right to enter this magic land, passed through the door to freedom and opportunity.

Safe in their carriage, driving away from the scene, Alice had turned to Chas.

'That was awful. I felt like one of those dreadful people who go to asylums to laugh at the inmates for amusement. I feel tainted.'

'Don't be so stuffy, Alice.'

245

'I'm not being stuffy. I felt angry for those poor people.'

'Poor people be blowed. They're being given the opportunity to live in this glorious land. What more could they want?'

'Not to be stared at like animals by the likes of us,' Alice found herself snapping. She loved Chas, she knew she did, but sometimes she would see in him an insensitivity that appalled her. She stared moodily out of the carriage. Poor Ia, she suddenly found herself thinking of her old friend. What she had just witnessed would have been part of Ia's dream of America – hardly a dream, more a nightmare. At least Ia had been spared the humiliation she had just witnessed.

In the weeks after that visit she found she thought more of her old friend than she had for years. Long ago Alice had found the memory too painful and had forced herself not to think of her Ia. But now it was as if she could not stop.

She had been in New York six weeks when the letter from Miss Gilby had arrived. Miss Gilby had apologised for how disjointed and confused her letter must appear but she had written it just as Mrs Trelawn had told her. Miss Gilby was far too discreet to say that Mrs Trelawn had been drunk but Alice guessed that to have been the case – she clearly remembered Mrs Trelawn's weakness for sherry. Apparently Mrs Trelawn had been visiting Miss Gilby in the schoolhouse when she blurted out that Alice had been cruelly deceived by Queenie. After much coaxing on Miss Gilby's part she was prevailed upon to continue: it transpired that Ia Blewett had not died but had been sent to the workhouse orphanage, though no one knew where she was now. The next day, however, when Miss Gilby taxed her with the story, Mrs Trelawn had denied everything and had declared that Ia had been dead these past three years. Miss Gilby had thought it her duty to report the somewhat muddled story to Alice.

As Alice finished the letter she found she was shaking with excitement. '*In vino veritas*' she knew from her Latin studies: so there might be a good chance that Ia was alive. But the knowledge while exciting was also shocking. How hurt Ia would have been at her apparent abandonment of her, what bitterness she must have suffered. And what hardships had she endured as a result? When Chas called for her he found her in a state of great agitation, talking with such speed that her words were jumbled.

'My darling, sit down, calm down and tell me slowly.'

Alice took a gulp of air and explained about the letter. 'She's not going through Ellis Island if I can help it. She must have a proper ticket and come second class.'

'Who, Alice?'

'My friend. I told you. I thought she was dead but there's a chance that she's alive. I must find her. I love her dearly, I want her to join me here. I must somehow arrange her fare. It was always her dream to come to America.'

'Why can't she pay for herself?'

'Chas, she's poor, probably a maid somewhere. She won't be able to afford the fare.' She laughed at the very idea.

'Steerage will suit her fine then,' he said laconically.

Suddenly Alice felt a flash of anger at his studied coolness: his disregard for other people's problems seemed almost callous to her.

'I thought this was supposed to be a democratic land,' she snapped back.

'It is, but within limits. Good God, we don't make friends of our servants.' He picked up his hat and gloves. 'Are you coming for a drive?' he added impatiently.

'No thank you,' Alice said, hurt and bewildered, as she realised they had for the first time come near to arguing.

Without even removing her hat Alice had sat down at the desk and had written to Mr Woodley in Penzance.

She requested him to instigate a search for Ia, no matter what the cost. When he found her, he was to buy her a second-class ticket. She was insistent that he buy the ticket, for she feared that if he sent the money Ia would be tempted to travel the cheapest way. He was to include enough money for Ia's needs on the trip. The remainder of her money, which she knew amounted to nearly £1,500, he was to transfer to Alice in New York. She had also requested that, should her father continue to pay her allowance, it should also be sent to her here. She then enclosed a letter to Ia, explaining how she had for these past years thought her dead. Out of loyalty to Queenie she did not mention her role in the catastrophe. She asked Ia's forgiveness for her apparent neglect; she sent her love.

As she had sealed the letter, across her mind flashed the scene outside her father's house the morning she had fled. The maid sweeping the pavement, the way she had lowered her head like a nervous animal . . . Suddenly she knew whom the gesture had reminded her of. But it was three years since she had last seen Ia, who had been only a child. That maid had been a young woman. All the same . . . she took another sheet of paper from the rack and started the letter she had so far avoided writing. To her father. She did not ask forgiveness; instead, she wrote of her need to pursue her happiness with Chas. She wrote of what a fine man he was. She asked for her father's understanding. As a postscript she enquired if Ia Blewett was one of his servants. If so, could he ask her to contact Mr Woodley. Looking at the letters lying on her desk she had felt a great contentment and found she was no longer angry with Chas.

All that had been over a month ago, neither had mentioned the incident again and it was easy for them to resume their close friendship.

There were times when Chas kissed her and she experienced the strangest but most delicious feelings in her body. She suspected that, had he asked her, she would have given herself to him – but he never did. He continued to be a perfect gentleman. To society she might appear to be a compromised and fallen woman, but in fact Alice was as pure as the day she had left her father's house.

On the yacht, crossing the Atlantic, they had had separate cabins. And when Mrs Waddell, their hostess, had suggested that the captain marry them, Chas had jokingly, and much to Alice's disappointment, refused. He wanted to marry Alice, he explained, at his parents' house. Everyone had agreed that such an arrangement was far more suitable and the exciting suggestion was dropped.

Now, three months later, Alice had still not met Chas's parents. There were days when she wondered why. And constantly she wished she was already Mrs Cordell, but shyness and convention prevented her from asking. There were days, also, when she wondered when Chas was going to look for a job. He never talked of it, and she was now frequently worried about their expenses. There, she turned from the window, her thoughts had gone full circle and she was back to worrying about that perplexing subject, money.

'Alice!'

She heard him call and at sight of him all the worries disappeared as they always did. She raced across the room and into his arms.

'I think you spend all morning in bed, Chas,' she teased.

'I've been extraordinarily busy this morning, I'll have you know.'

'Doing what, Chas?' she asked eagerly.

'At the crack of dawn we are off on an expedition. All of us, up into Bear Mountain for the whole weekend. Delaware's parents have a hunting lodge up there. You will love it, with the forest around us, peace and quiet, great log fires – I want you to see how my ancestors lived.'

'Chas, it sounds marvellous.' Her eyes shone at the prospect of a different adventure, and an escape from the city. 'But, Chas, there is just one thing.'

'Don't sound so worried, my dear. What is it?'

Alice twirled her hands with embarrassment. 'I don't know quite how to say this. But . . . could you perhaps lend me some money so that I could get something a little warmer to wear. I can buy it ready-made here. I wrote to Mr Woodley, my lawyer, weeks ago. I should be getting my money, from England, any day.'

'My poor darling. What a thoughtless brute I am. Of course, my sweet love must be feeling the chill. Get your bonnet this minute. We are off to buy the best that New York has to offer. Only the very best for my future wife.'

She snuggled up against him. She loved it when he talked like that, for it made her feel so secure.

2

The morning was a faint streak in the sky when their carriages set off. They had soon left New York behind. There was the added excitement of a ferry crossing and then they were in wild countryside – but countryside the like of which Alice had never seen. The autumnal colours of the trees were so rich, so deep in their crimsons and oranges it was as if God had reserved a special spectrum of colour for North America. The others who would not normally have noticed a tree or a flower took pride in her continual exclamations of astonishment. It seemed as if the hillsides were on fire, in a way which was almost frightening. But her need to be in the country was stronger than this irrational fear. She had always thought that this was where she belonged. Now she knew for certain that with such scenery so close to New York, she could never fully settle in that teeming city.

It was late afternoon and the sun had already set when they finally arrived at the lodge. The mountain itself was something of a disappointment. It was high ground rather than mountain, Alice considered, but she was too polite to comment. She had no complaints about the lodge, however. It was built of logs and was simplicity itself. A flight of wooden steps led up to a wide verandah on which stood tubs full of late-flowering geraniums. They entered a large sitting-room with an enormous stone fireplace. The floor was of polished boards on which were spread highly coloured hand-made rugs. The furniture was robust and simply made but comfortable as all the chairs had brightly embroidered cushions. Alice was entranced with everything, feeling that she was in a house from a child's fairy story.

Beth and Caroline were appalled and soon complaining. They found it too primitive and uncomfortable. Where were the servants? And, worst of all, they were cold. Delaware and Roger disappeared to get logs from the cord outside and soon a fire was burning. From the carriages they unloaded the baskets of provisions which they took to the kitchen. Here was a wood-burning range which Delaware had difficulty in lighting.

On the table was a note for Delaware which explained the lack of servants. There was to have been only one – a local woman who would have cleaned and cooked, but she had been called away to a family catastrophe.

'We'll have to go to a hotel,' Beth said, cheering up considerably at the prospect.

'There are no hotels for miles,' Delaware explained.

'This is dreadful!' Caroline stamped her foot. 'What on earth are we to do?'

'Well, we've brought provisions. Mrs Chambers will have got in milk and butter. The fires are now lit. You girls will have to cook.' Delaware grinned in satisfaction at the situation.

'I can't cook!' Beth protested.

'Neither can I,' added Caroline. 'Don't be ridiculous. What sort of hospitality is this, Delaware? What on earth must Alice think of us?'

'I think it's all splendid. It's lovely here, and so uncomplicated,' she replied, smiling.

'Who wants to live like white trash?'

'I've always thought how wonderful the simple life would be,' Alice sighed, but noticing Beth's irritated expression added hurriedly, 'Given that one were not too poor, of course. And, anyway, I can cook.'

This news seemed to transform her in the eyes of the other two women, as they bustled her into the kitchen and even helped to unpack the food. Then they stood about rather aimlessly.

'If you have anything else to do, please don't let me stop you. I'm better on my own. I get flustered if I'm watched,' she explained, tying a large white apron about her.

Alone, she could not have been happier as she peeled and chopped and tended the fire. She made a vegetable soup; she decided to stuff the trout with fresh herbs and to bake it. The meat was perfect for roasting, and she could make an apple pie for pudding. Mrs Trelawn would have been proud of her, she thought, as she mixed the Yorkshire pudding. She only hoped that they would not find the meal too simple for their very sophisticated tastes. If only she and Chas could live like this, in a similar lodge, with land on which to grow their vegetables and raise chickens and perhaps a cow. It would be a perfect way to bring up their children.

'Happy?' It was Chas, gently kissing the nape of her neck as he handed her a glass of champagne the men had chilled in the stream that ran alongside the cabin.

'Isn't it wonderful?'

'You never told me you could cook. Rich and able to cook – what a lucky man I am.'

'Oh, Chas, I'm not that rich.' She laughed but at the same time she wished he wouldn't mention her money so often. 'We could live like this, you and I. Think how perfect it could be, Chas. I'd have enough money. You would never need to work: it would be idyllic.'

'Alice, what a sweet innocent you are. This life is not for us. We need riches, you and me. Fine clothes, jewellery, perfect carriage horses. Excitement. I want an apartment in the Dakota building – now that's real chic. And a large house at Newport, that's what we shall have.'

'I'm not sure if that is what I want.' She frowned.

'Why not?'

'I'd always planned on living the rest of my life at Gwenfer, as you know. I never envisaged living in a city. I don't even know if I could be happy living permanently in one.'

'Of course you will, my goose, Newport isn't the city. And in any case you'll be happy wherever I am.'

'That's probably true.' She laughed at him, conscious of how happy and secure he could make her feel.

Her dinner was a huge success. The compliments circulated as rapidly as the wine. The praise, however, did not stretch as far as any offers to help with the washing-up. Alice did not mind, in fact she preferred to be alone to play out her fantasy of what life might be like, as she washed, dried and stacked the dishes, while the others continued to drink and joke.

The task completed, she opened the back door and stood for a moment on the verandah, breathing deeply the clear air. She looked up at the great canopy of the sky and, remembering Gwenfer, was filled with longing for the place she loved so dearly and had never thought to leave. She sighed.

'Alice, you're sighing. You must be tired after all that

work. What inconsiderate brutes we are. Beth was right, we should have gone to a hotel.'

'I told you all, I really don't mind. I'm not martyring myself, if that's what you think. I've enjoyed doing it.'

'God, Alice, you look so beautiful tonight.' Chas advanced towards her, a strange husky catch to his voice and an odd look in his eyes. Alice wondered if his expression had been caused by too much wine; she did not know for she had never seen him drunk. 'I need to kiss you.' He took her in his arms and kissed her passionately.

'Where are the others?' she asked, anxiously peering over his shoulder.

'All tucked up, my little one, as we should be,' and without saying more, he swept her into his arms and carried her across the large sitting-room and into a bedroom at one side of the hallway. Alice looked nervously at the large pine bed, covered with a sensible patchwork quilt.

'I've waited so long, Alice. Forgive me, I can wait no longer.' Chas placed her gently on the bed and began to undress her. She lay there, her heart pounding. She knew she should protest but she wanted him to possess her though she was afraid. Alice knew nothing of men and women: there had been no one to tell her. She knew that within her was a great need but how that was to be satisfied she was unsure. Naked now, she slid quickly between the sheets, gasping involuntarily at their chill. Rapidly Chas began to undress. In the light of the candle she saw his body for the first time. For the first time also she saw a man's erect member and was shocked at its size. Chas did not look like the Greek statues she had seen: Chas was several times larger.

'Dear, darling, little girl.' He was beside her and whispering into her ear as he licked the ridge of it. His kisses were like butterflies' wings upon her skin. When he took her breast into his mouth and softly began to suck upon it she felt faint from the sensation of pleasure it gave her. She heard herself moan as he caressed the whole of her body. She began to feel that all her body was alive for the very first time, as if the ends of her nerves were exposed to the air. She had not dreamed that such feelings were possible.

Talking to her all the time, telling her of his great love for her, caressing and stroking, he carefully began to enter her. She could not resist, did not wish to resist. Now she understood. She wanted him, wanted him to be part of her.

When he began to thrust within her she found herself rising to meet him, ignoring the pain, wanting more and more of him within her. Her body was moving of its own accord, as if it had always known what to do and had been waiting for this to happen. Suddenly Chas shuddered. A long convulsive shudder and then he lay still and heavy upon her. She was puzzled and scared. She held him tight and feared for him.

'Alice, my precious. Thank you. That was so glorious,' with relief, she heard him say eventually.

His voice broke the spell for Alice and she had to face the enormity of the step she had just taken. 'Chas! What have I done? What must you be thinking of me?'

'That I love you.'

'But I should never have allowed this to happen. It was wrong. It was . . .'

Gently he placed a finger over her lips. 'Shush. How could it be wrong, darling? We love each other. We are to marry. It was the most natural thing to want each other.'

'Then you don't think less of me?'

'Less of you?' He laughed. 'I love you more.' He settled her in the crook of his arm and contentedly lit a cigarette. 'I wish we had made love ages ago.'

'Why did you wait so long?' she asked quietly, breathing deeply, enjoying the masculine smell of his tobacco and his body.

'Respect for your feelings. And there were things I had to arrange.'

'What things?'

'Nothing of importance. I hope they are settled now. Shall we marry at Christmas, at my parents' house?'

'Please let us. I do so want to meet your family.' She sat up eagerly, but was suddenly shy of her nakedness in front of him and lifted the sheet to cover herself. 'But what if they don't like me?'

'They'll love you. Who could help but love you?'

For the rest of that weekend Alice forgot the kitchen and the food. Let the others feed themselves, she thought, as she lay in the big bed with Chas. Reassured by his words she allowed him to make love to her so many times that she lost count of the number.

It was with sadness that on the Monday she packed their bags to leave.

They returned to the hotel in the late evening. There were letters waiting for them both. Chas went to his room leaving Alice to rest before dinner.

Alone in her room, Alice tore open the envelope from Mr Woodley with impatience. The letter was long and detailed, apologetic but blunt. Her father had removed her money from Penzance. He had indicated to Mr Woodley that he would not continue to pay her allowance to her; instead, it would accumulate until her thirtieth birthday when, by the terms of her mother's will, her inheritance was hers to do with as she wished. Regretfully, therefore, Mr Woodley had been unable to fulfil the instructions she had given for a ticket to be sent to Miss Blewett or indeed to finance a search for the young woman. If he could be of any assistance . . . etc., etc.

Alice sat down hard on the nearest chair, a wave of despair flooding over her. She reread the letter: there was no mistake. How could her father do this to her? What right had he? Apparently he must have every right or surely Mr Woodley would never have allowed it. With shaking hand she poured herself a glass of water and sipped it. What was she to tell Chas? He joked about her money, but she knew it was more than a joke to him. Of late she had made herself realise that he was depending upon it.

Chas entered the room. 'Ready?' he asked, but his voice was short, almost as if he knew already.

'You know?' she asked.

'Know what, darling?'

'About my money?'

'What about your money?'

'But you sounded so stern, Chas.'

'I'd had some news that did not please me. What about your money?'

Alice gave him the letter. He sat down, holding it to the light and read it. Then he read it again.

'The bastard!'

'I'm sorry, Chas.'

'Can he do this?'

'I don't know, but Mr Woodley is my lawyer. He has known me all my life and has always been kind to me. I think it must be so. My father is my trustee as well, you see.'

'You must get a lawyer here. Who's to say that this Woodley fellow isn't in league with your father?'

'Oh, no, Chas. You don't know Mr Woodley.'

'We must find a lawyer tomorrow, I'll ask Delaware, he'll know the best.'

'How would I pay him?' She looked at him helplessly, willing him to find a solution.

Chas put his head in his hands and sat silent. Alice watched him anxiously. Eventually he looked up at her, smiling his wonderful lopsided smile. 'Hungry?'

'Oh, Chas, how can you think of food at a time like

this? No. I'm too upset. I think, if you don't mind, I would prefer to go to bed.'

'Of course, darling.' He kissed her gently on the mouth. 'We had a perfect weekend, my love. No one can take that away from us, can they?'

'No, Chas. You made me so happy. I'm yours now, aren't I?'

He stood at the open door of her room and looked across the room at her for such a long time that Alice laughed with embarrassment. 'What are you staring at, Chas?'

'I love you, Alice. Never forget that.'

'I love you too, Chas. What does money matter?'

Chas stepped from the room and the door closed.

3

The next morning, after a restless night, Alice rang for her breakfast. On the tray was an envelope. She opened it and looked with dismay at their hotel bill. It amounted to over a thousand dollars. There must be a mistake, she thought. How angry poor Chas would be that they had sent it to her. Carefully she added it up: the figures tallied. She checked the items; she had not realised they had drunk so much champagne or that it was so expensive. She must tell Chas they could not afford it in future. And so many flowers, all those bouquets and orchids he had given her – what a silly, generous man he was. She would have to explain to him as gently as possible that she could do without flowers. And the chocolates! She exclaimed at the cost – there was a ridiculous expenditure that must stop forthwith.

The size of the bill had taken away her appetite. She collected her bath robe and made her way to her favourite bathroom, the one with pink tiles. This was the only part of staying in a hotel that she did not like, this undignified scurry along the corridors, so improperly dressed, always fearful of being seen. She did not shower this morning but instead lay for a long time soaking in the hot water and thinking.

It was obviously proving difficult for Chas to find a job. Maybe it would be easier for her to find one. In a shop perhaps, or she had heard there were women these days who worked in offices. She would have to investigate the possibility. She knew it was going to be difficult to persuade Chas to allow her to work. It would be against all his principles, but what other alternative was there? And she would insist that they move out of this hotel. The expense of two rooms was now unnecessary and in any case she was certain that they could get a room in a cheaper hotel; or perhaps they should rent a small house? This thought made her slip back into the water with contentment. How perfect that would be, a small house with a verandah and a garden, pretty curtains at the windows, and she waiting for Chas to return each evening for the perfect dinner that she would have cooked for him.

Back in her room she began to pack her cases. They must leave today before the bill grew larger. She looked at her little gold watch: it was still only eleven. She sat down and wrote a long letter to Miss Gilby. She wrote regularly to her governess, at least every two weeks, describing her new life and the wonders of this city. She told her of the vivid autumn colours, of the sweet log cabin. She smiled as she wrote: poor Miss Gilby, if she only knew what Alice had really done that weekend! She found herself blushing at the very thought. She explained that she was moving and that she would write again soon with her new address. She wrote to Gertie, her other regular correspondent. This letter was similar but with the addition of a rash of exclamation marks as clues, for she wanted her friend to understand what had happened, and how happy she was.

The letters finished, she sealed them and saw that she had plenty of time to post them before Chas awoke. In the foyer of the hotel she smiled at the receptionist who hurriedly looked down at the ledger in front of him. The hall porter held the door open for her but he did not look his usual cheery self. Alice thought that when she returned she must ask him if he felt unwell.

It was a glorious day, the air crisp, the sunshine clear and bright as it blazed in a last defiant gesture at the advancing winter as she walked briskly to the post office. Her cheeks felt quite pink as she clutched about her the new warm red cloak that Chas had bought her. She stopped dead. Oh dear, she had forgotten about the clothes he had bought last week – he had, despite her protest, spent a fearful amount upon her. She re-entered the hotel. The doorman was busy; she would speak to him next time, she thought. She was half-way across the foyer when she heard her name called. She swung round half expecting to see Chas.

'Miss Tregowan, if I might have a quick word?' It was the hotel manager beckoning her to his office. Puzzled, she followed him, glancing at her watch and noting with vexation that it had just passed noon and Chas might be wondering where she was.

'Mr Hulme?' She smiled pleasantly at him.

'It's about your account, Miss Tregowan.'

'Good gracious, Mr Hulme, I received it only this morning. Do you normally expect your guests to pay so promptly?' She managed to laugh, while her stomach was churning alarmingly.

'Of course not, Miss Tregowan, but it is a very large bill, I'm sure you'll agree, and in the circumstances . . .'

'Mr Hulme, I have not seen Mr Cordell this morning to show him your account. I should imagine that he will not be pleased that it was brought to me.'

'But, Miss Tregowan, we acted on Mr Cordell's

260

instructions. I should not otherwise have considered presenting the bill to a young lady like yourself.'

'Mr Cordell's instructions . . . ?'

'Yes, when he checked out last night.'

'Checked out? What does that mean?' she asked, quickly, her pulse beginning to beat rapidly.

'When he left, Miss Tregowan,' Mr Hulme said, in a kindly tone of voice. He crossed the room to a decanter of brandy and poured a small measure into a glass with the practised ease of one who has experienced this situation before. 'A small restorative, Miss Tregowan?'

Alice waved it away irritably. 'I don't understand.'

'No, Miss Tregowan.' Mr Hulme sighed, sat back at his desk, making a steeple of his fingers, and avoided looking at her. 'Mr Cordell said last night that he had received an urgent letter from home . . .'

'He did get a letter last night.' She leaned forward eagerly.

'That he would not be coming back to New York and that you would be settling both bills.'

Alice felt the room begin to close about her. She seemed to be looking down a long dark tunnel at the hotel manager. She took a deep breath.

'Yes, of course, I'd quite forgotten, his father has not been at all well. He probably did not wish to wake me. I must arrange to follow him,' she managed to say with superhuman effort.

'Would you like me to make the arrangements for you?'

'Arrangements, what arrangements?' she asked, vaguely.

'Your travel arrangements to . . . ?'

Alice felt she was trapped as her mind went blank and she could not remember the name of a single town she had heard of in America. 'Delaware,' she heard herself say. 'No, thank you, I'll make my own arrangements. If you would kindly excuse me, Mr Hulme.'

'So, you will be paying the bill, Miss Tregowan?'

'Of course I shall, Mr Hulme. What do you take me for?' She rose with as much dignity as she could muster, left his office and, aware of the staff looking at her as she crossed the hall, she virtually ran up the stairs. She passed Chas's room without looking in at the open door where a chambermaid was working. In her room she unlocked the drawer in her dressing-table where she kept the small amount of jewellery she had. She allowed herself a moment of anger as a picture of Daisy Dear floated into her mind, decked in her mother's jewellery. 'That won't get you very far, Alice,' she said aloud. She scooped up the pearl choker, swung her cape about her and, with head held high, walked down the stairs, across the foyer and out into the street.

She walked for several blocks before she found a jeweller. She did not pause – she did not dare to – as she opened the door and walked in. The man offered her $1,500. She had no idea of the choker's worth. All she could think of was the hotel bill and the shame if she could not meet it. She accepted, quickly, and tucking the money into her purse she made her way back on to the sidewalk.

Next she went to each of the restaurants that she and Chas had frequented. Not one of their friends was there.

She felt as if she were moving in a dream as she walked back to the hotel. It had to be a dream, a bad one, from which, at any moment, she was going to wake. How Chas would laugh when she told him.

At the hotel she paid her bill and asked for her luggage to be taken care of until she returned. Back to the street she went, thinking how odd it was that she should be behaving so efficiently in this nightmare.

By four o'clock she had taken a room in a boarding-house a good twenty blocks away from the hotel. She returned, collected her luggage, called a carriage, and by five was installed in her new room.

It was a far cry from the elegance of the hotel. But it was clean and neat, the bed was soft, and the woman seemed kindly. She looked about her and she began to shake. She hugged herself but the shaking would not stop. She felt sick, a dreadful nausea ... Suddenly she began to cry, a dreadful wail, like a wounded animal. She could hear the noise as if it were outside herself and, though she knew that she made it, there was nothing she could do to stop it.

4

For four days Alice kept to her room. She sat on her bed knees drawn up to her chin, her arms about them as if seeking comfort. She did not sleep but she was not truly awake. Instead, she sat gazing, eyes glazed with fatigue, in a world of her own. She longed for the safety of Queenie's arms, she longed for her rock by the sea; her despair appeared limitless.

Three times a day Mrs Feinstein, the lodging-house owner, knocked tentatively on her door, enquiring if she wanted food. Alice never answered.

On the fourth day, Mrs Feinstein, a caring soul, had decided the child had been on her own too long and sallied up the stairs, her master key in her hand. As she reached the door of Alice's room, it opened and a perfectly groomed Alice emerged.

'Ach, Miss Tregowan, I was very concerned. Too long you've been not eating. You eat now?' Mrs Feinstein had lived in New York for thirty years but still her voice was heavily accented and word order meant nothing to her.

'I'm so sorry I worried you, Mrs Feinstein, I've not been feeling well.' Alice smiled bleakly.

'Ill! Then you should have called me. Ill alone no one should be.' The fat little woman threw her hands up in horror.

'I'm better now, really.'

'Then some of my nice chicken broth you have?'

'I'm out to luncheon. You're very kind. But what I would like to do is to pay you for two months in advance.'

'Two months?' Mrs Feinstein's eyes glittered with interest. 'That long you stay?'

'If you don't mind.'

'Mind? Why be minding should I, a nice gentle girl like you?'

Alice dug into her purse and counted out the money for her full board. That done, she felt more relaxed. It left her precious little but at least she would know that the roof over her head was secure for that time.

She walked resolutely up-town to the four favourite restaurants. At each she enquired of the head waiter if her friends had been in. The answer from each restaurant was that none of them had been there for at least five days. Alice was puzzled – she could understand Chas disappearing but why the others? She felt relieved and disappointed, both at the same time. Relief that she would not have to face the shame of asking them where and why. Disappointment that she was not yet going to find out the truth.

Her next call was to an agency that found jobs for young women such as she. On her way to the address she had cut from a newspaper, she passed the jeweller's where she had sold her pearl choker. Idly she looked in the window; there it was for sale at $5,000. She felt so angry that she would have liked to break the window and snatch it back. She turned as if to enter the shop to accuse the man of cheating her. But she stopped. What would be the point? It was her own ignorance that had allowed her to be cheated. He probably would deny it was hers anyway. She felt too demoralised already to deal with such an argument.

She thought that educated, smart and presentable as she was, it would be the easiest thing to find employment. Confidently she climbed the stairs of the employment agency. The stiff-backed, severe receptionist took her name and she was told to join the crowd of young women waiting to be interviewed. Her entry caused total silence to fall upon a room that previously had been a buzz of chatter. She looked at the others and immediately felt out of place. Her white silk dress, with its high, pearl-trimmed collar, its large puffed sleeves, its matching hat, and the scarlet cape which Chas had bought her made her look like an exotic bird compared to the other women. Without exception, all were dressed in neat black or grey, no jewellery, their hats sensible and untrimmed, boots black and flat, in stark contrast to her own heeled, white kid, pearl-buttoned boots. She smiled but no one smiled back; instead, they glared at her as if she were an intruder.

It was finally her turn to enter the office of Miss Blackwood, the agency's principal.

A stern woman, dressed from head to toe in black, gold-rimmed pince-nez perched on the end of her nose, looked at Alice with distaste. Alice sat down on the chair in front of the desk.

'I was not aware that I had asked you to sit, Miss Tregowan,' she said, studying the list of names in front of her.

'I'm sorry, Miss Blackwood.' Alice jumped up in some confusion.

'And what can I do for you?'

'I'm looking for employment. I thought I would enjoy office work. My English is good, I can speak passable French, and –'

'Can you file? Can you use a typewriting machine? Can you add up figures?'

'A typewriting machine? I did not know such a

265

machine existed,' she laughed nervously and inconsequentially. 'I'm not sure about filing, and I suppose I can add up.'

'You would not appear to have the skills that I require to place you.'

'But . . .'

'Thank you, Miss Tregowan.' The woman returned to the papers in front of her.

'But I need work.'

'So do all those young women out there in my waiting-room. And they are qualified for the work and look suitable,' Miss Blackwood said scathingly, examining Alice from top to toe.

'These are the only clothes I have.'

'Then I suggest you buy yourself others which are more fitting for your station in life.'

Alice turned towards the door, determined to keep her head high and her back straight. Having paid Mrs Feinstein, she did not have the money to buy anything more suitable. Her prettiness was clouded by worry, and even the stony heart of Miss Blackwood melted sufficiently for her to suggest, 'Perhaps work in a shop might be more suitable for you, Miss Tregowan. A dress shop perhaps.'

Back on the pavement, Alice walked aimlessly. 'More fitting for your station in life . . .' What a chilling expression. It was correct though. Her station in life, in the scheme of things, had taken a dramatic jolt. She had started the year as the indulged daughter of an English lord, perfectly clothed and without a thought for money or where it came from. The year would close with her alone, almost penniless, apparently unemployable and unsuitably dressed. She managed a small smile – what a pity she did not have some of the dresses Queenie had made for her, which would have been so eminently suitable now. Feeling sorry for herself was not going to solve anything, she told herself sternly, and began to search for shops that might consider employing her.

Two hours and six shops later she knew the truth – that none of them would. Each time her appearance had worked against her. What was the point of her being better dressed than the clients? It was a reasonable argument, one which she had been unable to counter. The further down-town she roamed the more unsuitable she looked. She felt like a donkey caught in a treadmill.

She was nearly home when she saw a handwritten note in a haberdasher's window asking for counter staff. She looked at the shop; it was rather seedy, it was not in a good area and she would doubtless be shown the door, but she would try. Ten minutes later she had a position and was due to start the following Monday.

That evening she went to Delmonico's and waited outside. It was not a pleasant experience since men eyed her up and down and some were bold enough to direct remarks at her. The doorman stared at her suspiciously. It was only because she was an old customer that he did not move her on. She had almost given up hope when a carriage drew up and Roger leaped out and helped Beth and Caroline to descend.

'Oh dear,' she heard Beth say as she caught sight of her.

'Hallo, everyone.' She stood in their pathway.

'Alice, how are you?' Delaware asked, kindly enough.

'I'd like to talk.'

'Don't get involved, Delaware,' Caroline snapped.

'I just want some questions answered.'

'Of course you do.' Roger took her arm.

'Well, we're not having anything to do with her. It's her own fault.' The two girls swept in front of them into the restaurant.

Roger spoke to the maitre d' who led Alice and the two men to a table set in a secluded alcove; the girls had disappeared to the ladies' cloakroom. She waited patiently while the men ordered wine; she refused any for herself.

'Why?' she asked, simply.

'He didn't want to go,' Roger protested anxiously.

'He was at his wits' end. He couldn't see what else to do,' Delaware added.

'Why?' she repeated. Roger looked at Delaware; both seemed to have found fault with their stiff white ties and Roger appeared suddenly to be fascinated with the label on the wine bottle.

'He's already married,' Delaware said eventually.

It was not the answer Alice had expected. She felt as if Delaware had slapped her face. Involuntarily, her hand went to her cheek as if he had.

'Married?'

'Yes, years ago, when he was at Yale. She worked in a restaurant in the town. It was a totally unsuitable match – he got drunk one night, you see, and asked her. Once he had asked her, he felt he couldn't back out and she, the tart, wouldn't let him.'

Both men peered at her anxiously, with the male fear that she might be about to make a scene.

'Then why did he ask me?'

'Oh, he loved you, Alice, there's no doubt about that. He felt wretched about you, he really did. He never lived with her. No, no, there was nothing sordid like that,' Delaware said hurriedly.

'I don't see anything sordid in living with your legal spouse,' Alice said sharply.

'But she wasn't the sort of girl you could introduce to respectable people. It would have been like me marrying Beth.'

'If you don't intend marrying Beth, then why do you take advantage of her?' Her voice was becoming colder.

'Beth and Caroline don't expect marriage.' He laughed at the very idea. 'They're good-time girls, they understand the rules.'

'I don't think I do. I presumed you cared deeply for them . . .'

'Well, yes, but . . .' Delaware looked at the table-cloth intently, finding that he felt like a small boy who was being chided.

'But what made Chas leave when he did?' Alice asked in a calm voice which surprised her as much as it surprised the two men.

'Well, he had hoped to get a divorce.'

'A divorce?' Alice said, shocked. 'But marriage is for life.'

'It's different here.'

'I very much doubt if it is,' she retorted sharply.

'Anyhow,' Delaware ploughed on relentlessly, 'he had finally, after months of negotiation, got her to agree to a divorce. The night we returned from Bear Mountain he had a letter from her. She had got tougher. She said she was willing to agree to a divorce provided she received $20,000. She put a high price on herself, you see,' he laughed weakly.

'Yes, I do see. I see everything,' she said bleakly. 'And where is Chas now?'

'He said he was going out west, to California. He said he would be in touch,' Delaware replied after a long pause as if he had been weighing up the wisdom of telling her.

Alice stood up, feeling intensely cold. She shivered and collected her purse from the table. 'Thank you. You've been honest with me. I appreciate that.'

'What about you, Alice? What will you do? Go home?'

'No, Roger, I can't go home, there's no place for me there any longer. You see, English society fears nothing more than those who have compromised themselves, as I have. It is as if one has the plague.' She laughed harshly. 'I have a pleasant room, a kind landlady. I have even found work. It was most interesting knowing you both.'

She ignored their outstretched hands and, with head held high, walked from the table and out of the restaurant.

'Phew, what a woman! Now, that's class, Roger, real class. I wish I'd asked for her address.'

'We'll bump into her again. Beauty like that will surface somewhere or other, don't worry. Best be quiet, here come the girls . . .'

Alice might have appeared calm but inside she was seething with disappointment and anger. She had thought she knew Chas and, it turned out, she knew nothing about him. She loved him in the only way she knew how. She had given herself to him, and for her that meant for life. But perhaps he had never loved her, had only pretended; maybe it had been only her money that was of interest to him. Had he laughed at her behind her back? Had she been a joke amongst his friends? Had those two women known all along? Despite her anger, she knew she would never love like that again. She walked for hours in the freezing November night. It began to rain. The hem of her long skirt trailed on the wet pavement; unaware of it, she did not even bother to loop it up over her wrist. She walked and walked, ignoring the passers-by, ignoring the odd ribald remark. She found herself at the river – there was no further to go.

For a long time, she stood watching the swirling waters of the Hudson. How easy it would be, she thought, looking down at the blackness. Is that what her mother had thought? Is that what she, in her despair, had done? Had it been easy for her? Would it take long? Would there be pain?

She laughed a short, hollow laugh which, had anyone heard, would have chilled them. No, that was not the way. What would Queenie have said? She would have been furious, told her she was wicked and weak. Weak she was not. She had allowed herself to trust – but she would never do that again. She stood watching the water and, as she did so, she began to harden her heart against Chas and others like him. Rejecting self-pity, she searched for her pride. She would survive: she was determined to do so.

5

'I'm six cents short.'

'I'm so sorry, madame. It's my fault.'

'Of course it's your fault. You tried to cheat me last week, too.'

'Madame, I didn't. If there has been a mistake I assure you it was a genuine error.'

'If Mr O'Hare expects people to continue to shop here, then he should employ assistants who can add up, not young women who are playing at the job.' The hard-faced woman, her long jaw jutting aggressively forward, glared at Alice, drummed her fingers on the mahogany counter with exasperation, and looked as if she were still waiting for an explanation. Alice was flustered. She had apologised, what else was there to say? She began to rewind the ribbon on its cardboard reel but her fingers fumbled clumsily with the bright red satin. 'Six cents,' the woman repeated.

'Yes, of course, madame.' Alice delved beneath the counter for her purse and counted out the money. This was the third time today she had given the wrong change. She dare not go to Mr O'Hare again. She counted the money into the woman's outstretched hand.

'Would we be having a problem here?' Mr O'Hare had appeared from his tiny, ledger-filled office, at the top of the shop stairs, squeezed between household linen and baby clothes, in which he spent most of his day. He ventured out just once or twice during trading hours. Then he would prowl about his emporium, his hands

271

folded behind his faded frock coat, fussily rearranging the displays of lace, the cards of buttons, the reels of ribbon on Alice's counter. In the six weeks she had been here Alice had rarely had cause to speak to him. When she had, she was struck by how vague he was. He appeared kind and she had not heard any of the other shopgirls complain about him, but he was her employer and, as such, she was afraid of him.

He stood beside his client. Beneath a straight mop of hair that had faded from deep copper was a long face with skin so pale it had a bluish hue, its light freckles the only pigmentation. His watery grey eyes, ringed with straight ginger lashes, peered at them over his half-moon spectacles. They were eyes that looked as if they had stared too long at the sun – a paradox, since for over thirty years Mr O'Hare had spent each day hunched over the ledgers that chronicled his life in this little empire.

'A fine day, Mrs Greenslade, a fine day wouldn't you be saying?' He smiled, rocking back and forth on his highly polished boots which squeaked with each motion as if they too were joining in the conversation.

'Fine if you're not being cheated, Mr O'Hare,' the woman replied ominously.

'I made a genuine mistake, Mr O'Hare.' Alice looked at her employer, her eyes full of anxiety, her voice shaking slightly. To lose her job over as little as six cents would be too cruel, she was thinking.

'Then why did you take the six cents from your purse? Why did you not go to Mr O'Hare here and ask for it? Regular like,' the woman said with a degree of triumph.

'I didn't want to bother him.'

'A likely tale. You were afraid to, more like.'

'You now have your money back – does it matter where it came from? I've apologised. And I resent your accusations that I am a cheat and a thief.' She might be afraid but Alice was now beginning to feel very angry.

Mrs Greenslade gave Alice such a look of contempt

that, had she not been desperate for her wages, she would have walked out there and then. 'If you take my advice, Mr O'Hare, you'll employ assistants who can add up, you don't know how often she undercharges and cheats you.'

'Miss Tregowan I'll be admitting is not the most efficient assistant when it comes to the mathematics of haberdashery, Mrs Greenslade. But then look at her beauty. I ask you, could we be expecting the good Lord to make her a mathematician too?' Mr O'Hare's smile was a study in placidness as he spoke.

'You men are all the same – give you a pretty face and your senses go flying out the window,' Mrs Greenslade huffed.

'You never spoke a truer word, Mrs Greenslade. As an old man, all I can do these days is to admire. You wouldn't be wanting to deprive me of me little pleasure, would you now?'

'Well really, Mr O'Hare. I never heard such stupid talk in all my days. You can't expect people to patronise you if you have such an attitude.'

'If the choice is between your purchases and Miss Tregowan's wonderful smile, then, Mrs Greenslade, I'm sorry, but 'tis the smile would be winning.' Mr O'Hare gave an elegant little bow.

Mrs Greenslade's mouth sagged open with astonishment and disapproval, she turned on her heel, and with every inch of her seething with indignation, stalked out of the shop vowing never to return.

'Mr O'Hare, you shouldn't have spoken to her like that. She'll never come back now.'

'So?' He shrugged his thin shoulders, and smiled at Alice. 'So, what did she buy?'

'Two feet two inches of that satin ribbon, and one yard and three-eighths of elastic. It was the three-eighths that caused me the trouble.'

'Now, don't you be worrying yourself. For years that

woman has been coming here and if she spends twenty cents it's a good month. I'm growing tired of the Mrs Greenslades of this world who feel they have the right to treat people like clods of earth. You'd think she was a Vanderbilt the way she carries on. No, I meant what I said to her.'

'But I have to confess, there have been other mistakes too. I never mastered mathematics. My gover –' Alice stopped abruptly in mid-word. She had told no one about herself. She wanted no one to know who she was or what her background was. Having managed to remake and dye two of her dresses, she no longer looked as out of place as before. She did not want anyone getting the idea that she regarded herself as superior; nor did she want pity. 'I have dreadful trouble with sums,' she finished, lamely.

'Poor Miss Tregowan. Maybe you would be happier arranging the merchandise? The window display perhaps – no sums necessary. The filing in my office seems to have run amok. And with that fine hand of yours, perhaps you could help me with the letter writing.'

'Mr O'Hare, you are too kind to me.'

'No, I'm not. I meant what I said. You give an old man great pleasure with your pretty face as fresh as the morning and your lovely voice that, to be sure, is like music to my ears.'

Alice smiled and blushed at the same time. She could feel nothing but relief that she would no longer have to battle with the feet and inches, the dimes and dollars.

In the ensuing month, Mr O'Hare was pleased with his new arrangement – his windows had never looked so eye-catching. And, within days, his fusty office had been transformed into a model of tidiness and efficiency.

Daily Alice thanked heaven for the way her life was turning out. Each morning she set off happily for work, instead of, as in the past, approaching the shop worrying about what mistakes she would make that day. Mr O'Hare was a pleasure to work for, thanking her constantly for all she did. He made her laugh with the flowery compliments she knew he realised were as ridiculous as they sounded. They were a joke between them. Best of all, she was happy at Mrs Feinstein's.

Alice's metamorphosis from lodger to honorary daughter had been a subtle affair master-minded by Mrs Feinstein. Once Alice had emerged from the shock Chas's treatment of her had caused, the woman had seemed to be lying in wait to help her back to normality. She had never pried, never questioned why a young English woman should be alone in New York with apparently little money and no friends. She had conquered Alice's reserve with bowls of flowers in her room, a sachet of lavender on her pillow, an extra dollop of cream in her coffee, and the largest slices of her apfel-strudel for which she was rightly famous in the district. There were two other lodgers apart from Alice, both male, one a Pole who spoke little English and whose life and occupation were an enigma, the second a large German with whom Mrs Feinstein enjoyed talking in her native tongue. But with these two there was a barrier of Mrs Feinstein's making: they were never invited in the evening to join her in her private sitting-room, as Alice was.

This room was extraordinary. Mrs Feinstein had a weakness for things that glistened and glowed. Consequently walking into the room was like walking into a glittering treasure house. All the lamps were of glass, but of coloured glass so that the light which shone through was transformed into jewel-like colours. The overstuffed chairs, all with ornate carved and gilded legs, were upholstered in tapestry work, which in turn was draped with antimacassars. Vases, ornaments, candlesticks, were all chosen, it seemed, for the brightness of their colouring, the amount of gilt upon them. The carpet was deep scarlet heavily patterned in blues and greens, and its red matched the thickly embossed wallpaper. Not that much of the paper was visible since the walls were covered with paintings, lurid landscapes of mountains and streams with grass far greener, skies far bluer, and water more turquoise than God intended.

Each evening in this warm, glowing room, Mrs Feinstein would go to the cabinet in the corner, which was crammed with Venetian glassware. She would select a different coloured glass each time and carefully she would measure out their schnapps. Then she would take a box of chocolates and settle herself in the chair on the opposite side of the fireplace from Alice.

'Now it's comfortable, ja? Now let's talk.'

In this room Alice had learned of the hard life of her landlady. Her husband, a German immigrant as she had been, had worked all the hours in the day to build up his business as a tailor.

'Hard it was, Alice, my God it was a hard life. Every tailor in Europe, it seemed, had moved to this little corner of New York.'

Their life's ambition had been to buy the best house they could afford. For fourteen years they had toiled and then, two weeks after they had purchased the lease on this house, her husband had dropped dead.

'And six suits not finished.' Mrs Feinstein shook her head at the memory. Left with three children, no money and the six unfinished suits, Mrs Feinstein had been determined to keep their home at any cost. She had risen each morning at four to make apfel-strudels to sell to the local bakers, and she had taken lodgers. Now that her children had left home, she made the apple pies only for pleasure – her lodgers gave her sufficient money for her needs, she declared.

When Mrs Feinstein spoke of her sons her face glowed with pride as brightly as any of the objects in her room. Her constant sadness was that both had gone to California to make their fortune and she had seen neither for five years. The great tragedy of her life, after the death of her husband, was that her only daughter had married a Gentile and moved to Brooklyn. She seemed equally angry about both occurrences – a goy in her family, and Brooklyn which, as far as Mrs Feinstein was concerned, might just as well have been on the other side of the world. To her, only this corner of New York mattered and it was a continual puzzle that all her children should have chosen to leave it.

She lived now for the anxiously awaited letters from California, consumed by a deep longing to see the grandchildren she had never known.

Night after night, Alice would listen to her tale, her reiteration that life was a curse sent to try us all, her conviction that nothing could ever get better. Alice listened patiently and was always moved by the courage she saw in this unprepossessing woman and feared that, should she be put in the same position, she would find herself lacking.

Alice had expected long, lonely evenings in her room – not this warm home-coming when she returned from work.

She liked the area she lived in. It was noisy and crowded but everywhere in New York seemed to be the same. Alice adjusted to the noise and bustle. She discovered that the large city, daily growing outwards and upwards, was, in fact, a series of villages. Each village had its own noise, its own smell. She had, it transpired, wandered into what was left of a once large German village. As the builders had moved in, many of the inhabitants had uprooted themselves to the outer suburbs away from the noise and dirt but still enough Germans were left to make it possible to live here and never need to speak a word of English. These intrepid souls, like Mrs Feinstein, refused to move and regarded the changes in their area with horror. They lived in a welter of noise and dust as houses were torn down and larger ones built. Alice learned that at frequent intervals Mrs Feinstein was offered large sums of money to move. She always refused.

'And have my Mannie's house knocked down? Never!' she explained to Alice. 'Then it would be he toiled for nothing.'

Alice loved the Italian village which was larger and noisiest of all. Every street seemed to be a market, and there was laughter and even song here which was missing from other districts. There was one Jewish quarter where the men wore long black coats, strange hats, with flowing beards and hair that made her feel she had stepped into the Bible. No doubt there was a ghetto for every language ever heard at Ellis Island. It was a comfort, this close community spirit which the immigrants had managed to create for themselves, and one that she was happy to enjoy at second hand. On her walk to and from work she had come to know many of the local people. Mrs Feinstein had a bad leg, so Alice always did her shopping for her and was well known now to the local shopkeepers.

Alice was a figure of curiosity to the inhabitants. They were not used to English aristocrats such as Alice in their midst. Not that she had ever told them who she was. She had no need to: it was obvious in the way she walked, in her impeccable English and in the gracious courtesy of her dealings with everyone.

Everything in Alice's new life was running smoothly until the day she toppled from the top of the small ladder, in the stock room, and fainted. Coming to, she sat up, relieved to find nothing broken and that no one had seen the incident. She should eat more, she told herself sensibly.

A fortnight later, faced with the hot chocolate and bread rolls that Mrs Feinstein had placed before her for breakfast, she found, not for the first time, that she did not want to eat. She took one sip of her chocolate, dabbed her mouth with her napkin and asked to be excused.

'Alice, sit down a minute,' Mrs Feinstein kindly ordered. 'You can't go to the shop with no food in you. It's not good.'

'I'm just not hungry these days.'

'In this cold January weather, everyone's hungry.'

'Well, not me.' Alice laughed, collecting her bag and the box of sandwiches Mrs Feinstein insisted on making for her lunch.

'Alice, do you want to talk with me? I like you, you know. A lot I like you.'

'Why thank you, Mrs Feinstein, I like you too. But really, I must be getting to work, I shall be late.' She stood in front of the mirror and placed her hat upon her head.

'You know you're going to have a baby, Alice, don't you?'

Alice's hand was poised in mid-air holding the hat-pin which wavered as her hand shook. 'A what?'

'A baby. Maybe, a nice young girl like you, you don't know much. I do.'

'But, Mrs Feinstein . . .' Alice turned to face the woman.

'You can talk to me. I know men . . . I don't stand in judgement on any woman, for sure that is,' she said, firmly.

'How does one know, Mrs Feinstein?' Alice asked in a little voice, as she slid back on to her chair, feeling suddenly as weak as a kitten. She had fainted three times recently, she could not face food and she had begun to fear she was ill; she had never thought of a baby.

'Your monthlies, how long since you had one?'

Alice blushed furiously at the mention of the unmentionable. 'Last October. But what was that to do with a baby?'

'Ach, my poor child. As I thought, it is. That and the look in your eyes. I'm always right. And you're thicker round the middle these last few weeks. You didn't even know? Such innocence, such innocence it comes from God.'

'No, Mrs Feinstein, I didn't know,' Alice replied, feeling sick with fear and apprehension. 'What do I do?'

'You have it, of course. What else is there to do? A baby in the house, now that I should be enjoying.'

6

For a week Alice was stunned. The following week she felt fear and confusion. The week after that she felt a strange and calm acceptance of what had happened to her.

Throughout this period she continued to work. She confided in no one at the shop. This was not from natural shyness and embarrassment but rather because she had never been able to form a friendship with any of the other girls. At first she had tried to be friendly but her overtures had been met with stony resistance. She was puzzled; she had never before found getting on with people to be a problem. She put her lack of success down to the fact that she was English and most of the staff were of Irish extraction. In fact the reason was not political, simply that the other young women were jealous of her – jealous of her looks, her figure, her easy charm, her educated voice, her general demeanour. All this had come to a head when Mr O'Hare had selected her to work in the office with him. Now, as her waist thickened, the other assistants began to whisper and to give her sly and knowing glances. She realised that she could no longer keep her secret.

The problem was how to tell Mr O'Hare. It was not her embarrassment she feared but his. In the weeks of working with him she had learned what a devout and ordered man he was. If she told him she was pregnant, her unmarried state, she was certain, would shock him to the core, and his fondness for her would make him sorely disappointed.

'Could I have a moment of your time, please, Mr O'Hare?' she asked finally, a good five months into her pregnancy. Her dress was now let out so far that it could go no further and her swelling stomach was straining the seams.

'Why, Miss Tregowan, you're welcome to all the moments of my dull old time you'd be wanting.' He smiled at her over the top of the pince-nez which always lodged on the end of his large, somewhat doleful, nose.

Alice paused for a second before taking a deep breath and, in a rush, before she could change her mind, said, 'I'm sorry, Mr O'Hare, but I'm going to have to leave you.'

'Oh, Miss Tregowan, never.'

'I'm afraid so.'

'It wouldn't be anything we have done, would it? There's no one here upsetting you?'

'No, nothing like that. I've been very happy working for you and I shall never forget your kindness and patience with me.'

'Could I be persuading you to stay?'

'No. I have to go.'

'Very well, Miss Tregowan, I shan't be asking why, but, I'm telling you, I'm hearing this with a heavy heart.'

'If you'd excuse me –' Alice said abruptly, and, stumbling from the cluttered office, raced up the iron stairs that led to the female assistants' cloakroom. There she slumped on to a bench among the clutter of shopping bags and coats, her eyes filled with tears. She knew for certain that her heart felt far heavier than his did. A rustling of a skirt made her look up. It was Paula who, when Alice had worked in the shop, had run the counter opposite, serving hat trimmings. Apart from morning and evening greetings they had barely spoken to each other.

'Well, you're in a right pickle, aren't you?' she said, looking closely at Alice.

'I beg your pardon?' Surreptitiously Alice wiped her eyes and wondered if Paula had come as a friend or as an adversary.

'Oh, come off it, Alice. We all know, you know – have done for weeks. We're not blind.' She flicked open her bag and took out a mirror in which she closely studied her heavy features. 'Most were surprised – someone like you, butter wouldn't melt in your mouth. I'm not. I never trust stuck-up types like you,' Paula sneered.

'I can't think what I have done that gives you the liberty to talk to me like this, Paula.' Alice sat up straight, strengthened by anger at the other girl's impertinence.

'Not much point in talking to me like that, not now there isn't.' Paula gave an unpleasant laugh. 'My, how I enjoy to see the mighty fall. You and your airs and graces. You can't add up and then get promoted to the office over girls who have worked hard for years. It's always the same though, isn't it? Those with a pretty face and figure always get the best jobs. Not that your figure will be much to talk about now.' Again her unpleasant laugh rang out.

'If you'll excuse me, I have work to do.' Alice got up abruptly, smoothed down her skirt with short sharp movements and prepared to leave. She felt shocked that someone could have been harbouring such unpleasant thoughts and resentment towards her.

'No, no point in you going. The old man said as to give you this. He doesn't want you back in the office it seems. And quite right too. A good Catholic, Mr O'Hare, he hasn't time for girls who have fallen that's for sure.' She handed Alice a buff envelope. Alice took it, stuffed it in her bag and, with head down so that Paula could not see the tears that were now rolling down her cheeks, quickly

282

put on her cape and hat. Without another word she hurried from the room, down the steep stairs and, her head still down, across the shop floor to the back of the stores and the staff exit. As she walked she was convinced she could hear a rising babble of gossip following her like a malignant fog.

Her hand was trembling so violently that she could hardly get her key into the lock of Mrs Feinstein's front door. She felt she was scuttling like some animal into the safety of its lair as the large, stained-glass door at last swung open and she was safely in the hall. She leaned against the wall and fought her anger and despair with big gulps of air.

'Alice, my dear, you look as if a ghost you've seen. In here come. Tea, I'll get, with a little schnapps.'

'No really, Mrs Feinstein, I'll be all right in a minute – it's quite hot out there for April, you'd think it was summer. The heat made me feel a little faint, that's all.'

'Tut, you are not all right. You are coming in here with me, sitting down and drinking the tea. You've the little one to think of. Now do as I say – do you want that we are all at a wake to be?'

'I'm being stupid. I know that I'm going to have to expect things like this.'

'What things?' Mrs Feinstein was shocked at the frightened expression on Alice's face.

'It was one of the girls at work. They've known for ages about my condition . . .' Her hands fluttered protectively across her stomach. 'It was dreadful. She was gloating. She was pleased this had happened to me. It was such a shock.'

'And her face looking like the bottom of a cow, I'm thinking.'

'She's not very pretty. She was the girl on hat trimmings.'

'Ach so, like the cow, with the teeth like the horse. Of

course she was bad with you. She's jealous. She's a shicksa – ignore her.'

'I know deep inside that her opinion of me doesn't matter. It was other things too. I found it so hard to give in my notice to Mr O'Hare, that was bad enough. But, after Paula had spoken to me, I realised that she was probably the first of many who will be unkind. And as I was hurrying home, I was so ashamed, meeting people I knew and realising that they must know as well and perhaps were saying awful things about me too.' Alice felt close to tears again as she confessed to her landlady.

'If people bad things say it's because they never your friends have been. Those who like you, they'll be in sorrow for you. Bad luck you've had. That's all that's happened. For any girl the bad luck is always lurking.'

'You are sweet to me, Mrs Feinstein. But I was wrong. I should not have done what I did, I know that. Now I have to pay for the sin.'

'Sin? A baby a sin cannot be. That's no way to be thinking. It's done, that's all.'

'I thought he was going to marry me, you see.'

'Ach, the men!' Mrs Feinstein threw her hands up in horror.

'I think I should leave here. I couldn't bear the whispering – the people in this street, at the market. If I go somewhere new, I can lie, say I'm a widow. Here everyone knows me.'

'I've been thinking too, Alice. What about your family, at a time like this you need them. Maybe a good idea to go home, no?'

Alice looked steadily at her landlady. 'I have no family.'

'No family!' Mrs Feinstein's hands, normally active, now surpassed themselves as they windmilled her horror. 'Uncles? Aunts? Cousins? No one can have no one.'

'The only person who would have cared and forgiven

me was a woman called Queenie and she died a long time ago.'

'You English, you're so strange, you don't guard your families. So, no family but you have me. Leaving you are not. Why care about the gossip? I will defend you.'

'Oh, Mrs Feinstein . . .' Alice began to cry in earnest and was rapidly scooped up and clasped to Mrs Feinstein's ample bosom.

Her tears mopped, tea and schnapps drunk and with a good slice of apfel-strudel inside her, Alice rested in her room. It was then she remembered the envelope that Paula had given her. She tore it open; inside were not only her wages to date but a 20 dollar bill – 'a bonus', the note with it explained. Alice felt tears pricking again and with exasperation shook her head: she seemed to have spent the whole day crying, and that was no solution to anything.

From her dressing-table she took the thin suede roll in which she stored what was left of her jewellery. She looked at the cameo, the small garnet ring, the string of jet beads she had worn in mourning for her mother and the cross and chain of gold and wondered what they were worth. This time she would consult Mrs Feinstein. Her landlady would surely have a friend who knew about jewellery and would give her a fair price. She would not be cheated again. From the chocolate box in which she kept her savings, she carefully counted out her money, adding the wages and Mr O'Hare's bonus. If she were very careful, perhaps if she ate only light meals and not Mrs Feinstein's normal gargantuan meals, she could stay here at least for the next year.

But then she would have to find other work, which with a child would be more difficult. It was kind of her landlady to insist she stayed, though the sensible thing would be to leave here and find somewhere cheaper to lodge. But she felt a strange lethargy as if making such plans was all too much for her.

Her feeble attempt at planning her future was interrupted by a knock on her door. It was Daniel, the Polish lodger who never spoke to anyone. He stood, large, blond and awkward, on the landing. He rotated his cap nervously in his hands as if it were a wheel. He shuffled his big, booted feet and coughed.

'Excuse please, we talk.'

'Of course.' She smiled, uncertainly, not opening her door too far, for Daniel was an unknown quantity who had excited Mrs Feinstein's normally fertile imagination to all manner of mysterious possibilities.

'You no work?'

'Yes, that's right.'

'You me teach.' Daniel pointed at her and then at himself.

'Teach?'

'The English. You English, you teach me like you.'

She paused before replying, looked at the handsome serious face above her. 'I could,' she said cautiously.

'I pay. I pay good.'

She looked at the clear grey eyes that stared anxiously at her. How could a person with such innocent eyes be guilty of the crimes wildly alleged by Mrs Feinstein – that he was a master criminal, a spy . . . 'Tomorrow morning, at nine,' she said firmly.

'Nine?'

Alice unpinned the brooch watch she wore and pointed to the figure nine. 'Nine, we work, yes?' She smiled up at him: it was a broad smile, a smile that was etched with relief. Of course, that was the answer, there must be thousands of Daniels in this city. She would teach them. She could earn money and care for her child. It was a perfect solution. She raced down the stairs, her feet light now compared with the feet that had dragged her up to her room an hour before.

'Mrs Feinstein,' she called gaily as she rushed into the kitchen. 'I'm going to be a teacher.'

'Now a teacher, that's a profession to be proud of. To think, me with a teacher for a lodger, that makes me proud too.'

'It's Daniel, he wants help with his English. Maybe I can find others to teach.'

'Difficult that won't be. Mrs Heiner's son and Mr Lector's daughter they come too . . .'

'It was you, wasn't it? You told him to come? You arranged it all.'

Mrs Feinstein grinned broadly. 'And where would I be finding another lodger like you I was asking myself?'

7

Finding pupils had been easy – Mrs Feinstein saw to that. Each day for a fortnight young men and women arrived at their door. It had quickly reached the point where Alice had had to refuse to take any more candidates.

As the pupils arrived so did their money. There was a hunger in them to learn which made teaching them a pleasure. Knowledge of this strange and difficult language was a necessity for them all if they were to get employment, if they were to advance themselves beyond their various ghettoes. Frequently it was one member of a family who had been selected for the lessons, their meagre budgets not stretching to lessons for all. These pupils would then return home and teach what they had learned to other members of their families and their friends. Alice felt like a spider in the centre of a linguistic web as each week more of her native language was instilled into her pupils. She liked to think of the vocabulary she taught spreading in ever-widening waves across the great city.

As her savings grew, so did Alice's confidence. She

finally decided that she had sufficient money to risk buying the nice things she wanted for her baby. It was Mrs Feinstein who suggested that together they should go to Mr O'Hare's emporium to buy the bassinet, a *papier-mâché* bath and, most exciting of all, a baby carriage with a fitted parasol. At first she had been reluctant to go but Mrs Feinstein was insistent she should, just to show that Paula that she was not ashamed. And also – but Mrs Feinstein kept this thought to herself – she would be sure of a fine discount from Mr O'Hare.

The shopping had been a triumph. Paula had looked suitably embarrassed and the other girls for the first time had been forced to be pleasant to Alice 'the customer'.

'You were right, Mrs Feinstein, I feel better now. But did you see the scowl on Paula's face? Oh, that was worth seeing,' Alice laughed gaily.

'That was good, but why you no take that nice Mr O'Hare's discount he you offered?'

'I could not do that.' Alice stopped dead in her tracks on the sidewalk and turned to her landlady, her expression one of dismay.

'Why ever not? He's a business man, he understands. You did good business with him today. He expected to give good terms.'

'Oh, Mrs Feinstein, the very idea. He's already been so kind to me giving me that bonus. I'm only glad I was able to repay him a little.'

'You'll learn, Alice, you'll learn,' Mrs Feinstein said, nodding sagely.

Alice had never felt fitter. Her hair shone, her skin was flawless and though she ate every morsel that Mrs Feinstein put before her she remained slim and only her swelling stomach grew.

There were times, however, when she was alone, waiting perhaps for another pupil to appear, when she would feel such homesickness that it was almost a physical ill. When she had first arrived she had expected to feel like this, but she had not – life had been too exciting with Chas and after him she had had to work such long hours that fatigue had saved her from emotion. But now things were different, now she had time, and the homesickness, as if sensing these idle moments, crept into her and pained her. It was a longing that would come with no warning, at any time of the day or night. She would wonder why it came. Was it the noise and dirt of the city making her long for peace and solitude? Was it the way that Mrs Feinstein so often reminded her of Queenie, with her endearing bossiness and desire to organise her? Was it the longing for Mrs Trelawn's game pie that since she had become pregnant often haunted her? Whatever, it was an uncomfortable experience and one which she had learned there was no escaping. No matter how firmly she spoke to herself, or how much she tried to keep busy, the memory of Gwenfer would flood her mind and it was as if she could smell the place, hear it even. Sometimes she thought, if she put out her hand, it was as if she could touch it.

Helping Mrs Feinstein clear out a cupboard one day she came across an old box of water-colour paints. She fell upon them with the excitement of a child and begged to be allowed to use them. Mrs Feinstein had laughed at her pleasure in finding them.

'They my Samuel's. He does not need them, now he is in California. You have, you take pleasure.'

That night, from memory, she drew and painted three pictures of Gwenfer. She was pleased with them and was unaware of how exact in detail they were. She had painted the house from the front, she had painted Oswald's rock with the house in the background, and she had painted the roofs of the house as seen from the long, twisting drive, with the rhododendrons in bloom. When she had finished them she laid them on the table for Mrs Feinstein to admire.

'You paint good, Alice. That's a grand place. Where's a grand place like that? Like a house for a prince.'

'It's a house in England. I knew it once and loved it.' Alice spoke quietly and Mrs Feinstein looked at her quickly. 'Ah well, I doubt I'll ever see it again.'

'Is that you?' Mrs Feinstein pointed to the painting of the rock on which sat a slim girl, her long blonde hair blowing in the wind which came off Alice's carefully executed sea.

'No,' Alice laughed. 'It's not me, it was a friend of mine, Ia. I thought she was dead but then I heard she might be alive. I'd always hoped she would join me here, but now . . . If she is alive, I don't think I'll ever see her again.'

'You write?' Mrs Feinstein suggested practically.

'But where should I write? I asked my father but he did not reply. I cannot afford detectives. Probably I shall never know.'

'Strange that you should paint her?'

'Yes, Mrs Feinstein, very strange I suppose.'

From her precious store of money Alice had the pictures framed and hung on her bedroom wall. Now, when the longing for Gwenfer came over her, she would take one of them down and hold it to her and in a strange way it lessened her suffering.

One evening she studied her painting of Ia. It was very like her, as she remembered her. Had her father received her letter, had he given the message to Ia? As it had turned out it was a good thing that Ia had not come, for then she would have had the responsibility of her as well. She wondered what Ia had been doing in the intervening years. Had she been happy, or had she been sad? She was alive, Alice knew it from the way she thought about her – not with sadness now but curiosity. She often wondered what had made Queenie lie to her – so unlike her, she who had always been kind and honest. But then, she would think more practically, what if she did find her?

What could she do for Ia now? Nothing. It was almost as if Queenie had known what was to happen, that it was better they had parted.

Alice had finished teaching for the day and stood in the little study in which Mrs Feinstein allowed her to give the lessons. She rubbed the small of her back. She had been surprised to find just how tiring teaching could be. Mrs Feinstein bustled into the room.

'A visitor, you have,' she announced, opening the door wider to show the smiling face of Mr O'Hare behind a large bouquet of flowers.

'Mr O'Hare, what a lovely surprise. Please come in won't you, take a seat.' Alice indicated a chair and hurriedly collected her books together.

'I hear you're giving lessons?'

'Yes, I'm enjoying it . . .'

'She too hard works, Mr O'Hare. Resting she should be, instead of all this . . .'

'Oh, Mrs Feinstein, I enjoy it, you know I do. I have such lovely pupils, they are so keen to learn, Mr O'Hare, that sometimes it makes me sad. They set themselves impossible targets, you know.'

'Enjoy you might, but now rest you should. A cup of tea, Mr O'Hare?'

'Why, is it a mind-reader you are, Mrs Feinstein?'

Mrs Feinstein scuttled off to the kitchen.

'It's kind of you to call, Mr O'Hare.'

'You're looking well, Miss Tregowan.'

Conscious of her large belly, Alice blushed with confusion and looked down at the floor. 'You too, Mr O'Hare,' she muttered.

'My name's Patrick, but my friends are calling me Packy. Would you be doing me the honour . . . ?'

'Only if you will call me Alice.'

'These are for you . . . Alice . . .' Mr O'Hare held the

flowers out awkwardly, saying her name as if it were a foreign word to him.

'How very kind.' Alice buried her nose into the flowers breathing in their scent. 'June gives us such lovely flowers, doesn't it? Roses and freesias, my favourites, Packy.' She smiled broadly at him and was surprised to see that this smile made Packy O'Hare blush to the roots of his hair.

'Alice, I've been thinking,' he said with a sudden urgency.

'Yes?' She looked at him expectantly.

'I'm not one for beating about the bush, I'll be getting straight to the point. I know I'm a lot older than you – I guess as much as thirty years older. But I would be good to you, you know what I'm meaning, I wouldn't be bothering you, not unless you wanted me to. And I've money enough. And I love children and I'd be a good father and . . .' He paused for breath. 'And I'm lonely, Alice, dreadful lonely.'

'Mr O'Hare!' Alice said, a mixture of shock and surprise in her voice. 'Mr O'Hare, I don't understand.'

Before she could stop him he was down on one knee in front of her. 'I'll be asking you to be my wife, Alice, sure and I am.'

'Mr O'Hare . . .'

'Packy please. Even if you're about to say no, at least say "No, Packy".'

'Packy, it's a great honour, but I'm afraid I cannot say yes.'

'But why, Alice? You need a man to care for you and the baby. I could be that man. You'd not be wanting for nothing. I've worked hard all me life and I'd looked forward to a retirement with my Mary but the good Lord needed her more.' He crossed himself. 'I'd not be standing in judgement on you, ever – nothing like that. I want to help, I would regard the child as my own and God help anyone who said otherwise.'

Alice sat silent a moment, overwhelmed by what this kind man was offering her. 'I fully appreciate what a wonderful solution you are giving me to all my problems. I assure you of that and I am grateful. But I could not marry you. I'm sorry.'

'Is it me age? Is it the way I'm looking?'

'Neither. You're a fine figure of a man and age is unimportant. I don't love you, Packy, and I could never marry without love.'

'I wouldn't mind, I've love enough for the two of us. You might grow to love me one day.'

'It has to be there at the beginning for me. How could I vow to love, honour and obey if there was no love there to vow? And you are not being fair to yourself. You deserve more: you can't choose a woman because you are lonely. One day a good woman will come into your life, I'm sure. One who will love you as you deserve to be loved.'

He hung his head in disappointment. 'I knew you wouldn't,' he said in a muffled tone. 'But Mrs Feinstein she said I should ask.'

'Mrs Feinstein?' Alice felt an unfamiliar flutter of irritation that she should interfere in something so personal and important. 'Of course you should have asked. I'm honoured that you did. But I want you to remain a friend. We can be good loving friends, can't we?'

'Perhaps if I had not waited so long, perhaps if I had plucked up the courage and had courted you properly instead of being too cowardly to ask a grand lady like you to be considering the likes of me?'

'Packy, my dear, it would have made no difference.'

'Ah well, then. There doesn't seem much point then in me waiting for me tea.'

'No, not much point really,' Alice said gently as she stood up and opened the door for him.

293

As the front door closed Mrs Feinstein re-entered the room. 'Gone he has? What a nerve he has!'

'I thought it was very sweet of him. The poor man meant well and he's very lonely. Maybe I should have said "yes". I'd never have any problems then.'

'Sweet. Disgusting more like, an old man like him with a pretty thing like you, disgusting.'

'Then why did you tell him to ask me?'

'Because he kept asking me if you would be in a mind to be marrying him. I said to him, how can I be answering for Alice, you must ask her yourself.'

'I see. Oh dear, and the poor man took that as a hopeful sign?'

'Poor man? Stupid man. Tea?'

'Thank you . . . aahh . . .' As she took the cup and saucer from Mrs Feinstein's hands a pain deep within her made her double up, the cup and saucer clattering to the floor. 'Oh, Mrs Feinstein . . .' she gasped, looking at the older woman through eyes blurred with pain. 'It's too soon.'

Mrs Feinstein moved with a speed that defied her bulk. She half carried Alice to her room, and then lumbered down the stairs, calling for the neighbour's boy who was idly playing ball on the sidewalk to run to fetch the doctor. By the time the doctor arrived she had water boiling, the bassinet made up, a mountain of clean sheets ready and tea once more on the boil. 'Men,' she kept muttering to herself over the next twelve hours.

During her ordeal there were times when Alice cursed out loud at Chas and what he had done to her. She screamed at God for allowing this to happen to women. There were many moments when she wished that she could die . . . and then she heard her baby cry and all that was forgotten and almost everything was forgiven.

Chapter Seven

1

Because she was six weeks premature the first month of Grace's life was an anxious time. Alice, still confined to bed, would spend hours gazing at her baby, fearful that something so small could not possibly survive. But she need not have feared. Grace, after lying quietly for a month as if conserving her energies, began suddenly to grow and strengthened with each day.

The force of her feelings for the baby came as a surprise to Alice. Of course she had assumed that she would love her but it was the depth of that love which caught her unawares. Like so many who have been unloved as children she did not understand about familial love. So it was that all the love which had lain dormant in her during those years of neglect now burst out in a torrent upon this small child.

During her enforced confinement in her room, Alice began to fret that she should be up and giving her English lessons. The need to earn money now that she had Grace to support was an even stronger incentive. But Mrs Feinstein was as firm as any wardress and forbade Alice to move from her bed for three weeks, during which she fussed and cosseted the young woman, thoroughly enjoying every minute of it. During the following two weeks she was allowed to sit in a chair by the window for short periods. She looked forward to these treats for it was now early August and the heat was intolerable. After five weeks Alice was finally allowed downstairs but was still not permitted to give lessons. Feeling fit and quickly back to normal, she found this enforced invalid state irksome and alien to her nature.

Alice had been overwhelmed by everyone's kindness. Many of her students had brought presents for the baby, though she knew they could ill afford it. Mr O'Hare had sent a fine cross and chain for the little one and had even plucked up courage to call once Alice was up and about. After the first five minutes, made awkward by his embarrassment, Alice had been able to make him relax. His proposal was not mentioned but when he departed he was insistent that, should she ever need help, she must not hesitate to call upon him. The owner of the delicatessen had sent a mug and plate, the greengrocer a silver-plated spoon, the butcher's wife had embroidered a pillow-case and cover. Alice had feared that she would not be able to give her baby everything she would like, but she found that her baby wanted for nothing.

It was a proud Alice who finally ventured out with Grace in the baby carriage for her first airing. She had intended to be out for an hour, a gentle stroll around the park. Instead, it was three hours before she was back home – everyone in the neighbourhood wanted to stop her and admire the baby.

Apart from her blonde hair, no matter how hard Alice scrutinised her child she could see no one's likeness in her. There was nothing of Chas nor of Alice, not her father nor her mother. She searched assiduously for a likeness to Oswald her long-dead brother, but peer as she might, the baby's features would not oblige. Unless she favoured Chas's parents, it seemed that Grace looked like herself.

She found that her pleasure in her child had made all bitterness against Chas fade. She could think of him now and enjoy remembering him and the happy times they had had. Some days, she realised, she missed him. But, most of all, she felt sorry for him that he did not know his daughter.

Winter roared in with a vengeance, a hard and bitter winter as winds howled around the tall buildings and snow swept by in great drifts. But Alice felt safe and sheltered with Mrs Feinstein, and she had begun her lessons once again. Grace was a perfect baby – she rarely cried but lay in her bassinet as Alice taught her pupils, gurgling happily at the ceiling.

At last spring arrived. 'Alice, come quick!' The urgency in Mrs Feinstein's voice made Alice's heart miss a beat. 'Alice!'

'Excuse me,' Alice said hurriedly to her pupil and ran towards the sitting-room. 'What is it, Mrs Feinstein? You gave me a start,' Alice asked as she entered the room to see Mrs Feinstein flopping on to a chair and frantically fanning herself with a letter.

'Quick, Alice, schnapps,' Mrs Feinstein ordered. Concerned by her behaviour, Alice quickly poured her the drink and, to her astonishment, saw Mrs Feinstein gulp it down in one swift swallow. 'Such a shock.'

'What's a shock, tell me quickly.'

'My son, my Samuel. A letter . . .' The agitated fanning continued.

'Yes? But you always get a letter around this time of the month.'

'He's asking to California for me to go. Imagine, my son, oh such a good man he is.'

'That's wonderful, Mrs Feinstein. You could do with a holiday, this winter has been very trying for you . . . '

'No holiday. He asks for me to go and live there with him and his Sarah. He's sent my fare. I'm to live with my family, oh Alice, such happiness I never thought to know again.' Tears tumbled down the older woman's face. 'You see, he tells me, he always planned this but until now he did not the money have. He has a good job now – an attorney he is, you know.' Alice nodded: Mrs Feinstein must have told her this a thousand times. 'Now they have a new house, in San Francisco, a big house –

large enough for me also,' and the tears started in such volume that further speech was impossible.

Alice raced back to the study to explain to her pupil that there was to be no further lesson today. She picked Grace up and returned to Mrs Feinstein who was trying to control herself while frantically searching for pen and ink to reply to her son.

'So much to do, so much to decide.' She flapped her hands urgently. 'Lists, I make lists. I take. I sell . . .'

'I can help you.'

When Alice spoke it was as if Mrs Feinstein suddenly came to her senses. 'Alice. What you do without me?'

'Miss you, Mrs Feinstein, I shall miss you dreadfully.'

'You come too. That's the solution.'

Alice smiled at the woman who had been such a friend to her. The idea was one of the most appealing she had ever heard. It was on the tip of her tongue to agree to the suggestion when she remembered Chas. California was where he had gone, she did not know where, but in all probability, knowing his preference for city life, he would be somewhere like San Francisco. What if she should meet him? He would think she had followed him. She would rather take her chances here.

'It's kind of you to think of me, Mrs Feinstein, but I don't think so.' She managed to smile though she felt wretched at the prospect of losing this staunch friend.

'Then what you do? Alone in this city you cannot be.'

'To be honest, Mrs Feinstein, it is only your kindness which has kept me here. If you are no longer here then . . . well, I might go back to England,' she lied with a bright smile.

'Ah, now that is good thinking. Home you should be. Grace to meet her family, ah, that I'm understanding.'

The next few months were chaotic. Mrs Feinstein was not the most decisive of people and whether to sell or to pack was the endless question of the day. No decision was taken lightly. Every object she owned was studied and twisted and turned, its full history related to Alice, while the poor woman endeavoured to decide its fate. But slowly large packing chests were filled with the treasures to be transported across this great land.

In the midst of her packing and sorting, Mrs Feinstein insisted, in June, that Grace should have a birthday party – the last thing she should have been doing, Alice argued to no avail.

'Pity you go, really, you could have all this stuff I don't need.' Mrs Feinstein waved at a pile of furniture which Alice would have given anything to own since she had no real plans for her own future.

'I shan't go until the spring – it's too late now for this summer, I'd never get a berth. And I don't fancy the rough seas of winter. Perhaps I could have some of it until then to make do with,' she said, hastily.

'Bah, what you want to lumber yourself with rubbish for? No, I call Mr Schenk, he'll sell it for me.'

With heavy heart Alice watched the furniture go. Only two rooms were still partly furnished. Alice's room was stripped of all but her bed, wardrobe and Grace's things. They had moved a bed into Mrs Feinstein's sitting-room, now denuded of all its glitter. The lodgers had gone and in their place each day a long stream of callers came to inspect the house with a view to buying.

Alice had not been idle in these weeks of packing. She had left the baby in Mrs Feinstein's care as she had searched for accommodation. She had decided with regret that she could not afford to stay in this area. Each week, in a fruitless search, she walked further and further away from the district she knew and in which she felt safe.

The problem of course was money. In the year she had been with her landlady rents had jumped alarmingly and the available accommodation was not keeping pace with the endless stream of immigrants who poured into the city like a lava flow. Frequently she arrived to find a room already let. If she found a room she could afford, she was always thwarted by the demand for one month, three months, in one case six months rent in advance. She had travelled further and further down the East Side.

It was only on the day before Mrs Feinstein's departure that at last she found a room. It was in the 10th ward on the East Side, the worst ward of all. She was glad it was so late. There was no chance that Mrs Feinstein would have time to come and inspect it as she no doubt would have done otherwise. Alice would have been too ashamed to let her see what she had found.

It was on the fourth floor of a tenement. The street was narrow, dirty and unlit – it would be a nightmare when winter came. Across the street washing hung in criss-crossed lines, not lines of billowing white washing, but grey and tattered garments which hung listlessly in the still air. The smell, in the high summer heat, from the rotting rubbish in the streets was overwhelming. There were no garbage cans; instead, putrid piles of decaying waste lay where they had been thrown from the windows of the houses. The noise was deafening: babies squalled, children screeched and adults argued and shouted. The hallway was dark, its only source of light coming from a filthy skylight six floors above. If anything, the stench was worse in this ill-ventilated stairwell. The room she was shown into was small and filthy, no more than nine feet square. Her first expenditure would of necessity be on a bucket and soap. The faded wallpaper was peeling from the walls which were spotted with the black specks of damp which would be far worse in winter. The one window, which had a broken pane of glass, opened on to a fire escape which hung precariously from the back of the building. The landlord's agent, in between leering at her, had pointed this out, saying how safe she would be – there were not many houses with the luxury of a fire escape, he explained. Perhaps it was the fire escape which had persuaded her to take the overpriced and unsuitable room. She had been in New York long enough to have read of the dreadful fire tragedies which occurred with sickening frequency. The agent claimed the room was furnished – Alice looked about her with a cynical smile. A rickety table, two chairs, a greasy gas stove which she wondered if she would ever dare to use, and a mattress on the floor – that was its furniture. On the outer landing was a lavatory used by all the tenants on that floor. She had no choice. She counted out the month's rent in advance. She stood alone in the room and felt a deep depression flood over her. This was the city equivalent of Ia's home, she reflected before pulling herself together and starting the long walk back to Mrs Feinstein.

'Did you find a room?'

'Yes, at last. I've been too fussy that's been my trouble.'

'You can't be too fussy with Grace to consider. Is it comfortable, is the landlady nice?'

'She's very nice,' Alice lied, and seeing Mrs Feinstein begin to pout hurriedly added, 'But of course, not nearly as nice as you. It's very clean and comfortable. We shall be fine there.'

'How I wish I could it see. Just to make sure.'

'Oh, Mrs Feinstein, you don't trust me to do anything on my own, do you?'

'It's not you I don't trust, it's the bad people out there. You be careful, Alice . . .'

'I'll be careful.'

The next morning all the second thoughts which Mrs Feinstein had had at regular intervals throughout her packing, surfaced with a vengeance. She could not go. She could not leave the house that her Mannie had loved so much. She was deserting him; she was deserting Alice. She loved New York; she would hate San Francisco, she knew it, she felt it in her bones. She had become a selfish old woman, thinking only of herself . . . The litany was long and tearful. Since Alice wanted her to stay it was hard for her to persuade the woman she must go. They both cried copiously. With difficulty Alice persuaded her to get into the carriage they had ordered to take her to the station. It was a long task settling Mrs Feinstein into her train seat and stowing away the many bags, boxes and cases that she had refused to trust to the carriers. She kept getting out of the seat while Alice pushed her back into it. She must have kissed Grace a hundred times. Finally with a further torrent of tears from Mrs Feinstein, promises to write, assurances that she would take care of herself, Alice got off the train and waited for its departure. The great steam engine began to pull, the train began to move and Mrs Feinstein's anguished face appeared at the window.

'I don't want to go . . .' she wailed but it was too late. The train accelerated out of the station.

Alice stood on the platform feeling desolate. It seemed to her that everyone she loved left her. Either death or circumstances took them away from her. Maybe it was better if she did not love. She hugged Grace to her fiercely and for the first time feared the love she had for her child.

2

Keeping clean was a nightmare. Keeping warm was an impossible dream.

When Alice had lived with Mrs Feinstein she thought she had come down in the word. She laughed now at such a notion as she realised she had been living in a respectable middle-class environment. Now she did not have words to describe where she was – hell seemed the most accurate description.

She had seen that the city could be divided into its various villages, each with its own nationality. What she had not known was that there were other villages. She had been living amongst the successful, those lucky ones who had found happiness in the land of their dreams. Most of them had lived in America for many years, many were already second- and third-generation Americans. Now she was to learn that unless you arrived in this city with family or friends already established who would take you in and help you on your way, there was no alternative but to live in the tenement areas such as this. There was no neat division here, she lived in a melting pot of many different nationalities. No one had money, few had hope.

What made the other inhabitants different from Alice was that many had come from conditions that were even worse. Here they were delighted to have a roof over their heads, lights and lavatories that, even if they did not work or flush, were an awesome novelty. Some had escaped from religious persecution, some from political, and all had run away from the soul-destroying poverty which had been their lot in their homelands. There was a fierce loyalty between the different groups which she admired and envied. But she could never belong: the language barriers saw to that – here there were no English or French speakers.

Language apart, there was another intangible barrier. Initially she had smiled at the other women in greeting but each time her smile was rewarded by a stony stare or a turned back. As an attractive woman, alone, she was a threat to these women who, if beautiful as girls, had lost that beauty with an alarming rapidity once married and with children. Alice, despite her lack of money, managed to keep clean, to be neatly dressed, and these women, with instincts honed by years of fighting to survive, sensed that she was an alien, that she was not one of them – they did not need to articulate such conclusions. As to the men, she never dared look at one of them in case a glance should be misinterpreted. Instead, she walked about with her head down, her eyes averted, in a purdah of her own. Her sense of isolation therefore was acute.

When she had first come to this district, she had blithely assumed that she would be able to teach again, once she had settled. But here the people struggled simply to survive where they were. They had no ambition to acquire jobs out of the ghetto. They therefore had no need for English and, in any case, there was no spare money for the luxury of learning the language of this strange land. She put a notice in a local shop window advertising that she was willing to teach students all that was necessary to take the oath of allegiance – but it seemed that here no one even applied for naturalisation either.

She never went out once darkness had fallen: it was too dangerous. She would crouch in her ill-lit room and listen to the noises all about her. Through the paper-thin walls she could hear her neighbours fighting, eating, making love. From the street came noises more fitting to the jungle. She had sat in this room and had heard innumerable gang fights, she had listened to two murders, several rapes and robberies too numerous to count. She resented the cowardice that was imposed upon her – for there was nothing she could do to help anyone.

But in the daytime her cowardice shamed her. She had several times stood immobile with the other tenants and had watched whole families being evicted on to the sidewalk. She had closed her ears as she had heard them begging the agent, in their broken English, for more time, for understanding, for pity. She had heard and had not helped, she the only one here whose language it was. But she had learned far too quickly that the chief rule of survival here was to be unnoticed. Despite her shame, it was one she adhered to closely.

Winter had arrived – a cold, mind-numbing winter. Despite the agent's promises to mend her window, he never had, and precious cents of her store of money had to be spent on having it reglazed. She had intended to ask him for a refund but, since he never came to the building, she waited in vain. The last of her savings had long gone on essentials such as bedding, towels, a washing bowl, enough china for herself, a saucepan. Then her jewellery had had to go. This time she had been more sensible and had visited half a dozen shops before selling to the one who had made the highest offer. This she had used to eke out their food and to pay the rent. She had tried to find work but, with Grace, it was impossible. She knew no one with whom she could leave her. Undoubtedly there were women who would have looked after the baby for a fee but Alice could not afford one. She had travelled across town when she had seen a cleaning job advertised only to find that the job was gone and, in any case, the woman had explained, there were plenty looking for work without a baby in tow.

After nearly five months in these conditions she was permanently tired – the noise and the fear that was always with her prevented deep sleep. Dirt seemed to seep through the very walls of this building so that, no sooner had she scrubbed her room clean, than it was full of grime again. At least the scrubbing and cleaning gave her something to do, she reasoned with herself. Her greatest trial was the lavatory. Beside it was a jug and a tap to be used for flushing since the cistern was long broken – but the people in this building did not appear to understand the necessity of washing their evacuations away. Day after day she had to steel herself to brush the pan out before she could use it, gagging at the stench and averting her eyes from the piles of excrement on the floor from those who misunderstood its function altogether. When the catch on the door broke it was Alice, the only one of the tenants with a sufficient need for privacy, who paid to have it mended.

The winter was so cold that she could no longer take

her daily walk with Grace – the cloak that Chas had bought her was too thin to withstand the fierce chill of a New York winter. There was nowhere for Grace, now attempting to walk, to play but on the floor of the tiny room. From her own petticoats she had made Grace dresses. And the woollies which Mrs Feinstein and her friends had knitted, once outgrown, she had laboriously unpicked and reknitted into larger garments for the baby.

Alice would spend hours alone staring vacantly at the pictures she had painted of Gwenfer. She would look at them and there were days when she began to wonder if she had not dreamed it all, almost believing that her life had always been like this, made up of misery and despair, and that she had invented that other world of beauty to sustain her.

There were days when she looked at the gas taps and prayed that she could one day find the courage to turn them on and end it all. But always there was Grace to think of. Even if she could kill herself she knew she could never kill her baby.

It was late November. Alice lay asleep, Grace, her bassinet almost outgrown, asleep beside her. A shout from outside woke Alice and she sat up with a start. Feeling something heavy on her feet, she felt for the light switch which hung over the bed and pulled it. She looked with horror at a giant rat which lay asleep at her feet. She swung round in the bed to check that Grace was safe. The child slept fitfully. Gingerly she moved her feet, the rat stirred, lifted its head and settled back to sleep again. Alice slumped back against the pillow. Dear God, what was she to do? She had heard tales of sewer rats in this city which could, with one bite, kill a man ... It was huge! She shuddered. She sat in the bitter cold, her blanket round her, and watched the rat, fearful of disturbing it and yet too afraid to sleep lest it attacked them. As dawn came the rat suddenly awoke, looked at her with black, inquisitive eyes, that she realised with mounting horror held no fear, stretched and slid from the mattress. It scurried across the floor and down a hole in the wainscot which she had not noticed before. Alice jumped from the bed and then stuffed all the paper she could find down the hole before hauling a heavy box across it.

She sat at the table, her head in her hands. How had she come to this – to share her bed with a rat and to be too afraid to do anything about it? She shook herself. This had gone on long enough. She had to do something: she owed it to Grace. What on earth had she been thinking about? Why had she not tried harder to get herself out of this morass? She was too proud, that was her problem. She had been too proud to go to California – with Mrs Feinstein to protect her she would have been safe there. She had been too proud to go to Mr O'Hare and ask for the help he had freely offered. She was too proud to write to her father, beg his forgiveness and ask to be allowed home. What was she to say to her daughter when she was old enough to understand – 'Well, darling daughter, it was my pride, you see, which enabled us to live in these doleful conditions'; she smiled in the half-light at the absurdity of having to explain thus to her daughter.

And where was the Alice Tregowan who had fought for the miners? What a shadow of that creature she had become, allowing her own daughter to live in conditions like this. She sat at the table as the weak winter daylight began to filter through the thin curtain she had sewn for the window. She banged the table with her fist. She must find a solution, she must give Grace a better life, she told herself firmly. She almost felt grateful to the rat for jolting her out of the self-pity in which she had been wallowing.

She picked up her purse. There were two dollars and 30 cents inside it. That, and her meagre possessions, were all she had. She had to find a solution. She began logically to list her abilities. She must search in particular for optimism, that most precious of attributes which she seemed to have lost.

By nine she and Grace were dressed and had taken the horse-bus up-town. She strode purposefully up Broadway, past Barnum's theatre, past the new hotels, looking for possible shops.

She went to four shops before she could find anyone who would listen to her. Finally in the fifth shop, a large, busy grocers', she was lucky: the owner was in his office and was willing to see her. She was shown in. She could have burst into tears of relief when he spoke – he was English.

'Mrs Tregowan, isn't it? Can I be of assistance?'

'I do hope so, Mr Osborn,' she replied, reading the name in gold lettering displayed on a small wooden sign on the front of his desk. 'You see,' she began and coughed nervously. He smiled at her encouragingly; she realised that he too was reacting to her own English accent. 'I've been thinking. There are so many ethnic groups in New York and they all have their own cuisine. And though there must be many English people, we don't seem to be catered for.'

'That's true, I suppose. You don't see any crumpets or Dundee cake,' he said with a laugh.

'Exactly. And with Christmas coming I was thinking that they must be missing Christmas pudding and cake.' She looked at him earnestly.

'I know I do – my wife's American, of Swedish extraction,' he explained.

'There must be hundreds like us. My idea was to make them and for you to sell them.'

He rubbed his chin thoughtfully, at the same time

studying the beautiful woman sitting before him. Despite her shabby clothes, she had an air of quality which one noticed before she opened her mouth, and those pure accents announced her station in life. 'You have a point.'

'And I hadn't even thought of Dundee cake though I did think about marmalade. I've never seen any here, have you?'

'We do import it, from Keillers.'

'Oh,' she said disappointed.

'It's very expensive, mind you. It would be cheaper if we could find a source here.' He found he wanted to reassure her.

'So you're interested?' She held her breath, waiting for his reply.

'I'm more than interested,' she was relieved to hear him say.

'Of course, it's really too late for the puddings and cakes – our cook always made them the year before. But I could make sufficient for now and some to "lay down" as it were, for next year, like good wine.' She laughed. It was a small laugh but it was the first for months. 'And then we could try all the other things.'

'We could only take small batches at first – until we saw how they sold,' Mr Osborn hurriedly interjected.

'Of course, Mr Osborn, I understand that. But you'll let me try?'

'I look forward to testing the produce, Mrs Tregowan.'

'There's just one thing. I need some money.'

'Money?'

'I've worked it all out: the equipment I would need and the ingredients. My stove is rather old so I thought I should buy a couple of primus stoves. I shall need larger saucepans and a steamer. And of course cake tins and pudding basins – different sizes I thought, to give more variety to the stock. Eventually I should like to replace the stove but . . .' She stopped, fearful that her list might sound too much. 'It's only until I start earning, you understand. A loan really.'

'Should you not go to a bank for a loan?'

'I suppose so, but don't they ask for collateral? I don't have anything, you see.' She looked anxiously at Mr Osborn and noticed his deep frown with a sinking heart. 'The truth is, Mr Osborn, I have nothing. I've sold the last of my jewellery. If you cannot help me, then I don't know which way to turn.' She found to her surprise that swallowing her pride and being truthful with this man was far easier than she had dared to hope.

'How much?' he asked suspiciously.

'Forty dollars,' she said quickly, as if saying it fast could lessen the amount.

He laughed. 'Good heavens, Mrs Tregowan, I was expecting you to say at least 200.'

'Oh, gracious, that won't be necessary.'

'All right, we have a deal – as our hosts would say. I lend you 40 dollars and you pay me back out of what I pay you for your produce?'

'If you wouldn't mind.'

'It's an odd way to do business, but I've always been an odd business man. Shall we shake on our deal?' He offered her his hand. She shook it solemnly and from his desk he took a cash box and counted out 40 dollars for her.

Alice tripped from the shop with a lighter step than she had had for months. It was not until she had disappeared into the swirling crowds on Broadway that Mr Osborn realised what a fool he had been. He had not even asked her address.

A week later Mr Osborn was making his morning round of inspection. He felt truly ashamed of his misgivings as Alice Tregowan struggled through his shop door. This time, as well as the baby, she had with her two large wicker baskets she had barely been able to carry, and which he took from her and carried into his office. He was impressed by what she produced. Ranged before him were a dozen Christmas puddings, each pudding basin wrapped in a gingham cloth, on each a neatly printed label with cooking instructions. She had made six cakes, all iced and with a thick wodge of marzipan beneath the icing. Each cake was carefully decorated with seasonal greetings.

'And just one, Mr Osborn, but it's for you.' With a flourish she removed the cloth from a perfectly baked Dundee cake, glowing golden against the mahogany of his desk.

'My word, Mrs Tregowan, you have been busy.'

'Yes, it took a long time since I haven't cooked for ages and of course I had to sit down and remember the recipes.'

'You didn't have the recipes?'

'No, but it was no problem in the end. I have a good memory and I have watched these being made so many times. I'll be able to make double next time with ease. Because the puddings and cakes are so fresh I have put more brandy in than normal, to keep them moist. And here,' she delved once more into the cavernous baskets and produced a dozen small pots, once again neatly labelled, this time with the words BRANDY BUTTER. 'You can't have pudding without the butter, can you?' she said smiling shyly at him.

'Have you your costings?'

'My what?'

'If I'm to pay you a fair price, you have to know how much they cost you to produce and then add a figure that gives you a small profit.'

'Oh yes, of course. I've written it all down here.'

Mr Osborn studied the neatly printed list. 'You have not put down travelling or labour costs, Mrs Tregowan.'

'Should I?'

'Of course, delivery costs can add a lot to the price of a commodity,' he explained kindly, aware that this young woman was making him behave foolishly once more. He was certain that had she been ugly or middle-aged he would not be going to this trouble. It was an uncomfortable conclusion to reach.

Once her fares had been added, and Mr Osborn had explained what amount she should add for her labour and then for her profit, Alice was more than satisfied with the amount of money that changed hands. She dutifully counted out half to begin paying him back.

'No, Mrs Tregowan, I don't want you worrying about money at this point in your business. We'll leave the little question of the loan for a few weeks until we see how things go.'

'You are most kind, Mr Osborn. It must have been my lucky day the morning I walked in here. And I've been doing some more thinking. After Christmas there are other things I could make. Steak and kidney pies, game pies, Cornish pasties, for example. There are so many things people must miss if they cannot make them, or if their cooks aren't British.'

'Let's see what happens with these first, shall we?' He pressed a bell at the side of his desk. 'Harry, put these in a prominent position in the centre of the shop, with some holly round them. Make a big notice, something like . . .' He thought deeply for a moment. 'How about ENGLISH FARE FOR ENGLISH FOLK?'

Alice was delighted with the arrangement. She lingered for a while in the shop, pretending to be intent on other produce as she jealously watched her display. At first she was very disappointed, as no one seemed interested. But then she held her breath as a stout woman, whose haughty manner convinced Alice that she was English, paused at the display. The young assistant waited patiently as she studied Alice's instructions. 'I'll take four,' boomed an impeccable English voice and the assistant scribbled the order down before they moved on.

That day as she walked home, she found that she had rediscovered hope.

The next day a messenger came from Mr Osborn with an order double the size – Alice was in business.

3

Although her food was a success and Mr Osborn kept reordering, and although she had been able to celebrate Christmas, albeit in a modest way, life continued to be hard.

Lack of capital was her main problem, that and too much success too soon. She needed better equipment, she needed an assistant but, despite the increase in her business, she could afford neither.

It was becoming impossible to move about the small, tenement room. Every available surface was covered with her cooking paraphernalia. Sacks of vegetables for her pasties and pies littered the floor. With pots continually bubbling on the stove, the only safe place for Grace was in the newly acquired cot with the bars firmly in position. Alice loathed seeing her daughter's patient little face peering at her between the cot bars, like a miniature prisoner. The room was always full of the smell of her cooking. But it did not stop there, it permeated her clothes, her hair and, though she frequently washed, even her skin smelt of food.

After four months of work she began to know real exhaustion. She would rise at five and rarely fell into bed before one. She began to look ill and wan and she realised that she had replaced one kind of deprived life for Grace with another. Now there was no time for her to play with the child, let alone go for walks. Their only outings were to the shops to get in more supplies or up-town to Mr Osborn's emporium when they took their deliveries. It was not fair on Grace who, at nearly two, needed far more activity than she had the time to give her. Alice found herself being short with the child, snapping at her, and once or twice longing to slap her – the thought of which she would have abhorred before.

'You look tired, Mrs Tregowan, you should take a holiday.'

'I can't afford a holiday, Mr Osborn.' Alice was aware of the sharp way she responded to what had been meant as a kind suggestion.

'Then you should get an assistant, one who could help ease the load.'

'I can't afford an assistant either,' she snapped in reply, unable, it seemed, these days to speak to anyone normally.

'Sit down, Mrs Tregowan . . . please . . .'

Reluctantly she sat, holding Grace on her knee and glancing edgily at the clock. She wanted to be back within the hour to get the following day's pies under way.

'Just for a minute, then.' She managed to give him a wintry smile.

'I fear we are asking too much of you. It was never my intention when we embarked on this venture to have you look, well, if you'll forgive the impertinence, Mrs Tregowan, rather unwell.'

'I manage. Am I ever late with my orders? Is there a fault with their quality?' she asked defensively.

'No, no, everything is perfect. But there must be something wrong somewhere. You came into this office a young woman full of determination and energy. I don't see that any more, Mrs Tregowan. If you cannot afford an assistant, there is something very wrong with your marketing and I fear you cannot go on this way.'

Alice slumped into the chair. She gave him a look of such despondency that his concern strengthened. Grace slipped from her mother's knee and began to crawl about Mr Osborn's office. Alice, for once, was too upset to notice.

'I don't know where I'm going wrong, Mr Osborn. I'd hoped I would be able to afford help by now and a larger oven so that I could bake more in one batch and not have to stay up waiting for things to be cooked . . .'

'Where do you buy your ingredients?'

'There's a shop around the corner from where I live. The man is very good and always makes sure he has my needs in stock.'

'And meat?'

'Why, from the butcher, where else?'

'From a wholesaler, Mrs Tregowan, from a wholesaler,' he replied patiently. 'No wonder you are not making sufficient profit.'

'But I could not afford to pay out large sums, you see, and I do not have facilities for storing food.' She thought of the rats and shuddered.

'The wholesalers will allow you credit, my dear Mrs Tregowan. You pay them after you have sold your goods to me. That is how business is done.'

'Really?' she replied incredulously and looked at him with admiration as if he had explained the secret of the universe to her. As her spirits rose she became aware of her daughter, deeply engrossed in the contents of Mr Osborn's waste-paper basket. She swooped on the child, hurriedly picked up the scattered papers and returned to her seat, keeping a firm hold on Grace.

'I'm sorry, Mr Osborn, I did not notice what she was up to.'

'It's only paper, Mrs Tregowan. Now,' he continued once he had Alice's attention again. 'Until you can afford proper premises – which I think you should begin to consider – the size of your order will not matter, provided you can give trade references which I will be happy to supply.'

'Mr Osborn, what would I do without you?' Alice turned on him a smile of happy relief which quite unnerved Mr Osborn who, in all the years of his married life, had never noticed another woman. He found he was very conscious of this young woman.

'I think we should have some tea,' he said abruptly, coughed, and rang the bell. 'And I think we should begin to think how you can expand. There are shops other than mine you know!' he went on. 'Other large grocers, food halls in the department stores, delicatessens . . .'

'But you wouldn't like that, would you – my goods in other stores?'

'I don't know, perhaps if the label were altered to GWENFER OSBORN or vice versa? Perhaps you would like to consider having a partner?' He gave her a quizzical smile.

Alice was stunned. 'I don't know what to say,' she managed finally to blurt out.

'Think about it, Mrs Tregowan. Ah, the tea . . .'

That day Alice returned to her wretched room as light-heartedly as she had done after first meeting Mr Osborn. She did not snap at Grace once on the long horse-bus journey home; she even bought the child a bag of candies – normally forbidden – and she lingered in the small park close to the tenement for half an hour while Grace played on the sparse grass and Alice sat on a bench mulling over the implications of her talk with Mr Osborn. She would have liked to be independent of anyone but she saw that this was a luxury she could not afford. She liked the man and she felt she could trust him where advice and money were concerned. And, she could share the worry – that must be a good thing in favour of a partnership.

Her good humour was short-lived. She returned to her room to find the pastry she had mixed – and in her haste had forgotten to put into a tin – half-eaten. The rats! Recently the rats had become an obsession with her and were another reason why she was so tired – when pies and cakes were ready in the evenings for delivery the following morning, even though they were safely sealed in tins she hardly dared to sleep for fear the rats would crawl out of their holes and somehow prise off the lids. Reason could not take hold where her fear of these rats was concerned – she was convinced they were capable of anything. Her gas bill was enormous, not only from her cooking but because she left the gas mantle burning all night in a vain attempt to frighten them. It did not. These rats appeared to be afraid of nothing. She would lie in bed at night and listen to them as they scurried busily about the whole building.

But today her reaction was different. She did not sit dejected with frustration as she would have done the previous day. She swept out of her room, a confused Grace in tow. She knocked on every door and managed with difficulty to elicit the information that every room, every apartment was alive with rats as well as bugs and cockroaches. She knocked and knocked until she found one man who knew where the landlord lived.

Out of the building she stormed with Grace. In her fury she threw economy to the wind, hailed a cab and willed the driver to get the horse to go faster in case her anger had time to subside into timidity. Finally the carriage stopped at a fine mansion on Fifth Avenue. Angrily she mounted the steps and rang the bell. She swept past the astonished footman before he could stop her.

'Get your master,' she ordered and so commanding was the tone of her voice that he obeyed her.

She stood in the imposing hall, so like those of a dozen houses she had known in the past. Then she would have idled the time away admiring the decoration and the *objets d'art*. Now the rich hangings, the huge chandelier, the sweeping staircase with its deep red carpet, the stained-glass windows – the beauty, the luxury, the expense of it all fuelled her anger, like great logs on a fire, so that by the time her landlord appeared she was ready for him.

His face was the colour of good claret. The large gold watch-chain across his middle emphasised his corpulence. She swept immediately into the attack. 'The building I live in and which you own is alive with rats and other unspeakable creatures. I insist you do something about it, forthwith.'

'I beg your pardon, madame?' Alfred van Hooven, self-made millionaire replied quietly. He did not sound astonished, concerned or angry; she had not expected this calmness.

'I'm sure you heard me, Mr van Hooven. The conditions that we are forced to live in are intolerable. I demand attention.' As if sensing her mother's upset, Grace began to wail. Alice jigged the baby up and down in a vain attempt to pacify her.

'And your name is?' He had to raise his voice this time, just to be heard.

'Tregowan, Alice Tregowan.'

'If you would excuse me a moment, Mrs Tregowan. Perhaps you would care to take a seat . . . .?' With irritating slowness the man crossed the hall and disappeared into a room. Alice paced up and down, softly crooning to Grace who finally calmed down; now, the only other sound in the house was the ticking of a grandfather clock on the stairs. He reappeared with a large book in his hands which he opened and consulted. 'Ah, yes,' he eventually said. 'I see you are prompt with your rent, I like that.' He smiled at her and Alice found she relaxed slightly. 'However, I don't think, young woman, you are in a position to demand anything. No one asked you to live in that building. If you don't wish to, there are many who would be only too pleased to take your place.'

'Of course, and remain silent. Well, I refuse to remain

silent. The others are too afraid to make a fuss, I'm not. Unless you do something, I shall be forced to go to the authorities.'

'Oh yes.' Mr van Hooven gave an infuriating smile. 'And which authorities had you in mind?'

'Well . . .' Alice faltered; she had not thought this far ahead. 'I shall speak to the Tammany Precinct captain.' She said it without conviction – she had heard of the precinct captain, she was aware of his political runners who infested the area and who supplied him with the intelligence about who was doing what. She had heard rumours of pay-outs and corruption, but she had also seen the man – a fat jovial character who looked as if he might help. 'Yes, I'll speak to him.'

'Ha! And you think he will listen to a slip of a girl like you? No, madame, he won't. You see he works for me. They all work for me. There's nothing you can do.'

'Then I'll go higher – I'll go to the ward boss.'

'Have you not been listening to me?' he asked, still speaking in the quiet tone, devoid of emotion, that sent a chill down Alice's spine. 'I should not waste your energy, if I were you. You obviously have little understanding of how this city works. While we are talking of irregularities, I should point out to you that my agent has reported that you are in fact engaged in a business on my property. That is not allowed, Mrs Tregowan, by the terms of your lease.'

'I don't have a lease.'

'You do now, Mrs Tregowan, oh yes, you certainly have a lease now.' He smiled again but Alice realised that it was not a smile, as such, but rather the exercise of a particular group of muscles on his face.

'Aren't you ashamed? Do you think it right that fellow human beings should be forced to live as we do?'

'No, it doesn't shame me. Why should it? I cannot help it if people have failed in life. All that concerns me is that they pay their rent on time. The door is this way,' he said with insufferable politeness.

'You'll be hearing more of this. I shall go to the mayor,' she threatened.

He laughed, a laugh devoid of all humour. 'You do that, Mrs Tregowan. A very pleasant fellow. But I doubt if I shall hear any more of this, or you, come to that, Mrs Tregowan. Good day to you.'

Alice found herself once more on the sidewalk and confused as to how she had got there so quickly. Holding her bewildered daughter Alice marched resolutely towards City Hall. She stomped up the long flight of marble stairs. In her fury she did not even notice the famous and beautiful entrance hall. She might just as well have requested an audience of God. For an hour she ranted and made scenes which later made her feel hot with embarrassment. No one wanted to listen to her, no one cared; the mayor was unapproachable by the likes of her. She was not a citizen, she had no vote and, more important it seemed, she had no money and thus no patronage.

Exhausted, defeated, she made her weary way home. As she approached her building she saw a commotion on the sidewalk. Curiously she approached. All her neighbours were shouting and gesticulating in a dozen different languages to two burly men, who stood impassive, with arms folded, apparently oblivious to the rage swirling around them.

Scattered all over the sidewalk were her possessions. Her precious pots and pans had been thrown out and now lay dented in the mud. Her clothes and those of Grace lay in a jumble. Grace's perambulator, her pride and joy, was twisted on one side.

'Those are my things,' she screamed at one of the men.

'You Mrs Tregowan?'

'Yes.'

'Then they would be. Orders of the landlord. He don't want you as a lodger no more.'

'You can't do this,' Alice stormed, and to her surprise was aided by a chorus of protest from her neighbours who, for once, were united in indignation.

'We just have,' the man replied.

At the man's feet Alice saw one of her paintings of Gwenfer, the glass broken, a large black mark where a foot had trodden on it. It was the sight of the picture that was her undoing.

'Oh no,' she wailed and slumped on to the pavement, her shoulders heaving as she began to cry.

'Mummy.' Grace put her small arm about her mother to comfort her. It only made Alice weep all the more.

4

It was Mr Osborn who yet again came to Alice's rescue. After she had left his office he had sat a long time in thought. The more he thought, the more he was tempted by the idea of going into partnership with Alice. He liked the young woman, that was true. He admired her, that too was true. He felt they could make a success of the venture. But most of all, he found he wanted to help her.

He made a long telephone call to a friend who dealt in real estate. At the end of the call he and Alice had twenty-four hours in which to make a decision.

He called for his carriage and gave his driver the address. As the carriage approached the area of the city where she lived, his anger for Alice became greater. Like many prosperous people in New York he was only vaguely aware of the poverty that lurked far from their fine mansions and houses. They knew it was there, but it was a problem which none of them, secure in their own success, cared to dwell upon. He had never had cause to venture into these parts but now, as he looked about him and saw the overcrowding, the dirt, the poverty, he felt fury mingled with shame. Even so, his anger was for Alice and her misfortune rather than for these unknown immigrants from God knew where. The tall blocks of tattered tenements loomed above him; the carriage had difficulty manoeuvring through the street, crowded with shabby people, its sidewalks covered with stalls which sold, it seemed, everything from potatoes to clothes and second-hand furniture. The noise was tremendous as people shouted their wares and bargained vociferously in a dozen different languages. Worse was the stench rising from the refuse in the gutter.

The carriage drew to a halt in front of Alice's building, where a large and angry crowd was milling on the sidewalk. Mr Osborn leaped down and pushed his way through the throng; in the centre he found the cause of all the consternation. Alice, sitting amidst a tangle of clothes, pots and pans, and a child's paraphernalia, was sobbing. Her small daughter, clutched in her arms, was wailing. They were watched impassively by two large, silent men.

'Mrs Tregowan!' He knelt down in the dirt beside her. 'What has happened?'

Between sobs Alice attempted to tell him. Her account was disjointed, not helped by her various neighbours' interjections in barely comprehensible English.

'These men did this?' he said eventually, glaring angrily up at the two men, who looked at him not coldly but with eyes which showed a total lack of interest in this personal tragedy which they had instigated. 'We'll see about that.' He stood up and faced them. The crowd fell silent but pressed in closer to hear the outcome. 'How dare you. On whose authority, may I ask?'

'Mr van Hooven, bud,' the larger of the two men replied.

The crowd was to be disappointed. Mr Osborn said no more. Instead, he helped Alice to her feet, called his carriageman to give him a hand and loaded her pathetic bundle of belongings into his carriage. Finally he helped them both in and squeezed in himself.

'I'm so ashamed you should have seen all that, Mr Osborn. I had hoped to keep my living conditions secret . . .' Alice said miserably, as the carriage pulled away from the crowd.

'It's not you who should be ashamed. It's that villain van Hooven.'

'What can I do? I complained about the rats, you see. He did not like it. Then he used the fact that I did my cooking there as an excuse to have me thrown out. I was very careful, though, I do assure you. I covered everything, I scrubbed everything . . . What am I to do?' she looked at him, her fine grey eyes clouded again with tears which were close to brimming over.

'I fear there is nothing you can do, Mrs Tregowan. The van Hoovens of this city are impossible to fight. And it is dangerous even to try. All the officials are in their pay, probably the mayor also. Wherever the weak are there are rich men like him waiting to prey upon them.'

'Oh dear God, just as everything was getting better . . .'

'Please, Mrs Tregowan, don't upset yourself. I'm hopeful that I might have a solution. But first we will go to my home. There you must eat and have a good night's sleep and tomorrow, why tomorrow we shall make a new start for you.' He smiled at her gently.

Alice woke the next morning and looked about the pretty room. The walls were painted white, the furniture an attractive green decorated with white and gold flowers. White muslin curtains lifted in the gentle breeze from the window and outside she could just see the branches of a tree nearly in bud. She heard children laughing and the occasional horse trotting by. She pinched herself; she must be dreaming. She closed her eyes and opened them again. But the room did not disappear. Life could still be pleasant for some, she thought; there were people who still lived like this in clean, sweet-smelling rooms. During the past few months she had begun to think that there was no more quality to life anywhere. Last night his wife had insisted that she have a bath – oh the luxury of it! Alice remembered the acute pleasure it had given her to feel the perfumed hot water on her skin, the luxurious-smelling soap, the sheer joy of a clean, spotlessly white towel to wrap herself in. After a bowl of soup and a mug of warm milk laced with rum, the woman had insisted she go straight to bed where she had fallen into a deep sleep almost immediately, too exhausted to worry any more. She sat up. What had Mr Osborn meant last night? A new start? She had been too tired even to think.

Hurriedly she dressed, checked that Grace was still asleep in the cot they had put up for her, slipped from her room and down the stairs into the hallway, following the sound of voices.

'Ah, our guest is awake. You slept well, Mrs Tregowan?' Mr Osborn leaped to his feet as she entered the room.

'Thank you, yes. Like a baby. In fact my baby is still sleeping. I can't thank you or Mrs Osborn enough.'

'Some food?' Mrs Osborn, a slim, blonde-haired woman, in her forties like her husband, smiled at her, indicating a tray of fish and salad, a plate of meat sliced as thin as paper, and another of cheese.

'Some bread and coffee would be wonderful – nothing else, thank you.'

'We have tea, Mrs Tregowan. I may not have bacon and eggs but my wife allows me tea with my Swedish breakfast,' Mr Osborn laughed.

'Tea would be marvellous. Where am I? I feel as if I am in the country.'

'It's quieter, isn't it? You're in Brooklyn.'

'Brooklyn? Oh, how funny. A landlady I used to have

was so angry her daughter had come here to live, she talked as if it were Outer Mongolia.'

'Some people think it is. I prefer it to the city – all those straight streets, the people scuttling about, make me think of rats in a maze . . .' Mr Osborn instantly stopped talking as he noticed Alice shudder. 'I'm sorry, Mrs Tregowan, no more talk of rats. Here it is like living in a country town, almost like England I feel, that's why I choose to live here. Once the Brooklyn Bridge was built – about ten years ago – it made getting out of the city so much easier. Of course I have a long journey to the shop each day but I think it is worth it, don't you?'

'Oh, it must be.' She accepted her cup of tea from Mrs Osborn. 'Last night you said about . . .' She stopped in confusion, not wishing to appear too forward and anxious that in her distress she might have imagined it all.

'I most certainly did say you were to have a new start. I have been busy since our talk yesterday. There is a property, not far from here, that I think might be suitable for our plans – that is, if you want me as a partner – and provided you don't mind moving out of the city?'

'Mr Osborn, how can you even ask?' She laughed at him. The laughter seemed to banish momentarily the grey look that had worried him and she looked young again.

An hour later, accompanied by the Osborns, she was pushing Grace's baby carriage along wide tree-lined streets. The houses on either side were large and spacious, each with its own garden to the front and back. All were new and all were well cared for, the lawns were close-cut, by summer flowers would be growing in profusion. Children played in the street with their hoops and balls, and she could hear birds singing. It was as if she was a million miles away from the horror of her tenement.

'It used to be a baker's: it has everything you need,' Mr Osborn said with pride as they stopped outside the solid red-brick building. There was a pretty bow window at the front and outside a small magnolia tree.

'We had a magnolia at Gwenfer. A giant one. Maybe that little one will grow.' Alice swung around to face him smiling broadly. 'It must be an omen.' And he realised it was only the second time she had said anything about her life in England.

Inside, the building was perfect. The shop was small but the kitchen beyond was big. The ovens were still in situation, there were large bleached pine tables to work at, the walls were lined with pine cupboards and at the back, amongst the various store rooms, was a cold store.

'You haven't seen the best part.' Mr Osborn opened a door like a conjuror and led them up a narrow flight of stairs. 'You see, room enough for you and Grace and, if you look out of that window there, you'll see a fine garden for the young lady to play in.'

Alice explored the apartment with delight – two good-sized bedrooms, a large sitting-room, a small neat kitchen with running water that gushed into the white sink. Mrs Osborn took Grace to play in the garden. She watched from the window as her daughter ran about the grass squealing with excitement at the unaccustomed freedom.

'But how much is all this?' she asked anxiously, realising that her initial enthusiasm might be short-lived.

'I shall buy it and our partnership will rent it from me – a simple arrangement, my dear.'

'I have no furniture and no money to buy any.'

'Our loft is full of furniture that I've been telling Mrs Osborn for years we must get rid of.'

Alice looked at the kind face smiling at her. She had reached such a point in her life that when good fortune faced her now she could no longer believe in its reality. She was afraid to accept, fearful that if she did, something would inevitably go wrong.

'I don't know.'

'Mrs Tregowan. Here you can produce far more, you

can have your own shop, you will make enough money to engage assistants, then you can spend more time with Grace. It is good business sense.'

'I'm not Mrs Tregowan, it's Miss,' she blurted out.

'Why are you telling me?' he asked after the shortest of pauses.

'Because, if I don't, you might find out. Perhaps then you would not wish to know me. I would understand. I'd rather know now before . . .' She indicated the pretty room. 'Before I got used to all this.'

'Your past is not your present. I'm sure this misfortune was not entirely of your making. Perhaps it will be more comfortable for you, and Grace, if we continue to call you Mrs? And perhaps it would be better if we did not mention this to my wife.'

'I'm not ashamed, Mr Osborn. I know I should be but I can't feel shame for something as wonderful,' she pointed to her daughter, 'as that.'

'Yes, of course.' Mr Osborn looked embarrassed and somewhat out of his depth. 'We have until four o'clock to decide if we want this building.'

'You don't mind then?'

'I didn't say that. I'm a godfearing man, but . . . I admire your honesty.'

'Perhaps it would be simpler if you both called me Alice?'

'Maybe.'

An awkward silence descended. For her own protection Alice had felt she must be truthful about herself. But now, having done so, she wondered if she had not made herself vulnerable. She knew him only as a business man; otherwise she knew nothing about him. There had been moments when he had looked at her, smiled at her, in a way that had reminded her oddly of Chas – what if he had other ideas and plans? What if he thought she had loose morals?

'Why are you doing all this, Mr Osborn?'

'Business.'

'Just business?'

'Of course. That and the fact that I like you and would like to help you and Grace.'

'As simple as that?'

'I don't quite understand, Mrs . . . Alice.'

'It's difficult to explain. But I have to. I have to be reassured that there is nothing else . . . that, well, that I should be under no other obligation . . .' She found that she was blushing furiously at her own presumption and forwardness. 'You see, Mr Osborn, I have learned a lot in the last few years and I want everything understood at the beginning.'

Mr Osborn looked out of the window at his wife playing with Grace. 'Then I shall be straight too, Alice. Yes, there is something about you that I find very attractive. But I love my wife. Whatever it is, it remains in my mind only. I would never insult you, and I would not dream of hurting Greta. I should like to have the honour of helping you. We are two people of principle, you see.' He smiled at her.

'Thank you, Mr Osborn, for your openness. I should very much like us to become partners. Shall we shake hands as we did once before?'

'I feel we shall be most successful, Alice. And if we are to work together then please call me John – and my wife is Greta. But tell me something that has fascinated me about you: how on earth did a young woman such as you find the strength to survive in this city over the past years?'

Alice looked at him and laughed. 'I'm a daughter of a land of granite. It gives us a very special strength, you see.'

'I wish one could bottle it and sell it. I'd make my fortune.'

Six months later, the shop was busy. GWENFER AND

OSBORN was painted in gold letters on the dark green background of the shop board. Alice had not one assistant, but four.

It was as if the move had restored her luck. Not only did she have her own shop to serve the immediate district, she continued to supply John's store and three others in the city. But this was not the only reason for her increasing success. One day, a month after the store had opened, the new telephone – which John had insisted she have installed – had rung. It was a woman asking if Alice could supply a steak and kidney pie and an apple pie large enough for a dinner for twenty. Alice never knew what had made her suggest she should come and discuss the dinner with the customer in person.

Alice had found a frightened young Italian woman eager to explain her dilemma. Her husband was succeeding brilliantly in the New York building boom. An important client was to be entertained and her husband had forbidden her to cook Italian food. He wanted to impress his guests, he wanted Anglo-Saxon food.

As gently as she could, Alice advised that the chosen menu was inappropriate for the time of year – far too heavy, and never two pies on the same menu. She had suggested an alternative of a light soup, a fish mousse, stuffed chicken breasts in a cream sauce with a choice of small vegetables, a tender lamb roast with mint, and a selection of puddings all following a summer theme. The woman agreed eagerly to her suggestions. Alice was shown the dining-room where she counselled against the heavily encrusted gold dinner service, explaining that the menu they had decided upon would look so much better on the simpler second dinner service. They went on to talk of the wine and it seemed logical, finally, that Alice should tentatively enquire if perhaps madame would like her to cook the meal for her.

That was the simple start of Alice's home-catering business. By word of mouth Alice was recommended. As the city grew, she found that there were many such young women, frightened by the success of their husbands. Women who were desperate for advice and help in situations for which life in their home villages had never prepared them. They needed advice on every aspect of entertaining and, given Alice's quiet, considerate attitude, they trusted her. This side of her business had grown at such a rate that soon the number of assistants would have to be doubled.

Alice still worked long hours but she could begin to see that her life was improving. She had a carriage, in green and gold livery, for transporting her food and equipment. She had a young girl who helped to look after Grace, now over two and a half and very active and mischievous. She was able to buy pretty dresses, toys, books for her daughter. She had even bought two new dresses for herself. And for the past couple of weeks Alice had had her eye on a small house with a wooden verandah and a garden – just the kind of house she had once imagined living in with Chas. Now if she could manage to rent it, or better still, to buy it, it would be for her alone. Alice had learned one thing – she could live alone. Apart from Grace, she needed no one.

Part Three

Chapter Eight

1

The morning Alice left her father's house there was much drama. George Tregowan's anger and Daisy Dear's hysterics could be heard even in the basement. The police were called, private detectives arrived, lawyers swarmed in. The telephone rang constantly. An endless stream of callers came, ostensibly to offer sympathy, but in truth to find out as much as possible to fuel the fires of gossip already sweeping society. But Daisy could receive no one – the callers were told she was prostrate with grief; nearer the truth was that she had whipped herself into such a state of anger that she had made herself physically sick.

Ia was amused by the activity. She listened in silence to the staff's assessment of what had happened and their guesses as to where Alice was. She could have told them that she had seen her leave. She preferred not to – why should she help the Tregowans? Best of all was to overhear the remarks about Alice's character and the astonished surprise that the perfect young lady could do anything so shocking as to run away with an imposter such as Cordell. Ia could have told them what she knew of Alice's hypocrisy, but what was the point? She got on with her work, her ears, however, attuned to any new scraps of information.

The Tregowans went to Rome. Daisy felt unable to face society. The talk about Alice began to diminish belowstairs. There was a new topic of interest to occupy the staff when the Tregowans returned from their travels, in October – was her ladyship with child? The staff were in for a fine time: not only was she *not* pregnant, but it

333

appeared that his lordship had been banished from her bed.

Upon his return George Tregowan had disappeared into his study to sort through his accumulated mail. There was one letter from New York – he recognised the handwriting as Alice's. Without opening it, he tore it in two and flung it into the waste-paper basket.

The house settled back into its normal routine. Alice was rarely mentioned.

A year later, in October, Ia was sick. She assumed she had eaten something which disagreed with her. But the next morning, when she was sick again, suspicion began to dawn. A week later she was certain.

She kept her secret for another month. She had never felt fitter or happier. The idea that a baby was growing within her awed her, excited her. She longed for it to be born so that she could express her love for it: she would smother it with love – all the love she had to give.

She waited in the dark for Frederick. Tonight she had decided to tell him and she was bubbling with anticipation. She loved Frederick. She had told him frequently of her love for him. He had never said he loved her in return, but she was sure he did. Why else would he risk having her in his bed night after night? And she knew there were times when he had to bribe Robert to go out or to bunk down with the other footman. If she were honest, she wished that Frederick would talk to her more – once he had made love to her he always went straight to sleep. He was certainly energetic enough in bed, perhaps that was what made him so tired. After all these months she still could not honestly see what pleasure there was to be had from the exercise. Maybe women were not meant to enjoy themselves. She doubted whether her mother had enjoyed it much either, from what she could remember hearing as a small child.

Frederick was very late tonight. Lady Tregowan had

taken to staying out later and later and one of the downstairs staff had to stay up to attend to her needs when she returned. Ia wondered what she got up to until two or sometimes three in the morning. At last, she heard Frederick coming along the corridor. She sat up eagerly, her long blonde hair glimmering in the light from the candle, her face glowing with anticipation.

'You look pretty tonight, Ia,' he said, barely glancing at her as he pulled off his shoes.

'I've got a secret,' she said, smiling slyly, as he hastily removed his clothes.

'A secret, and what would that be?' He climbed into bed beside her, took her roughly in his arms and at once began to feel between her legs.

'Wait, Frederick. I want to talk, I want to tell you.'

'Be quick then, my prick is bursting.'

'I'm going to have a baby, Frederick. Our baby.'

Frederick's penis shrank visibly before her eyes. 'You what?' he shouted.

'You heard,' she giggled. 'Isn't it wonderful?'

'No it bloody ain't. What the hell do you mean getting pregnant? Don't you look after yourself, you stupid bleeding cow?'

Ia felt her skin tighten with shock and disbelief. 'Look after myself? I don't understand.'

'Douche yourself, of course.'

'I don't know what a douche is.'

'Then you bloody well should have found out. You'll have to find someone to get rid of it for you.'

'I can't do that. It's our baby.'

'*Your* baby, Ia. It ain't nothing to do with me.'

'Of course it is. You know it's to do with you.'

'I don't know what you get up to when I'm busy upstairs.'

'Frederick, you know there's only you. I thought you loved me.' She felt tears begin to form behind her eyes.

'Love? Don't talk daft. I like screwing you, that's all.'

'You bastard.' She swung at him with her arm, anger sweeping through her. He caught her arm and twisted it behind her back, making her wince with pain.

'Don't you call me names, you guttersnipe. You call me names, I'll wallop you, and that's a promise.'

Ia fought the tears she longed to shed. Her eyes were brimming. 'Oh, for Christ's sake, don't start blubbing. Get out. I don't want nothing to do with you. Get out,' he shouted, slowly picking up his belt.

Ia had seen that look on her father's face: she knew she had to get out of the room. Rapidly she grabbed her clothes. 'Cry? I'm not crying. Who'd waste tears on scum like you,' she shouted angrily and quickly slipped from the room before he could lunge at her. The noise she made as she stumbled up the stairs to her attic woke Fanny. That was when Ia, distraught, made the mistake of confessing her predicament to the other kitchen maid.

The next morning when Fanny took the cook her early morning tea she told the tale. By seven thirty Ia had been dismissed and given half an hour to leave the house.

In a daze she packed her clothes. Her lips set in a hard line as she folded her new blue dress and packed the pretty bonnet she had bought to please Frederick. Then she gently wrapped her azure bowl in a blouse and tucked it safely into her bag, the bag with which she had left the orphanage. She crept down the stairs fearful of being seen. Then, at the bottom, she placed her bag on the floor, thought for a moment and then flicked her hair over her shoulder and marched into the kitchen.

'I told you to get out.' Mrs Longman pointed her large kitchen knife at Ia.

'Is he to get out, too?'

'He?'

'Frederick. He *is* the father no matter what he says.'

'There's no proof of that and, no, he is not to be dismissed.'

'That's not bloody fair,' Ia shouted angrily at the cook.

'No one asked you to sleep with him, you slut. Why should the likes of you ruin the career of a fine young man like him? Mr Phillpott will no doubt have a word with him. As for you, out of my sight before I calls someone to throw you out.'

'I hate you. I hate all of you,' Ia screamed as she rushed from the kitchen, and sped along to the footmen's room. There she dug deep into her bag and found the pair of scissors she had bought for her dressmaking. With quiet deliberation she shredded Frederick's velvet evening uniform. She felt remarkably better once she had done that.

Ia did not walk along the street, she stalked. She was furiously indignant. Their hypocrisy and callousness enraged her. She touched her stomach. Still, she thought, now she was on her own, the baby would belong to her alone. She crossed busy Park Lane, dodging between the carriages, and made for the familiar territory of Hyde Park. Here she had slept all those months ago before she went to the Tregowans; she spat with disgust at the thought of that family. Here she had spent many deluded hours with Frederick; again she spat. 'Right fool I made of myself there,' she muttered. Never again, she vowed.

She sat on the grass, her knees hunched up to her chin, and wondered what on earth she would do. She could sleep here, she supposed, but shivered at the thought. Sleeping here in April was one thing, in November another. She had been a fool to buy that material to make clothes to please that bastard: now her savings were seriously depleted. She felt herself begin to fill with hatred, not just for Frederick but for all men.

'Hallo, are you lost?'

Ia looked up vaguely to see a tall young man standing over her.

'No. Resting.'

'Mind if I join you?' Without waiting for her reply he sat himself down beside her.

'I didn't say I wanted you to sit there.'

'Go on, I didn't think you'd mind. You don't look the hoity-toity type to me,' he said in a voice which proclaimed him a Londoner. He smiled, flashing perfect white teeth. She looked at him more closely: he was elegantly dressed in a suit which she reckoned would have cost over a year's wages. He wore a large gold ring in which a diamond glittered in the weak winter sun. 'It's not the ideal day for sitting in the park, is it?' He grinned disarmingly.

'Not really.' Finally she smiled back. She had made up her mind. If she were going to have to do it to make money, at least he would be a good start. He looked as if he had a bob or two, she thought. 'Why are you doing it then?' she asked, cheekily.

'I can't resist a pretty face, that's why. You working?'

'I was. Until this morning.'

'Got the push?'

'None of your business,' she retorted.

'Are you looking for another position?'

'Of course I am.' She sat up with interest.

'I think I might know the ideal place for you. Fancy coming with me?'

What had she to lose? She scrambled to her feet and together they walked out of the park. A few minutes later Ia was walking up the front steps of an imposing house behind Piccadilly. She had automatically made for the area steps but he had taken her firmly by the elbow and steered her up the main steps. Ia felt like a queen and wished someone she knew could see her.

The door was opened by a footman dressed in a smart grey livery. Ia did not look at him: she had had her fill of footmen. She looked round the large marble hall; a staircase swept to the floors above, its brasswork gleaming in the sunlight which shone down through a glass cupola.

'You wait in here.' He held a door open for her. 'I shan't be a mo. By the way, what's your name?'

'Ia Blewett.'

The young man disappeared, leaving Ia to take stock of the small sitting-room decorated in gold and white. The white carpet was finely woven with a delicate pattern of pale gold flowers. 'Bet that's a bugger to keep clean,' she muttered to herself. The curtains were of yellow shot silk and she touched them gently, twitching them into place in the ornate loops which held them back. The room was filled with vases of heavily scented flowers. There were many paintings on the walls, all of which showed naked or scantily clad women, she noted. Behind an ornate desk, inlaid with gilt, were french windows, leading to a perfectly maintained garden. This was certainly a fine house. She had never seen the upstairs of the Tregowan mansion but she doubted if it was any better than this. She wondered what sort of position they would be offering her – hardly that of a kitchen maid if they'd let her in by the front door. There was a rustle of silk behind her and as she swung round she caught a waft of heliotrope perfume.

'Hallo, Ia. I'm Blossom December.'

2

Many had attempted to describe Blossom December's particular charm, none had succeeded. There was a magnetic quality, an aura of energy about her not normally found in the average Mayfair drawing-room.

'The night sky', 'a summer storm cloud' – these phrases and more had been used to describe her luxuriant hair whose curls performed an exuberant dance of their own as she moved. The most accurate description had been the one likening her hair to a black panther's coat for it was more blue than black and had the same sheen. And the man who had compared the electric blue tinge at the tips of her curls to glow-worms had been duly applauded. She held her head high on the smooth column of her neck – giraffe-like, it had been said. Her strong chin jutted forward and she moved her head from side to side with short, sharp, inquisitive movements that reminded many of an exotic lizard. The enormous brown eyes, flecked with gold, their pupils large and velvet, were ringed with a double row of eyelashes and had so frequently been likened to a member of the cat family – wild or domestic – that the comparison was now considered banal. The same was true of remarks which described her movements as leonine, feline, fluid. Her nose with its faultless sharp profile had caused her to be likened to a rare and exotic bird. Fruits, usually cherries, were called upon as similes for the red fullness of lips covering small white teeth which, naturally, were 'pearls'. A large black mole at the side of her mouth disappeared charmingly into a dimple when she smiled – 'like a small black moon setting' one admirer had written. Poems had been composed to the perfection of her skin – molasses, hot chocolate, honey; food here was in the ascendancy.

Ia stood entranced as this magnificent woman approached her dressed in a fine pale yellow peignoir which flowed loosely over her body. A long slim hand, heavy with gold and diamond rings, was held out in greeting.

'Never seen a darky before?' The question was asked in a low husky voice bubbling with laughter.

'Well, no,' Ia said, studying the hand that had just been shaken.

'It's permanent. It doesn't rub off.' Blossom laughed, a loud joyous sound.

'The Queen of Sheba must have looked like you,' Ia said, her voice tinged with awe.

'I don't think I've ever been told I looked like her. Other queens, but not that one.' Blossom smiled, not displeased with the comparison. With one smooth movement she sat down and the folds of her peignoir settled about her as if in a pre-arranged pattern. She patted the seat beside her. 'Sit here, Ia, and tell me all about yourself.' She flashed the smile that had ensnared a thousand men. 'Shall we have some champagne while I listen?'

'Champagne?' Ia repeated as if she had misheard. The door opened and the footman appeared with a silver tray, bearing a bottle of champagne in a silver wine cooler, and two fine crystal glasses with air-twist stems. The footman served the champagne, and Ia took her first tentative sip as the man silently left the room.

'Best breakfast in the world, don't you agree?'

'If you can afford it,' Ia smiled.

'Would you like to be able to afford it?'

'Who wouldn't?' Ia took another, larger sip.

'So, Ia, how old are you?'

'I'm not sure, but I think I'm fourteen, maybe fifteen.'

'And why is your voice so pleasant and so out of keeping with your clothes?'

Ia settled back into her chair, sipping her wine almost nonchalantly now, and found herself explaining everything, or nearly everything. It was not difficult for Ia found this woman easy to talk to, almost as if she had always known her. Blossom leaned forward in her chair, her beautiful face concentrating on Ia and making her feel that she was, for this moment, the most important, the only, person in Blossom's life.

'You realise this is a brothel?' Blossom asked without more ado.

'I wondered.'

'It gets called a place of assignation, a pleasure house,

Chez Blossom, a lot of different names. Me? I call it a brothel, that's what it is and I'm not ashamed of my calling.'

'No, Mrs December.'

'Blossom, please. I like my girls to call me by my name. There's nothing special about me, I was like you once. What do you think then, finding yourself in a whore-house?'

'I think it's very beautiful here and it's warm. And I like the champagne.' Ia smiled slyly.

'When you worked at the pub, did you go on the game?'

'No, I didn't.'

'Why not?'

'The men weren't good enough,' Ia said with a defiant shake of the head.

'Am I to take it, then, that you are not against the idea of becoming a whore – if, that is, the clients are "good enough"?' Blossom asked with laughter in her voice.

'I want nice things, Blossom, pretty clothes, hats, possessions, a home of my own one day that's all mine – a cottage somewhere. I don't want to live in a slum, I don't want to spend the rest of my life washing other people's dirty dishes. This seems to be the only way that I'm going to get that life. Being a hard-working girl hasn't got me much so far.'

'In our business, Ia, with that attitude you'll succeed. I get girls who are ashamed, who feel it is all beneath them: they make a living but they are not my successes – the clients sense it, you see. Are you a virgin by any good chance?'

'No, I'm not. I fell in love, more fool me. And . . .' Ia paused; this would have been a good moment to explain her predicament, but she was enjoying herself, she would play this charade a little bit longer. She didn't want to be thrown out into the cold winter street just yet.

When Ia did not continue, Blossom smiled at her,

patted her hand and said, 'I shan't pry. No one's past matters here. It's a pity, but then you're still young ... You'll have to change your name, though.'

'My name? Why?'

'Ia's fine, but really, my dear, whoever heard of a good-time girl called Blewett – it doesn't sound right. Me, I'm Blossom Fish, really, I ask you ...' She laughed loudly again. 'So, I changed my name to December – the month I was born. How about you? Let's think. Ia Dubois, that has a classy ring to it.'

Ia wrinkled her nose at the thought. 'No, I don't think so, sounds foreign. Could I call myself St Just?'

'Ia St Just?' Blossom let the name hang in the air a moment. 'That's good, very good. Now let me explain my rules. You get no wages, you keep half of everything you earn – how much you earn is up to you but I expect a minimum of £100 a week from you.'

'How much? Did you say a hundred pounds?' Ia could hardly get the questions out and her mouth dropped open with surprise.

'With your looks you'll make double. I'll have you taught our techniques.'

'Techniques?' Ia wished she did not sound so much like a parrot.

'Li Po, she's from China, she worked for many years in Shanghai. The Chinese are wonderful with their techniques. A man who has been impotent for years is never impotent in my house. It's all a matter of touch, massage – of mystery. You will be taught how to use your hands, your mouth, even your feet with all the gentleness of a butterfly's wings.' Blossom's eyes glinted with excitement as she explained to Ia. 'I like to supervise your clothes – I shall have your gowns made for you by my dressmaker. You pay me back from your earnings. I insist on cleanliness, you will bathe each day.'

'Each day?'

'Of course. The doctor will examine you every week.

343

We are proud of our health record here: our clients can come and know they won't pick up the clap – it's important. Should you become ill, we will look after you for two weeks, after that you are out – this is not a hospital and I am not a charity. You will not fraternise with the clients outside these four walls – it means instant dismissal if you do. I expect you to behave with decorum. Just because you're a whore, there's no need to be vulgar. There, that's all, I think. I like to show my cards right at the beginning – that way there are no misunderstandings later.' She smiled broadly at Ia. 'So, what do you think? Would you like to join us?'

Ia slumped back in the chair. She frowned, she knew she had to explain and now felt nervous at the prospect. It was no longer a charade, Blossom had talked as the professional she was; she would be irritated with Ia for wasting her time.

'What's the problem, Ia?'

Ia looked into the dark-brown eyes that now studied her with concern. The eyes were so kind, perhaps she would understand.

'I'm afraid I've been wasting your time and your champagne, Blossom. You see, I think I'm pregnant . . .'

A frown appeared on Blossom's face. She looked at the beautiful child hunched in the seat before her and wanted to shake her with exasperation. What a waste, she thought. The ticking of the ormolu clock was the only sound in the room.

'How far gone?'

'Two months I think.'

'I could arrange for you to get rid of it. No old woman with knitting needles, but a doctor friend of mine who helps us out in these odd emergencies.'

'No!' Ia jumped to her feet, spilling her champagne as she did so, and placing one hand protectively across her belly. 'No, I'm not killing it. It's my fault . . .' She felt the annoying prick of tears and looked away quickly.

Blossom stood up and crossed the room. She looked out of the window on to the winter garden. A faint drizzle was falling now. Such a beautiful child with such a dignified quality to her. It seemed a shame to lose her. What on earth was she thinking of? What if the girl became fat? She was slim now – she did not look the sort who would run to fat. She could make sure she didn't, of course. But then what had she just said? She wasn't a charity. She pulled the peignoir closer about her: it was chilly away from the fire – how much colder it must be outside. Where would the girl go? And Blossom knew only too well what would befall her. A winter alone in London, pregnant, no money, no friends . . . Blossom shivered, she hugged her arms about her, her hands moving restlessly up and down the sleeves of her dress. After all this time she could still remember her own winter out in the cold uninterested city streets. The agony of hunger, the pain so intense it was as if her belly was full of animals gnawing away her insides; the cold that had made her bones ache, that had made her mind blank; the rats that had crawled over her, as hungry as she was, at night when she had lain huddled in shop doorways. She could remember the disgust she had felt – disgust with herself and with the men who abused her body, heavy with child. But there had been no choice: either she sold herself or she would have died. Blossom closed her eyes, trying to erase the memories . . . Abruptly she swung round.

'Until you begin to show, you can work as a maid. It will not be time wasted. You can watch the other girls, see how they work, learn how the establishment is organised. But as soon as your belly shows, you'll have to go behind the scenes – a pregnant woman would hardly be the best advertisement, would she?' She laughed now, her decision made.

'You mean it? You'll keep me?'

'Yes, Ia. Don't ask me why. I must be getting

sentimental in my old age.' She laughed again as only a woman can who is confident that she does not look her true age. 'I shan't pay you, however. You must rely on your tips. You can pay the doctor out of those – you'll get your food and uniform free. But . . .' She paused and studied Ia's face for what seemed an age. 'But, if I do all this, when the baby is born it must go.' Ia's hand shot to her mouth to suppress the exclamation of pain that was close to the surface. 'I know of an excellent family at Blackheath who will look after the child for you. I've used them before, in the past . . .' She swallowed hard, knowing full well the agony of indecision Ia was suffering.

'Will I be able to visit my baby?'

'No, Ia.'

'Then thank you for your kindness, Blossom, but I don't think I could do that.' She bent down to pick up her sack.

'Ia, sit down, listen to me. What other alternative do you have? How do you think you can survive in London before the baby is born, let alone afterwards? How will you support it? You'll have to work the pubs or the streets – there isn't a whorehouse that will take you and your child. Where would you leave the child? With some gin-soaked old crone? And what future is there for the child? A boy – does he become a thief, a pickpocket? A girl – how long before you're selling her virginity to the highest bidder because by then, Ia, you won't look as you do now. Your skin will be grey and covered in sores, your body will be sagging from lack of food. No doubt you will be dying of syphilis. You will be in constant pain from the beatings you'll receive because, let me assure you, you can't survive out there alone and you will have a pimp sucking your money from you, hitting you when it isn't enough. Believe me, Ia, I know what I'm talking about. This city is a cesspit for the likes of us if we are not lucky. And today you have had more luck than you will ever be aware of. Don't throw it away.'

'I can understand that the child must go away, but why would I not be allowed to see it?'

'Because it hurts too much, Ia. It hurts to see your child preferring the woman who is bringing it up, who regards that woman as her mother and not you. These people are respectable, good people, how would you explain to the child what you do? It is you I'm thinking of, Ia. I know. I've been down this path . . .' Blossom took a lace handkerchief from her pocket and blew her nose. 'Ia, I had a child when I first came from Jamaica – like you I was a fool, my head full of dreams of love. I insisted on seeing her, I cried for days every time, I worked in a brothel just like this and I lost my job because of my misery. It took me time to get back on my feet. When I did, when I was finally successful, I searched out my daughter – and she spat in my face, Ia.'

Ia reached out a hand towards Blossom.

'It's all right, Ia. It was a long time ago. But if I had my time over again, I would have had that child, farmed her out and forgotten her – in our profession it is the only way. And what's more,' she straightened her back, gave her shoulders a little shrug as if wiping this painful memory away too, 'it's bad for business. I can't have girls who are sad and depressed. Babies and whorehouses do not mix, you must see that.'

'I'll try. I can't promise that I will succeed.'

'Yes you will, Ia. You have courage, and you have sense. My way you can give your child whatever you wish. Come.' She took Ia's hand and led her from the room, across the hall and up the staircase. She opened the door of one of the rooms. 'This could have been yours,' she said, 'but when it is all over you will have one just like it.'

Ia looked stunned as she took in the beautiful room. In the centre was a large four-poster bed, its curtains made of embroidered damask. The wallpaper was handpainted with peacocks. The curtains at the long windows matched the hangings on the bed, and her feet sank into a thick, scrolled Chinese carpet. 'Come,' Blossom ordered again, leading her through a well-fitted dressing-room and bathroom and into a small, elegantly furnished drawing-room with french windows opening on to a balcony that overlooked the garden she had seen from the room below. A curtained alcove held a dining-table and a velvet-covered banquette. 'Sometimes you will have clients who will want to dine with you and frequently to take you whilst they are dining – a strange English habit that, I always found it too distracting, as if one were an extra course. Now, I shall take you to your own room.'

They climbed up two flights of stairs and into the attics. Ia was not prepared for the room she was shown into – white-painted furniture, pretty blue-flowered curtains at the windows, a pale blue carpet on the floor.

'This is a maid's room?' Ia said with disbelief.

'I like everyone who works for me to be happy. I have been poor too, Ia, probably far poorer than you. My mother was born a slave – no one I employ has to live like one. Here's your uniform. Be downstairs by one o'clock; we begin to get busy after two when the men leave their luncheon clubs and before they go to their "At Homes". We get even busier after they've been to them.' She laughed good-naturedly. 'The society ladies are my best allies: they whip them up into such a state of frustrated passion with their silly flirtations and then we get the business . . . One of the other girls will explain to you what to do.'

Left alone, Ia unpacked her bag. Carefully she placed her azure bowl on the dresser beside the wash-basin and ewer. She sat on the bed and looked about her. To think that maids could live like this, and whores in the sort of luxury she had seen downstairs – which could be hers if only she could let her baby go. Would she? Could she?

She lay back on the pillow and looked up at the ceiling. In her heart she had known since she left the orphanage that this would eventually be her way of life. Blossom had asked her if she minded. The truth was that she did not care. She knew that, if she stayed here and worked, she would feel nothing when she gave herself to the clients. She would be like an actress, an actress with a bed for a stage. There was no alternative. What had her year of working as a kitchen maid given her? – chapped hands, a bun in the oven and a hatred of men. She smiled at the ceiling, at the ambitions she had once had of sailing to America to find her fortune. What fortune? Undoubtedly the same fate would have awaited her there. Money – that was the key to everything. One had to be rich to survive, to feel safe. God, how she longed to be safe.

But to lose her child? There was much truth in what Blossom had said: it might be best for the baby if she could bring herself to let it go. But why should Blossom be so kind to a complete stranger? No one was that kind to someone they did not know. What would be expected of her in return, she wondered.

3

For a month Ia had worked for Blossom and in that time nothing had been asked of her, demanded, or expected beyond the normal duties of a maid. There were ten girls in the house: most of them were friendly, a couple kept very much to themselves but none seemed to have been ill treated in any way. The food was good, she was warm, never lonely and, compared with her duties at the Tregowans, not overworked.

She was never expected to be up at dawn, which was lucky since she rarely got to bed before the small hours. Provided she had dusted the main salon by eleven, it did not seem to matter what time she rose. None of the heavy work was hers, there were other maids, less pretty than she, who did those tasks. She helped with the flowers, which could in fact take several hours for flowers were everywhere, some in vases so large and heavy that it took two to move them. Blossom was very particular about the arrangements and insisted that they were done every day. Ia often wondered what her florists' bills must be like but the effect and the all-pervasive scent of the blooms were worth it. The tea and coffee-trays were her responsibility and she was taught how to make coffee in the French style. There was a large bottle of ink with which she refilled the inkwells on the escritoire and then checked that there was plenty of writing-paper and envelopes available. Blossom, with much amusement, had told her that to be allowed into her establishment held a certain cachet for the young bloods about town and it amused them to pen notes on her headed paper to their various friends who did not have the entrée.

When the clients began to arrive, usually after two, the door would be opened by two footmen who, Ia discovered, were not merely footmen but were there to prevent anyone undesirable from entering and on occasion to throw out someone who misbehaved and annoyed Blossom. Ia would stand demurely in her black maid's uniform with a crisp white apron on and a cap with long black ribbons sitting jauntily on her head. Blossom had taught her how to bob in a way that was respectful but at the same time slightly suggestive, and many of the clients eyed her, she noticed, with more than a passing interest. Ia's job was to take the hats and coats. It was important to memorise who owned which for she quickly learned that, after the visit, to return the correct garment and present it with her saucy bob ensured a good fat tip. It amazed her that there were people with so much money that they could tip her a shilling or even a florin just for giving them their coat. All this money she consigned to her azure bowl in her blue bedroom.

She enjoyed most the evenings when they were very busy and Blossom would order her into the great entertaining salon to help serve the drinks and the canapés, and to run messages. Ia loved this room. It was on the first floor and ran the full width and length of the house. The walls were covered in gold wild silk, the lighting from the small lamps scattered about the room was always subdued. All the furniture was white, even the grand piano. The comfortable sofas – large enough only for two – were upholstered in rich brocade and in this room the flowers were only ever white and yellow. And then there were the girls to admire. Each evening they appeared in different gowns, astonishing creations of silk and satin, sequined and beaded. In this room it always appeared as if there were a party under way.

The atmosphere was always relaxed since most of the men had been coming here for a long time and Blossom always knew their particular fancies and which girls pleased them most. Blossom would talk and joke with her clients. Anyone seeing her would have assumed that these were friends she was entertaining but, Ia noted, Blossom's glance was everywhere, watching all her girls, all her customers. She would signal discreetly to Ia, whisper in her ear which girl was about to take a customer to bed, and Ia would race up the stairs to tell the maids which bedroom to prepare.

Sometimes she was called upon to assist the upstairs maids. Ia did not mind: she wanted to learn all there was to know. So she had learned the correct way to turn the beds down; she was told how important it was to keep the temperature of the rooms warm since this helped the clients' libidos. Some rooms had to be scented with joss-sticks, others with Blossom's own specially prepared perfume sachets burning in a small brazier. One man, the maids told her, always insisted that a fresh bucket of horse manure be standing in the corner of the room. When the client had finished it was the maids' job to fill the girl's bath or her bidet while the head maid measured the vinegar into the douches which each girl administered between each encounter. At last the douche which Frederick had talked about was explained to her. They would help the girl to dress again before she ventured downstairs in search of another patron. Then they would strip the bed and remake it with fresh linen. There were girls whose beds were stripped six, sometimes ten, times a night. They always appeared cheerful, a fact that surprised Ia. There were times when one client stayed the whole night. Ia would have loved to know what was the difference in the rates.

Everyone adored Blossom. The only criticism she had heard, and that from only a couple of the girls, was that Blossom would allow no whips or instruments of bondage in her house. The girls balked at this, feeling that they were being cheated out of extra earnings, but Blossom was adamant. In fact, Ia was told, one girl who had smuggled her own whip in had been summarily dismissed. There was much speculation abovestairs as to why Blossom had this ban, whereas any brothel worth its salt always had a 'correction room'. Ia, remembering the beatings she had endured from her father, thought she understood – Blossom must have suffered too in the past.

Now she learned that Jimmy, the man who had brought her here the first time, was in fact Blossom's lover – she never entertained clients herself. But it was woe betide any girl who so much as looked at Jimmy for it transpired that Blossom did have a fault – an uncontrollable jealousy.

Ia regarded this period as a time of learning. She did as she was told and watched the girls at work with an eagle eye. She noticed how they flirted, how they teased, how every man's degree of anticipation could be heightened by the girls' expertise. She noted how cleverly they plied their clients with drink; she had learned that from every bottle of champagne which was bought each girl earned a shilling. But they never allowed the clients to drink too much and so complain in the morning that they could not remember what had happened the night before. There was always music, sometimes played by one of the girls who was a skilled pianist, but usually by a professional performer. Sometimes the girls sang to the guests; they played games with them, charades and guessing games. Each evening resembled an elegant party, but a party with no ugly women, and a party where one guest would suddenly disappear upstairs to be replaced by another guest. The house was superbly run.

Ia had been here for two months. Everyone was tired. Christmas had been fairly quiet but at New Year they had been run off their feet.

Ia entered Blossom's study quietly, the room in which she had first been interviewed, a large trug of flowers in her hands. Blossom was seated at her desk, her head in her hands, a look of dejection on her face.

'Blossom, are you unwell?'

'Ia, my little one. No, I am well. But I am sad.'

'Can I help?'

'No, it's Emily, she has to go, and I always hate it when I have to tell a girl.'

'Why? What has she done wrong?' Ia asked, concerned. She liked Emily particularly, a red-headed girl, a bit scatter-brained but one who was always kind to her.

'I fear she is getting too old.'

'Too old?' Ia asked in surprise. She did not know how old Emily was but she was sure she could not be more than twenty-two.

'She is twenty now and is asked for less and less by the clients. You see, Ia, the men prefer young girls, the younger the better. The fact that Emily is still a beautiful woman is irrelevant. And unfortunately for her, she has not managed to acquire her own group of patrons who want only her. I had one girl here, who worked until she was almost thirty simply because Lord Keble would have no other and was willing to pay extremely well for her. She worked here until he died.'

'I hadn't thought of that. How long do most girls last, then?'

'If I get them at fourteen – four years on average, five if they are lucky. So, really, Emily has done well. It's just that I like her – perhaps more than I should. Now she will have to go to an inferior house – of course I shall recommend her most highly. In a couple of years she will be told to leave there and go to another further down the scale. It is a gradual descent to the streets.'

'But surely she must have savings, from all she has earned here?'

'Not everyone's like you, Ia, saving like a little squirrel. And you know Emily. Money slips through her fingers like water – she spends more on clothes than any other girl. She likes jewellery too. At least she has some of that she can sell.'

'Why don't you start a saving scheme for them so that when they leave they have a start in the outside world?'

'Ia, that's not a bad idea. But would they trust me with their money?'

'Everyone trusts you, Blossom,' Ia said, carefully removing the dead flowers from an arrangement and putting them on the sheet of newspaper she had placed on the priceless carpet. 'You could "invest" it for them, make it grow. Isn't that how some of your clients make their money?' Ia stopped, aware that she was being indiscreet – she not only listened to conversations but recalled and understood them.

'You never fail to amaze me, Ia. You are such a quiet little thing and yet so intelligent.'

'Me quiet?' Ia laughed at the notion. 'Only because I'm too busy learning at the moment.'

'You've made up your mind to stay then?'

'Yes. It's a bit of a shock to hear how short a time I can

expect to be here. I'd hoped for more like six years. I've been talking to the other girls, you see, trying to work out how much money I could expect to make. I want to save it and then, well, I think I'd like to do this too – though obviously on a more modest scale.'

'What? Be a madam?'

'Yes. I don't really like men very much, but I think I understand them. So, I'd like to save and be like you, entertain them and let other girls sleep with them.'

Blossom threw back her head and laughed her loud joyous laugh. 'And I took you in thinking that you looked like a naturally born whore. Now you tell me you don't like men! I must have been mad.'

'It doesn't mean I can't pretend to like them,' she said quickly, in case she had given Blossom the wrong impression.

'You know, Ia, I agree with you, and that is exactly what makes me a good madam. I know what they want, I make sure they get it, and I never feel at all involved with them – I never did, even when I was having to sleep with them. I used to lie there and think of other things, of my homeland, of my retirement!' Her laugh rang out. 'You're right, Ia, the first requisite of a good whore is to be a good actress and a good liar. A woman I once knew gave me the best advice for anyone in this profession. She told me to tell them they are the best you've ever had, and that their cock is the most magnificent thing you have ever seen. They always believe you.'

There was a gentle tap at the door and a frightened Emily appeared. Ia excused herself, and went into the hall. There, as she did the flowers, she mulled over the conversation. It had been a valuable one. She had little time, that was apparent, to earn large sums of money. She would need a group of patrons of her own willing to go with her when the time came. And she must never allow herself to become involved with the girls in the way that Blossom did.

*

355

A client commenting on what a fat maid Blossom employed hastened Ia's removal to the back of the house. Here she helped clean the silver and mend clothes and any linen that needed it. The other staff and the girls were kind to her, especially the girls – forever bringing her little presents and clothes for the baby. It seemed that the birth of her baby was a source of great interest and excitement to them. But Ia found the work boring and repetitive and longed to be in the front of the house.

It was quite by chance that one day in March, in Blossom's study, she discovered that Blossom had difficulty reading and writing. She had been relying on Jimmy, her lover and the brothel tout, to do her books and paperwork – she had trusted him completely. This arrangement had ceased abruptly the week before when Jimmy had been found in bed with one of the girls, a new arrival. Blossom's fury had been awesome and within the hour Jimmy and the girl were out on the pavement, in the pouring rain, with their baggage.

Blossom threw a sheaf of papers angrily to the floor as Ia entered the room. She was battling with the books, afraid of finding that Jimmy had cheated her financially as well. Picking up the papers, Ia couldn't help noticing how ill formed Blossom's handwriting looked.

Since she could read and write, Ia had immediately offered to help. Alice had taught her the basics of arithmetic. Now, to her pleased surprise, she discovered she had a natural aptitude for figures. She quickly learned the rudiments of book-keeping which Blossom could explain but not execute. And nothing gave her greater pleasure than to admire the neat columns of figures when they tallied. She quickly had the paperwork organised, the clients' monthly accounts ready to be presented, the list of debtors and the list of bills ready to be paid. Suddenly she was no longer cleaning silver and sewing; she had become Blossom's assistant.

In large red-bound books Blossom's clients were listed.

How often they came, what they spent, their preferences. Ia studied them with interest – it seemed anyone of any importance patronised this house. Out of fun she looked up the name of her former employer. There was no account for George but to Ia's amazement she saw the name of Daisy Tregowan.

'Blossom, there's a *woman* listed here.' Ia swung around from her desk to face her employer.

'We have several.'

'Women?' she said, disbelieving.

'I thought you liked to think you knew everything, Ia.' Blossom chuckled.

'I thought I did.'

'Well, two of them come here for men. I always know in advance when they are coming and arrange handsome young men to service them. Of course it has to be done very discreetly – they come in the back way, that's why you've never seen them.'

'The others?'

'I've two who like women and one who likes to watch.'

'Like women?'

'Yes, it's very common. You get a lot of whores who prefer women to men. Not surprising really, is it? Maybe you're one,' Blossom said.

'Not likely, not me. I think that's disgusting,' Ia said firmly.

'Remember Ia, in this job nothing's disgusting. We don't stand in judgement – ever.'

'No, Blossom, sorry, of course you're right,' Ia said meekly while thinking the opposite. 'This Lady Tregowan,' she went on with studied casualness, 'what's she?'

'Daisy Tregowan? She's trouble, very demanding but she likes boys, the younger the better. Why are you interested?'

'It was the name. I think I must have seen a postcard of her . . . you know, those of famous beauties you can buy.'

When Blossom left the room Ia took pen and paper and noted down the dates that Daisy had been in the house, whom she had been with and how much she had spent. She did not know why she did it but, having done so, she folded the paper carefully and slipped it into her pocket.

As she understood the inner workings of the house, as she totalled up the figures and saw the fortune that Blossom was amassing, so she was more than ever determined that, once she had served her apprenticeship here, she would start her own establishment.

Now she could hardly wait for the baby to be born so that she could begin to work in earnest for a better future for both of them.

4

It was on a hot June morning, just after she had consumed a large bowl of strawberries and cream, that Ia went into labour. For the rest of that day and well into the night Ia did the inconceivable – she caused total disruption to the smooth running of Blossom's brothel. Between clients the girls, instead of reporting back to Blossom, were sneaking up to her room to see how she was, to hold her hand, mop her brow and ask if there were anything they could do. 'Have the bloody thing for me,' she groaned in answer. Blossom herself, while pretending to be annoyed with the girls for neglecting the clients, also spent much of her time running up and down the stairs. She found she was consumed with anxiety. Finally the tension became too much and for the first time since she had opened her establishment, Blossom closed it. Firmly she shepherded a crowd of disgruntled clients to the door and left instructions that no one else was to be admitted. Between pains Ia thought how ironic it was – all this excitement in a house where procreation was a dirty word, where pregnancy was a serious impediment to a career, and where the abortionist rather than the midwife would normally be called.

Ia cursed and roared through her labour. She did not like what men did to women, and she liked this even less.

The baby was a girl. It was impossible to move in the small attic bedroom as everyone crowded in to see. They sighed, cooed and kissed the baby and several cried at the first sight of her. Ia, amidst all this adulation, was disappointed by her reaction. She had expected to love the baby immediately; in fact, she looked at the child quite dispassionately, thought she was the ugliest child she had ever seen, was annoyed by her crying, and knew she would never forgive her the pain she had caused. When the midwife handed her the baby to put to the breast she felt only repugnance. The only consolation that she could see in such an attitude was that she would not mind in the least when the baby was taken away from her.

A week later matters had changed. Without warning Ia found herself entwined in a thick blanket of maternal love. She was besotted with the baby she had called Francine. She wanted her awake all the time and would frequently poke her when she slept just to see her eyes open again.

The plan was for the child to be removed after two weeks, for Ia's breasts to be bandaged, to dry up her milk, and for her to go on a strict diet to regain her figure so that she could be back at work in at least a month. But now she begged Blossom to let her have her a few weeks more. Blossom should have refused; haunted by the memory of how she had felt when her own baby had been taken from her, Blossom relented. Ia had Francine with her for three happy months.

It was a grave error. When the time finally came for the baby to be taken to the family in Blackheath, Ia pushed the heavy chest of drawers against the door and refused to open it. It took the combined weight of the two large footmen to push the door open. They found Ia crouched on her bed, clinging to her baby and looking at them with the wild eyes of an animal at bay. Ia screamed and ranted with rage at Blossom; the baby, sensing the drama, added her screams. The other girls, collected in the passageway, stood with tears pouring down their faces begging Blossom to let the baby stay. Blossom, her face rigid with anguish, wrenched the baby from Ia, wrapped her in a shawl and swept hurriedly from the room, with Ia's screams echoing in her ears.

Ia refused to see anyone for a week. She would not venture from her room, she would not eat. She lay on her bed gazing at the ceiling, her heart, she felt, turning to ice inside her. For that week Blossom was patient. At the end of it she confronted Ia.

'This will not do, Ia. You must get up, dress and come downstairs.'

Ia turned her head to the wall.

'Ia, I don't want to get angry with you but I have been patient long enough. Either you get up and come downstairs and begin work or I must insist that you vacate my premises.'

'You wouldn't do that.'

'I would and I will. When you first came here I told you I was not a charitable institution. I have waited long enough for you. If you cannot live without your child, then here is the address.' She produced a piece of paper which Ia grabbed from her and read eagerly, memorising. 'Go and get her, then what will you do? Where will you sleep tonight? How will you feed her? Go on the streets will you, and who will have you with a child in your arms? The decision is yours, Ia, no one else's.' She turned and walked resolutely from the room; she felt nothing but pity for the girl but she could not allow her to see it.

'I hate you, you mean old cow!' Ia screamed desperately after her.

Ia read and reread the address so many times that soon the piece of paper was tattered. Then she lay consumed with a burning hatred for Blossom, for life and its cruelty. Round and round in her mind anger and hatred chased each other . . . Abruptly she stood up, and crossed to the mirror to study her face. What was happening to her? She didn't hate Blossom, how could she hate someone who had tried only to help her? Blossom was right – if she collected her child, they were both doomed to no future whatsoever. And if she lay here sulking and grieving, she would never earn enough to be reunited with her child.

She bathed quickly. Hanging on the side of her wardrobe was one of the dresses that Blossom had had made for her once her figure had regained its normal slimness. She slipped the silk gown over her head and called for one of the maids who was cleaning in the corridor to come and help her with the unfamiliar dress. She wore no stays or pantaloons; she wanted to be naked beneath the fine dress – she wanted to be different from the other girls firmly laced into their corsets. She brushed her hair, letting it flow loosely down her back – she wanted to *look* different too, from the others with their elaborate coiffures. She pinched her cheeks to give them some colour – not for her the heavy make-up of the others. From a shoebox she took the scarlet slippers she had ordered. She was proud of her small feet and had decided that red shoes were to be her trademark. Then she stood back and studied herself in the mirror. She liked what she saw. The pale grey silk dress matched the grey of her eyes. It fitted tightly showing off her breasts, fuller now since the baby, and then flowed loosely, while the silk clung to the contours of her body. She had fought long and hard with Blossom as to how her dresses were to be made. She had rejected pleating, beading and ruffles, and had known instinctively that she should be simply dressed. That would accentuate the air of innocence which, though false, still shone in her face. Ia twirled in front of the mirror and remembered another mirror, another new dress, another transformation, so many years ago. She grinned at her image.

'Bain't I blooming lovely,' she said out loud before she swept from the room, down the long staircase and into the salon. It was too early for clients but the room was already full of the girls, Blossom also. Her entrance was met with a gratifying silence followed swiftly by a whispered hum.

'Good evening, Blossom. It's a beautiful evening,' she said smiling.

'Ia. I knew you would be sensible. So, you're ready?'

'Yes, Blossom. I want as many men as you can arrange for me. I want my daughter back.' She flicked her hair back over her shoulders in her usual gesture of defiance.

Overnight Ia was a sensation. All the girls who worked for Blossom were beautiful but none of them had Ia's strangely innocent beauty, that of a child-woman. Within the month, Ia had her own group of clients who would have only her.

Her success led to problems. She lost favour with the other girls. While she had been no threat to them, they had liked her but now she was so popular and had taken men from several of them they were no longer friendly. At first she had been hurt and had tried to make overtures to them to put their relationships back on the old easy footing. But she saw that her efforts made no difference. It began to make her miserable. Then the professional she had already become determined to ignore them – a long face would not bring her the clients and their longed-for money.

But she had Blossom. Blossom was proud of her and enjoyed her company. Not only were they employer and employee, but they became friends. She continued to do all Blossom's paperwork. And she still made a note of each of Lady Tregowan's visits.

Sally, one of the older girls, had been told to leave and Ia, who had already been moved into a fine room, was selected to move again, into her room, one of the grandest in the house. It was at the front and bigger than the other rooms, more opulent in its decoration and with the most luxurious bathroom. It had once been Blossom's room in the days when she had entertained customers. This new privilege did nothing to endear Ia to the others.

Ia had all manner of men. They were young and old. They came in all shapes and sizes – she did not mind who they were or what they looked like. She did not care. It was as if, when Francine had been taken from her, her mind, her body and her soul were left in a state of limbo without feeling. The men were objects to her, objects to be used for her ambitions. While they mauled her body, while they sweated and grunted as they heaved up and down upon her, she sighed and moaned and screamed with simulated pleasure while all the time she thought of other things. As they rolled off her she would smile at them, sigh with pleasure, assure them it had never been like that before for her – 'ever'. And when they left the room, the door was barely shut before she was quickly noting down in her little book the fee she would get. She bathed after each client. She would rub her flesh vigorously to rid herself of their smell, of anything to do with them. She would put on her dress again, she would descend the stairs and, her face glowing, she would glide into the salon in search of another body to use for her own ends.

Ia was a consummate actress.

And then Ia fell in love.

The evening had started much as any other. Ia prowled about the room assessing the customers. She had learned quickly: if they did not look affluent enough, she avoided them. She had warned Blossom she was interested only in the rich and the large tips she could expect from them on top of the fee. She had presumed she would get a lecture, but Blossom acquiesced – Ia was bringing in such earnings that she was not about to argue with the girl, and Blossom was dependent on Ia's expertise with the book-keeping.

The door opened and with a flurry a large party of men entered in high spirits after an evening at the theatre and a long and drunken dinner. Blossom fluttered up to welcome them, coaxing, controlling – parties who had been drinking heavily were always difficult to handle, the bonhomie could so easily deteriorate into a brawl, arguments and threats. The Earl of Holt had brought the group, several of whom had not been here before.

Ia watched the party with predatory interest. She did not mind the drunks as Blossom did, in fact she enjoyed them. Her policy was to choose the one who was the worst for wear. Then she would persuade him to have every embellishment in the book. She would take so long with the initial foreplay that, if she were lucky, he would fall asleep. This meant that Ia could have a whole night's undisturbed sleep herself. In the morning, when he awoke, she would purr over him, telling him what a superb lover he had been – the strongest, the most enduring of any man she had known.

'When? Oh when will you visit me again?' she would ask breathlessly, caressing him, twirling her legs about him. Invariably such talk excited the man to such a degree that he would take her there and then which, of course, was duly added to the bill.

Ia was a consummate whore.

The party milled about the room eyeing the girls, talking, laughing, flirting with them before they made their final choice. One man stayed back, leaning against a pillar, his arms folded, watching the proceedings with an ironic smile that played about his mouth. Strangely, his dress suit seemed darker, his shirt-front whiter, his collar stiffer so that the other men paled into insignificance beside him. Ann and Faith both tripped across the room to engage him in conversation, he bowed, he smiled, he laughed but, with looks of disappointment, they moved away. Flora attempted to interest him, then Iris, but to no avail. It appeared he was not interested in anyone in particular but was content to stand, a little apart, and survey the company. Ia watched all this with mounting interest aware that it was as if, in the whole crowded room, there was only this man. He had an aura of superiority that was like a challenge, an air of dominance that was a tangible thing. Ia, conscious that she was staring, and with no intention of being spurned like the others, averted her eyes, but, as if they had a life of their own, she found herself looking at him again. He was tall and slim and carried himself well. He was not conventionally handsome but there was a brooding strength in his face that made him attractive. His dark hair had the merest curl. There was no beard or moustache covering his skin which was tanned as if he had just returned from abroad. It was his large, dark-brown eyes which were his finest feature. They watched everything, registering all, amused by what they saw of life and its foibles.

To her intense surprise Ia discovered that she was looking at him as a man and not as a client. That had not happened to her before. What was more, she realised with mounting alarm, she wanted to talk to him, wanted to know him, and wanted him to choose her. She lifted a glass of champagne and abruptly turned her back on him. This was not what she wanted. Feeling flustered by her reactions she forced herself to laugh and joke with the shortest, fattest, youngest member of the group.

'You'll find no satisfaction there.' She knew it was he for the deep, strong voice was how she had known he would speak.

'Perhaps I do not look for satisfaction,' she said, lightly, half turning, but not looking at him. Suddenly she found she was afraid to look in case she saw the same faintly bored look of indifference she had seen on his face with the other girls.

'That would seem a pity. Such beauty should be satisfied.' She listened for laughter in his voice but it was not there. Now she turned and looked up at him; she became aware, as she did so, that she had such a longing for this man that it was totally illogical. 'Come,' he said and held his hand out to her and she, taking it as if mesmerised, followed him.

Ia knew she would remember that night for the rest of her life. He made love to her with such sensuality, such gentleness, such ingenuity, such ferocity that she realised that, despite her experience of men, she had never once known physical love. He seduced her, coaxed her body, played with her, made demands of her. But always he waited – determined that she should climax again and again.

Ia who had moaned, cried and sighed in false ecstasy, now did the same with genuine passion. As he lifted her senses yet again and she approached the oblivion of total release she screamed, 'I love you!'

Later, she lay back against the pillows, her body soaked with their sweat, her eyes half closed with exhaustion. He sat at the end of the bed facing her, watching her intently. She hoped to see tenderness in his eyes but it was not there; instead, he looked at her with the half-amused expression she had seen downstairs.

'Satisfied?'

'Um . . .' She cuddled down into the bed and lifted her hand towards him, longing to touch him again.

'You said you loved me.' He moved up the bed towards her. She smiled, expecting an embrace but he moved to one side.

'I know.'

'Do you always say that?'

'Never.' She smiled again, enjoying the languorous

366

pleasure of her own body. She looked at him and marvelled that she had ever thought him not handsome.

'I didn't know that whores were capable of love,' he stated, turning towards the bedside table and pouring them both a glass of champagne. Ia, who had for the first and only time found pleasure in a perfect sexual encounter, felt her brief happiness collapsing about her and knew there was nothing she could do. She was a whore. He was her man only for this one night. How could she have been so foolish as to allow emotions she had thought she did not possess to take hold of her? She felt the pricking of tears behind her eyes and her skin tautened with sadness. She fought the feelings and the tears, with all the strength the years had taught her. She picked up her shawl and wrapped it about her, feeling suddenly chilled.

'I didn't feel like a whore when I said it. I'm sorry, I didn't mean to embarrass you. Forget I said it,' she said bravely, raising her glass of champagne as she felt her heart shattering inside her.

'I took it as a compliment.' He smiled at her and she wished there were a way she could clutch at that smile and keep it with her always.

'I wish I weren't a whore . . .' she heard herself whisper.

'So do I,' with disbelief she heard him reply.

In the morning she informed Blossom that she was leaving.

5

'Peter who?'

'Peter Willoughby. He was in the Earl of Holt's party.'

'I don't give a damn whose party he was in. Who is he?'

'I didn't ask.'

'Ia! Ia, have you lost complete control of your senses? You walk in here, you tell me you are leaving, that some man has asked you to become his mistress and then you tell me you don't know who he is.'

'I love him.'

Blossom ceased pacing up and down the room, which she had done non-stop since Ia had given her the news, and slumped into a chair, not elegantly this time, but with a sagging of her body, a drooping of her head. 'Love? Whores don't love, you fool. Have you learned nothing here?'

'He makes me feel as if I'm not a whore.'

'And of course he told you he loves you?' Blossom sneered.

'No, he didn't. But I know he likes me. He doesn't want me to work here. He wants me entirely for himself.'

'What wage is he paying you?'

'We didn't discuss money. He has a house he is going to set me up in, he said. I can have a maid and my own carriage. I don't want anything else from him.'

Blossom looked at Ia with exasperation. 'And what happens, young woman, when he tires of you, as he will; they always do. A year, I give you, and then he will be looking for a new excitement. You will be a year older and he will be looking for something younger and fresher.'

'I've my savings from here,' Ia said staunchly.

'How long do you think they will last? How are you going to get Francine back when the savings have all gone? Oh Ia, of all the girls who have passed through my hands in the past thirty years, you are the one I credited with some sense. I watched you with the men, your totally professional approach, your ambitions, the way you saved your money. Now look at you. You look like a lovesick moon-calf.'

'I can't help myself, Blossom. It's happened. I didn't

want it to, but I can't not go to him. If I stay, I know I shall regret it for the rest of my life.'

'In that case, I think you're an ungrateful little chit and I wash my hands of you.' Blossom stood up and faced Ia, her brown eyes flashing with anger. 'I take you in off the streets. I put a roof over your head while you have the baby. I even let you stay here for three months not working . . .'

'You've earned plenty from me in the nine months I've been working. And before that I did the books for you and never asked for a penny – and I could have done, you'd have been lost without me.' Ia's voice rose in anger.

'You are an ungrateful, selfish *bitch*. You needn't think you can come back here when he's discarded you, that I can promise you.'

'He won't discard me.'

'You bloody fool, of course he will.'

'I thought you disapproved of vulgarity?' Ia snapped.

'How dare you speak to me like that. Go and don't you ever bloody well come back.' Ia stepped forward as if about to speak. 'Get out of my sight . . .' Blossom screamed.

'As you wish.' Ia shrugged her shoulders and left the room. In her room she hurriedly packed her bags. She expected that she would be angry at Blossom's reaction but instead she felt sad: she knew she had lost a good friend. She said goodbye to no one at the brothel but let herself silently out of the door and stood with her cases on the pavement waiting for Peter. It was not until she was there, with her bags at her feet, that she suddenly wondered if he would come, or whether she had imagined it all. For an instant she was afraid but the fear disappeared as a spanking phaeton, pulled by two black horses, drew up. The minute the carriage ground to a halt the horses were pawing the ground impatient to be off again.

Peter leaped down, swung her into his arms and kissed her soundly on the lips while Ia laughed with happiness and wonder. From an upstairs window Blossom watched the scene. She was crying. She was angry with herself for caring so much. She had never become so involved with one of her girls before; she knew it was a mistake but she could not help herself. She loved Ia and she feared for her as if she were her own flesh and blood.

Peter took Ia to Rules for lunch. Ia had never been taken to a restaurant before and she sat on the plush seat, glancing this way and that, enjoying the bustle, the famous names, and quite forgetting, in her excitement, to pretend to a sophistication she was not feeling. She sipped her champagne and toyed with the food, more interested in her surroundings. But, while she was enjoying the experience, she wanted to be away from here, she wanted to be alone with Peter, in bed.

'What are you thinking, Ia?'

'That I want to be in bed with you.'

He laughed loudly. 'Was last night not enough for you, my darling?'

'I don't think I shall ever have enough of you.' She smiled, her heart jolting at the endearment. No one had ever called her darling before – it must mean he loved her, too.

'Are you naked beneath that dress?'

'Yes.' To her astonishment she found she was blushing. She could not remember doing that for years.

'Be like that for me always.' His voice, normally deep, was even deeper. The expression in his eyes was a look full of longing for her, his voice so full of passion, and Ia knew that all her body needed was the sound of his voice, one glance from him, to be ready for him.

Her wish was not granted immediately. He continued to linger over his food, then a brandy, then another. Ia was tormented with frustration, and he, appearing to sense her discomfort, seemed to enjoy it and prolonged the meal further by ordering a savoury. At last he stood to leave and eagerly she collected her bag, but then he went from table to table greeting friends. Ia, despite her eagerness to be alone with him, would not have missed this for the world. For her to be introduced as an equal to his friends, to have them stand to greet her made her feel so proud. In the carriage she sat as close to him as possible enjoying the lean feel of his body. To her dismay, he ordered the coachman to drive to Bond Street.

He bought her a fur cape, new hats, shoes, petticoats – no pantaloons, no corsets, no night-dresses. She knew that her nakedness beneath her gown shocked the vendeuse who measured her for the ten gowns which Peter had selected from their pattern book. Ia just smiled and flicked her hair over her shoulders. If he wanted her naked, naked she would be.

It was early evening before the carriage slowed down in a tree-lined, peaceful road in St John's Wood. Neat villas in equally neat gardens stood on either side. They stopped in front of a small, white-painted cottage with latticed windows and gothic gables, and with a large wrought-iron knocker. The small front garden was a riot of summer flowering – roses climbed the walls of the house and the scent of syringa filled the air. Taking her hand he led her up the cobbled path. The door was opened by a smiling maid, Jennie, who bobbed a curtsy which made Ia both blush and giggle. Peter, with mock solemnity, lifted her and carried her over the threshold while she laughed and laughed until she ached.

'Peter, it's wonderful.' She swung around to him, her face glowing with excitement as they stood in the sitting-room. The room was large, in total variance to the outside of the house which gave the impression that everything in it would be on a small scale. It was decorated with bold paisley-patterned wallpaper. Deep claret-coloured velvet curtains, with gold-trimmed pelmets, hung at the windows to the front of the house and at the windows which opened on to steps leading to the back garden. The furniture was new and in the latest black lacquer. 'I fear it's all a dream and I shall wake up any minute.'

'It's no dream. And if you don't like anything you can change it.'

'I don't want to change anything. It's all perfect.' She looked about the room. She had never given houses and furnishing a thought, beyond that vague dream of one day having a cottage of her own. Now she was standing in it and it was as if, when Peter had chosen everything, he had already known what her taste would be. She continued with her excited inspection of the room; she admired the gilt clock which chimed prettily at that moment. Suddenly she stopped dead in her tracks. Everything was perfect, decorated with sure taste by a woman, she was certain of it. But who? Had there been a mistress here before her, whose choice this was? If so, what had happened to her? Had he tired of her, was she to take her place?

'Bored with admiring?' He grinned at her.

'No, no. Can we see the rest?' She managed to smile back. She could not ask him. She realised she could never ask anything. As his mistress, it was not her place to enquire about his past; he would tell her only what he wanted her to know and she would have to accept that.

He led the way on the tour of inspection. Into the dining-room, small but large enough for six to dine in comfort – though she could not imagine whom they would ever invite. There was a study for Peter. Compared with the other rooms, this was too austere and too functional for her taste. But she had no such complaints about their bedroom which had red-and-white striped wallpaper. White silk curtains hung at the windows; there was a fine brass bed with a large white counterpane, there were rugs on the floor, intricately carved Indian furniture, and a door which led into a bathroom with running water and a large gas geyser. The bedroom and bathroom extended over the whole of the first floor – there were no spare bedrooms. A small pine staircase on the landing led to the attic where Jennie slept.

'So, you like it?'

'I love it, Peter. I know we'll be happy here. And I shall look after you so well, make you wonderful dinners – I hope,' she giggled. 'I can't cook. I never have done, you see.'

'Jennie will cook. I don't want you to get tired from cooking and cleaning for me. You have a different purpose in my life.' He led her to the bed and began to undress her. 'I shan't be living here, of course.'

She sat up, disappointment etched on her face. 'You won't?'

'No, I can't think what made you think I would.' He pushed her back on the bed, his head nestling at her breast. Tense with an unaccustomed anxiety she felt nothing; she wanted only to ask him where he lived, with whom; most of all she wanted to know if he was married. But she dared not ask. He looked at her, puzzled. 'What's the matter? Where's the passionate Ia of last night?'

'I'm sorry.' She touched his face, gently. 'It's all so strange.'

'Ia, no man lives with his mistress, you must know that.'

'Of course I do, I was just being silly. It was the excitement.' She lay back on the pillow willing herself to forget, and to react to him as he wanted. She must learn to control her feelings, forget her dreams. She was his mistress, nothing more; she turned her head into the pillows as he made love to her. Her eyes began to fill with tears. She was his mistress; she wanted to be his wife.

'Ia!' He stopped fondling her body, sat up and looked at her with exasperation. 'Ia, you're like a lump of wood. I shall begin to be annoyed, I expect better than this.'

373

She too sat up, and looked at him anxiously. 'I'm sorry, Peter, I just don't know what's wrong with me.'

'Perhaps you're jealous?' He looked sideways at her.

'Jealous, me?'

'Yes, you. You're all the same, you women.'

'No, no, it's nothing like that,' she said, hurriedly. 'Why should I, of all people, be jealous? I'm grateful for what you are giving me.'

'I think you're lying, Ia St Just. I think you began to wonder downstairs who had decorated this house, who had chosen the furniture, who had been here before you.'

'What on earth gave you that idea?' She tried to laugh, but with little success.

'So, to put your mind at rest and so that I can enjoy your body before I go, I shall tell you. I bought the house ready-furnished. You are most definitely the first.'

'And the last.' The blonde hair was flicked back as she looked him boldly in the eyes.

Chapter Nine

1

Ia had looked forward to having a maid. After years of being told what to do, she wanted to enjoy the privilege of ordering someone else about. But Jennie was a rule unto herself. When Peter was there she always had an air of submissiveness about her, she was respectful to Ia, bobbing at every opportunity, smiling and willing. But when he was not there, Jennie did very much what she wanted to do and not necessarily what Ia wished. Her insolent attitude and her idleness were bad enough but Ia found after the first two weeks that she resented Jennie. She resented her for having known Peter longer than she. She resented the fact that Jennie had lived in this house before her, that she knew better what Peter's preferences were, how he liked things done, what he liked to eat and how to launder his shirts. Ia had never loved before. She realised now that the feelings she had had for Frederick had been the product of a desperate need for love and approval. But now, having found love, she had also found jealousy.

It would have been impossible to find fault with Jennie when Peter was in residence – the house was spotless, the food excellent, his laundry perfect. Ia had once tried to explain to him that things were not as they should be when he was away but he had become irritated that she should bother him with complaints about the servant. Why on earth couldn't she solve the problem herself? he had asked shortly.

Ia was aware that she herself was, in a way, responsible for the maid's attitude. Since meeting Peter she appeared to have had a complete change of personality. Whereas once she had known exactly what she wanted and where she was going – and to hell with the world – she now found she was haunted by a hundred insecurities. She was certain he would tire of her. She was convinced that she did not amuse him enough. She spent hours at her mirror studying her face anxiously. She ate little when he was away in case she grew fat. She read every new book published, even if she did not enjoy it. She forced herself to study *The Times* daily, though it bored her, for fear that, if she were not well read, she, in turn, might bore him.

Peter had caused this change in her. Not only did she not know when he was coming, but she could never be certain what he would be like when he did appear. There seemed to be several Peters. There was her favourite, the joking, relaxed Peter, who, when he made love to her, did so with tenderness and unselfishly. Then there was the silent Peter, who would sit brooding, a glass of port in his hand, as he stared into space and seemed not to hear a word she said. This Peter frequently left without touching her. And there was the Peter she dreaded, who would arrive and find fault with everything, her appearance, the meal, her conversation. On these occasions he would quickly order her to bed and take her roughly with no thought for her pleasure. These constant changes in him reduced her to a state of acute anxiety in her need to please him.

Ia was aware of the changes in herself and they worried her. For she realised that the nervous, jumpy creature she had become was a different woman from the one he had invited to live with him, and therein lay the very real danger. And yet, as honest as she was with herself, it was as if she could do nothing about it.

She wished she knew more about him. After months of living in this house she knew nothing, for she never asked. She waited for him to tell her what he wanted her to know, which was little. One or two small clues he dropped by accident: that he had been in India for the past two years but whether in the army, in the diplomatic corps, or in business, she did not know. She had learned that he loved heliotrope and immediately bought herself a large bottle of perfume, the kind that Blossom used. She feared that the perfume reminded him of some lost love, but her need to please him was greater than her fear of a woman from his past. By chance she heard that he had been to Oxford, that he knew the Prince of Wales, that he hated onions and loved ice-cream. But where he lived, and with whom, and how rich he was were still mysteries to her.

She spent too much time alone. There was no regular pattern to his arrivals. In one week he might see her five times and then he would not appear again for ten days or so. And he never stayed the whole night. It was her dearest dream at the moment that one night he would sleep with her until breakfast time. There was never any warning when he was about to arrive, just the sound of his carriage – one she had learned to recognise from any other – and the sound of his key in the lock. She did not dare go out. He had offered her a carriage of her own, but she had rejected the offer. It would have been pleasant to bowl into the city in it, call on Blossom to show her how well cared for she was, join the parade of carriages in the park. But it was a long ride to Hyde Park and, if he should come and find her out, might he not look for someone else to entertain him? She would sit at her window, willing the next carriage to be his, or playing games with herself – that if five black carriages went by in the next five minutes he would come. It was from the long hours spent at her window that she realised that she was not alone in this street, that in the other houses there were other girls such as she. She presumed this from the way the carriages arrived, stood maybe for two hours, and then sped away to return at the same time the next day. She saw the other girls leaving their houses, dressed for a walk, for shopping or the theatre, for all she knew, and she envied them the routine they had with their lovers.

And then one day Jennie sniffed. It was only a little sniff but one that indicated such disdain that Ia finally lost her temper.

'What do you mean, sniffing at me like that? I asked you to press that dress for me, so do it.'

'Do it yourself.'

'How dare you speak to me like that?'

'You should have said "Please".'

'Maybe I would have done, if you weren't so insolent. Now do this dress.' She thrust the dress towards the maid.

'I've Mr Willoughby's laundry to do. That comes first.'

'What I tell you to do comes first.'

'Ha.' Jennie stood arms akimbo and sneered, her expression saying exactly what she thought of women in Ia's position. Her attitude was a continual puzzle to Ia, since the maids at Blossom's had respected the girls, liked them, even envied them.

'I suggest you pack your bag, Jennie, and leave. Now.'

'I beg your pardon?' Jennie laughed.

'You heard.'

'Mr Willoughby hired me, likes of you can't sack me.'

'That's where you're wrong. Get out this minute.'

'I bloody well won't.'

Ia streaked across the room, slapped Jennie hard across the mouth and frog-marched her, protesting shrilly, up the staircase and then up the pine steps into her own room. 'You've five minutes to pack or I'll throw your things out on to the pavement.'

'I shall go and see Mr Willoughby about you.'

'Fine. And how will you do that?'

'I'll go to his house in Cadogan Square, that's what I'll do.'

'Good, you do that.' Ia slammed from the room. At last she knew where he lived, she thought, as she skipped down the stairs full of excitement that she was finally to be rid of Jennie. Jennie did not pack fast enough for her. Ten minutes later Ia was back to find the maid lying on her bed with her shoes off, looking at the ceiling.

'So, this is how you want it?' she said, angrily stuffing the maid's clothes into a carpet bag.

'You can't do that.'

'I am doing it.'

Three bags she packed and then lugged them down the stairs, with Jennie in hot pursuit. She opened the front door and with all her strength hurled the first bag into the roadway causing a passing horse to shy. Jennie, wailing, raced after her bag.

'And this one, and this,' Ia said triumphantly as she hurled the bags over the gate towards the maid.

'I'll get you for this, you whore!' Jennie shrieked.

'Having trouble with the servants?' an amused voice said from the other side of the hedge. Ia peered round to find a girl of her own age, who was holding her sides with laughter at the spectacle of Jennie hurtling down the road in fury.

'I've loathed her ever since I got here. She's rude and lazy and ... She had to go ...' Ia said, a shade defensively.

'You needn't make excuses to me, love. If she isn't doing her job, then boot her out is my advice. You'll soon get another.'

'I'm not sure I want another. Snooping about, listening at doors.'

'Don't be daft. You get a new one. You don't want to end up skivvying yourself, do you?' and she laughed loudly at the idea. 'Fancy a mug of gin?'

Ia looked anxiously up the road. 'I don't think I can.'

'Expecting your toff?'

'Not really, I'm never sure when he's coming.'

'Come on in, then, I could do with a bit of company. You can watch out the window just in case.'

'Well, yes, why not?' Ia followed the elegantly clad form up the garden path and into a house which was almost identical to her own: the wallpaper was the same, the furniture similar. 'Are all the houses in this road the same?' she asked uneasily.

'Mostly. The gents buy them furnished, usually. Bubbles up at 25 is different, her fellow came with a lorry-load of stuff, and Chloe didn't like it and her man got her all new. I like it meself, it certainly beats what I'm used to. What's yer monicker?' The girl's voice was strange. At one moment genteel, with each word carefully enunciated. And then suddenly, sometimes on only one word, the accent would slip and pure Cockney rang out. It was as if her guard fell momentarily to be hoisted up again hastily on the next word.

'Ia.'

'I'm Florrie. Here's your drink.' She crossed the room and with a gracious gesture handed Ia a large glass of neat gin. Ia took it doubtfully; she liked a drink but not in such quantities. 'Sit there in the window. You can see whoever comes up the road from there,' said Florrie, seating herself opposite. Once she had a clear view of the street, Ia relaxed. 'Bloody hell, look at that fire, the lazy cow . . .' Florrie crossed the room, and opened the door. 'Mary, get your arse up here, you lazy scut. Do this fire or I'll hit you,' she bellowed into the hallway with all pretence at refinement gone. A white-faced maid appeared blubbering with apologies as she knelt on the hearth rug and tended the fire.

'I couldn't have spoken to Jennie like that, she'd have taken no notice,' Ia said, unsure whether or not she was impressed by Florrie's abuse.

'You have to show them who's boss from the word go. Get one younger than yourself, it's easier. Mary, have you got a mate looking for a job? There's one going next door.'

'Oh, I . . .' Ia attempted to interrupt.

'Mary's all right, ain't yer, girl?' Mary nodded dumbly. 'We understand each other, Mary and me. I shouts at her a bit but she don't mind, do you?'

'Not really,' Mary giggled. 'I have got a friend as a matter of fact. We was in the orphanage together. I'll pop and see her.'

The fire roared in the grate, Mary left them, and the two girls sat sipping their gin. And Florrie started on the serious task of finding out more about her neighbour.

'I'd begun to think you were a bit of a snob – keeping to yourself all the time.' Florrie's number one accent was back.

'It's Peter. I never know when he's coming, you see. I daren't go out.'

'Oh, you've got one of them. I suppose he comes days on the trot and then leaves you without sight nor sound for a week or two.'

'Yes, he does. How did you know?'

'You know what that means, don't you?'

'No.'

'He's keen on you, that's what.'

'I don't understand.'

'When they are regular like a train – Mondays, Wednesdays and Fridays for three hours on the nest – then they're not really interested. You're just a body, a bit like a public convenience to relieve themselves in. Could be anyone. But when they keep you guessing, like yours does, that's a sure sign they like you, that they're smitten. He's keeping you on the hop, you see. You never know when he's coming so you don't go out – that way he can be certain you won't find no one else. See?'

'Oh, I don't know about that,' Ia said uncertainly, yet secretly elated at what Florrie was saying.

'I'd put money on it.'

381

'Well . . .'

'What you doing for Christmas?'

'I don't know, he hasn't said.'

'There's distinct disadvantages to fellows like that. How can you plan? How can you have any life of your own?'

'I'm not sure I want any life of my own.'

'Don't fall into that trap, girl. You could come really unstuck if he dropped you.'

'But you just said . . .'

'That doesn't mean he'll stick with you, love. It just means that he's possessive for the time being,' Florrie explained airily, completely destroying Ia's initial elation. 'Anyhow, Christmas is next week. Several of us are having a knees-up here – all our fellows spend Christmas with their families. You just pop in if you feel like it. I think . . .' But Florrie did not have time to finish her sentence for coming up the road, heard before it was seen, was Peter's carriage.

'He's here,' Ia exclaimed, jumping to her feet and with a rush and quick thanks for the drink, she ran to the door.

'She's heading for disaster,' Florrie shook her head and said to the empty room.

2

'If a servant is to be dismissed then I will do the dismissing,' Peter was saying sternly as Ia helped him out of his greatcoat.

'I'm sorry, Peter, but she had to go.'

'Why didn't you tell me you were having problems with her? I would have spoken to her. Good servants are difficult to find.' Ia followed him into the sitting-room where, to her mortification, the fire was almost out. 'And

I was not pleased that she should arrive at my home. It was very awkward for me.'

'I did try to tell you, but you became irritated. I thought it best not to mention it again.' Ia tried to hide the sense of injustice that she was feeling. Instead, she poked the dying embers with more force than was really necessary.

'We shall have to find a replacement.'

'I'm not sure I want one. I prefer it here – just you and me. I can look after you just as well.' She knelt back on her haunches and looked at him as he settled himself in the wing chair beside the fire.

'How do you propose to manage? Who will help you dress?'

'I don't need any help. All my clothes fasten at the front or sides – not the back. I can dress myself easily.'

'And undress yourself with equal ease for me,' he laughed, leaning forward and, to her relief, kissing the nape of her neck. His anger appeared to have dissipated.

'Of course.'

'But what about food? And the cleaning?'

'I've found this book in the kitchen, look.' She hauled the heavy household tome, written by a Mrs Beeton, on to the table. 'It explains everything. I can learn. And cleaning is no problem, any fool can clean. Think of all the money it will save you. Let's try it, Peter, please.'

'No,' he said after a long pause, which to Ia seemed to go on indefinitely. 'I prefer you to have someone here.'

'But, Peter . . .'

'No "buts". We will look for a new maid. As to this evening, we shall go out to dinner. Get your cloak.'

Ia felt despondent. She knew that would mean a long carriage ride and then an equally long one back. It would mean at least two hours less of his company here, and two hours less of him in her bed.

'I met the girl next door. She invited me in,' she said as

they rode along in the carriage, a heavy fur rug tucked firmly about them against the winter chill.

She could see Peter frowning at her from the glow cast by the gas lights in the street. 'I don't think that is a good idea.'

'Why ever not?'

'She is unlikely to be suitable company for you, a woman like that.'

'She's fun, and at least it would be company for me when you are not there – as you so often are not . . .' Her sentence trailed off. She had not meant to say that.

'Are you complaining?'

'No, no, of course not. But I can't see the harm in it. It's nice for me to have other people to talk to. Her maid can get a new maid for us, too,' she added hurriedly.

'I'll choose the servants. I don't regard the recommendation of another whore as adequate,' he said shortly and Ia turned her face away from him so that he would not see the tears that had sprung into her eyes. In one breath Florrie was not good enough for her and in the next he was lumping them together as whores. She did not understand him nor the way his mind worked.

Dinner was a long and mostly silent affair. She would have liked to be light-hearted, she dearly wanted to conjure away the frown that was marring his features. But she could not think what to say. She felt restless. There was none of the placid contentment she normally felt, just to be with him. She felt peevish, hard done by. After just half an hour of talking to Florrie, a little of the old Ia was returning.

In their bedroom, as he dressed to leave, she plucked up the courage to ask him about Christmas.

'I shan't be seeing you now until after the New Year. I'm leaving for my uncle's in three days. Why?'

'Oh, nothing, I just wondered.' She had decided it was better not to tell him of her invitation from Florrie.

'I shall send a new maid. You won't be alone.'

'Thank you, Peter.'

'Are you being sarcastic?' He glared at her

'No, I just said thank you.'

He tossed a packet across the bed to her. 'That's for Christmas.'

'Thank you, Peter. I'm sorry, I didn't get you anything. I didn't think . . . I don't like to go out.'

'No matter.' He turned towards the door. She had hoped he would kiss her goodbye.

The next morning she was knocking on Florrie's door. The little maid showed her up to Florrie's room where she lay still in bed, her lip gashed and a black eye just beginning to show.

'Florrie! What happened to you?'

'My bastard Weasel, that's what happened to me.'

'You mean . . .'

'Yes, he's a right little short-arse with a pecker the size of an acorn. They're always the worst, aren't they? Beating you up, 'cause they can't get a good poke . . .' She laughed and winced at a pain in her chest. 'He's going to have to go. I've had enough. I don't mind the odd bit of roughing up, but not this.'

'What will you do?'

'Find another shift monger – that's the easy part. Getting them to do what you want – that's the difficult part.' Again she laughed, one hand darting to her torn lip, the other to her ribs. 'Cor, lummy, I must stop laughing.' Ia looked at her with admiration, that she could make so light of catastrophe – on the one hand to be beaten up and on the other to risk losing her protector. But looking at her with the mop of golden hair that curled prettily about her perfectly heart-shaped face, Ia could see that it was unlikely to take long.

'How many protectors have you had?'

'Five. And he's the worst. He's meaner than any of the others and he smells something shocking. So, Ia, what

385

can I do for you?' Today there was no pretence at gentility.

'It doesn't matter now. I just wondered if you'd like to come to town with me.'

'What's this then, spreading your wings at last? Did you listen to what I said, then?'

'I've learned where Peter lives, I just want to go and see what it's like. But don't worry, you're not fit to go anywhere.'

'I'll be right by Christmas, if it kills me. You're coming I hope. But take my carriage, I'm not using it. Have it all day if you want. I'm staying here with a pint of gin.'

An hour later Ia sat in Florrie's carriage at the entrance to Cadogan Square, wondering which house was his and what had been the point of her coming.

'You just want to sit here, miss? It's cold enough to freeze the balls off a brass monkey, today.' Florrie's coachman peered through the window at her. Despite the rug, and a foot-warmer which Florrie had insisted she bring, Ia was shivering as flurries of icy fog began to swirl about.

'I just want to find out which house someone lives in.'

'Your fellow? Deserted you, has he?' The coachman spat out a wad of tobacco in a dark stream. 'What's his name? I'll find out.'

'Willoughby.'

'You sit tight, ducks. Dutton will find out for you,' and he disappeared into the murk of the fog. He was back in a few minutes. 'Number 4. No problem. Very respectable young man, just back from two years in India, with the viceroy, no less. Lives with his widowed mum and unmarried sister, and is filthy rich. Anything else you want to know?'

'Mr Dutton, you're a marvel. How on earth did you find that out?'

'Asked in the stables at the back – they always know

everything about everyone. Coachmen, we're a wonderful breed.' He laughed at his own joke. 'Can we go now? I'm bleeding perished.'

'Can you just drive by, very slowly, please?' She smiled at him.

'For you, ducks, I'd drive to Timbuctoo,' he said cheerily as he leaped into his seat and, whistling, urged the horses on. Ia looked eagerly out of the window as they approached the house. Dutton pulled the horses to a stop right outside. With beating heart, and covering the bottom of her face with her cloak, Ia peered out. There were lights in the window and Ia could see figures moving about in opulently furnished rooms. She ducked as the front door opened, but Dutton was pulling away before she dared look to see who it was. 'See enough?' Dutton's cheery face appeared in the slot behind her.

'Yes, thank you,' she said settling back happily on the cushions. He was not married! 'Home, Dutton.' She warbled her voice to sound like a dowager and hugged her arms to her, suddenly cold no longer.

The next day the new maid arrived. Lizzie was short, fat and forty. She was boss-eyed and had a fair sprinkling of hair on her face. Her eyes made her look sly, something of which, Ia reasoned, she had no proof. She was not friendly but she was not unfriendly either. She would never be a friend but, on the other hand, Ia could not imagine her an enemy. She was not insolent and her work was adequate. Perhaps she had been foolish to think that she would have enjoyed life without a maid.

She went every day to Florrie's; her neighbour had now decided to stay with the Weasel at least until after Christmas.

'With a shiner like this who the hell is going to look at me? And in any case he might get generous with Christmas coming. You never know yer luck.'

'Or guilt-ridden,' Ia suggested.

'Not that sadist,' Florrie grunted. 'So, have you decided about Christmas?'

'Yes. I'd love to come.'

'Good. No point in mooning about on your own, is there? I like this Christmas thing, I didn't even know it existed when I was a kid, did you?'

'In the workhouse we celebrated a Christmas of sorts but not like the others . . .' There she stopped. She did not know why but, even when she was in the orphanage, she had denied the Christmases she had spent at Gwenfer, with presents from Alice and each year a knitted scarf from Queenie and so much food that each time she had made herself sick. Odd that she should suddenly think about them now when she had given neither Alice nor her betrayal a thought since meeting Blossom. Alice had let her down and now she herself had let Blossom down. It was odd the way life went.

'What others?' Florrie asked.

'Oh, nothing. Just something that happened a long time ago and I've only just remembered it.'

'I don't like thinking about the past, gives me the frigging frights. What you going to wear?'

Ia was pleased that Florrie had apparently changed the subject.

'Lizzie, have you got a home to go to?' Ia asked later that evening as she helped Lizzie fold the linen.

'What you mean, miss?'

'I wondered if you would like a holiday. Mr Willoughby won't be back until after the New Year. I can look after myself.'

'Oh, I don't know as I should, miss. I mean it would be nice to see me mum, but . . .'

'Haven't you got the fare?'

'Lor', it ain't that, miss. I lives at Whitechapel, not far on the bus. It's just that I promised the master I wouldn't leave you alone.' She glanced sideways at Ia who, irritated by the squint, was unsure if the look was as sly as it appeared.

'He need not know, need he? I shan't tell.'

'Thank you very much, miss. I'd like that, then.'

'Whitechapel. Do you know the Feathers?'

'Cor love you, miss, it's just round the corner from us.'

'You don't happen to know a Gwen Roberts who was going with a Johnnie Flocks, do you?' Ia asked idly as they finished the linen.

'I knows Johnnie, everyone knows Johnnie. But I don't know a Gwen. He's married, got two kids but I don't know his wife's name.'

'I expect it's the girl I used to know. That's nice,' Ia smiled. 'She was kind to me when most weren't. Right, Lizzie, you'd best be packing if you're going.'

3

At the start it did not appear as if Florrie's party would be a success. As the other guests trooped in they each behaved in a parody of a grand lady. The language they spoke was almost incomprehensible as they painfully tortured the vowels out of all recognition. Their mannerisms, the affected giggling, the exaggerated fluttering were wholly false. But, as the excellent meal progressed with course after course, each accompanied by a different wine, so they began to relax. The more drink they drank, the less affected they were. One by one they began to speak normally and their robust humour showed itself.

Dinner finished, they made their way unsteadily to the sitting-room. There they sat, in a semicircle, around the fire, their skirts flicked up over their knees, the fire-light warming their thighs. Each had a tankard of gin in her hand.

'Imagine.' It was Florrie holding forth. 'There's the heroine dead as a door nail, lying on the stage. The hero's wringing his hands with grief. "What shall I do?" he wails at us. "Fuck her while she's still hot!" I yelled . . .'

'Florrie!' In unison the others exploded with laughter.

'What did your Weasel say?'

'He thumped me – right there and then. No sense of humour, that's one of his bloody problems.' She began to pick her teeth with a fork.

Ia wiped the tears of laughter from her eyes and attempted to focus on the others.

'This is the best Christmas I've ever had,' she slurred, and shook her head, concerned to find that she could see not four other girls but eight. 'I think I'm very drunk,' she announced with a giggle.

'You don't drink enough, my girl, that's your problem,' Florrie admonished.

'Truth is, I don't like it,' she explained to them as if imparting a secret.

'Blimey, I couldn't survive without my pint of gin,' Doris said with feeling.

'I quite like champagne,' Ia said, not wishing to offend.

'Who doesn't prefer champagne? Love a duck, you ain't half hoity-toity. You've been here six months and this is the first we've seen of you,' Primrose said sharply.

'Come on, Prim, that's not her fault. Her bloke don't like her to go out.' Florrie leaped to her defence.

'Why she talk so posh then?'

'I dunno, ask her.'

'Go on then, tell us,' Primrose demanded.

'I didn't always talk like this. I had a friend, Alice, she taught me how to talk like her,' Ia explained, carefully enunciating her words.

'Come orf it. I'd believe a man taught you, but a woman? What decent woman would associate with the likes of us, eh?' Primrose was not about to give up, convinced as she was that Ia, for some reason or other, was not one of them but was masquerading.

'It's true.' Ia glared belligerently at Primrose. 'My

friend Alice, she lived in the big house and she taught me to read and write and talk . . . well, properly . . .' Ia said heatedly.

'Then what you doing as a kept woman with such posh friends?' Primrose sneered.

'Leave her alone, Prim, stop nagging. What's got into you?' Florrie handed round the jug of gin once more.

'She went away and she didn't write.' Ia paused and stared deeply into the fire. 'The bitch deserted me.' She looked up at the assembled company. 'I hate her.' A tear escaped and trickled down her cheek; angrily she wiped it away and turned her head so that the others could not see the other tears in her eyes.

'You poor little cow,' and Primrose burst into tears. 'Not much of a friend then, was she?' She blew her nose noisily on the hem of her skirt.

Ia flicked her hair over her shoulders and faced them. 'No, Primrose, you're right. She wasn't my friend, not like all of you. Now you are real friends.' Suddenly she laughed, flung her arms wide to encompass the group and spilled the remainder of her gin, all down her front. 'Oh, lor', look at me.' She jumped to her feet and stood swaying. 'I think I'd better go home.'

'You lie down there, Ia, my love. You're in no fit state to walk up the garden path. You sleep it off, there's a good girl.' Florrie led her to the couch and laid her down. By the time she had covered her with a paisley shawl, Ia was asleep.

'Poor little mite,' Florrie said as she returned to her chair and settled herself again. 'I think she's in love with her man.'

'The fool. Was she fresh?'

'I doubt it. She don't say much but I reckon she's been on the game some time.'

'Boris saw her the other day when he arrived. He says she was at Blossom December's for a while,' Doris, who had been longing to impart this new information all evening, informed them proudly.

'Blossom's!' The others sat bolt upright in unison.

'Yes, Boris says she was there for about a year.'

'And she left Blossom's for this? She must be mad. You can make your fortune at Blossom's. I'd give anything to have got in there.'

'But if she fell in love . . .'

'My Boris says he's very rich.'

'But it don't matter how rich he is, he ain't going to set her up when he wants a change, is he?' Primrose had quite forgotten her initial antagonism towards Ia and now felt genuinely angry for her.

'I nicks what I can. I've good arrangements with the butcher and the wine merchant, and the Weasel hasn't discovered yet. I'm determined my old age is going to be all right.'

'Why do you call him the Weasel, Florrie?'

''Cause he stinks, that's why. He's bloody useless, honest – all he can do is piddle through it and then blames me. I'm off in the New Year. I only hung around 'cause of this party and 'cause I hoped the mean old bugger would give me something – jasmine water, that's what I got, I asks you.'

Ia slept while the others worried about her future and moaned enjoyably about the protectors in their lives.

Slowly the influence of the other girls began to work on Ia so that she started to question her relationship with Peter. She realised that not only were the others given allowances, generous ones at that, but any money they saved from the housekeeping was theirs too. She did not approve of the way that, despite this, they cheated their protectors. She knew that she could never do that to Peter. But when he returned she would ask for money of her own. And also, at the others' insistence, she was going to request that their relationship be put on a more regular basis. It was not fair that she was a virtual prisoner; she began to wonder how she had allowed the situation to occur in the first place.

But then Peter returned. And in his arms, his kisses raining down upon her, his mouth on her breasts, all such intentions evaporated and she settled to her routine of acquiescent waiting, of snatching visits to Florrie and sitting in the window to wait. She was convinced now that Lizzie was spying on her, for Peter always seemed to know when she had seen Florrie. Her reaction to this knowledge was confused. Initially she had felt angry but then she began to feel pride. It meant he cared for her. Maybe it even meant he loved her. She wrapped the idea of his jealousy about her with joy, for at any indication that he had feelings for her she grasped like a hungry beggar.

And so the strange lethargy which Peter instilled in her returned. The fiery Ia became once again the docile mistress, fearful of offending, afraid of losing the man she adored.

Ia was sitting in the garden reading. She had joined the penny library and now read, voraciously, anything she could get her hands on. It was a beautiful spring afternoon, the blossom just beginning to show on the cherry tree in the garden. Ia was happy. Last night she had tentatively mentioned to Peter that she would love to have her daughter to stay occasionally. She had expected an immediate refusal. But he had smiled at her and said that, provided the child did not get in his way, he had no objection if she visited at weekends – a time he rarely came.

'There's a man to see you, miss,' Lizzie had appeared at the french windows.

Ia jumped to her feet. 'Mr Willoughby?'

'No. He didn't give his name. I put him in the study, there's less to pinch there.'

'Oh, Lizzie, you are funny.'

'I'm just going to the shops, anything you want?'

'If you could change this book for me. Miss Walters the librarian will know what I want.'

She gave Lizzie the book and hurried into the house curious to find out who her caller could be. No one ever called on her. She opened the door of Peter's study.

'Hallo, Ia. Still as pretty as ever.'

'Frederick!' Ia's hand shot to her mouth with shock at seeing this man from her past here in her present.

'Thought I'd look you up for old times' sake. Good times, weren't they, girl?'

'How did you find me?' She did not smile.

'The usual belowstairs grapevine. There's a Boris Janovitz got a doxy up the road. His valet drinks in the Grapes, same as me. It was easy.' He looked about the room. 'Well, Ia, my friend, you appear to have done well for yourself, I must say. Nice house, pretty dress, you're looking well.' He put out a hand to stroke her face but Ia dipped away from his touch. 'Too good for the likes of me to touch you now, is it?'

'You still with the Tregowans?' She sat down and decided it would be better if she tried to engage him in conversation rather than antagonise him.

'Not for much longer.'

'Any news of Miss Alice?'

'What you want to know about her for?'

'Oh, just curious. I was still there the day she eloped. I just wondered what had happened.'

'Gone to America. The old man got a letter from her. He tore it up, I saw him do it.'

'Poor Alice,' she murmured, surprised by her own reaction.

'Poor Alice, be buggered. I could do with being as poor as her.' He sat down opposite her. 'I'm getting married,' he said, suddenly, glancing at her slyly as if to gauge her reaction.

'Congratulations,' she replied in an equable voice. She looked at him now and saw only an ordinary young man, too flashily dressed, in a suit that was cut a little too tight, and with jewellery that was vulgar in its size. She sat there calmly, observing him, and wondered why she had ever thought she loved him or wanted to marry him.

'Yes. A nice widow woman, got a little pie shop, in Camden. Will do me very nicely. No more waiting on the likes of the bloody Tregowans.'

'That's good, Frederick.'

'Course she's an old grabem pudden. Fat and forty. But then you can't have everything, can you?' He put his hand out again as if to touch her. Ia pressed herself back in her chair to get as far away from him as possible. 'So you had the kid? What was it?' He sat down opposite and leaned towards her.

Ia looked at him sharply and felt suddenly threatened. An older wife, one perhaps past having children; with alarming speed Ia realised what Frederick was after – their child. 'She died,' she said coldly.

'Oh, pity. I had plans. Never mind. Perhaps I wouldn't make a good father.' He shrugged his shoulders and Ia relaxed at the ease with which he had swallowed her lie.

'I thought you were so certain that it wasn't yours.'

'Me job was on the line, Ia. You couldn't expect me to accept it as mine, now could you?' he whined at her.

'Didn't you wonder what had happened to me?'

'Course I did. There were nights I couldn't sleep worrying about you and wondering what had happened to you.'

'How thoughtful of you, Frederick.' He looked up sharply at her tone, but she was smiling at him.

'Christ, Ia, that smile of yours! Always made me prick rise.' He laughed and leaned across the divide between them, attempting to take her hand.

'Don't you touch me,' she hissed at him.

'That's not friendly, doll. Not friendly at all. I'd heard

you were on the game. What about giving one to me for old times' sake?'

Ia jumped to her feet. 'I think you had better go, Frederick. Now.'

'Too grand for your old friend? I can pay, you know, I don't mind paying for it. A shilling, will that do yer?'

Ia crossed to the door and held it open. 'I would appreciate your leaving, Frederick, and I don't ever want to see you again.'

He got up and walked calmly towards the door. 'Not so fast, Ia. Not so bleeding fast.' He grabbed her and his mouth came down hard upon hers. She punched him with her fists, kicked his shins. He stood back and laughed at her. 'You always was a fiery little devil, weren't you? I liked that ...' He lunged towards her, grabbed the front of her dress and with one vicious tug tore the silk in two. Her breasts were exposed. 'Oh, naughty, naughty. Is that how the gentleman likes you? What about down below then?' He flicked her skirt up as she twisted in his other hand. 'Even better, your little muff all ready and waiting.'

She lashed out with her foot but missed as he darted nimbly to one side. He grabbed her hair and, twisting it in his hands, dragged her out of the room towards the stairs. She slapped, she punched, she spat, she tried to bite, as relentlessly he pulled her behind him up the stairs. He kicked open the door on the landing. Once in the room he threw her on the bed and jumped on to it. Standing with one heel on her stomach to prevent her escaping, he began to unbuckle his trouser belt. As he loomed over her she turned her mouth away. He slapped her hard across the face, jolting her head. 'That's for being so unfriendly,' he shouted. His hand lashed out and he struck her again, 'And that's for my best velvet jacket you cut up.' He punched her on the breast. 'And that's for my velvet breeches, you slut. Too good for me, are you? I'll bloody well show you.' He ripped the rest of her

396

dress from her, the material cutting into her flesh as he did so. He lunged on to her and entered her roughly, as she flailed beneath him, impotently punching him with her fists. He was too heavy for her; she was trapped. She lay still, her eyes wide open, staring at the ceiling, forcing her mind to be blank as he tore into her body.

The door crashed open. 'You whore!' Peter shouted as he strode across the room. Hauling Frederick from her, he kicked him hard on his behind. Frederick, his trousers hanging around his ankles, hopped from the room with speed.

'Thank God, you came, Peter. I thought he was going to kill me.' Ia was clutching at the shreds of her dress attempting to cover her nakedness.

'You lying trollop. You were enjoying it like the tramp you are.'

'Peter, I wasn't.' She looked at him, horrified. 'He was raping me.'

'I should never have taken you in: once a whore always a whore.' He slapped her hard across the face, his blow falling where Frederick had already bruised her.

'But Peter . . .' Again he lashed out. He stood above her throwing at her every filthy name that he could call to mind. Every time she tried to defend herself it was as if the sound of her voice drove him to greater fury. Only when her face was puffed beyond recognition, only when she could no longer speak through her swollen mouth, only when the blood dripped from her nose on to the white coverlet did he stop.

He hauled her from the bed, wrenched open the wardrobe and threw a dress at her. 'Put that on, slut,' he ordered. Fighting back the tears that were close to the surface, she fumbled with the dress. He took a bag and, like a man demented, began to throw her possessions into it. Last of all he threw in her azure bowl.

She slipped and tumbled as he pushed her ahead of him

down the stairs. As she lay on the floor he kicked her hard. 'Get up. Get out of here.'

'Peter . . .' She spoke in a thick, blood-clogged voice.

'I loved you. God help me I loved you,' she heard him say.

She swayed, clutching at the wall for support. She felt the cool breeze on her battered face as he opened the front door. As if regretting his moment of weakness, he pushed her towards the open door and shoved her out on to the path. 'Go, go now,' she heard him shout. She fumbled her way blindly down the path, her sight misted by blood. As she reached the gate, he threw her bag after her. It landed with a thud at her feet. The front door slammed shut behind him.

She stood in the roadway, swaying, only vaguely conscious of the curious stares from other houses, from other girls. Wildly she looked about her and picked up a large stone. With all her might she hurled it at the window and watched the glass panes shatter.

'You bastard! Why wouldn't you believe me?' she screamed in anguish.

4

Ia sat slumped in the corner of the dark and crowded police cell. She had no idea how long she had been there. She could recall only the barest details of the scene she had made outside Peter's house as she had screamed hysterically, throwing stone after stone, while all the time pleading with him to take her back. Only now did it strike her how ridiculously illogical her behaviour had been. Florrie had come rushing out and Ia had pushed her away, sending Florrie sprawling in the road. She did recall the arrival of the police van pulled by a tired and sagging horse for she remembered feeling pity, in the middle of her own despair, for the poor beast. She was

dragged by two burly policemen and hurled unceremoniously into the back of the van with only the smell of urine
for company.

At the police station she had been stripped and
searched, the cold, rough hands of the wardress delving
into her most intimate parts. Her bag taken from her, she
had stood and allowed herself to be pushed first one way
and then the other as if nothing mattered any more. She
could not see the other occupants of the cell into which
she had been shoved. She seemed to have moved into a
world where one was only pushed, thrown or hurled. It
was as well she could not see the other women. Young,
old, middle-aged, they all stank, they were all covered in
sores and lice. On her arrival they had set upon and
searched her just in case she had anything of value worth
stealing. The occupants urinated and defecated where
they sat: the stench was intolerable, but luckily for Ia her
nose was too swollen to smell anything. Rats scuttled
about the floor and crawled over the women as they
attempted to sleep, though the noise of screaming,
cursing, begging made sleep impossible. Ia wondered if
she had been taken to Bedlam. Now as dawn broke, she
lifted her head, aching beyond endurance, and looked
about her at the grey, tattered bundles that bore little
resemblance to fellow females.

She felt as if she had been drunk. She felt as if she had
died. She wished that she had.

'Ia? Ia, is that you?' a voice whispered urgently.

Wearily, she turned her battered face towards the
sound of the voice. 'Yes,' she croaked.

'Cor, lummy, who got at you? What a mess. Hold on.'
One of the grey bundles crawled towards her, delved into
the shapeless prison clothes, produced a rag and, spitting
on it, began to try to clean Ia's face. With a shudder she
lifted her head away from the offensive cloth, the action
making her head feel as if it was about to split into two.

'Don't do that,' she ordered.

'I was only trying to help.' The voice sounded aggrieved. 'Suit yourself.'

'It hurts so badly.'

'I'm sorry.'

Ia peered at the face through swollen eyes. She saw a woman whose age it would have been impossible to guess – she could have been young and prematurely aged, or she could have been old with still a touch of youth. Her hair, which might have been red, was dark with filth and plastered to her scalp. Her eyes were marred by the conjunctivitis which made them permanently weep, and a collection of cold sores about her mouth glistened in the pale dawn light.

'You don't recognise me, do yer?'

'No, I don't.'

'It's Gwen. You remember – from the Feathers down Whitechapel way?' She smiled, which had the unfortunate result of making her sores ooze.

Ia sat up with interest forgetting, momentarily, her own aches and pains. 'Gwen Roberts! But I thought you were married and had children.'

'Me married? That's a joke,' she snorted with laughter.

'Fuck off . . .' one of the grey bundles complained.

'Fuck off yourself,' Gwen aimed a kick in the complainant's direction. 'Who was I supposed to be married to?'

'Why, Johnnie, of course.'

Gwen spat in disgust. 'What, that bleeder?'

'I'm sorry. It didn't work out then?'

'Nar. He used me like all the other sods. Got me to give up the Feathers which made old Bert furious. We moved in together – but he didn't want me, not as his wife. He made me go back on the game – on the streets – then he took all I earned. When I didn't earn enough he beat me. When he beat me, no one wanted me, so he beat me again.'

'Couldn't you have gone back to Bert?'

'You didn't hear him when I left, there was no chance

there. Wish I'd had the chance to kick him in the jelly bags like you did. Cor, we didn't half laugh about that. He was walking about like a cripple for days and, of course, he couldn't fuck neither, what put him in a real mood.'

'But you had no children, I hope.'

'Nar, I got done up, didn't I? Went to old Mabel the greaser with her knitting needles. That did for me forever I reckon, probably for the best.'

'Gwen, I'm sorry.'

'Mind you, I did get to Margate. I did see the sea. It's just like you said it was, all clean and lovely. I'll never forget it as long as I live.'

'Maybe you'll see it again one day.'

'How? God knows when I'll get out of here. I've been here a week already. I can't pay me fine and, if I don't, then it's Holloway for God knows how long. Then I'll go back on the game and I bet you I'll be back in here in a trice.'

'How much is your fine?'

'Five shillings. Where the hell I'm supposed to get that from, I don't know.'

'What did you do?'

'Bit a rozzer.'

Despite the pain Ia laughed.

'He was moving me on and there was no need, I wasn't doing nothing. Some of those bloody Temperance people were about, that was the trouble, they likes the street tidy when the do-gooders are about. What did you do?'

'I can't really remember. I think I broke someone's window.'

'Drunk?'

'No, angry.'

'I know the feeling.' Gwen shook her head. 'You been up in front of the beak yet?'

'No.'

'Expect you'll go this morning. I hope they bring you

401

back here, I don't like this lot one little bit, thieving cows all of them.'

The one gas light that had been burning in the corridor, barely filtering into their cell through the bars, was suddenly joined by a row of other jets as a wardress went along the corridor between the cages lighting them. One by one the other prisoners, with much moaning, began to awake. There was a noisy jangling of keys and the sound of a metal door being swung open.

'Breakfast. Or that's what they call it,' Gwen said helpfully.

One of the wardresses thrust a couple of bowls through the bars. Gwen grabbed them. Ia looked with disgust at the watery grey porridge, more like slops than food.

'Here, if you don't want that I'll have it.' Eagerly Gwen took the bowl from Ia and ate with relish.

As Gwen busily devoured the breakfast Ia put up her hand to her face and gingerly felt the swelling.

'God, I must look a mess. How on earth did you recognise me, Gwen?'

'Oh, it wasn't your face. It was the way you sat and shook your hair over your shoulder. All proud like. I've only ever seen you do that.'

'I think I'm lucky I found you, Gwen.'

'Well, I sorted you out once before, didn't I?'

'Yes, you were kind then.' She looked fondly at Gwen who, despite these surroundings, despite everything that had happened to her, could still be cheerful. 'What is it about us, Gwen, why are men so cruel? Why do they hit us, abuse us and tell us too late that they love us?'

'Ha,' Gwen snorted again. 'Love, what's that? I haven't heard too much talk of love in my life I must admit. As to why do they hit us? 'Cause they're useless bastards, that's why. When I die, I'd like to go to a heaven where there's only women, I really would. But then I bet you, if we get there, you'll see, God's a man and he'll be bossing us about just like them wankers down here. Don't seem much point in dying really, does there?'

'Oh, Gwen. I wish I could find some of your spirit.'

'You will, love. You're just feeling a bit low at the moment.'

'St Just?' a sharp female voice bellowed, making both Gwen and Ia jump.

'Here,' Ia said uncertainly.

The wardress approached their cage with her large bundle of keys. 'Who's the lucky one, then? The charges against you have been dropped. Come out here. Not you lot,' she shouted as some of the others tried to force their way out of the open grille. 'Get back or I'll get the bloody whip.' Cowed, the others returned to their squatting positions.

'Lucky you,' Ia heard Gwen shout as she was led out to an anteroom. She was given the clothes she had arrived in and her bag was restored to her.

'Get dressed and you're to wait here.'

'I thought you said there was no charge,' Ia retorted, more confident now and anxious to be out of this hell hole even if she did not know where she was going.

'Don't be in such a hurry. I was told you were to wait here and wait here you will.'

For two hours Ia sat alone in the paint-peeling, musty atmosphere of the room. There was nothing to look at, there was no clock, the barred window was too high to see out of, only a scrap of sky visible – just like in the workhouse, she thought. She longed for a book, anything to keep her mind from racing and hoping. If he had dropped the charges maybe he had forgiven her, maybe he was on his way now to collect her . . .

'This way.' The wardress ordered Ia out of the room and pushed her along the corridor. She opened another door and shoved Ia through it.

'Good God, Ia. What a mess. What on earth have you been doing?'

'Blossom!' Ia stood speechless 'Blossom!' was all she could find to say.

'Oh, Ia, my love. Who did this to you?' Blossom's arms were about her and she was holding Ia tight. Ia's throat felt stiff with a longing to cry but, as in the past, she could not cry, could not allow anyone to see her pain and grief – not even Blossom.

'I thought you never wanted to see me again?' she eventually managed to blurt out, giving Blossom a wan smile.

'I'm a fool, that's me.'

'I should never have left you.'

'I shan't say it, but I'm thinking it,' Blossom smiled. 'Don't ever do it again, that's all.'

'I promise.'

The wardress appeared with a box of money. 'You sign for this,' she ordered, still unable to speak pleasantly even though Ia was now a free citizen.

'Count it first,' Blossom said.

'There's no need for that, miss. That's what you brought in with you last night and that's what's there. See.' Angrily the wardress stabbed her finger at a figure on the paper beside which was Ia's signature.

'We'll count it all the same, if you don't mind.' And with the dexterity and practice of years Blossom soon made the total tally to her satisfaction.

'Blossom?'

'Yes, dear?' Blossom looked up from her task.

'Do you need a maid?'

'I'm not wasting you as a maid. You're far too valuable for that.'

'I didn't mean me.'

'No, I don't need a maid, I've plenty.'

'A kitchen maid, a scullery maid?'

'What do you want, Ia?' Blossom asked with a patient smile.

'There's an old friend of mine here. She's down on her luck, she kept me sane last night, I'd like to help her. I can pay her fine.' She counted out five shillings from the pile of loose change. 'Blossom?'

'I always seem to lose my senses where you are involved.' Blossom laughed. 'All right, but she had better be honest.'

It took them an hour to pay Gwen's fine and obtain her release. It was as if the authorities were loath to lose her. At sight of her in her filthy rags and with her hair alive with lice, Blossom muttered that she must be mad and refused to let Gwen travel in her carriage. She gave her the address and the fare for the hackney.

'That's the last we shall see of her,' she announced as she and Ia settled into the luxury of Blossom's coach.

They were half-way home before Ia suddenly sat up and looked at Blossom. 'How did you know I was there?'

'Peter Willoughby called at dawn – I ask you. He was full of remorse and asked me to go and find you.'

'Did he . . . ?' Her voice leaped with relief.

'No, Ia, he doesn't want you back.'

'I was raped, Blossom. I was not lying. It was Francine's father. I haven't seen him since I was dismissed from my old job, then he turned up out of the blue. And Peter found us.'

'I didn't for one moment think you had lied, Ia. As to that young man, Frederick, he seems to cause nothing but disaster in your life.'

'Peter didn't believe me.'

'Men never do where rape is concerned, Ia. Never.'

Blossom was wrong about Gwen, though. As the coach drew up in front of her house, there, panting from her race across town and grinning from ear to ear, was Gwen.

'Here's the hackney fare back, miss. I saved yer money

and ran.' She held out the money to Blossom.

'Keep it, child. But we've got to do something about those sores, what will the customers think?' Blossom fretted as she swept up the stairs into her empire.

That night, up in the attic room she had occupied when she first arrived, and where she was to sleep until her bruises faded and her cuts healed, Ia unpacked her bag.

On the top of her clothes, in pieces, was the azure bowl. Gently, Ia removed them, one by one, and placed them on the table before her. She studied them for a long time, picking the pieces up to see if there was any hope of mending it.

Alice, Frederick and Peter. Three people in her life whom she had allowed close to her, people she had thought could love her, and each of them had betrayed and rejected her. It was a dangerous thing to love. It was a risk she was determined never to take again.

She picked up the largest shard of her bowl on which was one complete rose, undamaged. Tenderly she outlined it with her finger and then one by one she dropped the pieces into the waste-paper basket. Like the love she had felt, she thought, her bowl was shattered too. As the last piece slipped from her fingers Ia, alone, and in the night, began to weep.

She wept for lost love. For shattered dreams. For hope that had disappeared. And she wept for her beautiful azure bowl.

5

'My old room? I didn't expect that, Blossom.'

'Why not for my favourite?'

'I didn't know you had favourites.' Ia grinned at her.

'I don't. It's our secret,' Blossom smiled back. 'Face the window, let me see you.'

Ia turned towards the light which flooded into the room. Blossom studied her face carefully. 'It's amazing, completely healed. You wouldn't think anything bad had happened to you.'

Three weeks had passed and Ia's face had fully recovered from its battering. Her body had healed but her mind had not. Before she had despised the clients; now she was certain she hated them. She was unsure how she would feel about starting work again.

'And this is for you.' Blossom held out a neatly wrapped parcel.

'A present? For me?' Ia ripped the paper off the package. She peered into the box and there, nestling on a bed of tissue paper, was her bowl. 'Oh, Blossom!'

'You have Gwen to thank for that. She rescued it just as the broken pieces were about to be thrown away. She brought them to me. We both knew how important the bowl was to you. It's a welcome-back present.'

'I wouldn't have thought it possible for it to be repaired.' She turned the bowl in her hand: it had been as skilfully mended as possible with wire clips holding the many pieces in place. It looked battered but, at the same time, even more precious to Ia. 'It was my mother's. It was the only pretty thing she ever owned and it's the only memento I have of her.' She felt that she owed Blossom an explanation.

'Then I'm even happier we had it repaired. But, Ia, sit down a moment, I have to talk to you.' She fussed over Ia until she was settled. 'My dear, you might find it difficult at first with the men – I want you to know that I understand, it's quite natural after your experience. Now, I'll tell you what I've planned. I shall not allow anyone who has the least tendency to violence near you. You can rely on that. And look.' She crossed to the bedside table, lifted the cover, and pointed to a small button. 'It's an alarm bell should you become frightened. We had a bad experience here while you were away. One of the girls was badly beaten – I've had them put in all the rooms now.'

'I think you must be the most considerate madam in the world.'

'I do my best,' Blossom laughed.

Whether it was the presence of the bell, or the clients whom Blossom selected for her, she did not know, but Ia did not find the adjustment as difficult as she had anticipated. She could not stifle the hatred she felt but, as she had acted a part in the past, so she found the ability to do so again. Her ambition to make money as quickly as she could returned, and with it the little notebook in which she entered her earnings. She was annoyed when she calculated how much she had spent when with Peter – on perfume, flowers, presents for him. It was money wasted instead of invested – a stupid error she would never repeat.

In the three months she had been back there had been one amusing interlude with Boris Janovitz. He was, she discovered, a mild, elderly man who most of all wanted to talk and admire Ia's naked body. When she had asked after Doris he had become so embarrassed and confused that it was as if she had asked after his wife. She apologised but wished she could have asked him to send her greetings to Doris and the others.

At last she had seen Lady Tregowan. One night, late, she had swept past Ia in the corridor icy with diamonds and hauteur. Ia had not minded the jewellery but resented the arrogant way she had flattened her against the wall. What was the difference between them? Ia had wondered as she stared at the retreating figure of her former employer. Ia was paid; Daisy Dear paid. But wasn't she as much a whore, reduced to climbing the back stairs and scuttling along corridors at dead of night in pursuit of lust? But her arrogance, her discourtesy only served to fuel Ia's hatred for the Tregowans which, despite the passing of time, never lessened.

Ia had settled back reasonably content into her old life when one evening, unusually, Blossom herself appeared in her room between clients.

'Ia, it's Peter Willoughby. He's downstairs and is asking for you. You need not see him. But I think you should. There's something about him, I'm not sure what it is but I think he *needs* to see you.'

'Not here.' Ia looked about her room as if trapped.

'No, I've shown him into my study.'

Ia took some time in dressing and doing her hair. It seemed vitally important that she look as beautiful as possible. She was determined that he should not know how deeply he had hurt her.

Her heart was thudding alarmingly as she entered Blossom's room. He was sitting in the wing chair and jumped quickly to his feet the moment she appeared.

'Ia . . .' He put out his hand.

'Peter,' she replied, ignoring the hand. She swept across the room to the side table and poured herself a large glass of madeira.

'You look well, Ia.'

'As do you, Peter. Please sit.' Ia herself took the chair on the other side of the fireplace. 'Isn't it a wonderful evening?' She looked to the window which was open in the summer heat.

'It's over a year since we first met here, Ia.'

'Is it?'

'I've missed you.'

'Have you?'

'The little house is so empty.'

'Haven't I been replaced?' she said with a small bitter laugh.

'There's no one with whom to replace you.'

'My dear Peter, the streets of London are full of young women who would leap at the chance.'

'You deliberately misunderstand me.'

'I don't think so.'

'Will you ever forgive me?'

'For what?'

'My behaviour. I had never hit a woman in my life before. I behaved badly.'

'Yes, you did, Peter. Very badly.'

'I've often regretted it.'

'And it's taken you three months to decide to tell me in person?'

'I didn't think you would want to see me.'

'What on earth gave you that idea? Beating one's mistress is quite a common sport in your circles, I gather, from the friends I made.'

'I would never do it again, ever. I apologise, Ia. Forgive me.'

'You miss the important issue, Peter. A beating one can recover from, but the damage to one's soul takes longer.'

'I've come to ask you to return.'

'And you think that will make me feel better?'

'I will do anything, give you anything to make you love me again.'

She looked at him steadily. 'Yes, I did love you, didn't I? And did I imagine it, or did you not say, just at the end, that you loved me too?'

'Yes, I did.' He leaned forward towards her so that she could smell the sandalwood balm he always wore. His nearness made her clutch her hands firmly together. The worried look on his face had been replaced by one of eagerness. 'It was true, maybe I should have told you sooner.'

'Oh, I don't think that would have been a good idea. I might have made unreasonable demands upon you, Peter. That was a risk you could never take.'

'I have made you bitter, my darling. But please, Ia, try to understand how I felt. I love you, even if I had not told you. When I saw you, in my bed, with that lout, my

410

control snapped. I felt like an animal. I wanted, I needed, revenge.'

'You certainly had your revenge.' She touched her face as if to remind him. 'My night in prison was an interesting experience too.' She looked at him coldly.

'Ia, I need you. I can't live without you.'

'Oh, come, Peter. Aren't you being a little melodramatic?' she snapped because as he spoke of his need for her the memory of their nights together wormed insidiously into her brain. 'It was lust, nothing more.'

'Come back, I'll give you whatever you want, a large allowance, a bigger house, your daughter can live with you permanently. I'll pay for her schooling.'

'You can't use my child as a bargaining point,' Ia said sharply.

'Ia, I'm not. I truly want you back and I want you to be happy.'

'Would you marry me?'

'Ia, you know that's not possible.'

'What security would I have then? One day you'll marry a suitable young woman and then you would no longer need me.'

'Yes, I would. I would still visit you.'

'Oh, thank you. How nice . . .' she laughed softly and flicked the long blonde hair back over her shoulder. 'I think I'm safer here. I have more security than you can offer. I can plan my future here.'

'I could assure your future. I am quite willing that we should have a contract drawn up by my lawyer to arrange for an annuity to be paid to you.'

'You don't understand anything, Peter. Love got in our way. In my heart I wasn't your mistress.' Dramatically she pointed to her chest. 'There, where one cannot lie to oneself, I thought of myself as your wife. I could not share you with a legal wife, Peter.'

He crossed the room and poured himself a large whisky and another madeira for Ia. As he handed her the

411

glass he gently touched her hand. She moved it away sharply. With a light touch he traced the outline of her mouth.

'Such a lovely mouth. How well I remember the joy it gave me,' he said huskily.

She moved her head back against the chair trying to escape the excitement that the feel of his hand was giving her.

'Peter, please . . .' There was a hint of desperation in her voice.

'You love it, my darling. Remember what it was like? Remember how I used to make you scream with passion . . . Come, quickly, to bed, now . . .' Taking hold of her hands he began to pull her to her feet.

'No, Peter.'

'But why not, if you love me?'

'I did not say I still loved you. In fact, Peter, I hate you. I hoped never to see you again. You are only a fragment from my past.'

He let go of her hands, picked up his hat and cane and looked at her coldly. The knuckles round his cane were tense and white. 'I understand.' He bowed to her and left the room without another word.

As the door closed on him Ia began to shake. She clutched her arms about her in an endeavour to control the shaking but she could not stop. Tonight she had surpassed herself as an actress. She loved him; nothing had altered. She would always love him. It had taken every ounce of self-control not to rush into his arms. She wanted him as she had always wanted him. But she could not risk the pain. Never again.

Part Four

Chapter Ten

1

'Alice Tregowan, at last!'

Alice looked up questioningly from the ledger she had been working on. She shielded her eyes the better to see the figure which loomed over her. A woman, perhaps a little younger than herself, but fatter than she. The dress she wore was of deep blue silk, tightly swathed across her full breasts, and over it was a long sable coat. Beneath the large matching blue hat, on which several ostrich feathers swayed, several deep red curls had escaped. There was something familiar about her. Alice stood and found herself looking into the dark-brown, amused eyes of Gertie Granver.

'Gertie!' she exclaimed.

'The very same – but Gertie Frobisher now. As large as life, well unfortunately a little larger than life since the last time you saw me! Babies . . .' she laughed loudly.

'You married Basil? How wonderful. But what on earth are you doing here?'

'Oh, we come to America frequently,' Gertie said, airily. 'Why did you stop writing? I've written you dozens of letters but they always come back. Your father has been impossibly mysterious about your whereabouts.'

'He doesn't know where I am. I wrote to him once but he never replied so there seemed no point in writing to him again. But how on earth did *you* find me?'

'Almost an impossible task. Is there nowhere we can sit and talk? It's unbearably hot in here.'

'It's the heat from the ovens, it's always like this. Let's go to my house, it will be quieter there, too.'

Alice collected her coat and after issuing a list of instructions to her staff, showed Gertie out of the door. They walked, talking non-stop, around the corner to the next street. Alice stopped outside the neat house with its little garden and verandah.

'You live here?' To her confusion Gertie found that she had not successfully disguised her shock.

'Yes, Gertie. This is mine. Pretty isn't it?' Alice smiled as she walked along the path and up the shallow flight of steps. She opened the front door which she held wide for her old friend. 'Welcome.' She bowed Gertie ceremoniously through the door and into the sitting-room which opened directly off the porch. She crossed the room to the door that led to the kitchen and popped her head around it. 'Merry, I have a guest. Could you bring us some tea in the sitting-room, please? Let me take your coat, Gertie.' She took the coat and hung it, tidily with her own, in the large walk-in closet.

Gertie stood in the room, its size making her hat seem much bigger than it really was. As if conscious of this she began to remove it. 'Do you mind if I take my hat off?' she asked as her red curls leaped free from the confines of the hat.

'That's how I always remembered you, that wonderful hair flying about all over the place.'

'Oh, rats, it's always been the same.'

'And the way you say "rats". Oh Gertie, it's so wonderful to see you again. I can hardly believe you are here.'

Gertie stood awkwardly, looking about the sitting-room which was large enough only for two armchairs, one small sofa, a desk and chair with a matching bookcase, and a whatnot on which stood a potted plant. A fire burned in the grate; over the mantelshelf was a small plain mahogany mirror, and on it a wooden clock and some sea-shells. The only picture was a water-colour of a granite house by the sea.

'How sweet,' Gertie said as she looked from one chair to the other, uncertain on which one to sit.

'It's all right, Gertie. You needn't lie. I know it's not much, but it's all mine. It's what I've worked for.'

'It's very um ... compact. And as you know I abhorred Mother's clutter.'

Alice laughed. 'The Americans, I've discovered, are clever at not wasting space. You should see the cupboards we have upstairs, they are enormous.'

'It's very cosy.'

'I've just had a boiler installed for central heating. But, as you see, I'm still English enough to be unable to do without an open fire.'

'Central heating? How luxurious.' At last Gertie sounded impressed. 'But Alice, your money . . . ? I mean, I don't wish to pry, but . . .'

'My father refused to let me have any. I have to wait another three years, until I'm thirty.'

'That's disgraceful. The law is a complete ass, and the sooner we get female suffrage the better. Once we get the vote then men like your father will have to stop regarding us as "chattels".'

'I'm sure Basil doesn't treat you as a chattel?' Alice interrupted the tirade.

'No, but then he's one in a million. That's why I married him.'

'That and his estate in Scotland,' Alice said wickedly.

'Ah, yes, and that too.'

'I really don't mind, Gertie. I'm very happy really. It's amazing what you can do without when you have to. I doubt now if I will change the way I live even when I do get my inheritance. I might buy a slightly larger house but it would still be here in this area.'

'I'd no idea. I don't think anyone has. I mean, everyone just assumed you'd married and, well, that you had your income and . . .' She leaned forward with an anxious expression. 'I think this is scandalous.'

'Please don't worry, Gertie. I'm perfectly all right. It's been hard but I've fought my way through. I know this little house has come as a shock to you. But I can assure you that compared to where I have lived, this is a palace. But when I look at it I don't see only bricks and mortar – I see five years of working nineteen hours a day. And everything here, every stick of furniture, every pot and pan is mine, earned from my labour.'

'Nineteen hours a day?' Gertie's face was etched with shock.

'Not any longer; that was in the beginning. Now I only work twelve, I have a great deal of help.'

'I begin to understand what you mean. You see your achievement.'

'Exactly. Everything I own is mine alone. I get such joy from buying a book or, very occasionally, a new hat, when it's my own work that has given it to me not someone else's. I am completely independent of a father, of a husband.'

'You should be in politics. We need women like you in our movement.'

'Oh, darling Gertie, that's a luxury that only the rich can afford. I'd never have the time to campaign for anything.'

'And what about Gwenfer?' Gertie nodded towards the painting. 'That's Gwenfer, I assume?'

'That sadness will never leave me. I've resigned myself to never seeing it again, but I still long for it . . .' She shook her head. Still, after all this time, the memory of Gwenfer hurt. 'But, you still haven't told me, how did you find me?'

'Last night, Basil and I were taking a walk down Madison Avenue. I can't imagine why, I don't think I've ever been so cold in my life. This city is positively arctic. However, there we were after a particularly large dinner in need of some exercise and, well, we were looking in the shop windows like a pair of housemaids.' She laughed. 'It's very strange: I could never get Basil to walk down Bond Street but here he's quite happy . . . strolling past a grocer's shop of all places, I saw a pot of jam and it said "Gwenfer and something" . . .' She waved her gloved hand in the air vaguely.

'Osborn.'

'That's it. Well I screeched when I saw it. There's only one Gwenfer, I said to Basil, and that has to be something to do with Alice. I could barely wait for the shop to open this morning. I telephoned – don't you think these American hotels are marvellous the way you have a telephone apparatus in your room? We've only got one in the castle and you have to jolly well run like the wind when it rings.'

'Yes, Gertie, marvellous.' Alice gave a wry smile.

'Of course they would not tell us a thing. Really, you would have thought I was a spy or something. Basil suggested we get Pinkerton's to find you but then I had a wonderful idea: I went to the shop in person. I met the most dreary man, who refused point blank to tell me where you lived. Ridiculous! I said I was your oldest friend in the world, but still he wouldn't – English too, you'd think an Englishman would have believed me. Stuffy old toad.'

'He's my partner actually and he's really very charming. He was protecting me, that was all.'

'I outwitted him though, I bought a pot of jam which had an address on the label and here I am. Do you realise this is my fourth trip, and to imagine all that time you were here and I didn't know. We were in Canada for Christmas, Basil's youngest brother lives there – quite primitive, not like farming at home at all. But what are you doing? In a bakery?' The door opened. 'Oh good, tea, real English tea will it be?'

Merry, Alice's maid, entered the room. Carrying a

heavy tray she manipulated the door with a judicious use of ankle and behind. Gertie watched the girl's gymnastics with wide-eyed interest.

'I hope it will be all right, Alice,' Merry said as she deposited the tray. 'I boiled the water like you said and let the tea stand. If it's awful you'd best have coffee.'

'Thank you, Merry, it's kind of you to bother. I'm sure it will be perfect.'

'Right you are. There are cookies on the plate. Shout if you want anything else,' and, smiling broadly at Gertie, she slipped from the room. Alice began to pour the tea.

'Was that a friend of yours?'

'Merry? Yes, she's my friend, she's also my maid.'

'She called you Alice?'

'Yes,' Alice laughed. 'She always does. Things are different here. She works for me, she doesn't serve me. We eat together . . .'

'Mercy!'

'It works very well. After all, the house is hardly large enough for her to have separate quarters. They are proud people, the Americans. And this is the land of equality, you know.' She laughed at the incredulous expression on Gertie's face. 'It's why the rich tend to import their servants from abroad. Haven't you noticed?'

'Well, now I think about it, yes. Heavens, I always prided myself on being the modern one, but here you are streets ahead of me.' She accepted her tea from Alice.

'You asked what I do. I'm a cook.'

'A cook!' Gertie nearly choked on her tea. 'Did I hear right?'

'Yes, Gertie. When I needed a job it was the only thing I could think of that I could do. All those hours I spent in the kitchen at Gwenfer, you see, weren't wasted.'

'And you can make a living?'

'Oh, yes. I'm very successful. I make pies and cakes as well as jam. And I have an outside catering department that does dinners and weddings. I employ twenty people altogether.'

'But what about Chas?'

'He left me soon after we arrived here – when our money ran out. I had nothing. I had to find something to do – or starve. And I have a child, Gertie. Now, if you don't want to know me any more I'll quite understand. But I don't intend to lie to you and say I'm widowed or anything silly like that.'

'My poor, dear friend, how awful for you. Is it a boy or a girl? How old?'

'Oh, Gertie, you are wonderful; you never were like anyone else I knew. A girl, Grace, she'll be eight in June. She's at school at the moment. I live for her.'

'They are fun, aren't they? I've two, Richard and Gerard, but I do long for a girl.'

'How's my father?'

'Truth?'

'Truth.'

'Unhappy. Daisy Dear is the disappointment of his life: no heir and she flits around all over the place dripping with *your* jewels and spending *his* money.'

'Poor Papa.'

'He probably regrets losing you now. Could you not write?'

'No, I don't think so. There wouldn't be any point. He never cared, and now there's Grace. In any case, I love my work. It's not nearly as hard as it was in the beginning. I admit there was a time when I nearly gave up. But I've been very lucky, I manage to make a pleasant living – I don't miss the luxuries.'

'What about men?' Gertie grinned archly over the rim of her teacup.

'Sorry to disappoint you, Gertie, but no, no men. Who would want me with Grace?'

'Someone will, one day.' The clock chimed the hour. 'Lord, is that the time? I have to fly. Now, I insist you come to dinner with us tomorrow and we shall all go to a party afterwards. Eight o'clock at the Waldorf?'

'I'd like that, Gertie. I'd like to see Basil again. But just the dinner. I really don't want to go to a party.'

'Nonsense, why ever not? It sounds as though you haven't had any fun for years.'

'That's true. But how can I go if I haven't been invited?'

'Don't be silly. As soon as I get back to the hotel I shall arrange for you to be invited. Have you forgotten how things can be done?'

'But I've nothing suitable to wear.' She looked at her friend. 'Oh rats, as you would say, why not? I'll get something.'

'Isn't it amazing in this country how you can buy clothes already made. I love it, no fittings or fuss. I always go back with trunks full of things.' Alice smiled, knowing that if Gertie did return with trunks of new clothes they would have been made for her by the best couturiers in New York. She knew this was Gertie's way of making her feel equal. 'Now, wear all your best jewellery,' Gertie ordered as she pinned on her hat.

'But Gertie, I haven't got any jewellery.'

'Of course, Daisy Dear's got it all hasn't she?' Her laugh rang out. 'Never mind, you can borrow something of mine. I'll send a carriage for you at half past seven.'

Gertie was still talking as Alice walked with her to her carriage.

That afternoon Alice felt almost guilty as she took a bus up-town to buy a new dress. It was the first purely extravagant thing she had done in all her years in New York. She found she was excited at the prospect. So much for all her grand talk to Gertie that one did not miss such things, she thought to herself.

She had forgotten how much was involved in dressing up. She began to regret her first enthusiasm as she had to buy shoes to match the new emerald-green evening dress which needed only a small alteration to make it perfect. And then there were the gloves and evening bag at such expense that she decided that she would have to make do with her old cloak.

That evening she dressed in all her new finery for Grace and Merry to admire. As she twirled around in front of them she realised that, pretty as her new dress was, compared with the other guests she was going to look very plain and undistinguished.

'Mummy, you look like a princess,' Grace exclaimed, her face glowing with pride at seeing her mother dressed up like a lady.

2

Gertie did not send a carriage. Gertie sent an automobile. The noise of its arrival could be heard long before it appeared, followed by a long line of chattering, excited children. Despite the chill wind, heads appeared at windows, and front doors opened as Alice's neighbours crowded to see the display. Grace's plump little face was pink with pride as the vehicle drew to a spluttering halt outside their house. Clouds of acrid smoke belched from the engine and its oil lamps flickered and died. Alice surveyed the contraption with a degree of trepidation. It was typical of Gertie, she thought, with her passion for things modern. Seeing the shining-eyed excitement of her child, Alice asked the chauffeur to drive the three of them round the block. Grace's face grew even pinker as the car navigated the streets and Merry, still in her apron, sat upright, her nose in the air, waving at the staring crowds, as grand as any duchess.

As the motor spluttered and rocked its way up Fifth Avenue Alice held firmly to the strap. She looked anxiously at her watch: it would have been much speedier by horse and carriage, she thought. And then she smiled, imagining how much Queenie would have disapproved of this form of transport.

Alice had seen the Waldorf Astoria but she had never before been through its doors. Crowds of expensively dressed women and their elegant escorts milled about her as she stood in the entrance hall. It had been so long since she had been in such sophisticated company that she found it rather intimidating. No one looked at her in her plain, grey, wool cloak and for a moment she had the extraordinary feeling that she had ceased to exist. She dismissed the fancy and with difficulty made her way through the throng to the busy reception desk. Patiently she waited her turn.

'Would you please –' she started to say to the desk clerk.

'Mr Toohey, your key, sir?' The clerk ignored her.

'Excuse me –' she tried again. This time his attention was centred on a large fat couple who had just arrived in a flurry with a pile of luggage. She began to tap her foot with exasperation.

'Would you –'

'Mrs Hoffer. How very nice to see you again. Are we dining in the Palm Garden tonight?' The clerk smirked obsequiously over Alice's head at the latest arrival.

Alice pushed forward. 'Excuse me . . .'

'Young woman, wait your turn,' Mrs Hoffer blustered at her.

Alice banged her gloved fist on the counter. 'If you don't mind, madame, it *is* my turn.' She swung round to the glowering clerk. 'If you could possibly find the time to tell Lord and Lady Frobisher that their guest Miss Tregowan has arrived, I should be more than obliged,' she said sarcastically.

At the mention of the Frobishers, the change in the clerk's attitude was instantaneous. 'Ah, Miss Tregowan. His lordship requested that you be shown to his suite the moment you arrived.'

'Precisely eight minutes ago, I believe,' she said sharply, looking at her watch.

'Yes, well . . .' With as much dignity as he could salvage and with a flick of the wrist and a flourish the clerk banged the bell for the bell-hop.

The boy escorted her up in the lift. It rose so swiftly that Alice felt her stomach had been left in reception while the rest of her arrived on the fifth floor. Gertie must have been informed she was on her way for her head was poking out of the door to her suite, red curls bobbing as she loudly greeted Alice.

Basil took Alice's hand firmly and declared how shocked he was about Chas and that he would like personally to horsewhip the fellow and when was she going to bring her little girl to tea? Alice felt such warmth from her friends that she now regretted all the years she had not written to them for fear of their censure. She should have known better. Society might spurn her but she should have known that the Frobishers would not.

Gertie, still talking, swept Alice into her sumptuous bedroom for the serious task of sorting through the five leather, crested jewel boxes.

'I don't want to borrow anything too valuable. What if I should lose it?'

'Don't be silly. Choose what you want: it's all insured.'

Since she was wearing green taffeta Gertie suggested emeralds. Alice looked at the matching set of necklace, brooch, ear-rings and bracelet and rejected them, knowing that she would feel uncomfortable in such grandeur. To Gertie's disappointment she chose a simple pearl choker with a diamond clasp, mainly, she realised, because it reminded her so much of the one she had had to sell.

Gertie looked magnificent in fiery red silk which should have clashed with her hair but which made it seem only richer and redder. Her many diamonds glittered as she moved.

'Dreadfully vulgar, isn't it?' she laughed uproariously, catching sight of herself in the full-length mirror. 'But it's New York and here everyone seems to wear every jewel they possess all at once. I always bring the whole Frobisher collection with me on these visits. One can hardly let the side down, can one? Are you sure you're happy with that choker? The other women will be looking like Christmas trees.'

'Perfectly, thank you.' Alice smiled. She was unaware that, by refusing her friend's generous offer, in her simple emerald green dress, she would look dramatically different from the other women.

'At least let me put these little pins in your hair,' Gertie pleaded, showing her a set of pearl and diamond hair clips shaped like flowers. Alice smiled agreement and sat on the dressing-stool while Gertie pinned the flowers about the pleat into which Merry had dressed her long hair.

'You seem happy, Gertie, I'm so pleased.'

Gertie plopped down on the stool beside her. 'Aren't I lucky? Basil is more than I deserve. We have so much in common and he doesn't disapprove of my involvement with the suffrage movement.'

'And who didn't believe in love?'

'Ah well, we can all say silly things when we're young. But I didn't love him when I married him. Love grew. It can, you know.'

'I envy you.' Alice smiled at her as she rose to pick up her plain wool cape.

'You must borrow one of my furs,' Gertie insisted.

'No, thank you. My cloak is a symbol for me. I like to observe and I can in this, no one takes any notice of me.'

Downstairs once more, they walked down a corridor of amber marble. Along its length the sofas were crowded with people who sat and watched the passing parade, as though they were at the theatre, as brilliantly attired women and their escorts strutted up and down. Everyone stared at everyone else, assessing, calculating their worth, and then commenting on their conclusions to their companions. The air was full of the swish and sweep of gowns, the light from the chandeliers played games with the sparks from the jewels on display. The atmosphere was heavy with the scent of a score of different perfumes.

'Isn't this fun?' Gertie clutched at Alice's elbow. 'They call it Peacock Alley. I could spend hours here just gaping at the spectacle. That's what I like about America. What is rude in England is normal behaviour here. Good gracious, look at that woman over there – she can hardly move she's so weighed down with baubles.'

They made their way to the Palm Garden and were fussed over by the maître d' as he showed them to their table.

'I am impressed,' Alice said. 'I gathered that one had to book weeks in advance for a table here.'

'One does but they do so love an English m'lord that Basil always gets us in.'

Alice smiled at Gertie's childlike enjoyment and found that it was catching. She looked about the enormous room, at the full-sized palms growing in pots, which made her feel she was in an exotic jungle. There was an exuberance about the decor and she found she felt a strange pride in her adopted country that it should have produced such opulence as to impress even these two, used as they were to castles and large country houses.

'Lincoln! At last, we had almost given you up,' Gertie yelled across the room, making all heads swivel in their direction. Approaching them across the wide room was a very tall, broad man, tanned and with an unruly shock of corn-coloured hair which reminded Alice of a lion. She was disappointed that they were to be joined by a fourth person; she had hoped that it would be just the three of them. Impossible now to gossip about old times and acquaintances.

'Alice, may I present a friend of ours, Lincoln Wake-field? Lincoln, this is a very dear friend of mine, Alice Tregowan.' Alice found her hand being firmly shaken by one so large that her own disappeared completely into it.

She sat silently watching as a small army of waiters flurried about them. As one discussed the food, another consulted Basil about the wine. A third rearranged their perfectly aligned cutlery. Yet another altered the positions of the glasses. Four others stood silent, watching, like acolytes at a communion. She took the opportunity to study her fellow guest who was in expansive conversation with Basil and the wine waiter. Her first suspicion was that Gertie was match-making, for why else was he here but to escort her? He had a strong face not a handsome one, the sort of face that, she was certain, would look more relaxed in the open air than here in this artificial setting. His hands were those of a worker not a drone and he was old, at least in his mid-forties. He was more likely to be a business associate of Basil's, she decided finally.

He turned to her and asked her where she lived. She looked him square in the eyes, suddenly struck by how blue they were, like a Cornish sailor's eyes. 'Brooklyn,' she said firmly, steeling herself for the surprised look, the inevitably superior reaction of those who lived in New York to those who lived outside. Instead he smiled a warm generous smile that made the skin around his eyes wrinkle into a mesh of laughter lines.

'I hear it's very pleasant there, quiet and peaceful compared with the city,' he said in his deep attractive voice.

The meal began. The food was delicious, of a standard which Alice had not enjoyed for years and, as course followed course, she began to fear for her digestion. The conversation was general and easy until, to her horror, she heard Gertie announce they were going to Mrs Astor's annual January ball after dinner.

'You said we were going to a party. I can't go to the Astors' ball!' Alice exclaimed.

'I thought that's what you would say, so I fibbed.' Gertie grinned at her.

'Why do you not wish to go, Alice?' Basil asked.

'Well, look at me! I'm not dressed for a ball.' She began to feel agitated.

'I think you look beautiful, ma'am,' she heard Lincoln say.

'But it's so select.'

'You mean the Four Hundred?' Lincoln asked.

'Why, yes, that and . . .' she paused, not knowing what to say, not certain why she so vehemently did not want to go. 'I just don't think I should go,' she finished lamely, conscious that they were all staring at her.

'Tell me, where did this expression, "the Four Hundred", come from?' Basil asked Lincoln, deliberately turning the attention from Alice's confusion.

'At Mrs Astor's previous house – which used to be next door to this hotel – her ballroom would hold only four hundred guests. So if you were not invited to her ball, you were nobody,' Lincoln explained with a quizzical air, certain that Basil must already know the reason; everyone did.

'Gertie, you can't just turn up with me and murmur in your hostess's ear that you've brought an old friend with you,' Alice whispered urgently at her friend.

'Really, Alice. As if I would do anything so impolite.'

'But, Gertie, the invitations went out weeks ago. Those who don't get one leave town rather than not be seen. It's completely exclusive.' Alice continued speaking quietly, but with exasperation, to Gertie.

Gertie clicked open her handbag and produced an engraved card. 'See.' She flashed it under Alice's nose. In large black copper-plate she could read 'The Honourable Alice Tregowan.'

'Oh Gertie, I'm sorry,' she said sheepishly.

'Gertie is a marvel, Miss Tregowan. She acquired an invitation for me, too, and I can assure you I am certainly not one of the famous Four Hundred.' He laughed loudly, an uninhibited laugh which showed all his startlingly white teeth. When Alice looked at him again she wondered if he were as old as she had at first thought.

'It really is the most striking coincidence – and I can assure you both that I did not plan it – but do you know that you two have the *most* amazing amount in common.' Alice and Lincoln looked at each other and then expectantly at Gertie. 'You both make pies – now isn't that extraordinary?'

'Really, Miss Tregowan?' he asked politely.

'Well, yes, in a small way.' Her eyes widened with surprise. 'Good gracious, you must be something to do with "Wakefields"?' she said with mounting interest.

'Something to do! Alice, he *is* Wakefields.'

'Then we don't really have much in common, Gertie. Don't be silly.' Not only was 'Wakefields' one of the largest and most famous pie-makers in America but they also made soups, sauces, pickles and jams, which put her small efforts very much into the shade.

'You wouldn't be anything to do with Tregowan of "Gwenfer and Osborn"?' it was his turn to ask.

'Oh, I am enjoying this. She is *the* Tregowan, Lincoln. Isn't that the most extraordinary thing, Basil? Two friends and they both make pies.' Gertie laughed her hooting laugh which never failed to make those sitting nearest jump out of their skins. They all joined in her amusement for, coming from Gertie, the statement was one of genuine pleasure and had nothing snide about it.

'Your products are excellent, Miss Tregowan. Your Dundee cake the best I've ever eaten. And what is the secret of those little pies you make, the triangular ones? Delicious.'

'The pasties? Nothing really, but we use the best meat and it's important to get the potato and onion in the right proportions.'

'Careful, Alice, you'll have him pinching your receipts. Our Lincoln's a ruthless cove when it comes to business aren't you, old sport?' Basil said.

'I would never steal from such a charming competitor.'

'Ah ha, Alice, I sense danger. Lincoln has plans for you.'

'I can think of nothing more pleasurable,' Lincoln replied with a serious expression and looked at her so intensely that Alice, to her confusion, found herself blushing furiously.

3

The crowd standing in the freezing weather outside the Astor mansion moved and spoke as one. At the arrival of each new carriage their bodies moved forward in a wave, necks were craned and the 'ohs' and 'ahs' were expelled in unison. At each break in the spectacle their feet were stamped like an approaching army in an effort to keep their circulation going.

'It makes one understand how royalty must feel being stared at like this. Ghastly!' Gertie said, staring moodily out of the carriage at the crowd as they remained halted in the long line of carriages which spread down Fifth Avenue as far as the eye could see. Gertie might enjoy staring but obviously found it irksome when she was on the receiving end.

As she descended from the carriage and saw the large white stone house ablaze with light, Alice felt nervous. The last ball she attended had been her own. She trailed along in Gertie's wake, conscious of what a bitter disappointment they were to the sightseers – Gertie clutched her furs about her closely so that no jewels were visible, and Alice in her plain cloak looked like Gertie's maid scuttling along behind her.

Blue-velvet-suited footmen took their coats and solemnly handed them on to other footmen who, with measured tread, escorted them through a series of rooms each one decorated in various combinations of white and gold. The main salon was a blaze of rococo and here everyone, it appeared, momentarily forgot they were sophisticates to admire the carpet of peacocks' tails. Gertie nudged Alice and pointed out the furniture, telling her that the pieces were copies of those in the Trianon. Alice was unsure if Gertie were intrigued, admiring or censorious. It did seem strange to have so much money and then to furnish your house with reproductions, Alice thought.

Standing beneath a portrait of herself, Mrs Astor welcomed her guests. Alice found herself shaking the hand of a woman who, compared with the image in the painting, had a kindly expression and, she thought, a rather sad smile. Her rather commonplace face, the kind one would pass in the street without a second glance, was at complete odds with her appearance. She glittered with diamonds from head to toe, as if on fire. From the diamond tiara on her wig – shockingly black – and the long strands of diamonds wound around her neck and cascading down her front, to Marie Antoinette's large brooch on her bosom, she outshone and outsparkled any of her guests. It must all have weighed an enormous amount, was Alice's irreverent thought.

Gertie led the way into the ballroom, a large room which spanned the full length of the house and which by day was the picture gallery. Gertie peered up at the walls which were completely covered with paintings. Beneath the ceiling was a heavily decorated frieze. On this, at intervals, larger than life statues stood poised on their plinths, their bodies arched ominously over the throng below, like divers about to leap.

'Somewhat municipal, isn't it?' she said with the confident and unselfconscious air of one whose home was hung with Reynolds, Rembrandts, Velázquez and the odd Holbein. 'Such shiny frames,' she added in what she, no doubt, took to be a whisper.

'Gertie!' Alice admonished, conscious of the frowns of those about them who could not help but hear.

'What have I done?' Gertie looked surprised.

'You're being rude.'

'Am I?' Gertie said, astonished, her red curls finally breaking free from her tiara and bouncing around in her agitation.

'Yes, Gertie. I'm sure everyone here thinks this is beautiful.'

'Oh, rats. I meant it, such glittering frames. You should see our Rembrandts' dingy frames. In any case, I was only talking to you; I didn't know anyone else was listening. They shouldn't listen to other people's conversations,' she said, loudly and defensively, glaring at the affronted Americans as if they had been at fault. 'Let's get some wine punch.' She bustled over to a group of seats and their party sat down. Within a second Gertie had seen some long-lost friends and was on her feet again and, with Basil in tow, was careering across the ballroom towards them.

'The English aristocrats have such a natural arrogance about them.' Lincoln laughed good-naturedly. 'But it is almost childlike, so one cannot be offended for a moment.' He beckoned to a footman to bring them refreshments.

'Centuries of ruling, I suppose,' Alice smiled.

'You don't approve?'

'Of Gertie? Who could remain cross with her? She's so outspoken, always has been, but she doesn't mean to give offence.'

'No, I meant of the system in your country?'

'I think it's wrong that only the top stratum of people have the chance to succeed – in the church, in the army, in politics. I think it is stupid, and equally unfair, that if you are "in trade" you are not socially acceptable. Why, you and I, we pie-makers, wouldn't be invited anywhere!' She rolled her eyes in mock horror and laughed at the silliness of it all.

'Don't for one moment, Miss Tregowan, think this is a true democracy. In our way we are as socially restricted as your society, here the "Four Hundred" rule with a rod of iron. The nouveaux riches are not welcome. I'm here only because of Lady Frobisher – I gather the Astors stay with her and Basil in England. I'm sure Mrs Astor takes their friendship with a parvenu such as myself as proof of their aristocratic eccentricity.' He laughed with such confidence that it was obvious he was not in the least concerned with society's strictures.

'But that's worse. I'm not making excuses for the English but at least they have had centuries of ruling. I mean, how long have the Astors had money, or the Vanderbilts, or any of them – they all started in trade, didn't they?'

'Of course, but, like your aristocracy, it is something that after a few generations they would prefer not to be remembered. We are not so different after all, you see. But, Gertie tells me your father is a lord,' he went on, 'and yet you have radical views.'

She looked up at him, sharply, annoyed that Gertie should have told him about her background and fearful of what else Gertie might have said. 'I didn't have a conventional upbringing. I was once, but I'm no longer, a lord's daughter,' she replied enigmatically and there was a coolness in her voice that made him look at her closely and change the subject.

'Would you care to dance, Miss Tregowan?' he asked

as the orchestra resumed after an interval and dancers drifted on to the floor to take up their positions.

'I'm afraid I can't dance the cotillions – they're unknown to me.' She smiled apologetically, afraid now that she might have sounded too sharp with him. 'But please don't let me stop you asking someone else.' And as she said it she realised, with a start, that his dancing with someone else was the last thing she wanted.

'There's no one else I wish to ask.' She heard his reply with pleasure. Again Lincoln looked at her with the same intensity as he had in the restaurant. And once again Alice found herself blushing and, worse, beginning to feel a strange agitation. He sensed her confusion. 'Might I confess? I'm greatly relieved. The good Lord may only have given me two feet but out there on the dance floor it's as if I have four,' he joked and Alice felt safe again.

'So,' he continued. 'You're a political lady, as is Lady Frobisher?'

'Me? Good gracious, no. I never have any idea what is going on in the world. I'm so busy, you see, that I never read a paper. When the new century came in I was in my kitchen making a rush order of pies!' She laughed. 'And, two years ago, the Queen of England had been dead for a fortnight before I knew and then it was only because my partner mentioned it. No, I'm sorry, I'm very ignorant.'

'I find that difficult to believe.'

Gertie fluttered back and forth, alighting with them for a moment before flashing off to greet another friend whom she would then lead back to meet Alice and Lincoln. Despite what he had said about not being acceptable, Alice noticed that, at the mention of his name, those being introduced looked at him with a keen interest – money did matter, whatever he said. But as to herself, she felt as she had at the Waldorf, as if she did not exist. Time and again her hand was politely shaken, but the gaze of those to whom she was introduced quickly flitted about the room, past her shoulder, no doubt on the look-out for someone of more consequence than this plainly dressed young woman. Only a couple of young men, taken by her beauty, met her gaze. But even they did not linger, casting about for richer and more acceptable prey than one who looked like a dressed-up governess.

She watched Gertie as she effortlessly joked and gossiped, talking of nothing of any consequence and yet making whomever she was talking to lean forward with anticipation. Alice wondered if she had ever been so relaxed in society. If she had ever had it, the ability had gone. She felt gauche, underdressed and tongue-tied. She might rack her brains but still she could think of nothing to say; she had lived too long without the need for social repartee.

Alice surveyed the glittering throng, the fortunes displayed in jewellery. She noted the great banks of flowers all forced in a hot-house at goodness knows what expense. There was food enough for an army and a battalion of servants stood ready to serve it. She found the overstated opulence distasteful. And it smelt. She had forgotten the smell of ballrooms – that combination of perfumes, tobacco, mothballs and sweat.

She felt an arm gently touch her elbow. 'Perhaps you would like to walk a little?' It was Lincoln. She agreed, far too quickly she realised, and tentatively took his arm as they moved from the noisy ballroom. 'I find these occasions very irksome, don't you? Everyone so busy saying nothing to each other. And such displays of wealth are overpowering.'

'It wasn't just me, then?'

'No, I think your friends are far more used than we to such gatherings.'

He led her towards a sitting-out arrangement in an alcove decorated with banks of blue and white flowers, the blue matching exactly the footmen's liveries. He held the gilt and expensively upholstered chair for her to sit down at an exquisite marquetry table.

'I think the last time I saw such opulence was at Buckingham Palace when I curtsied to Queen Victoria.'

'There are those who say that Mrs Astor is our queen, so it would seem fitting.' He laughed. 'Would you like an ice, or something?'

He might not be socially acceptable but he had such presence about him that he had only to look in the direction of a footman for the ice to materialise as though by magic.

Alice was enjoying the sorbet, but even more she was beginning to enjoy his company. She found him easy to talk to, easy to laugh with. To her surprise she found she was completely relaxed with him.

She was laughing at a joke he had made when she looked up and saw coming towards her Mr van Hooven with a large, complacent-looking woman on his arm. It was as if a jug of ice-cold water had been thrown over her. She began to shake, the spoon slipped from her fingers, which seemed suddenly lifeless, and clattered on to the floor. She stood up, her face rigid at the sight of the man who made her recall things she had hoped she had forgotten. Lincoln spoke to her but she did not hear him as she took shocked stock of herself. What on earth was she doing here in this company? What did she mean by accepting the Astor hospitality? The champagne she had drunk, the sorbet she had been eating, the music she had listened to, the flowers she had admired – all had been paid for by the misery of the people in the tenements. Paid for from the pathetic sums they had had to work for, beg or steal to pay their paltry rents. She was being unfaithful to all those poor souls trapped in the hell from which she had escaped. She did not belong here, not with these people.

'Excuse me,' she said in an almost inaudible whisper to Lincoln and, snatching her bag from the table, ran from the room. She sped down the stairs, ordered her cloak and, still shaking, was let out of the great door. She fought her way through the throng of sightseers who still clogged the sidewalk and was soon running down Fifth Avenue.

She sped along, oblivious of the snow that was beginning to swirl about her, totally unaware of the cold that was seeping through her thin cloak. She felt only anger with herself that she had not stood firm. Worse, she knew why she had not and despised herself the more. She was just like the sightseers crowded on the sidewalk; she had been curious, she had wanted to see what it was like inside the great Astor château. Maybe she had even, despite herself, hoped that she would be accepted, would find herself back where once she had belonged. And all the time she had known full well that next to van Hooven the name of Astor was the most hated name amongst the tenements.

She was unaware of an automobile slowing down beside her as she raced along the sidewalk as if all the demons in hell were after her.

'Miss Tregowan. Please, what is the matter? Did I offend you?'

She swung round to see Lincoln Wakefield, a worried expression on his face, leaping from the motor and running towards her.

'I'm sorry. You did nothing.' She put her head down and continued to hurry, crossing an intersection without looking to left or right.

Lincoln grabbed her arm. 'Miss Tregowan, you will kill yourself at this rate. Get into my vehicle, please.'

'Leave me alone. I want to be alone.' She wrenched herself free.

'No, now stop,' he ordered, and despite herself the tone of his voice made her slow down. He took her arm and turned her towards his motor car which had been slowly following them along the street. 'In you get, you'll die of pneumonia in this cold.' Unceremoniously he bundled her into the vehicle. As soon as she was safely inside, her teeth began to chatter; the shaking which had started at the Astors' house returned and she found speech impossible. Lincoln ordered his chauffeur to drive on. He turned to her to ask her what the problem was and to his horror, and hers, she burst into tears. Without saying more, he carefully draped a fur wrap around her, put his arm about her and cradled her against him as she continued to weep uncontrollably.

Gently he stroked her hair, saying nothing, waiting for the storm to subside. Her sobs became less. He let go of her for a moment to lean forward and open the travelling cocktail cabinet. From the silver-topped decanter he poured them both large brandies.

'Drink this slowly, it will help,' he ordered gently. 'And when you're ready, tell me. I want to know what frightened you so.'

'I didn't belong there.'

'Why on earth not? Because you make pies? Because they wouldn't think you good enough? Oh come, Alice.' He smiled and she did not even notice that he had called her by her name.

'I hate those people. I should never have gone. I betrayed my past by being there – I should not have been in the same room they were,' she exclaimed dramatically, looking at him with anguished eyes.

'Alice, try to calm down and tell me what happened.'

She gulped the last of the brandy and he poured her another one and waited patiently. She looked at him, at his kind and concerned expression, and, slowly at first, and then more quickly and finally with an almost desperate speed, she began to tell him of her time in the tenement, of the rats, of the poverty, of her dreadful fear that one day, unless she worked and worked, she would return there.

'Never, Alice, as long as I live,' he said and, leaning towards her, kissed her gently on the mouth.

439

Alice had overslept. For the first time in the six years she had been working she was not the first in the bakery. It was Merry who, having woken her, sped round to the bakery to give the staff the day's orders. And it was Merry who persuaded her, just this once, to have her breakfast in bed.

Alice felt quite decadent as she lay in bed waiting for Merry to bring her tea and toast. She knew she should be up but on the other hand she felt an unfamiliar lethargy. She blamed the wine and the rich food. There had never been enough money left over, after she had met the interest on her house loan, had paid Merry's wages and Grace's expenses, to waste on the luxury of wine and exotic food. But also she was tired, for last night she had found it difficult to fall asleep. Once in bed she had found her mind a helter-skelter of thoughts and ideas.

She had been shocked at how vehemently she had reacted to the van Hoovens and Astors of this world, at how much the opulence had disturbed her. Where did it leave her? Once she had been one of their company, but no longer. And yet, the women she worked with, as much as she liked them, were not her friends. There was always the barrier of employer and employee between them and she knew that, sweet and kind as they were, she had nothing in common with any of them. This morning she saw that her reaction last night was due largely to the shock of realising that she did not belong anywhere now. She had not made friends in this new life; now she was faced with the prospect that it was doubtful if she ever would. The knowledge emphasised her loneliness, something she had not allowed herself to face until this moment.

And there was Lincoln. When he had leaned over and

kissed her she had not resisted, she had allowed it. What a fool she had been: she had liked him very much, he had been a good companion and now she had spoiled it by behaving like a servant girl in the back of his automobile. What must he have thought of her? But in any case, she thought as she settled back on her pillow, there could be no friendship. He might like her now, but what would he feel when he found out about Grace? How would she appear to him then? Even if she had not had her daughter as an impediment to their relationship there was another – Lincoln was wealthy. Having known poverty, she could no longer contemplate life with a rich man. She smiled at herself. One kiss and here she was, just like the servant girl, dreaming of a future with him.

But if last night she had discovered how violently she resented wealth, what was she to do when her own inheritance came? She did not know how much it was; she had never enquired for she had learned about it in those far-off days when money had meant nothing to her. She always had plenty of it. So, how was she to reconcile having a fortune of her own with the way in which she felt about the injustice of life? She sighed. She would have to give it away – that was the only possible action. She would pay off what she owed on this house, get new ovens for the bakery, perhaps set a little aside for Grace's future, but there was nothing for it, the rest would have to go.

She was greeted in the bakery by sly glances and much giggling which increased dramatically when a large bouquet of flowers was delivered. Her hands were shaking as she slipped the card out of its envelope to see that it was from Lincoln with the request that they dine together this evening. She telephoned the number on the card.

'Thank you for my flowers, Mr Wakefield, they are beautiful. But I'm afraid I cannot dine with you tonight.'

'Why not?'

'I can't. That's all.'

'Have you a prior engagement?'

'No, it's not that, I . . .' She wished she could have lied and said she had.

'Then I shall be at your house at seven, Miss Tregowan.'

'But –' The telephone was dead. She shook it, annoyed that he had cut her off, annoyed at his arrogance. She would not go; she would show him.

She could not settle to work, she made mistakes, she found her mind wandering alarmingly and finally she handed over to Marie, her senior assistant. She returned to her house, collected Gertie's pearl choker and, catching a horse-bus, started on the long journey across the bridge and up-town to Gertie's hotel.

She asked for Gertie at the reception desk, part of her hoping to be told that she was out.

'What on earth happened to you last night, Alice?'

'I felt unwell,' she lied, wondering how she could so easily lie to Gertie and yet had not managed it with Lincoln.

'Are you well now?' Gertie was concerned.

'Yes, very. It was the excitement I expect.'

'What did you think of Lincoln? I think he rather liked you.' Gertie grinned.

'He's very pleasant.' Alice looked fixedly at the carpet.

'Ah ha, Basil said he was sure something was afoot! When are you to see him again?'

'He's invited me to dinner tonight but I'm not going.'

'Why ever not?'

'I don't want to.'

'Why? What's wrong with him? He's very personable and very rich.'

'I don't want to see him again, that's all.' She felt herself becoming annoyed with Gertie's insistence.

'Then I'll find you someone else. New York is full of the most unsuitable men.'

'Oh, Gertie.' She laughed. 'You are sweet. But I have my life arranged; I don't want any complications. I don't want to be hurt, if you must know.'

'Lincoln won't hurt you.'

'Gertie, I have a daughter, remember. No one will want me once they know that. Meeting Chas compromised my life for ever. It was kind of you to take me out with you last night. But I don't belong in your world any more, Gertie. I found it unsettling, I found being escorted by a man equally disturbing, and the sooner I return to my own life the better.'

'It all seems so dreadfully unfair. I expect that Chas is quite merrily married now and no one thinks the worse of him.'

'You'll never change the attitude of the world, Gertie. I was a fool and my daughter and I have to pay the price. I'm used to the idea now.'

'But don't you feel bitterness towards Chas?'

'How could I? It would mean I was bitter about having Grace, and that I cannot be.'

'Well, I think you are a saint. I would be screaming injustice from the roof-tops.'

Despite all her protestations to Gertie, despite her determination not to dine with him, Alice found that as the evening approached she was excited. It was an excitement that she had not felt for a long time and one that she had not expected to feel again. It was a feeling to which she finally gave in. By seven o'clock she was dressed and waiting. One evening of his company, a pleasant dinner, good wine, there could be no danger in that, she had persuaded herself.

They sat at a discreet table in a discreet restaurant and Lincoln smiled at her in such a way that Alice felt she had made a grave mistake. She should not have come; she was in danger of caring too much for this man. It would be better if she finished it now.

'Mr Wakefield . . .'

'Could you not call me Lincoln? You are so formal.'

'I'm sorry, it's the English in me. Lincoln, I have something to tell you.'

'Yes?' he looked expectant.

'Eight years ago I eloped with a man. That's why I'm here – he was American, you see. There was a slight problem in that he was married and did not see fit to tell me,' she said, attempting to laugh light-heartedly and failing miserably.

'What was his name?'

'Oh, his name is unimportant.'

'Not to me. I would like to know.'

'I would rather not say. I was very young and very stupid.'

'He deserted you?'

'Yes. And left me with the hotel bill.' This time she did manage to laugh. 'A very large bill: he had expensive tastes.'

'I see,' Lincoln frowned and she did not know at whom he frowned, at Chas for deceiving her or at her for being so foolish. 'A sad tale.'

'It becomes sadder. I had a child.' She sat back in her chair and closed her eyes so as not to see his expression. It was done now, she could get back to her old life. She felt her hand being taken and she opened her eyes to see him lift it to his mouth and to kiss it gently.

'I want to marry you, Alice.' He looked at her tenderly, but it was an expression that she did not see.

She sat stunned. 'Marry? Me? Oh, really . . .' Her laugh this time was a short bitter one. And then she felt a flash of anger. 'I've never asked for pity from anyone.'

'You think my proposal is out of pity? I'm not a fool, Alice. I would not contemplate marriage for that reason.'

'Then why?'

'Who can tell? Just that last night, as I crossed the floor of the Palm Garden and I saw you, I resolved there and then that you were the woman I wished to marry. I don't know why. It's illogical but it happened. I can assure you I do not make a habit of proposing to young women I have only just met. If it is a shock to you, it is also one to me.' He laughed. She frowned. 'I had not intended to speak so soon. But just now . . . it seemed, oh, I don't know, it seemed the right moment.'

'Haven't you been listening to anything I have said, Lincoln?'

'I knew already.'

'Knew what?'

'That you had run away from your family and country and that you had a daughter. Grace is her name, am I not right?'

'Who told you?'

'Does it matter? It was not your friends if that is what you're worrying about.'

'Then you found out?' He nodded. She pushed her plate of uneaten food from her and stood up. She adjusted her dress with a nervous flick of her hand and looked proudly at him. 'I don't like people who pry into the lives of others, Mr Wakefield. I find it most unattractive. No doubt you think you are doing me a great favour in offering me marriage. Well, you are mistaken. I don't need anyone in my life, thank you, and certainly not someone who, without knowing me, has the temerity to think that I would consider him as a husband. Good evening . . .'

And with head held high, Alice swept from the restaurant and from Lincoln Wakefield.

5

Walking out of the restaurant dramatically was easy. Rejecting Lincoln Wakefield was to prove far more difficult than Alice had realised. She was bombarded with flowers, trinkets, letters and telephone calls. The letters, the flowers, the trinkets, all were sent back unopened. In self-defence, Alice stopped answering the telephone in the bakery. Instead she had one of her assistants do it for her and, when Lincoln called, she was instructed to say that Alice was not available. It made her feel very foolish in front of her staff.

Luckily for her sanity, during the next few days she was very busy. She had two important dinners to arrange, which involved her in much supervision and work. And the following week there was a large wedding for which she was to do the catering. Work, she had decided, was the answer to everything.

Then his automobile began to appear. Whenever she came out of her house, in the early morning, it was there. In the evening, when she left work, there it was again across the road from her bakery. As the days passed it ceased to be an innocuous automobile but became a sinister collection of black metal which began to make her fearful of looking out of the window. He never got out of the vehicle; he made no attempt to speak to her, did not even acknowledge her. He simply sat watching her. After a week of this she began to wish that he would approach her; it would be less menacing.

Eventually she could stand the strain no longer and one evening, after work, crossed the street purposefully and banged on the window. With insufferable slowness he wound the window down and, as his chauffeur sat impassively gazing ahead, Lincoln smiled at her.

'Alice!' he said as if he were surprised to see her.

'Really, Mr Wakefield. I should appreciate it if you would stop spying on me. Otherwise I shall be forced to call the police.'

'Then let me see you, Alice. Let me take you out to dinner. Accept my gifts, at least speak to me on the telephone.' He smiled at her and she was struck by how much softer his face became when he smiled, almost handsome, she decided. And then, conscious of her treacherous thoughts, she shook her shoulders and stood upright, as if her posture gave her more control.

'I thought I made myself clear to you the other evening, Mr Wakefield. I want no more to do with you.'

'You made yourself painfully clear, Alice. But we have a problem, you see. I have decided that you are to be my wife, and I never give up when I want something – not, that is, until I have it.' Again he smiled, the warm all-embracing smile which for some inexplicable reason made her look at his mouth and remember the feel of his lips upon hers.

'This is ridiculous.' She turned hastily to go, but his hand moved quickly to grab at her arm and stop her.

'Alice, please listen to me, I beg you.'

She looked up and down the street; curtains were twitching at a couple of the windows. 'We can't talk here, like this, it is too undignified. You'd best come to my house. But only for a minute,' she added, pointedly.

Lincoln's size made her sitting-room seem even smaller. He seemed uncomfortable and looked even more so when she asked him to sit down. He perched awkwardly on the edge of one of her chairs.

'I wish you would leave me alone, Lincoln, to get on with my life.'

'But I want you to be part of my life. I realised that I was heavy-handed the other night. I had not intended to speak my mind so quickly. I regret what I said.'

'I did not ask you in to start all that again,' she said sharply, seating herself as far away from him as she could. To her consternation, she found that here, in this room, his close proximity made her feel strangely elated.

'You must listen to me. If you don't you could be about to ruin both our lives.'

'Don't be so melodramatic.'

'I love you, Alice. Perhaps that is what I should have said. I loved you the moment I set eyes on you. What has happened in your past is no concern of mine. I want to

447

look after you and your little girl. I have the wherewithal to give you both a good life . . .'

'I don't want your money. I don't approve of money.'

'Oh, Alice, don't be so high and mighty.' He chuckled.

That chuckle annoyed Alice more than anything else. 'You haven't lived as I have had to,' she said angrily. 'People like you know nothing about life in parts of this city. I could not live like you: my guilt would be too strong.'

'That is foolish talk. I can promise you anything you want, but I cannot pledge you poverty. I am rich because I have worked to be so, I feel no shame for my wealth. It was honestly gained.'

'On whose suffering? I wonder if your workers would agree with you?'

'What do you know about me or the way I work? How can you condemn me simply because I employ people? You employ people – do they resent you?' He was not laughing now, she was pleased to note.

'Of course not. I'm a fair employer and I work harder than anybody else in my establishment.'

'So, what makes you think you are special? I had no idea you were so conceited.'

'That's because you don't know me.'

He glared angrily at her and she began to relax, feeling that at any moment he would storm out of her house and her life. Instead he sighed, settled back into the chair and studied her for what seemed an age. She found his stare more than disconcerting.

He leaned towards her and she found herself pushing further back into her own chair. 'Look, Alice. I can understand how you felt the other night at the Astors, after your experiences in the tenements. But I'm not one of them. I have a huge manufacturing complex as you know, and you are welcome to come and see it, to talk to whomever you like amongst my workforce. But for God's sake don't turn me down because I'm rich. What would we gain if I gave it all away? Thirty thousand people would be out of work, or employed by someone far worse than me. That would be the outcome.'

Alice looked steadily at the pattern on her carpet and said nothing, for the simple reason that she could think of nothing to say and was beginning to feel rather stupid.

'I want to make you happy, Alice. You and your little girl. I could adopt her, she could take my name.'

'She's got a name. Mine,' she flashed at him.

'Then mine could be added to it. Be reasonable, Alice. What has happened is unfortunate for you, but it is worse for your child. She will carry the stigma for ever – what sort of marriage can she hope to make? But as our daughter her future would be secure. You can reject me for a thousand reasons, but can you reject me for your daughter?'

'That is unfair, Lincoln.'

'I know. But to make you my wife I will fight any way I can.'

'I don't love you.'

'Perhaps not, but you find me attractive. You weren't averse to my kissing you the other night . . .' He gave her one of his charming, lazy smiles. 'If you had remained in England in high society, would you have loved the man you married? Probably not. Like most society women you would have married someone suitable and, if you were lucky, you might have learned to love him. Like our friend Gertie, for example.'

'I would not have married.'

'You cannot say that, Alice, with any certainty. I realise that there have been intolerable burdens in your life. I want to relieve you of those. I want to make the rest of your life a happy, secure one.'

'I have a considerable amount of money of my own to come soon. I will be secure then. I won't need any money from anyone.'

He laughed. 'So who's lecturing me on wealth? At least I worked for mine. Where's yours coming from?'

There was no answer to that remark and Alice, feeling outsmarted, asked him if he would like some tea. This question reduced Lincoln to such laughter that soon the tears were rolling down his cheeks. Alice sat perplexed, unsure what it was she had said that was so funny. But his mirth was infectious and soon she too was laughing even if she did not know why.

'Oh, Alice,' he was wiping the tears away with a handkerchief, 'I love you. In the middle of discussing our whole future you ask me if I want tea? That is so beautifully English, so wonderfully foreign. And, you know what? It's a sure sign that I have just won the argument.'

'I don't understand.'

'Who ever heard of an Englishman sitting down to tea with the enemy?' And he was laughing again. 'But I will make a pact with you, Alice. No more talk of love and marriage. We shall be friends, if that will make you happier.'

'It would,' she replied, and to her annoyance and confusion found that her voice held a tinge of disappointment.

She had told him she did not love him but, as the weeks went by and she saw him nearly every day, she realised that she had not been speaking the whole truth. What had confused her was that she did not feel, as she had with Chas, that overwhelming sense of excitement, the thrill of knowing she was to see him that had made even breathing difficult. This emotion was different, it was calmer, it was easier, it was more comfortable.

Now the daily flowers and trinkets were joined by toys for Grace who, the moment she had met Lincoln, had been swept off her feet far more quickly than her mother.

On Sundays when the bakery was closed they spent the whole day together taking Grace with them, to the zoo, the park, the museums. Alice enjoyed those Sundays. She would watch Grace and Lincoln walking hand in hand, would smile at their childish jokes and pranks. At such times she would allow herself to think of them as a family, she let herself dream.

But if she enjoyed the Sundays, best of all were the evenings when they did not go out but dined at home, just the two of them. After dinner they would sit in the fire-light and she would listen as he talked about his life. He had been a poor farmer's son who, with his mother, had decided to augment their income as she had done. In their case they made a pickle, the recipe of which had been handed down through generations of his family. He told her how, after its success, they had increased their range of products. Now, she learned, although Wakefields were one of the largest manufacturers of sauces and pies, he had invested shrewdly in rail, in real estate, in cattle and the stock market – no tenement blocks, he was at pains to assure her.

One day he took her to one of his factories. The professional woman in her was more than impressed with what she saw. Long production lines, efficient methods, clean, well-lit and ventilated working conditions, smiling workers. She noted how he greeted them, and with what easy familiarity they responded. He showed her the nursery he had installed for the married women workers. He took her to see the community hall he had built and, last of all, he took her to the small town, most of which he owned and whose inhabitants were his employees. She admitted quite openly how foolish she felt.

In turn she told him of her past life. She spoke of her parents and the lack of love. He learned of Oswald, her mother's madness. She was surprised she had told him

451

about her mother; she had never told a living soul that, not even Chas. She could even confess to him her fear that the same madness might strike her. He took her hand gently and reassured her that she was the sanest person he had ever met. And suddenly the nightmare that had been part of her life for as long as she could remember faded in that moment. She talked of Queenie, and of her years with Ia who, apart from Gertie, had been the only friend she had ever had in her strange life. Frequently she talked of Gwenfer. She became frustrated at her inability to convey in words its beauty and what it meant to her. She expected him to laugh at the idea of loving a house so much, but he did not; he seemed to understand. Invariably, he noticed, when Gwenfer was the subject, her eyes would fill with tears.

They were becoming good friends just as he had promised. And Lincoln kept his other promise. He never mentioned love, let alone marriage.

The summer came and their trips included boat journeys, picnics and enough ice-cream to satisfy Grace for a lifetime. But he never touched Alice in a way that could be construed as over-familiar, and never attempted to kiss her.

She seemed to be in a permanent state of confusion these days. She did not have Gertie to confide in, for in the spring Gertie and Basil had sailed for England and would not be back for two years at least. She was relieved that Lincoln made no advances and yet found she was bitterly disappointed that he did not. She wanted to see him but also she wanted him to stay away. During those evenings she had to work in her business she found herself racked with jealousy, wondering where he was and with whom.

At the same time she was perplexed by her emotions. This was not love – not as she remembered it. Nor was it friendship – she felt far more for Lincoln than that.

Above all he made her feel content; she found security when she was with him. But was it enough?

She knew she must not love, because when she did disaster and death followed her like a shadow. She knew her fear of catastrophe was not for herself alone, it was for him.

6

'Are my ladies ready?' Lincoln called up the stairs as Merry let him into the house. 'You must wrap up warmly, we have a long journey ahead of us,' he said as Grace and Alice descended the stairs.

'A journey? Oh, Mr Wakefield, how exciting, where?' Grace hopped from one leg to another with excitement.

'I have a secret I want to show you.'

'A secret? Can Mummy know too?'

'Oh, yes, most definitely.' He smiled over the child's head at Alice.

'I like your coat, Mr Wakefield. So warm it looks.' Grace's chubby hand stroked the nap of the beaver fur he was wearing.

'I shall have to find one just like it for you, shan't I?'

'Please!' The hopping increased in intensity.

'Lincoln, you must not. You spoil her.'

'I like spoiling her, at least she lets me – not like her mother, always angry with me for my little gifts.'

Outside was a gleaming new automobile. This one, with a fixed metal roof, was a decided improvement on the last whose top had been of fabric which never fitted properly. No matter how tightly Alice tied a scarf over her hat she always arrived at their destination dishevelled from the draughts that sneaked in. But today it was so cold they would still need the fur wraps that the chauffeur tucked about them.

'Is this the surprise, this new car, Mr Wakefield?' Grace asked, a shade disappointed.

'Good heavens, no. My surprise is a giant one.'

The car bumped its way across the bridge, up the wide avenues which were as always clogged with traffic. As, these days, half the vehicles were automobiles and half were horse-drawn the resulting tangle became worse each month. The horse drivers felt they should have precedence over the motors. The automobile drivers felt differently. Both groups were not inhibited in their abusive defence of their position.

At last they were out of the city and in the country. The sight of the trees in their gaudy autumn colours made Alice shiver. She remembered another October, another trip into the country. Then the colours had seemed joyful; now she found them threatening in their blood-red intensity. Lincoln looked at her, concerned.

'Are you too cold, Alice?'

'No, Lincoln, I just thought of something silly.'

'May one ask what?'

'Nothing of any importance.' She managed to smile back.

Despite Grace's entreaties Lincoln remained tight-lipped, refusing to say where they were going. It was a good hour later that the car finally left the main road and chugged along a dirt track, panicking every living creature they passed, much to Grace's amusement. Children ran screaming for their mothers, horses' hooves flicked in the air with panic, herds of cattle stampeded and dogs barked hysterically before slinking away, their tails between their legs, from this noisy, smoke-billowing monster. After crossing a wooden bridge over a wide river they finally turned in between large gates and up a long drive along which maple trees in their scarlet livery stood as sentinels. The drive ended in a great sweep before an old white house. Great trees, oaks, beeches, and more maples, surrounded it, as if holding the building protectively and the red, orange and yellow of their dying leaves made the house with its simple pillared portico stand out in dramatic contrast against this fiery backdrop. The long sash windows glinted as if in greeting. The large white door with its fan-shaped window at the top reminded Alice of her father's house in London.

'That's the surprise.' Lincoln sat back and watched their reactions with a satisfied expression on his face. Grace tumbled out of the car and raced up the flight of steps that rose from the gravel in a graceful curve.

'Mummy, I can see the sea,' she shouted with excitement.

'Lincoln, it's beautiful. Who lives here?'

'It's not as grand as Gwenfer, I know. And I also know that no house can ever replace it. But Grace is right, you can see the sea and that's one thing in its favour.'

'But Lincoln . . . ?'

'For us, my darling. I needed to find the perfect position for a house for you before I dared once again to ask you to be my wife.'

'Oh, Lincoln.' She felt her heart racing, she wanted more than anything to say yes, but perversely found she could not. What was it? What was stopping her now? All she knew was that today the memories of the past seemed more intense. Perhaps it was her silly reaction to the colours of the trees that made that other time, and its catastrophic consequences, keep returning to her mind. She looked around almost in panic. Grace raced back to the carriage.

'Mr Wakefield, it's a pretty house.'

'Would you like to live here?'

'Lincoln! This is not fair,' Alice admonished.

'Please. Our house is so tiny and shabby. This one is lovely.'

'Then here you shall live.'

'Can I have a pony?'

'Yes.'

'And a governess's trap?'

'My dear Grace, you can have whatever you want.'

'Lincoln, you are impossible.'

'I told you I would use every weapon at my disposal to have what I want. But look,' from a briefcase on the floor of the car he took a sheaf of papers, 'these are the plans I've had drawn up for the new house.'

'You're not going to knock that one down?' she asked, horrified.

'Of course. It's far too small, it has only six bedrooms, and it's too simple. I want a mansion for my Alice.'

'I think it is perfect as it is. I don't need a mansion, Lincoln.'

'Does that mean – yes?' he asked eagerly, taking her hand in his. Alice looked at this man, this honourable man. She thought of the confusion in her mind and wondered if by agreeing she might make it all disappear. The trees threatened her and that, she rationalised, was illogical. Then she had been an innocent young girl at the mercy of a scoundrel. This time she was a woman with a man of a different calibre altogether.

She laughed softly. 'I suppose it does,' she said eventually.

Controlling Lincoln over the matter of the house proved difficult. She had managed to persuade him that to knock it down would be sacrilege and so he had appeared with another set of plans which, using the original house as its core, added large obtrusive wings. She feared that the result might be an unfortunate *mélange*. But there was no stopping Lincoln. He had compromised once, but it did not appear he was willing to do so again. Finally, for the sake of peace, she agreed. It transpired that he had bought the whole island – Dart Island, named for its shape. Lincoln wanted to rename it 'Gwenfer Island' but here she was adamant. As kindly as she could, she explained that there could only be one Gwenfer. So Dart Island it remained.

It was a pretty island, heavily wooded, with a farm, a handful of small dwellings, a minute school, and an even smaller church built of wood. But best of all for Alice there was the sea. Not the towering cliffs of her childhood, nor the great cruel rocks jutting from the water, but it was her Atlantic all the same even if it rolled in in great sweeping waves and seemed altogether a more gentle beast than the Cornish one. When they visited to supervise the building work she liked to sit beside it and fantasise that the water at her feet might, just might, have once been a great wave that crashed on Gwenfer's cliff.

The house's position was ideal for Lincoln. Many people were moving out of the city. Their migration had little effect since the unending flow of immigrants continued. The rich might live outside but their work was in the city and so they travelled to work on the excellent train service. Lincoln could be in the city in just over an hour. Ideally she would like to have lived here all the time but Lincoln had decided to keep his town house too, a large, somewhat gloomy brownstone on the upper East Side. She was learning that once Lincoln made up his mind nothing would change it. Saving the core of the house had been a personal triumph and there were days when she wondered if it would be the only one she ever managed to achieve in their life together.

Alice had been concerned about her business. She did not want it to close – she had worked too hard for that. And what would happen to her faithful assistants if she did? Lincoln wanted to close it, arguing that, as his wife, she would have other pressing duties. But Alice knew too much about life now and its way of suddenly turning everything upside-down. With her own business she would always have that independence she had learned to prize. A compromise was required. Marie, who had worked longest for her, was promoted to manageress.

Alice would work three mornings a week and more in an advisory capacity. But if he were to agree to these arrangements, Lincoln insisted that John Osborn be bought out.

'But why? He worked hard too. And it's thanks to him that I succeeded as I did.'

'He's more than happy with the figures I have suggested to him. I don't want him involved. He's from your past. I want to expunge that past entirely.'

'You can't expunge everything,' she laughed. 'Grace is a little bit too big and boisterous.'

On her wedding day she felt sad as she looked about her little house, so long her refuge and security. But Grace could not leave it fast enough as she nagged her mother to hurry to the automobile.

The wedding was small. The Osborns, two women from the bakery, Merry and an old friend of Lincoln's called Frank Petersham. As they signed the papers which made them man and wife Lincoln also signed the papers which made Grace his daughter. Her name was now Tregowan-Wakefield and she was inordinately proud of the hyphen.

Since the main part of the house had been completely redecorated and furnished at what seemed to Alice terrifying expense, they had decided to delay having a honeymoon. In any case, she teased him, he would only fret if he could not supervise the progress of the building work.

That night she moved into the house – The Dart it was called. With her came Grace and Merry from her past. Lincoln, her future, carried her over the threshold.

She had thought when Chas made love to her that never again would she know such feelings. She was wrong. Lincoln was a consummate lover. In his sensitive hands, beneath his sensuous mouth, she was to discover that her body could be easily aroused to greater joy. She thought she should not feel this way. Not loving Lincoln as she had Chas, she felt almost wanton when she enjoyed their nights in bed. But, without doubt, the great feeling of security that Lincoln gave her made the painful memories of the past begin to fade.

Part Five

Chapter Eleven

1

At almost twenty-three Ia was far and away Blossom's oldest girl. Apart from her time with Peter, she had been in the brothel for nearly seven years. The life she led had in no way diminished her beauty. It would be truer to say she was more beautiful. She might have lost the look of innocence which in the past had so excited the clients, but it had been replaced by a mature beauty which most found more beguiling. Her skin was as clear as a child's, its colour never needing any artifice. Her large grey eyes had a more guarded look now, but she had learned how to use them with devastating effect. Her hair, despite living in the grimy city, was still silvery blonde. And her figure, like her face, had matured also, so that her breasts were full above a small waist from which her hips swelled voluptuously and fashionably. Her looks, her profession-alism, her humour and Blossom's dependence on her as a book-keeper were the reasons she had outlasted so many others.

Though she was able to amuse the customers with her quick wit, she was not happy. However, it was an unhappiness that with all her experience of sadness, she was able to hide. She would sometimes look back over her life and think there had only ever been two truly happy periods. Those wonderful years with Alice, the first few months she had spent with Peter Willoughby. She had reached the decision that so many have to accept – that lasting happiness was not for her – and she resigned herself uncomplainingly to the life she had.

Money gave her the greatest pleasure. It was the one passion in her life which never diminished. She had a bank account now. One of her clients had introduced her to Hoare's Bank as a woman of private income – they would never have taken her if they had known the nature of her work. It amused her – a whore banking at Hoare's. It was a great source of mirth to her that frequently the money she brought to the bank had been removed from it only days before to pay for her services. Her financial interests were not restricted to banking, however: she had a strong portfolio of shares. She had been advised initially by another client who was a stockbroker. She had learned quickly and soon displayed unexpected skill in the management of her own investments.

There was nothing that Ia did not know about running a brothel. When Blossom was unwell it was Ia who was in charge and everything ran as smoothly as if the madame were there herself. She often thought that she could probably do it better than Blossom who was nearing fifty and obviously getting tired. When she added up her worth it was obvious that she could easily leave Blossom's to start her own establishment. But Ia's need for security kept her here. She was resigned now to staying until she had sufficient finances to establish herself in a brothel as opulent if not better than Blossom's, a modest 'house' would not do at all.

She spent much of her spare time making plans for what her own 'house' would be like, what services she would give, how she could improve efficiency. She wasted nothing: any scrap of information that came her way about clients and their preferences she noted in her book – she now had three of these notebooks full of her scribblings. She had lists of customers she was certain would come with her when the day came. And at the back of the little black books, she continued assiduously to note every visit of Lady Tregowan, who had serviced her, what she had paid. Ia could not see what use the information would ever be, but it had become a habit.

Apart from her clothes, her red boots and shoes, creams, soaps and perfume she spent no money on herself. Her only other expenditure was on Francine's keep, with the family in Blackheath, and on the many presents she sent her daughter. She delighted in shopping for these gifts which were always dispatched with a note from her 'Aunt Ia' and the promise that they would meet one day.

She had once gone to the house where the child lived. Her intention had been to knock on the door and ask to see the girl but when it came to it she found that she couldn't. Suddenly she felt shy and nervous at the thought of the encounter. Instead she sat in Blossom's carriage, which she had borrowed on the pretext that she was going shopping, and waited. For over an hour she sat, while the coachman and the horses became restless, outside the small villa with its neat garden and white-painted fence. Her patience was rewarded when a middle-aged, plump and comfortable-looking woman appeared with a boy holding one hand and a girl the other. She did not even have to wonder if it were Francine for the young girl was the image of herself from the long, blonde hair to the large, clear eyes, though they were green not grey. She was about to get out of the carriage when Francine said something to the woman who, laughing, bent down and picked her up and hugged her. Francine threw her arms about the woman, nuzzled her neck and kissed her. There was an ease in the movement, a naturalness, which showed it to be a common occurrence. Ia watched the obvious affection between them and knew that she was an outsider and, in a way she did not fully understand, that she had no right to interfere with the child's security. Instead Ia had settled back into the shadows of the carriage and ordered the man to drive her home. The outing had upset her far more than she would have thought possible and she was depressed for some time. It affected her work to the point that Blossom asked her if anything was wrong. She had merely replied that she was a little off-colour and resolved there and then not to attempt to see her daughter again for several years. She contented herself with sending presents, and receiving reports from her guardian.

Peter Willoughby had re-entered her life once more. After their last encounter she had assumed she would never see him again and she had done all in her power to try to forget him. She had failed. Over a year later, he had arrived and insisted on having Ia. Blossom, loyal as always, had said this was not possible. But it was too late, Ia had seen him in the hallway. It was enough. All the old longing, the old feelings returned and, as if in a trance, she moved out into the hall to greet him. A year before, she had successfully rejected him and had suffered months of longing for him. This time she knew she would say 'yes'. Would always say so, now. No other man had ever made her feel as he had. No other man could change her personality as he did. And no man had her love as he had.

She gave one of her best performances that night. She pretended she was light-hearted as she had mounted the staircase with him, conscious of a worried Blossom watching them. To reassure her friend she had laughed lightly, and smiled up at him, despite a thumping heart. And holding his hand she allowed him to lead her to her room.

It was just as it had been before. She had been without him for a year and in that time no man had made her body react as he could. Time and again he brought her to a climax of joy and love – though now she did not cry out her love. And in that great bed, in the dim lighting, she could for a few precious hours forget what she was.

'It always was marvellous with you, Ia. Always,' he said dreamily, slumped back against the pillows.

'Yes, for me too,' and she crept closer to him, inhaling deeply the smell of his fresh sweat, sweat that she had made him shed. He held her in the crook of his arm and she lay wondering what she would say when he invited her back, as she was certain he would.

'That's my farewell to the past,' he said, releasing her from his arm.

'I don't understand.'

He stood up and began to dress. 'I'm getting married tomorrow. I was curious, that's all.' He smiled his lop-sided smile and she could not believe him, could not believe that he too had not experienced the same.

'Is this some form of revenge?' she asked in a level voice.

'No, I just told you. I'm burying the past, that's all. You really are just a whore. Just as I always said. I can forget you at last.'

'If that's what you want to think, Peter, so be it.' She surprised herself with the dignity of her answer when her soul was screaming with pain.

'Don't you believe me?'

'Of course I do.' She smiled. 'But why should you have to forget me? At least you will always know where this whore is in future, should you feel like reminding yourself again.'

'How interesting.' One dark eyebrow arched quizzi-cally. 'I'll bear that in mind.'

She watched him cross the room and smiled at him while all the time her mind was begging: Don't leave me, please don't desert me, I love you . . . And the door closed quietly.

There was no dignity now: Ia screamed and raged. A

fearsome jealousy filled her for the woman who tomorrow was to be his bride. A dreadful anger overwhelmed her for what might have been, but for Frederick. Finally she was beside herself with grief, but it was not a grief which sought release in tears and wailing, it was a grief which made her feel that part of her was dead, never to be reborn, and that the rest of her had turned to stone; a grief which made her sit for the next two days gazing silently into space while a worried Blossom tried to find the cause.

But, as always, Ia rationalised her emotions and decided what she was to do. She loved him and would always do so. She needed his body, for when they made love it was the only time her senses were alive. She knew she could never have him, not as once it had been. For the present she was willing to grasp what happiness she could: she would always be here waiting for him. She needed him.

She had never enjoyed what she did; now she liked it even less. She hated these men for touching her, wanting her, lusting after her. She could not make it easier for herself by thinking of him during those repugnant acts for that would have been a betrayal of her love. She endured. Only the thought of the money, which was to be her eventual passport away from this, enabled her to carry on.

It was another year of intolerable waiting before she was to see him again. As before, he appeared suddenly. He asked for her and led her to her room. As before, he was the only man who could bring this consummate whore to a passionate climax and, as ever, it increased her need for him.

She knew this time that she could not survive another year without him.

'You come here so infrequently, Peter,' she said casually.

'Should I take that to mean you would like to see me more often?' He leaned on one elbow, his chin cupped in his hand, looking down at her as she lay beside him in the bed. He smiled.

'Yes.'

'Are you becoming short of customers for your favours?'

'No.'

'Then why?'

'I find, Peter, that I need to see you,' she said in as calm a voice as she could muster. 'You are the only person who gives me any pleasure . . .'

'Maybe you should be paying me.' He laughed.

She frowned. She knew she was dealing clumsily with him. She would have preferred to talk of her love for him rather than her physical needs but she feared that, if she did so, she would frighten him away for ever. Talk of love was not part of a mistress's vocabulary.

'I don't expect anything from you, Peter, just to see you more frequently. If you can't see your way to doing that, I would prefer that you did not come at all.' She held her breath. There, she had said it. She realised that her heart was thudding as she waited for his answer.

'I think I could probably arrange that.' He leaned towards her, took her breast into his hands, toying lazily with her nipple, and laughed softly at the expression in her eyes which told him that, as always, she was ready for him.

So for these past six years he had been her lover, the one she waited for, the one she hoped each evening would be there. She was certain that this must mean she loved him. But, devoid of love all her life, she could not fathom its complexities. She did not know that with love went caring, anxiety, giving; that love was not only the meeting of bodies but of minds also. She needed him, of that there was no doubt, but it was his body heavy upon hers, thrusting into her, that was her need. She thought herself in love, little realising she was a victim of infatuation, that sad, kissing-cousin of love.

Sometimes she would have to wait a month, sometimes only a day for him to come and find his whore.

2

'Blossom, imagine what I've discovered?' Ia rushed into Blossom's study flinging her hat on to the chair and swinging round to face her, eyes sparkling with excitement.

'Gwen has managed a whole morning without breaking anything?' Blossom smiled. Gwen they had soon discovered was a disaster, china seemed to fly into pieces as she approached, coffee pots fell out of her hands, staining carpets and furniture with depressing regularity. But, every time that Blossom said she would have to go, Ia would leap to the girl's defence and insist she was kept. Admiring Ia's loyalty, and despising her own weakness, Blossom invariably gave in.

'Poor Gwen, you're hard on her. She can't help being clumsy, and the more you shout at her the worse she will get.'

'Poor Gwen, I like that! What about poor Blossom?' she said with a good-natured laugh.

'Blossom, you're not listening. The house next door is for sale,' Ia said, breathlessly.

'So? I know.'

'You must buy it.'

'What on earth for?'

'To expand, of course.'

'Why should I expand? I'm quite happy with my business thank you, Miss St Just. I don't want it any bigger.'

'But, Blossom, it's such an opportunity. Just think. We

could double the number of girls and double your income.'

'And where would we put them all? I could not have two salons: it would not work. And to have people rushing from this house and up the steps of the house next door would not look too dignified, would it?'

'No. We get builders to knock the dividing walls down,' Ia said so eagerly that Blossom laughed. 'Oh, please listen to me. We can make the salon here larger by extending it next door, which would mean that all the girls could entertain in the one room and you could supervise it. We would have extra bedrooms. And ... this is the best bit, I think, we could make a restaurant on the ground floor next door.'

'A restaurant? What on earth for?'

'They nearly all come here after they've eaten, don't they? Love on a full stomach. Well, we could feed them, *we* could make the money from their stomachs as well, and for the wine, everything! They'd stop going to the supper clubs, their clubs, they'd eat here. They could dine the girls and then you wouldn't be feeding them either. It's so logical, Blossom.'

'You make my brain whirl.'

'Think how often they ask for food in the bedrooms. They like it. But you always give the food to them included in the price of the girl. We could give them a choice of a restaurant or dinner in the rooms and they would have to pay for either. We could have entertainment in the dining-room – a pianist, a singer, something like that. Oh, Blossom, isn't it exciting?'

'It's very interesting, I must say. But I'm not sure that I want all the bother and the anxiety.'

'We could have a gaming-room. A small one, think of the money.'

'No, no gambling. The laws are too strict, the fines too high. In the old days when I started there wasn't a brothel that didn't have gambling but now ...'

'Oh, Blossom, don't be such a misery. We can bribe the police. We already pay them enough to keep out of our way – what's a bit more?' As she spoke Ia was moving restlessly about the room, her mind whirring with ideas and excitement. Blossom watched her with an indulgent expression on her face. She remembered, watching Ia, how ambitious she herself had once been, the excitement she had once felt at the idea of building a business. She had not felt like that for years, she realised.

'How would you like to be my partner?'

At Blossom's suggestion Ia stopped dead in her tracks, in her hand a bowl she seemed to be examining but which, in her excitement, she was barely conscious of holding.

'Your partner? How?'

'Fifty-fifty.'

Ia's brain was working at lightning speed. She had only just found out about the house next door. She did not yet know the price. But, in this area so close to St James's, the cost would, no doubt, be prohibitive. And then there was the cost of the alterations? Blossom was a business woman; she was not offering her a present. Ia realised that Blossom would expect an investment from her. Even if she sold every share she owned, drew all her money from the bank, she was sure she would not have enough.

'I don't have enough money for a plan as large as this.'

'Then borrow.'

'Who would lend it to me?'

'I can think of a lot of people, Ia.'

'But how would I pay back?'

'You've done my books for long enough to know what the profits are here. We shall no doubt double the business and thus the profits. We divide them in half, as I suggest, and I can assure you that you will have enough, with your modest expenses, to service any loan you need.' Blossom sounded very confident. Ia listened. Blossom might not be able to read and write easily but when it came to business she knew exactly what she was doing. Despite caring for Blossom as she did, Ia's mind raced, searching for the disadvantages. What was there for Blossom's advantage? What catch was there? What was she missing? She could not see anything – only advantages for both of them.

'Blossom, I would love it.'

'It would mean you need not work with the clients any more.'

'But the loan?'

'Come, come, Ia, you would have enough, I promise you. Your savings must be considerable now and the loan won't be so enormous. And you know how you hate what you do. Think! No more of that, ever again.'

It was that prospect which finally decided Ia to take the risk.

Blossom arranged the finances for her. When she saw the figure involved – £15,000 – Ia had one short moment of panic that she might be making the biggest error of her life. Then she shook her hair defiantly over her shoulder, berated herself for her cowardice and signed the forms.

As soon as the next-door house had been purchased in their joint names, Ia stopped work. Her regular clients pleaded, cajoled and offered her more money than she had thought possible. As she refused them she despised them all the more. She was glad she had been born a woman and was not ruled by her sex organs as her clients were.

The money they offered was attractive but Ia wanted to use every ounce of her energy for the conversion of the house. It was a major undertaking. Blossom's one proviso had been that she did not wish to be involved with any of it, that it was Ia's responsibility, and the work must be done with the minimum of disruption to the orginal business.

Luckily for Ia, Christmas and the New Year were approaching – traditionally a quiet time for the brothel.

The customers spent the festive season sanctimoniously in the bosom of their families instead of on the bosom of one of the girls.

Like a general Ia laid her plans for the builders to knock the wall down between the two great drawing-rooms to make one giant salon for entertaining. This work was the main problem and the one that would most likely interfere with business. When she had informed the builder that he had forty-eight hours to complete the work and have both rooms redecorated, he said it was a total impossibility. Ia told him he spoke nonsense, that he must employ more men. When he explained that the decoration would have to wait because the plaster would not be dry, Ia flapped her hand at him with irritation. He was summarily instructed to decorate over the new plaster, allowing extra paper for rehanging after it had dried out. She also prowled around the shops until she found some large tapestries which would hide all manner of temporary work. When the drawing-room plaster was finally dry they could hang on the stairwells.

The tapestries were only a small part of her purchases. All the rooms had to be decorated and furnished to Blossom's exacting standards. Initially Ia was nervous.

'I don't know about such things, Blossom,' she complained. 'You'll be furious with me if I make mistakes.'

'I'm trusting you to succeed. Do you really think I'm so stupid that I would let you attempt it if I didn't think you could? Good God, girl, if I could do it as well as I did – a simple girl from Jamaica – surely you can.'

Ia need not have feared, she had lived long enough surrounded by the luxury and the good taste of Blossom not to make mistakes. The new 'house' was going to be even better than the old one.

The bedrooms were comparatively easy and soon completed. The new restaurant she had furnished in mahogany and red velvet with discreet lighting so that it was almost impossible to see who was at the next table.

She chose white and red china, ordered the best plate available, and had the damask napkins embroidered with a great, swirling 'B'. She wanted it to look luxurious – that went without saying. She also wanted it to look like a more sybaritic version of a club dining-room – a parody of one – and it worked. But her pride and joy was the salon which stretched across the first floor of both houses. She wanted a dramatic setting for the beautiful girls. Blossom's room had always been elegant but it was also so ornate that it was as if the room was in competition with the women in it. Bravely she had the gold damask ripped from the sofas and chairs and had them upholstered instead in black or white silk. The carpet she had woven had a white background with a black and scarlet motif. The walls she had covered with white silk and then hung on them Blossom's brightest paintings. The great flower vases were only ever allowed to hold red or white flowers. It was the perfect, simple backdrop for beautiful women. It looked dramatically modern and was a great success.

She was also thorough in her researches. She took a job at Belle Simpson's in Mayfair. Belle was Blossom's legendary rival and her house boasted more dukes than any other brothel in London. Ia was there only for a day. There was no need to stay longer – Ia had seen enough. Not only was Belle drunk, so were some of the girls. The silver was tarnished. The flowers in the vases needed changing. There were no clean sheets after each customer. The place smelt of cigar smoke. There was no competition – Belle's was a far inferior establishment.

'You've put your money in,' Blossom said, 'you've done all this hard work, we should change the name, use yours as well as mine.'

'No. It wouldn't sound right at all. It's always been "Blossom's" – no doubt it always will be.'

'You've enjoyed doing it, haven't you?'

'I'll let you into a secret, Blossom. I never realised that spending money could be such fun.'

'I'm more than pleased with the result. Even the salon. I thought that might be a mistake, but you're right. It's nearly 1904, we must move with the times, I suppose.'

Ia was proud of the brothel but her greatest joy was that she now had a small flat completely private, and hers alone. It was over the stables at the back of the house across the enlarged garden. Tucked away in the mews, it was like a little cottage. She had her own sitting-room and a bedroom and small bathroom. There was no need for a kitchen since, if she was not on duty, she had her meals sent over.

The night that she entertained Peter for the first time she was like any young housewife about to have her first dinner guest. She checked with the kitchen so many times that eventually the normally placid chef had hysterics and imperiously ordered her out. No one, not even Ia, argued with Alphonse. She often wondered how surprised he would be if she mentioned that she had worked for him at the Tregowans'. It had amused Ia greatly to poach him away from Daisy Dear, bribing him with an almost doubled salary.

'Ia, this is charming.' Peter stood in her small sitting-room, a large bouquet of flowers in his hands and a small parcel which he gave her. Eagerly she unwrapped it. Inside was a bisque sculpture of a naked couple embracing.

'Thank you, Peter, it's so perfect.' Gently she put it on a chest beside her azure bowl.

'What a strange bowl, hardly in keeping with the rest, is it?'

'Probably not, but it's the most precious of all the objects in this room.' She offered no explanation.

After dinner they lay in her new bedroom.

'So, now you are a madam? No more clients?'

'That's right, Peter. Are you pleased for me?'

476

'Very, but even more pleased for myself. I never liked your life, Ia. I hated what you did. Now I can have you completely to myself.'

'If you like.' She looked thoughtfully at him. He had been her lover for so long now, but he had never before commented on her way of life nor said that he disliked it. It was a subject they had never discussed.

'I love you, Ia,' he said, suddenly serious.

Twice now he had said that he loved her. Twice! She wanted to reply that she loved him too, she wanted the words to form of themselves to help her explain her feelings for him. But they did not, would not, come. Instead she clung to him with a quiet intensity, all her life's need for love distilled into this embrace.

3

The pattern of Ia's life had changed. Six nights a week she worked supervising the girls, overseeing the restaurant, entertaining the clients, falling into bed far more exhausted than when she had been one of the whores. And bed was rarely before four in the morning. By ten she was doing the paperwork, by noon she was ready for lunchtime clients.

But one evening a week Blossom suggested that she should be free. That evening she always spent with Peter in the little mews house. Gwen looked after her now. It was Gwen who served them, and it was she who saw Ia's happiness. Blossom frequently told her she was a fool, that she should use that time to go out, to go to the theatre, out to dinner. But Ia wanted nothing of the world. She was content with her work and she was happiest with Peter.

Their relationship had changed. Or rather Ia had changed, for Peter was very much the same. She knew that her love for him was her one weak point but she was resigned to this one vital weakness. She never knew what mood he would be in each time he called. Would he be relaxed and easy? Or would he be moody and difficult, hardly speaking to her but quickly taking her to bed? Ia found she was no longer jealous of his wife – how could she be when the poor woman was cheated week after week? She never asked about his wife or whether he was happy or sad with her, it did not matter to her. What mattered were these evenings they spent together. He had never again spoken of love. She could wish he did but it was not his way, she told herself. So, she did not burden him with her own talk of love. His moods still filled her with fear but time and familiarity had enabled her to hide that fear. She had learned when to be quiet, when to cajole and tease. There were times she felt she knew him better than she knew herself. But of one thing she was supremely confident: she could always be certain that he would come to her. As he was a drug to her, so was she to him. It was as if their bodies had been made for each other. After all these years they could still excite each other; each time it was as if it was the first.

Once, just before the new brothel opened, Peter asked her to move, to be his mistress in the little house he still owned. He too had noted the change in Ia and was certain that this time, if she came, she would continue to be the Ia who intrigued and fascinated him.

She refused the offer. She had long ago decided this was a risk she could not take. She told him that if they tried to return to the past, the magic that they now had might die. It would only be a matter of time before she was like a second wife to him. It would then follow that he would begin to haunt the brothels again. He denied this vehemently. But Ia was wiser now, and knew far more about men than Peter did about himself.

There was another reason, but one she did not tell him. She liked being successful, she liked being her own mistress, and she did not want to give up the security of her new life. Despite her loans, despite the fearful expenditure on the new brothel, Ia could see that her earnings in the future would, if she was sensible, be considerable. She could not ignore this fact for she was determined, with a fierce all-consuming passion, that never again would she be poor, never again fear for the future or where the next meal was coming from. And she was determined that her daughter would never know such misery. Men tired of women, she had seen it; not for her the streets and a slow and painful death. He was a man: she did not trust him. That was one lesson life had taught her.

The grand opening of the enlarged brothel was held at the end of January. Blossom gave a party which was to be the talk of London for a long time to come. Everyone who was anybody was invited. Over 200 people crowded in and there was a moment when Ia feared the floor might collapse.

The champagne never stopped flowing; Ia had it served by young girls who were naked under diaphanous shifts through which could be seen their rouged nipples. The men became so sexually aroused that Blossom was forced to put a limit on the time they could spend upstairs with a girl – it was the first time that such a restriction had been brought in. No one complained. Ia noted this and wondered if it wouldn't be a good idea to bring it in permanently; she must speak to Blossom about it in the morning.

Ia had arranged performances for their amusement. There was a girl who did a dance and remarkable things with a snake. There were two girls who made love to each other. As Ia watched the viewers' mounting excitement, she shook her head, doubting if she would ever understand men and their appetites. A naked trapeze artiste followed some female clowns: Ia watched with a smile on her face but inside her she despised them all.

In the midst of more new arrivals was a man she thought might be George Tregowan. She could not be certain since she had only seen him a couple of times and always at a distance. None the less she found herself hiding behind a pillar in confusion. She laughed. How stupid, she told herself, what did it matter if he saw her? She crossed the room.

'Lord Tregowan, I believe,' she smiled brittly at the tall man and was shocked by how old he looked. The fine face she vaguely remembered had disappeared completely to be replaced by a deeply lined one, with eyes that were hooded as if hiding an expression of despair from the world. His face had an expression of such decadence that it made even Ia shiver. He looked like himself only from a distance, she realised. She supposed she should have felt sorry for him, but instead the pain of the past came flooding into her mind. She remembered her father's fear and exhaustion, the mind-destroying poverty, the agony of her mother's deathbed, and her buried hatred of the Tregowans flared up again like the embers of a dying fire rekindled by a sudden blast of air. He looked at her quizzically. 'I used to work for you a very long time ago, m'lord,' she explained.

He frowned. 'I beg your pardon, miss? I regret . . .'

'There's no need for regrets, m'lord. I worked in your kitchens, you would hardly have seen me, would you?' She laughed gaily, amazing herself by the ease with which she was dealing with him.

'I wish I had. Such beauty hidden in my kitchen. What a pity I did not know,' and he smiled, but it was a cruel smile which made Ia feel she was very glad he had not known.

They lapsed into silence.

'Your daughter, m'lord, do you hear from her?'

'I have no daughter,' he said coldly.

'I'm sorry. I should not have asked.' So, she was not alone in her bitterness towards Alice. Good, she thought.

'It's no matter.' He took a glass of champagne from one of the young girls and Ia noticed with surprise that he seemed oblivious to her smile and her attractive body.

'We're very honoured that you are here at last. We've never had that pleasure before.'

'We?' He sipped his wine, all the time looking about the room with a bored, uninterested expression.

'Blossom December and I, we are partners. I'm Ia.'

Solemnly he shook her hand. 'I've heard of Blossom's of course, I don't know why I never came.' He frowned, the lines on his face deepening and making him look even harder and older. 'Ah, yes, I remember. You don't do all, how shall I say, services?'

Gambling? Sadism? Masochism? Which was lacking for his lordship? Ia wondered to herself. Which was he? He looked like a sadist but then, frequently, those who did were the masochists.

'It's Blossom's policy, Lord Tregowan.'

'Pity. Well, if the policy ever alters, perhaps you'll let me know. You obviously know where I live.' His attention was drawn by a man across the room, and he made his excuses courteously enough. Ia watched his tall figure move away, and hated him.

It was five in the morning before the last of the guests had left. Blossom, Ia and their twenty girls sprawled exhausted in the great salon drinking tea as the maids scurried around clearing the debris.

'What a night!' Blossom said. 'How can people drink so much champagne and still be standing? They're gluttons.'

'Not just the champagne either. That Cyril Bottersham, I had him twice.' Rowan complained. 'I wouldn't mind but he ain't no good.'

'Lummy, I had him twice too,' Marthe exclaimed. 'You're right, Rowan, he's got a prick like a stallion and don't know what to do with it.'

'Did you see that girl with the snake, Blossom? She was

481

in the linen cupboard doing it. When I asked her what she was up to she told me to "fuck off". "Charming," I said. "Don't you let Blossom hear you talking like that, she don't like vulgar language." And do you know what she said? "Fuck Blossom too." '

'The cheek of her!' Blossom said. 'I'm not paying her fee then if she was messing about in my linen cupboard, whatever next?'

'Just as well she was, Blossom. The girls were hard pressed as it was to accommodate everyone,' Ia said.

'Bloody hell, my feet are killing me.' Lizzie massaged her feet.

'I'm surprised it's your feet that are tired,' Ia chuckled and everyone began to laugh with the hysteria of fatigue. 'Did anyone have Lord Tregowan?' Ia asked as if she was not really interested.

'Oh, he's not interested in sex, not any more. He gets a hard prick from gambling. You'd have to disguise yourself as the Queen of Diamonds to get anywhere with him,' Dot said knowledgeably.

'I think he's tried everything else. He used to go to Belle's for years, I saw him quite a lot when I was there. You imagine it, he did it, and then suddenly he stopped and the cards took over,' Mavis added helpfully.

'Does he know his wife is a client, Blossom?'

'Good gracious no, I hope not. We pride ourselves on our discretion.' Blossom looked shocked at the very idea. 'Well, young ladies, if you're going to be fit for business later today, I suggest you all get off to bed. We shan't be busy today, not after last night. So, I suggest that you divide into two shifts, one lot do the afternoon and the other half do the evening. And thank you for your hard work, I was proud of you all. Now, off you go,' she shooed them away like an indulgent mother whose children have behaved particularly well.

Ia stood up too, suddenly overwhelmed by total exhaustion.

'Don't go, Ia. I want to talk to you.'

'Could it wait until after we've slept?'

'No, I'd rather talk now. Pour us both a brandy, that will keep us awake.'

Reluctantly Ia poured the brandy, longing for her bed and hoping whatever it was Blossom wanted was not going to keep her from it too long.

'I'm going back to Jamaica, Ia.'

'Oh, that's nice for you, a holiday will do you good. How long are you going for?' She yawned discreetly. Her eyelids seemed made of lead; she could barely keep them open.

'For ever.'

'Blossom, you can't.' Ia was awake now and her mind in panic. All that money she had borrowed, what on earth was she to do? How could Blossom desert her like this?

'I've had enough, Ia. I'm fifty, I want to retire to my homeland. I've written to my brother and he has found me a nice house, with land. I've enough now that I can look after my whole family; none of them need ever worry again. It's been a momentous task – we Jamaicans have large families,' she said contentedly.

'But why now? After we've done all this. After I've borrowed so much money. What the hell do you mean, Blossom? What the hell am I supposed to do?' Angrily Ia stood up and began to pace the room.

'I want you to buy me out.'

'What? Oh really, Blossom, how on earth could I do that? I'm up to my ears in debt and now you suggest I sink further.'

'Calm down, Ia. Now listen. I'll sell you 50 per cent of my share now. The other 50 per cent I retain for the time being. You buy that part of my share when you can. Until then you pay me interest – I shan't ask for the moon, 6 per cent will be sufficient. My living costs in Jamaica will not be nearly as high as they are here and I have my savings.'

As always, when money was discussed, Ia's mind became needle-sharp. There was not a shred of fatigue left in her now. She was wide awake and alert. She crossed to the window and looked down on the street. In the winter's gloom the gas lights glowed. The milkman with his fat piebald horse clattered into the street. She could just make out a couple of kitchen maids wearily mounting the area steps, large brooms in their hands. How she had hated these bitter cold mornings when she had had to do just as they were doing. She was afraid. What Blossom was offering her could make her fortune, make her rich beyond her dreams. It could also ruin her so that she might end up sweeping area steps again. Her mind raced. She disagreed with some of Blossom's rules – if a man wanted to be beaten, why shouldn't he? They paid double for it. And if a girl didn't mind being beaten, why shouldn't she? They earned double for it. She had watched the faces of the men when the half-naked girls had served them – she could sack the waiters, have the girls serve the men dressed like that. Blossom had not liked the prices she had suggested for the restaurant, wanting only to cover her costs, Ia would put up the tariff and make it profitable. The champagne was too cheap – twelve shillings for a bottle was ridiculous when they could easily ask fifteen. And there was the gambling – that's where the big money lay. She could turn Blossom's elegant study into a gaming-room. Perhaps she could get another four girls in. She could have cabaret evenings at double the normal rate. She could . . .

'But where would I get the money from?'

Blossom smiled. She had not been mistaken: she knew that Ia would want what she had to offer. 'I've already spoken to some of my oldest and most trusted clients. I've explained your present loan arrangements. I told them that I thought you were likely to run the whole operation on a far more commercial basis than I have. They are more than interested. And then I wondered about Peter Willoughby. Perhaps he would be interested in financing you?'

'No. I don't want him involved.'

'Very well, it was just an idea. I've arranged for these men to come at noon today. What do you say?'

'What's the alternative?'

'I shall sell my share to them. You could manage the whole operation for a wage and be responsible to them.'

'I wouldn't like that.'

'I didn't think for one moment you would.' Blossom chuckled.

'I'd like to talk to them. Noon, you said?'

4

Ia had been concerned when Blossom had told her she was booked on a 'banana boat'. To Ia it sounded a primitive way to travel; Blossom should be booked on the best liner. It was an amused Blossom who explained it was by far the best way to travel to Jamaica. Ia was not reassured until she saw the comfort of Blossom's cabin.

Ia thought her heart would break when she said goodbye to Blossom. She travelled with her to Tilbury. The farewell was not easy for Blossom either. She had last seen her home as a child of thirteen. She was returning as a woman of fifty, her parents dead, her brothers and sisters strangers to her. And she dreaded her farewell to Ia. Ever since she had met her that day, so long ago, when Jimmy her tout had brought the bright-eyed, intelligent girl back with him, their relationship had been more than a professional one. Blossom knew that in Ia she had heard echoes of herself at the same age, the same courage, determination and yet humanity. Gwen was a case in point. No one would have kept the girl for more than a couple of days, but Ia had fought for the friend she loyally protected. Blossom realised that Ia was the daughter she had lost. She loved her. But she left with a conviction that Ia would succeed beyond her own achievements. They kissed tearfully. They promised to meet again even if, as they said it, they both knew that this was highly unlikely.

With Blossom gone, to relieve her sadness Ia threw herself into her work. She had to keep busy every possible moment, for, if she did not, the enormity of her debts would frighten her into mind-numbing stupidity. The nights were the worst. On those nights when Peter was not with her, if she could not sleep she would lie awake and worry. So she made certain that she worked as late as possible, worked until she was almost dropping with fatigue for that way she would fall quickly asleep and the demons of worry were cheated for one night.

Blossom's boat had not left the Thames estuary before Ia was visiting every hotel of significance, and every club. There she spoke to the hall porters and did deals. For every man they sent to her she would pay an introduction fee. She visited the hansom-cab ranks, left her card and promised a similar deal. Blossom, in the way of the old madams, had run a discreet house, more like a gentle-man's club, where society searched for its pleasure – the list of clients was limited, the aristocracy reigned supreme. But Ia had seen that society was changing. The new king numbered manufacturers and bankers amongst his friends, trade was no longer such a dirty word. There were rich men from the north who came to London on business. She would welcome them whereas Blossom would not have done so. Nor did Ia object to the middle classes, the lawyers, the doctors, the business men. Blossom, she realised, had been a snob.

But she did not want to lose the old clients. What she needed were extra attractions. She did everything she had planned. Her naked waitresses were a great success. She put up the price of food and champagne and, strangely, found she sold more. She had padded rooms constructed in the basement for 'correction'. Ia understood the predilections of the English males brought up by strict nannies followed by their public schools. At Ia's establishment they could howl and yell to their heart's content – all for double the cost. Blossom would have been appalled but Blossom was half-way across the Atlantic by now.

Lastly she had Blossom's study enlarged, and opened a small gaming-room. She employed a croupier who had worked in Monte Carlo and who knew all the tricks of the trade. He showed her how a roulette wheel – the latest craze – could be tampered with so that the house would win by a larger percentage. He was disappointed when Ia refused his suggestions. She might have a lust for money but she had always been fair and she had no intention of cheating her clients. In any case it could be dangerous. What he was doing was illegal, a disgruntled client would be a danger. She would build her reputation on honesty.

Within a week she discovered that the gaming-room took twice as much as the brothel. The men liked to drink more as they gambled. When they won, the first thing they wanted was a woman. When they lost, they sought consolation in sex. So one activity fuelled the other.

Only Ia decided what credit was to be given and what the limits should be. She found that she enjoyed the sense of power this gave her, realising that, should she wish, she could financially ruin any of her compulsive gamblers.

By the end of the first quarter she found that she could not only meet her interest payments but could also begin to pay off lumps of the principal she had borrowed.

The place was still called 'Blossom's'; her partners frequently suggested she change it to 'Ia's' but always she refused. They thought she refused out of sentiment. She didn't. It was out of superstition. Blossom had brought her luck: she hoped her name would continue to do so.

At the end of her first six months when she added up her figures, she felt that perhaps she could worry less; but she would still have to work as hard, that was obvious.

'Ia, why this mania for money? It's so unattractive in a woman. You need not work as you do. It's ridiculous – you'll make yourself old before your time.' Peter was lying on her bed watching her as she hurriedly dressed to return to the main house. She did not take nights off now; she took only odd hours.

'Only someone who has always had vast amounts of money could make a remark like that.'

'But it's a greed with you. It's unattractive. I don't like it.'

'Then you'll have to try and ignore it, my darling. I can't stop now. I owe too much. I want to clear all my debts, buy everyone out, and own everything myself.'

'Let me buy them out, let me be your partner.'

She stopped as she was slipping her garter up her leg to secure her silk stocking, and looked across at him. 'That's very kind of you, Peter. But no thank you.'

'Why not, for heaven's sake? It makes sense.'

'It doesn't to me. I want to own it – myself.'

'Don't you trust me after all these years?'

'It's not that. I'm just bloody independent, surely you've learned that – *after all these years*?' She smiled across the bed at him.

'It's more than that. It must be.'

'Do you really want to know? I want to be so secure that I never even *risk* being poor again. I never want to feel that agony in my stomach when the acid pours in and begins to eat you away from inside because you've had no food for days. I never want to live with lice, rats and filth. My daughter will *never* live that way. I fear poverty,

Peter, I have nightmares about it. That's your reason, simple when you know it.'

'I could cushion you from all that.'

She shook her head, flicking her hair back over her shoulder. 'Oh, Peter, you don't understand. I don't want a cushion against poverty. I want a huge, gigantic feather bed!'

Daisy Tregowan was still a regular customer. Her beauty had not been of the type to last. She still, though now in her thirties, dressed and acted as the young giggly girl she once had been. But the pose was becoming grotesque. As her beauty faded so she used more and more make-up to deceive. Her face was a mask of paint and powder. Her lips might smile but her eyes never did. And the pretty little mouth was always set in a spiteful line. Her clothes, however, were magnificent. Each winter she arrived with a different fur. It amused Ia to try to guess just how much she was costing her husband in clothes alone – a small fortune annually. Her appetite for Ia's expensive champagne was becoming legendary. Her appetite for young men was becoming insatiable, the younger the better. Ia enjoyed welcoming her former employer with all the graciousness she could muster whilst hating her in her heart. She double-checked all her bills so that every item, even a rare cup of tea, was accounted for.

She had not contacted George Tregowan for she was certain that, once news of her gaming-room became common knowledge, he would come. He did. She also gained a high degree of amusement from knowing that he would be downstairs quite unaware of his wife's presence upstairs. A strange couple. She doubted if he would have cared one jot had he known. And his wife, provided he gave her everything she wanted, cared even less about his gambling.

He played like a man demented. He came frequently at lunchtime and was still there playing at three in the morning. He would bet on anything, she discovered – whether the next carriage along the road was a phaeton or a hackney, or how many motor cars, still fairly new but increasingly common, would pass along in the space of half an hour. He would have bet on the proverbial flies climbing the wall, had there been any – but Ia's house was spotless. No flies survived to bet upon.

She encouraged him. She would stand and watch him stake £100 on the turn of a card, and she despised him. She despised all men who had such little respect for money.

When Lord Tregowan asked for an account to save the inconvenience of carrying money, Ia immediately agreed. She gave instructions to the manager that there was to be no limit to his lordship's credit.

There had been a time when she saved pennies in her azure bowl. Now it was Lord Tregowan's IOUs.

5

For over six months clients and their money had been pouring in. But then trouble began.

The police were the first. All the time that Blossom had been in residence, she had had arrangements with certain police officials. These arrangements could take all manner of shapes and forms, from free service at the brothel and cases of whisky or champagne, to assistance with doctor's bills. One inspector had enjoyed a holiday at Brighton with his wife and family at Blossom's expense. And, of course, Blossom's contribution to the 'Widows and Orphans Fund' was the largest of any of the local residents. That was the only money which changed hands. In return Blossom had never been prosecuted for running an illegal house and the police had guarded her premises and her person assiduously.

The threat, when it came, was quite charmingly put by

the chief inspector who called on Ia. Better arrangements would have to be made, or he would have no choice but to report to his superiors that there was a brothel and gaming-house on his manor.

They sat in Ia's small office sipping her best champagne while they parried and argued the case. There was no point in Ia threatening to go to those selfsame superiors with the complaint that certain of the police force were blackmailing her, since what she did was against the law. She could only negotiate the amounts involved. He wanted money now; gifts were of insufficient importance. They argued the sum for over an hour. Ia succeeded in reducing slightly the original figure asked, and she refused point blank to continue simultaneously with the old system of presents.

Once she had calculated from Blossom's books how much she had given away, in a year, to the police in presents, Ia had not been displeased with the sum that she had now negotiated. It was only a few hundred more than Blossom's and, given the increase in business and inflation, she felt she could not complain.

The sum had been set, at least Ia thought it had, until the neighbours began to cause problems.

When Blossom had run the brothel like a discreet club, the number of clients was restricted by its size, and also by their aristocratic preference of being unobserved in pursuit of such pleasures. But the new clients had no such inhibitions. Many had come from hundreds of miles away – those rich northern business men whom Ia had been so pleased to recruit – and had no inhibitions for they knew no one here. Many were the noisy scenes which occurred in the street as they argued with hackney-cab drivers, or drove up in carriages which announced on their doors everything from department stores to breweries, whereas the old clients, preferring to keep their anonymity, had arrived on foot or in hackneys rather than in their own emblazoned coaches.

491

The neighbours, who for the most part had been prepared to turn a blind eye to Blossom's activity, working on the principle that such establishments were necessary for the protection of their own womenfolk, found they could no longer do so. In fact, it was not until a petition of local residents was taken, that it was discovered that four of the householders had had no idea of Blossom's occupation, so discreet had she been. They complained to the police.

The police, in return for calming the neighbours by pointing out to them that at least with Ia the situation was controlled – would they prefer to see prostitutes walking up and down the street affronting their daughters? – demanded more money. They also pointed out to Ia that it might be expedient if she in turn gave the odd gift to her long-suffering neighbours. So, she was back to distributing what seemed like endless cases of whisky and champagne. Several of the householders took up her offer of free services – the most eager being two residents who had not known what was going on in the first place. Not only was her financial outlay heavier, she was back to distributing largesse. All this went deeply against the grain with Ia and the extremely healthy profits of the first six months were sadly depleted in the second.

To cover this added expenditure Ia put the prices up. This led to a near revolt by some of her clients who had been paying Blossom the same amount ever since their fathers had brought them there in the first place.

'I'm sorry about it. But it's to cover my added expenses. It's not going into my pocket, if that's what you think,' Ia explained to an irate earl and a furious baron one evening.

'Blossom had to pay the police, too, but she didn't rob us.'

'She didn't have to pay the enormous amounts that I do. And in any case she had been undercharging you for years.'

'Belle Simpson's is cheaper. We'll go there en masse unless you do something about it, Ia.'

'Then go there, Lord Borough, do,' Ia smiled sweetly, 'and get the clap for your economy,' she added sharply as she opened the door for them.

They muttered, they continued to complain, but they did not leave.

And then the girls themselves started to make trouble. They had chosen Emma to be their spokeswoman as they stood one morning in the large salon in which they had requested a meeting.

Ia sat patiently waiting as Emma stood tongue-tied in front of her. It took several 'Go on Emma's from her colleagues and an 'I shan't eat you' from Ia before the quivering girl, swallowing hard, began.

'We're not happy, Ia.'

Ia waited for the girl to continue. She said nothing, but her hands were twisting and turning with nervousness.

'Yes?' Ia asked eventually.

'We're not happy.' There were mutters of agreement.

'So you said, Emma.'

'Get on with it, Em, for God's sake,' Sally shouted from the back.

'Perhaps you can help her, Sally,' Ia called across but Sally merely blushed furiously and was silenced. 'Oh come on, Emma, I haven't got all day.'

'You've got double the clients, and the restaurant and the gambling, and we ain't got double the money and we don't think it's fair and we're not happy about it,' Emma said in a rush and she too blushed to the roots of her hair.

Ia stood up. 'Is that all?' she asked coldly.

There was a collective, 'Yes.'

'You're the best-paid whores in London. You have free medical attention. Wonderful food. You certainly have the best accommodation. Have you seen how they live at Belle's? The rooms, those luxurious rooms in which you entertain your clients are yours, yours alone, aren't they?'

There was a reluctant mutter of agreement. 'At Belle's they work a shift system. Have you seen the filthy, cold dormitory the girls live in when not on duty? You want that, you'd prefer to live in those conditions?' She looked angrily about the assembled company. No one said anything. 'Are you listening any of you?'

'Yes, we are. It's lovely here, but it don't alter the fact that you're making money hand over fist and we're not getting any of it.'

'Not getting any of it?' Ia's voice rose dangerously. 'Not getting any of it? There's not one of you making less than £100 a week. Haven't you any intelligence? If I'm taking double it also means that my expenses are double too.'

She was faced by a row of blank faces. 'It's not fair,' a voice from the back whispered. Assent rippled along the rows of girls.

'Then if it's not fair I suggest you all go and pack your bags and be out of here within the hour.' She crossed the room aware of the consternation she was creating. 'Within the hour, I said.' And she slammed the door behind her.

She slammed the door of her office with even more vehemence.

'What's got into you?' Gwen asked, looking up from the flowers she was clumsily arranging in a vase from which she had dripped water all over Ia's desk.

'Stupid little bitches. I've sacked the lot of them. We'll have to put you into glad rags, Gwen. At this rate you'll be back on the batter tonight.'

'Cor, love a duck. Bit past it, ain't I?' Gwen cackled. Her laugh was interrupted by a knock at the door. Ia swung it open to find the girls standing there looking sheepish.

'We're sorry, Ia.' Sally had finally become official spokeswoman. 'We didn't think it all out.'

'Don't blackmail me again like that ever, any of you. Is

494

that understood? I don't like it. Genuine complaints I'm willing to listen to, not that sort of rubbish. Get changed the lot of you, the first toffs will be here in a minute.'

She closed the door behind them, leaned on it and let out a soft whistle.

'Close shave there, Ia, my old love,' Gwen said with a grin.

'I won't have any more trouble from them,' Ia replied. And she did not.

But the troubles of these past weeks had taught her one lesson. Nothing in life, it seemed, came easily. She had always thought that she knew more than Blossom, knew better how to run things. Now she was not so sure.

6

Ia had a small boudoir in the main house rather than an impressive study as Blossom had. It was simply furnished, a couple of armchairs, a small desk, a chaise-longue, vases full of flowers and a selection of paintings on the wall, all of the same theme – the Cornish coast.

She used this room when business was quiet to do her accounts or sometimes, if she were lucky, to read. At some point in the last eighteen months odd favoured clients had got into the habit of dropping in to chat to Ia. Frequently they brought her flowers, small presents, and occasionally a painting of Cornwall. She did not let everyone in.

Why he should have thought he was favoured was to remain a mystery to her, but within a couple of months of his coming George Tregowan had also started to visit her. Her initial reaction had been to be quite cool so that he would go away and leave her in peace. And then, again she was never to know why, she changed her mind, held her door wide in invitation and offered him a glass of champagne.

From then on he was a frequent visitor. He obviously regarded her as a friend, for he would often stay talking to her long after the gaming-room had closed. He began to tell her of his loneliness, of the failure of his marriage. Had he not been who he was, she might have felt sorry for him.

His marriage, it seemed, had failed on his honeymoon – the delayed holiday he had taken in Rome, when Alice had run away. It was in that city that he had discovered that Daisy Dear had been pregnant before they left England and, fearing for the loss of her figure, had had an abortion, one that rendered her sterile. His longed-for heir was not to be. Perhaps he could have forgiven her had she not, in a moment of anger, coldly informed him, in her childlike lisp, that he disgusted her because he was too old, that the feel of his skin upon hers nauseated her. She wanted only young men to touch her, she said. As she spoke he found all desire for her ebbing away.

'You should have divorced her,' Ia suggested with her usual pragmatism.

'Tregowans do not divorce,' he replied coldly, thus quelling her momentary sympathy.

So, he had continued, upon their return, their lives had taken different routes. He confided that her extravagance was enough to try even the most patient of men. He talked frequently and with longing of Etty, the wife who had died. Occasionally he spoke of Oswald, his dead son, and how different, how full, his life might have been had he not drowned. Ia nodded sagely and, if she felt a twinge of compassion for him, she reminded herself whom she was listening to. She would sit seeing memories of her childhood cottage, of her mother, of her father's crushed legs, in her mind's eye.

What she most wanted to hear about was Alice but, to her frustration, he never mentioned her. The way he had shut his daughter from his mind as if she had never existed was chilling.

Although from the beginning he had known that she had worked for him, he never asked Ia about her life, or how she had arrived where she was. She often expected him to comment on her paintings of Cornwall. But he never did; he did not appear ever to have noticed them. Ia was no fool and realised that he did not care a jot about her. He was using her to unburden his misery. Maybe he wanted to make her feel sorry for him.

Ia was now twenty-five, her beauty undiminished, and with a confidence in herself forged by her success in business. For nearly two years she had run the brothel single-handed and business kept improving as her fame spread. The majority of men who visited London, be it from the North or from abroad, regarded a visit to Blossom's as an essential part of their itinerary. And always there were her regular customers. Her repayments to her backers not only pleased but surprised them; they had never imagined that she would manage to return the money so fast. She was offered more money to invest in whatever she wanted. Ia had become that phenomenon in circles where money ruled: she had the kiss of good fortune upon her, and many would have liked to be involved with her luck. She always declined. Her goal was that the brothel should be entirely hers. Then she would look about for other forms of investment.

Christmas was approaching and Ia was collecting her papers and figures together to work on before the New Year. Ia was punctilious about her paperwork. To a penny she knew the sum of George Tregowan's IOUs. Over £50,000. Perhaps it would be a good idea to call some of them in; it was too much to have outstanding. She had been foolish to allow them to accumulate, but she had so enjoyed seeing the pile of debts growing in her bowl. She would keep some back; it was a good idea to have him constantly in her debt. She wanted to damage him. She was not sure how she was going to do it, but she felt that the money must be the key.

She left instructions for George to be invited to her room the moment he arrived.

'You wanted to see me, Ia. I hope it's not for long. I've just seen old Rotherman come in, I'd like to take him on, a big gambler that one,' he said, smiling as he sat in the chair opposite her. It was always Ia and George now, she could not remember when that had started.

'It's about these, George. I don't want to hurry you, but they are mounting up.'

She bent over the papers on the small table beside her and looked slantwise at him to see his reaction. He had gone white.

'How much are they?'

'Fifty-five thousand, five hundred and forty pounds, six shillings and sixpence.'

'Good God!'

'It's a large sum, George.'

'But why on earth did you let me run up so large a debt?' he asked accusingly.

'Could I have stopped you, George?' She smiled sweetly at him, her heart beginning to race as with dawning comprehension she realised that he was not as rich as everyone thought him, including herself.

'I don't have it.'

'I beg your pardon?' Still she smiled sweetly.

'I don't have the money to repay you,' he spoke sharply.

'Excuse me, George. But when I accepted these IOUs I accepted them in good faith. I had assumed you were a man of your word as well as of enormous wealth and that there would be no problem with regard to settlement. I cannot afford to carry a debt of this size.'

'What you are doing here, Ia, is illegal A gaming debt cannot be sued for.'

'I'm fully aware of that, George. But then I assumed I

was dealing with a gentleman. And, of course, it goes without saying, gentlemen always pay their debts.' She spoke in a calm, cool manner yet her heart was racing with excitement. She still did not know precisely what she was going to do but she knew instinctively that revenge, such sweet revenge, was within her grasp.

'Of course I will pay them. But you will have to give me time, Ia.'

'The problem is, George, I don't think I can. I have obligations, too, you know, pressing ones.'

'I just don't have it. And that's that.'

'What about your London house?'

'Mortgaged up to the hilt.'

'Your silver, your valuable possessions?'

'Pledged.'

'Oh dear, George, we do seem to be in a bit of a pickle don't we? Surely you own a large estate in Berkshire?'

George groaned and put his head into his hands. Ia sat waiting patiently.

'When my gambling became as it is …. my wife insisted that I gave her the house in Berkshire, and its contents, plus some shares I had.'

'An astute woman, your wife.' Ia was surprised that someone who appeared as empty-headed as Daisy Dear should have been so shrewd. 'And you don't think she will help you now?'

'There's no question. She would refuse. I do have another property.'

Ia leaned forward and then, fearing she might appear too eager, sat back again. 'Another property?' she asked innocently while her heart pounded to such a degree she felt it must burst.

'In Cornwall. Gwenfer. I might be able to sell it, the problem is that property in Cornwall is very cheap. There were mines there once but they are no longer worked; they are worthless.'

'How much land?'

'Now, a mere thousand acres, mainly moor and cliff top. I've been selling off what I can here and there. There's a village, a disused mine, a farm – poor land you understand, and the house.'

'Is the house furnished?'

'Oh yes, neither of my wives liked it, nor its contents. Too old-fashioned, d'you see?' He smiled weakly, Ia's interest in his house had given him a faint glimmer of hope.

'The problem is, if it is as bad as you say, it might take a very long time to sell. I mean who would want a property so far away from London?' She shrugged her shoulders. 'What would you think it was worth?'

'In the region of £30,000, I'd say.'

'That leaves us very short, doesn't it?'

'What do you mean?'

'I'll take the house. I'd quite like a house in Cornwall, for personal reasons. I hear your wife has some beautiful jewellery. What about that?'

'She made me give it to her. It wasn't even mine to give, it was my daughter's. She will be thirty in two months. Somehow I have to be able to raise the money to buy it back, and then there's her fortune too.'

'You don't mean to say, George, that you've frittered your daughter's fortune away as well? That *is* naughty.' As she spoke Ia felt that at any moment she was going to burst out laughing. She could not remember when she had felt so elated. 'What is your estimate of the value of your daughter's jewellery?'

'At least £25,000.'

'Then I should have it, don't you think?'

'But I've explained to you, my wife will not let it go. She says it is hers.'

'I see. Ah well, George, we must arrange what we can. I'll instruct my lawyers in the morning to contact you about the property in Cornwall. Then I suggest that you give up gambling, George.'

'I can't. I have to have money. I have two months in which to get back my daughter's fortune.'

'It's not long, George.'

'I do have credit elsewhere. They're not all vultures like you.'

'Oh come, George, that's hardly fair, is it? However you won't be gambling here any more, if you don't mind.'

'I shan't even be coming here again, I can promise you that.'

'As you wish,' she smiled sweetly as she held the door open for him. She slammed it shut and hugged herself with glee. She could not believe it. Gwenfer belonged to her.

7

'Mrs St Just! Of course. When my butler said there was a Mrs St Just needing to see me urgently, I had no idea . . .' She laughed nervously. 'I never knew your name, you see, just Ia.' Daisy Tregowan fluttered across her drawing-room. 'Thank you, Phillpott, that will be all.' She waited until the door closed and they were alone. 'I hardly think it is right that you should come here, Ia. However . . .'

'You haven't been to my establishment for over a week, I wondered what had happened to you. I wondered if you had decided to stop patronising us.' Ia looked about the ornate and cluttered room for somewhere to sit. How she disliked this predilection of Mayfair hostesses for such a jumble of possessions, as if the amount they could cram into a room was an indication of their wealth. She looked at Daisy and then at the chair by which she stood. Daisy did not invite her to sit.

'I've had a slight cold. I find the winters most trying. In fact I'm thinking seriously of going to Egypt next winter.' She dabbed her nose prettily with a small scrap of lace

501

which did service as a handkerchief. 'Your concern for me is most touching, but I should have preferred it if you hadn't come. You do understand . . . ?' She smiled archly at Ia and sank gracefully on to a chair, sighed and brushed her forehead with a limp hand.

Since she was obviously not going to invite Ia to sit, Ia sat. Daisy frowned, 'I was not aware that I had asked you to be seated.'

'I know, it seemed you were never going to invite me,' Ia said pleasantly.

'I can't imagine why you are here.'

'I'm here to collect the jewellery which belongs to Alice Tregowan. That's all.'

As if her spine had been replaced by a rod of steel, Daisy sat bolt upright. Her mouth sagged with astonishment as she stared at Ia, her head to one side as if she had not heard properly. 'I beg your pardon?'

'The jewellery, it's mine. Your husband owes me a considerable amount of money. The value of those jewels will cover the debt. I've arranged it with Lord Tregowan.'

'They're not his to dispose of. You most certainly cannot have them,' Daisy trilled shrilly.

'If I do not leave this house today with the jewellery, Lady Tregowan, I shall take your husband to court and I shall sue him for the money.'

'Ah! You can't,' she said triumphantly. 'No one can sue for gambling debts.'

'I shall sue your husband for his unpaid bills in my restaurant for the past two years.'

'Who would believe that his bills could be so large? Don't be stupid, woman.'

'You would be surprised what bills can be run up entertaining friends and with patrons who have, shall we say, peculiar appetites. I'm sure you would not want any of this made public for your husband's sake.' Ia spoke quite calmly.

'Do what you want. What happens to my husband does not concern me.'

'I think it might, Lady Tregowan. You see, with a clever counsel – and I can afford the best – I'm sure that it will be the simplest thing in the world to introduce in our evidence the fact that you have been an even more devoted and loyal client. Of course, the fact that you prefer such young boys will be of enormous interest to the newspapers and your friends.'

Daisy did not merely go white, she appeared to become transparent, as all the blood drained from her face. Her pretty little hands with their pink-tipped nails flew to her mouth. A stifled scream issued. 'Who would believe you, who?' she was almost shouting.

Ia dug into the large cloth bag she had brought with her and produced not only her small black book with every visit of Daisy Dear carefully noted but also the receipts and several unbanked cheques which she had kept back as an added precaution. 'This will be sufficient, I'm sure.'

'This is blackmail, no more, no less.'

'Yes, that's right. I agree.'

'You are a sly, loathsome person.'

'I haven't much time for you either, Lady Tregowan. Now if you would just collect the jewels, I can be on my way?' she said briskly.

'If you think that I'm going to give you a fortune in jewellery and family heirlooms, you can think again. I shall call the police.'

'I gather you still see the King socially, even if your husband is not often part of the charmed circle. I should think he would be most interested to know, don't you? It would be the easiest thing for me to inform him.' Again Ia gave the enigmatic smile that was increasingly infuriating to Daisy Dear. 'Of course you should not just hand them over to me; you should check with your husband first. I don't mind waiting.'

Mustering a stare which she hoped would kill, Daisy

rose to her feet and stalked out of the room with as much dignity as she could salvage.

Ia sat and waited patiently. She was disappointed. She had spent the last week planning in minute detail every aspect of this interview, only to find that in its execution she was not experiencing the pleasure that she had anticipated. Daisy Dear was an unworthy opponent; she almost felt sorry for her. How bereft she would be without her baubles. She flicked her head; the hair that in the past would have cascaded over her shoulders was now firmly pinned up in a becoming chignon, but the mannerism remained. Still, she thought, money is money. She must not weaken . . .

Half an hour later a tear-stained Daisy Tregowan re-entered the room with a large leather box in her hands which she thrust unceremoniously at Ia.

'I hope never to set eyes on you as long as I live!' she said angrily, with no trace of a lisp.

'Thank you for your understanding of the situation and your time. Good day, Lady Tregowan.' Ia slipped the leather box inside her large carpet bag without checking the contents and without looking back, crossed the room. As she shut the large mahogany door it was to hear Daisy emit an ear-piercing shriek of rage.

In her small room, Ia finally opened the box and looked at the glittering display of jewellery. Everything was in a tangle. Daisy, in her temper, must just have thrown all the pieces into the box, higgledy piggledy. She dug her hands into the tangle and, lifting a handful of pearls, gold chains and a diamond choker, she held them up to the light, enjoying the way the gems sparkled. What on earth did she want with them? She never wore jewellery; she had always made simplicity her hallmark. The logical thing would be to sell them. She let the jewels slip through her fingers, reminded of water as they shimmered out of her grasp. She picked up a sapphire and diamond ring and suddenly remembered the child she had been, staring into the jeweller's window her first day in London and vowing that one day she would have one of each. An emerald brooch caught her eye. It seemed her wish had been granted.

She spent a long time staring at the gems wondering what to do. Oddly, she found, she did not want to sell them, but she did not want to wear them, so why should she keep them? With a start she realised that most of all she would like to return them – to Alice. What on earth had made her think that? Why should she care about Alice's jewellery after what she had done to her?

It had been a magical time, though, those years she had spent with Alice. And she was honest enough to realise that much of her success was due to the way Alice had taught her to speak. Thanks to her she could read and write – otherwise what a pickle she would be in now! Yes, to be fair, she still had much to thank Alice for.

She shut the lid of the box and locked it. She removed from the wall the painting of Lamorna Cove which was one of her favourites and behind which was her safe. She unlocked the safe and stowed the box of jewels away. She would put off making a decision for the time being. Since she did not need the money desperately, she would give herself time to decide.

She poured herself a glass of madeira, and sighed. She had dreamed of revenge, but the reality had been disappointing. She felt tainted by what she had done and could almost wish she hadn't.

It was late evening on 15 February 1906. George Tregowan sat at his desk, in his study, in the house that no longer belonged to him but to his creditors. His wife had left him, the day that Ia St Just had claimed the jewels, promising never to return. He was completely alone.

Above the fireplace hung a portrait of Etty. A portrait which captured her beauty, her joyous nature, a portrait which, despite Daisy Dear's objections, he had refused to remove. He looked up at his long-dead wife and as so often in the past pondered on how life could have been, if only . . . He studied the beautiful face, her smile captured for all time, and wondered if Alice still looked like her mother. Did she look like the image hanging above him? He regretted now what had happened. He regretted that he did not know his daughter, the last of the Tregowan line. He felt bitter that his anger had prevented him from finding her, so that now he did not know whether she was dead or alive, married or single, fertile or barren.

He looked again at the papers on his desk and the long letter from Mr Woodley of Penzance which detailed Alice's inheritance – the fortune that by rights should be hers tomorrow, her thirtieth birthday – except that there was no fortune left for her to inherit.

From his key ring he selected a key and slowly unlocked the drawer to the left of his desk. From it he withdrew a revolver. He checked it, cocked it. He waved, a strange gesture, half wave half salutation, to the portrait of his wife. He put the gun in his mouth and with eyes still open and gazing at the one woman whom he knew he had loved, he pulled the trigger.

George, 7th Baron Tregowan, slumped forward, a large gaping hole in his shattered head.

Chapter Twelve

1

The cumbersome Tregowan coach made its way from Penzance railway station and along the Promenade. Ia looked with interest out across Mount's Bay. She had not known Penzance well, but Alice had brought her here a couple of times, in this selfsame coach she was certain. She was sure that then the bay had been full of sailing ships with tall masts. Now there were mainly steam boats riding at anchor – not nearly such a romantic sight. She looked at her watch wondering if she had time, before dusk, to go by Newlyn to see if the fishing-fleet was in. That she could remember from her childhood as if it were yesterday. Holding Alice's hand tight in the crowd which had gathered to watch the fleet return. She had jumped with surprise at the great cheer that greeted the first sighting of the ships, low in the water from their heavy cargo of fish and with swirling, noisy seagulls in attendance, like bridesmaids fussing over a bride. They had rushed to the quayside to see the size of the catch, to marvel at the baskets full to the brim with their silver-scaled treasure. They had peered with pounding hearts in the hope of seeing a monster from the deep caught in the nets by mistake. She remembered the excitement, the noise, the wonderful sea smell of the fish, and looking at her watch, peered up at the sun and decided she would come another day. She had set her heart on watching the sun set on the sea at Gwenfer. She leaned out of the coach and ordered the coachman to go by the shorter route.

She could not make up her mind which was worse – the slow snail's pace as the horses strained up the hill to

Mount Misery, or the cracking pace down the other side, when the swaying of the coach made her feel sea-sick. One of the first things she must do was to get rid of this antiquated contraption. She looked at the plush, buttoned interior as she bounced about and decided it must be at least a hundred years old. She would get a more sprightly vehicle; it would be kinder on the horses too. Maybe, if she could afford it, she would get an automobile. That would cause a stir – there did not appear to be many in Penzance.

She leaned forward eagerly as if she wanted to devour the view with her eyes. She had been only a child when she had left and yet she found that she remembered every turn in the winding road, each cottage and every farm they passed. In the hedgerows campion, ragged robin, the last of the primroses, swathes of bluebells, the crisp white of the wild garlic and some whose names she had forgotten, bloomed as if in riotous welcome. She had forgotten the beauty of Cornwall in May; she had been right to delay her visit until now.

They were close to the village and she leaned out of the swaying coach. There was the church, the hated school, the cobbled main street with its hodge-podge of houses of differing sizes and periods. Strangely, she found that her heart was beating quickly as they approached the miners' cottages. They passed rows of neat new-thatched houses and then they were out on the scrub. So, where was her cottage? She leaned dangerously out of the coach, peering back the way they had come. Surely that was where the cottages had stood? She had remembered everything else so clearly, she was unlikely to forget where her own home had been.

The coach slowed so as to swing into the gates of Gwenfer.

'Stop a moment,' she ordered, and the coachman pulled up the horses with difficulty. They were tired, they knew their stable was near and they were eager to be home. Ia slipped out of the coach, dropping to the ground before the coachman could help her. 'I'll walk the rest of the way, thank you.' She smiled up at him and he decided, there and then, that she was the most beautiful creature he had ever set eyes on.

She walked slowly down the drive shocked by how overgrown and neglected it had become. If the house were in as bad a state she was going to need every penny she had to restore it. The rhododendrons had spread their branches over the driveway, meeting at one point so that she found herself walking through a tunnel of their dark-green, shiny leaves. The mophead hydrangeas had not been dead-headed so they wore a crown of lacy brown, dead blooms above the thrusting bright green of the new shoots.

Ia turned the last bend in the drive. Before her stood the house. Her house. She paused for a moment. The old house was in every way just as she had remembered it, at any moment she half expected Alice or Queenie to appear in the doorway. She felt proud and she felt shy. She felt as she had that very first day when Alice had brought her here and she had looked up at the great building, at the windows watching her blankly. Then she had been afraid of the building, as if she should not be here. That was how she had reacted then and that was how she felt today. It was as if she should not be here, should not be the owner of this place and that the house knew it.

She tossed her head. What nonsense she could sometimes think! Of course she had every right to be here: she had acquired the house legally. It was not her fault that George Tregowan had been an idiot, neither was it her fault that he had killed himself. From what she had gathered he had never liked the place anyway. And his rejection of Alice was so complete that he would have been unlikely to leave it to her.

'You're mine now, and I've every right to be here,' she

said aloud and stood, hands on her voluptuous hips, looking belligerently up at the granite building.

But she did not enter the house. Instead she walked down the long flight of shallow steps that led to the garden below. The great stone urns that guarded the steps contained a fine crop of weeds. The garden had never been neat and tidy but now it was a jungle. Roses, freed from the gardeners' secateurs, trailed over every available wall, every fallen tree. The lawn was covered in daisies, buttercups and primroses. Clematis had taken up residence on every tree. It was wild and it was beautiful.

With difficulty she made her way through the garden until she came to the small river which, crystal clear, still tumbled towards the sea. She reached Alice's rock and as she looked at it she felt immeasurably sad – sadness for lost dreams and hopes but most of all regret for the little girl who had had to learn that it was dangerous to trust. She sat down on its smooth surface and faced the sea. She drew her knees up close to her and hugged them as she watched the great globe of the sun sink gently down the heavens and over the rim of the ocean. The grey granite rocks glowed red and pink; the sea was changed into a great pool of molten gold in its dying rays. She waited patiently for the green flash of light as the sun finally sank below the edge of the restless sea. How often she and Alice had sat here longing to see the flash that many spoke of and few had ever seen. Had it existed at all? Nothing had changed, she thought to herself: there was still no mystical spark of green.

She breathed deeply the pure, unadulterated air. All she could smell was the sea, the scent of the wild flowers, the pungency of the wild garlic – no fumes, no smoke. The noise of the sea gently slapping against the rocks, the light breeze rustling the new spring leaves, and the evening song of the birds were the only sounds; no traffic, no coughing, spluttering motor cars, no shouts from the costers or the newspaper boys. She had forgotten how peaceful life here was.

How perfect this would be for Francine. She could have such a wonderful childhood here. But it would be difficult for a time. It had been easy to acquire the house, but maintaining it was going to be a problem. That would be her goal now, to make enough money as quickly as possible so that she could retire here with her daughter and live the life of a lady of leisure. She laughed softly at the idea.

Suddenly she felt chilled. She pulled her fine grey cloth coat closer to her, stood up and made her way back to the house.

''Ere 'er comes. Cor she be handsome.' Flo swung back from the window of the great hall. 'Er's been down to the rock. Bain't that peculiar?'

'I don't see anything peculiar in that. You come here, young woman. Just watch your apron, we don't want no marks on it, do we?' Mrs Malandine ordered. The staff were few but Mrs Malandine knew what was proper and had lined everyone up with clean aprons, scrubbed nails and brushed hair. It had been a trying time for Mrs Malandine. The Tregowans had neglected this house for so many years that to make it presentable for the new owner had been a long and hard task. She looked about her, fretfully noting a lump of plaster which had fallen from close to the hammer-beamed roof since this morning. Well, there was nothing she could do about it now. She crossed to the great door and noted with relief, as it opened, that Mr George, the coachman, had oiled the hinges which had lost their eerie squeak.

She dropped a low curtsy. When she rose she was surprised to find herself looking at a very young and beautiful woman. Maybe there had been a mistake. The woman smiled at her but said nothing.

'Mrs St Just?' she asked cautiously.

'Yes, Mrs Malandine. I wanted to look at the sea. I'm sorry if I've kept you waiting.'

'Oh, please, Mrs St Just, we don't mind waiting for you. Not at all,' she said, realising how flustered she sounded. This woman was not at all what she had expected. Not only was she much younger, still in her twenties she hazarded a guess, but so beautiful. 'If I might introduce the others?'

They crossed the wide flagged hall to where the servants were lined up beside the long refectory table. She went along the short line; first Mrs Trelawn, Flo, Sal, Mrs Butters who helped out with the heavy cleaning, Mr George whom she had already met, and Zack the odd-job man. To their surprise she shook each of them by the hand and her smile seemed to be on the point of laughter. They did not realise that their bobs and bows were amusing Ia to the point of near hysteria – especially Flo's, the girl who had refused to touch her.

'There don't seem to be many of you for such a large house,' Ia said finally, in a controlled voice.

'Oh, we manage. No one has been here for years, you understand, Mrs St Just. So really we have only had to try and maintain the building, keep it aired and dusted.'

'Ah, I see.'

'Would Madame be wanting some tea? It gets chill these early spring evenings, I've lit a fire in the small parlour for you.'

'A whisky and water, please. And perhaps you could arrange a bath for me. I should like to dine at about nine. Something fairly light, if you could, Mrs Trelawn.' Ia crossed the hall towards the small parlour, opened the door and smiled at them before closing it behind her.

'Well, who ever heard of a lady drinking whisky?' Mrs Malandine was quite puffed up with shock.

'Er knew your name, Mrs Malandine, did you notice that?' Flo said, wide-eyed. 'And she knew where the parlour was. Bain't that peculiar?'

'Of course she knew my name, you silly girl, Mr Woodley would have told her.'

'But 'er knew where to go . . .'

'I must have nodded my head in that direction.'

'And don't 'er look like Miss Alice?'

'What a fanciful girl you are, Flo. Whatever next? She doesn't look a bit like Miss Alice. And I can assure you that Miss Alice would never have ordered whisky. Come on everyone, what are you thinking of? We've things to do, we've someone to look after at last.' And she bustled the others towards the back of the house and the kitchens.

Ia stood in front of the fire in the small parlour, the logs cracking, giving off their sweet apple smell. Sometimes in winter she and Alice had done their lessons here when the schoolroom had been too cold. She had loved this room then, she loved it even more now. Nothing had been moved. When she had acquired the house lock, stock and barrel from George she had half expected to find, when she got here, that the furnishings would have been moved. But everything was in place. She remembered these paintings, these books, that chair; even the fire-irons were the same.

She still felt that she was in a dream from which at any moment she would awake. She must be careful, though: she did not want people to know who she was, in case her occupation might also be discovered. She wanted the slate to be clean for Francine when she joined her here. She would pretend to be a wealthy widow. She had already made a couple of slips – knowing the housekeeper's name for one, and she wondered if they had noticed that she turned automatically towards the parlour door without being directed. She was certain none of them had recognised her, though. Why should they? Who would think that that ragged child had become the elegant woman she now was? It was a shame that she could not let them know. Would there ever be a day when she could confess? What fun that would be. She could just imagine the gossip in the village. 'Imagine, that Ia Blewett, the drunken miner's daughter, lady of the manor!'

2

Ia had slept fitfully in the great oak four-poster bed in the main bedroom. She lay against the fine, lace-trimmed, linen pillow and looked about her. She thought she had seen every room in the house but she could not remember having been in this one before. Perhaps it had been Alice's parents' room and for some reason, that she had not chosen to explain, she had not wanted Ia to see it. Last night, in the candle-light, she had been unable to see the dimensions of the fine room. She looked about her and admired the tapestries which hung on the plain white walls. There was a carved, dark-oak blanket chest, a matching cupboard, and two high-backed chairs on either side of the huge fireplace whose carved overmantel reached to the heavily plastered ceiling. She liked the solid simplicity of the room's furniture in contrast to the elaborate ceiling with its plaster flowers, birds and crests – all with some symbolic connection with the Tregowans, she presumed.

It was a strange feeling for Ia just to be lying in bed with nothing to do all day except what she chose. She lay back to enjoy the experience and found immediately that she was worrying about her business. It had taken a great deal of planning to be able to leave. Blossom had been luckier than she, in that Blossom had had Ia to trust and so she had often been able to get away for a rest. But Ia had no one whom she trusted. It had been Peter who had insisted she travel to Cornwall to inspect her property. For months she had resisted and she was still unsure if that resistance had been totally to do with her work or whether, in a strange way, she had been nervous of returning. Eventually someone had recommended a retired madam, who could come in during the week she planned to be away – she refused point blank to go for longer. But, here she was, one day into her holiday, fretting that she might be losing money – the woman had had a distinctly shifty look. Gwen had undertaken to supervise the girls for her and there she had no worries. Gwen was quite capable of being as tough as Ia was, and would defend Ia's interests like a tigress. Peter had promised to drop in to keep an eye on the takings, especially the gaming-room.

This, she realised, was the first holiday she had had in the whole of her twenty-five years, and she wondered what people did on holiday. She wished that Peter could have come with her. But she had not suggested it, and nor had he. Over the years, she had become a perfect mistress, making no demands on him at all.

She slid from the high bed and, slipping into her robe, let herself out of the room and padded along the long main corridor that stretched the width of the house. The corridor was lined with portraits of Tregowans: it was like looking at a pictorial costume history of England, she thought, as she made her way between them. How strange it must have been for Alice to have been able to see what each of her ancestors, back to the sixteenth century, had looked like. Unlike Ia who knew only the faces of her father and mother and had no pictorial souvenir of either. The wide corridor had antique rugs on its oak-planked floor, and beneath the portraits were more oak chests, an Armada chest; and on the walls were the Tregowans' instruments of war. There were so many swords, knives, shields, that one could have withstood a siege, she decided. The light poured in from the great oriel window at the end. She ran towards it and looked out to see the sea, just like any child on the first day of her holiday – it looked to be a perfect day.

She retraced her steps and opened the door at the other end of the corridor which led to the winding stairs to the upper floor and the nursery wing. The housekeeper and her helpers, presumably thinking she would not be interested in the upper floors, had not got this far with their cleaning and she left footprints in the dust on the bare boards of this long, narrow corridor. The door of the old schoolroom squeaked as she pushed it open and stepped back into the past.

Nothing had been moved. It was as if Alice and she had just left the room for tea or to go to the sea-shore. She crossed the room to what had been Alice's desk. Lying open on it was the register she had kept with Ia's name in it. A pencil lay on it as if the writer was about to return to fill in her attendance. She picked up the pencil. The last entry was '24 August 1891'. She made a new entry: '15 May 1906', and laughed softly as she marked herself present.

She crossed to the desk where she had sat, lifted the lid and took out her books. Opening the one marked 'English Composition', she remembered the essay at which the book fell open. 'When I grow up', it was called. She smiled at the childish writing. She had written of her dream of going to America on a great boat, of how, once there, she would work in a shop, a cake shop she hoped. That much she could recall but she had no recollection that she had day-dreamed of marriage and four children, two boys and two girls. She wondered, chuckling to herself, if she had chosen the names. What a strange little girl she must have been with her dreams of another land. She closed the exercise book. What if she had gone, what would have happened to her, what would she now be like? A shopgirl or a whore? Well, one thing was certain, a shopgirl would never have owned Gwenfer. She shut the desk and looked about the large sunny room, at their paintings on the walls, at the globe where she had first learned where America lay. She sniffed the air, even the smell was the same as she caught a distinctive whiff of chalk.

She stood up from the desk, crossed the room, took the key from the lock, and opened the door. Once on the other side, she shut and carefully locked the door behind her and slipped the key into her pocket. She wanted nothing changed here, ever. For within those walls were the only happy memories in a childhood devoid of happiness.

In the garden of the schoolhouse Philomel, the schoolmistress, pottered about. She was not there by accident. She had heard that the new owners of Gwenfer had arrived last night, and she was rather hoping that they might pass by so that she could see them. She could not remember when there had been such excitement in the parish as the arrival of these new people. The rumours, of course, were rife and she had heard that an Indian princess had bought it; that the owner of a Durham mine was the new incumbent and intended to open up the tin mines; the latest information had been that it was to become a boys' school. Whichever was true, none filled Philomel with joy. She had spent the last thirteen years longing for her dear Alice to return. In Philomel's eyes, Gwenfer belonged to the Tregowans. Whoever owned it now was a usurper.

She was not simply being nosy, though she admitted to herself that there was an element of that. Most important, she wanted to see them so that she could report to Alice. It had been such a worry when the letters from Alice had so abruptly stopped and her own had been returned, marked 'Gone Away'. Years of worry, in fact, and then suddenly the letters had started again with no explanation of why they had stopped in the first place. Once in regular correspondence again Philomel had not enquired about those lost years. If Alice wanted her to know, she would tell her in her own good time. She was overjoyed to read that Alice had married and appeared happy. They seemed to have adopted a little girl which, while typical of Alice's kind nature, was sad if it meant she could have none of her own. Alice would have made an ideal mother.

Philomel tugged at a particularly recalcitrant piece of bindweed. She was most distressed at the reply to her latest letter. Philomel had written expressing her condolences on the death of Alice's father. She was shocked to the core of her tiny frame when the reply had been to thank her for letting her know. It was shocking that no one more official than she herself had seen fit to let Alice know that her father had died. Philomel had heard dreadful stories of the manner of his death, none of which she had passed on to Alice. No doubt it had all been servants' gossip and if it were true, then she would have been the last person to have wished to impart it.

A thistle that she was certain she had dug up last week, was the next to be attacked by Philomel. How much she would have liked to see Alice's face when she had written her own news. How surprised she would have been, almost as surprised as she herself had been – that she was married. Every day Philomel sank to her knees to thank God for his goodness in bringing Ralph Trenwith into her life. Philomel Trenwith: still, after five years, she experienced a thrill every time she signed her name.

She settled back on to her haunches, her trowel idle in her hands as she remembered the day they had met. She often spent time reflecting on it as if to reassure herself that it had really happened. She had long given up the idea of marriage. Not only her looks but her age had been against her until Ralph came, as the new curate, and he did not seem to notice how she looked, nor that she was two years older than he. He liked to talk to her. After a year he had proposed to her and she had nearly ruined everything by bursting out laughing for, of course, she had thought he joked. But he hadn't. They lived together in such compatible bliss in the schoolhouse which Alice had arranged for her, and now all they longed for was for Mr Reekin to retire and for Ralph to take his place. Such a good vicar he would make, far better than that dreadful cold, cheerless soul, Reekin. How Alice would approve.

Spying a particularly virulent crop of groundsel Philomel swooped on it and thus missed Ia as she passed by.

It had been such a glorious day that after a breakfast of bacon and eggs, the like of which she had not eaten in years, Ia had set out on foot to explore. She had trudged up the drive, getting very hot in the process. She had forgotten how very steep it was. She had walked the cliff, pausing now and then to admire the wild flowers. Soon the foxgloves would be marching over the cliff like an army of cerise soldiers. She wondered if the books of pressed flowers that she and Alice had made were still in the schoolroom. She must look; there were so many flowers' names she had forgotten.

She wanted to see the cottage she had lived in with her family and, at the same time, was afraid to do so. She felt so happy and relaxed she was convinced that at sight of the hovel all the anger of the past would come roaring back into her mind to disrupt her equilibrium.

She paused at the new houses. If only they had had a cottage like that, then her mother might still have been alive. Maybe then she would have had the pleasure of moving Ada Blewett into the big house she had once scrubbed. Ia looked about her, puzzled. This must be where her house had been. She was certain of it. Yes, it was: when one reached the top of the alleyway one had been able to see the Brisons, just as she could now. She wandered down the pathway between the rows of houses, noting the well-tended gardens, the neat thatch, the windows upstairs as well as down. In the centre of the row there was a date on the wall – 1893. She stopped in her tracks. So, her mother had not died in vain, obviously even that bastard Tregowan had been sufficiently shamed by the conditions in which his tenants had lived to rebuild the hovels not long afterwards. She was not certain if she was pleased or angry.

She retraced her steps and walked up towards the village proper. The women were out with their shopping baskets, there was a bustle about the place that she could not remember from the past, the people smiled, she could not recall that either. She realised there were no ragged children about, children with sores and undernourished bodies, even the few dogs she saw seemed to be well fed.

She skirted the church, there was nothing for her there and never had been. There was no point in going into the graveyard, she did not even know if her mother was buried there. She wondered if her father was alive or dead, found she did not care either way, and resolved that she would not bother to find out. She walked past the school – empty today, it must be a holiday – and passed the schoolmaster's cottage. She certainly hoped that that pig Featherstone was under the ground.

Then she stopped dead in her tracks. Ahead of her stood a row of almshouses. Window boxes glowed with daffodils and narcissi, curtains billowed at the clean latticed windows. But what made her stop, what made her put her hand to her mouth, what made her virtually stop breathing was the inscription carved into the granite of the cottages, in large swirling gothic letters. THE IA BLEWETT MEMORIAL ALMSHOUSES, 1893, she read with disbelief.

3

Ia leaned against the schoolhouse wall trying to catch her breath. She felt faint. What did the building mean? A memorial to her – but one could have a memorial only if one were dead! Who had built them, who had thought she was dead? George Tregowan had not known her in those days, which left only Alice. Could she have had them erected? Had she for some reason thought her dead? What could have happened to make her think that?

'Can I be of assistance?'

The voice made Ia jump. She swung around to find the ugliest woman she had ever seen poking her head over the wall of the schoolhouse. 'I . . . I felt a little faint, it's the heat, I think . . .' she said, smiling weakly at the strange little woman.

'Would you care to come in for a drink of water, or maybe some tea?' Philomel asked, wondering who the stranger might be, and at the same time whether it was safe to invite someone one did not know into one's house. But the woman looked innocent enough and was extraordinarily beautiful. Philomel peered at her, wondering if the clothes she wore were fashionable, since she knew little of these matters. She decided that exotic might be a better word to describe her outfit. Her dress, turquoise silk covered with emerald green chiffon, hung loosely on her body and yet to her surprise Philomel found she was more aware of the woman's contours than if the dress had been tight-fitting. A matching long scarf was wound about her blonde hair and like the dress was wafted gently in the light breeze. In fact, Philomel thought, the combination of the turquoise and green made her look as if she was clothed in moving water – Philomel shook her head at such a silly notion and padded to open the small white gate.

'That would be most kind, thank you.'

Philomel held the gate open and, taking her arm, led her guest up the garden path and into the small house.

'You were lucky to find me here. It's a school holiday you see, I'm the teacher. Normally I would be in the school with my pupils. I'll get you a glass of water first and perhaps some sal volatile? Then I'll make some tea.

Oh, silly me, I'm Philomel Trenwith.' She held out her hand, conscious that when she said her name she never said it in a normal tone of voice but rather as if it should be accompanied by a fanfare of trumpets.

'Mrs St Just.' Ia took the proffered hand.

'St Just. That's unusual, there's a town here with the same name. Are you from there?'

'No,' Ia could answer honestly. 'I live in London.'

'How distressing for you, I hated living in London. It's so much more congenial here, as my husband is always saying. But the water . . .' She bustled from the room. Ia looked about the tiny room crowded with badly executed water-colours, cheap figurines, books on every surface and . . . Ia crossed the room to a cluttered desk on which stood a sepia photograph. It was Alice, there was no mistaking her face, older but still the same sweet expression, the fine blonde hair. There were other photographs, too: one of a rather plump little girl, her hair the same blonde colour but twisted into fat ringlets held up with a large bow. And one of Alice with a tall, broad-shouldered man who stood with his arm proudly about her. Ia studied the photograph carefully but she could not make out his features; they were blurred as if he had moved. She was so used to thinking of Alice with venom that her initial reaction was one of anger that she obviously had a husband and security, and her child was with her – not like Ia's. Then she remembered the almshouses and looked at the photographs and felt confused.

'Ah, you're admiring my darling Alice.'

'Is that her name?' Ia hoped she sounded sufficiently uninterested to allay suspicion, but at the same time not too much so, for she was curious.

'Yes, Alice Tregowan. Her family owned everything here, even the village. The large house in the valley, Gwenfer, that was theirs. I haven't even dared write to her to tell her it is sold. It will break her heart to think of

522

strangers in her house. I know she always hoped to return one day.'

'Is that her husband and child?'

'Yes, that's Lincoln, a fine man I gather. I haven't had the privilege of meeting him yet. He's American you understand, that's where they live. But Alice promises me that they will be visiting shortly, if not this year, the next.'

'Lincoln?' Ia said thoughtfully and wondered what had happened to Chas. 'And the child?'

'That's Grace. Adopted, I understand . . .' Philomel lowered her voice as if the information was not quite nice. 'She's eleven this year.'

'Eleven?' Ia was aware that she sounded like an idiot, the way she kept repeating things. She took the glass of water and sipped it but refused the small bottle of sal volatile.

'I've put the kettle on. I've some nice fresh scones, my husband loves my scones. Do please be seated, Mrs St Just. Are you here on holiday?'

'Just a week.'

'I do hope you don't think me impertinent, Mrs St Just, but it's quite extraordinary how you remind me of Alice. It's the hair I think, the same colour, and your eyes,' Philomel giggled, afraid the woman might take offence.

'I take that as a compliment. She's a very beautiful woman.' Ia looked about her, unsure how to continue, wanting to find out as much as possible without frightening the schoolmistress off. 'This village is very pleasant. I had expected it to be very poor, but everyone seems quite prosperous.'

'Oh, that's because of dear Alice. She started a little factory here for the poor miners who had no work when her father closed the mines. They make Cornish pixies from copper – you can still find small deposits hereabouts which we have smelted – tourist souvenirs, that sort of thing. Dear Alice was so clever. You see, she foresaw that with the trains being so fast and efficient, people would come here for their holidays. Dear Queen Victoria came to Penzance, you know, stayed in the Queen's Hotel – good gracious, do you think that's why it's called that? I've never thought of that before. But the Queen coming helped the area enormously. The factory is most success-ful – it belongs to the people who work there, you see. Alice wanted nothing from it – she's a wonderful woman. And then she arranged equipment for making butter and cream in large quantities – you've no doubt heard of our famous clotted cream?' She smiled, at least Ia presumed it was a smile, but on Philomel's poor misshapen face it was difficult to tell. Ia wondered why, in the face of this avalanche of information, she ever feared that Mrs Trenwith would not be forthcoming. 'With the visitors coming, and so many hotels opening, we supply them.'

'We?'

'The village again, you see. Those who work in the factory or creamery share in the profits – almost every family here is involved. Alice felt it was only right that those who did the work should benefit the most. She is so advanced in her political thinking, it really is a shame she's not a man. My husband,' Philomel paused and uncertain if Ia had heard, repeated with pride, 'my husband, the curate, is one of the trustees.'

'A most fortunate village.'

'Oh, yes. It was dreadful here, you know, when I first came. The poverty was painful to witness.' Philomel shook her head at the memory. 'Alice was appalled once she was old enough to be aware how wrong it was. She asked her father to rebuild the miners' cottages but he refused. Imagine, all that money and he wouldn't do it. Such a small amount of money for a rich man like him. Oh dear,' her small hand shot up to cover her mouth, 'oh, perhaps I shouldn't be speaking ill of the dead but,

524

oh dear . . .' She flapped her hands anxiously and sat for a moment frowning. 'Well, anyway,' she said, brightening up as if she had managed to placate her conscience, 'Alice used her own money. She had the vermin-filled cottages burned to the ground, and then had those dear little cottages put in their place. Everyone was very pleased. Have you seen them?'

'Yes, they're delightful. And the almshouses?' She felt her pulse beginning to race.

'That was Alice too. She worried about the old people who could no longer care for themselves. Years ago there was a dreadful epidemic here and there was a little girl of whom Alice was particularly fond who died in it. Alice had the almshouses put up as a memorial to her. She could not find her grave, you see. Such a sad story I've always thought.' Philomel paused as if making up her mind whether to say more. Ia waited, silent, fearing if she spoke that the little woman might change the subject. Philomel leaned forwards in her chair conspiratorially and glanced over her shoulder as if to check that no one was listening. 'It's all very strange, if you ask me, Mrs St Just. Years ago, Mrs Trelawn, who cooks at the big house, came here for tea. Of course she's not of the same class as my dear friend Mrs Malandine, the housekeeper. Mrs Trelawn did not seem to know when to go, if you know what I mean?' She grinned meaningfully and Ia nodded in sympathy. 'In desperation I offered her a sherry – presuming of course that she would refuse as a lady would have done. She accepted. In fact she accepted rather too many. Oh dear, it was unfortunate; perhaps I shouldn't be telling you.'

'I shan't breathe a word to anyone, Mrs Trenwith.' Ia smiled becomingly at her.

'The story she told me was quite extraordinary. She told me that Ia Blewett had not died. That the nursemaid Queenie had not approved of the friendship – well, quite rightly, too – and had told Alice the child had died in the epidemic.' She looked at Ia to gauge her reaction to this news.

'Really?' Ia said with difficulty and with what she hoped was a fairly controlled degree of interest.

'Of course my first reaction was to write immediately to Alice and to tell her the good tidings. But then, I thought perhaps I had better check. It would be too cruel to have written her a falsehood and I cannot begin to describe to you the condition of Mrs Trelawn when she told me ...' Philomel tutted at the memory and Ia clucked in sympathy. 'So I asked Mrs Malandine. She told me that there had been such a silly rumour but that sadly it was not true. All the same, I felt duty bound to tell Alice of this rumour. But, just about the same time she stopped writing to me. Maybe she did not even receive my letter – such a long way for a letter to travel, to America, don't you think? Really, it's a miracle any get there at all.' Ia nodded agreement, fearing that the woman had lost the track of her conversation. 'And then, strangely, a couple of years later a woman in the village told me the same story. I did not know what to make of it all. Should I perhaps institute an investigation? But my husband counselled me. After all, the building was up, no one knew the truth it seemed, and if she were alive, goodness only knows what she was doing. Best to leave things as they were.'

'Of course,' Ia muttered through the gall that was rising inside her.

'She had a lonely life, my Alice, I'm so happy that she seems to have found contentment now.'

'You seem to know a lot about Alice,' Ia said with difficulty, for her voice had suddenly become very thick and she felt tears pricking behind her eyelids.

'I was her governess. A wonderful pupil, the best I ever had. And when she went to London for the season she arranged for me to take the position of teacher here. I've been most contented.'

Ia felt she needed to be alone, she needed to think. 'Thank you for the water. I feel much better now.' She stood up abruptly.

'Are you sure? You still look pale to me. And you've had no tea.'

'I feel well, now, thank you.'

Philomel walked to the gate with her. She leaned on it and looked up the village street. 'Good gracious, you've brought back so much of the past, Mrs St Just. I've become so used to how everything is now that I had quite forgotten how dreadful it all was when I first came here. Of course, whether it continues like this . . . ?'

'Why shouldn't it?'

'The new owners.' Philomel shook her head and tutted fussily. 'No one knows anything about them and of course the village is part of the estate. Perhaps they won't allow things to continue as they are. Perhaps they will charge large rents. It's all most unsettling.'

'I don't think you need have any worries about that, Mrs Trenwith. You see, I'm the new owner. I shall not be changing anything.' She enjoyed the mixture of surprise, pleasure and concern that flitted across the woman's face.

'Oh, good gracious. Oh dear. How rude you must think me, oh dear.' She fluttered her hand in agitation.

'I don't think anything of the sort, Mrs Trenwith. I'm just pleased to see everyone so happy.'

She turned from the gate and made off through the village. Philomel did not even wait to collect her bonnet before she rushed from the cottage in search of her husband to give him the wonderful news.

Ia went straight to her room and lay on her bed refusing lunch, tea or any refreshment. She lay looking up at the carving on the ceiling above her and felt only misery and overwhelming regret. She had spent all those years hating and planning revenge, a wicked, useless, futile emotion. And when she had finally achieved her revenge, she had not enjoyed it as she had anticipated. It had been an empty thing. Now she found that her hatred for Alice had been badly misplaced. Alice had been her friend, and Alice had loved her, not only to what she had believed was her death but beyond the grave.

How would her life have been, had Alice known she lived? To what would she have put her considerable mental energies with no need to fill her thoughts with hatred and revenge? What sort of person would she be now? The possibilities of what could have been filled her with a bleak despair.

Should she herself contact Alice, try to make some sort of amends for the lost years? The thought brightened her, but only for a second. How could she approach her now? Alice was a happily married woman, living a life of total respectability. How could she, the most famous whore-house keeper in London, make contact with her old friend? Imagine Alice's embarrassment. She could not do that to her old friend. She smiled. She had thought of Alice as her 'friend' again, a much more comfortable way of thinking about her than all the thoughts in those hate-filled years. No, for Alice she must always remain dead: it was the only solution.

Listening to the little teacher and her litany of praise for everything Alice had done for the community, Ia had now to consider how she would behave to her tenants. She knew herself, she knew how much the insecurities of her earlier life had made her obsessional where money was concerned. She could never imagine herself giving it away as Alice did. However, Alice had set an example as a model landlord. Should she not follow her? She would have to think about it.

That evening, after dinner, she summoned the staff.

She told them what work she wanted done about the house and the gardens. She explained what arrangements she had made about their wages. She then ordered Mrs Malandine to pack her cases. She was returning to London, she explained, to their astonishment. She was not sure when she would be back, she told them.

It was late. She could not sleep but lay in her bed watching the shadows cast by the candle-light, listening to the sound of the sea and to the noises of the old house. It seemed to Ia as if the house were talking to her. Gwenfer was hers, when by rights it belonged to Alice. The house had known last night as soon as she arrived. The house had known she had no right to be there.

4

Almost three years after Ia's visit to Gwenfer she and Peter had one of many arguments about it.

'How much did this place, Gwenfer, cost you?'

'I don't see that it's any of your business,' Ia snapped.

'On the one hand you ask me to advise you with your finances, but when I try to do so you bite my head off,' Peter replied, exasperated.

'I have no recollection of asking you to help me with my affairs. You just presumed that I would,' Ia retorted; she had been feeling irritated most of the day and this intrusion into her affairs did not please her. 'In any case, it has nothing to do with the business.'

'Of course it does. You took it in lieu of a debt. It's very much to do with the business.'

'If you must know, I wrote off £30,000 of George Tregowan's debts against it.'

'You did what?' Peter swung round and looked at her with astonishment.

'You heard.'

'You were cheated. You paid too much. Properties such as that, with a small amount of land, situated in the back of beyond, go for next to nothing.'

'I'd have settled double to get it.'

'Then you would have been an even bigger fool.'

'It's my money. I'll do what I bloody well like with it.' She crossed her small sitting-room and poured herself a large whisky, spilling half as she did so.

'You drink too much.'

'Oh, mind your own business. You counting up the cost of that too?' She glared angrily at him.

'Ia, what is the matter with you? You told me you want to buy the house which is for sale on the other side of this to make the brothel even larger. You need capital but you have far too much tied up in a ridiculous house you've visited only once. I was merely suggesting that you see sense and sell it.'

'It's not a ridiculous house. It's the most beautiful house in the world,' she said, petulantly.

'Then why don't you visit it more often? You could go at least once a year . . .'

'It's none of your business why I don't go there. In any case it was not my idea to buy the house on the other side. It's everyone else telling me what I should do – including you. You all treat me as if I was a machine which can just go on working and working, and I'm sick to death of it. I'm fed up with the lecherous men, the hysterical women, the bitching, having no life of my own, the worry . . .' Ia was pacing up and down the floor angrily sipping at her glass of whisky.

Peter snorted with laughter. 'You ask me to believe that *other* people are forcing you to do this? Oh, come, Ia. When have you ever allowed anyone to influence you?'

'I'm tired,' she shouted at him, irritated that he should see through her protestations.

'Then retire, you've plenty of money to keep you in comfort for the rest of your life if you give this up.'

'And do what? Live on my own in Cornwall?'

'No, with me. Together.'

'What?' Ia stopped dead in her tracks.

'We could live together. I could manage the estate. My wife wants a divorce. I've been meaning to tell you.'

'You've been meaning to tell me?' Her voice was rising dangerously. 'You sit there calmly telling me that you're about to be divorced and have only just got round to telling me?' Her voice was shrill. 'And how long have you known, may I ask?' she added sarcastically.

'A couple of months. There did not seem to be any point in telling you until I knew she was serious. I thought she might change her mind.'

'On what grounds?'

Peter looked long and hard at his highly polished shoes. 'Adultery.'

'With me?' Ia laughed. 'I don't count. What does the stupid woman think she's doing? You don't sue for adultery over a whore. There wouldn't be a marriage left if *we* were regarded as a threat.'

Peter had stopped studying his shoes and was now taking a deep interest in the state of his cuticles. 'It's not you.'

Ia felt suddenly cold, a chill not on the surface of her skin but one which had its source deep within her. 'Would you repeat that?'

'I'm sorry, Ia. That's why I didn't tell you straight away.'

'Who?' Ia's voice was dangerously calm.

'You wouldn't know her.'

'Who?'

'Her name is Rose Fitzgerald. Old Lord Fitzie's daughter.'

'She's not a day over eighteen.'

'I know.' He hung his head with embarrassment.

531

'How long?'

'A year.'

Ia flung her glass of whisky across the room, it caught Peter on his forehead and smashed. Blood began to pour down his face. 'You bastard! You stinking heap of garbage. How could you? You had me – was I not enough? Or am I getting too old for you, just as Blossom predicted? Get out, you hypocritical Judas. I never want to see you again.'

'But, Ia, I thought . . .'

'Run away to Cornwall with me, that's what you thought, did you? Well your thinking was wrong. I don't like hypocrites or people who deceive. I trusted you. I've never made demands upon you. Outside your marriage, I expected you to be true to me. I loved you, you bastard. I never want to set eyes on you again.'

'You'll regret this, Ia.'

'All I regret is that I ever allowed you back into my life again. I hope your wife goes ahead with this. I hope she ruins you and your little maiden. I hope you're never accepted by anyone decent again. Now get out . . .' she screamed at the top of her voice.

After he left her temper was awesome. She stood in the centre of the room and screamed until her throat hurt. She kicked the furniture, she threw all the glasses at the wall, and she hurled the bottles after them. She ripped the curtains from the window. It was as if she wanted to destroy this room where she had thought she was safe with him. And then she slumped on the floor sobbing with anger and grief that he should think so little of the love she had given him for so long with no reservations. She wept for all the lost years, the lost investment of emotion in a man who had cheated her as she had never cheated him. She wanted to love, to be loved. All her life it was what she had wanted, and needed. Now she knew that it could never be.

Six months later the emptiness that Peter had left in Ia's life and soul was still a constant presence. It was like the dull ache of a slow-growing cancer – it never went away. She worked all the hours she could stand but still it remained and in bed, alone, some nights the longing was unbearable.

At first she had thought her need purely a physical one and, to his immense surprise, Ia had one evening invited a client to bed with her. Flattered, he had accepted. She had chosen carefully, having listened to her girls talk about the various men and their attributes and performance. It had been a vigorous night and not a wholly unenjoyable one, but it left Ia feeling more empty inside than before so she did not repeat the experiment.

Peter had called several times but each time she had her doormen send him away. He had sent her flowers, presents, tried to contact her by telephone, but she always refused to speak to him. This refusal was the hardest thing to do, but her hurt went too deep for forgiveness, although it seemed her body was unaware of this. Often when he called, she would find herself hiding behind a curtain just to catch a glimpse of him. She knew her behaviour was ridiculous but did not seem able to help herself. After each such occurrence she would sternly counsel herself. Just because she was a whore it did not mean that he had the right to deceive her. She had been more than a whore to him. In any case, whores cost money and she had not cost him a penny for years. He had destroyed her trust in him and that, she knew, would never return.

There were days when she felt immeasurably sorry for herself. She had no one. She had lived twenty-eight years, and, if she faced reality, she knew that only Gwen would care if she lived or died. The girls who worked for her respected her, but she did not think they liked her. She was too strict with them to expect that. Her daughter did not even know she was her mother and Alice, her one friend from so long ago, presumed she was dead.

All this was her private misery, for Ia, the consummate professional, never allowed a glimmer of her personal unhappiness to show. To her clients Ia was fun, glamour, wit. It was to Ia that they poured out their own misery and dissatisfaction with life; none of them ever suspected the loneliness of her own.

It was November, a bitter cold night with a freezing fog outside. In this weather business would be slow, only those desperate for sex and companionship would venture out on such a night. Ia sat in her small office, a whisky beside her, working on her books. The fog was so thick that barely a sound reached her room from the streets outside. Gwen poked her head around the door.

'There's a young girl to see you.'

'Say we aren't taking any more on at present. Tell her to try Mog's behind Drury Lane – she's taking on girls.'

'She insists she sees you.'

'Does she now,' Ia laughed. 'Well if she's very young, beautiful and a virgin I might consider it.'

'She's young and beautiful, I'm not so sure about virginal!' Gwen laughed loudly. 'No, it's not that, Ia. She says she's a relation. She says to tell you her name's Frances Blowit or some such.'

'Francine?'

'Yes, that's what she said.'

'Oh, my God.' Ia's heart lurched and she felt the room pressing in upon her. She crossed to the window and, despite the cold and the fog, opened it and took a deep breath of the freezing air. 'Where have you put her?'

'She's in the hall. What on earth's the matter, Ia, you've gone as white as a bleeding sheet.'

'Pour me another drink, Gwen, a large one. What do I look like?'

'I just said, like a sheet. Cor, love us, what's the matter?' Gwen poured the whisky, all the time looking with concern at Ia. So distracted was she that half the drink poured over the silver tray. But for once Ia said nothing.

Ia drank in one gulp the drink Gwen handed her. 'Send her up, Gwen.' She pulled the window down. 'I'm all right now, I just felt a bit faint.'

'You sure? Will you be all right with her, on your own, I mean? You don't half look peculiar.'.

'Yes, I'll be fine. It was a bit of a shock, that's all. She's a niece of mine, you see, one I never expected to meet,' she lied.

While she waited she inspected herself in the mirror. She fiddled with the ends of her hair, pinched her cheeks to a suitable degree of pink, moistened her lips. She wished now that she had made the girl wait and had changed into something more decorous than this revealing, diaphanous gown that was one of her work clothes. What would she think of her?'

'Come,' she said to the barely audible knock on the door. It opened. The first thing she thought was how beautiful the girl was. The same long blonde hair that she herself had and the same enormous eyes, not grey like hers but a beautiful green, true dark green, like the leaves of the ivy. How exhausted and bedraggled she looked, was her second thought.

The girl's coat was torn and filthy, spattered with mud from top to toe. Her boots were scuffed. There was mud on her face, her hands were scratched and what looked suspiciously like a bruise was beginning to show on her cheekbone.

'Francine . . . ?'

The girl paused a second. 'Are you my Aunt Ia?'

'Yes, I am. Oh, Francine . . .' Ia held out her hands in welcome.

The girl raced across the room to Ia. Gwen, her face

wreathed in smiles, silently closed the door on the happy pair.

Ia could not believe that she was holding her daughter, that it was her child in her arms clinging to her like a limpet. She could not believe it was her baby's fine hair that she stroked nor that they were her tears soaking her fine silk dress.

'Hush, my little one. Hush. What is the matter?'

It was a good five minutes before the sobs subsided sufficiently for speech, and even then it was almost incomprehensible. Gently Ia prised the hands from about her neck. She helped the girl out of her sodden coat and, crossing to the tray on which her whisky decanter stood, poured a small one for the girl. She made her sit in a chair, beside the roaring fire, and handed her the drink.

'This will help you, sip it slowly, there's a good girl. Now tell me, what has happened to make you so unhappy?'

'You won't make me go back?' The girl clutched the stem of the glass, her enormous eyes looking anxiously up at Ia.

'Back where?'

'Back to those 'orrid people. And their filthy 'ovel.'

She would have to get rid of that accent, was Ia's inconsequential thought, upon hearing the dropped aitches, the vowels of a cockney. It was imperative if she was to make a good marriage that she spoke well. She should have thought of that; she should have been sending the woman money for elocution lessons for her. Francine must marry well. Ia was determined that her daughter should never lead the life that she led.

'I thought you were happy there.'

''Appy?' The voice rose shrilly. ''Appy, it was a living hell.'

'Oh, my poor darling. But I always had such glowing reports about you from Mrs Prendleby, she always said how happy you were.'

'She would. Otherwise you might have taken me away, then she'd have lost the money you sent. But I couldn't stand it no more, Aunt Ia. I couldn't. Night after night he was at it. It was more than a girl could stomach.' She shuddered dramatically.

'What do you mean?' she asked with dawning horror.

'That beast, that Alf Prendleby. He was always after me, always interfering with me. I want to be a good girl, Aunt Ia. I do. Like the vicar says. But he was so 'orrid to me. And he 'urt me, oh, Aunt, he 'urt me so bad. I had to come to you. I don't have another soul in this whole world that I could turn to: I won't be a nuisance nor nothing, honest I won't.'

With shaking hand Ia poured herself another large whisky. She felt sick, she felt filled with such a dark hatred that she wanted to kill. Her child molested! She downed the drink as Francine began to wail again.

'It's all right, Francine. You're safe here with me. Are you hungry?' she asked, practically. The girl nodded mutely. Ia tugged the bell pull. The speed with which it was answered implied that Gwen must have been at the door, if not listening at it.

'Gwen, get Francine here some soup and a large steak. Would you like that, my darling?'

'That would be lovely, Aunt Ia.'

'Then order my carriage, Gwen.'

'What, on a night like this? You must be bleeding mad. You ain't going nowhere, I'll see to that.' Gwen stood in the doorway, arms akimbo, as if to prevent Ia leaving.

'I have to, Gwen. Something dreadful has happened, I have to go immediately and see these people.'

'No! Don't leave me. For the love of God, don't leave me –' Francine screamed, flew across the room and clung desperately to Ia, her shoulders heaving with sobs.

'Cor love a duck,' Gwen exclaimed.

Ia looked anxiously over the child's head at Gwen, who, nonplussed, shrugged her shoulders. 'There, there. I shan't go. Not tonight then. You have your supper and then I'll get Gwen to make a nice bed up for you. Won't you, Gwen?'

'I ain't sleeping alone. You won't make me sleep alone, will yer? Please.' The tear-stained face that was turned towards her was heart-rending to see.

'No, of course not. You can sleep with me, in my bed. I have a little house across the garden. We shall be safe and cosy there, shan't we?' Ia found herself speaking to the girl as if she were a tiny child and not the same age as Ia had been when she had left the orphanage for London to seek her fortune.

Much later, after she and Gwen had watched with astonishment the speed with which the girl ate her enormous supper, she had personally washed her, dressed her in one of her own night-dresses and tucked her into bed. She sat beside the girl, holding her hand, until her even breathing indicated that she was fast asleep.

Ia sat for a long time and watched her sleeping daughter. It was quite extraordinary, the depth of her feeling for one who was really a stranger. She had felt like this when she had held Francine as a baby; this was how she had felt the day Blossom had taken her from her. All those years the love had been awaiting her return. But then, she reasoned, for more than twelve years everything she had done, every penny she had earned, every shilling saved had been for this girl. There could not have been a day when she had not thought and worried about her, the memories sustained only by her monthly letter from Mrs Prendleby, listing her progress and state of health. And now the object of all that love and concern was here in this very room. It seemed unbelievable.

Ia stretched, stiff now from sitting too long in one position, and gingerly she drew her hand away from Francine's. It was too late to go and see that bastard Prendleby tonight. She would go first thing in the morning. She had to make plans now. She could not keep the child here. She was determined that Francine never find out what she did, even though she thought Ia was only an aunt. She would send her away to school: that would be the ideal solution. She would ask some of her clients about the best schools, those which would teach her to be a lady, to speak properly, to learn all the social skills.

Eventually she climbed into bed beside her daughter and gently took her in her arms. She lay in the dark, cradling her. Ia felt totally at peace. She felt such love within her for this little stranger and such a desperate need to protect her from any other hurt. Without doubt, she thought, holding Francine in her arms in this bed was the happiest experience of her life.

6

It was still dark when Ia slipped from her bed and dressed silently. She had to arrive at the house in Blackheath early, before Alf Prendleby went to work. Gwen complained loudly when awakened by Ia and asked to sit with Francine so that the girl would not be alarmed when she awoke. The thick freezing fog was still swirling about and, although she told her coachman to hurry, speed was impossible in the winter murk. It was nearly three hours later, and nine o'clock was striking, before she arrived at the house in Blackheath where for all those years she had fondly assumed Francine was well cared for.

'All right, all right, keep your hair on,' a voice muttered at Ia from behind the closed door, in answer to her loud and persistent knocking. There was much scraping and rattling of bolts and chains and the grinding of a key in a long-unused lock before the door eventually swung open. 'Yes?' A short, stout woman, whose body was swathed in an apron of blinding whiteness, peered quizzically up at Ia.

'I'm Mrs St Just, come to see you about the treatment of my daughter Francine Blewett,' Ia announced as she swept, imperiously, into the narrow passage that served as a hall. There she stopped and had to wait with impatience while the woman laboriously refastened all the bolts and chains on the door.

'Can't be too careful these days,' she said pleasantly. 'But I'm glad to see you, missus. Worried out of my mind, I've been. If you'd care to come this way?'

She opened a door and squeezed herself back against the door jamb in order to allow Ia to pass. The room was small but crowded with furniture and ornaments, so that passage across it was fraught with difficulty. It was also filled with the leaden silence of a space unused to sound. And, although all surfaces were highly polished and there was not a speck of dust to be seen, it had the musty, damp smell of one that was little used.

'I'll just get the fire going. We don't normally light it until teatime, you understand,' the woman lied as she bent to put match to paper that had been laid for weeks and was sodden with damp. Half a box of matches later a weak puff of smoke was her only reward.

'Mrs Prendleby, leave the fire. It's not going to catch anyway, and I need to talk to you,' Ia finally said with exasperation.

'Tea?'

'I wish to talk, Mrs Prendleby. Would you kindly sit down and listen to me . . .'

But Mrs Prendleby was across the room moving, despite her bulk, with amazing agility between the pieces of furniture. She lifted the heavy velvet curtain on the door, opened it and, 'Alf, tea,' she bellowed down the corridor. 'There, it'll be here in a trice. Best to talk with a cup of tea inside you. It always helps, don't it?' She smiled kindly at Ia and patted her gently on the arm as if comforting her. 'I expect you're as worried as I am. Why don't you sit down, take the weight off your feet.' She began to puff up the many cushions on the larger of the two armchairs energetically and, smiling encouragingly at Ia, made her sit though she would have preferred to stand.

'Mrs Prendleby . . .'

'She's run off before but never for this long. A right handful she's become and looking like butter wouldn't melt in her mouth . . . Oh, that's not fair,' she tutted to herself rather than to Ia. 'Poor little thing, she wants so much and is in such a hurry to get it all. I haven't slept a wink these last four nights, I can tell you.'

'Four nights?'

'Yes, since she did a bunk. I know I should have contacted you, Mrs St Just, but as I says, she'd done it before and I just hoped she'd be back before we knew where we were. But my Alf he said as how I should go and see you today. I've had the police looking for her, of course. They was very kind, but since she was over twelve there wasn't a lot they could do, they said.'

'Over twelve?'

'Yes, age of consent, you see. Nothing no one can do then if a girl gets a silly idea into her head. And I must admit that Albert Swallow at the butcher's is a fine strapping lad . . .'

'Albert Swallow?'

'Oh yes, that's where she ran off to, we found out in the end. But he walloped her, said she'd nicked a sovereign, and off she went again. I didn't believe that, real angry I got, I can tell you. Not our Francine, I told him straight, she wouldn't steal. High-spirited she is, but not a thief.' Mrs Prendleby was puffed up with indignation at the very idea.

Ia had sat listening with mounting anger until she thought she would burst from it. She stood up and confronted Mrs Prendleby. 'How dare you malign my daughter in this way?' she shouted. 'I very much doubt if you've been anywhere near the police. I doubt if this

541

Albert even exists. You're just saying these filthy things to mislead me.'

'I beg your pardon?' Mrs Prendleby sat down heavily on the other chair, shock etched on her face. 'I beg your pardon? I don't know what I've done makes you think you've the right to speak to me like that, I'm sure.'

'I quite expected you to say you didn't know. I would have believed you, there was no reason why you should know – it could have happened at any time, when you were out or asleep. But all this talk of going to the police only proves to me that you knew and you're trying to protect that monster of a husband of yours.'

'Monster, my Alf? What on earth are you going on about?'

'Oh, come, Mrs Prendleby.' Ia was pacing the room in agitation. 'Don't pretend innocence with me. I've come to complain about your husband interfering with, molesting, my little girl.'

'Interfering? Molesting? Your little girl?' Mrs Prendleby repeated idiotically. 'Well, I never. What a wicked thing to be saying. I don't understand you, missus. That I don't. What do you mean coming here and saying nasty things about people what have done you no harm? I've a good mind to call the police, that I have. Bloody cheek I call it.' She settled her chins on her chest like a turkey as she rested after such an impassioned sentence. She took a deep breath and started again. 'I'm sorry about your daughter, but as I says, she'll turn up in her own good time and when she does this time, with your permission, Mrs St Just, I'll let her feel the rough side of my palm, that I will. What an upsetting time. I'm so sorry, that I am.' During the course of her speech it was as if Mrs Prendleby had forgotten half-way through that at its beginning, she had been angry with Ia, for she finished it in sympathy with her. At this point the door opened and a young girl, cleanly dressed and smiling broadly, entered carrying a tray of tea and followed by a huge man who loomed in the doorway and smiled at everyone. Despite a nose which had been broken in at least three different places the smile was in truth a very pleasant one, the sort of smile it was difficult not to respond to, as Ia found when she attempted to stare stonily at him. The sight of her husband brought Mrs Prendleby back to her conversation with Ia.

'Alf, this here is Mrs St Just, Francine's mother. She's come looking for her and she's saying you're a monster, that she is.'

Alf Prendleby lumbered across the room and held out his hand to Ia. Such was his size that Ia found herself backing away from him until she was against the chair and, with nowhere else to go, she plopped back into it.

'A monster, me?' His laugh began in the lower regions of his stomach and rumbled up, echoing around his barrel of a chest, before being emitted in a great bellow. 'Me?' he repeated and Ia found herself pressing further and further into the chair to get away from him. His enormous size filled the room and made even his wife, who was as wide as she was tall, appear small. The deafening laugh subsided into a wide but questioning smile. 'Me a monster, why?'

'My daughter is at my house. She arrived last night in a dreadful state . . .'

'Last night?' husband and wife chanted in unison nodding sagely at each other across the room.

'Yes, last night. She has accused you, Mr Prendleby, of interfering with her and hurting her.'

'My Alf? My husband wouldn't hurt a fly. That's God's honest truth. You ask anyone hereabouts. Oh, this is silly –' Mrs Prendleby interrupted, and with a mighty heave got up from her chair and then, as if uncertain what to do next, promptly sat down again.

'That's not nice, that's not a nice thing to say at all.' Her husband nodded his head mechanically.

'Nor is it a "nice" thing to do, Mr Prendleby. I've come

here to tell you that I shall make it my job to see that decent people don't bring their children here ever again. The children already here I shall have moved from your evil presence. You're not fit to be near children.' Ia found she was shaking with fury.

'Now, hang on a minute, missus. I ain't interfered with no child, I can assure you of that. If Miss Francine says I did then she's bloody lying, that's for sure.'

'Well, of course you'd say she was lying. I hardly expected you to admit it.'

'I don't lie, missus, never!' Alf said quietly as he moved towards Ia. He paused in front of her chair and looked down on her. 'Let's get one or two things straight, shall we? We're the decent folk here, missus, you just ask anyone. We don't run no brothel for toffs up west, we live quiet and respectable like.'

'What I do doesn't enter into it.'

'Seems to me it does if you're trading insults. You're in no position to come here accusing me of this and that pretending that you're whiter than white. You can't go about saying these wicked things, depriving me and my wife of our livelihood, just because it suits your daughter to lie.'

'How dare you say my daughter lies. You who stole her virginity, her innocence. You bastard!' Ia hissed venomously at him.

Alf leaned forward and, putting one hand on each arm of the chair, peered down at Ia who was now trapped. 'Let me explain one or two things,' Alf said in his slow and ponderous voice. 'For one, your daughter lies, frequently. Two, your daughter steals –'

'Oh, Alf, I don't like you saying that, we're not sure,' Mrs Prendleby fluttered nervously from the depths of her chair, like a giant white bird trapped in a cage too small for it. Alf continued in his slow, reasonable voice.

'As I was saying. She steals. Your daughter's virginity went the year before last – eleven she would have been.

And it wasn't me, it was the boy from three houses along, Arnold Beam. I've no doubt she seduced him but his father gave him the belting of a lifetime for all that it wasn't his fault. As for me, I ain't touched her but it's anyone's guess how many have around here since then.'

Anger gave Ia sufficient strength to push the huge man out of her way. She sprang from the chair and rounded on the husband and wife, eyes flashing with her fury and indignation. 'You're both filthy liars. I believe my daughter. You are an evil man. I have influential friends and I shall make it my personal duty to see that you and your wife are ruined.'

A high-pitched squeal issued from Mrs Prendleby. 'Oh, Mrs St Just, how could you be so unkind to us, what have been nothing but kind to your little girl? We did our best, it's not been easy, lovely little thing though she is. It's true what my husband says. She's a dreadful handful, I promise you. There have been times . . .' She took one of her deep breaths and started again. Refreshed by the added oxygen the words tumbled out in a torrent. 'If you want to know the honest truth, I'm glad to see the back of her: she's been nothing but trouble since the day she came here. Always upsetting the other children. They're happy she's gone I can tell you. You've a lot to learn about that little madam one way and another. Mind you, the way she's going she's ended up at the right place. I'm sure you can find her a nice cosy position there.' This time, Mrs Prendleby, from starting her speech in a cajoling whine had, half-way through, suddenly lost her temper. But so had Ia, who quickly crossed the room knocking a whatnot and a small table flying. She slapped Mrs Prendleby sharply across the cheek.

'Don't you dare talk about my daughter in that way. Don't you dare . . . You haven't heard the last of this,' Ia said as she swept from the room. Balked by the confusing array of locks on the front door she went out to the back through a room where half a dozen clean and happy-looking children were sitting down to a large breakfast.

Ia seethed all the way back to her house. If only Francine had been a little bit younger she might have gone to the police. But would they have listened even then? She knew men and the police too well to believe that they would take the word of a young girl against one of their own. But somehow she would find a way to ruin the family.

Francine was peering anxiously out of the mews house window as she crossed the garden. Gwen had found her some clean clothes to put on and she had breakfasted well in Ia's rooms.

'Aunt Ia, I asked you not to go.' She had thrown herself into Ia's arms the minute she entered the room. 'I expect they said horrid things about me. They're lies, Aunt, I promise you, on my mother's soul, they lie.' Tears spurted into the great green eyes. 'I ain't going back, never.'

'Don't upset yourself, Francine. I didn't believe them for one minute. I know you speak the truth, you're a Blewett. Don't be afraid. I'll look after you.'

'Can I stay here then?'

'No, my dear. It's too difficult.' At sight of Francine's dejected face Ia sighed, resenting the life-style which prevented her from giving her daughter a proper home. 'Dear Francine, it's only that with the . . .' she paused, frowning, 'with the . . . hotel . . . I'm always so busy, I would not have sufficient time for you.'

'I wouldn't get in your way, honest I wouldn't. I told you last night.'

'It would be too restrictive for you here in this little house. It really is only big enough for me. I think I know what we should do. I want you to go to a good school –'

'I don't want to go to school. I hate school.'

'Let me finish, Francine. I want you to go to the sort of school where you can learn to be a real lady.'

'A real lady?' Francine looked up at her with renewed interest. 'Cor . . .' She grinned and then remembering herself added, 'But I'd rather stay here with you, Aunt,' and she smiled winsomely at her.

'Oh, my dear, Francine, you are so sweet,' Ia put out her arms to her and hugged her close.

7

Having Francine with her helped Ia to forget Peter. It was ideal having someone important, not concerned with the business, to occupy her mind.

Ia planned her days so that she could spend as much time as possible with Francine. On these mornings no book work was done and the backlog of work built up. She had initially tried to interest the child in the art galleries and museums. Francine was interested only in shopping. So, most mornings they would dress against the cold and set off to the shops. Down one side of Bond Street, up the other; it seemed Francine was never bored with what there was to see. Indulging her daughter gave Ia more pleasure than anything else in her life. She quickly realised her generosity was not completely altruistic: she loved to see the expression of pleasure on Francine's face. She became adept at noticing the flickering expressions of interest shown by the girl in various objects. Ia would then swoop and purchase whatever it was that for a second had taken her fancy, her reward being the almost hysterical reaction that it was sure to inspire.

When they lunched together Ia would take the opportunity of beginning Francine's education, teaching her about wine and food. Then, while Francine had a rest, Ia would slip across to the main house to check that all was well. But she was always back in time for tea which they would share beside the fire, toasting muffins and giggling at the silliest things, more like friends than mother and daughter. It was not surprising that at such times Ia often thought of teas taken years ago with her other friend, Alice.

Each evening she was late to the brothel for she could not leave until her daughter was asleep. Regularly, Francine made dreadful scenes if she thought Ia was about to leave her, sobbing pitifully and clinging to Ia's skirts. Ia was flattered that she was needed so badly, so she did not mind having to wait until the girl was asleep before she slipped out to her clients. As she was rarely in bed before three and since Francine was prodding her awake at seven, Ia was exhausted.

She knew it could not go on like this. There were days now when to lift her feet from the bed took all the will-power she had. She was fully aware that she was neglecting her business. She was certain she would find the takings were down, when she got round to doing her books. And it could only be a matter of time before the clients complained, or the girls began to cheat her. And it was bad, she knew, for Francine to be cooped up in the little mews house. When spring came she would want to be out in the garden. That would not do at all – not with the propensities of some of her clients.

However, she could not send her away to school yet, not before Christmas, not when she had just found her. In the new year when the weather was a little warmer, in March maybe, or perhaps April, that's when she would relinquish her.

'Why can't I go into the hotel, Aunt Ia?' Francine asked for what seemed the hundredth time.

'I've told you, dear. We are very busy and our clients would not be amused if young people were to get in their way.'

'I wouldn't, Aunt, I really wouldn't.'

'Either you stay here, Francine, in the mews, or you

will have to go away again. I shall have to find another Mrs Prendleby until we find the right school,' she teased.

'Oh, you wouldn't, Aunt. You couldn't do that to me, please.' Tears swamped the huge green eyes. Ia felt like a monster for making her cry and quickly took her into her arms to hug her.

'Silly me, it was only a joke. No more Mrs and Mr Prendleby for you, my precious. I'm going to look after you.'

'No school?' Francine sat up eagerly.

'You must go to school to learn so many things that I can't teach you. But we'll look for one close by so that we can see each other frequently. I promise.'

Ia loved promising Francine things. She loved the eager expression, the uninhibited way the girl would throw herself into her arms to thank her. At first Ia had found such spontaneous affection difficult to accept; for too long her own displays of affection had been stage-managed, false, of no importance. Having been used only to displays of anger in her childhood, it had taken her time to adjust to Francine's exuberant affection. And, when Francine's arms were about her and she was smothering her with kisses, it was even harder for Ia not to tell her who she really was.

Christmas was approaching. This was to be a Christmas to remember. Ia used the time in the afternoon, when Francine was resting, and when she should have been with her clients, to return to the shops and to buy secretly things which she remembered her daughter admiring in the morning. She had purchased dresses, a fur muff, a gold bracelet, dolls, a sewing-box, satin slippers, a small fob watch, piles of games, a miniature theatre and, best of all, on a whim of her own, a puppy.

For the first time she had a Christmas tree in the sitting-room of her mews house. By the time she had finished, the floor was completely covered with presents – all for Francine.

By the time Christmas Eve arrived Francine was sick with excitement. In fact Ia feared that she might have to cancel the lunch she had ordered for the following day. She was disappointed for she had planned to take her daughter to Midnight Mass. Ia had not been in a church since she was a child. But this Christmas was different, this year she had something for which to give thanks.

She need not have feared. By Christmas morning Francine was fit as a fiddle and eager for the festivities to begin. Ia too felt as excited as a child and as she listened to Francine chattering about other Christmases she had enjoyed, Ia felt an illogical burst of jealousy for, from what the girl said, even if Alf were a monster, they had always had wonderful Christmases. Ia so badly wanted to make this Francine's best Christmas ever.

'Now, you wait here, I just have to go and give the staff their presents. I shan't be long – and no peeping,' she laughed as she let herself out and, huddled against the cold, quickly ran across the garden to the main house.

All the girls were assembled in the main salon awaiting her arrival. Here there was also a tree, but a huge one. Beneath it was a present for each member of her staff, from the girls to the kitchen maid. Ia had never forgotten the bleakness of the kitchen maid's lot. There were also gifts from clients to their favourite girls and presents for Ia too.

It took two hours before the last of the presents had been opened, and the last of the kisses had been exchanged, and Ia stood up to leave. The girls were disappointed she was not to stay with them for lunch. Christmas here had its own traditions, one of which was that everyone ate together. Ia was touched as they begged her to stay. But she had to resist and, as she hurried back to the mews, she thought how impossibly divided her life was becoming these days.

'Why did you take so long?' An angry-faced Francine

awaited her. Ia was shocked, she had never seen the child anything but sweet and loving.

'I'm sorry, my dear, but there were so many presents to distribute and open. But I'm here now.' She smiled, forgiving the disgruntled expression. How could she expect one so young to wait with equanimity to open her presents?

'You shouldn't have gone and left me all on my own,' the pretty little mouth pouted.

'Oh, my dear, it was just for an hour or two. And you were hardly alone, you had Gwen here with you.'

'Gwen don't count.'

'Francine, that's not very kind.'

'She don't. She's only a maid.' Francine glowered at Gwen who stared impassively back. Ia looked from one to the other. In the past couple of weeks she had sensed a growing animosity between these two that she was at a loss to understand.

'Gwen is my friend, Francine. I'm sorry if I upset you but I had no choice, I had to go.'

'You love them more than me!'

'Of course I don't. What a silly thing to say.' Ia longed once again to tell Francine who she really was. If she did, surely this jealousy would fade. Was it jealousy that stood between her and Gwen too? Was Gwen suffering as well?

'It's true though. And I expect you gave them lovely presents . . .'

'Of course I did, but not nearly as fine as yours. When shall we open them? Now or after we've had our luncheon?'

'Now.' Francine managed a weak smile.

'Very well, Gwen, we'll eat in an hour. Pull a chair up.'

'She's not staying, is she?'

'Of course Gwen's staying, she's got to have her presents too, look I brought them over from the hotel.'

'She ain't got more than me?'

'Of course she hasn't, and you must stop saying "ain't". It's not proper in a young lady.'

The present-opening began. The difference in approach to the presents was startling. Gwen carefully unwrapped each parcel, smoothing the paper straight, winding the gaily coloured string up for another day, while Francine tore into the paper, pieces of it flying to left and right in her haste to see what was inside. Gwen savoured each gift, turning it this way and that, holding it to the light, admiring it. Francine, having inspected hers, almost in a cursory way, flung them to one side before beginning on the next one. Ia smiled indulgently at her daughter thinking that, for all her thirteen years, she was really only a little girl after all.

The best present Ia had kept hidden until last in her bedroom. She made Francine close her eyes as she went to collect it. The puppy peered cautiously over the side of the basket which Ia had, with difficulty, wrapped in paper.

'A dog!' Francine screamed. And stood looking down on the little creature.

'Pick him up – they love to be cuddled. He'll be a comfort for you when I have to work. He won't bite,' Ia laughed.

Gingerly Francine picked up the puppy. She held it a second before it seemed to slip from her hands to fall on the floor with a thump. Immediately she returned to work on her model theatre.

'You mustn't drop it like that, you'll hurt it,' Ia admonished, patting the puppy which lifted one paw to her as if it hurt. 'See, I think you've damaged its paw.'

'I didn't drop it, it slipped.'

The puppy slunk across the floor, and sniffed at one of the new dresses Ia had bought Francine. In a flash Francine was on her feet, had dived after the dog and kicked it sharply. The puppy gave a high-pitched howl.

'You filthy beast,' she screamed and kicked it again.

The puppy scurried under the table and sat there quivering with fright.

'Francine, you must not be so cruel. The puppy had done no wrong.' Ia, on all fours, crawled under the table after the dog and taking it in her arms cuddled it to give it comfort.

'I hate dogs what are filthy. I'm sorry, Aunt, I got quite carried away then. Mr Prendleby, he had a dog, and they just let it mess everywhere, nothing was safe, and I forgot. It brought it all back to me, all the horror. Forgive me, Aunt.'

'Poor Francine. Of course I do.' Ia lifted the small dog up. The puppy snuggled up close to her. She buried her face in the puppy's coat, hiding from Francine the guilty expression which she always had when her daughter remembered her past. It had all been Ia's fault, that was the cruel truth she could never escape. In doing so she did not see the expression of distaste on Francine's face. 'What shall we call it?'

'Dog,' Francine replied.

'That's not much of a name. We must think of another one.'

But whatever name Ia suggested Francine did not like and 'Dog' it remained. From then on, each night the puppy curled up to sleep as close to Ia as it could get.

By February Ia's exhaustion at trying to please her customers and not upset her daughter had reached a peak. One evening, Ia simply collapsed with fatigue and Gwen had to help her to bed.

'You're doing too much, that's your problem. Making yourself ill,' Gwen nagged as she helped Ia into bed.

'But what can I do? Poor little thing, she needs me so,' Ia whispered in return, looking tenderly at the sleeping form of Francine, curled up like a baby beside her.

'Do what you decided ages ago to do – send her off to school. That's what she needs, a good dose of schooling.'

553

'What do you mean?'

'You're spoiling her, Ia. Mark my words, she's getting difficult.'

'Oh, don't be silly, Gwen. What's a child for but to spoil?'

'She ain't that much of a child any more,' Gwen sniffed.

Pointedly Ia turned her head away and switched off the bedside light. She had no intention of arguing with her old friend on how best to bring up children.

A week later Ia thought her heart would break as she loaded Francine and her baggage into the carriage.

'I've arranged with the headmistress – I shall see you this weekend.'

'It's too long.' The tear-stained face looked at her with desperation.

'It's for the best, Francine, it really is. Please don't make it more difficult for me.' Ia was fighting her own tears which were just below the surface. 'I'll see you on Saturday, we'll go for tea somewhere nice ...' The carriage started and Ia waved goodbye, the tears she had struggled not to shed pouring down her face as if she would never see her again.

She picked the puppy up and held him to her. 'Just you and me tonight, Dog, my friend.'

In her office she worked like a demon. This was not just to get the memory of Francine's tearful face out of her mind but also to catch up on neglected work. Since Francine had come, the paperwork had become a dreadful mess. Gwen had also warned her that several of the clients were complaining that they never saw her these days, and that some of the girls were getting slack. So Ia set to with gusto. And everywhere she went, Dog padded along behind her.

She did not have to wait until Saturday to see Francine.

Two days after her departure she was back on Ia's doorstep.

'I hated it, Aunt. They was all so stuck-up, and they laughed at me and the way I talks. Don't make me go away again, please, for the love of God.'

But Ia hardened her heart and she sent her away, not once but, in the following year, a total of six times to six different schools. Sometimes Francine stayed a day and sometimes a month but sooner or later she would run away. At first Ia had believed her tales of woe – of snobs who were unkind to her, of cruelty, of beatings, of starvation. But eventually, when the sixth school, like the others before it, informed her that under no circumstances did they want her 'niece' back, Ia had to face the fact that Francine might be at fault. The idea sent Francine into such a state of hysterics that Ia did not persist with her interrogation but wearily began the search for another school. For Ia had fallen into the trap of many a mother of a spoilt child – she was afraid of her and of her tantrums. But most of all she was afraid that if she did not please Francine she might lose her love.

At all these schools, apart from a marked improvement in her accent, Francine appeared to have learned nothing.

'I've decided to send you to Switzerland to a school there,' Ia finally announced after a great deal of research into schools in France and Switzerland.

'But you can't do that.'

'Gwen will accompany you there to make sure you arrive,' Ia said pointedly. 'And once there, you might find it harder to run away.'

'You couldn't be so cruel.'

'I'm not being cruel, Francine. I want the best for you.'

'Why? Why do you spend all this money on me? I don't appreciate it. Don't you understand? I don't want to go to school. I want to be a dancer.'

'I'm aware of that, Francine. But one day you might appreciate what I'm trying to do for you.'

'Let me stay here, Aunt Ia, I can work in the hotel for you, help you, I'd enjoy that.' She looked up slyly at Ia.

'It's out of the question, Francine. I've told you before.'

'Why? Because it's a brothel?'

Ia abruptly stopped counting out money and looked up sharply at Francine. 'Whatever gave you that idea? What a thing to say.'

'It's true, though, isn't it? And you're the madame.'

Ia paused for only a second. 'Yes, it's true. Now perhaps you understand why I can't have you over there?'

'When did you start, how?' Francine leaned forward, her face alight with interest.

'A long story and not one for your ears.' She smiled at her. 'So, if you know, that settles it.'

Francine grinned triumphantly from ear to ear.

'You've definitely got to go to Switzerland now.' Ia snapped the lid of the money box shut briskly. She turned her face away from Francine's sulky expression.

8

The dog Ia had given Francine was no longer a puppy. Ia knew nothing about dogs and had never owned one. She had not intended to buy this one, but when she had walked through the market in the drizzle and seen the poor bedraggled figure for sale that Christmas Eve, it had reminded her of another dog in another rain storm – old Domino on the totter's cart which had really been the cause of her coming here to Blossom's in the first place. So, for two and sixpence she had a dog, a pedigree spaniel she was assured, hence the expense. But the seller had lied to her. Dog was no more a spaniel than he was a unicorn. His head was far too big for his body, which in turn was far too big for his spindly legs. Furthermore, his paws were far too large for legs or body and were a far better match for his head. His antecedents were a cause of much amusement to Ia's clients who would spend long hours arguing his possible parentage. But Ia, to her surprise, found that she loved the dog, ugly as he was. She had not thought it possible to feel such emotion for an animal. But then, she had never known a creature as devoted as he was. When she worked in her office he slept under her desk. In the salon he sat alert and upright at her side. No one would have dared argue with Ia when Dog was there to defend her. At night he slept on her bed. At the foot of the bed was a special basket on a stand that she had had made for him, but Dog disdained to use it, certain in his own mind that Ia much preferred that he sleep with her. Ia had attempted to break him of the habit but, as with most of her battles with Dog, he won. His love which asked for nothing but to be allowed just to be with her, meant much to Ia, and he was a constant comfort to her in Francine's absence. She wished now that she had always had him and vowed never to be without him.

Francine had been in Switzerland for three months. Ia had received only a couple of letters. She did not fret when no more came, presuming that Francine had settled and was happy. It was a shock, therefore, to receive the letter from the principal enquiring when they could expect Francine back from her grandmother's funeral.

The picture which emerged from the long series of telegrams which flew between Ia and the school was that, within a week of being there, Francine had received a telegram from England saying her grandmother had died. There was nothing about the telegram to make the school think it was anything but genuine. From the principal she had received a large part of the allowance which Ia had deposited with her for her expenses. And nothing had been heard from her since.

Ia panicked. She did not know which way to turn first. She contacted clients who worked in the Foreign Office, those in the Home Office, all the Members of Parliament she knew, a French count who always called in when in England, and of course the police who, for once, were going to have to do something in return for her. She could not sleep for imagining that Francine was dead or had been kidnapped.

And then one day, a week after she had been reported missing, Francine turned up.

'Where on earth have you been? I've been worried sick about you. I've had the police in three countries looking for you. You owe me an explanation.' Beside herself with anger Ia shouted at her daughter standing forlornly in the middle of the room.

'Oh, Aunt Ia. I knew you would be cross, I just knew it. I would not be here now but I ran out of money and, Aunt, I'm so hungry.'

'I don't care if you are starving. I want to know what you have been doing all these weeks.'

'I've been travelling, Aunt. Trying to get back to you. It was hard, I had to cross France, I don't speak any French.' The large eyes watched Ia's reaction: Ia was too angry for sympathy and, as if on cue, large tears began to well up in them.

'It can't have taken you three months,' Ia snapped.

'I kept getting lost. I was so frightened. Please don't be cross with me . . .' The tears escaped and rolled down her perfect, smooth cheeks.

'Stop snivelling, Francine. I'm very disappointed in you.'

Francine looked shocked at Ia's cold dismissal of her tears which normally moved her so quickly. 'Oh, Aunt, I'm . . .' And before Ia could stop her, Francine was on her hands and knees at Ia's feet clutching at her knees. 'I can't bear it when you are angry with me.'

'Don't be so ridiculous, Francine. Let go of my skirt.' She shook the girl off. 'What did you expect? I've done everything I can to help you get a good start in life. This school was the best . . . Oh, you silly girl. You could have made such useful friends there.'

'Don't send me back. Please don't. I nearly didn't come here, I was afraid to come back, I really was.'

'What do you mean, afraid to come back?'

'I thought you would not believe me. I was truly afraid. That's the truth.' And she began to sob uncontrollably.

'What wouldn't I believe?' Ia's voice had softened, her hand went out to touch the girl, to comfort her, and then she withdrew it, sharply, as if annoyed with her hand for acting so.

'It was dreadful, Aunt. I had only been there two nights when the principal's husband, he . . .' Francine shuddered. 'Please don't make me talk about it.' She looked up at Ia, her eyes full of anguish. Ia looked at her, saw the expression; all anger disappeared, and she knelt beside her.

'Oh no, he didn't! Oh, my poor darling . . .' She put her arms protectively about Francine, held her close and rocked her back and forth as she would a baby.

'What is it about me, Aunt? What is it makes these men attack me, it's always me . . .' Fresh tears began to flow.

'It's your beauty, my sweet. It seems to be the price you have to pay. Don't cry. I shan't send you away, we can't risk this happening again.'

'Oh, Aunt Ia, you are so kind to me.'

A fortnight later, Dog disappeared. Ia looked everywhere for him. She did not even know when he had gone missing, she was so used to him always being there that she had not noticed when he wasn't. She had the doormen out in the streets searching half the night for him. She called the police, she posted a reward. Three days later he was found, locked in an outhouse, his back legs bound together, his fur matted where the blood from a severe beating had clotted and hoarse from whimpering.

'Oh, my poor Dog, who could have been so unkind to you?' Ia bathed the dog's wounds and he struggled to lick her hand in gratitude. Gently she wrapped him in a soft blanket and bedded him down for the night.

'Can I speak to you, Ia?'

Ia looked up from settling the dog to see Gwen standing, grim-faced, over her.

'Of course, Gwen, what is it?'

'I don't know how to say this, Ia, not without you getting all worked up. It's about Dog.'

'Yes?' Ia looked up expectantly.

'One of the girls – and don't ask me who, 'cause I promised not to mention her name – says she saw your Francine acting real peculiar like round the outhouse a few days ago.'

'What do you mean, Gwen? Speak plainly,' Ia was aware how sharp her voice must sound.

'Well, it's obvious ain't it? It was she what did it to the poor little bugger. She's jealous of it and the way you love it, any fool can see that.'

'Gwen! You spiteful bitch! What a dreadful thing to say!' Ia was beside herself with anger. 'Francine loves Dog, he is her dog after all. It's the girls who are jealous of her . . . they have been ever since she came here. I'm surprised at you, Gwen, listening to such malicious gossip. I expected more loyalty from you of all people.'

'That's why I'm telling you. I *am* being loyal. I thought you ought to know, that's all,' Gwen said stolidly.

'I don't see much loyalty in repeating lies to me.'

Gwen stood, arms crossed, as if fending off Ia's remarks. 'There's something else,' she said resolutely. 'There's been money taken from several of the girls and two have lost items of jewellery. Now I'm not saying –'

Ia was on her feet in a flash and confronting Gwen.

'No, Gwen, you had better not,' she said in a steely voice. 'And I suggest you leave this room before I hit you.'

The door slammed loudly behind Gwen. Ia found she was shaking. She crossed to her decanter. Gwen of all people, to talk to her like that. With an unsteady hand she poured herself a drink and sank into a chair.

She did not like what she had just heard. Least of all did she like the fact that it was Gwen who had spoken. She had never known her to lie or cause problems; she had always been her staunchest ally. Why should she suddenly change? The drink finished, she poured another. She looked for a long time at the golden-coloured whisky. She shuddered. The truth was that there was much that was already worrying Ia. The last thing she had wanted was to hear such accusations from Gwen.

She had to acknowledge that Francine did lie. She would lie about silly little things such as saying she had eaten one chocolate instead of four, or what time she had got up. But she told larger lies too. Ia, in her initial indignation, had checked out several of the schools that Francine had maligned, determined to have them closed – none had been the dreadful, cruel places she had described.

Also, though she had not mentioned this to Francine or Gwen, she had not pursued her threat to ruin the Prendlebys. She could not, for the more she thought about them, the more she remembered the air of solid decency about them, their immaculate little house with the row of happy children eating their breakfast. And she found that, despite what Francine had told her, she liked the couple. And, worst of all, and she hated herself for this, she very much doubted if Francine had been attacked by Alf. Ia knew men too well. As soon as a man walked into her establishment, Ia would know what his pleasures were. In Alf she had seen a kind, rather simple family man, not a pervert.

Worst of all, in the past year and as recently as last

week, Ia suspected that money had been taken from her office. Once she would have known for certain, but she was so behind with her books these days that she could not be sure. It could have been anyone, of course, but she had never had that trouble before. Not, that is, until Francine came.

And, then, she had seen with her own eyes how the dog shivered and cowered if Francine entered the room. That evening she could stand the uncertainty no longer.

'Francine, was it you who beat Dog?'

'Me? Oh, Aunt, what a silly question.'

'He does seem very frightened of you.'

'All dogs are like that with me, Aunt Ia. It's difficult to tell you this but I really don't like them very much and they seem to know. You see I'm frightened. Mr Prendleby had a huge dog and when it bit me once, they all laughed. Now, when I see a dog it reminds me. I never said, not when you had given me Dog as a present – it would have been rude and unkind of me.' She smiled at Ia.

'Ah, I see.' Ia felt relieved at Francine's explanation and angry with herself for doubting the girl, for allowing Gwen's gossip to filter into her mind. It was so typical of the child to hide her fears rather than hurt Ia's feelings.

That night, in bed, Ia resolved that Dog would have to go; she could not have Francine living in fear. But the next morning she could not find it in her heart to let him go. Who would love such an ugly creature as she did?

9

Keeping Francine out of the brothel proved impossible. She was always sneaking in, always curious, forever asking questions. Finally Ia capitulated and allowed her into the office to help with the sewing and the flowers. But she insisted that she had no contact with the clients and as little as possible with the girls.

Ia, alerted to the possibility of missing money, was now more careful. But she was not mistaken: money was being taken, and regularly. She always had a large float of cash. This was kept separate from the takings which were always locked away immediately in the safe. The thought of the missing money made her feel sick but what made her feel worse was that someone she trusted had taken it. There could be no question of a customer stealing from her. When clients were in the house she was either in her office or it was locked while she entertained them. The only time the room would be unlocked was in the morning before the clients came – it had to be one of the house's occupants.

She set a trap. Even as she set it, she knew that she was doing so reluctantly, as if she did not want to know the truth, as if deep inside her she already knew the answer. She looked at the money laid out before her and wondered if it mattered, when she had so much. Of course it matters, her inner voice said. You have to know, otherwise everyone is under a cloud. In the petty cash box she had the usual collection of notes with which she could do little. But the coins were a different matter.

The next morning she announced quite loudly that she was off to the shops and expected to be out for two hours. She asked Francine if she would like to accompany her but the girl said she wanted to tidy her room.

When Ia returned it was to find £10 missing from her office. For five minutes she sat at her desk staring into space. She picked up her cloak, swung it about her shoulders and marched across the garden to the mews house. Dog padded along beside her. She slammed the door.

'Francine, I want to talk to you,' she called up the stairs.

From the small bathroom she heard the splashing of water. She tried the handle; the door was locked. She banged on the door. 'Francine. Come out. I wish to talk to you.'

'I'm in the bath.'

'Then get out and come here this instant.'

She waited five minutes before Francine appeared, wrapped in her bath towel, her face glowing, her long hair snaking in damp tendrils about her face. Ia thought she had never seen the girl look more beautiful.

Without saying a word, she picked up Francine's hands and looked at them. On both were the marks of the Indian ink with which she had marked the coins, faded now, and surrounded by red flesh where Francine had evidently been frantically scrubbing.

'I knew it was you and I prayed to God I was wrong.' Ia looked sadly at her daughter. 'Why?' Francine stood, a belligerent expression on her face, and stared out of the window. 'We can stay here all night if you like. But we stay here until you answer.'

'If we stand here all night, what about your precious clients? You wouldn't like to lose money, now would you, Aunt Ia?' Francine said unpleasantly.

'Why?'

'You can afford it.'

'If there was something you wanted why did you not ask me?'

'And get an inquisition? Not bloody likely. What I do is my own affair, thank you very much.'

'How long have you been stealing?'

'Thought you always knew to the last penny what you were worth? You were forever telling me how wonderful you were with money.'

'I want to know how much you've stolen from the others. I have to replace it. And the jewellery.'

'They get enough.'

'That's not the point, Francine. I can't tell you how dreadfully ashamed I am of you. I shall have to punish you severely.'

'Calling the police?' Francine sneered.

'No, we don't want them involved. But you will stay in the mews for four weeks. You are not to go to the house. You are not to go out. I shall give you no money during that period. You can spend your time sewing . . .'

'You're my mother, aren't you?' Francine looked at her slyly.

Ia sat down abruptly. 'Who's been talking to you?'

'That stupid old cow, Prendleby, who you dumped me with. I got her drunk: it was easy to get that old lush drunk. That's when she told me. That's when it was easy to nick from her, too.'

'Francine, you didn't? How could you?'

'Because I wanted things and no one and nothing was going to stop me getting them. Don't *you* understand?'

'I can understand you wanting things but not stealing to get them. What else did she tell you?'

'Your address, that's how I knew where to find you. Who my father was. That you deserted me because I interfered with your social life,' Francine said bitterly.

'Oh, Francine, that's not true. I did not desert you, ever. I could not keep you: it was impossible. I did what I thought was for the best. Mrs Prendleby came highly recommended.'

'Why did you never visit me?'

'I couldn't. It was too painful to see you. I came once and I watched you, it nearly broke my heart. You seemed so happy that I didn't want to interfere with your security with Mrs Prendleby. You obviously loved her . . . I couldn't have you here. It seemed better that I did not try to see you, for both our sakes.'

'Loved that old bag?' Francine snorted. 'She neglected us, she used your money for her gin. Highly recommended, Christ, that's a laugh.'

'I don't believe you, Francine. They are good hard-working people. You are lying again. Her husband didn't attack you, did he?'

565

Francine snorted with laughter. 'I wouldn't have let him touch me with a barge pole. I had other interests, myself. Seems I must be taking after you.'

Ia quickly crossed the room and slapped her daughter hard across the face. 'I went to those people, I accused them of dreadful things – because you lied, and because I could not believe that my daughter would lie,' she shouted at her, hurt and angry.

'I want some money,' Francine said, rubbing her cheek where Ia's blow had fallen.

'You already have plenty of my money. Why should I give you more? What for?'

'It's none of your bleeding business. You owe it to me for all the things I've been deprived of.'

'You've not wanted for anything in your life. Just look at the dress you're wearing. And your education, your singing lessons, piano, painting classes . . .'

'And why not? The daughter of a lord should be properly dressed and have all those other things.'

'Oh, Francine, who's been telling you silly things like that?' Ia said, her voice no longer angry but full of compassion.

'I didn't need to be told. I know. Look at me, I'm bloody beautiful. That's breeding, that is.'

'Francine, sit down. I can assure you, your father was not a lord.'

'You're lying so's I won't go and find him.'

'I'm telling you the truth. Why should I lie to you?'

'To protect him.'

'I'm not protecting your father. I'm protecting you, you silly girl. I can understand why you want to invent this fantasy, in the circumstances . . .'

'What? Being illegitimate? Oh, I just love being a bastard, it's wonderful.' The laugh which rang out was hard and cold. 'Don't make things worse by lying to me. I know the truth, don't you fucking well deny it to me.'

Ia looked with horror at her daughter's venomous

expression. The foul language coming from such a beautifully formed, young mouth made the vulgar words sound more obscene.

'Your father was a footman. I'm sorry to disillusion you. A footman in a lord's house, perhaps that's where the confusion came from –'

'You lying old whore.' Francine leaped at her mother and shook her fist at her. 'I won't listen to you. It's not true, it's not sodding well true. Mrs Prendleby, she always told me I was from the quality,' Francine was screaming at her.

'Then she did wrong,' Ia replied, desperately trying to keep calm.

'Then look at this place, it's luxurious. You live like this and all those years you forced me to live in that hovel.'

'It was not a hovel, Francine. It was a pleasant respectable villa. Look, I can understand your bitterness, I'm sorry, I was fifteen when I had you, your age now. Your father deserted me and I lost my job. I could not have managed, we'd probably both be dead by now if I'd tried. You must believe me, Francine. Try to forgive me, please . . .'

'Money.' Francine held her hand out to her mother. 'I need it and now.'

'How much? What for? Francine, tell me, are you in trouble?'

'Five hundred pounds.'

'I can't give you that, Francine. It's an enormous sum of money. And certainly not if you won't tell me what it is for.'

'You can afford it.'

'Even if I could I wouldn't give it to you. It's far too much for a girl of your age. You could be cheated out of it.'

'I'm no fool.'

'I didn't say you were.'

The two women glared at each other like antagonists, both determined not to give in.

'Give it to me. If you don't you'll never see me again and that's a promise.'

Ia looked at the spiteful expression on Francine's face and knew with a heart-sinking certainty that she meant her threat. She needed Francine; she was all she had in the world to love. Ia realised she was in a trap. She who had had to learn to be strong was, where her daughter was concerned, weak. She might feel love for the girl but there was nothing in return. But why should there be? What right had she to expect it? She wrote a cheque. Even as she signed it she knew that what she was doing was wrong, that it would solve nothing. All the same, she handed it to Francine. 'I'll give you £100. That's all. I hope it's for something worthwhile.' Francine snatched the cheque. 'I can't buy your love, Francine. I'm aware of that. I should like us to be friends but I do not want even that, or to see you, if you resort to emotional blackmail.'

'Bloody grand for a whore, aren't you?'

'Yes, Francine, I'm a whore. I wish I wasn't but it was the only way I knew how to make money, how to give you the things in life that I did not have myself. I make no apology for that.'

'Mind you, makes the story perfect, don't it? My mother a bloody whore. In the circumstances I'm not so sure I want to see you again. Why should I? You're not exactly someone I can be proud of, are you?'

'At least you won't have to do what I've had to, to survive.'

'Too bloody true, I shan't. I'll be back for more money.' Francine stood up and waved the cheque at Ia.

'Then you won't get it.'

'I hate you – *Mother* – I hope you rot in hell . . .' was Francine's parting shot as she slid out of the door and Ia heard her slam into the bathroom.

Ia sat dazed. She had loved the child at a distance all

those years. She had had such dreams. She remembered how she had imagined them both at Gwenfer. But she had expected too much. How after all these years could there be a normal relationship between them? She couldn't blame the girl for being ambitious – hadn't she always had a lust for money herself? Had her own mother been wealthy, no doubt she would also have felt it her *right* to have money. So Ia sat and invented excuses for her daughter. She had been living in a dream these past two years, though, to be sure. She had showered affection and gifts on the girl, all the time refusing to allow herself to see what her daughter was really like.

This would not do, she thought, standing up and returning to the safety of her brothel. Work, that was the solution, she told herself sensibly.

Hours later, Ia felt suddenly old as she crossed the garden to her mews house. She opened the door and held it open for Dog to follow. He was not there. When had she last seen him?

'Dog,' she called out into the gloom of the garden. He did not come. 'Dog,' she called up the stairs.

She entered her sitting-room. There on the carpet lay Dog, in a pool of his own blood.

Part Six

Chapter Thirteen

1

Four years were to pass before Alice could keep her promise to Philomel to visit England. Plans had been made often enough, tickets had even been bought, but time and again something turned up that prevented their departure. Twice it had been Grace who had prevented them, once with measles and the second time with mumps. Then Alice herself had suffered a miscarriage and had been confined to bed for two months so that all thoughts of a journey were out of the question. And, if there was not a problem with Lincoln's business empire, it seemed to Alice that he manufactured problems – anything to prevent their departure. Lincoln could not delegate, that was his fault. He was one of those men whose large personality was closely accompanied by an equally large ego, which took the form of a conviction that only he could manage his business and that all those around him were congenital idiots.

Since her marriage she had learned to contain her impatience with Lincoln and his frequent intransigence. She had found this particularly irksome after living on her own and being her own mistress for so long. What contained her impatience was her gratitude to Lincoln for the security he gave her, not merely financial but emotional too. For he loved her, there was no doubting that. She only wished that she could love him with equal intensity. She felt guilty that she didn't. She seemed always to be taking from him – the luxury in which he surrounded her, the security he gave his family, his love. She felt she gave too little in return. If only she could feel more but always something stopped her. She knew why. It was that, for all the past bitterness and rejection, Chas or rather that light-headed happiness he had given her remained solidly in her memory. And also that old fear which had never left her, that if she did love him, he would leave her or be taken from her.

If she were ever to see her homeland again, Alice had to take matters into her own hands. She went to the shipping company herself and booked their staterooms. Then she informed Lincoln that they were going, that this time there was to be no cancellation. If Grace were to catch chickenpox then she would have to travel with it. Alice was going home for a visit. Lincoln was so surprised that his acquiescent wife should be quite so dogmatic that to everyone's surprise he agreed like a lamb.

Grace was finishing her studies in school in New York and since they were to be away for some time Alice engaged a governess for her. With Lincoln's valet, and Merry to help Alice, there were six in the party. Merry was sick with excitement and the ship's doctor advised that she take to her bed. The governess, without even consulting the doctor, took to hers before the ship had cleared the harbour, prostrate with sea-sickness. And Grace, because she had spots, refused to leave her cabin. Only the valet, Harold, seemed likely to enjoy the voyage.

'We should have come on our own, Lincoln.'

'When I think what it's costing!' He laughed. He always laughed in the face of misfortune, she had discovered. During a crisis on the stock market when fortunes were disappearing overnight, Lincoln was one of the few who kept his head, a sense of proportion and humour, and emerged relatively unscathed. It was Lincoln who, when she finally heard from Mr Woodley that her own fortune had been dissipated by her father, had shrugged his shoulders, taken her in his arms and said,

'It's only money. But I do hope the old bastard enjoyed himself while he spent it.' He could not placate her, however, over the loss of Gwenfer. She had wept when she had heard of the sale of the house. She had always presumed that somehow she would return, that it was at Gwenfer her life was destined to end. She felt bereft at its loss and still, after four years, her bitterness over the house was such that she found it difficult to talk about it.

She had wept for Gwenfer; she had not wept for her father when Philomel's letter had arrived. Nor had she wept when in his guarded, solicitor's jargon, Mr Woodley in his letter had hinted at the manner of his death. But as he was a peer of the realm the true facts had been neatly hushed up and George's death had, miraculously, become an accident. Alice had been through too much in her own life to feel anything but contempt for her father. As far as she was concerned, he had taken the easy way out.

She had heard from Gertie that Daisy Dear had remarried and had shocked society by choosing a young man of twenty-one to her thirty-four. As Gertie had caustically written, the fact that he was an enormously wealthy 21-year-old undoubtedly helped the match. Since he was so wealthy Alice could not help but think that Daisy should return her mother's jewellery to her. Lincoln had laughed at her naivety.

These matters apart, Alice was reasonably content. In Lincoln, despite his belief that he was always right, she had found a man who understood her feelings about life and her guilt at being wealthy while so many suffered. In the time she had spare from running her business, which had grown from strength to strength, he had encouraged her to help with the social welfare of his workforce. He never queried why the large dress allowance he gave her seemed sufficient only to buy a very modest wardrobe each year. She gave much away and had been relieved once more to be able to send an annual sum for the help of the old people in the almshouses she had built.

Alice had longed for another child but after three miscarriages Lincoln refused to allow her to try again. He loved her too much and feared for her safety, he explained. He took the responsibility of making sure she would not become pregnant again. Unlike most men, he never made her feel guilty that she had been unable to provide him with the heir he must have longed for.

If there was a shadow in her life it was Grace. She had known nothing but love, and Lincoln had been more than a father to her. In truth he was too indulgent to the girl, showering her with gifts and pretty clothes. The child had only to say she wanted and she received. But for all that she had a sulky disposition, and an unpleasant temper. She could have been pretty but the endless boxes of chocolates that she ate made her fat and ruined her complexion.

'Puppy fat, that's all it is. She'll slim down, you'll see.'

'But you spoil her so much, Lincoln. It's making her such a discontented person.'

'That's what children are for – to spoil. She'll grow out of her moods, it's her age,' he continually counselled her.

At thirty-six Alice had matured into a beautiful woman. The prettiness of her youth had not deserted her, although she had been through too much for her experiences not to have left their mark. So there were lines on her face and already a sprinkling of silver in her hair. But the upright, slim figure remained and, if anything, the lines on her face added to its dignity while no adversity had been able to remove her sweet expression.

'Would you like to go and see Gwenfer?' Lincoln asked the evening before they docked at Tilbury. They were both leaning on the ship's rail peering into the dusk as Alice tried to catch sight of the land of her birth.

'Lincoln, I couldn't. I've thought about it but I've

decided it would be too painful for me. You do understand? I wondered instead if we could invite Miss Gilby – gracious, I keep forgetting – Mrs Trenwith to London with her husband? I must see her, but not at Gwenfer.'

'As you wish, my darling. I'll arrange it. Excited?'

'I can't believe we are so close. You know, this ship must pass by my cove. If it were daytime and if we had a telescope we would be able to see the house.' She looked up at her husband, her eyes shining with joy. 'Do forgive me, Lincoln, I'm happy in our life together, our lovely homes, but, well, England means something very special.'

'I know. And I've been thinking that perhaps we should look for a small house to purchase here. We could come over each year then and Grace would learn of both her heritages. What do you think?'

'Lincoln? You mean it? But what about your business?'

'We've enough money to live as we want for the rest of our lives. I've built a team of good men I can trust. We can escape for a few months without too much harm.'

'Oh, Lincoln, I can't believe you would. Not *you*, you'd never trust anyone else to run your affairs.' She laughed.

'No, you're wrong, Alice. This voyage has given me time to think. I work too hard and I see far too little of you. I've not been fair to you. It's time I eased up, enjoyed myself, with you.' He stroked her cheek gently and then clasped her in a great bear hug.

Philomel had been in a state of perpetual flutter ever since she had received Lincoln's letter with their tickets for the train and hotel reservations for a whole week in London. Of course it had not been easy to arrange. Mr Reekin had made such a fuss. As they would be away for one Sunday Ralph would have to cancel both a Bible class and a confirmation class. When Ralph had gone up to the vicarage to argue his case, Philomel was quite resigned to their not being able to go. But when her husband had returned it was with an uncharacteristic strut and the information that he had told old Reekin they were going and that was all there was to it.

Philomel had not been out of the county once since she had arrived to teach Alice, and was quite puce with excitement as they boarded the great train for London.

Alice had arranged a beautiful room for them, in the Ritz Hotel, overlooking the park. Philomel thought she had never seen such luxury in her life. The train had not arrived until nine and so she had to contain herself until the following morning to see Alice.

The two women fell into each other's arms and cried, much to Lincoln's amusement, and Ralph's concern. Miss Gilby looked exactly the same to Alice; Alice looked older to Philomel. Alice had trouble with Philomel's name and blushed with confusion each time she got it wrong. But neither Philomel nor her husband was insulted and in fact, when she finally said 'Trenwith' with no prompting, it was they who led the cheers.

'My dear Alice. After all this time maybe it would be much simpler if you called me Philomel?' she suggested.

Grace was brought in by the governess to meet them. Philomel was not impressed by what she saw. She felt that here was a young woman who was running wild, who needed a good dose of discipline, and she did not approve of the governess at all. The woman appeared too timid, almost as if she were afraid of the girl, and with a few judicious questions Philomel reached the horrific conclusion that the governess appeared to be gravely undereducated. For the first time in her married life, just for a fleeting moment, she wished she were free – to take on Grace's education herself.

Loving young people, Philomel was shocked to find herself relieved that Grace was not to be present at luncheon. The meal was to be served in the Wakefields' suite, so that they could talk more easily, Alice had explained.

They talked of everything under the sun, politics, travel, Lincoln's work. Philomel was full of pride when Lincoln told her of the catering business that, virtually single-handed, Alice had built herself. Alice had found London greatly changed with so many motor cars and the buildings much begrimed and the streets shockingly dirty. They talked of everything, it seemed, except Gwenfer. Sensing that Alice would find the subject too painful, Philomel kept off it as well, even though she longed to tell Alice all the gossip, and how well the factory was doing.

As the meal progressed Philomel felt nothing but admiration for Lincoln: an intelligent man, a fair one, but most important of all, he obviously cared deeply for Alice. She would never have to worry about her again.

'Gwenfer,' Alice suddenly said, which made everyone almost jump with embarrassment as if she had talked of someone recently dead.

'Yes?' Philomel asked uncertainly.

'How is it? How is everyone? Who owns it now, are they looking after it? You see,' she smiled around the table at them, 'in the end I have to know.'

'Ah well!' Philomel sighed with happiness as she allowed the dam of information to open. 'Everyone is well. Mrs Malandine has become a particular friend. And Flo is well. You remember her of course? Mr George is still the coachman but he's getting so old that Mrs Malandine worries for him. Mrs Trelawn is even fatter. Oh, dear, perhaps I shouldn't have said that, I didn't mean it unkindly.'

'Of course you didn't, Philomel. She always was. And how is the house?'

Philomel's unfortunately placed eyes flickered nervously. 'It's very sad, Alice.'

'Sad?'

'No one lives there. I hate going; that great beautiful house, sometimes it's almost as if it's crying out for company.'

'I used to think the house talked to me, too. How nice that you feel that as well, Philomel. But the new owners, if they don't live there, do they visit?'

'It's most peculiar.' Philomel leaned forward, eager at last to tell Alice. 'She came, just the once. The message had been that she was to stay a week,' Philomel paused for dramatic effect, 'but . . . she stayed overnight only. In the morning she was away and has never been back, and that must be three . . . good gracious, no, four years ago. Just like that, most odd. Of course the servants were fearful that they had offended in some way. But it seems not: their wages are paid by Mr Woodley every month as regularly as clockwork.'

'She?'

'Yes, a Mrs St Just. Very young and beautiful, a rich widow we presumed. We wondered if she was Cornish with a name like that but she said she came from London. I gave her tea, we talked for quite a while. She was very interested in what you had done for the village, Alice.'

'And you never hear from her?'

'Nothing. A place like that should be cared for, loved as you used to love it, Alice. There was one odd thing, though: Flo said she thought she had been there before. But then Flo was always a fanciful child, wasn't she? Champagne? Oh, Lincoln I shall giggle,' she said happily.

2

Ia was disillusioned. All her life she had thought that with money she would be protected, with money she would be happy, that money was the solution to life's ills. She had been wrong. Money had not kept Peter or made her daughter respect and love her. She had everything and she had nothing.

She had never seen Francine again. She could have forgiven her many things – the lying, the deceit, the stealing, her waywardness – but what the girl had done to poor innocent Dog, Ia could never forgive.

Dog lay buried in the garden, an inscribed marble slab marking his grave. It was a rare day that Ia passed the spot without thinking of him and missing him. She had made no attempt to replace him.

She would often think how all the beings she had loved had slipped through her fingers – Alice, Peter, Francine and Dog. Loving was obviously not for her. Loving was a dangerous pastime.

Although she had not seen Francine, she had heard about her. It was now apparent why she had demanded so much money, for she was in residence in a smart new flat with a French composer, whom no doubt she had met on her adventures through France. His tunes though 'popular' had not yet brought him fame. But, because of Dog, Ia made no attempt to contact her daughter. She did everything possible to expunge from her mind the fact that she had a daughter at all.

After three years Peter still called infrequently. She refused to see him but she admired his tenacity. There were days, when the loneliness was at its worst, when she wondered if the argument had been worth the bleakness of her life without him. But then she would remember how she had made a fool of herself over him. She had been right all along that men were not to be trusted; she had wavered in that belief and now was having to live with the turmoil caused by her mistake. Never again would she take a man into her heart. She might use one in bed, but nothing more.

And then, during this sad and confused period in her life, came further bad news. After cutting Francine out of her mind Ia had felt a deep need to find out if any of her family remained, any, that is, except her father whom she had no desire to see again. So, for some time she had had detectives searching for her brother Paul and sister Mary in America. Their report lay on her bureau. Mary had died fourteen years ago in poverty and of Paul there was no news.

She had worked all her life, for what? She had a daughter whom she disliked. Her hope to be able to help the remaining members of her family had come to naught. Even her faith in money had deserted her. So what was she working for? She wondered if, as Peter had suggested, she should sell up? The money from the gaming-room continued to pour in; all her debts had long been cleared and she had achieved her ambition – she owned everything here. She had more than enough for her needs for the rest of her life. Perhaps she should return to Gwenfer, and do good works like Alice. She smiled to herself.

She fought this depression with all her old courage but she seemed unable to lift it. And, until she decided what it was she was going to do, she still had her responsibility to the girls who worked for her. Once again the actress in her was called upon to pretend a gaiety she was far from feeling.

Ia sat in her small sitting-room in the main house doing the task that had once given her such pleasure and now seemed empty – her books. Gwen came in to announce that there was a man to see her. Though irritated by the interruption she agreed to see him. A stranger, Gwen had said, but perhaps he wished to become a client – Ia was not one to turn her back on a potential customer.

'Thank you for seeing me, Mrs St Just. My name is Lincoln Wakefield.'

She shook his proffered hand as she looked at his pleasant face, the intense blue eyes, and noted the humour in his expression. There was something vaguely familiar about him as if she had seen him in a shadow somewhere. In a trice the professional in her summed him up as an uncomplicated but lusty lover.

'A drink, Mr Wakefield? Lincoln Wakefield? You know, I'm sure I've heard mention of your name. You've not been here before?'

'This is my first trip to England, ma'am. I can't imagine where you could have heard tell of me.'

She crossed to the drinks tray and poured them two large whiskies. 'How can I be of assistance? Are you looking for entertainment?'

He laughed a loud bark of a laugh. 'Nothing like that. You have a property that I'm interested in.'

'I have?'

'Gwenfer, in Cornwall.'

She placed her glass carefully on the table beside her. 'May I ask how you found that I was the owner of this particular property?'

'It hasn't been easy. It's taken me nearly six weeks to establish the ownership. You're a woman of great mystery, Mrs St Just.'

'Not really. I just don't like everyone to know my business. Understandable in the circumstances.' She smiled at him and he was struck, as so many had been before him, by her outstanding beauty, and the lack of hardness in her face, unusual in one of her profession.

'I am very discreet, Mrs St Just.'

'Obviously someone wasn't. There are very few people who know that I own Gwenfer. I cannot imagine that Mr Woodley would have divulged my secret.'

'Woodley? No, not he. I tried him but he was as close as a snail.' He laughed again; lifting his glass to his lips he saluted her with it. She studied him: he was obviously a man who was well content with his life and confident that whatever he wanted he would get.

'You have not been a client here, so no one here could have told you.'

'A Mr Willoughby informed me.'

'Peter Willoughby?'

'I met him at a friend's club, I told him I was looking for a property. He told me of several. Then I told him I knew the one I wanted but I just could not locate the owner. When I told him its name, he laughed and exclaimed over an extraordinary coincidence.'

'He would,' she said coldly. 'I trust you have not been making difficulties for me in Cornwall.'

'I haven't even been to Cornwall.'

'A moment, Mr Wakefield. Do I understand you correctly? You want to buy my house and yet you've never seen it?'

'That's right, ma'am.'

'Isn't that somewhat odd?'

'Not really. I want it, that's all. The reasons why are irrelevant.'

'They're not to me. But you're an American.'

'I guess that's fairly obvious, ma'am.' He grinned.

'So why would an American want an old house in Cornwall? Do you live here?'

'No, I live in the States. I want it as a home here when I bring my family over.'

'Are your antecedents Cornish, Mr Wakefield?'

'No. My ancestors came from the North.'

Ia crossed the room and poured them each another drink. She was enjoying herself. She did not like the arrogant way he seemed to assume he could buy the property – he needed to be taught a lesson.

'Is it for sale?' he asked, accepting the glass she gave him.

'No.'

'I'd pay you double what you paid for it.'

'I'm not interested.'

'Three times . . .'

'Really, Mr Wakefield, that is rather rash of you. It's not worth what you are offering.'

'That's my concern.'

'I'm sorry to disappoint you – you're obviously a man who is used to getting what he wants – but, this time, I'm afraid you're not going to get your wish.' She smiled sweetly at him.

'I won't give up, Mrs St Just. I shall keep on offering until I wear you down.'

'You can't wear someone down if they are determined not to give way. I like getting my own way too, you see, Mr Wakefield. I don't wish to appear rude, but I do have rather a lot of work to do.'

He stood up, collected his hat and cane. 'Very well, Mrs St Just, for the time being . . .' And he turned towards the door.

He was about to leave the room when her curiosity got the better of her. 'Tell me, Mr Wakefield. Why? Just tell me why you are so determined.'

He turned to look at her. 'It's not for me. It's for my wife.'

'What a fortunate woman. Can't you find another house to suit her?'

'No. It was her home, you see. She loves it, almost as if it were a living thing. Her father sold it. It has broken her heart.'

'Your wife's name is Alice, then.' She was surprised at how calm she sounded.

'Why, yes, how did you know that?'

'I think you had better come back in, Mr Wakefield.' She rang the bell and ordered lunch for herself and her guest.

To his frustration she refused to discuss the matter further until their lunch had been brought in and the champagne poured. She was not being contrary; she needed these minutes to collect herself and to put her thoughts in order, to decide what she was going to do.

'Mr Wakefield, you can have my house but on two conditions.'

'Any.' He leaned forward eagerly.

'I don't want your wife to know that it was I who sold it to you.'

'If that's what you want, ma'am.'

'Secondly, I never want you to divulge to her that you have met me. That is important.'

'Might I ask why?'

'No, you may not. As to the price. I must warn you I paid too much for it. It was in settlement of Lord Tregowan's gambling debts. I had a moment of weakness, rare I would like to point out.'

'Gambling. So that was it. You know he frittered her whole fortune away?'

'So I gathered. But at least she has you. It appears you are making things better for her. So, to the price.'

'I said, I would pay you three times what you paid. The price does not matter to me. My wife's happiness is more important.'

'No. I don't want three times the sum.' She smiled. Her initial reaction was to let him have it for what she had paid for it, but Ia had not saved and toiled and enmeshed herself in money all her life to allow a good deal to pass her by. 'Give me 10 per cent above what I settled for.'

'Done.' He shook her hand on the agreement, and she poured more champagne to seal it. He studied her over the rim of his glass. 'You're the child she befriended, years ago, the miner's daughter, aren't you? Don't deny it, there's no point. You see, Alice did a painting of you from memory. It's a remarkable likeness.'

'Yes, I was Ia Blewett in those days. My time with Alice was without doubt the happiest period of my life. I thought she had deserted me. It's a long story of muddle and confusion. But I must insist, Mr Wakefield, on the terms of our agreement. I do not want her to know who I now am.'

'I know she would be overjoyed to see you again.'

'Mr Wakefield, I hardly think I'm an ideal friend for your wife now. Do you?' She chuckled softly.

'Perhaps not. It seems sad, however. But, I promise, your secret is safe with me, Mrs St Just.'

3

Alice's return to Gwenfer was a triumph.

Ever since Philomel Trenwith had received the news that Lincoln had managed to buy back the property for his wife, she had been in a turmoil of planning. From her own meagre savings she had bought material to have each girl at her school dressed in a bright new white pinafore. She requested that on the great day each girl should have large white ribbons in her hair. There was not much Philomel could do with the boys – such scruffy creatures! But she had travelled into Penzance and had purchased twelve red-spotted kerchiefs for them to wear around their necks. She had sent a note to the mothers insisting that they have clean white shirts to wear on the great day. And for a week before Alice's arrival she had held daily inspections of boots and fingernails.

She had composed a song of welcome which the children were to sing. And, convinced as she was that one of the first things Alice would want to do would be to inspect the school, she had the cleaner scrub the school out, and had hung the best artwork on the walls.

Lastly, in the attic of the church hall, she discovered boxes full of bunting which the older members of the community told her were last used for Queen Victoria's Diamond Jubilee. There was no shortage of volunteers to wash and launder the bunting which she then had the men string across the main street.

Alice's train was due into Penzance in the late evening which did not suit Philomel's plans at all. With difficulty and an appalling expenditure on telegrams she had persuaded Lincoln to arrange for Alice to spend her first night back in Cornwall at the Queen's Hotel.

Once she had arrived, Alice was beside herself with impatience to see the house which Lincoln had bought. For a time, when he had said he had found a property, she had thought it must be Gwenfer since he was being so mysterious about it. She had wheedled and begged to be told the truth.

'But I want it to be a surprise,' Lincoln said.

'Just tell me, is it Gwenfer?'

'Oh, my poor love. I'm sorry, it isn't. But I've found a beautiful property and at least it is in Cornwall,' he had lied. And at sight of the dejected expression on her face and the brave way she had tried to hide her disappointment he had almost relented and told her the truth. Fortunately he had not, and as they dined at the Queen's Hotel, at a table overlooking Mount's Bay, he was glad the secret had been kept. She sat opposite him impatient to know which property he had acquired. She kept going over the names of all the prominent families in the area and could not think of one who would have agreed to sell. Lincoln just sat and smiled.

The following morning Lincoln hired a carriage and they set off. It was a glorious August morning as the carriage left Penzance. Three miles outside the town Lincoln pulled down the blinds so that Alice could not see out.

'It's too hot, Papa,' Grace whined.

'I don't want Mama to see where she's going,' he gently explained.

'I think it's silly,' Grace continued.

'Well, I don't. I think it's charming of your father,' Alice gently chided the child. She wished Grace did not always complain, no matter what they did.

The carriage pulled up. 'Right,' announced Lincoln,

'you can look now.' Dramatically he snapped up the blind.

Alice looked out on the main street of Gwenfer transformed with bunting and with all the inhabitants, it seemed, lining the roadway and looking uncomfortable in their best clothes. As she stepped from the carriage, Philomel raised her arm and with a flourish and a loud 'one two three', led her pupils into the song which had been written for Alice.

Alice stood in the sunshine, with tears pouring down her cheeks, clutching Lincoln's hand tightly, as she listened.

'They're flat,' Grace sneered.

'They're beautiful,' her mother replied.

From the crowd of schoolchildren emerged the youngest pupil, carrying a bouquet of flowers so large it threatened to swamp her. With a much-rehearsed curtsy, she presented it to Alice.

'What can I say?' Alice started shouting above the general hubbub. There were many shushes, angry glares at the noisiest, and several children received sharp slaps before any semblance of order was restored. 'I just want to say that this is the happiest day of my life . . .'

'What about when you met your husband then, Miss Alice, don't 'e count?' one youth shouted and everyone laughed.

Alice smiled. 'Very well then – I've had two happiest days in my life and this is one of them.' Everyone cheered. 'I never meant to go away. And then I always hoped and prayed that I would return. I wish we could live here permanently but it can't be. But we shall be here each year, I promise. And one day . . . I believe we shall be here all the time.' This information was greeted with an even louder cheer. 'I've missed all of you more than I can express . . . and if you'll excuse me . . . I . . .' She fumbled in her pocket for a handkerchief.

'God bless her, her's a beauty.'

'Don't 'e cry, my 'andsome.'

'You'm home now, my lovely.'

All of which only made Alice cry the more.

'Good God, I didn't realise my little surprise would cause you such grief,' Lincoln said, putting his arm about her.

'I'm so happy, Lincoln. You're very good to me.'

'Look, look what they're doing.' Lincoln pointed to the carriage, from which the young men of the village were unharnessing the horses. Putting themselves in the traces they lifted up the shafts of the carriage and with the villagers running in front and bringing up the rear, Alice was borne home in style.

Mrs Malandine, forewarned by Philomel, had purchased barrels of beer and cider and Mrs Trelawn had been cooking for days. The resulting picnic on the terrace and lawns of Gwenfer was voted the best ever.

Four hours later they watched the last of their guests wearily weaving their way back up the drive.

'Come with me.' Alice took Lincoln's hand and led him down the steps and through the garden, along the river and to her rock. 'This is the rock I told you about. This is where I used to spend hours as a child.'

'On your own?'

'Always, until Ia came. Oh, Lincoln, if only she had been here today, how wonderful it would have been.' Lincoln said nothing but looked out at the sea. 'That's Oswald's rock. That's where he died.' But now, with her husband beside her, she could say it in a steady voice and find that there was no grief for her brother any more. 'We must visit his grave tomorrow. There can't have been any flowers on it for years. Nor on my mother's.'

She leaned against Lincoln and they sat for some time and watched the sun setting over her cove. This rock had seen her sad, lonely, but now it witnessed her content and happy.

With the sun set they returned to the house.

'I don't like this house,' Grace complained, as she met them in the doorway of the great hall.

'Why not, Grace? It's a beautiful house.'

'There's no electricity, there are no bathrooms, it's horrid.'

'But wait until Mrs Malandine lights the oil lamps – they are beautiful and make such a lovely hissing noise as they burn. And you will bathe in your room, in front of the fire. You'll love it.' Alice laughed at her daughter. Not even her disgruntled little face was going to ruin this day for her.

'I hate it.'

Lincoln ruffled Grace's hair.

Alice was up before anyone else the next morning. She had not slept well. Mrs Malandine had put her and Lincoln in her parents' bedroom, and she could not sleep easily there. After all these years, she could still remember her mother's dreadful screams coming from this room the day that Oswald had drowned. She decided they should move into one of the other bedrooms.

She slipped out of the room quietly so as not to wake Lincoln and went to inspect the other bedrooms.

She chose the room four doors along. It was not as large as her parents' but was spacious enough and, best of all, had windows on two sides. And it was just as beautifully furnished. How lucky they were that nothing from the house had been sold, she thought. No doubt she could go down into the kitchens and find everything exactly in the same position as on the day she had left. She wandered along the corridor checking that each of her ancestors was still there. She paused in front of the twin portraits of her parents painted at the time of their marriage. She could look at them and think only what a fine couple they had made. Within her was no emotion. She did not feel hatred and she did not feel love. There was no bitterness but neither was there gratitude. Nor was there any guilt – she had expected guilt. She shuddered at her emptiness. What if Grace should feel nothing for her, have no fond memories either when, in her turn, she stood here and gazed at Alice's portrait, one day to hang here with all the Tregowans? She turned her back on the paintings.

At the end of the corridor she opened the door that led up to the old nursery wing. At the top of the stairs she paused and looked at the trail of bare footprints in the dust. They must be quite old, she reasoned, for on top of the imprints was another thinner film of dust. She placed her own foot beside one of the footprints and laughed at the game. How small that foot was, she thought, wishing she had tiny feet like that.

She turned the handle of the schoolroom door but it did not open. She tried the other rooms and all of them opened. She spent some time wandering about the old nurseries, looking at her old toys. To her astonishment, she found all her old clothes still hanging in the cupboards. She looked at the fussy garments, miniature adult dresses really, at the minute buttoned boots, and decided that little children were much more sensibly dressed these days than she had been.

She returned to the schoolroom, puzzled that this was the only door which would not open. Looking about her she found in the day nursery a knitting needle, one of Queenie's she presumed, and returned with it to the door. It took her nearly five minutes of fiddling with the lock before the door opened.

She stepped into the room and felt she was stepping into her past. Everything was the same. Nothing had been moved, it was just as if she and Ia had left the room to go for tea or to the beach.

She walked across and sat at her desk, the big one she had used as the teacher, and looked over at Ia's pupil's desk. How pompous of her, she thought laughing softly to herself. It was strange but she felt so close to her old friend here that she would not have been in the least surprised if the door had opened and Ia had walked in. Idly she picked up the register which lay before her, a pencil upon it. She read the register, smiling as she did so. And then the smile disappeared in a flash. She rubbed her eyes and looked again at the page. She could not believe what she saw. She held her breath as she studied it more closely holding the book up to the sunlight. She felt her skin tingle, felt her heart pounding and fought a wave of dizziness. She took a deep breath. She was elated. Ia was alive, Ia had been here. Ia had marked herself present . . .

'Lincoln!' She tore into their room waking him from a deep sleep. 'Lincoln, it's Ia, she's been here. Look in the register we used to keep. It's written, see, she was here on 15 May 1906. Look!' She shook him with impatience.

Lincoln sleepily rubbed his eyes and hauled himself up the bed. 'But, Alice darling, anyone could have done that. Children playing, perhaps?'

'No, it's Ia. I knew I could feel her there in the schoolroom. She's been in that room recently, I know. Oh, Lincoln, I must find her, please help me,' she begged.

4

Ia had finally decided what she was going to do. She was going to sell up. She had paid off her creditors, she had the money from the sale of Gwenfer, and she owned a highly successful business. She would buy herself a house in the country, not Cornwall, but by the sea, Devon, maybe. She could not return to Cornwall. The desire to see Alice again might prove too strong. She would look for a little business. A shop, perhaps. It would be interesting to see if she could make as big a success of that as she had of the brothel. She would take Gwen with her. Gwen had been a good and loyal friend to Ia. But first she would take a holiday. She would go to America, she liked that idea. Finally she would see that great land but she would arrive in style – a stateroom would be her accommodation not the steerage that had once been her dream.

She had thought a great deal about Alice since the papers on Gwenfer had been signed. She did not have to wonder if Alice would be happy there; that went without saying. She would have loved to see her face when Lincoln had told her that Gwenfer was theirs. How she would have enjoyed being there when Alice returned. Returning her ancestral home to Alice was one of the most satisfying things she had ever done in her life. But no doubt Alice was back in the United States by now and planning her next visit to Gwenfer. Ia was certain of one thing: her friend would never get the longing for Cornwall out of her blood – no one ever did.

Despite her decision that she could not live in Cornwall because of Alice, illogically she still wanted to see her. She frequently planned their reunion, what they would say to each other, how it would be. She did not regret telling Lincoln not to divulge her identity or her whereabouts. How could Alice welcome her, a retired harlot, a practising madam, with open arms? But when she had sold the brothel, when she had another business, a respectable one, that would be a different matter. Then she could meet her old friend on equal terms and with pride that, against the odds, she had survived. Yes, that was the solution: she must sell now.

She peered out of the window. It was a freezing November day, fog was beginning to swirl about the streets coating everything with its dull, yellow-green tendrils. It was in November that she had first come to this house; strange that it should be in the same month that she should decide finally to sell. Much as she would have preferred to stay in by the fire on a day like this, she had to venture out. It was Gwen's birthday tomorrow and she wanted to buy her something special. She would go to Cook's too and find out about sailings. Tomorrow, when she gave Gwen her gift, she would tell her about her plans, of the new life they were about to venture out on, the holiday they were going to take.

She bundled herself into a fur, pulled her felt hat low on her head, and set out for Knightsbridge.

Alice felt harassed. The six months they had planned to stay had stretched into nine months. Lincoln had finally put his foot down. They must return to New York for Christmas or he would be bankrupt. Gwenfer would be there next year, he had teased her. Even then Alice had delayed their departure from Cornwall to the last minute; she was loath to drag herself away. They should have returned to London the previous week, not last night. She had to shop: there were so many presents to buy for Christmas – they would all expect something from England. She had only today for the ship sailed on the morning tide. She also had an appointment with a private detective. She had asked Lincoln time and again to arrange for an agency to search for Ia, but he always seemed to forget. She wanted to arrange it before leaving, for, she hoped, upon her return, that her friend would have been found.

With a complaining Grace in tow she set out. Everyone had recommended that she go to Knightsbridge for the best shops.

Ia stepped from the motor cab. As she paid off the driver she idly glanced across the street. She smiled as through the swirling fog on the opposite side of the wide road she saw a woman, swathed in furs against the freezing weather, arguing with a young girl who was scowling in disagreement. So like Francine, she found herself thinking. The fog closed in as she waited for the driver to sort out the change. When she looked again the fog had lifted sufficiently for her to see the woman more clearly as she lifted her head from talking to the girl and looked up to the heavens as if making an exasperated prayer. It was Alice! She was sure of it. She did not bother to wait for her change but to the man's astonishment thrust it all into his hand.

'Why not?' she muttered to herself. She had decided to sell; she was almost not a brothel keeper. It would be stupid of her, with Alice so close, not to speak to her.

'Alice,' she called and dashed into the road.

At the sound of a blaring motor horn, Alice turned in time to see a woman, well wrapped up, her hat pulled low on her head, standing as if frozen like a statue in the middle of the road. Everything happened so quickly and yet as if in slow motion as the car skidded on the icy surface, and Alice found herself lifting her hand as though in warning; but, like the other woman, rooted to the spot. The car slammed into the side of a stationary horse-drawn carriage. The horse reared in panic, its ears laid back, its eyes rolling in terror, and bolted. The carriage rocked dangerously before toppling over upon the woman who was dragged beneath it along the road until someone caught the head of the bolting horse. All that could be seen of her was a pair of small, red-leather boots, which stuck out incongruously beneath the shattered woodwork of the carriage. Alice stepped forward to go and help and then remembered Grace who, engrossed in a window display of sweets and chocolates, appeared oblivious to the commotion. She put her arm protectively about her daughter, with her body shielding the accident from view. Hurriedly she led the girl into the shop and away from the sight.

A crowd had gathered around Ia. A man had bundled his coat beneath her head. Gently they lifted the coach from her legs. She smiled at them and thanked them politely, unsure what she was doing lying in the middle of the road. 'Alice,' she said quite distinctly and wondered why she felt so strange, as if she were floating.

'Was there someone with her?' a man demanded of no one in particular. 'Is there an Alice here?'

'I didn't see no one, guv. She was alone in my cab. She didn't speak to no one as far as I know.'

'She just ran out into the road, there was nothing I could do, the ice, the fog . . .' The distressed driver stood wringing his hands, completely ignored by everyone; they were all concentrating on Ia.

'Alice.' This time she found it difficult to say the word. 'Alice,' she croaked and a thin trickle of blood appeared at the corner of her mouth. A woman knelt and gently wiped the blood away. 'Alice,' she said but by then no one could understand and all thought she groaned as she tried to speak through a blood-clogged throat. 'Alice,' she mumbled as the dark blanket of death wrapped itself about her.

This is the last Will and Testament of Ia Blewett (known as St Just), spinster of 22–24, Grenadier Street, St James's, London. It is my wish and intention that upon my death all properties, shares, all possessions, all goods and chattels belonging to me be sold. After the payment of my debts and funeral expenses I wish that 25 per cent of my fortune be used to purchase annuities of equal value for all members of staff at my establishment who have been in my employ for more than two years. For my friend, Gwen Roberts, a double annuity is to be acquired. From my estate sufficient money is to be used to purchase a building for the sole use and occupation of young women alone and unattended in London. A matron is to be employed for their care and protection and the residue of my estate to be invested for the running costs of this establishment. The large black leather box to be found in my safe and containing the Tregowan jewels is to be returned to their rightful owner Alice Wakefield (née Tregowan). To my daughter Francine Blewett I bequeath my azure bowl. It was all I had at the start of my life in London. Let us see how well she does with it.

☐ **Advances** £5.99
ANITA BURGH
0 75280 931 8

☐ **Avarice** £5.99
ANITA BURGH
0 75281 641 1

☐ **Breeders** £5.99
ANITA BURGH
0 75280 691 2

☐ **Clare's War** £5.99
ANITA BURGH
0 75284 290 0

☐ **The Cult** £5.99
ANITA BURGH
0 75280 929 6

☐ **Distinctions of Class** £5.99
ANITA BURGH
0 75281 066 9

☐ **Exiles** £5.99
ANITA BURGH
0 75284 409 1

☐ **The Family** £5.99
ANITA BURGH
0 75282 772 3

☐ **Lottery** £5.99
ANITA BURGH
0 75281 640 3

☐ **On Call** £5.99
ANITA BURGH
0 75281 695 0

☐ **Overtures** £5.99
ANITA BURGH
0 75281 684 5

☐ **The Azure Bowl** £6.99
ANITA BURGH
0 75283 744 3

☐ **The Golden Butterfly** £6.99
ANITA BURGH
0 75283 758 3

☐ **The Stone Mistress** £6.99
ANITA BURGH
0 75283 759 1

All Orion/Phoenix titles are available at your local bookshop or from the following address:

Mail Order Department
Littlehampton Book Services
FREEPOST BR535
Worthing, West Sussex, BN13 3BR
telephone 01903 828503, *facsimile* 01903 828802
e-mail MailOrders@lbsltd.co.uk
(Please ensure that you include full postal address details)

Payment can be made either by credit/debit card (Visa, Mastercard, Access and Switch accepted) or by sending a £ Sterling cheque or postal order made payable to *Littlehampton Book Services*.
DO NOT SEND CASH OR CURRENCY.

Please add the following to cover postage and packing

UK and BFPO:
£1.50 for the first book, and 50p for each additional book to a maximum of £3.50

Overseas and Eire:
£2.50 for the first book plus £1.00 for the second book and 50p for each additional book ordered

---

BLOCK CAPITALS PLEASE

name of cardholder ....

address of cardholder ....

delivery address
(if different from cardholder)

....

....

postcode ....   *postcode* ....

☐ I enclose my remittance for £.................................

☐ please debit my Mastercard/Visa/Access/Switch (delete as appropriate)

card number ☐☐☐☐ ☐☐☐☐ ☐☐☐☐ ☐☐☐☐

expiry date ☐☐☐☐   Switch issue no. ☐☐

signature ....

prices and availability are subject to change without notice